Praise for

The Death and Life of Zebulon Finch, Volume One: At the Edge of Empire

◆

One of the Ten Best Books of 2015
—*Entertainment Weekly*

"A splendidly rendered, macabre picaresque—muscular and tender,
imaginative and grotesque, cynical yet deeply moving. This tale may be told by
the dead, but what's rendered here is life itself in all of its absurd glory."
—Rick Yancey, *New York Times* bestselling author of *The 5th Wave*

"Morbidly fascinating."
—*Publishers Weekly*

"An absolutely sweeping tale of brilliance that drowns its reader
in an intoxicating tale of death and degradation, with an absolutely masterful
ending. Kraus has a beautifully twisted mind. More, please!"
—Zac Brewer,
New York Times bestselling author of the Chronicles of Vladimir Tod series

"Kraus's careful prose gifts Mr. Finch with a voice that retains a sheen of elegance
even as it repulses readers with macabre imagery. And still, when his occasional efforts
at reform fail, Mr. Finch becomes an oddly pitiable character."
—*Kirkus Reviews*

"Wild, intense, creepy, gross, and impeccably written."
—Andrew Smith, award-winning author of *Grasshopper Jungle* and *Winger*

"Taking on the big questions of the meaning of life, the purpose of death, and
good versus evil, this first half of a giant-size epic skillfully blends historical fiction,
dark humor, and horror to push readers right to the brink."
—*Booklist*

THE DEATH AND LIFE OF
ZEBULON FINCH

VOLUME ONE

AT THE EDGE OF EMPIRE

Also by Daniel Kraus

The Death and Life of Zebulon Finch,
Volume Two: Empire Decayed

The Monster Variations

Rotters

Scowler

Trollhunters (with Guillermo del Toro)

THE DEATH AND LIFE OF
ZEBULON FINCH

VOLUME ONE

AT THE EDGE OF EMPIRE

AS PREPARED BY THE ESTEEMED FICTIONIST,

MR. DANIEL KRAUS

SIMON & SCHUSTER BFYR

New York | London | Toronto | Sydney | New Delhi

An imprint of Simon & Schuster Children's Publishing Division

1230 Avenue of the Americas, New York, New York 10020

This book is a work of fiction. Any references to historical events, real people, or real places are used fictitiously. Other names, characters, places, and events are products of the author's imagination, and any resemblance to actual events or places or persons, living or dead, is entirely coincidental.

Text copyright © 2015 by Daniel Kraus

Cover illustration copyright © 2015 by Ken Taylor

All rights reserved, including the right of reproduction in whole or in part in any form.

SIMON & SCHUSTER BFYR is a trademark of Simon & Schuster, Inc.

For information about special discounts for bulk purchases, please contact Simon & Schuster Special Sales at 1-866-506-1949 or business@simonandschuster.com.

The Simon & Schuster Speakers Bureau can bring authors to your live event. For more information or to book an event, contact the Simon & Schuster Speakers Bureau at 1-866-248-3049 or visit our website at www.simonspeakers.com.

Also available in a SIMON & SCHUSTER BFYR hardcover edition

Cover design by Lizzy Bromley

Interior design by Hilary Zarycky

The text for this book was set in Adobe Jenson Pro.

Manufactured in the United States of America

First SIMON & SCHUSTER BFYR paperback edition October 2016

2 4 6 8 10 9 7 5 3 1

The Library of Congress has cataloged the hardcover edition as follows:

Kraus, Daniel, 1975–

The death and life of Zebulon Finch. Volume one, At the edge of empire /
as prepared by the esteemed fictionist, Daniel Kraus.—First edition.

pages cm

Summary: "The story follows Zebulon Finch, a teenager murdered in 1896 Chicago who inexplicably returns from the dead and searches for redemption through the ages"
—Provided by publisher.

ISBN 978-1-4814-1139-4 (hardcover : alk. paper)

ISBN 978-1-4814-1141-7 (eBook)

[1. Murder—Fiction. 2. Dead—Fiction.] I. Title. II. Title: At the edge of empire.

PZ7.K8672De 2015

[Fic]—dc23

2014039293

ISBN 978-1-4814-1140-0 (pbk)

TO

MR. GRANT WILLIAM ROSENBERG

OF CHICAGO, LATELY OF PARIS

THIS BOOK,

WHICH OWES GREATLY TO HIS FRIENDLY COUNSEL,

IS

Respectfully Inscribed

BY

THE AUTHOR

OVERTURE

———◦«(◦)»◦———

Beneath the World Trade Center
New York City, New York

L ET US BEGIN WITH THIS:

I am seventeen years old.

And also this:

I have been seventeen years old for over a century.

Even as I lay down these first few lines of what I intend to be the definitive chronicle of my miserable existence, I can hear Héctor apply the final blanket of cement to my tomb. Héctor, it turns out, is the long-awaited hero of this tragicomic opera. It is he who agreed to wall me inside of this chamber, first with plank-wood, then cement, then brick, and, at last, cement again. It is the greatest favor a human being has ever paid me and it shan't go unremarked upon, not even by a degenerate of legend such as myself.

My dear Héctor. Such men were rare when I was born in 1879. More than a hundred years later, I find they are rarer still. He is built like a wardrobe, his boxy torso denotive of his Mayan heritage, his slicked onyx hair and brushy mustache testimony to his laudable ignorance of fashion. He has nobler concerns. His wife. Their five children. Squirreling enough away to graduate the lot of them from an apartment that, he has told me in broken English, chatters at night with *cucarachas*.

So it is for virtuous reasons that he accepted my substantial cash offer. The windfall for him and his family will be great; so, too, is the

3

risk. Should we be discovered, both of us would be imprisoned posthaste—of piddling consequence to me but a dire situation indeed for Héctor's family, who would swiftly fall victim to the vilest cockroaches the city has to offer.

But we shall not be discovered. Héctor may be without formal education but he is most assiduous. What's more, the man is purehearted; not once during our delicate process of negotiation did he recoil at my yechy stench or wrinkle his nose at the leathery skin showing beneath my long hood and betwixt my cuffs and gloves.

Before he sealed the final fist-sized hole connecting me to fresh air, Héctor peered inside and asked once more if I wished to call it off. It was compassion I saw in his somber brown eyes; I recognized the emotion even though, for decades, I'd kept a lion tamer's distance from it. Meanwhile, emotions far more familiar to me fought like the lions themselves: my zeal for life clawed to shreds by a paralyzing confusion of purpose; my pride of independence gnawed away by shame for those left behind; my confidence of character swallowed down by frightful realizations, always arriving too late, that I'd failed myself, and others, again and again.

"Thank you," said I. "But no."

"I wait a day. Come back, knock-knock. You change opinion, maybe."

"Do not think of me again. That is an order."

"You're the boss, Mr. Finch."

But his reluctance was obvious. To him I seem like a teenager with a lifetime still ahead of me. He cannot fathom my motivations and I know that my entombment will forever haunt his dreams. Why else do you think I made his payment so handsome?

"Good-bye, Héctor. Take care of your family."

He gave quite a pause before nodding.

"*Que le vaya bién. Adiós.*"

Héctor knows how to build a wall. In seconds he was gone. And so was the world, every last wicked, wonderful speck of it. For a time I did not stir, so laden was I by the disappointment that manacled my remaining three limbs. I had hoped—so fervently had I hoped!—that the darkness of this chamber would be indistinguishable from the darkness of Death that has claimed every person I have ever known, ever hated, ever loved, ever killed. Alas, no. It is just dark. And only I, as usual, have been called upon to serve a never-ending sentence.

Calling this final home of mine a *closet* would be generous. It is a rhomboidal surplus shaped by accident from the steel girders and concrete foundations propping up the skyscraper above. I am lower than the lowest subway level, deeper than the deepest culvert of electricity and sewage. This is a netherworld restricted to those underpaid drudges like Héctor who have earned security clearance. It is a space so narrow that, just shy of six feet, I cannot lay outstretched, so foreshortened I cannot stand. No matter. Héctor's penultimate favor was to run a power cord into this locker, and from that cord dangles a single lightbulb.

There is something brave about this bulb. I think it shall endure. My task here, after all, should not last more than a few measly months. Before me, on a child's school desk that Héctor installed, is a box of pencils (ink pens I deemed too vulnerable to the subterrestrial chill), a cheap plastic pencil sharpener, and a stack of brand new spiralbound notebooks, the same kind children tote to school; oh, would that I had known such a conventional life!

My right hand, the only one left, is supple enough to grip these pencils. This is what matters. The rest of me—well, I am long past the point of narcissism. The vandalized condition of my skin no longer infuriates me; my missing chunks of flesh are irrelevant; the wounds suffered from a hundred conflicts serve as plot reminders, nothing more. Down here it is dreadfully cold and I can feel—as much as I "feel" anything—the chill where my leg bones are exposed to open air.

But that leg has lost its wandering wont; it does not itch to kick free of Héctor's barricade and walk once more upon the face of the Earth, and for that I am gladdened. Too much harm has been wrought by me in your overworld of sunshine and noise. What, I ask you, is the foremost attribute of youth? It is hope—but not for me it isn't. What buds of that emotion I once had have frozen over a hundred winters.

My hunch is that your schoolmarms repeated to you the same old saw mine repeated to me: history, they chanted, is written by the victors. Thus the contributions I've made to your world, debatable though their worth, have been all but wiped from the records. Any accounts that you've read of me were, at best, unauthorized, and at worst, spurious and hateful, none more so than those centering around what they now call the Savage Tragedy of 1983. You are better than those muckrakers. You deserve the naked truth.

For that reason I have enshrined myself here in order to set the record straight, to fashion for you a complete autobiography before I commit myself to an eternity of darkness. It is a record of what I lost: Death. Of how I lost it: Pride. Of what I sought: Redemption and Peace—and Salvation, too; was that too high for me to reach? Of what I found: Failure. Of how I failed: in every way possible. When this tomb of mine is discovered following some entertaining future apocalypse, I will be but powder that an archaeologist blows from the topmost notebook before turning the page with an antisepticized tweezer. What a relaxing fate for me, don't you agree?

But soft! Can't you hear the orchestra reach its crescendo? This overture is finishing. Héctor, that most complaisant of ushers, has closed the odeum doors. Dearest Reader, slip your gloved hand over my elbow and allow me to escort you to our box—a cramped one, to be sure, but with a view unrivaled. It is time to find a comfortable seat befitting an epic telling. You shall complain to me that the composer is indulgent, the librettist mad. I shall encourage you to give the drama time to bloom before passing final judgment. Many urgent questions will be raised as the opera progresses. Will they be answered? Oh, Reader, you charm me. Would it be good theater if they weren't?

PART ONE

1879–1896

———◦《◎》◦———

In Which Your Hero's Life Of Crime Is Confessed;
Includes Meditations On Love And Violence;
Also, Your Hero's Callous Murder.

I.

AWAKENING FROM DEATH WAS like standing aboard a canoe amid the keeling swells of the Great Lake Michigan. Indeed, that selfsame lake was storming before me on the seventh of May of 1896, at both 7:44 in the evening when I was murdered and at 8:01 in the evening when I was resurrected, a fact I am sure of because the last (and first) thing I saw was my Excelsior pocket watch, an object that had no equal when it came to putting a smile on the old mug.

It was but a year prior, at age sixteen, that I had stolen the watch off a fat innkeeper who should've known better than to play dumb, which he did, and right at the moment that I was loosening a few of his teeth with my most talented knuckles. I was thus compelled to not only leave him as I did, with his blood and piss dribbled merrily about, but to go the extra step of filching everything he had on his person, which included, to my astonishment, the Excelsior, the precise model I had pined for in shop windows for months.

Never had I owned anything so fine (and never would I again), with its sun-dappled gold plating, machinery delicate as grasshopper legs, and a *tick, tick, tick* like the sound of a man's fibula before it shatters from pressure. It made me feel good just to look at the Excelsior, particularly during fretful periods, which is exactly why I was fondling it on the foggy beachfront of Lake Michigan when some no-good bastard son of a bitch did what he did and murdered me, crept up and shot me in the back, a bullet through the heart, and down I went, into the sand, dead as meat.

Let us not fritter away another second.

I shall describe to you what it is like to die.

Most humans conceive of the afterlife as a reward of stillness after a long life of continual movement. This is only half correct. Death, sad to say, is no blissful repose atop a cloud hammock, nor is it a carefree float amid the celestial ether. Death is a suicide dive off an incalculable cliff, a free fall of such pulverizing force that you become molten, brand new every instant. This, Reader, is the exhilarative glory of Death, a motion so perpetual that all sense of self is scrubbed away and you become a Nothing in Particular, rebirthed through the Uterus of Time.

Oh!—it was wondrous. Brief!—but wretchedly, painfully wondrous.

For me, this paradise ended seventeen minutes after it began. I awoke not with the candied liquors of an Elysium feast upon my tongue but the bitterest sand. My first breath with reawakened lungs was a wretched one; I felt, residual from my Death, the touch of Gød. The surprise was that His touch was so physical—it was right there in my stomach, tickling and scraping. I rose to custard knees and doggie-walked toward the surf to get away, but Gød's touch responded by abandoning the pheasant, gravy, and tankard-loads of ale in my belly and scaling my throat.

Gød—for what He has done to me, I shall forever deface His name with a slash.

No stranger to inebriation, I positioned myself to vomit up our Almighty Lord. I had a fancified notion that the Holy Vomit would shoot like sunshine through the gray fog and instead of the familiar sound of retching I would hear Handel's *Hallelujah Chorus*. A willing choirboy, I parted my lips.

What emerged from inside me was a damp and disgruntled mayfly. Dreadfully disappointing, no? Having moseyed into my open mouth during those seventeen minutes of death, the insect had panicked upon my resurrection and climbed its way back up my esophagus. I watched the beslobbered bug drop to the sand, be twirled by a lick of surf, and then fly away imperiously, as if I had called it a schoolyard name.

Pocket watch palmed, I collapsed to my side, scared and confused, helpless and friendless. I closed my weary eyes. Still, I could hear each thunderous roll of the lake and feel each passing second of the Excelsior. The tide washed o'er my lips. My clothes heavied. I asked the tide to drag me away to a fitting resting spot for a Nothing in Particular—the unreturnable depths of the Great Lake!—and, given a half hour more, it did just that.

II.

YOU MAY BE ASKING YOURSELF how a young man so gifted of language (thank you) and of obvious high breeding (you are too kind) found himself on the wrong end of a bullet. Brace yourself for a cruel shock, Dearest Reader. Near the end of the nineteenth century there were a great many people who would have accepted—nay, celebrated!—my premature death at age seventeen. One of them, it so happens, was a man whose very vocation was violence, and who, I came to believe, chose to turn that violence upon me.

His name was Luca Testa. He was the ascendant leader within a crime organization known as the Black Hand. I am not so conceited to presume that you are familiar. After all, there is no telling how many millennia these humble notebooks of mine have traveled. You could be reading this from your private space rocket in the year 3000! So let me explain how two men of wildly different backgrounds— but of similar rabid ambition—came to be acquainted.

It is stinging irony that my final act on Earth is to write a book. I still recall the second-floor study of my childhood, the shelf of spines lettered with the surnames of the damned: Brontë, Hardy, Dickens, Flaubert, Hawthorne, Dumas. The idea of imitating those loathed tormentors of my youth nauseates me. I am a young man utterly bereft of imagination, aside from imagining how a fellow's finger will sound when I break it or imagining the cut and hue of a girl's undergarments.

Writing was the bane of my youth, each letter and number learned at ruler's end while other boys my age rioted in alleyways within earshot of my cloistered study. My mother and the worthless coxcombs she employed as tutors never received so much as a cheeky word from me, the meek student. I was that overfed with knowledge, that sick with learning.

What's that, Reader? You doubt the exaggerations of a snot-nosed schoolboy? Permit me to provide specifics. 'Twas an hour of arithmetic before breakfast to stir the appetite for scholarship. (By age eight I knew the value of n. By age ten I had matured to know a harder lesson: that you cannot know the value of n—it changes its mind on you, the fickle bitch.) Then a break for fish and eggs, followed not by a final course of sweet rolls but rather the tasteless hardtack of algebra. Yes, back to the well-windowed second-floor child's study for me, where every infernal dash and dot bled the day of its bright promise. After that, classical studies—literature, language, history, music, art, archeology, philosophy—bracketed by the afternoon's dry climax of geography, economics, science, and religion.

The blame for my over-education cannot be placed solely upon the corseted back of Mrs. Abigail Finch. A savvy prosecutor would also finger my dear old pop, Mr. Bartholomew Finch, whose fault it is that we had so much goddamned money in the first place. I knew little about him beyond that he wore a waxed mustache and stylish chapeau, but word had it that he was a self-styled "dynamitier" who demolished everything from buildings to bridges to mountains, canvassing the country by rail alongside his famously delicate cargo, thrilling observers with the disregard with which he slung his explosives from one dray to the next.

Generally it is bad business to bomb too much of the city you call home, so the country's leading dynamitier had established residence in Chicago, purchased an enormous house, and inserted into that house, as one might two porcelain dolls, a young wife and, shortly thereafter, their first and only child. Bartholomew Finch then skipped town to go blow shit up, a lot of it, thereafter making only cameo appearances.

I find some satisfaction in this description of my pop. From all accounts, he was a man unburdened by the excessive vocabulary and needless dogma that would weigh down his heir. Had we been anything other than father and son, I suspect we might have shared a beer or a hooker or at least some randy stories in the back of the saloon. As it was, though, I'd have rather liked to strangle the fellow, for it was his absence that locked Abigail and me into fateful impasse.

Paintings suspended about our home depicted Abigail Finch as a toothsome bride possessed of a blushing demeanor, but these still lifes lied. It is my belief that Abigail felt wasted by her absentee husband; a lady of her standing could not gallivant about town unescorted. From these holes poked into her pride sprung bitter founts. Some mothers, or so I assumed, might enjoy observing their child at play. Abigail preferred to stare out windows. Some mothers might dress their child in silly costumes to motivate mirthmaking. Abigail took distorted pleasure in ordering the finest of gowns for herself, only to wrap them in bags and stow them inside a closet.

From time to time, she shuddered as if feeling one of Bartholomew's distant detonations. To her, the Chicago beyond our property lines was in perennial post-explosion, the streets filled with debilitating debris and the air unbreathable from nitroglycerin smog. Having lost a husband to these dangerous elements, she was determined to raise her son as a man of walls, chairs, desks, inkwells, and pens.

Each day I was laced into Little Lord Fauntleroy ensembles as restrictive as iron maidens: tight velvet jackets, hard ruffled collars, snug cuffed knee-pants, and buckled shoes. Though I looked as if attired for an afternoon outing, these were but dress rehearsals for an opening night that never came.

"You shall not drift about the country like your father," Abigail would declare while knotting some infernal bow about my neck. "You shall stay at hand and be a good boy. The best boy."

"But Mama," I'd plead. "I just want to go out and play."

My, the brutishness with which she raked a comb through my hair! Never would my sheer locks hold the girlish ringlets into which she ironed them. It was a source of perpetual guilt.

"The proper term is *Mother*," said she. "Not *Mama*."

"But can't you hear the other boys? It's so nice and sunny out."

"And dirty. The city is filthy. Do you want to soil your clothing?"

Debate never moved me an inch.

"No, Mama," said I.

"*Mother*, Zebulon. We are a proper family."

We were anything but! Our Sunday walks to and from church offered my best gulps of fresh air, and when possible I wiggled from my leash and rushed up to other boys with far dirtier knees than I, only to be too shy to ask to be taught their games of cards or jacks. The Chicago streets might as well have been the Galápagos Islands; I was a stranger there, but smuggled home rare specimens, from rust-burred bottle caps and teeth-scored horse bits to sticks.

Yes, sticks! How I adored a good, sturdy stick! So gnarled, even

17

vulgar they looked inside our scrubbed and laundered confines, so black were the shavings of bark they left upon white lace doilies. My favorite stick of all time boasted a ninety-degree bend and, having spied lads on Sundays doing their best cowboy or Indian impersonations, I recognized it as a prize. During bathroom breaks from my tutors, I rollicked about the house with the stick in hand, dueling famous outlaws and taking down creeping henchmen with impossible hip shots.

Confiscation was inevitable; I was a careless child. Abigail made me set the stick upon the floor before she pinched it through a handkerchief and flung it out back as you might a dead mouse. She then led me to the bathroom, filled the sink with scalding water, and waited for me to to lower my hands. Tears welled from dual pains—the burn of the water and the loss of my stick—but I did not let myself cry. I swore to my bright pink hands that one day I would find myself a better gun, even a real one, and oh! How I would use it.

Lend me your fingers, Reader, and your toes as well, so that together we might tally the times I weathered such sanctions. I so wished to please Mama—sorry, *Mother*; let us agree upon *Abigail*—but came to accept myself as a grave disappointment. Why else wouldn't this woman traffic in hugs or kisses, those currencies of affection so prevalent in my storybooks?

No cruelty leveled by Abigail Finch oppressed me more than French. It got so that I could manage but a few hours per night of sleep. My first duty each morn, after dressing, was to enter Abigail's room, stand rigid before her bed, and recite five minutes of memorized French narrative while she scrutinized every lilt of lip or curl of tongue. She frowned at each stuttered flub and snapped her fingers to make me start over. On bad days, I was there for an hour. But what glorious serenity felt I when I got it right! My mother appeared to float above the sheets, taken away by my expert telling.

For five years I believed that hogwash. At age thirteen, I misspoke an obscenity and my sonhood was forever altered. What I meant to recite was *Le garçon a regardé le soleil se coucher sur la butte* (The boy watched the sun set over the butte.). But *B* and *P* sounds are slippery, and the last word came out *pute*—a vulgar word for "whore." I nattered past it, perceiving my blunder only after beginning the next paragraph. At first, I thanked my luck that Abigail hadn't noticed. A mere minute later, I became irked. My sterile life frustrated me, and the idea of getting into real trouble was strangely enticing.

Again I smuggled the word into a sentence. Again she evinced no ill reaction. I used it twice in repetition: *pute, pute.* She nodded along. With an icy thrill, I began to insert into my monologue supplementary smut: *chatte, merde, connard.* She remained satisfied so long as I pronounced my profanities with pluck. When at last I was excused, I had to hide my trembling hands.

Abigail Finch did not speak French.

The language, as best as I could guess, had been chosen not for the practical purpose of a future business trip I might take abroad, but rather for the fantasies that French allowed her, of Parisian balls she'd never attend, of twinkling boardwalks along which she'd never stroll, of mystery, of romance, of love. My hundreds of hours of slavish study had nothing to do with me. I was just a knife in Abigail's silent fight against the deficiencies of Bartholomew.

So I was a knife, was I? Well, then, I would cut.

I started to fry my French in spite. *Vous êtes bête.* (You are stupid.) *Vous ne savez rien.* (You know nothing.) *Vous êtes méchante.* (You are mean to me.) *Je ne vous aime pas.* (I don't like you.) Abigail smiled gently and I felt rotten; she nodded wisely and I felt rottener. Loathing oozed from every pore, and rather than soak myself in its hot viscosity, I slopped it back upon her. *Je vous déteste, Maman, je vous déteste:* I hate you, Mother, I hate you.

From there the oaths only compounded.

Forgive me if I do not repeat them here.

These were the most hurtful things imaginable to say to a person, and I do not believe one can say such things day after day, and month after month, and continue to look into the eyes of the blasphemed. Nor could I look into my own—the reflection I saw inside every pewter teapot and glass clock face repelled me.

By the day I turned fourteen, I wanted nothing more than to escape the shame and guilt. Youth had served me only anguish; I was eager to leapfrog the teenage years, jump into the big, ugly boots of an adult, and do whatever it took to be, at long last, noticed. If I was fortunate, thought I, I'd become the antithesis of what Abigail wanted. I'd burp in public, guffaw rudely at burlesque, wear the same suit for days on end so that words (embarrassing to me for how stuffily I spoke them) became unnecessary to convey my surly nature.

That night, before I left, I tiptoed the path I'd taken to deliver hundreds of insulting French soliloquies and stood one last time at my mother's side. Even in sleep she was disgruntled. She clawed her pillow and gnawed her bottom lip. Curiosity got the best of me and I leaned over the bed, as careful as a lad of that age can be, and placed a kiss upon her troubled forehead. It was as nice as the books said, though a bit salty. I licked my lips clean and moved with some reluctance toward the door. I was sorry I could not be the boy that Abigail Finch had wanted, but glad that she might finally rest easy in my wake.

Au revoir, Maman.

III.

AND THAT, DEAREST READER, IS how I ducked the drab future aimed squarely between my eyes and began to ramble exciting ethnic neighborhoods, stealing every strange, spicy morsel I could, much of which fell out of a mouth agog in constant wonder. This boisterous, cantankerous, pugilistic city had hidden from me for too long.

Chicago of 1893 was a sensory carnival. The striped cloth awnings of taverns, druggists, and shoemakers snapped in lakefront wind; meat markets stank of hot blood; the glass bottles of milkmen made music as they were lifted from dairy wagons; locomotives coughed up oily clouds that settled as soot upon your skin; and horse-drawn undertakers' carriages clacked and clacked and clacked—the only sound that did not change in a town that was always changing.

Those first weeks were quite a challenge for the baby-fleshed Zebulon Finch! I slept in barns, on sidewalks, inside of factories that had left windows open. I became acquainted with creatures I'd never before met: lice, mice, roaches, and rats. Many a night I held back sobs while dreaming of my clean and comfortable bed, and yet I refused to go home. My sense of self-respect was a foundling, but born with a pair of strong knees.

Hunger gave me the boldness required to seek employment. I placed brick, scraped a hog-house floor, and scrubbed smelly horses.

My tender palms grew callouses of which I became obsessed. At night I'd stroke these rough patches in wonder. Look at me now, Mother! A proper hooligan at last! A lonely one, though, until a stint operating a paintbrush brought me into federation with a young Italian by the name of Giuseppe Fratelli.

Fratelli was my opposite. He spoke enthusiastic but patchy English and had no formal education at all, but possessed a rat's instinct for survival. After a long weekend spent painting a firehouse, he invited me to his uncle's tavern for a carafe of red wine, a drink with which I was unfamiliar. I found it sour, but Fratelli guzzled it like water, and soon enough we were arm in arm singing songs from the old country. It was my first bender, and despite the morning-after head-pounding, I enjoyed the hell out of it. My future, as I saw it, was filled with drunken binges and the resultant blotting away of unwelcome memories of my mother and father. I could not wait.

Never before had I a companion, and for a goodly while I behaved as Fratelli's shadow. He was but a handful of years older than I, but I idolized his fearless swagger, disrespect of elders, and forceful animalism, whether it be in pursuit of violence or *amore*. I endeavored to improve his English and in exchange he taught me where to find the nearest hostels, the cheapest markets, the warmest baths, and the least revolting outhouses.

Little Italy was a hazardous place for a boy of my refinement. Try as I did to ply the slang of the street, the truth was that I sounded like a blue blood looking to get mugged. Thus I took Fratelli's lead and focused upon the physical. I engaged in my first fist fight; the pummel upon my flesh was frightening, but when it was through each bruise panged in the most invigorating way. The desperado fantasies

I'd spun while shooting my stick-gun in Abigail's house had prepared me quite well for these rowdy new habits.

The painting work eventually dried up (so to speak) and I did not see Fratelli for many weeks. When next I did, he was looking fine in a Prince Albert frock and wide-brimmed fedora, and I asked him what business had so quickened his income. He looked about furtively before beckoning me into the shady sort of establishment within which two enterprising young men could have a confidential consultation.

There he told me of the dire lack of employment that had led him to risk the unthinkable. It was not difficult to find reports of the violent *La Mano Nero* gang in newspapers, but Fratelli revealed to me that the title of "the Black Hand" could be borrowed by anyone possessed of pen, paper, and desperation. He described the note he had written to a grocer demanding one hundred and fifty dollars or else the Black Hand would cut off the noses of his children. "A veil will not hide the wound," was the line of which Fratelli was proudest. I was in shock. Had he actually received the money?

"Every and each penny," replied he, flashing me a winning grin.

I was jealous, all right. By then, ambition to improve my social position burned so fiercely that I'd made it my purpose to understand the Italians among whom I spent my time. Largely, I found, they hailed from hamlets in southern Italy, and many wished only to generate enough wealth to return to Sicily or Campania and purchase land for their waiting families. Practical men, and yet *La Mano Nero* was on their lips, each utterance followed by a kiss to their crucifixes.

In other words, they were ripe for the picking.

Was I ever the nervous one! I had chosen as my first target a tailor and written my extortion letter a dozen times over. Finally I stamped it with the famous trademark—a fist rendered in black ink—and delivered it beneath the tailor's door with specific instructions regarding payment.

On the appointed day, the tailor indeed arrived, looking green. Taking a great breath, I walked past the tailor and paused to ask him the time of day—that was our signal. He mashed his lips as if dying to spit invectives. Instead he stuffed an envelope into my hand and charged away, eyes watering. My heart was an eager little woodpecker as I dove into the nearest alley and counted my winnings. The two hundred dollars was all there. I whooped. I couldn't wait to find Fratelli and flaunt it.

Instead what I found were a dozen new targets for extortion. The first purchase I made with my profit was a ream of paper and a flamboyant set of pens. My fantasies were a-flutter with the kinds of depraved acts I could describe, the astounding sums I could command. My second payment was for a room of my own, and nestled within, I sat at the furnished desk, cracked my knuckles, and set to writing.

What I had overlooked was that the Black Hand's clout came from a willingness to make good on threats. Few American thugs I had heard of would slash a man's face in broad daylight just to make off with his wallet. But these immigrants and their *mafiosi* were a different breed. Merchants began to neglect my limp ultimatums. My money dwindled. I became anxious. Still, I would not be forced to return to Abigail Finch. As tough as I'd become so far, I needed to become tougher, and be quick about it.

I set my sights upon Mr. Perfetta, a reputed saddlemaker and bridlemaker possessed of a comely wife and gurgling baby. I sent a letter, a strong one, full of phrases like "you have been adjudged to hand over money or life" and "woe to you if you do not resolve to comply." I demanded payment of five hundred dollars and specified a due date; Mr. Perfetta, however, ignored it. I sent a follow-up letter stating how I was "sick and tired of your dally" and that inattention to this second chance would "bring down your ruination" and in the margin rendered my finest black hand emblem yet. The new due date came and passed.

So it was that I girded myself for violence. Not wishing to prolong the wait, I journeyed to his shop. I was early and found this note upon the door:

Dear Mr. Hand—

Thank you for your notice of payment due. I regret to say that I am already obligated to another Mr. Hand, who has demanded from me the even more impressive sum of $1,000 and who has insisted I produce "every and each penny." I do wish that the various Mr. Hands would call a meeting to agree upon their figures. In the meantime I will resume the production of saddles and bridles, both of which I can offer at a fair price should you be in need.

With respect—
Louis Perfetta

Even before I gathered my dropped jaw I recognized the phrasing of "every and each penny" and identified my competitor as none other than Fratelli. The unfairness of it was too much to stomach. Fratelli possessed every advantage over me—he was, after all, Italian!—while I had been reduced of late to stealing windowsill baked goods. Fueled by a childish frenzy, I accosted every sleepy-eyed palooka on the block with the only word that mattered—"Fratelli!"—until rewarded by a pointed finger. By nightfall I had closed in on a café outside of which stood Fratelli smoking a cigarette with wine-stained fingers.

Humiliated, hungry, and tired, I challenged him. He responded with familiar oaths. *Ciuccio! Finocchio! Stronzo!* In retaliation I unleashed my full vocabulary. He could not keep up and that shamed him. He slapped my face; I slugged his head. There was a scuffle, the sort to which I'd become accustomed, and then, somehow, he got his hands on an empty wine bottle. This he used as a club, a capital idea had not a lucky snatch of my hand robbed him of it upon first strike.

Reader, I know not how to plead. Fratelli was bedecked in rings, fobs, and a pelisse, while I, Zebulon Finch, son of Bartholomew, could feel the crusted filth of my undergarments. How woefully easy was the act of lowering a blunt weapon! The bottle crashed upon Fratelli's forehead, driving him to a seated position. There was blood. His fingers clawed at my throat. To ward them off, I lowered the bottle again. More blood, this time arterial.

Bestial now, I hurried back toward Mr. Perfetta. I would show him *exactly* which Mr. Hand he was dealing with. Within minutes, though, I was intercepted by a hulking trio, two of whom gripped me by the arms, while the third relieved me of my weapon, removed a handkerchief from his coat pocket, and made a fastidious display of wiping clean his fingers.

Said he, "My name is Luca Testa."

His accent glided like lotion, quite at odds with a posture that made it look as if he hung from a coat rack. He folded the handkerchief, smoothed the center part of his otter-sleek hair, and offered a grin made up of identical round teeth.

"And I am the Black Hand."

Such rodomontade deserved the scornful laughter I gave it. Testa muttered "*andiamo*" and his men-at-arms ushered me several blocks south, down unlit stone steps, and into an underground trattoria populated by whispering men with gleaming pinkie rings. I was terrified, yes, but also thrilled. Even were my throat about to be slit, I was more alive than I'd ever felt inside Abigail Finch's prison.

We took seats at a corner table. Testa sat on one side with legs crossed and fingers laced upon a knee. I squeezed between the two heavies. Testa clapped his hands and a man brought over a bottle of wine and poured glasses, one for Testa, one for me. I bolted most of it in a single go and saw Testa's amused smirk. I was fourteen but felt half that; I urged myself to slow down, calm down, listen, and think.

Testa had a vision and with a liquescent lilt described it. The American offspring of *La Mano Nero*, said he, had carved itself a reputation, but how far could it go with sloppy firebombings, stabbings, and kidnappings? Centralization of power was the key to upward mobility, and it was he, Luca Testa, who would midwife this phase. Finding candidates for soldiers was easy, laughed he, for nothing was more difficult for a criminal to hide than success. Fratelli's gaudy costuming had recommended him highly, but his meeting with Testa had been canceled due to a random attack by a psychopath named Zebulon Finch.

Fortunately for me, my rash behavior warmed the cockles of Testa's heart. True, I wasn't Italian, but a young *animale* like myself was just what the man needed. I'd be supplied with several sets of smart clothing, the newest model of derringer, and money enough to throw at drink or women—provided neither got in the way of business. All I

27

had to do was fire the occasional bullet, break the occasional nose or finger or arm or leg. Could I do that?

Yes, thought I with some surprise. *I think that I can.*

Testa added that I'd also have to start the occasional fire. He asked if I knew anything about dynamite and I wondered if my old pop, wherever he was, could feel his ears burning.

Testina d'agnello was brought before us on a silver platter and Testa basked in the aroma. It was a fitting repast: baked lamb head, cloven in two, with both eyeballs still in place to monitor its own consumption. Abigail Finch would have fired the cook who dared place such a dish before her. I, therefore, was impatient to dig into the brains—the best part, insisted Testa.

My second bite was on my fork when I heard myself ask, quite gaily, if I might be allowed to compose extortion notes. Testa stopped chewing his brains. The shoulders at either side of me bristled. I filled the silence by saying that I fancied myself not half bad at writing and that my ink fists were coming out more realistic each time I drew them and if he thought he could use some help—

"*Che cazzo?*" Testa surveyed his associates. "Is this a playwright I'm hiring? Was that Willie Shakespeare giving the business to Fratelli? Was that a feathered quill bashing in that dago's head?"

I shan't forget that gut-twisting moment before he broke into laughter. His relieved colleagues chuckled back. Testa wiped at his eyes and shook his head in disbelief as he took another forkful of brains.

"This kid. This kid's all right. Look, you nut. No openings for playwrights at the moment. Not in the market for poets either. But do what you did tonight, when I tell you to do it, and you can fancy yourself whatever you like. *Capisci?*"

IV.

CAME TO KNOW THE ACRID smell of piss evacuated by the bladders of cornered men. I became attuned to the eggshell crunch of an Adam's apple giving way beneath my pressing thumbs. There is a certain force required to tear off an ear and I can describe it. Italian never made much sense to me but I came to recognize the words being repeated by victims during the same critical moments: *Salvami. Madonna. Rapidamente. Mi dispiace, sono molto dispiaciuto.*

Half of my cohorts were teenagers. I had a hunch that Testa liked his thugs young for the ease with which he could transfix them with danglings of reward. Most were runaways like myself, though from backgrounds more unwashed. I affected their boorish demeanors as best I could: contests of belching or urination, boasts about innovations in the thriving business of coercion, and meticulous chronicles of perversities shared with fast floozies.

Eighteen months after taking up with Testa's Black Hand, I met Wilma Sue. Do not think that I hadn't enjoyed other whores before her. Ridiculous! Fratelli had dragged me to a cathouse within a week of our first bread-breaking, and though I cannot say my performance there was laudable, my confidence and ability doubled—no, tripled!; no, quadrupled!—with subsequent visits. Identifying yourself as one of Testa's men had advantages. Rarely did I wait for service and often I was allowed to keep tabs. I was

29

tireless in my pursuit of orgasm. I was, after all, fifteen.

Wilma Sue lived and worked alongside three other demimondes on the second floor of Patterson's Inn, a serviceable club that sold their beer flat but in large quantities and encouraged their women to hold court near the first-floor balustrade. My first time with Wilma Sue was coming off a fabulous drunk and I fear that I was a bellering lout as she helped me up the stairs, sat me on the bed, yanked off my boots, and set to stripping my relevant half.

As a boudoir artist she was more than competent. Even in my sapped state she knew how to bring me to attention. I was in no condition for rolling over so she climbed on and did the work herself, though my most vibrant memory from the intimacy was her strange, tilted expression, as if I were murmuring something of great interest.

The next morning I was struck by how beautiful she looked brushing her brown hair in the peach rays of light, and so I brought out some more bills and asked for another go. Her fine pale face and darling underbite was untroubled at my request and I found myself comparing our ages (I estimated she was nineteen) and wondering if I was as proficient at my job as she was at hers. Finally she responded that another round would be acceptable, yet she continued to brush. After a spell she asked for my name. I told her and she frowned.

"Zebulon? So sophisticated for one so young."

I shrugged. "Last name's Finch."

"Like the bird? You're no bird. Puppy, maybe."

"Puppy?" It was my turn to frown.

The glissando of her laughter swept away my irritation like dandelion fuzz on a breeze.

"Fine, not a puppy. A proud, healthy horse." She brought a hand to her forehead, playing the fool. "Of course! I should've said that at first. All young men appreciate comparisons to horses."

In the off chance that you do you not frequent brothels (you poor thing), let me assure you that it is atypical of trollops to goad customers in this fashion. Wilma Sue, though, jabbed as if it were sport, and instead of gall I experienced a pleasant flutter of excitement. The corner of her lips climbed in anticipation of further skirmish. I was glad to oblige.

"Oh, yes, miss," said I. "A horse indeed. You'll want to find yourself a saddle if you don't wish to be bucked."

"Bucked?" She turned on her stool. "What kind of horse are you?"

"Just a horse like any horse. I see you've got a couple of apples there. Let me show you how well I nibble them."

Wilma Sue brayed like an ass and clapped a hand over her mouth as if that might retract the unfeminine sound.

"No, do not blush," said I. "It's good to know that you are a donkey. A donkey and a horse—this union might not be as unnatural as I feared."

"You're a cruel one." Her carriage was one of complete relaxation, her spine curled, the ruffles of her nightgown gathering over the soft dome of her stomach. It was the most fetching posture I had ever seen held by a professional. "Such cruelty deserves a name. I will not call you Mr. Horse, for fear that you'll call me Miss Donkey."

"The other girls call me Zebby."

She dismissed this with a wave of her hand. "You have a middle name?"

"Aaron."

The sardonic lines of her face smoothed and she placed both

31

hands over her heart. She nodded, struck speechless in a way I still do not understand, and I nodded back, glad that I had bumbled into an answer so favorably received. There was silence then; I shuffled my feet and discovered the money still in my hand. I held it out to her but for a time she did not look at it, as if hoping to sustain an alternate reality for a few more seconds. When she removed her garments and reclined upon the bed I found myself mad with desire, not just for her luscious body but for that unguarded smile and acerbic tongue.

From that day forward Wilma Sue became not just my favorite prostitute but my favorite person. Oh, I hear your doubt fulminating across the centuries. "But Zebulon, old boy," you chide, "had you a single other acquaintance with a woman to whom to compare this girl?" The answer: no, not really—and what of it? I required no parade of the fairer gender down Western Avenue (though that sounds like good fun) so that I might juxtapose and judge, not when Wilma Sue, with her every sweet breath, rebutted each adverse aspect of womanhood I'd learned from Abigail Finch.

Under Abigail, my every word of English—and for a time, French—required exacting evaluation for accuracy and suitability before I voiced it. I'd be a dead man if I played that slowly with Wilma Sue, whose conversation demanded a spry tit for tat. Where Abigail had shrunk from the outer world and each new day's fresh frights, Wilma Sue was nosy, posing inquiries and immediate follow-ups regarding all I'd done since last we met. And of my elocution, that stigma nailed into me by Abigail Finch? Wilma Sue found it charming, particularly when used for lecherous repartee.

Put simply, she *liked* me. Not because I served her purpose, as I had Abigail Finch and still did Luca Testa, but because I was Zebulon Aaron Finch—the one and only.

In the privacy of Wilma Sue's room I was bellied with butter-flies and rabbity of heart. My muscles ached all day, if not all week, to press her girl parts against me, and the tilt of her spine when I entered suggested she wanted those girl parts pressed. Behind her closed door I dropped every crude pretense, engaged in solicitous intercourse, and laid so that I might feel her heart beat like a clock— *tick, tick, tick.* It was a rhythm over which we spent nights uncoupling from our unpalatable professions and discussing which wonders of Chicago the two of us might one day enjoy together: an egregious supper at the famous Allgauer's Fireside, a clackety streetcar ride to the North Shore beach, a trip up the preposterous piston-powered invention dubbed the "Ferris wheel."

Now, it is true that other men cycled through Wilma Sue's room. It was not my business. Yet I yearned to find fault in how those arro-gant bastards looked at me when they passed through the bar so that I might find an excuse to flatten their noses. I had to be careful. For a Black Hander to display affection for a person was to risk that per-son's safety. So I doused my silly, chivalric urges in alcohol and tried to celebrate how I'd become my own man. I made a good show of gruffness: I snarled over Scotch, stewed over stew.

There was no hiding my vocation from Wilma Sue, so often did I come to her bruised and eager for her brown paper and vinegar poul-tice. It was a heady time for Zebulon Finch. Newspapers doted upon the Black Hand like a favorite child and I became a fanatic collector of their breathless accounts, pasting into a scrapbook any headline of which I felt partially responsible. I could not resist sharing the com-pilation with Wilma Sue, and while we dawdled in bed I gave each headline my most orotund tone:

33

THOUSANDS IN TERROR SINCE BLACK HAND ATTACK WAVE

SIX INJURED BY FIRE, RESIDENTS PLEAD FOR PROTECTION

MILLIONAIRE DRIVEN TO EXILE BY RELENTLESS BLACK HAND

ITALIAN CRIME ORGANIZING—A PERILOUS CONDITION

Was it so wrong, my pride? Does not every boy long to begin adulthood with prodigious success? Chicago teetered upon a fulcrum that, should it swing in the direction of Testa, could change the centers of power and influence of the entire country—and I was at the center of it! From time to time, I fluffed my feathers before Wilma Sue's mirror and flapped about her room in the excitement of it all.

On this single subject, however, she did not match my mood. Shall I be truthful? It stung. Everything else about me—the socks I purchased, the way I wore my hair, my posture when I peed—she challenged until she had me riled enough to tear off my clothes, then hers, between hiccups of laughter. But regarding my job she maintained the reserve befitting a paid courtesan. Let me be truthful again despite how it pains: I attempted to purchase her opinion with cash, tight rolls of Black Hand dollars that I doled out in gross overage. *See?* I tried to say. *Can my line of work be so bad if it pays for pretty new dresses or knickers to replace those worn ones?*

What else could a girl in her position do? She took the money. Never, though, did she submit a word of gratitude.

On occasion, late of hour, after the awkward matter of payment was lost behind us, Wilma Sue would play with my gun. (By that, randy Reader, I refer to my sidearm!) I lodged no protest; she was the one living soul I trusted not to shoot me. Two years into my Testa tutelage, I'd traded my derringer for what I fantasized would become my signature weapon: an 1873 Colt single-action revolver known colloquially as the "Peacemaker." I relished the nickname even if "peace" was obverse to the Black Hand objective.

One night, Wilma Sue languidly popped the cylinder and let the six golden .45 caliber bullets drop silently to the sheets. She then arranged the Peacemaker upon the mattress in odd fashion, with the butt and open cylinder propping it into a triangle. Over the barrel she draped the edge of the bedsheet.

"Look, Aaron," said she. "It's a wee little house."

Abigail Finch had boiled my hands upon catching me with a gun-shaped stick. Seeing Wilma Sue look with affection upon a gun of actual polished silver jangled my insides with optimism. She was adjusting, thought I, to my criminal obligations.

"A house?" said I. "I'm afraid your architecture is too primitive. A teepee at best."

She set one bullet on its flat end beneath the sheet overhang.

"Here is wee little Zebulon Finch."

"Oh, come now. Don't I rate a larger caliber?"

She set a second bullet next to the first.

"And here is merry little Wilma Sue."

"Were you that unshapely, I doubt either of us would be merry."

She took up the other four bullets and arrayed them in nativity configuration.

"Children," announced she. "Two of them."

"The spitting image of their mother. And those other two?"

She shrugged.

"A dog, I think. Maybe a chicken?"

"A pastoral scene," declared I. "I might feel remorse now when forced to fire them."

The conversation left me discomfited. I shifted upon the bed so that the gun-house collapsed. I chambered the bullets, secured the cylinder, slid the gun into the holster upon the floor, and made a series of jokes, the best garrisons I had against the gleam I'd glimpsed in Wilma Sue's eyes as she watched the transmogrification of our bullet proxies back into nameless utensils of death.

In the end, Dearest Reader, our sad story must pass through the thorny thicket of February 12, 1895. I was sixteen and stood at Wilma Sue's stove fixing us tea while the battened window fought a howling winter storm. She'd been swaddled in blankets to her neck since I'd arrived thirty minutes prior with my coat cottoned with snow. We were too cold to converse, preferring to wait until we could bring our bodies together for warmth. Finally I could wait no longer and brought her the cup. As she dipped into the candlelight to accept it I noticed her consternation. I sat upon the edge of the mattress to enjoy the tentative stretching of her lips. She saw me watching and glared.

"What's the matter?" asked I.

"Well, this tea, for one. Your tea is for children."

"Or those with childlike minds. Hence, your drinking of it."

"Don't forget I'm older than you. If I'm a child, you're an infant."

"Then you must bare your breast and suckle me."

She rolled her eyes and sipped the unsatisfactory liquid. I crossed my legs and arms; it was freezing and I wanted into that bed.

"Tell me what's wrong," said I. "That dour face of yours."

She held the cup so that its steam clouded her face.

36

"You have a cut over your left eye."

I lifted a hand to my brow and felt wetness. I'd assumed the laceration had scabbed over. Hours earlier, I had bludgeoned a storekeeper with his broom in front of his twin daughters. As sometimes happened, my prey scored a lucky blow. The snow was still light when I was finished, so I headed down the block and got myself a leg of lamb. The woman who served it said nothing about the blood gushing from my head. Afterward I crossed the street and drank two beers. The man who poured them said nothing about the blood, not even when it made patterns upon his counter. The walk to Patterson's Inn was a long one and not one I managed without several more interactions. Blood shows quite well in the snow and yet no one I met said a word.

It was only here, in a cold black box that stank of cheap perfume and cheaper sweat, that there existed a person who cared about my physical body and, by extension, the possibility that one day, in the course of my duties, I might die. Death was the last thing upon which I made a habit of dwelling, and yet shivering beside Wilma Sue I had the abrupt, surprising notion that not only did I wish to avoid death but I wished to avoid injury, too, if it meant the happiness of this girl.

But such an arrangement required a pledge of commitment. Had I not made a competing pledge to Luca Testa?

I stood, shaken by these ideas, and went for my coat.

"Aaron."

"I'll find a doctor. Have this stitched."

"In this weather? I will take care of it. Get in."

"Doc Wallace won't be under the table quite yet. I know his tavern of choice."

"I'm wearing no clothes," she pouted.

37

Her underbite was enticing. It filled me with sadness.

"Yes, you are. I can see your collar. As well as the cuffs of your sleeves."

I pulled on my boots, grimacing at the slush puddled inside, and opened the door to the hallway. Noises to which I was intimately accustomed—drunken mayhem, general depravity—swept inside. It was this *other* intimacy, the one in this low-lit room, that would require the effort, not to mention the courage.

"My Aaron," said she. "My stupid Aaron."

The Peacemaker latched to my hip was heavy—heavy as a house, you might say.

"I'll be back, Miss Donkey." Something caught in my throat. "Keep the bed warm."

V.

I NEVER SAW HER AGAIN. That night I failed to find Doc Wallace but found his favorite pub all right, and drank until I sweated alcohol, which slid down my temples, partner to blood. I awoke squinting into morning light with a tin stein in my hand and stumbled out into the street. Turning left would lead me back to Patterson's and unanswered questions. I turned right and checked in with Jonesy, the man who acted as liaison between Testa and boys such as myself. There was no work for me that morning but I bumped into two of my fellow heavies and together we banged on the window of a pub, wakening the wild-haired proprietor. We drank throughout the day; only during gaps in the gulping and shouting did I allow myself to think of Wilma Sue and how she wanted me to give up this life, and for what? To love her? Best to drink such thoughts away. The night passed in the same delirium as had the afternoon, and the new day brought new misadventures, new debtors, new opportunities to intimidate and extort. Another day or two passed. Jonesy supplied me with an envelope of money. I spent two full days perusing shop windows and dreaming about which kind of pocket watch I could afford if I could just get myself to save up, which I could not. Soon I was watchless but dressed as fine as you please, and though it had been a full week since I'd seen Wilma Sue, a part of my brain—she may have called it the stupid part—believed that my fresh duds would dazzle her and we might blame our recent discussion on winter fevers and fall again into comfortable rhythms.

It was my habit at Pattersons' Inn to go directly to Wilma Sue's room. I put my ear to the door and right away knew that something was awry. Without ado I threw open the door and found a man looking annoyed and a woman covering herself. She was as skinny as a coyote and had a light mustache. I demanded the whereabouts of Wilma Sue. The man told me to get out of the fucking room. The coyote said that she did not know any "Wilmy Sue" but if this was the kind of thing that happened at Patterson's Inn then she would have to reconsider her employment.

I believed that I might be sick. I charged down the hall, kicking open other doors and finding girls in all states of undress, though not one shoulder or thigh or breast belonged to Wilma Sue. Downstairs I ran and took the bartender's shirt from across the bar. He began shouting out the name of Mr. Patterson. Presently the innkeeper materialized, wiping his hands on a towel. He smirked and said that Wilma Sue was gone and good riddance, for she had had too many customers—he said this pointedly—who overstayed their welcome. I stood there trembling as he left the room. My paralysis dissevered and I careened after Patterson, finding him in a dim closet counting boxes of produce.

He was a large man and not unafraid. Nor was I. I threw him against the shelves. Tomatoes toppled onto his shoulders and erupted upon the floor. It smelled of food and I experienced a swirl of panic that I'd never gotten around to dining with Wilma Sue at Allagauer's Fireside, never traveled with her on that street car to the North Shore beach, never held her hand at the top of the Ferris wheel, never saw how she looked in any setting aside from this dank, stinking rathole.

Patterson never had a chance. Between blows I accused him of casting out an angel and replacing her with a toothless, syphilitic witch. When muscle ache forced me to quit, my enemy was a twitching pink lump. I did as trained and emptied his pockets.

That, Dearest Reader, is how I came upon my Excelsior—bright, clicking, indifferent. Its metronome provided me with hope. It had divided hours in its patient fashion long before Wilma Sue had arrived and would continue in the face of her absence. The Excelsior promised time, plenty of it, practically an infinity, and if I kept it near me it might be as if I had climbed into Wilma Sue's bed after all. I slipped the watch into a pocket and felt the familiar, contented beating of her heart next to mine: *tick, tick, tick.*

I bolted through the snow. It was simple when you looked at the evidence with a cleared head. A man like Luca Testa demanded the full attention of his army and it would not escape his attention when a promising young soldier missed an appointment, or two, or three, because of extended lounging within the limbs of a common tramp.

Never had I been inside Testa's home but I knew as well as anyone its location. Two men pretending to read newspapers guarded the entrance. They knew me and put on grins. I grinned back and then cold-cocked the bigger one in the face. He wailed and fell to his knees. The other guard spat his toothpick, elbowed me aside, and kneeled down to assess the damage to his friend.

"Finch, you piece of shit. You want to talk to Jonesy, why don't you ask instead of getting violent? Ah, look at his nose. That's gonna break his mother's heart."

The vestibule was gilded with candleless sconces and vacant art frames and opened into a parlor both lavish and empty. Unopened crates contained the majority of the furniture and finery. A wide staircase to my left swept upward but before I could go for it a set of double doors parted and out came Jonesy, a bald, pear-shaped man possessed of the unique talent of making bow ties look intimidating. His heels made heavy clumps across the marble.

"You busted Pavia's nose, you know that, you *testa di cavolo?*"

The speed with which he had received this news amazed me, though I resigned myself to letting that particular mystery go unsolved. I reached into my jacket and withdrew my Peacemaker. Jonesy slumped his shoulders in exasperation.

"Have you gone batty?"

"I want to see him."

"Why don't you put that thing away before you embarrass yourself?"

I lifted my head and shouted into faraway, curtained corners.

"TESTA! GET OUT HERE!"

"*Madonna*," groaned Jonesy. "You're going to be Swiss cheese if you don't knock it off."

I pointed the Peacemaker at a lamp and fired. Instead of exploding into dust, as had every other lamp I had joyfully demolished in my life, the bullet punched a hole through one side and exited the other, eliciting a carefree *ding* and a tulip of white dust. I stomped my foot like a child and looked for something noisier to shoot.

Five men arrived at the parlor aiming four snub-noses and a single bolt-action rifle. Among them was poor disfigured Pavia, who used a winter scarf to staunch the blood streaming from his crooked nose. I aimed my own weapon back at Jonesy. There was a clicking chorus of hammers being pulled back. I took a deep breath to shout out for Testa before things got loud.

Like magic he responded before I could do it.

"Kid. You're killing me."

He appeared at the same doorway from which Jonesy had emerged, draped in a shiny red kimono. He held a small gun, too, but it hung uncocked at his side. He waved back his retinue of triggermen.

"Everyone relax. This is Finch. Finch just recently went insane but we're going to see what we can do about that. Now—" He cut himself off, noticing something to my right. He narrowed his eyes into a red-hot glare.

"You shot my lamp?"

"Boss, I didn't want to tell you," said Jonesy.

"That was the only lamp in this fucking place that I liked."

My Peacemaker weighed a ton.

"Why not that davenport behind you?" asked he. "You could take target practice on it for all I care. It'd be a mercy killing."

"Boss," sighed Jonesy. "We'll send it back, I told you."

Testa swore beneath his breath and started back through the double doors.

"Come here. And put that pop-gun down before you murder any more furniture."

The door was closed behind me after I entered. We were alone, Testa and I, for the first time ever, in a room centered by a long, sculpted table and a crystal chandelier. No doubt it had been intended for formal dining purposes, but the notebooks and city maps, not to mention the combination safes lined up against the back wall, told me that Testa had repurposed the space as base camp for general operations. On the far side of the table lay a strange two-handled gun with the oddest-looking magazine. Testa wandered toward it and picked it up.

"Just a prototype. Thing's as useful as my nephew. But one day, Finch, when the smart guys figure out the mechanics, a gun like this is going to own this town. You wait and see. I'll have five hundred of these babies. You might have one or two yourself. Replace that lit match you're packing."

He bent his knees and curled his bottom lip like a boy playing cops and robbers and pretended to shoot. With his spiffy new toy and posh pajamas, he looked happier than I'd ever seen him. He scurried about the room, slaughtering squadrons of imaginary police with a clip of bullets that never seemed to run out. He ducked behind a few slender columns and peeked at me as if getting the drop.

"Bang. Gotcha, Finch."

"Where is she? What did you do with her?"

Testa leaned his shoulders onto two columns so that his amused face emerged from between them, begging to be hammered.

"You know how many *sciupafemmini* like you come to me moaning about a missing girl? You think I got a spare room somewhere where I stockpile them? That might sound like a fun idea to you, but when you get older, your priorities change. You expend your energy in different ways. What you don't do is go shaking your little *pistola* in the face of the guy who gives you your payday."

"Just tell me where she is."

"Where who is? You hear what I'm saying? Look, I don't like to get emotional. But you're emotional, so I'll make an exception. You're just a kid, Finch, but I like you. You think I'd let just anyone come in here and shoot my lamp? That's a compliment, free of charge—but it's the only one you get. Now be smart and back off. We got a lot of work to do together."

He could see as well as anyone the blood and tomatoes smeared across my suit. They say that a leopard cannot change his spots; neither, perhaps, can a gunman scrub his clothing hard enough to wash away the red.

My voice was no more commanding than broken wind.

"Is she okay? Can you at least tell me that?"

Testa caressed the columns.

"First off, I'm not saying I know anything about any flatbacker. But I might have heard by the by how you had a special one. Maybe she could screw the paint off a wall; if so, congratulations. Chances are—aw, look, Finch, it's a hard world. Chances are she caught herself the clap. Or met the wrong guy and he did her in. But, hey, why be pessimistic? How about some Arabian prince fell in love and whisked her off to a life of luxury? Shit, she probably just got tired of it. Walked away. Think of it this way: if she was smart, she left. Was she smart?"

I found myself nodding. Yes, that had to be it. I had not misjudged her affection for me. She'd simply made her overdue escape from Patterson's. I should, in fact, be glad about it.

"Well," said Testa, "there you go. We done here?"

Isn't it interesting how certain moments grow ever fatter in your mind, eating your other memories one by one so that, one day, they will be the last memory left?

I have long wondered if Testa was aware of the double-edged brilliance of his question. If I did not kill him in that room that very second, the only other option was to redouble a dedication to the Black Hand that had eroded since meeting Wilma Sue. There could be no second-guessing my choice between her and Luca Testa, not if I valued my sanity. Besides, how would I ever find her?

I had never bothered to learn her last name.

45

Said I, "Yes. We're done."

"Good." He clapped twice. The doorknobs rattled behind my back and I smelled the dusty inrush of parlor air. "Jonesy, fill in Finch about the De Gravio letter. We gotta deliver this one today. Wait till you see this *buffone*. I wouldn't change into a clean suit, not yet."

Jonesy gripped my shoulder. I became aware of a letter with the Black Hand symbol being pressed into my palm. Details were supplied regarding names, places, and times. Soon I began letting these facts displace the memory of that "flatbacker" of mine in bed with the covers pulled up to her chin. In lieu of her, I had her stolen heart, the Excelsior, which would now beat in replacement of my discarded original. Funny how long I have depended on the thing—for over a century. Like me, it is a machine of astonishing durability.

VI.

ITTLE MORE THAN A YEAR passed between Wilma Sue's disappearance and my offing, but oh, was it a fruitful time for Zebulon Finch. With Wilma Sue I had toyed with tenderness; in order to forget her, I mastered ferocity. What time was there to think of her, or where she might be, when there were so many lips to split and arms to break? Testa's fertile mind continued to bear blood-thirsty fruit, though as business accelerated, I saw less of the man himself.

His final, and most fateful, piece of advice came when he tagged along with Jonesy to question me concerning a roustabout from which I'd left with a busted lip. I attempted to collect the draining blood in a cupped palm while Testa repeated one of his favorite chestnuts, that so long as I insisted on entering into each confrontation as a dog bounds after a skunk, I would be no stranger to a spray of ass. He insisted that there was but one way to survive in this business.

"You don't need to show it, *bimbo*," said he. "But you gotta have fear in your heart."

It was a slip of advice I did not heed.

The job that winded the clockwork of my murder began in March of 1896. From out of the mist (so it seemed) had risen an enclave populated by good-looking immigrants from a tiny island off the heel of Italy. They lived at the elbow of two unremarkable streets

47

and had adopted a socialist lifestyle wherein each family took up the job most needed by the community. You need only visit the neighborhood on a Saturday to see these sturdy folk line their carts upon a wildflowered knoll and trade goods. Ne'er a penny changed hands.

We called them the "Triangulinos" because of the tattoos worn on their left biceps: a triangle made of triangles. This insignia lent the otherwise congenial immigrants the aura of a posse; one got the impression that they would be all too happy to die for their shared ideals. In short, they were not the sort of fraternity a man of intelligence would disrupt, which is exactly why the assignment ended up in my angry, idiot lap.

For days I strolled their borders, chewing jerky and spitting cigar butts and watching the insufferably handsome men tip their hats to their magnificent women. It would take a fine disaster indeed to bring down this bunch! I puzzled upon arsons; I mused over explosions; I considered the kidnapping of a beloved elder or some other such key figure. None of them sat right in my gut. The fires would be extinguished with awesome speed, the dynamite defused before damage was done, the kidnapped fellow eagerly self-martyred.

Jonesy claimed to sympathize with me but a man cannot sit on his hands forever. I delivered the Black Hand letter (the amount specified was extraordinary even by our standards) and waited the specified number of days for the Triangulinos to respond. Of course they did not pay, so that night I took up my club, waited in the darkened entryway of a bakery, and when one of their fine young men happened by, took out his knee with a good, swift blow. I muttered Black Hand boilerplate and made my exit.

The next day was spent urging my Excelsior to make the sun drop faster. At dusk I headed out with my club and busted an elbow.

Day, night: this time it was a rib. Sleep, wake: a collarbone crumbled. A Triangulino fell each night for two weeks. Could I extend it to three? Yes, I could: the snaps and pops of broken bones became my evening lullabies.

There was nothing innovative about my dark-corner thuggery, but the sheer number and regularity of the beatings began to bestow upon me the reputation of a phantom. Soon I came to identify this as the exact notoriety I'd for so long sought. What's more, I had achieved it without the management of Testa or the aid of additional muscle.

My experiment was closing in on a month when it came to a precipitous end. I was rambling along my now-favorite block, whistling and twirling my Excelsior, when a young man stepped before me with enough abruptness to bring me to a foppish halt. He wore his Sunday best though it was Wednesday, his hat freshly mended and his fingernails cleared of dirt. I prepared to deliver an admonishment ("I *say*, sir," or something of the sort) when my eyes were drawn to the triangles-within-triangles inked into his biceps.

His arm shot forward. At last, thought I, it was my turn to experience a blade to the stomach! But the object from which I flinched was an envelope so thick with cash that it had been girdled in twine. My first thought should have been how glad Testa would be to hear of my overdue success. Instead I found myself disheartened, as if this immigrant had made an exceptional offer on a prize calf I had yet to raise to full maturity.

This barbaric business with the Triangulinos would end up being the worst thing I had ever done, or would ever do. And that, as you shall see over time, is saying a mouthful.

Within the week I graced two separate "Wanted" posters. I heard the news as I was about to dig my mitts into a basket of shaved pork, and I left it for the flies so that I could rush out and see for myself. The first likeness made me look as if I had water on the brain, but the second lent me the lackadaisical glamor of a Jesse James or John Wesley Hardin.

I tore down one example of each and hurried home to award them proud positions within my scrapbook. It had ballooned since the days of Wilma Sue. Now that I slept alone, the collected posters of my fellow criminals had become my confidants. At night I'd whisper to them as though we shared a bunkhouse: "Good night, Butch 'the Rat' Higgins. Sleep well, J.R. Baker, Murderer. Until morning, Clyde Landsness, for Whom a Mighty Reward Is Offered."

The rise of my reputation did not escape the notice of the boss. "Testa sends his regards," said Jonesy, handing me a shiny new bottle of bourbon. But the twist of his mouth said something else: *You did fine. Enjoy it. Just remember, this ain't about you, Finch.*

In my mind, of course, it was. I came to view the Triangulino affair as a prime example of the major weakness of Testa's Black Hand. Namely, the extortion letters. They came from Jonesy sealed but I began to take peeks, only to find that they were just as I had feared: the novice jottings of the barely literate. I remembered that first meeting with Testa and how he'd mocked my offer to compose letters, asking if I thought I was Shakespeare. Well, next to these dilettantes, I was!

The first letter that I, if you will excuse the understatement, *revised* was for the prosperous entrepreneur butcher Salvatore Petrosino. What Jonesy handed me was claptrap: "Deny if you have Sufficient Courage this demand of $2,000 and risk all Future Happiness. Your Money or your Life is required at the following Day and Time and Location . . ."

It chagrined me as a fellow intellectual that savvy, successful Petrosino might read such solecistic drivel. I hid myself in the corner of a pub, withdrew a piece of paper, licked the tip of my pen for dramatic effect, and met the two in hopes that magic would alight.

Mr. Petrosino,

So you spear with hook your beef as it still kicks its hooves; so shall you kick when lifted by our beefiest men. So you slice your cattle from brisket to round with little thought of breath or soul; such operation to us is familiar, for we open bodies the same as we unbutton a shirt. So you collect innards within a fist; so we collect your TRUE innards, your loved ones, within ours, a fist much Blacker.

The price of meat today is high: $2,000 delivered this coming Sunday to a man with a yellow handkerchief outside of Molly's. Chew on this as would a child—quickly—and digest it rare if you can, for there is no time for the dithering of seasonings and peppers. We shall belch our gratitude.

Hungrily,
The Black Hand

To this day I know the paragraphs cold. Melodramatic? Yes, of course. You must agree, though, that it contains traces of genuine poetry! Proud was I to deliver it; prouder still was I to receive payment in full. Emboldened, I exercised my wrist in service of further flowery directives, for several weeks producing the most imposing collection of extortion letters in American history.

Lesser drafts were flung to the floor at the invention of more expressive metaphors. It was inevitable that one of my jealous colleagues would collect this dropped evidence and present it to Testa. I can see it as if I had been there: Testa pacing among his despised sofas and durable lamps, clutching a newer gun prototype in one hand as he rifled through my discards, following not so much the meaning of my nimble prose but rather the insubordination that fueled them. A man who could make threats as well as carry them out was a potential rival he did not need.

Here at last we come full circle. On the morning of May 7, 1896, I received an anonymous letter that, despite its rudimentary penmanship, preyed quite cunningly upon my vanity. The letter expressed admiration for my abilities and the desire to discuss a proposition. *Recognition at last*, thought I. I dined on pheasant and potatoes and ale. On balance, I believe it was a good final meal. I walked with full belly to the lake, as I had been directed; I checked my Excelsior by the tapering dusk; by and by it was 7:44 and through my heart passed a single bullet, and all because I had ignored the advice of a man I'd stubbornly refused to acknowledge as my cerebral superior:

You gotta have fear in your heart.

It is not difficult, you see, to understand why I had to be killed. The more difficult question is why I, of all people, was brought back.

PART TWO

1896–1902

———◦◦◦———

Containing An Account Of Your Hero's Assimilation

Into A Lot Of Unsavory Characters And Affiliation

With A Person Of Very Small Stature.

I.

MY NEXT MEMORY COMES TWO days after my murder. I was seated inside a tent. A man entered from a corner, parting the frayed yellow fabric with a shark fin hand. He took a single oversized step and then held that bizarre pose, legs scissored, while one hand weaseled into the folds of his frock coat and procured a cigar. His other hand held a chicken leg, undercooked and drizzling pink liquid. Masterfully, he lit the cigar without losing the chicken. Puffing away, he loped closer and sat with enough spirit to flare his low-hanging hem, which flung grit from the dirt floor into my open eyes. Quite oddly, I felt no sting.

He crossed a leg over a knee and bounced it; the scruff of his boot was slathered in cheap polish. He held his cigar with an actor's verve and with his other hand brought in the chicken leg, rotated it for best vantage, and took a rapacious bite. I guessed the man to be more than double my age and yet he gave off an impression of rakish good health. Beneath the scraggled beard his flesh was peach-hued; his lips were red, even too; the hair falling from under his top hat flowed across his shoulders in a womanish cascade. His pale green eyes were ringed with red, the kind that told of late nights and budget booze as much as it did the unshirkable responsibilities of morning.

I would come to know this man as the Barker.

He smacked his lips when he drew smoke.

"I'm a busy fellow," said he. "So out with it. Who are you?"

Speech was a revolting memory. I burrowed back into my quiet.

The Barker spat a tendon and hovered the cigar before his lips.

"Indeed. Very clever. Hold your cards, reveal nothing. Force the interrogator to ask the same question of himself. Who am I? Who are any of us? It becomes existential. Ah, you're a cleaver, sir. You're the sharpest object in the drawer. Indulge me a revision. What is your *name?*"

Being addressed was a torture. Did this mean I was not, as I'd hoped, a ghost? Dull sensations began to seep in from great distances: coldness, wetness, a discomfort in my neck. Also came the first twinges of curiosity. Where was this tented location? How I had arrived there? What was the reason for my paralysis?

"No name." He oozed smoke. "This, of course, opens up a host of possibilities. You're a thief, mayhap a feminine defiler, and what you seek is sanctuary. You realize that this changes our dynamic. If I lower myself—forgive me, sir, for the blunt words. But if I lower myself to deal with—ahem—Criminal Element, the only Christian method of proceeding is that I become the benefactor and you the benefacted. An awfully one-sided relationship, that one. No, it's better to be out with it. Tell me what it is you have done."

At this point our twosome became three. Slinking through the same corner opening was a tabby in the most destitute of states: down an eye, patchily furred, and pregnant. Her legs were mud-crusted, her tail crooked. She threaded herself about her master's ankles, opening her scabbed muzzle to mewl for chicken.

The Barker's eyes grew redder as he squinted.

"My, my. It was a child, wasn't it? Who you . . . well, I don't care to voice such perversities. And since you see no need to disavow me of this assumption, I am forced to presume it correct. That's a foul business, sir. Why, I could be jailed if I was found to be giving you asylum. Oh, no, sir. Heavens, no."

He flung aside the chicken bone and inserted his thumb into his mouth all the way to the root, withdrawing it with a slurp as he sucked it clean. He held aloft the glistening digit as if imagining one of the aforementioned perversities. The cat, meanwhile, eyed the grass for sign of the bone but displayed none of the gumption necessary for scavenging.

"Apologies for wasting your time, sir," said the Barker. "And I believe I shall stop referring to you as 'sir.' It is a gesture I make to honor the poor abused child, you understand. Children—defenseless angels! We adults are obligated to protect them."

He expelled a tragic sigh and brought himself to his feet. Despite the unfair scoldings, I longed for him to remain. I was a little boy— lost, confused, willing to cling to anyone possessed of orientation. The discomfort in my neck magnified.

The Barker had gone but two steps before he turned on a heel and jabbed the cigar in my direction.

"On the other hand, it is my belief that, as Jesus of Nazareth taught, we all deserve a bit of forgiveness. For who among us hasn't a sin tucked away in his darkest heart? Yes, by George. I believe an understanding can be reached between the two of us. Look! Even Silly Sally likes you. Don't you, Sally? Don't you, Silly Sally Kitty Catty?"

My lowermost vision caught the cat's matted tail as it swayed in the vicinity of my feet. Something about this creature's proximity upset me.

"You're a crackerjack listener, anyhow," the Barker continued, "and if you are to work for me, that is an asset. For I, as benefactor, will tell you to do things. And you, I'm afraid, will be required to do them. Discussion poisons the rehabilitation process."

I felt the cat's fangs tugging at my ankle. Through benumbed senses, I catalogued the quick, violent actions necessary to rid myself of this animal. But I could no more act upon them than I could form words or lift my chin from my chest. Oh, but this frightened me! Was this waking slumber the penance of the damned? Was this man Mephistopheles, this tent an antechamber of Hell?

"They tell me," said he with a simper, "that they fished you from the lake."

The man had called me a gambler but it was he who knew when to turn his best card. The bottom of the lake—yes, that's right, I had witnessed it! I had lain upon pebbles, blinked stupidly at the remains of a sunken boat, been kissed by a passing school of fish. Sand had shifted in such volume that the lower half of my body had been covered, then uncovered, then covered again. How long had I lain down there bereft of air? It had to have been hours. It was then that I remembered my murder.

Remembering it was worse than the act itself, I assure you.

The truth was, to say the least, difficult to accept. I was a corpse. I could feel the stagnant weight of internal organs no longer quickened by lifeforce. A bullet had pierced my heart—warm spring air now passed through the wound!—and I had suffered a hundred drownings. I believe I would have lost my marbles right there in that tent had I not heard the Excelsior ticking away inside my pocket, unfaltering despite its recent dunking, my steadfast beating heart.

The Barker observed my reactions with a biologist's dispassion. The cigar rolled from one end of his mouth to the other, a pendulum.

"My initial interest in you stemmed from a report we received from a satisfied customer of ours residing south of Chicago. It would seem that this gentleman, a Mr. Avery, hoping to catch breakfast,

58

borrowed a hook and rod and obtained himself a rowboat. On this particular morning he hooked a big one. He hooked you."

The Barker pointed.

"The webbing between your finger and thumb. Right hand. Take a look."

It was my first willed movement. My eyeballs, devoid of moisture, skipped across tacky sockets, and my elbow scuttered like machinery desperate for lubricant. A hand that looked very much like my own rose shakily from its dangled position. Carefully I rotated it.

There was an ugly hole ripped clean through the flesh exactly where the Barker had said. I brought the hand closer. The visible meat was a dull gray-pink. Blood failed to pump, even when I clenched and unclenched the fist. For a moment there were no sounds but the popping of my finger bones.

"Twenty years now I've fielded cockeyed stories from desperate milksops," said the Barker. "So when Mr. Avery returned to our grounds demanding an audience in regards to a man who breathed underwater, I motioned to have the sot escorted away. But then he mentioned the other thing and I knew I had to see it."

My expression was fixed, yet must have conveyed puzzlement.

Up went the Barker's eyebrows. "You don't know? Oh, my. My, my. I don't know how to say this." He winced and pointed with the cigar. "There—right there. On your—yes, right there."

I spider-walked my fingertips across the shirt slicked to my deadlocked chest, in and out of the collarbone hollows that no longer throbbed with pulse, and onto my cold neck, where I discovered something that was not flesh. Panic reared and I counted along to the Excelsior to calm myself. So *this* was the cause of my neck discomfort.

An iron fisherman's hook the size of my forearm was implanted deep into my jugular. I swallowed and there was a metallic *clink*. I probed with my tongue and tasted rust. With great effort I fiddled around and found two inches of iron pushing from inside my neck like a goiter. I took the hook's handle with fantasies of extraction but I was far too weak. Silly Sally, who continued to work my ankles, cocked her head in an inquisitive way. The weight of the hook pulled my head to the right, giving me, I imagined, a similar expression.

"I would be cross with Mr. Avery for gross mishandling had he not sold you to me for nothing more than what he'd lost at our Boardwalk the previous night. For this business, as you shall learn, is all about acquiring the New."

The Barker tossed his cigar and approached, frowning at my impalement like a doctor, which might have been comforting if not for his playful, mincing steps. He wiggled his fingers as if to limber them and spoke in the barest of whispers.

"When a man of my talents meets a man of yours, there are few limits. Of course, this grappling hook will have to be removed. We can't tip off the audience prematurely. Ah, that reminds me, I've already chosen for you a name, as you do not appear to own one yourself." He made a theatrical gesture. "'The Astonishing Mr. Stick.' What do you think? Handbills are being printed as we speak."

I felt him take hold of the hook's handle. The pressure inside my neck thickened and I braced for decapitation. His touch, though, was gentle. He of all people did not wish to see me further mangled.

His right foot kicked. Silly Sally moaned and waddled away from my ankles.

"Filthy cat. Adores dead things," said he. "But that does not stop me from loving her."

II.

FUN FACTS FOR YOUR ENJOYMENT, Dearest Reader!

I do not eat.

I do not excrete.

I do not sleep.

I do not bleed.

While I lived, these obligatory functions could be frustrations for how they delayed lustier pursuits. What shocked me in those first days following my slaying was how much I missed these signals of life. Without them, did I exist? My body had been sold to the Barker with no more ceremony than one might sell a goat or pig. Livestock, however, were luckier, for they could relax upon the promise of slaughter. What was in store for me was anyone's guess.

Before I achieved the scantest bit of bearings, the Barker's cryptic caravan hit the road. The comforts customarily extended to the Black Hand were lacking; I bounced about within a cage filled with straw. Each time the carriage stopped I was bombarded with insects eager to sup upon putrefied flesh. Within seconds they sensed the unholy coldness about me and never was I pestered again.

Gød above, pleaded I, watching the flies keep their fearful distance, *how can any of this be real?* I closed my eyes and composed epic odes to my squandered life, which now dangled just beyond arm's reach—age eighteen, age nineteen, age twenty, and onward; the varieties of women to be bedded; the varieties of lagers to be drank; all of it gone, gone, gone, slurped from my stein before I'd enjoyed one full swallow. And in return I got this? This coarse maltreatment? This migratory bazaar on the road to who knew where?

I was kept hidden from all eyes for days. The Barker's show, whatever it was, began a brief residency in Dale City, Illinois, and between lectures I could not quite hear, he sneaked into the supply tent, pulled back the blanket that covered my cage, and peered at my woebegone visage for ten, twenty, thirty minutes at a time, searching, I expect, for sign of breath or pulse that he had earlier missed. He, a man of great skepticism, still suspected that he was being duped.

Perhaps this is what led to his drastic change of approach. Early one morn, he employed two tattooed workers to remove me from the cage. (I lacked the power to resist or object.) They stripped me of my moldy clothes, took me by the ankles, and gave me a vigorous shaking. Lake water gushed from my throat, sinuses, and wounds. The smell was sour and the men recoiled. I was relieved, though, to be rid of the slop. The men dressed me in a suit ill-fit enough to make me miss Abigail's uncomfortable vestments and returned to me the Excelsior—thank heavens for that!

Scrubbed and suited, I was given work. I could not believe it at first. I was a vile demon fit to be expurgated, not some transient hireling! Yet I was propped into a sitting position inside my cage and handed through the bars a pile of soft cotton pads, a jar of red pepper, and a bottle of glue. I saw no connection between these curious peripherals until Little Johnny Grandpa, a tiny old man in filthy overalls, hobbled over, rapped his cane on the bars of my cage, announced in a graveled voice that he was to teach me the construction of "liver pads," and bade me to listen close so that he did not have to repeat himself.

But he was forced to repeat himself seven or eight times, so stunned was I by his irregular comportment. Little Johnny Grandpa, I discovered, was so dubbed because of a rare affliction, an outrageous disease that aged his physique at an accelerated rate. He had the sparse white hair, bowed back, bad gums, lax skin, and milky eyes of an ancient. Yet he was no older than ten years! Like any youngster, his conversational instinct was to fill silence, and as it so happened, silence was precisely what I had to offer.

"Lookie here," said he. "What y'do is y'put y'cloth on y'lap and then y'find the dead center with y'fingers, right?" He jabbed with his cane one of the cotton rectangles wadded upon my thighs. "Now y'take y'pepper and y'dab y'pepper on y'cloth—look, like so."

He reached between the bars as only a child would dare, and took my wrist. Before he'd moved my hand an inch toward the jar of peppers, he was aroused to the truth of my condition. His thousand wrinkles coiled.

"S'true," whispered he. "Y'cold. Y'cold as ice."

It was amazement, not horror, with which his cataracts gleamed. For the first time since my death I wished to speak, but my lips were capable of only a dismaying hiss. Little Johnny Grandpa sniffed at my odor; the long gray hairs of his nostrils fluttered. Right away he dropped my hand. It landed upon the cotton spread across my lap and that is where I fixed my eyes. I saw the lad's stumpy shadow rise on two legs and a cane and leave at full-speed totter. I could lay no blame at his fleeing feet.

Then came a miracle rivaling the one that resurrected me: the elderly little boy came back.

"I got what y'need!" A green bottle was uncorked and he commenced blessing me with an oily liquid. A drop hit my eye and welled like a tear. "Just a little perfume, see, and y'have ladies tearing off their knickers in no time. Y'see if Little Johnny Grandpa's not right."

The cologne did not mix well with dead flesh and stirred up a sickly sweet funk. Regardless, I nodded my appreciation and the boy became sheepish. He corked the bottle and jammed it into his pocket.

"Aw, don't y'get thankful on me. It's not even real cologne. Colonel Moseley's Halitosis Garg-o-lax is all it is. Comes ten cents a bottle."

He kneeled next to my cage, wincing at his weak knees, and snatched up my wrist. With arthritic fingers he brought my hand to the cotton upon my lap and showed me how to approximate its center. Next came the jar of peppers: he operated my fingers like chopsticks until we landed a pepper and then he showed me how to snap it in half and rub it against the cotton to create a splotch of red. Finally, a different finger was dipped into the glue and used to apply a dollop.

"Liver pads," said Little Johnny Grandpa. "Y'know, for y'liver?"

I most certainly did not know.

His sparse white whiskers curled into a grin.

"Well, I'll let you in on the secret, then! Folks r'worked into a tizzy over th'livers. Half what the Barker sells got the word 'liver' on it. 'The Great Organ' he calls it. 'The Magnificent Gland.' Y'got chills, sir? Evil lockjaw? Wretched biliousness? Wakefulness got y'spirits low? Why, it's y'liver that's to blame! Oh, we got pills and phosphates and snuff that'll do y'service, but nothing so fine as Dr. Whistler's Own Salvation of the Common Brute Liver Pads. Not convinced? Why, step up to th'platform, sir, and expose, if y'will, y'midsection. Now apply Dr. Whistler's pad, like so, and feel th'warm bloom of rebounding health! Yes? Y'feel it?"

I felt, at that instant, many things. First was an appreciative shiver at the deception: a man's body temperature would soften the glue and release the pepper, resulting in a short-lived burn of "health." Second was a pang of loss: my own body, cold as marble, had relinquished all such sensations. The third realization was the most distressing: after only a week of death, egads, how lonely was I for tones of camaraderie and cabal!

I molded a grin from my facial flesh.

My stiff fingers showed more dexterity while assembling the next pad, and the next. Little Johnny Grandpa hunkered down to work on his own quota. For once, nothing about my situation felt threatening. Hoping to perpetuate the moment, I enlarged my grin. Unfortunately, it peeled open the grappling-hook wound of my neck—not quite the overture of normality I'd hoped to make.

The boy halted his work and blinked at what had to be a hallucination. I let my mouth close and the wound, like a second mouth, closed also. Little Johnny Grandpa frowned with lips pappy from lack of teeth. He then fished from his pocket a red handkerchief and hobbled his small body into position behind me. One of his arms appeared at either end of my peripheral vision. Three years operating amongst base cretins had trained me to expect strangulation. All right, thought I, let us get this over with.

Instead his swollen knuckles and tremorous fingers tied the red cloth into a jaunty triangle that neatly hid my neck-hole. I gawked at it. The color gave my faded suit the kind of snazz I'd always preferred from my fashion. The Excelsior ticked in my pocket; the kerchief was red as blood; my hands labored at a task; were these not evidence of life?

"There y'go, Mr. Stick," panted he. "Sniff. Cough. Hack!"

That was the first time I heard Little Johnny Grandpa vocalize his choking, but it was far from the last. Though the boy suffered the infirmities of the old, he maintained the levity of the young, and by turning a cough into the word "cough," he made light of his chronic maladies. Not a day after he taught me the assembly of liver pads, his chest began to rattle with a sickness that sounded like dice in a cup. He undertook that day's lesson while struggling for breath.

"Morning, Mr. Stick. Hack—*hack*. The Barker's asked me—here comes a *hack*. Cough. Another *cough*. Wants me t'show you th'making of . . . Spit. HACK! Th'making of worm eradicator. Makes putting together liver pads look like yanking on your pud. But y'can do it, right, Mr. Stick? I know y'can. Snort. Snort!"

The Barker, or so I gathered, was a medicine vender of sorts, and nothing quickened sales like the suggestion that a tapeworm was coiled within one's intestines. In this endeavor, he had two chief weapons.

The first was the nostrum itself. Billed as The Infallible Indian's Tape-Worm Disgorging Lozenges, these little nuggets were the apotheosis of the Barker's genius and that week I constructed hundreds. The secret ingredient was not stomachic, not sassafras or aloe, but rather a gentle tissue paper that was sliced into long, thin strips and rolled into pellet shape before being dipped into a hardening syrup. Once swallowed, the syrup was digested, but the long strips of tissue were not, and showed up in feces as supposed evidence of the parasite's demise. Repeat purchases were guaranteed.

The second weapon was every bit as effective. It was a large jar propped upon the edge of the main stage, filled with formaldehyde and the most appalling congress of giant tapeworms ever assembled. Little Johnny Grandpa assured me that these abominations were actually purchased from cattle stockyards, which, as it turned out, had carved themselves a lucrative sideline providing gastronomical monstrosities to men like the Barker.

One would be hard-pressed to look at the jar and not feel certain of impending death from within. Unless, of course, you were me. I brooded upon those tapeworms quite a lot, wondering how easy or difficult one might be to swallow. Once a tapeworm was inside of me, you see, I could pretend that it was my organs, squirming and throbbing and going about the daily business of keeping me alive.

III.

D
R. WHISTLER'S, LITTLE JOHNNY GRANDPA explained, was what the Barker's traveling show was called by those relaxed to its lectures, performances, and product, though the traveling medicine show's full title, if you lingered upon the banner that stretched between the entry poles erected in each town, was Dr. Whistler's Pageant of Health and Gallery of Suffering.

You understand that this was before health commissions, before laboratory trials, before warning labels. Popularity of a given drug was based upon nothing more than the unsubstantiated claims on the packaging. Medicine lecturers I'd glimpsed in Chicago had sold their serums out of the backs of wagons, which folded down into clever little stages. Dr. Whistler's, however, required the entirety of a vacant lot and carried with it the atmosphere of a circus.

This is no surprise, given the Barker's history. It was said that he spent his early career stamping and hollering in front of a one-ring circus sideshow (hence the sobriquet; his real name was unknown). Despite the vaudeville and blackface acts overtaking the business in 1896, the Barker still believed in the gasps-over-giggles sideshow approach.

On a good day our bally would draw several hundred simps so starved for entertainment that they'd purchase product out of sheer gratefulness. Dr. Whistler's core company hovered around twenty, each of them pulling double or triple duty. It was not at all uncommon during periods of heavy merchandry to see a worker pitchforking horse manure throw aside his tool and leap to the stage to extol the virtues of Benjamin Franklin's Cocaine Tooth-Drops or Dr. Basil's Genuine Preparation of Highly Concentrated Fluid Extracts of Borneo.

Dr. Whistler's peddled roughly fifty different panaceas at any given time, most of which were mixed on-site in a bathtub. If business was brisk, we remained in town for up to a week. There was no hurry to leave; travel was hard, weather was unpredictable, and mud mired us. After we pulled up stakes, the company formed a convoy of five bulging, top-heavy, horse-drawn wagons. This was accomplished with a maximum of irritability, for the Barker was never satisfied with the take and his upset quickly filtered down to the lowliest soul. (That would be me.)

We packed four or five to a wagon and followed the harvest, playing central states in summer before heading to cotton towns with the onset of autumn. During travel, which was, shall we say, bumpy, I lay curled in fetal position within my straw; there was no sense in suffering another injury that would never heal. In a day if we were lucky—three days if we were not—we reached the town of our next destination. "Ideally not as small as a fly on a pile of dung," the Barker once said, "but not as large as the dung, either."

I was too weak to assist in the setting up of stages and booths. During those first weeks my proudest accomplishments were twofold: drawing myself to a sitting position and, from my cage, tearing a hole in my tent so that I could observe the company's activities.

Shows began at eleven in the morning, an optimal time for bringing out customers who did not want to miss out on special bargains (hah!) on limited stock (hah, hah!) and who would then be caught hungry around lunchtime and purchase our overpriced (and undercooked) food.

Every element of the show was this shrewdly designed. As townsfolk arrived, they were greeted with the sounds of four musicians tuning their instruments. Given our ensemble's middling faculty with mandolin, lyre, and hurdy-gurdy, their tuning session was preposterously belabored, which was precisely the point. Their atonal blurts and nerve-jangling shrieks served to put customers on edge while they absorbed the horrifying advertisements painted on sackcloth and draped at regular intervals:

O, Why Shall Ye Die? When The Never-Failing Remedy For That Deadly Scourge Of Infancy And Childhood, THE CROUP, Is At Hand?

YOU! Do Not Die The Most SHAMEFUL Way: The Sure-Killing Disease Of CONSTIPATION.

Look Upon This Picture! And Imagine Your Bodily Self Rid, Like This Girl, Of Dropsy And Scrofula And Gout. See How She Is Now?

The first thing the Barker did at any show was to isolate a boy in the crowd, beckon him close, and bid him to fetch a pitcher of water before the lecture began. For this paltry errand, the Barker gave the lucky lad the staggering sum of two dollars. Sometimes it was the last two dollars the Barker had, but the offhand way in which he bestowed it produced an expectant buzz among the commoners.

What a success this man's tonics must be to earn such disposable wealth! The people were snared; the Barker straightened his suit and noticed them as if by accident. Softly, then, he began.

"Welcome, welcome all. I am Dr. Whistler, A.M., M.D., former lecturer on nervous diseases and neurasthenia at the University of the City of New York, fellow of the Boston Academy of Medicine, author of *Every Man Is a Physician*, author of *A History of Groin Injuries*, Medicinal Therapist to the Massachusetts State Women's Hospital, and your most humble of servants. I arrive here with an esteemed assemblage of professionals eager to diagnose and prescribe.

"In the area to my right you see the Boardwalk of Chance, at which you may exercise the spirit with rousing tests of skill; to my left, the Gallery of Suffering, in which you will meet magnificent examples of those at the mercy of inexorable conditions, each of whom combats his or her affliction in a panoply of inspiring ways. It is our great pleasure to be here in Biddy Creek—" (or Sparrowville or Two-Bit Hill or Turd Town or what-have-you) "—and our great pleasure to cure every ailment that harasses you. Look this way—this way!—now!—for a medicine that you go without at great, great personal risk."

Thus began the choreographed bedlam. The old and infirm were helped to the stage to quiver before their neighbors. Liver pads were demonstrated. The inconvenience of ingesting tapeworm lozenges was weighed against the inconvenience of tapeworms. Fizzing healant miraculously closed a bloody wound that in reality was a glob of red paint. Twice a day they trotted out a harrowing display called the Museum of Venereal Hardship, during which a pitchman sold an ointment that I'd buy too, if still alive: Mumford's Cure-All for

Youthful Mistakes. Bottles, bags, vials, packets, jars—they streamed from stage to crowd as if they were bobbing along a rushing river.

There was but a single booth that offered no jumping and shouting. There, a well-dressed attendant used only a placid smile to take money from those at death's door. The oldest and sickest of townspeople, those past believing in cures, lined up to exchange their last few coins for cheap rosaries, poorly printed pictures of Jesus and the Virgin Mary, flimsy wooden crosses slopped with gold paint. They clutched these talismans with palsied fingers and prayed for a bigger miracle than the easing of whooping cough or the shriveling of piles. These are the faces that haunt me to this day, so desperate were they to stave off the same Death that had already claimed Mr. Stick.

Dusk seemed to convince folk, their pockets sagging with product, to pay out just a little more to enter the Gallery of Suffering. The lectures held within were but freak shows lent veneers of respectability by vague medical overtones. Little Johnny Grandpa was the opening act, and his routine revolved around the comic disparity of a withered old man promulgating the attitudes of the young. His "spontaneous" conversations were no doubt adorable but also scripted to the final word. Pills to ward off premature aging were sold afterward.

The other performers I shall mention in brief. Vera Diana was a lissome Romanian who dressed in a snug garment on which a diagram of the inner body had been painted. She sold salves for the betterment of joint health by twisting her body into an assortment of impossible contortions. The Soothing Foursome came next, a quartet of Negro brothers who helped sell throat and chest solutions with effervescent, four-part madrigals of minor-key melancholy. (Incidentally, they were well-muscled and adorned only in loincloths.)

The closing spot went to Pullman Larry, a loathsome devil who by day acted as our on-site dentist and by night put on a show of bullet-firing wizardry to help sell elixirs purporting to quell anxieties, spasms, and nervous afflictions. Little Johnny Granda shuddered when this man mussed the boy's wisps of hair. Mr. Hobby, the show's stalwart accountant, pushed his bespectacled nose into his ledger to deflect any dialogue. Professor Bach, the wild-haired cook/chemist who mixed our elixirs in his crusty cauldron, feigned chemical burn if the man wandered too close. Even the Barker ground his jaw when cornered for conversation.

Pullman Larry, they said, was a former Texas millionaire and world traveler who abandoned a life of luxury to perfect his skill at sharpshooting and master the art of dentistry. (Odd bedfellows, these enterprises.) Country folk traumatized at the hands of the local barber-dentist would try almost anything, and Pullman did brisk business. When the flow of patients abated, he drummed up more by pacing the grounds clad in Western regalia: a cowboy hat festooned with shark's teeth, a yellow-and-pink-dyed frilled leather coat, and gold-mounted .44 cufflinks.

For sure he cut a dashing figure with a long handlebar mustache serving as stage curtain to thirty-two impossibly white teeth. Lashed to his belt were two guns, which he liked to draw in tandem, spinning them this way and that before popping open the handles to reveal two sets of gold forceps. Presuming that he was as handy with teeth as he was guns, sufferers followed him to take their place in his adjustable chair. Musicians were always present and struck up a bombastic march as Pullman cranked open a patient's jaws.

The music was to cover the screams. For all his brilliance with a sidearm, Pullman Larry never mastered the dental arts, and this failure, according to Johnny, turned the ex-millionaire into a self-loathing Grendel who instead of admitting defeat chose to mask it with sleight of hand.

After swabbing a patient's mouth with his patented Gød of Pain, billed as the world's greatest numbing agent, Pullman took the patient's head in a grip that secretly constricted the vocal cords. The offending tooth was plucked quickly if bloodily and then an oversized wad of cotton was jammed in its place. It was only at this point that Pullman asked the patient how he felt. From behind the cotton came dazed, indistinct mumbles, which Pullman generously translated to onlookers as breathless praise.

So you see why I regarded the dark folds of the Gallery tent as a dirgeful last stop for mankind's most forlorn of specimens. Nightly I watched how the formation of the six o'clock queue sapped all energy from Little Johnny Grandpa. With resignation he would gather his cane and begin hobbling away so as not to be late for his performance, often forcing a grin and a parting quip: "Y'wrappin' those worm pills like y'stranglin' someone, Mr. Stick."

It was true. I was. As occupied as I was with my own horrific condition, I knew that there were some dens a boy should not be forced to enter, some lions he should not be forced to face. Particularly a child as bighearted as this one, whose doleful smile, I soon found, came not for his own sorry fate inside the Gallery of Suffering, but for mine.

There was a slot between the Soothing Foursome and Pullman Larry that had my name on it.

It was several months after my abominable act began that Little Johnny Grandpa crept into my tent and snuggled up alongside my cage. It was late and I was in the withdrawn state that typically followed one of my performances. The boy gripped the bars with sclerotic fingers while tears rode the canals of his aged skin. Under risk of being caught out past his curfew by the Barker, the boy whispered with haste.

"Beg y'pardon, Mr. Stick, but I have me a question. Are y'really dead like some of them say? Are ya? And if y'are, does that mean you're an angel? Would y'tell me if y'were? Because I figure I'm a person in need of one, Mr. Stick. Y'hear what I'm saying? Can't y'find the energy to speak? Can't y'show all them bastards what y'really are?"

He made a valiant effort to muffle the inevitable hack!, cough!, and spit! that followed. Yet I refused to respond. We were colleagues, yes, and as colleagues we exchanged periodic commiserations. Anything beyond that could not be permitted; Wilma Sue's disappearance had taught me the pitfalls of emotional involvement. I turned away so that the lad could feel the brunt of my disregard. I was a sack of rotting beef, could he not tell? The cheap tears and bucolic fantasies of a sick child would not distract me from the misery I so deserved!

After a good long stretch of this silence, Little Johnny Grandpa swallowed his sniffles, brought himself to leg and cane, and hobbled from the tent. *To hell with him*, thought I. I did not require a boy's weepy reminders of the heartlessness that made me a hateful being. Johnny had no idea that my teenage life had been spent doling out pain, lots of it, again and again and again.

Why the deuce should my death be any different?

IV.

YOUR DISPLEASURE, DEAREST READER, IS hot enough for me to feel across time and space. You find me sadistic. A reassuring smile, you think, was not much to ask to becalm a boy ravaged by rare disease and facing the dragon of Death without sword or scutcheon.

Yes, all right—I suffered the chigger-bites of guilt. Hopeless though I might have been, Johnny was more hopeless still. Does that confession change a single thing? Even had my seventeen years versed me in the ways of cooing and patting backs, which it had not, what comfort to a dying boy could be offered by a fellow who had already died? I was, and remain, the Damned, and for you to believe it, I need only describe what happened to me each night inside the Gallery of Suffering.

Note, though, that you were warned.

When I began my career as the Astonishing Mr. Stick, I spent the duration of my performances posing the question of *Why?*—to the gent in the front row and to the kids roughhousing at the rear; to the rodents scuttling backstage and to that biggest rodent of all, Gød. None of my addressees answered. The Barker himself accepted my existence with nary a care about heaven or hell. Rather than spiritual interrogation, he muttered to me the same statistic:

"Seventy-five million dollars will be spent on patent medicines this year, Mr. Stick. And I'll be damned if we don't take our share."

I learned to disassociate during performances. It is, I am convinced, the only thing that saved me from total neurosis. The Barker's tone was authoritarian and his manipulation of my body had a physician's fearlessness. I let myself be lulled by both. He is Dr. Whistler, I told myself, and I am merely Dr. Whistler's Subject, and what is happening to the Subject upon this stage is barren of emotion. I find it difficult to deviate from this perspective even in writing. Allow me this indulgence as we proceed?

Dr. Whistler takes the stage alone. The Gallery can squeeze in upwards of fifty people, but this particular show nets fifteen on a good night. These brave souls sit upon benches in darkness, though the stage is ablaze with such fervid torchlight that they are forced to squint. The Subject watches from backstage.

"'The great art of life is sensation, to feel that we exist, even in pain.'" Dr. Whistler surveys his audience. "Lord Byron gave us those immortal words. I am but a humble man of medicine, hardly the equal to such a poet, but I submit to you a thesis. When pain overwhelms our existence, the 'art of life' Byron spoke of becomes abstract. So says Thomas Jefferson: 'The art of life is the art of avoiding pain; and he is the best pilot who steers clearest of the rocks and shoals with which it is beset.' Now, those are the words of an American! A man whose breast, like my own, like yours, in dark days draws comfort from the steady march of science."

The Subject is unconvinced that the rural assemblage follows the good doctor's literary logic. Yet they nod along hungrily. Indeed, hunger is a quality that does not change from town to town. These people are lame and wracked; some of them are dying and know it.

"For twenty years, Dr. Whistler's Pageant of Health has been the pacesetter in the eradication of pain. Our agents scour the Earth for extraordinary individuals who have found ways to battle the ailments that beset mankind, and then we bring them to you, in this very gallery. Your time is precious and yet you come to us because you have watched your siblings, your friends, and your elders die with leeches on their faces—that awful medieval praxis prevalent even in this enlightened day.

"Gentlemen! We have ether now, we have chloroform. A man named Röntgen last year developed a photographic method of viewing bones inside the body! And ladies, one of your own by the name of Elizabeth Blackwell received an accredited medical degree in 1849. Others of your fair sex follow, and in a generation our country shall have a battalion of the prettiest doctors in the world! Our nation has not faltered when asserting with rifles and cannons our independence from the British. Nor shall we falter in this war against pestilence. We shall assert our sovereignty—with nerve, with audacity, with puissance!"

The Subject is unable to muster the strength required for the clapping of hands; otherwise, even he might find himself swept into the ecstasy of the saved.

"It is in this spirit of grand adventure and bold investigation that I bring before you a great discovery. Found shepherding cattle in our forty-first state of Montana, where he lived with bland parents in a small clay hut, this youngster represents a step in evolution that we can emulate with the clever application of known chemicals. I need say no more—you shall witness his fortitude with your own eyes. I present to you, distinguished guests, a most accomplished young man—the Astonishing Mr. Stick!"

Generally it comes as a surprise to the Subject when two of the pageant functionaries assist him into the brilliance. Things are in dizzying motion. A chair is being placed onto the center of the stage. A large easel is being positioned stage right and balanced upon it is a giant pad of paper painted with the Subject's pseudonym.

The audience recoils upon getting a look at the Subject. He is given to believe that he looks unwell under this lighting. To distract from the Subject's lifeless deportment, a small elevated box is positioned stage left. It is a tiny replica of the stage, upon which sways the doctor's beloved Silly Sally adorned in a tiny replica of Dr. Whistler's attire, complete with top hat tied with string around her chin. What elicits the sighs of adoration from the crowd, though, are the five kittens dressed like the Subject poking their pink faces from the lower half of the box. Collectively they are known as the Kitten Chorus.

Dr. Whistler plucks a pointer from the easel and taps it thrice.

"Mr. Stick is unlike the others you will meet in the Gallery of Suffering. He is not one given to displays of emotion. He comes from hearty Austrian stock and his time in the mountainous West further developed his stoicism. Mr. Stick's aloof demeanor is, in fact, evidence of his talent. Pain of head, chest, stomach, ear canal, extremities; burns and scalds; the bane of sciatica—you, too, can hold mastery over them! Mr. Stick is a prophet of a sorts; he shall lead each of us into salvation, right here on Earth."

The Subject has trained himself to look straight ahead, especially when hearing the squeal of hinges as the doctor opens the box. The Subject cannot see the needles within but he can imagine how they must gleam in the firelight. The turn of the page upon the easel is loud. So is the gasp from the crowd that follows.

Dr. Whistler touches his pointer to a colored medical illustration of a man flayed of his skin. His body is woven from vessels like a topographical map of red tributaries, and these lines thicken as they draw toward the heart, one of the many organs depicted. This plate is labeled "The Chief Arteries and Veins of the Body" and numbers from one to thirty match a list written down the edge of the paper.

"Oh, the human body," sighs Dr. Whistler. "How many pockets of wonder are contained within! How numerous the sockets of pain, how frequent the intersections of agony! We have notated here, honored guests, thirty threads of circulatory fabric, from major artery to superficial vein. If I were to invite the hardiest among you to take this chair, the piercing of a single one of these vessels would result in acute suffering and significant spilling of blood."

The Subject knows that the first needle is coming. He can see it flashing.

"The Astonishing Mr. Stick is made of sterner material. Part of it is nature; part of it is the combination of herbs, pollen, grasses, honeys, minerals, and cured meat juices that he has ingested since birth. See for yourself its power."

The tip of the needle touches the Subject's chest. The Subject has not lost his sense of touch. He wishes to make that abundantly clear. His senses have been but truncated, so that he feels what happens just beyond the point of pain. This manifests itself as a hard, heavy, sobbing sadness of the physical flesh.

"Number thirty." Dr. Whistler adopts a technical tone when reading from the list. "Branches of the pulmonary arteries, veins in the lung."

These are not sewing needles. The steel is thin as a whisker and as long as a child's forearm. The needle passes through the Subject's clothes and on into muscle. The audience gasps. The Kitten Chorus hears this cue and rescues the audience from overwhelming horror by mewling a parody of the Subject's tribulation. The Subject cannot fathom how the felines have been so well trained. In his experience only dogs are trainable; cats are but proctors of chaos. Nothing that happens upon this stage each night impresses the Subject more than this.

The doctor continues with the insertion. The Subject can hear the squeak of his own flesh as it resists the steel invader; he can feel the itch of a lung sac being lanced. Ofttimes the puncture releases trapped air and it feels like a bullet being shot from inside the Subject's body. Dr. Whistler stops the insertion. This needle is not withdrawn. This is important to the overall effect of the performance. He sifts through his box. It makes a pleasant xylophone sound.

"Number twenty-nine: kidney, renal artery and vein."

Dr. Whistler bobs about the stage inserting needles and counting down. (twenty-eight: the long saphenous vein; twenty-seven: femoral vein; twenty-six: iliac vein; twenty-five: median vein—the words are as familiar to the Subject as a song.) The Subject takes on a porcupine appearance; the evidence becomes irrefutable. Dr. Whistler moves ever upward. (five: common carotid artery; four: innominate vein; three: aorta; two: temporal artery.) Needles pass through the Subject's heart, his throat. The Kitten Chorus keeps up their uncanny comedy. The audience is sickened, then amused. The dramatic swings leave them exhausted.

"'Pain pays the income of each precious thing,'" says Dr. Whistler. The audience chokes on a collective breath as the point of the final lancet rests upon the Subject's eyeball. "William Shakespeare—he knew of what he spoke, did he not?"

Those in the front row are treated to a soft popping sound as the needle punctures the eye. The Subject's lashes flutter, he cannot help it, as the needle slides through the vitreous humour. Dr. Whistler, tired now, dripping sweat, nevertheless takes care to complete the insertion at an angle sharp enough to skirt the brain entirely. He is nervous about the brain. The Subject can tell. Dr. Whistler cannot afford a miscue that might turn his already taciturn attraction into a vegetable.

The Subject is helped to his feet and for thirty seconds he stands under his own power. It takes a while, but he raises an arm and waves while thirty inserted needles *click-clack* against one other. Women fan themselves. Men blurt expletives. The Subject is ushered offstage by the same two men who brought him in, one of whom, with little artistry, extracts each of the quills. The other worker leaves to join Dr. Whistler on stage to begin the bonanza of selling. "Pain" is a vague malady; anything with which the Pageant of Health is overstocked becomes the sale *du jour*.

Shaken but already loosening the caps from their medicines, the exiting audience is met by the Soothing Foursome, whose silken voices keen like the whistle of a far-off train. To the tune of "Auld Lang Syne" they transform that evening's commercial message into a jewel of four-part harmony:

> *So long as mortal ills endure,*
> *And mankind suffers pain,*
> *So long shall Apache Blood Purifier*
> *Its trusted name maintain.*

Now, Dearest Reader, I—the Subject of the above play—ask you: was I really so cruel to Little Johnny Grandpa? How could I come to his aid when I was unable to aid myself? My prose is flowery, that I cannot help, and so you project upon me sensitivity, gentility, compassion. You are wrong to do so. Any sensitivity or gentility that remained in my pallid corpse leaked out through thirty holes inflicted dozens of times per month, each drop of compassion drawn from me like a bulb of blood. You cannot see these holes from where you sit. Nonetheless, I guarantee you that they are there.

V.

LIFE, UNINTERESTED IN A CORPSE'S ashen daydreams, rolled on. Popular conversation topics among Pageant employees ranged as capriciously as unfed bison. For a time discussion centered upon the so-called St. Augustine Monster, the washed-up carcass of some fantastic sea beast workers saw during a swing through Florida. Then it was the late 1896 death of Alfred Noble, the inventor of dynamite, a substance all Pageant laborers held in high regard. (I, of course, wondered if my pop was out there somewhere raising a toast.) Then, for a spell, it was President McKinley's war with Spain off our southeastern coast that had our boys oiling their weapons and fantasizing of bagging a baker's dozen of Spaniards.

Were the degenerates of Dr. Whistler's valorous patriots or avid newshounds? Neither! These uneducated louts were more insulated from the real world than your typical Midwestern clodhopper. Their insipid chatter served one distinct purpose: to distract them from the deadly downturn of our business.

That is not to say crowds were thin. Southerners, especially, amassed like ants, spilling in incredible numbers from the smallest of holes. It was that few possessed the money to purchase product. The Barker slashed prices, slashed them again. Pitches were dumbed down to one-word bleats: "Health! Drink! Good!" We often moved on a mere two days after arrival, our passage from county to county marked only by the levels of mongoloidism and the irritating quirks of local patois.

By 1898, Dr. Whistler's Pageant of Health was as broke as the oafs before whom we danced. No one was happy. Vital repairs were delayed and the stage buckled mid-spiel more than once. Laborers, ornery after anemic payment, raised hell in local barrooms and landed in the clink. The chow served up by Professor Bach was reduced to a succession of ambiguous stews, each one underperforming the previous. The Soothing Foursome had it worst of all. Whites everywhere were disturbed by colored folk singing anything other than spirituals and the Foursome was greeted by thrown fruit, discharged tobacco, fierce invectives.

It was not long before I noticed the Barker looking askance. Oh, I knew what went on in his hateful head. My show, for all its sick thrill, was a resounding flop. Crowds were modest, to put it charitably, and it was becoming daily routine for the Barker to accuse me of sabotage. Without me showing a little *joie de vivre*, said he, the act was doomed! Naturally, I made no reply. If he felt that I was scaring away customers—the worst of sins—so much the better. Toss me to the roadside, why don't you? Leave me for dead and perhaps the wish would come true.

You will concur that the stressors about me were significant. Regardless, I had come damned close to relaxing late one night when Little Johnny Grandpa swatted aside my tent flap with his cane and entered, small chest heaving and face crimson from some newborn indignity. His cry was vehement:

"You can talk, sir."

For two unspeakable years I'd been cool to Johnny to little effect.

85

He spoke to me; I gazed into a neutral direction. He adjusted my red kerchief; I pulled away. But he viewed me as a fellow hopeless case—a dismal honor—and was determined to be the Damon to my Pythias! The Horatio to my Hamlet! The Panza to my Quixote! I worked hard to deserve none of these comparisons and still the child's fealty withstood erosion.

I favored Johnny with a minute shake of the head. No, stupid child, I could not speak, nor could I stand. I was powerless to better my pitiful situation and cursed him for suggesting otherwise.

"But y'can, sir. I know it. I been listening at night, y'see. Y'roll thisaway and thataway. Y'roll so hard there's straw all over the place. And from deep down y'chest come moaning up words."

Reader, I have taken pains to establish that I do not sleep, yes? When lucky, however, I could achieve a trancelike state in which my racing mind, for the most part, shifted to a quieter gear. But not once had I entertained the thought that the ramshackle bellows of my lungs remembered their former purpose.

"Sounds t'me like 'Chester.' Or 'Tafta.' Y'say it over and over again, Mr. Stick, honest y'do."

Testa.

This jolted me more than any boxful of needles.

" Y'got your bars and y'got your straw . . . but it ain't much, Mr. Stick. No, sir, it ain't. All y'need to do is talk to me. If y'can tell me what you want—this Chester or Tafta or anything at all—I'll get it for you. Have faith in me, sir. Don't no one keep watch on an old man like me. But I ain't run down all the way, not yet I ain't."

Quietude had long been my consort and to her, for the moment, I remained faithful.

"Don't think of it like no favor. There's something I want too.

Y'start talking better, walking better, and then you and me, we get out of here. I know, I'm slow. You ain't so quick on y'feet y'self. The two of us together, though? I figure we might surprise 'em all."

Still I said nothing. Too many radical ideas, too quickly.

The boy stabbed his cane.

"Ain't you sick of being quiet?"

He shifted the cane from right hand to left, left hand to right. Gradually his countenance grew stormy. Sullenness twisted his loose skin into a spook mask and summoned profilgacies of phlegm.

"Y'won't talk to me? Snort! Snoooooort! Y'won't even try? Hack! Hack! Spit! Why, y'must *like* it. Y'must *like* what the bastard does to you. Well, *he* can be y'friend, then. Y'go on ahead. Maybe when y'come back from having all that fun with y'friend, maybe I'll be gone! *Cough!*"

He exited with what passed for him as a righteous stride.

Six hours later, the sun not yet risen, Johnny tripped his way back to my cage.

I heard him puffing and grunting across the lot and prepared myself to endure the coldest of shoulders. But when the tent flap opened, the usual tapeworm supplies were not tucked under his arm. He limped up to my cage, lungs whistling like a punctured accordion.

"You're gonna talk," gasped he, "So help me, y'gonna talk."

He stuffed his hand into the front pocket of his overalls and foisted upon me a box of capsules branded with the slogan "Pleasant to Take, Magical in Its Effects!" The dear, dumb lad! He'd raided Dr. Whistler's supply of product in the foolish hope that one of the preposterous panaceas might actually work! With an exhausted hand I pantomimed the basic problem, touching my throat, then my stomach, then my bowels. Would the ingested material sit and spoil in my gut before leaking out of my bottom? No, thank you.

Johnny's lips quivered in a doughy frown. I braced for the worst. Instead, he dug from his pocket a final product that did not require swallowing: the Little Miracle Electric Mexican Stuttering Ring.

It was, indeed, a ring made from the cheapest tin, which one wore around one's finger to lessen instances of stuttering. Useless though the trinket was, I found myself pushing it onto the ring finger of my right hand, where, I had to admit, it drew the eye away from Mr. Avery's fishing-hook wound. I forced a wan smile and displayed the adornment for the boy's approval. Pride fired up his rheumy eyes.

Perhaps the ring contained some magic after all, for I realized that the pint-sized fool was correct. There was one thing that an unnatural beast like myself wanted quite badly. The clue had been in that single word Johnny had heard me mutter.

I positioned the dead worms of my lips and gave speech a try.

"*Re.*"

How snorting and swinish was the grudging grunt!

But how pleasurable was that second syllable, the buzz of a wrathful wasp.

"*Vvvvvvenge.*"

VI.

WE WERE ON OUR WAY. Shortly after the noon hour the following day, Johnny ducked into my tent. He had to tell me of his discovery, "Something to make y'talking go faster."

I held up the finger sporting the Little Miracle Electric Mexican Stuttering Ring, all the remedy I needed. He beamed at the gesture but asked if I'd ever seen Vera Diana stretch through her regimen of backstage gymnastics. Had I ever! Not even a dead man could resist gaping over a female form so erotically contorted. Well, said Johnny, he'd just overheard from a customer a ten-dollar word that would limber my vocal organs in the same way, so daring and multisyllabic was its composition.

"Don't know what it means," confessed he, "but it's got 'bout every sound y'need."

The word was "indefatigable."

It was, I had to admit, one hell of a word. Sized next to it, "revenge" was duck soup. For the rest of the day, I nestled the word to my breast as one might a shivering, wounded bird, for it was only at night that it might enjoy silence and space enough to fly. My initial attempts, though, were inhuman:

Unnh-zhunn-shaaa-kuuhn-unnh-wuhh.

A week more of practice and I had matriculated to another monstrosity:

Ehh-dehh-hwa-hee-uhh-wul.

Discouraging, yes, but what other path was there to pave? Over
the subsequent month I spent uncountable hours picturing my teeth,
lips, and tongue, going over in my mind how these organs had once
upon a time moved in intricate concert, and when next I attempted
my chorus there came from my mouth the frightful noises of ani-
malia. Rat clicks, raccoon gurgles, the wheeze of a nightmaring dog:

Inn-dehh-fweh-tee-ul-buh.

Steady work continued by the rooster and by the locust. Never
in my days as a tutored pupil, and certainly not as a Black Hand combatant, had I hammered so hard at an assignment. My reward was a
semblance of sense:

Inn-dee-fah-tee-guh-buh.

In the lonely darkness of my rehearsal sessions, I began to weigh
the wasted words of my life. Smug retorts to men whose bones I
split with my blackjack, empty flatteries to whores who were but pale
echoes of Wilma Sue, superficial solicitudes to the nameless bartenders who kept my steins wet. If I could have those words back, just a
few, I would return the blood, the sweat, the beer, all of it with due
interest:

In-de-fa-ti-ga-ble.

Indefatigable.

INDEFATIGABLE.

INDEFATIGABLE!!!

The word became my battle cry. Dawn's arrival no longer filled
me with dread, for I was indefatigable. The coin-jangle of the poor
giving their last pennies to hucksters no longer scoured me raw with

guilt, for I was indefatigable. The Barker could plunge all the needles he wanted into my torpid flesh and it would not deter me from my goal—I was indefatigable! Speech came faster; short sentences were within my reach. I could hardly wait for nighttime so that I could chant into the dark like a zealot.

It did not take a berobed scholar to valuate what these months meant to Johnny. He delighted in my developed whispers and clapped his palsied hands at each cunning new twist of my tongue. Every word I rediscovered was a scrap of hope thrown in his direction. Those scraps, I found, were large enough for me to nibble upon, too. Before long I believed that I had mastered enough speech to blurt a cold (if abbreviated) soliloquy to Luca Testa before murdering him.

Chicago was a vast distance to cover for two conspirators so lame of leg. My brainstorm was to bring the villain to me and force him to divulge all he knew of my murder, what black sorcery might have tainted it, perhaps even how to effect a cure. Then I'd repay him for his services by gunning him down with a sidearm Johnny would steal from one of our showmen. Firing a pistol would take a mastery of hand similar to my mastery of mouth, but there was time yet to achieve it. Finally, once the malefactor was dead, I would ride away in his trans-portation—and, yes, if possible, take this loyal little lad with me.

The Black Hand had functioned quite well via the deployment of written letters, so I would follow the example. I bade Johnny to gather some materials for writing and three days later he smuggled to me a composition book, the same brand as I'd used as a student. A disfavorable coincidence, but nonetheless I set pen to paper. How the first squiggle of ink emboldened me! Poets, librettists, and son-neteers, thought I, would shrivel in comparison!

That, it turned out, was overstating it. My hand was weak, my pencraft elementary. Johnny, though, was an absolute illiterate, so I had no choice but to proceed, albeit with brevity. Much humanity had I lost in death, but literary eloquence, ground to so sharp a point under Testa himself, lived on. To wit:

To Our Lord & Master Mr. Testa—

Dost thou remember May 7, 1896? On that day a fat tick dropped from your well-fed belly—a tick called Zebulon Finch. I hope you remember the name, for Mr. Finch now feeds from the blood of a traveling jubilee called Dr. Whistler's Pageant of Health.

Come see for yourself.

Exhausted by the effort, I dropped the pen with the melodrama of a Victorian heroine. Would the archvillain take the bait? Of this I had no doubt. It was a direct taunt and Testa did not trifle with matters of pride. He would spare no expense in tracking down the Pageant and taking a second shot at my murder.

On the opposite side I wrote Testa's Chicago address and passed the letter through the iron bars. I fixed Johnny with the heartiest expression of confidence and encouragement I could muster. It would be up to him to hobble to town and post the letter. He had already done so much; I had no choice but to wager that this, too, was within range of his abilities. A bad bet, as it turned out, but can you blame me for placing it?

VII.

THE DEVIL IN THE SILK hat stormed the tent at daybreak. He was shoeless, sockless, and stripped to the waist, his neck spotted with shaving cream and florid from the application of boiling water. (Incongruously, he was top-hatted.) With one hand, he pushed ahead of him my diminutive accomplice. The man's other hand, quite alarmingly, clutched a shotgun large enough to fell a rhinoceros.

The Barker pressed the remonstrating lad into the bars of my cage. Yours truly flinched—so human a reaction for a monster! Johnny's forehead took quite a knock and I believe he would have collapsed had not the Barker snared him by the neck and held him aloft.

The scoundrel touched his hat brim in greeting.

"Are you a sporting man, Mr. Stick?"

For all my language lessons, I was struck dumb!

"No, your present circumstances do not allow for it. Alas, nor do mine. In my younger years, however, I was a willing pupil, and my uncle taught me to track, to shoot, to dress my kill. I was not without some natural talent. The first thing you learn is that the hunt is best at dawn. What say we set this varmint loose, you and I, and see which of us can tag him first?"

Reader, do not fault me for thinking that the maniac meant each word. His very life was a twisted game; the Boardwalk of Chance

93

might as well have been the setting for his every interaction.

"Come now, Stick. Shall I send this boy up like skeet? Fly this boy who so wishes to fly away? No? Too bad; I feel the bloodlust churning. Maybe it is you, the bull in the cage, that ought to be set free for me to dodge and dispatch."

His grin, kept thus far at even keel, curled away as if eaten by fire.

"Should either of you fine young gentlemen operate under the belief that I can be made a pigeon of, let me take this beautiful golden daybreak, delivered to us from a giving Lord, to relieve you of that presumption. Do you not see that this pageant is to me as a child is to his mother? When it wakes, I know its sounds, its odors, the ways in which it wiggles. Something is awry, I attend to it. I give it either my breast or the back of my hand."

For emphasis he gave Johnny a shake and one of the boy's few remaining teeth rang off an iron bar. Johnny did not recoil, but for the second time I did. The letter had been my idea; this beating belonged to me.

"Stopping this child at full bore was no more difficult than stopping a mouse by stepping on its tail. They squeak the same, too. Crinkling 'twixt the lad's hand and cane was a missive bound for the local postman. He claimed the words were his invention. I had myself a chuckle at that. If there is one thing I am sure of regarding this particular entertainer, it is that he goes about life quite unhindered by intellect. But you? I had you pegged as daft. And now this exhibit of authorship! Jolly good show."

"Sorry, Mr. Stick, sir," slurred Johnny. "Sorry, sir, I'm sorry."

The Barker smiled.

"'Mr. Stick.' That *is* the name on the posters and fliers for which I have paid so handsomely. Strange that it is not the name referenced in this note."

He set his shotgun against a tower of boxed tonic—within my grasp, had I the strength!—and pulled from his trousers familiar stationery. It proved too delicate to unfold with one hand and so he heaved Johnny to the dirt. The boy attempted to mitigate the impact, but his brittle bones offered no more protection than a handful of twigs. His elbows went akimbo and his sternum landed with a crack. For the third time in short sequence I cringed.

The Barker cleared his throat, smoothed out the paper, and squinted through an imaginary monocle.

"Zeb—" He stretched out his lower lip, pretending to be stymied by the most exotic of spellings. "Zeb-yew-lon Finch." He straightened his spine as if becoming conscious of a dignitary standing before him. "So melodious a moniker for a man who wallows in straw, who stinks of the animal that occupied his cage before him. Is the name genuine? Or a *nom de guerre?* I wonder. So much I wonder about, frankly, after having read this letter."

Johnny moaned from his crumpled station in the dirt.

"Y'don't talk that way to Mr. Stick. Hack. No one does. Hack. *Hack.*"

"Mice are quiet," the Barker reminded.

"*Hack! Snoooooooort!* Spit!"

The sounds crackled with urgency. I glanced and saw red ropes of saliva stretch from the boy's whiskered lips. He was cradling his ribcage with an arm that ended in a dangling, injured wrist. I appealed to the Barker, but the rage baking from his bare chest was enough to compete with the uncharacteristic fall heat. The man's temperature had, in fact, been building steadily over the past year—the truth, Dearest Reader, is that Zeb-yew-lon Finch had chosen to ignore it.

The Barker leaned a naked shoulder against the cage, affecting nonchalance.

"Zebulon Finch, this letter boasts, is still alive. I suppose that's mostly true. It goes on to state that the aforementioned Mr. Finch is retained by Dr. Whistler's Pageant of Health. Another truth. You acquit yourself well, Mr. Stick. Aside from belabored metaphor, little else is communicated. I find that curious. This is but a simple declaration of existence. Who, I wonder, would care to know the true identity of Mr. Stick?"

"He's twice the man of you!" cried Johnny. "Thief! Sodomite!"

"Charming child," said the Barker. "Lucky for me, this memorandum is addressed." He gave the paper a dramaturgic perusal. "Marked to the attention of one Mr. Luca Testa of Chicago. Now, I am trying to recall. Do I know a Mr. Testa? Hmm. No. No, I think not, and I know every medicine show operator from Philadelphia to San Francisco. Yet there is but one reason you would send such an epistle. *Mr. Testa*"—his utterance dripped with disgust; at least we agreed upon that—"is the owner of a fledgling fair and both of you are planning to jump ship."

Here he'd made a pompous gaffe! The self-absorbed jester could not fathom a world existing beyond his profession. He beamed at the two of us as if we were darling children.

"When I think how the two of you must have huddled together, drawing these big plans in excited whispers, the poignancy is almost too much to bear."

"Up your ass," said Johnny. "Cough. Cough. *Cough*."

"I cannot imagine why this Mr. Testa would want to sew such troublesome warts onto his own flesh. The point is, Mr. Stick, you belong to me, and no one else shall have you."

"I don't want to belong to you!" said Johnny. "I'd rather die!"

Frustrated, I think, by my lack of expression, the Barker turned on the crumpled lad with sudden ferocity.

"You think I shall lose one minute's sleep over your fate, old man? Slobbering over my audiences nightly? Barely able to stand erect?"

"I don't care!"

"You were worth nothing in your first four years, something marginal the next four, and now very little indeed in your twilight. You say you wish to die? Be my guest, though I implore you to schedule it during our six o'clock show. Your funeral, if well promoted, could be your highest grossing event."

"I'll kill you," wept Johnny. "Someday I'll kill you."

"You'll what me? Hard to hear due to the slobber, the missing teeth."

"Help! Someone! Anyone! Help!"

The Barker looked surprised, as if he'd believed crying out for aid was a tactic below even this brat. Johnny was either too young, too old, or too afraid to hold to any such code. He ratcheted his blare and the Barker become aware of how the scene might look to someone answering the call: he half-dressed and armed, Johnny cowering, me looking on from my cage like the Marquis de Sade.

The Barker drove his foot into the boy's side.

"Quiet," said he.

Johnny yelped.

The Barker frowned and kicked again. It pained his naked foot and so when the boy next wailed he drove the butt of the shotgun into Johnny's shoulder. Johnny's response this time was more like a choke of surprise. I swear that the Barker giggled before he drove the gun again, using both hands to ensure that it popped against pelvis or knee or chest with just enough force to sting.

"You are never to speak to him again," said the Barker.

"What?" shrieked Johnny. "Who?"

"Far too loud." The Barker cracked the stock against the boy's shin.

"Ow! Please! Stop!"

On the chin this time—the bone did not break but must have come close.

"Mr. *Stick*," clarified the Barker. "You are longer to speak to Mr. Stick. Disobey and I will . . . well, I will come up with something. Tie you up in the woods by the feet, let the bears have at you. Are we understood?"

"Yes!"

This time the crotch. Johnny's fists clutched his groin.

"Quieter, mouse."

"*Yes.*"

That should have ended it. But the Barker was giddy now and as a punctuation mark he brought the shotgun down a final time onto the boy's ribs. The snap I heard was dry as timber collapsing in a campfire. Johnny gurgled. It sounded nothing like a man of seventy years or more. It was the sound of a child under savage assault, pure and simple.

What happened next is beyond my authorial acumen to describe. I had never harmed a child while working with the Black Hand, and yet had heard plenty of exclamations similar to those of Johnny. My mind raced to these aural memories and blindness overtook me, hot and silvery, like slipping into the mercury rivers of Hades. *Was this Death*, thought I, *come once more to claim me?* A hurtling backwards commenced: three years of performances, thousands of piercing needles; Mr. Hobby, the Soothing Foursome, the whole damned lot of rogues; Little Johnny Grandpa gifting me the kerchief to cover my grappling-hook wound; and then, as if it were in parallel time, brighter images of Abigail Finch and her nursemaids pressing stiff new shirts against my body; and then Wilma Sue, my Wilma Sue, tiptoeing across her room to watch a rainstorm rage outside Patterson's window, the lamplight curving around her naked hip like my caressing hand. These things were *life*, and I could have no more of it, had fribbled it away when I'd possessed it, and sweeping me up now was the vortex of oblivion, experienced once before upon that Chicago beach, those seventeen minutes of perfect perpetual motion. This fresh taste of Death would not last, that I knew, and so I muttered profanities to Gød the deadbeat Father in the same breath that I told Him that I loved Him for allowing me a quick, sweet lick of this dimness, this stillness, this silence when I needed it most.

La silenziosità—a phrase Giuseppe Fratelli had taught me.

The Silentness.

It was at that instant of *la silenziosità* that the Barker turned to me with a sunny grin.

"So, Mr. Stick, what say you to this—"

With every particle of psychic might I held to *la silenziosità* for four or five more seconds. It was long enough. The grin died on the Barker's face. Color poured from his neck as if loosed from a beheading. There was a slackening of his every muscle down to the tiniest of forehead and eyelid.

He was paralyzed by my Death-look.

What he saw inside of it, or so I came to believe, was Death in its wholeness, its hugeness, its inescapability, and the torment Death would deliver unto him should he not alter his behaviors. The Barker could not see such a thing and not be frightened. Nor could he fail to hate me for it afterward.

The Dearest Reader might presume I loved every second. To the contrary! 'Twas horrid—*horrid*. As candied had been my curtailed vision into the void, the bitter aftertaste of its absence was a thousand times worse. The Barker's eyes, you see, reflected back every atom of my own hideousness. So too, probably, had the eyes of the hundreds I'd pulped at the behest of Testa, but only now could I see with clarity how evil I'd been then and how very alone I was now.

La silenziosità slipped away. The Barker staggered in place, blinking and harrumphing, too shaken to reassemble his former authority. He reached to straighten a lapel that was not there. He tried on different expressions but discarded each as if it were an embarrassing bit of costume.

"You . . . Mr. Finch." He shook his head. "*Stick.* Mr. *Stick.*"

Even the beaten child sensed something unprecedented had occurred. Johnny peeked from his fetal coil as the Barker remembered his shotgun, snatched it with both hands, tried to use its weight to reestablish reality.

"We are not finished. You . . . you monster. You and I are not yet through."

The Barker wanted out of there. He hurried to the tent flap and lifted it. The light was far whiter than when he had entered. He squinted, looked to the dirt, and then whirled around to face us once more, fully awakened to a humiliation he did not even understand. Nothing was being forgotten, not my insubordination nor the immobilizing experience of seeing his own black future in my dead eyes. With a hand still clutching our doomed, undelivered letter to Luca Testa, the Barker gestured to Johnny.

"Come now. We will get Professor Bach to patch you up. After all, you took a nasty fall. You ought to take more care."

VIII.

ONE WEEK LATER IT WAS Halloween. As a lifelong entertainer, the Barker could not be ignorant of the holiday's roots in *dies parentales*, the Roman festival of the dead, in particular the midnight rites of Feralia in which the malevolent deceased were exorcized.

The date was ideal for exorcising me as well.

So lightless was the October sky that it slid into night without notice. The moment I was assisted through the back door of the Gallery of Suffering, the Barker locked eyes with me and I knew. This was to be the final performance of the troublesome, underhanded, secretive, and astonishing—though not quite astonishing enough—Mr. Stick.

It surprised me that my first regret was that I would not be able to say farewell and good luck to Johnny. As was the Barker's decree, the two of us had been kept apart since the morning our plot was uncovered, but from afar I had spied the bandages that sheathed his ribs as well as the sling that cradled his wrist. The Barker's fabricated explanations began the night after the injuries and I heard them repeatedly as I queued up abaft the stage.

"This cherished child hurt a rib whilst chasing his beloved red ball over a hill, running slower than the next child by a power of ten. This same sprightly cub sprained his wrist shooting marbles with his chums—but how he wanted that golden aggie! Ladies and gentle-man, I see your faces and we can, if you'd like, lament this child's frac-tures and bruises. But I choose instead to celebrate them! Youth will not be repressed, no matter how unfortunate and twisted its form, and for this I give all thanks to Gød."

The idiots clucked in appreciation.

"Oh, Little Johnny Grandpa? Look what Dr. Whistler has for you. I purchased it from a lad whose pockets were overstuffed with marbles. That's right—it is the selfsame golden aggie! No, no, child, do not waste words thanking me. You glow with happiness and that is thanks enough."

At least, thought I, as I was shoved on stage that Halloween night of 1899, I would not have to endure such lies much longer.

Ohioans proved themselves indulgent of the macabre holiday by amassing in unusual numbers. At least twenty-five pairs of eyes reflected our fiery stage lamps. This pleased the Barker. Their word-of-mouth would lend credence to the eulogy for Mr. Stick he would no doubt repeat as frequently as he bestowed the same golden aggie upon Little Johnny Grandpa night after night.

He was in rare voice, a baritone burr I'd not heard since my first months. I let it lull me. He spun his anecdotes with so much rel-ish that he smacked his lips. He brandished the first of the needles as if it were a rabbit pulled from a magician's hat while the Kitten Chorus hit every cue. He orchestrated like a conductor with the most resourceful of batons, alternating moods of scherzo and fugue; inserting commentary in both passionate glissandos and whispering nocturnes; sustaining impossible fermatas until the cliff-drop of his refrain of needles. The audience was his faithful, gasping chorale.

The music made me as delirious as any paying customer. We

broke the one-hour mark, a staggering feat, and began eating into the time reserved for Pullman Larry's sharpshooting show. In shadow against the side of the tent, I could make out the line of impatient ticket holders. They would have to wait. The final lance was slipped from the velvet casing. He held it up to the light. It was nigh time for the Barker to do what he had set forth that night to do.

The needle approached my eye. I felt it tickle my eyelashes. Then it became a dark wedge scribbling across the surface of my eyeball as it searched for a different entry point than usual, for this time the Barker meant to run my brain straight through, and afterward—who knew? Cremation? Burial? One way or the other I was finished.

The great, and possibly disappointing, surprise of that instant was how dearly I wished to live! Perhaps it was my desire for revenge upon the Barker, upon Luca Testa, upon Gød Himself, I do not know; or perhaps it was something Mr. Charles Darwin would have endorsed, a primordial slithering toward life, always life. Woe—I do not know! But in that climactic moment, the walls of fear (and dignity?) that I'd built about me collapsed and my mouth dropped open.

"Euri. Pides," said I.

The Barker pulled back an inch. His expression was something new.

"Euripides." This time I got the fifth-century tragedian's name out in a single breath. My voice was raw and multi-octave, not unlike the groaning of five rows of wooden benches when each person upon them leans forward in unison—which is precisely what happened.

For a moment I was as fearful as a child who has lost his mother. The Barker offered no solace. His face was a soup, churning and changing. The Kitten Chorus grew fidgety at the change in program and hissed to be set free. With trepidation I scanned the crowd of Ohioans. Moths danced near open flames like lingering particles of my spoken words.

There was nothing to do but complete what I had begun. Johnny, my patient English teacher, was owed that much.

"'No. One. Can con. Fidently say. That. He will. Still. Be living. Tomorrow.'"

With a snap, a moth perished in fire. A pair of tickets were dropped; you could hear the thin paper rustle past the lace hem of a dress. Not a single man or woman or child in Ohio, it seemed, had expected the final quote of the evening to come from the Subject.

Their stares drove me to panic. What was I doing in front of all of these good people? Yes, of course, finish the scene! I rose to wobbly knees and lifted a trembling hand in salute. It was the usual end to the usual act and it was to be met with the usual scattering of hand-claps.

Instead, this humble gesture was the coup de grâce of a performance of legend. Dozens of breaths expelled at once and the pandemonium began. Men of poise shouted "Bravo!" Women abandoned decorum by squealing. Applause lit somewhere stage right and in seconds consumed the entire tent. They were on their feet. They were stomping on the pews. Those in line outside began lifting the edge of the tent to see what was behind the bedlam. Children's faces appeared first; being monkeys, they smiled and clapped in imitation and crawled inside, and then their parents, those non-paying trespassers, streamed after in chase, clueless as to what had occurred but nonetheless bewitched, tipping their hats to the Barker, and to me as well.

I backpedaled from it and stumbled; a hand shot out to steady me. I followed the wrist, elbow, and shoulder to find that my rescuer was none other than my enemy. His mouth made a horizontal line that his forehead mimicked. I do not know if he'd guessed that I'd suspected my intended fate that night, but he could not get rid of me now, not after I'd generated this reaction.

The Barker and his fellows scooted me offstage with their hands at my back, as if congratulating me on a job well done. Once behind the curtain, they drew away as if I were boiling with contagion. Pullman Larry stood close tapping his spurred boot, gazing pointedly at a pocket watch that told of the late hour. Mr. Hobby was there, too, chewing at his mustache, his forehead slick with perspiration, a pencil behind each ear. The Barker held out my elbow to his most trusted associate.

"Remove the needles and take him to his cage. Make haste; our dentist is truant."

Hobby winced apologetically. "They demand another show."

The Barker blinked. "They—they what?"

Hobby winced again.

"The folks in line. They wish for Mr. Stick to give a command performance."

Pullman Larry crossed his arms. "This is cow shit."

"Our first audience," continued Hobby, "has cycled around to see him again."

"To see that comatose feller?" sputtered Pullman. "Y'all are pullin' my leg."

The Barker glared at me. This was my fault. I had put him in this position of having to choose between loathing and money. Really, it was no choice at all.

"Fine. We shall perform again. Send out word."

Pullman's hands gripped the handles of his twin pistols.

"This is a danged outrage!"

"You'll be paid per usual," snarled the Barker.

"I been playin' the final spot here for a coon's age and I ain't about to watch no dang voodoo doll take my place!"

"I make the decisions here," said the Barker. "You'll do well to remember that."

Pullman cocked and uncocked his triggers.

"You pack too many folks in there and whatever the secret is to his little trick? Mark my words, it won't last. Then you'll come crawling back to me and we'll see what percentage I accept then, won't we?" He planted his cowboy hat. "Make more coin selling my Gød of Pain anyhow. More than you'll ever see!"

With a flail of pink fringe he turned on his three-inch heels and was gone. In the resultant flap of tarp, I caught a glimpse of Johnny outside, his face slack with either shock or pride. When the flap closed, there was something about it, even then, that felt final.

The Barker massaged his closed eyes for a moment.

"See to it there is no chaos in our queue, Mr. Hobby. You there, boy. Come here. Remove these needles into this box." He sighed and gave me the flat look of an infantryman ordered to fight alongside a despised rival. "Yet another stupendous show is upon us."

IX.

HOW DO I BEGIN TO describe the months following my speaking debut? One night after that auspicious improvisation, the Barker delivered to me a terse directive. Our stock climax of a needle into the eye would heretofore be replaced with a short testimonial from Mr. Stick about how the product of the night (whatever it might be) had provided me with my enviable abilities. Sensing a subtle shift in power, I agreed and when the moment came I summoned verbiage memorized from one of the Barker's many pitches. The audience approved and out came the wallets.

Attendance surged. Pullman Larry's sharpshooting show did indeed find itself swapping with mine, and the dentist made no secret about his disgust at serving as my opening act. Even unhappier was the Barker. After years of dwindling income, his profits were on the rise, and yet he behaved as if each coin he counted was stippled with invisible barbs. Oh, how he hated me.

Mr. Hobby presented me with a suit so new it bore the indents of the manufacturer's rack. I was grateful to peel off the old one. The humans who lined up an hour in advance were not there to see my snappy suit; I knew that. They wanted to see me take punishment. But their interest in my verbal contributions was real, too, and by and by I found myself incorporating more speech into the routine, punctuating the Barker's anthology of over-trod citations with vapid interjections: "Hear, hear!" "Wise words, those!"

I was not above humor, either: "Golly, but that scratches an itch," I'd say when he drove a pin through my heart. One night I told an entire joke. After the Barker inserted a particularly long needle, I said, in the deadpan which was becoming my trademark, "I cannot think of what I would do without you. But it is worth a try." The laughter: uproarious! The Barker's blush: priceless!

You may wonder how I massed so many words in sequence. Every inch of progress I owed to Johnny, for he'd sparked what had become a regenerating need to speak. Still the Barker's decree held and the boy and I were kept distant. Worse, the lad had taken to drink; not before or since have I seen anyone take to it more quickly. His nose swelled, patches of strawberry veins invaded his cheeks, and he became shackled to the kind of headaches even a grown man struggles to bear.

I was resolute in blaming Pullman Larry. With each state boundary we crossed, the dastardly dentist would buy up local moonshines and amuse himself by giving them to Johnny to choke down. Pullman would clap the boy on the humped back and encourage bigger mouthfuls as remedy for his sundry ailments. Whenever Johnny fell on his face while crossing the yard, I needed only turn my head to find Pullman Larry bent over with the force of his guffaws.

It is helpful to remember that Little Johnny Grandpa had been a fixture in the Gallery of Suffering for most of his life. Doing his show stinking drunk did not present much of a challenge, not at first. Audiences were happy to chalk up his slurring to his medical condition. Scuttlebutt, however, had it that his show was swerving into unsafe territory. He moved about the Gallery with the stagger of a lush, not of an old man, and customers knew the difference. When he collapsed into the laps of women, no more did they twitter at his folly; rather, they recoiled from his breath.

But who had time to think about Johnny and our shared oaths of revenge when fame was within arm's reach? A riotous new millennium had broken open and I planned to be a prominent rioter, a mite paler and cooler of temperature, perhaps, though looking no older than I'd been at my death. The America I observed, meanwhile, aged by the minute. The stink of burnt oil and the pneumonic cough of petrol machinery heralded the approach of automobiles along the same paths down which our carriages lumbered. Telephone cables joined us, too, strung along the road like laundry lines. News of our arrival in each town traveled faster. So did the customers.

Mr. Stick's audience became dedicated in a way unfamiliar to Dr. Whistler's. Those forlorn buyers of our religious trinkets began instead migrating to my performances. A single show was often all it took to hook them, and the following night the same sad sacks would gather outside the Gallery with hymnals spread in an attempt to whip the assembled into a Sunday state. Once inside the tent, these fanatics would testify at irregular intervals, throwing the Barker off his script. One night in Kentucky a woman bolted upright and began gibbering in a nonsense tongue until she had to be removed.

Soon after rose a countermovement peopled by grave Evangelicals just as preoccupied with yours truly, though instead of singing they held aloft handmade signs lettered in severe black paint. Oh, but the messages were jolly!

THERE BE ONLY HELL THAT AWAITS
AND YE GUIDE IS MISTER STICK, LUCIFER'S HELPER!

WE ARE JOINING GENERAL STICK'S BEETLE ARMY, HARD-SHELLED FOR REVELATIONS!

These brimstoners did not cotton to their saved counterparts, and now and again the war of psalms escalated into physical melees. Remaining in any one town for too long became a risk; the Barker did not like to attract the attention of lawmen. The result was that we spent half of our days in transit, a disagreeable percentage if your name was Mr. Hobby.

It began to feel as if we were on the lam. The Barker woke each day with his ear to the ground and I oft heard him speak to Hobby of a growing animosity in Washington regarding the unchecked contents and unbridled claims of patent medicines. Rumors swirled about a trafficking law that would hog-tie interstate transport of food, liquor, and, more to the point, drugs. Even worse, there was serious talk of requiring drug producers to be accurate in their labeling of product.

Hobby stood alongside me backstage one night, raking a hand through his shedding hair while reading from what all indications was a most bothersome manuscript. By the by he put it aside and I struggled over to have myself a look-see. The book, published by some medical association or another, was over five hundred pages and focused upon the topic of "quackery." On one page I found a checklist of "notable humbuggers"; missing from this manifest was the Barker and I wondered if the slight would relieve or ruffle him.

In the winter of 1900, the highest compliment was paid me: three products emblazoned with the likeness of none other than your sheepish narrator. I shall let the labels of the first two speak for themselves: Mr. Stick's Suffradine, The Carbonated Cream For Numbing Those Scalds, Relieving That Stranguary & Bolstering All Muscle

Gimps; and Mr. Stick's Ambrosial Aegis Vegetable Compound (A Delicious Drink) For The Sweet Slaying Of Nervous Stomach & Neuralgia. These were harmless agents meant to distract the user while the body made its own repairs. Both had been offered at the Pageant for years, though not behind such handsome packaging.

Only the third product gave me pause, though I knew it should not concern me what the stupid of the world inflicted upon their stupider loved ones. It was a flat, thin box containing a slip of cheap purple velour and five needles neither as sharp nor as fine as the ones used in my act. They called this The Oriental Pin Therapy of the Astonishing Mr. Stick.

The simulacrum of my face on labels big and small magnified my import in the eyes of the audiences. Lines for my show stretched ever longer. I was delighted. By summer 1901 my program began to sell out on a regular basis. Mr. Hobby passed by my cage one morning discussing with a worker how to rejigger the pews so as to squeeze in more paying customers. I'd been ruminating on the same and called out to him. He stopped and I explained my idea for placing boards perpendicular to the pews so as to add up to twenty additional seats. Hobby nodded in the most peculiar way.

Only later did I realize that by offering a suggestion for improving the show, I no longer considered it a debasement. This, you will agree, was psychological headway. I dwelled on it overnight, wondering if my brain had begun to sour as had my flesh, yet began the following day with a sense of anticipation. Can you make sense of this, Reader? People were traveling from miles away, often on the backs of mules, with the express purpose of seeing me, and the drawings of me on our handbills were more flattering than any "Wanted" poster. That's it—I was *wanted*.

A week later I was helped back to my tent by Mr. Hobby only to find that my cage had been pushed into a corner, where it loomed like a gargoyle. I gave Hobby a querulous look. He inhaled hard enough to flutter his mustache and gestured his forehead at the center of the room. There sat a derelict cot, as well as a narrow chest of drawers. I was speechless. I nodded my appreciation, forgetting that Pageant administrators were the ones who'd caged me in the first place.

That night I lay on the cot staring straight into the rippling darkness of the tent top. I heard enough pissing and smelled enough cigarettes to know that some marplot had been posted to ensure that I did not flee. It was wasted labor. Escape and revenge, the promises that had once kept my foul body kicking, no longer held appeal. Oh, 'twas a long night of pondering imponderables only to end up in the same spot: right there, where I was getting every damn thing I ever wanted.

Freedom from the cage provided excellent opportunity to work on physical rehabilitation. At night, while sentries kept watch, I took advantage of the tent, pacing up and down and lifting heavy objects (a foot stool, a box of tonic) as well as delicate ones (a teacup, a spoon). My progress was swift. Resurrecting muscles, I found, was akin to resurrecting speech. The ability swirled above my head like a firefly and I had only to learn how to reach out and snag it.

It was a beautiful autumn morning when I limped out to the road with my walking stick to watch the erection of a Pageant banner inscribed with the show's new full title: Dr. Whistler's Pageant of Health and Gallery of Suffering Featuring Defier of Death the Astonishing Mr. Stick. I hope you do not find it too unattractive that I took from the moment a good deal of pride. I breathed deep, a behavior I simulate though it serves no biologic purpose, and felt the burrs and pollens of a new season adhering to the dry surfaces of my interior. I tapped the Little Miracle Electric Mexican Stuttering Ring against my stick and thought of Johnny for the first time in weeks.

I turned and there he was, squinting at the same banner from a distance. His eyes fell upon me, but when I gave him a friendly nod, his expression became one of anguish and betrayal. My good feeling sogged with shame. For a time I'd lent the lad's accursed life purpose. Now that I'd taken ownership of my role here, he had no hope. Some mornings I would spy him kicking around old bottles in a dispirited search for one more swallow. On scattered nights I would notice him slumped by the communal fire, drooling and crying. Our most promising intersection was the Gallery of Suffering, and one evening I did stumble across him. Sadly, it is a literal statement: the lad was passed out and face down in the grass where his disgusted handlers had left him.

It was October when our caravan paused outside of a small town that would loom large in the strange history of Zebulon Finch: Xenion, Georgia. We were met at its outskirts with the dismal sight of two men lynched among the Spanish moss of a single oak; the limb creaked at the weight. These men were white. No, not exactly white; they were plum from a week's rot. Pinned to each of their chests was a card sporting a one-word warning:

CHARLATAN

The Barker gave the order, reins were pulled, and the front horses began to circumnavigate. By then, I had graduated to sitting at the front of a wagon and I had my driver whip our animals so that we caught up with the Barker. I gave him a piece of my mind, which he bore with his special brand of barely contained contempt. Shall we be intimidated by cheap scare tactics, asked I? Do not the good people of Xenion, Georgia, need their liniments and extracts and soaps and snuffs? What shall they do about their whooping cough and clubfeet and varicose veins and flatulency? Plus, what about my new forty-dollar velvet-and-corduroy suit and sixteen-dollar hat? For what had they been procured if not to show?

Truly, my boundless stupidity is something to behold.

X.

IG DEEPLY ENOUGH INTO YOUR microfiche, your archive of yellowed newsprint, and you shall find it. Historical record shows that on November 11, 1901, the Astonishing Mr. Stick was arrested in Xenion, Georgia, for Ungodly Acts.

It was not quite night when I heard the ruckus. I was sitting on the edge of my cot picking the lint from the suit of which I was so proud. Shouting in and of itself was nothing unusual at the Pageant—some folks were feverish with sickness, others were discovering Gød, still others were nettled about being sold a product yesterday that evidenced no results today. But the shouts grew nearer and I began to make out specific oaths. My stage name was among them. *My fans,* sighed I, *how rabid they are.*

Next came the scuffling of feet and the meaty sound of fists to flesh. Moments later the tent flap shot open and wild-eyed men with sleeves rolled to the biceps came at me and placed their rough hands upon my person, three to an arm. Without the aid of my walking stick I was dragged across the dirt on my knees straight out of the tent.

There were torches all about even though it was but dusk. There were also pitchforks and shovels, enough to make a man nervous. On the main stage Professor Bach was faking a rather heroic Georgian twang in hopes of keeping the eyes of the locals fixed in his direction, but that battle was lost; those curious about liver pads were already drifting to the superior distraction of a brewing fight.

Grabbing for me was an assortment of Pageant bigwigs, which I appreciated, though they were no match for these burly Georgians, who were in no mood for negotiation. I caught only glimpses of telling detail: Mr. Hobby's spectacles askew; one of the Soothing Foursome doubled over and bloody of lip; and the Barker, screeching vitriol at a slender man in a cleric's collar and a fat man wearing a copper star.

As I was dragged in the direction of town, I realized that my last hope was Pullman Larry. With but a few quick shots from his fine-tuned firearm, he could blast the garden tools right from the abductors' hands. But he did not interfere. Either he was off yanking a tooth (there were twenty or thirty still left in Georgia, from what I could tell), or was enjoying the degradation of his unworthy successor, flashing his big white choppers in the troubled torchlight.

By the time we reached the local jail, the knees of my beloved new suit were ruined and the dead flesh below embedded with gravel. I was lifted across a threshold and shoved into a counter, behind which appeared Sheriff Nelson (I had gleaned his name as assorted bumpkins offered their congratulations on a varmint well trapped). He was in affable spirits, grinning as he took up a pen and ledger and asked for my name.

"Mr. Stick."

"Full name, please."

I thought for a moment.

"The Astonishing?"

Sheriff Nelson winked at a man to my left and a fist drove into my kidney. On instinct I reacted as does a living man, curling into the impact and crying out. There was, after all, no gauging the sturdiness of my dead body. Enough blows like that and I might get to see that kidney of mine when it plopped onto the floor.

Still, I managed a fib.

"Aaron. Aaron Stick."

The sheriff raised an eyebrow.

"Not 'The Astonishing Amazing Dingdonged Aaron Stick'?"

Plenty of laughter from that gibe! All at once I felt quite dejected. I shook my head to concede that, no, I was not quite astonishing. Sheriff Nelson began talking far too rapidly for me to follow. It was legal pap he had regurgitated countless times in the past and when it was through, my coachmen picked me up by the armpits and transported me to the jail's only cell, a six-by-six-foot box where I was dumped onto a wooden bench. My first thought upon landing was a dismal one. *My hat*, thought I. *I've lost it, and it so well matched my suit.*

The door slammed loud enough to vibrate the wood beneath me. How many wrongful deeds had I performed under the Black Hand? Yet never had I fielded a warning from a lawman, much less an arrest. Now I let *others* hurt *me* by trade—and into the pokey I went? The irony was cold.

Presently I became aware that I was not alone. Sitting on the opposite bench was a bearded old man with wild hair and a magenta complexion, clad in tattered military regalia. I nodded acknowledgement before detecting his snore. The man's naked feet were swollen and muddy and somehow obscene; they twitched within a rectangle of segmented moonlight. I followed the beam to a small, barred window near the low ceiling. Captured in the light was my second cellmate, a colored man. He was a few years my senior and stood with his forehead against the wall as if trying to follow a faraway song.

I found myself tied of tongue. My experience with Negroes was limited. Abigail Finch had barred their kind far from home and grounds, so afeared was she of their coarse looks and thieving hands. They had been a rare sight in Little Italy as well, though when I ventured farther into the city I saw them plenty, ambling along the side of the road, mouths moving with a confounding tempo, having devised a method of speech that prevented white men from reading lips.

Well, I had to distract myself somehow, didn't I?

"What did you do, boy?" asked I.

His eyes flicked toward the moon.

"Stole."

A-ha! So Abigail Finch had been right.

"And what did you steal?"

"Corn."

"A cob of it?"

His lips thinned.

"A bag."

"Why did you go and do that?"

He shrugged.

"You don't have any idea?" pressed I.

A dream-snort ripped through the body of the wild-haired man. I flinched and I thought I saw the ghost of a smirk grace the Negro's lips. That angered me! I manicured for him a pointed glare.

"Tell me, boy. What's the punishment for stealing a bag of corn?"

"A fine."

"That's it?"

He shrugged.

"What else?" I pressed.

He frowned out the window. "Got to pay for the corn."

"Very reasonable. You have the money?"

"Already paid."

"Then why are you here?"

The Negro pushed the sweat of his forehead into the stiff crinkles of his hair. Moonlight made the pinks of his palms glow white. This time he did not respond, which I attributed to either his disbelief that I would understand or to general antipathy. This did not help mollify my growing affront. I had not risen from caged aberration to premiere attraction to be given the cold shoulder by a mulish colored!

"Then allow me to guess. You are here because you are pigheaded. Your mood is churlish. You refuse to apologize. Come now, grade my guesswork. Am I correct?"

He stared out of the window for a time before responding.

"I guess so."

"I guess so, what?"

"I guess so, *sir.*"

That final word hissed like a blade across flint. I leaned back to take full measure. He was broader than I and could doubtlessly pluck my limbs from my torso as a child does a fly. But the night's battery had inured me to such fears and instead I found myself intrigued by this monosyllabic brute, the middling interest he showed in his own fate, his pensive study of the autumn eve.

"Ever loquacious, aren't you?"

"Sir?"

"You do not talk much."

"No, sir."

"Four coloreds travel with my company. Voices clear as crystal water. Mannerly. Obliging. Agreeable. They are a credit to your race. Too much, I think."

"What are their names?"

The question came with confrontational fleetness. My mouth opened with retaliatory speed—the fighting instinct, I guarantee you, had not vacated Zebulon Finch along with his physical vitalities! But I could not strike. Indeed, what *were* the names of the Soothing Foursome? One of them had taken a punch for me that very night. My cellmate blinked his thick eyelids with the insouciant patience of a boxer.

I did not like this Negro.

Thus I played the childhood game of Name the Presidents.

"Their names are George, John, Thomas, and James."

My cellmate weighed that for a moment.

"Fine names, sir."

"And you," asked I, "have you a name?"

The boy loved long pauses.

"John," said he. "John Quincy."

Have you ever witnessed such impertinence? Detecting my lie, the boy chose for himself the name of the president next in line! I became hotheaded, all right, but what could I do in quarters so confined? Lifting myself above this childish squabble would be advisable (the snoring wild man maintained more dignity than I!), but I could not disengage myself from this so-called John Quincy, the President of Thieves.

"Will you not ask what *I* did? Is your mind so incurious?"

"Already know, sir."

"And how is that?"

120

He managed a shrug.

"All day folks been on about catching the Devil."

"I see."

"Yes, sir."

"And you've no fear of the Devil?"

Moonlight made his lips gray against purple skin. There, a smile.

"Met the Devil already. You ain't him, sir."

The hooligans who'd torn me from my beloved cot had been convinced that I was profanity itself, so while it might be simple recalcitrance fueling John Quincy's opposite assessment, I was nonetheless grateful. I searched about the cell to find a topic less stressful for us both.

"You know this man?" I gestured at the sleeper.

"That's the General, sir."

"A true general?"

"Yes, sir."

"A secessionist? One of Lee's?"

"Fought at Fort Wagner, sir. Gettysburg, too. Folks hereabouts mighty proud."

"Yet he is caged with a Negro and the Devil."

John Quincy shrugged.

"He in here each week. He gone battle-headed, sir."

"Battle-headed?"

"Just wait, sir. You'll see."

XI.

CONCURRENT WITH THE COCK'S CROW came the foul noise of the General choking upon the bile of the habitual drunkard. With arms a-flail to dispel a horde of invisible bats, he leapt to his feet and expectorated onto the stone floor a wad of caramel mucus. Groaning, he stumbled toward the window, shoved aside John Quincy, and clung to the bars with both hands. The tips of his toes made him just tall enough to lodge his chin over the sill so that he could gasp at the fresh dawn.

"UNROLL THE MORNING MAPS! LICK THE WICKS! COLD MEAL FOR FEAR OF STEAM! BEST FOOD GOES TO THE HORSES, FOR NERVOUS MEN WILL ONLY SICKEN!"

The energy with which he ejected this rot was astounding. The man was over sixty but had been one to be reckoned with in his prime. You could tell by how the iron bars shook within their sockets; the way his wide back stretched his sundered blouse; and, of course, that voice—that crackling, full-throated blast that would carry quite well across a field of cannon booms and musket fire.

He severed his tirade and I heard a woman calling to him from the street. The General hooked one of his arms through the bars and, sure enough, withdrew with a block of cornbread, which he began smashing into his mouth even as we heard the parting blessings of the woman on the street. Sixty seconds later the cornbread was demolished, with equal amounts residing in the man's stomach and beard. Then he was back at the window blabbering and it was not long before another passerby gave him a package, this time a pyre of warm bacon swaddled within a monogrammed handkerchief.

It was midmorning when a visitor at the window began speaking to the General in a distinctive manner. No comforting tones were adopted, no foodstuffs gifted. Instead the tone was low and urgent, and I watched as the General's eyes grew ever wider. At last the message was complete and the General scurried away and planted his back to the far wall. For the first time he looked at me.

"GET THEE BEHIND ME, SATAN! THOU ART AN OFFENSE UNTO ME, FOR THOU SAVOR NOT THE THINGS THAT BE OF GØD!"

The fervor was curdling. Even John Quincy edged away. I held up what I hoped was a becalming hand. Of course I had expected to suffer superstitious oaths before my adventure in the slammer was complete, but not from inside my own cell.

"HE WAS THERE IN THE WILDERNESS FORTY DAYS, TEMPTED OF SATAN! AND WAS WITH THE WILD BEASTS AND THE ANGELS MINISTERED TO HIM!" His shaggy face twitched as if beaned by a pebble. "NO, NO, I AM NOT READY! NOT PREPARED FOR THIS LONG JOURNEY OF ISCARIOT!" He flung his body against the cell door and reached through the bars with claws extended. "LET ME OUT! OH, SWEET SERVANTS OF JUSTICE, LET ME OUT! I AM NOT READY FOR THE IRON CHAIR UPON WHICH MY NAME IS BRANDED! LET ME OUT OF HERE, I BEG YOU!"

John Quincy gave me a concerned look. I could not tell if he was sharing in my discomfort or if his belief in my status as non-Devil was beginning to founder. The old man wagged an accusatory finger.

"I REMEMBER YOU!"

Every person in Xenion, Georgia, seemed to have formed an opinion of Mr. Stick before taking in a single performance. It struck me as unfair.

"We have not met, General. My name is—"

"GIVE ME NO FALSE NAMES! I KNOW YOU, DEMON! FIRST YOU CAME FOR ME IN THE GRASS! THEN YOU CAME FOR ME IN THE MUD! THEN YOU CAME FOR ME IN THE SOOT—THE SOOT THAT DRIED THE BLOOD! BUT YOUR HOOVEN CLUTCH SHALL NOT TAKE ME! I BELONG WITH HIS LORD ON HIGH!"

Suffice it to say that this ranting continued along the same lines for hours, though I admit exaggerating time is easily done when one is being assailed as a diabolical reaper. Around noon, a deputy slid beneath the cell's lowermost bar a tray holding three bowls of stew and as many hunks of stale bread. The General yielded his filibuster, snatched up his share, and retreated to his corner to pour the stew down his gullet. John Quincy took his bowl and bread and dipped the latter in the former, eliminating the food at a pace that betrayed neither hunger nor relish.

I, of course, had no interest in my portion and instead looked up to find the deputy still standing there, giving me injurious consideration. After a time he plucked a folded newspaper from his back pocket and tossed it through the bars.

"You made the papers, Stick."

The *Atlanta Constitution* included on its front page an item about the sellers of patent medicines. The author treated these bottle-mongers harshly, but so too were the denizens of Xenion, called out by the journalist as "shameful" in their unjust jailing of an apparent innocent. Even more notable was a full-page advertisement on the following spread taken out by none other than the Barker, who must have scrambled all night long and spent stupefying amounts of cash to turn this nightmare scenario into a publicity coup. I managed to pocket the relevant page and would you believe it has survived with me all these many years? Here I insert the yellow, crackled evidence for your pleasure.

DR. WHISTLER'S PAGEANT OF HEALTH
Under the auspices of the above a

MASS MEETING

WILL BE HELD ON
Tuesday, Noon, November 12, 1901,
AT THE
PAGEANT GROUNDS OF DR. WHISTLER'S

(Xenion, Near Working-Men's Club, Morris Avenue, NW Lot)

To Protest the Unfair Imprisonment on Nov. 11th, 1901, of

THE ASTONISHING MR. STICK.

Friends of the Beautiful State of Georgia,
Hundreds of times have I placed advertisements in your fine publications—for

my popular halitosis cure, my liver pads, and my much-appreciated loosener of catarrh—delightful remedies of which many of you are familiar and fond. 'Tis the first time I find myself in the pitiable position of calling out your brothers and sisters in Xenion for barbarity exercised upon one of my most esteemed lecturers. Mr. Stick is a benign man of good standing and yet was afforded none of the luxuries of complaint or trial the night of Nov. 11 when a group of ruffians led by SHERIFF JOSEPH P. NELSON ambushed Mr. Stick—asleep in bed!—and dragged him away as if he had participated in Physical Aggravation or otherwise displayed Maniac Tendencies. Friends, I do not need to tell you why this is an Outrage Most Severe and why Immediate Action is yours to be taken. If you are gutted with worm, you take our best-selling Infallible Indian's Tape-Worm Disgorging Lozenges. So it is now: SHERIFF JOSEPH P. NELSON is a disease and you, Friends, must serve as Tonic. If you are the rare soul unfamiliar with our Large Repertoire of Humane and Effective Products, come see us Today (address above) to confirm for yourself our generous nature and good behavior. —*Dr. Whistler*

COME EARLY TO SECURE BEST SEATS

Doors Open (Special Time) at 10:30 a.m. Gallery of Suffering Opens (Regular Time) at 6 p.m.

ALL ARE INVITED, INCL. CHILDREN (THERE WILL BE CANDY).

Not since the days of reading aloud Black Hand headlines to Wilma Sue had my heart so happily hammered. (A figure of speech; my circulatory organ is a wad of hamburger.) Here was a legitimate newspaper with cross-state influence. At that very moment, my stage name might be on the lips of thousands!

Vigorous rereadings of the advert commenced. Only after a time did I become conscious of a growing commotion—shouts, thrown objects, and so forth. The jailers delivered warnings for the crowd to disperse, but the screwballs did no such thing. By sundown the jail was under siege. We smelled the smoke of a great many torches and our concrete box began to fill with heat and ash. John Quincy and I cowered in corners as one does during such unpredictable events.

The General, though, paced in circles, patting at his belt as if expecting to find pistol or saber. As night fell, the chants became organized and I was shocked to pick out the refrain:

"FREE! STICK! FREE! STICK!"

A tear or two might have dropped, had my reservoir not gone dry.

The commotion must have sounded to the General like the charge of the Union Army. He wailed and dropped to his knees. Duly chilled, the colored fellow and I looked at each other for clues of what to do next. As it happened, there was no time for plotting. The General scrabbled about so that he was facing me, and then—horrors, it was a distressing sight!—began to spider-walk in my direction, eyes bloodshot and rolling, saliva flowing in multiple strands from his lips. I secured myself into my corner but there was no avoiding this feculent, broken-clawed hobgoblin who looked to have slithered from the bowels of Hell.

Of course he thought the same thing of me! When he was but a few feet away he pounced, wrapping his muscled arms around my thighs. I thought he meant to wrestle me to the floor to, for instance, put out my Devil eyes with his righteous thumbs, but instead his fingernails dug into my slacks as if afraid that we might be separated before he could say his peace.

"JUDGE THE PENNYWORTH OF MY BLACKEST GUTS, DEVIL! TELL ME NOW IF I MUST JOIN YOUR OGRE CIRCUS SO THAT I MAY STRIP AND PREPARE MY FLESH FOR THE FLAYING! OR—PLEASE, I BEG YOU!—SET ME FREE SO THAT I MIGHT YET KNOW SOFT DANDELION FIELDS!"

What strange things worm their ways into the human brain at the oddest of times! Beset by a mob's bedlam and facing down a filth-encrusted madman, my thoughts hopped to Little Johnny Grandpa. My most recent sighting had been a typically morose one: he falling to the dirt, me a mile away yet extending a hand as if to catch him. Just as vivid was my memory of the lad hunkering against my cage years prior, whispering through tears some piffle about whether I might have been sent back to Earth as an angel to guard him. A preposterous idea; the General's assessment of me was closer to the mark.

Perhaps that is why I reached out to the raving old-timer. I took firm hold of the General's wrists; his pleading dribbled away. I brought him closer. I knew not what I was doing. Soon the fronds of his matted hair were batting my face. I relinquished his wrists and his hands took my shoulders for balance. My own hands, freed, found themselves holding the old man's grubby cheeks. Things had turned out badly for Johnny, and it had been my fault. In the little boy's honor, if for no other reason, I owed this man absolution.

Outside, noises raged. Horses screamed. Gravel rained from our walls. I lowered my chin so that my cold forehead touched the General's sweltering one. Our eyes were but inches apart and his lashes, when he blinked, interlocked with mine. Again: I did not know what I was doing.

"You fought bravely," said I.

Where was this coming from? I grimaced, fearful that I had spoken flapdoodle.

"I ran," replied he, "while they died like dogs!"

His bludgeoning rout had withered to a timid whine. It gave me hope.

"What else could you have done?" asked I.

128

"I could have died! I could have poured my guts like a proper soldier."

A *hurrah* shook our walls. Some victory was being celebrated. John Quincy rushed to the window and I wished to do the same, but the General was in a piteous state. My nerves, too, had shipwrecked among waves of turmoil equal to anything happening outside. I let myself be the old man's anchor.

"Look at how you eat," said I. "Clearly you do not wish to die."

"I slop like a hog because of bed-pissing cowardice! My men cradled their livers in their laps like newborns, do you understand? They held their eyeballs like doubloons for me to admire! Yet I ran because you, Devil, were there and your legs are so very long. This time there is nowhere for me to run."

There came gun blasts, nicks of stone rebounding from the jail facade. I surprised myself by slapping the General's cheek to keep his attention. Because, what was this? Yes, I could feel it! The shuttling backward through the years, the lifting of my soul like garbage caught in a storm, the marvelous dimming of the physical world—'twas *la silenziosità* rolling like dribbled honey just out of tongue's reach!

The General's buckram beard became cotton in my hands. The sooty cell walls took on a whitewashed splendor. The slick, sliding, swirling re-entry into the Uterus of Time lifted me upward before I was caught like phlegm in a throat, allowing me no more than a few seconds of pure Death to show to the General before my focus was broken by sights of my own reflected revelations.

Unlike the Barker, who'd been forced to acknowledge his incurable malevolence, *la silenziosità* gentled the General's distress—it was not for me to understand how. He pulled from me until we clung but to each other's forearms, his pink eyes blinking to reveal a startling clarity, his lunatic fever washed away. His lips worked into an unpracticed smile and he nodded, first once and then a hundred times, his gray locks dancing about his shoulders.

"I will not forget you, Devil."

"The name," said I, "is Finch."

Our strange embrace was interrupted by an affrighting crash. The cell door was thrown wide. The General shaded his new, clear eyes and John Quincy lifted a shoulder as if expecting the lash. I turned toward the door and saw a big, round silhouette throttling a key ring. This was it, thought I, the scene where my soft corpse was rent, bit by bit, by noisome little projectiles of metal. Another man, taller and hatted, was moving into position behind the first.

"Stick, Aaron, whoever." Sheriff Nelson spat on the floor. "It's your lucky dingdonged day."

The second man leaned into the light with a smile as silken and cunningly knotted as his scarf, lifting a finger to touch the brim of his hat. I recognized the gesture all too well. I stood and followed, just as I always had, throwing one final look at the strange cellmates upon whom I was sure I would never again lay eyes.

But the planet is not so big as it seems when you're still new at being seventeen.

XII.

THE BARKER AND I WERE directed to a chaw-spattered chamber no different from the cell except that the barred window had been upgraded to glass, which, regrettably, had been shattered at some point during the day's uproar. I was relieved to see that the door, at least, had no locks. Sheriff Nelson closed it anyway after telling us to wait as he did some dingdonged paperwork and spoke to the dingdonged crowd so that we could get our butts on our dingdonged way.

In a reversal of our act, I stood while the Barker took the seat. He brushed dust from the bench and collapsed upon it with a great sigh. It was no act. His eyes were scarlet and his energy sapped. He took a meditative moment to catalogue my torn slacks and scuffed jacket, the topsy state of my shirt and hair.

"How like our first meeting, eh, Stick? It is quite a challenge, you know, reconciling this ignoble jailbird with the proud martyr of my invention."

"I am sure you are up to it," said I.

"Tut tut. Do I detect a lack of gratitude?"

"Impossible. You have been so good to me."

He chuckled.

"Mr. Stick. Even at this hour, you think so little of me."

"It is a talent of mine."

"Do you know how much sleep I have slept since your arrest?"

"I was not aware that vampires slept."

"I've had not one wink, haggling with news editors and papering the town with handbills and whipping up the requisite frenzy. Do you care to know how much money I have generated for my trouble?"

"Enough to line your coffin with silk?"

"Money has been *lost*, Mr. Stick. What these rubes are interested in is an overthrow of the local government, not buying what I have to sell. I did nothing more than pat their asses to encourage them to action. Hundreds of dollars, Stick. Those are my losses. In a single day. And I have done it willingly in exchange for the publicity. Publicity for you. Can you not appreciate that?"

"Which hand shall I kiss first?"

The Barker withdrew from his jacket a cigar retarded with piebald skin and a midsection crease. He showed no mercy for its birth defects. He bit off the end. A match was struck across his heel. He gestured his chin at the window as he puffed the cigar to life.

"Take no satisfaction in their arousal. You bring an animal to meat and the animal eats."

He closed his eyes and relished a deep mouthful before letting the smoke slither out like blue eels. The cigar was the prize he'd saved until the completion of his thankless mission.

"You friendly with history, Mr. Stick? No? You have heard, though, of George Washington? The founding poppa of our fair democracy? Good boy. It's his wooden teeth you likely know of. His chop-chopping of yon cherry tree, all that hokum. But the story of Washington that stirs me most is lesser known. Listen, Mr. Stick, in these few moments we have. See what you learn. About your country. About your place in it."

"My place, I thought, is beneath stage light, behind bars—"

"Your mouth. Trained at last, it hops about like a dog after treats. Now. Cast your mind. Washington lays suffocating at Mount Vernon. Men of medicine are gathered, those with the know-how to carve tunnels through mucus, those with hands steady enough to lop off the president's tongue if it comes to that. Together they release their combined powers. They practice phlebotomy, bleeding thirty-two ounces from our brave leader. Special jars are on hand to catch the blood, maybe keep it, examine it. They pour into him mercury to vacuate his bowels; there are special jars to catch that, too. Finally they blister the man, applying ungodly amounts of heat to scald away the sickening spirits. Washington dies, of course, a hero. And these men who lanced and emptied and burned him, unafraid of taking the most extraordinary of measures? Why, they are heroes, too, each of them the recipient of a kiss from the mournful Martha."

With a shirt cuff the Barker blotted at his still-closed eyes.

"What these unsung heroes performed, in short, were stage acts, the same end-of-life celebrations we, too, perform. Our sleights of hand, all of them, are offered in appeasement of Dionysus, or, if you prefer, the One Gød Almighty. He appreciates a good show, too, if that play upon Calvary Hill was any indication."

His exhaled smoke was the exact color of ennui.

"It is not long for this world, this showmanship of ours, this unbound creativity, all of it so much more satisfying than the rote pokings and sewings demanded by"—and here he snarled the word—"*science*. Lives in the future will be saved, or not saved, like beads slid this way or that across the abacus. But life itself? I think it shall not be worth living. One day, Mr. Stick, our brains and hearts will be but engines powered by steam and only because that is the

133

latest innovation engineers have come up with in their drab, dull-minded colleges."

His eyelids split, revealing coruscating orbs.

"You hear them out there? Ask those people about me and they will rush to answer. Dr. Whistler, why, he can cure anything. And, in my own way, I can. Anything except, I think, you."

"I wish that you could."

Instantly I recognized my words as the truth.

He pushed them aside with an impatient hand.

"Save me your melancholy. You are not the first to feel it. The paper this morning said fifteen percent of our men are jobless, a fact born out by the townspeople outside these very walls who have nothing better to do than pelt the local jail with rotten vegetables. These same men, in better days, would have paid a full day's wage to gaze upon those worse off than they. No more. Now the only way into their wallets is to raise doubts about their livers. I do it. I am happy to do it. But the thrill, the sheer thrill of discovery, the heroism of it . . . it is not nearly the same. My lot, for better or worse, is here with you, Mr. Stick."

He raised an eyebrow and waited to see if I would do anything but play with the tin ring around my finger, and when I did not, he smoothed his beard in distaste. From the other side of our wall we could hear Sheriff Nelson address a hissing crowd. The Barker took to his feet, slapping the dirt from the seat of his pants and adjusting his hat in the surviving window glass.

"They fear you and that is good. But anymore you do not seem to fear them. If that is the case, this jail is only the beginning. Some advice, if you will accept it. You have got to have fear in your heart."

Those were his exact words!

So shaken was I by this repeat of Testa's most indubitable counsel that when the door opened and Sheriff Nelson beckoned, I could nary move. The Barker apologized and gave permission for the sheriff to drag me. Just short of the front door, Sheriff Nelson turned to block our exit. His prodigious, damp belly bumped into my own.

"You walk through those dingdonged doors, you ain't my concern. All right, Mr. Astonishing? If there's any shootin', if there's any killin', we plan to be on the winning end."

Two deputies turned their heads to their boss and drew their revolvers, and no wonder, for outside awaited a field of torch-wielding Xenionians shouting in anticipation of my release. Here, this hooting aviary of jubilant hillbillies, was the Barker's publicity. I went through the motions of inflating my lungs with air in case the inhalation might steady me for our victorious march. Despite what the Barker had suggested, this was fame. How could it not be?

XIII.

I T WAS AN UNREMARKABLE DAY in December when I met the man who would shape the next hundred years of my life.

I was meditating upon my cot several hours after that night's performance when I heard a scraping in the dirt outside my tent. Were it an attempt at ambush, it was a clumsy one. I could have fired upon the creeper with leisure enough to fashion a smiley-face pattern from the holes, provided I still had my good old 1873 Peacemaker.

Instead I said, "Do come in."

The sly noises stopped, there was a pause, and then the curtain parted to allow the curt entry of a short, fresh-faced man of the most unexpected trappings. He wore a top hat of distinguished altitude and a silk frock coat tailored to such specifications that he looked as well-folded as an envelope. He wore black gloves, fine buttoned boots with white uppers, and carried a leather doctor's valise. More striking than any of this was that his cheeks were shorn of hair, a style you did not see on Pageant grounds unless upon a child, woman, or, well, me. He was twenty-six, twenty-seven—no older.

He cleared his throat and offered me a polite grimace. Where were my manners? It had been some time since I'd shared space with a nobleman.

"Please," said I, nodding an invitation.

He took all sorts of liberties at once, snatching a crate of salve

136

to sit upon. The top hat came swooping off, the valise went between his seated feet, and one of his hands dove into his coat pocket to retrieve what I identified straight away as my favorite edition of the *Atlanta Constitution*. He slapped it smartly against his opposite palm and gave me a thin-lipped smile.

"Dr. Cornelius Leather, at your service."

Two details were of note. He spoke with an English accent. He did not offer his hand.

"Mr. Stick," replied I.

Irritation sundered his forehead.

"Please. Time is short."

The truth was drawn straight out of me. I steadied myself.

"Zebulon Finch. At *your* service."

Leather's eyes flashed in the moonlight.

"Men of uncivil disposition are threading the grounds as we speak. My guess is that these men will not look kindly upon my unannounced appointment."

"You guess correctly."

Again that smile: tight, nervous, but pleased. It was my impression that this was a rare outdoor adventure for an indoors gentleman. He vibrated with the thrill of trespass.

"As I said, time is of the essence. Permit me to be terse. I am a surgeon. I teach anatomy at the Medical School of Harvard College. You have no doubt noticed my elocution. The British Empire lost me for the same reason it loses so many: to the pursuit of freedom, of both idea and practice, and not at the behest of a crown nor a royal society of physicians, which will hold back, indefinitely if possible, exploration into the dark matter where resides the greatest of secrets. Forgive me. I am no longer being terse. I shall only say the following.

137

For such opportunities I gave up an enviable position in society, stockpiles of gold, and the woman of high standing I was intended to marry. All for the chance, Mr. Zebulon Finch, of conjuring miracles from science. Indicate to me that you are following along."

I was but barely. The man needed to be slowed.

"Making miracles from science," said I. "We do that here every day."

Leather drew a face of such repugnance that I believed he might spew vomit.

"Games take time to play, Mr. Finch. We have not that luxury. What you do at this hell-hole is stir fevers, irritate skin, rot intestines, and, in worst cases, incite the mortal arrest of vital organs—nothing, I assure you, about which to jest. If we have to discuss this moronic point we will get nowhere. Can we move along?"

Fascinating, no? I crossed my arms and nodded.

"America has been good to me. My students listen, or at least stroke their chins convincingly, and when during dissection I sever something that their texts say is not to be severed, rarely do they rush for the constable. That is much appreciated, as I rather despise explaining gross anatomy to men whose greatest accomplishment is firing a nugget of metal into living tissue so that men like me are tasked with extracting that nugget and massaging that tissue back to life.

"Again, I find I am not being terse. Let me skip ahead. I have a laboratory in Boston. It is mine alone. It is situated on the top floor of my home on Jefferson Street. Half of my time is dedicated to my experiments. Half of my time, Mr. Finch! It was the crux of the deal struck with the college. Up there I do what few men of the saw dare, which will make me the *cause célèbre* of the medical world if allowed to reach completion or will have me swinging from a noose should it be discovered tomorrow. Indicate that you understand."

"I do," said I, a bit flustered.

"Doctors read journals written by other doctors. I do not begrudge it. It is helpful if what you seek is a tighter suture or a smarter dose of ether. But doctors staring at doctors will result in what, Mr. Finch? Imitations. Replications. We shall see more veins, more vessels, not the hands that wove them in the first place. So I extend my reading to the shameful. Magazines filled with fantastic tales, attacks of Himalayan ape-men, clairvoyance, the dashing rescue of women from the clutches of exotic monsters. I seek out the rare diamonds of truth among the dull stones of these concocted fabrications, and then I do what men like myself ought to. I stick those diamonds in my gas flame, submerge them in liquids both corrosive and peptic. Report, Finch, report."

"Yes," sputtered I. "I am listening."

"The article about your jailing was rubbish. But the advertisement. Now, that carried with it the breath of conviction. So I took a leave from the college to travel, tracked you down, bought my ticket, and spent the intervening hours walking the countryside, so disgusted was I by the lethal concoctions being bottled and sold by your army of crackpots. Every one of you should be behind bars. I digress. I took in your show. I sat in the front row."

"I am following along."

"Stop interrupting. I watched carefully. I know where needles can be inserted without harm. This man working on stage with you, he is no doctor. He is a butcher. You should be dead, Mr. Finch. You should be drowned in your own blood. What I saw tonight was so aberrant, so unprecedented, so bloody insane, that I found myself *non compos mentis*.

"It is *your* insanity I have waited for. You are *my* lunatic. Let me

139

be terse. Come with me. Now. Under this cloak of night. Not a mile away waits a driver, four horses, and a carriage. Come to Boston, let me study you, and let us make the world at last retch religion and superstition and embrace science as the successor to Gød. We shall save humanity. Listen to those words. Compare them to your current mission. I repeat, Mr. Finch: *We shall save humanity.*"

Leather paused and raised his eyebrows.

"Indicate that you understand."

"I—well, yes, but—"

"Then there is nothing more to discuss. We move now. Are you ready? Is there anything you wish to bring?"

He was already on his feet, situating his top hat and ducking toward the tent flap to scout for the Barker's night soldiers. Now that his tautologous assault was finished, up swept my pride. This palaverous crank wished to remove me from my livelihood of being prodded with needles in order to—what? Prod me with *other* needles? The Gallery of Suffering at least offered the warm pleasure of rapt eyes, the sustaining promise of stardom.

"I will not come," said I.

Dr. Leather let the flap fall. He looked surprised, even wounded. Were I one of his students I felt sure he would deliver a stinging retort. But this was not a highfaluting Harvard dissecting theater. This was the Pageant of Health in all of its gritty, grueling glory.

"Nonsense. Up from that bed."

"I will not rise."

He chewed on his cheeks for a moment.

"I see you use a walking stick. Do not let that be a deterrent. I will assist you."

"I regret you have traveled so far, Doctor."

"No more interruptions. I told you about the carriage. The moon is clouded. Now is the time."

Dr. Cornelius Leather was nothing if not perceptive. It did not take long for him to recognize his fateful disadvantage. Everything about his attitude wilted, though he kept his shoulders high in a final effort to turn the tide. His smile, though weakened, remained shrewd.

"Too bad, Mr. Finch. I so wanted to show you my People Garden."

So unexpected was this phrase that it jarred me from my vow of silence.

"People Garden?"

It was coy how he angled his head.

"You will have to come and see for yourself, now, won't you?"

Light jocularity did not suit a man of such forthright dynamism. The twist of his lips, meant to be razzing, came off as petulant. Still, I admired the effort. I reverted my expression into one of cool patience.

Leather drew himself to full height, which was not much, and nodded, a gesture I took as a bit of self-encouragement. He slipped his manicured fingers into his coat and removed a business card of creamy ivory flecked with gold and textured with the subtle striations of maplewood. In embossed letters were printed the doctor's name, title, and home address.

When I tore my eyes away from it, the doctor was peeking through the tent flap.

"My truest hope is that we meet again, Mr. Finch. Forget nothing that I have said."

Sensing an ebb in watchmen, Leather forwent further farewells and darted away like a doe. The wall of the tent rippled for a minute as if he had instead dived into dark waters. Indeed the whole conversation with Leather had the atmosphere of a strange dream. I let the four sharp corners of the business card bite into my palm. Dr. Whistler's did not travel to populous cities. Boston was not in my future.

Yet I kept the card in the same pocket where resided the Excelsior and the page from the *Constitution*, perhaps because the card was of quality and I wished to have printed some of my own. Or perhaps as a reminder of alternate futures, and indignities, left unrealized.

XIV.

CHRISTMAS EVE FOUND ME IN passable yuletide spirits. I had managed to slip into one of my subaqueous night-dazes when the front wall of my tent was ripped to shreds with the charge of a dozen multilimbed monsters. They dove upon me with fangs dribbling over my face and claws ripping at my bedclothes and the most awful of grunts and cackles emitting from their bottomless throats. I rose from this half-delusion as I rose in real life—lifted into the air not by monsters but by men whose faces I recognized as Pageant employees.

From beyond the tumult boomed directives—*Take his arm, idiot; somebody do something or other with that foot*—and there was no question from whom these directives came. The Barker stood at the doorway, a familiar libertine vision: fist to hip, scarf whipping like a flag, cradling his big-game gun in his elbow like a proud poppa. His eyes were ablaze with victory. The men began to transport me and I was struck by the similarity of this scene to my kidnapping by Sheriff Nelson, except in one fundamental aspect. My defenders had become my assailants.

The cage, that ravenous mouth, awaited me with its iron teeth and straw tongue. With all the strength I could muster, I grasped for a handhold to halt my consumption, and for a glorious instant my fingers tickled the embroidered edge of my bedsheet, the very texture of civilized man. Of course there was no stopping this cruel retrogression. The cage door groaned and I was tossed in as a log to a fire.

The Barker twirled the key ring about a finger and grinned.

"You have a visitor, Finch."

Finch, he said. Omens do not come more foreboding.

He spoke over his shoulder to the throng of winded men.

"Everyone back to your candy canes and eggnog. Mr. Hobby, fetch our guest from my quarters, there's a good man."

The Barker positioned himself before the cage as the men filed out.

"What a wonderful feeling it shall be to be free of you at last. The money? It has been good, that I admit. But even money is not worth the rank indignity of being dependent upon one I loathe with unholy fire, year after insufferable year."

Rather than meet his exultant eyes, I monitored the tent flap.

"Who has come?"

"I renamed the show for you. I *changed* the show for you. How we operate, where we devote our resources. Pornographic amounts of money were spent in ways I am ashamed to recall. Well, no more, and I am glad, so very glad. Now I shall profit from the spectacle of your demise and parlay that into more profit. Propaganda: it is, after all, what I do."

"*Who?*"

Footsteps approached the tent. The flash of a torch made bright coins of Mr. Hobby's spectacles before he turned aside to make space for a group of others to enter.

"Here is the gift-giver himself," chuckled the Barker. "The most unexpected of Saint Nicks."

Luca Testa had changed. You could tell by looking that Chicago had at last lifted its famous fists and punched back. I took some solace from that. His forward hunch was more pronounced, as if he had grown accustomed to hiding his face. His hair, always so smartly parted down the center, now twisted in unintentional braids across a pale scalp. Most tellingly, a pink scar, no more than a year old, I'd say, ran from the corner of his left eye down to the tip of his chin, the trail of an acid tear.

But that night he appeared exuberant. The Barker bowed and excused himself and Hobby followed. Testa, absorbed with the pleasure of seeing me alive and captured, did not appear to notice their exit. The three well-dressed men who traveled with Testa, none of whom I recognized, hovered near the tent flap, but Testa came closer. I pushed myself into the far corner of the cage and titled my chin to hide the grappling-hook wound of my neck. Here was my murderer, back to finish the job, and what I felt most was not fear but shame for what I'd become.

"*Madonna.*" The accent was as slippery smooth as ever. "The kid hasn't aged a day. Kinda pale in the face, though."

He wiped cobweb from the top of the cage and chuckled as he shook clean his hands.

"You guys see what it says here?"

One of the men read aloud in a voice just barely literate.

"Highly. Intelligent. Monkey."

The other two soldiers burst forth with laughter and Testa's shoulders shook until I could see tears of mirth sparkle at the corner of his eyes. My humiliation burned all the greater. Oh, but it was unbearable!

"Jonesy and me used to say the same thing. 'Our boy Finch— pretty sharp for a trained orangutan.' Probably thought you were quite the playboy, right? So do all the young hoodlums. Make a little dough and suddenly you're looking up sculptors to carve you in marble."

More titters from the peanut gallery. Bulges in the right places told me that each of them was armed, and Testa made no effort to conceal the revolver strapped inside his coat. He leaned in and wrapped his hands around the bars. It was an image familiar from the day that I, the silly monkey, had demanded Testa tell me what he'd done to Wilma Sue while he'd danced about, pretending to shoot me. Tonight there would be no pretending.

"Seeing you again? Makes me sentimental. Those were fun days, weren't they? We got a lot of laughs from you, me and Jonesy. Our little Billy Shakespeare. Our little Charlie Dickens. You think we didn't know about the letters you were writing? Full of poetry tripe that confused the hell out of whoever you sent them to? Those were immigrants, Finch. Poor, uneducated. *Mannaggia*, it took a lot of time to fix the damage from those letters, but we couldn't bear to let you stop, not right away. They were so damned funny! Jonesy would fall on his ass. Ah, I miss that guy. Jonesy's not with us no longer. Came to a bad end. But that's life. We all come to bad ends eventually, right?"

One needed only look at the two of us to know he spoke the truth.

He frowned; the line of his scar deepened.

"Things back home are prickly. You do too much boom-boom and damn if the boys with badges don't start paying attention. Raided my place—you remember my place? Hated that goddamned place but now I'm in some *stronzo* apartment where I can't even— ah, what's the use. Better than a cage full of straw, right? Point is, I needed a vacation, needed to wait out some of the heat. And it just so happened, for the first time in my life, there was someplace else I wanted to go, someone I wanted to see."

There had been a time when I would have traded anything for this moment. A chance at revenge! The ticket to a better life for myself and Johnny! That old rageful passion, when measured alongside the empty hunger for fame that replaced it, seemed purer than fire.

"Me," said I.

"Craziest thing in the world. Year back, the postman brings a letter. Jonesy, rest in peace, was still handling deliveries and nobody had a sense of humor like Jonesy, so he showed it to me. It was—well, it was like it was written by a child. Somehow this child had gotten my address, which is a feat in itself. He'd spelled the city and street all wrong and the whole thing looked like garbage, but by God there was postage paid and everything. And that's not even the strange part. There was a little scrap of paper inside, same little-kid scribble, with just three words. Confused the hell out of us. What it said was, 'Finch is Stick.'"

Johnny had pulled it off. The same period during which I'd turned away from him to pursue conceited fancies beneath the spotlight, the resourceful kid had followed through on our plan. Let me assure you, Dearest Reader, that bloating at the bottom of a lake or being driven full of needles were jolly diversions next to this moment. The villain could shoot me all he wanted; any blossoms of meat that popped from my corpse would be welcome—less weight I had to carry to Hell.

"Jonesy and I couldn't make heads or tails. Then a couple months back, I'm reading the paper, like I do every day now since they put me

147

in that *giamoke* apartment, and there's an editorial about, what-you-call-'em, medicine shows, how they're no good and all that. The fuck I care, right? But alongside it is a story they picked up from down South and there's that name again: Stick. And there was a picture, too, a guy being led out of jail. It was a shit photo. Wouldn't have given it a second look if not for that crazy note. 'Finch is Stick.' Holy shit, you know? I had to come see for myself. Because I was sure, *mi amico*, one hundred percent fucking positive, that you were dead."

"Should have shot me twice."

His lips pursed in genuine interest.

"I always wondered. Who did it? One of them *Italiani* with the triangle tattoos?"

From my gut crept an icy sensation.

Gød, no, thought I. *No, no, no.*

"Do not lie." I fought for a steady voice. "You had me shot."

The scoundrel shrugged.

"No. *Mi dispiace.*"

"Through the heart. On the beach."

"Sorry, Finch. Wasn't me."

"You lie. You *lie.*"

"Hey, I don't mean to disappoint you. But come on, you really think I'm gonna execute my smartest monkey for a few funny letters? You don't know me better than that? I was going to have some words, sure. I was going set you straight, you bet. Shit, if I wanted to shoot you I would've done it that day you killed my favorite lamp."

Everything was aswirl. I braced my arms against the bars of the cage. Beyond the cloud of wasps that had taken up residence in my skull I heard the insufferable cretin begin to chuckle.

"What, you been depending on that or something? Guess you

wanted to return the favor, huh? And now I've gone and ruined your hopes and dreams. Kind of wish I *had* shot you, just, you know, so you didn't look so pitiful. Look at you, kid. You're white as paste. Looks like you've got a hole in your neck. You're in a cage. And now you don't even know who to blame for—ah, gee. That's gotta be rough."

It was too much then; it's nearly too much for me to write about now. Johnny had laid waste to his own life after helping me exact revenge upon a man *who'd not even been the one to kill me*. Mr. Finch's lack of vision was far more astonishing, I thought, than anything ever accomplished by Mr. Stick.

With languorous motions Testa reached into his coat, unsnapped the holster, and removed the revolver.

"I do have some good news for you, Finch. I don't know who shot you, but they sure did a lousy job. Unless you got a ventriloquist hiding back there, I can guarantee you that you survived. That's the good news."

He took a backward step equal in length to the space required to lift the revolver to full extension. The hammer pulled back with a soft *tick*. Farther away I heard the rasp of clothing that indicated the cautionary readying of additional handguns. I gazed into the muzzle of Testa's gun and let my body go limp like the puppet Testa had suggested I was.

And then the sadistic bastard returned the hammer to peaceful position.

The long pink scar served as the extension of his grin.

"The bad news—and it's real bad—is that I'm not going to do you any favors. Bottom line is you ran from me. No one does that to Luca Testa. You're messed up in the head, I can see that, thinking how you're already dead and whatnot. So what I'm going to do is leave you this way. Crazy as a loon and at the mercy of whatever your boss's got planned, which from what I can tell ain't gonna be good."

The coat was buttoned around the reholstered gun, sealing away its merciful promise. Testa walked toward his men and I noticed him shudder as if surprised by a wintry gust. This halted him and he gave me a last look from across the tent.

"I was going to say it was good to see you, Finch. To make sense of that note, see what happened to you, all that. But that ain't the truth. It wasn't good to see you. Feels bad in here. Feels like a nightmare. Something's not right with you and I got no idea what it is, except that I don't want to spend another goddamned second finding out. I'm on the next train to Chicago. They're reversing the goddamn river there, you heard that? Worth seeing, I suppose. Some unpleasant shit in that town, for sure, but nothing that feels any worse than this."

The soldiers exited first, taking a quick survey of nefarious lurkers. Testa spoke his final words without looking back.

"Have a shit life, Finch. *Addio*."

He needn't have worried about that.

XV.

BEG YOUR INDULGENCE IN THIS brief detour from our usual lecture series, but I am obligated as a doctor of distinction to tell you of a recent event that has shaken our humble company to its core. It is with heaviest heart, ladies and gentlemen, that I tell you of the fall from grace of the Astonishing Mr. Stick—yes, the very same Mr. Stick whose name is lettered upon the banner under which you entered. Mr. Stick's tenure at the Pageant of Health was a triumphant one and one in which I took particular satisfaction, as it was I who discovered the young man scrounging a life among the slag heaps of a Tennessean smeltery. I will not name the town, as they do not deserve to be held accountable for this scalawag.

"Ladies and gentlemen, Mr. Stick is not who he claimed to be. It devastated me to discover that he is no less than a cutthroat trained to carry out the brutal whims of one of the big-city criminal masterminds about whom we read far too much these days. And this villain most vile had infiltrated my pageant! I wasted not a second impounding Mr. Stick on the premises. Only then did I became aware of an accordant tragedy. This maggot has obscured his past deeds so that the law is powerless to convict.

"Esteemed friends of mine, that will not do. For years I have protected you and your loved ones by offering rare nostrums at fair prices. I shall not betray that trust now and let this assassin run wild

151

across your own backyards. That is why, on February fourteenth, at first light of dawn, near the village of Janus, Virginia, I shall meet Mr. Stick in a duel of pistols.

"Please, please! Men, grab hold of your women so they do not faint. I know the duel is a fading tradition, frowned upon by local agencies. But you and I know a deeper truth! There remains, in the small towns of this good nation, an honor that answers not to elected officials but to Gød Himself. And though Mr. Stick is a trained killer, I fear not, for the Holy Light of the Lord on High shall shine upon me and protect me, and we, all of us, will find in Mr. Stick's just demise peace and glory. The fee to attend, of course, will be nominal—nominal! I remain, as always, your servant, Dr. Whistler."

How many times did I endure this magniloquent sermon? How many times did I have to suffer to the fanatic applause that followed? I had nothing else to do during those weeks in which the Barker marshaled his hoopla. That did not mean I was out of the public eye. For ten cents, you could come see this Highly Intelligent Monkey sitting comatose in his cage. And so they did. The public. My people. Acolytes and brimstoners alike, and practically overnight. Even back then, Americans relished nothing more than seeing the meteorically risen fall back down.

The Barker, whose hatred of me was embedded into his soul as solidly as coal into bedrock, had done what he'd promised, devising a baroque and potentially profitable method of slaughter. But I cared not a whit. I did not intend to raise my pistol in defense. Rather, I intended to be filled with lead, up to and including the brain that the Barker had long avoided penetrating—and that, hoped I, would be the end of me. If not, why, I'd play dead until I was buried.

Two regrets made misery of my final days in the Pageant of

Health. One, that I would have no opportunity to apologize to Johnny for my mishandling of his brotherhood. It tore at my heart, piece of mud that it was, that I had given so little to he who had given so much. Two, that the Barker would likely emerge from our duel a hero. It took balls to enter into any gunfight and his reward would be the reputation of a swashbuckling daredevil. Oh, the villain knew better than anyone how best to engineer my torture!

'Twas a select group that rendezvoused at the so-called field of honor the morning before the duel to review the rules. I'd not been out of the cage since Christmas Eve and my legs were like a newborn calf's; I was carried to the clearing in arms I did not bother to identify. Once in place, Mr. Hobby opened his omnipresent ledger and paged with a gloved hand until he found the relevant notes.

My, they were dull. He said something about how he himself would inspect the revolvers beforehand. Jibber-jabber, yakety-yak. The Barker and I would stand back to back, walk fifteen paces each, turn about, and on Hobby's command of "Fire!" draw our weapons. There would be no taking of turns, no limit to the number of shots fired, and neither of us would be allowed to show up with his dong hanging out—well, who knows, I'd stopped listening. Hobby, ever the efficient one, licked his pencil and asked for the Barker to name his second, and when that was done, he waited for me to do likewise.

But I was off gazing above their hatted heads and past the rising plumes of breath. My companions began bouncing upon their heels, freezing and impatient. They snapped their gloved fingers and demanded again that I name my second. It was an unkind request. They knew that I had no friends. I shrugged, feeling rather low, when I heard a soft baritone over my right shoulder say, to my surprise, "I will be his second."

The voice came from the man supporting my weight, the same who'd carried me from my cage. I twisted my neck and identified him as one of the Soothing Foursome. He, too, shivered, but remained tranquil of expression, as was hallmark for his brethren. Along the underside of his chin I saw a pinkness of wound and surmised that this was the same colored who'd been bloodied during Sheriff Nelson's raid. I'd never thanked this fellow and now I owed him doubly, but when I parted my dry lips, I remembered the truthful taunt of the jailbird John Quincy. Still I did not know this man's name.

I nodded my assent. Hobby sighed in relief, snapped shut his ledger, and everyone made haste to return to their trays of sausage and tins of coffee. This Negro, my pledged second, carried me back to my cage. I climbed in and by the time I'd turned around he was gone and Hobby stood there instead, sifting through his keys. When he'd isolated the proper one, he secured my lock and took a step back. He did not leave right away. He breathed steam and pulled at his mustache.

At length he chose to speak.

"Your numbers, sir." He indicated his ledger. "They were exemplary."

This greatest of all compliments voiced, he exhaled mightily and took his leave. I was alone. This is not to say paying customers did not file in once an hour to get a last look at the man in the once-pretty suit who would take on the dapper doctor come morn, for they most certainly did. But I paid them no mind. I closed my dry eyes and held the Excelsior to my cheek and pretended the *tick*, *tick*, *tick* was the beating heart of Wilma Sue lying next to me in that cold little room on the second floor of Patterson's Inn.

XVI.

WHEN THE LIGHT FROM OUTSIDE the tent brightened from gray to pearl, they came. Mr. Hobby was the only figure of note; the others were shiftless, nameless young men, cracking their knuckles as if expecting the thrashing of a man being lugged to the gallows. I wished to disavow them of this belief; I nodded good morning to all as Hobby unlocked my cage. Upon the dirt my legs felt more or less solid. Hobby offered me my walking stick but I declined. I shook the straw from my hat and was optimistic. This exit from Earth would be cleaner than my previous one.

It was difficult to stifle awe upon seeing the size of the crowd at our field of honor. They looked to me like a herd of leering inbreds, spread across both sides of the field as if for a game of football, jostling for position despite the dampening drizzle. I kept my eyes on my boots as they squished through the black mud that one day ago had been windblown dirt.

When we reached the center of the field there were four other sets of boots I did not care to identify, save for one that I knew by heart. These boots belonged to Mr. Hobby and they tapped at the mud with even more impatience than was typical. There was a delay of some sort and he muttered about it. Were not the nerves of the participants already stretched thin, asked he? Not to mention the rain, which might unload in buckets at any moment? Why, he had a mind to take the bull by the horns and call the whole thing off. It took me minutes to realize that the tardy character was the Barker himself.

The rain went from faltering to resolute. I heard the popping of dozens of umbrellas but kept my eyes on the gray water that streamed from my chin. Then a shout cut through both the rain and the dissatisfied murmurs of the crowd.

"Here! I am here!"

Even I could not resist. I turned to look, as did every man, woman, and child in attendance. Of course it was the Barker making his grand entrance. It was dramatic if unorthodox. His appearance upon the field of honor did not take the shape of a stalwart stride but rather a lean, lurch, and limp. He doubled down on his handsomely tormented grimace.

In place of his right boot were wrappings of gauze. Hurrying after him was none other than Professor Bach, toting a satchel that I knew from experience to contain medical supplies. Bach caught up to the Barker and offered an elbow, but the Barker flung it aside and charged onward. The crowd gasped in unison.

The Barker reached our circle out of breath and shuddering with cold. His face was as pale as mine and he ground his teeth as if fighting off pain.

"Forgive my lack of punctuality."

Professor Bach arrived soaked and panting.

"He cannot duel. He has been shot in the foot."

We all looked down at the foot in question. Shot *before* entering into a duel? It was preposterous. The bandages, however, were wet enough that we could discern the outline of the naked foot beneath, trace the sizable gouge carved just down from the littlest toe, see the blood welling thick before the rain turned it pink.

Mr. Hobby was aghast.

"*How?*"

The Barker lifted his chin. "A thief."

"But I don't understand."

"You don't have to understand." Bach pointed at the injury. "You can see his foot plain as day."

Hobby wiped his wearied face with the crook of his arm.

"Please, sir, tell me how this happened."

Bach waved away the request. "There's no time for *that*." He unbuckled his satchel. I expected him to withdraw additional gauze, a tourniquet, painkiller mixed on-site in his favorite tub. Instead he removed a bullhorn. A bullhorn—it was the only thing in the satchel. He indicated the huge crowd on both sides of them. "Them. That's who you need to tell."

For an instant Professor Bach's eyes met mine.

He blinked and all at once I knew.

It was a lie.

Before I could determine the exact breadth of the deception playing out before me, the Barker snatched the bullhorn from Bach, planted his wounded foot bravely into a puddle, and pressed his mouth to the apparatus.

"Ladies and gentlemen! Ladies and gentlemen, all! Your attention, please! Thank you for your patience this morning. I know it has been a trying one. It has been trying for me as well. Not one hour ago, I, Dr. Whistler, A.M., M.D., of the University of the City of New York, was ambushed in my private quarters by a common hoodlum and shot."

Cries! Moans! Sputters of disbelief! Not because a man they admired had been injured—do not give them so much credit. It was that they had traveled so far to see the spilling of blood.

"Please! I beg your attention! This thief, no doubt, sought to take advantage of this important event. He knew that our Pageant would be well stocked with fantastic and rare product, knew that our coffers would be filled for making change. It is my suspicion that had he succeeded in dispatching me, he would have come after you good people next, your wallets or your lives, for he was a savage, unclean and ruthless, without compunction when it came to killing."

The truth: there was no thief.

"Though unarmed and outsized, I fought this man. How we raged about my quarters! He may have been fueled by the need of the desperate, but I was fueled by a mightier power! The men with whom I work are as close as family and I protect my family as you protect yours. So I beat this thief back, I did, though before he fled he was able to get off a single shot and with that shot took off much of my foot."

The truth: the shot was self-inflicted.

"Ladies, gather yourselves! Gentlemen, listen to what I have to say! This morning we gather beneath stormy skies bound to one another by honor! You have honored us by coming from far and wide. We honor you by carrying through what we have promised. But this contest is not about me! I am merely a stand-in for any of you who would doubtlessly take my place! With our Extract of Viper, Rival to Startling Infection—available for purchase today—I shall be back to my regular exercise regimen in seven days' time. In the meantime, as I so often say, the show must go on. I must hand over this morning's duties to my sworn second."

The truth: his second had always been the man I was going to face.

"Ladies and gentlemen, our gentle dentist, Pullman Larry."

I found the raucous applause that followed rather unseemly. Yet clap and stomp and whistle these people did, as the Barker dropped the bullhorn into the mud and collapsed (convenient timing, no?) into the arms of Professor Bach. Pullman Larry stepped up and his mustache elongated in a lackadaisical grin as he tipped his shark-toothed hat to the crowd. The dentist—or, more to the point, the sharpshooter, though the Barker had omitted that bit of his biography—had been standing beside me the whole while, waiting to play his part.

Professor Bach bent down to pick up the bullhorn and satchel. From his new position slung upon the chemist's back, the Barker opened his eyes. His green eyes shone with more cunning than one should possess while losing precious lifeblood. Weak and wet though the plotter was, he took a moment to bask in the extravaganza he'd produced. To Pullman Larry he issued a final charge.

"Fill his brain with bullets."

Pullman adjusted his gold-mounted .44 cufflinks and flicked the rain from the frills of his leather coat. His easy grin was his only reply.

A thundercrack shot from the black sky. Children cried out.

Mr. Hobby, sensing time was of the essence, took both myself and Pullman Larry by the arms and brought us back to back. So quickly it happened that I caught but a glimpse of Professor Bach hustling the Barker from the field. Something cold was in my hand. It was a revolver. I lifted it.

Hobby pushed my hand back down.

"*No.*" He had to shout it, for the rain had become a downpour and splattered to the mud with such force that it sounded as if the crowd itself had decided to open fire. "Fifteen paces. *Fifteen paces.* At my word. Then you turn, face each other. You lift your guns and fire at my word. *At my word.* You each have six bullets. *Six.* Understand?"

Lightning split the sky over the Boardwalk of Chance. For a moment the rain was caught in the air, a million silver daggers. Against my neck I felt the scrape of a shark's tooth as Pullman Larry nodded. It was all I could do not to lift the gun again to re-establish its reality. I wondered if Pullman Larry was using his personal pistol equipped with the golden forceps. After I was shot down, perhaps he would kneel in the mud and as a finale pluck me toothless.

"Begin!" shouted Hobby. The word lost volume as he scrambled for the perimeter.

Pullman Larry pulled away and I realized I must do the same. I lifted a knee and my foot came down and rumbled the Earth—no, it was thunder, crashing about the black jar that contained us like bugs. My second step was just as shattering, a series of explosions as finely sequenced as if set and triggered by Bartholomew Finch himself.

I lost count. Five steps, six? Lightning flared, revealing chthonian dimension to the mountain ranges of the clouds, and then came down at us like bolts from Zeus, drawing patterns clean as chalk across a blackboard. I found myself absorbing the energy and the anger of these dark heavens. Much had I done to earn this long-awaited final meeting with Death and I'd entered into it readily. That was before the Barker had exited the drama with unfathomable cowardice. Dying like this was no different from being shot in the back on the shores of Lake Michigan and I could not allow that, not again.

Ten, eleven, twelve steps? The rain became the manifestation of the cold hate exuding from my extremities; the mud sucking at my soles became the self-disgust of my betrayal of Johnny. As I reached my fifteenth step—the correct count came to me through the fire-work blasting of thunder—I turned and laughed at the abrupt understanding that crashed over me in a tsunamic tide.

It was not anger that was required to summon *la silenziosità*; not *just* anger, I should say. It was the repellent melange of fury and regret and, most important of all, fear, an ingredient that, though foreign to me while working for the Black Hand, I had discovered anew when defending Johnny against the Barker's assault and while liberating the General of his wartime guilt.

They had been right, both Testa and the Barker.

You gotta have fear in your heart.

Pullman Larry was impossibly distant, his features smudged through the downpour. Yet his bright eyes dulled as he recognized in *la silenziosità* the Death that must come for us all. His practiced squint widened with childlike dread. His laconic smirk loosened into a gawp. When Mr. Hobby shouted "Fire!" there was but a startled jerk from Pullman's shoulders before he halfheartedly raised his gun through some scrap of ingrained instinct.

The sight of his revolver made visceral the abstract truth: I wanted to survive, at least past this deceitful joust. Of course I could never hit anything from this distance and under such foul conditions. But—what was this now?—I was moving.

Thunder burst and spectators wailed. I was hurtling across the field. The gun, the full thousand pounds of it, was rising up with my arm and the speck of my being not lost in the weightless spiral of *la silenziosità* experienced great satisfaction from the wielding. I felt rainwater spilling out of my mouth and realized that I was grinning.

At twenty paces I fired a shot; the bullet lost itself in the curtains of rain. I kept careening forth and now that I could see the whites of Pullman's mesmerized eyes and the quivering of his bottom lip, I fired again. Horrible—a lightning bolt lashed out like a lizard's tongue and ate it.

The shot was close enough to have an effect upon Pullman's stupor. His face crinkled into the blubbering mug of a terrorized toddler and his arm lashed out and the revolver discharged, but there was no aiming involved and it went directly into the seething crowd to his right, and now there was real screaming, male and female alike, as hundreds of people tore themselves away from their stations and began scrambling into the maelstrom of stroboscopic light and the ocean of falling water, diving into the woods or burrowing into the mud or stupidly dashing right into the line of fire, elbows locked around their heads.

Still I advanced. A man bounced off my elbow and in retaliation I fired a third shot. Not only did I miss but the sound further oriented Pullman. His gun swung across the field—more screaming—and fixed upon me. The dentist was sobbing and dancing in place, but his arm was a trained animal, steady enough on its own when the trigger was squeezed.

The bullet lodged in my left abdomen. I was spun around and the world became a tornado seen from inside the funnel. But at circle's end I found myself facing the correct direction and kept moving. Pullman fired two more times and both bullets passed through my body, one through my right shoulder and one through my right thigh. Not the head shots he'd promised the Barker, but not bad under the circumstances.

For a moment or two I teetered sideways, then backward, then dug my heels into mud and sprung forward with a rush of euphoria, for here at last I was taking full advantage of my corpselike state. The new holes in my body lightened me and allowed me to move with real purpose. I was *running*.

My fourth shot missed from a distance of five feet. Pullman let loose with a high-pitched shriek and fired, hitting me again in the right shoulder, but by then I was crashing into him and he went down into a puddle with all four limbs wiggling so that he resembled an overturned beetle. His gun was lost in the storm and I advanced until I straddled his waist. His cowboy hat lost, Pullman Larry blinked into the rain that pounded his face. His eyes were clear and so, I discovered, were mine; *la silenziosità* had slipped away and I was back in this real world, wet and gored and exhausted and emptied of fear.

I leaned over, supported myself with hands on knees, and took a closer look at the dentist. He was no longer crying or crapping himself and instead sneered, having never lost a contest before in his life. I wondered if in some squirmy part of his brain he appreciated the unforeseen turn of events, how the Highly Intelligent Monkey, the Nothing in Particular, had gunned down the only man who could never be outgunned.

I fit the muzzle of my revolver against those handsome white teeth.

Where was his Gød of Pain now?

His death sounded like more mud splashing about. Felt like mud, too, when it hit me. No matter—I wiped it away along with the rain and wheeled about to absorb the scene. It was as if a military campaign had been conducted while my back was turned. The mud was scored in countless furrows. Thousands of footprints evidenced the frenzy. Dozens of people still flopped about in the mud, injured or immobilized or unable to tear themselves from the disaster of historic proportions.

One felled body loomed larger than the rest, even though it was, truth be told, a very small body indeed. Twenty feet behind me lay Little Johnny Grandpa on his back, his blue overalls and white arm sling blackened with mud and his face taking the hard rain without cover.

A feeling of great unease lowered upon me as I shoved the revolver into my trouser pocket and started toward him on legs far less steady than those under the influence of *la silenziosità*. My feet slithered away and I found myself on all fours, my hands disappearing into the mire. I crawled the last few feet until I could collapse at the lad's side. So hunched, I could feel the rain weep through my body's newest holes.

Johnny had been shot twice in the chest. The shudder that gripped me nearly tore my limbs asunder. Reader, do you not see? These were the very two bullets that had passed through my dead flesh before being stopped by the smaller target of his body. That meant that this boy had been directly behind me as I charged Pullman Larry. Unbidden the vision came to me: Johnny hobbling across the sloppy field in his three-point foot-cane shamble, crying my name against the storm because he was certain of my doom and had to try to stop it—and why? Because the drunken, jealous, protective, lonely, gracious, foolish little boy had loved me.

Rain cascaded down my cheeks like the tears my eyes were incapable of producing. I pressed my palms against the lad's punctured torso in the stupid hope of damming the bubbling blood and felt beneath my fingers the brittle tremor of a breath. This lad had given me my words back, so I placed my mouth at his ear and gave back all that I had left: lies.

For a few magnificent seconds, I believed them.

164

"We did it," said I. "We got our revenge."

Johnny's cataracts swam with rain.

"We can leave now," said I. "Find a place to live, you and me, where no one will bother us."

His mouth opened, filled with water.

His arms stirred and I shook my head to tell him that he was under no circumstances to move, that I was strong enough for the both of us. I cradled his mud-spattered cheek in a cold hand, and even drowning in rain his eyes gleamed at this tender touch. His old, coarse lips inched upward into a smile and a thin glaze of blood cascaded down his neck, and then, so sudden for a boy who had lived so long, he died.

I rested my head against his chest. It was reasonable, thought I, that I might remain in that pose forever. But before long a hard nodule began bothering my chin. I figured it to be a bullet, snagged against one of the boy's shattered ribs. But when I investigated the pocket of his overalls, I discovered the golden aggie used each night in his Gallery performance.

Oh, Gød! This boy! His spirit had not been nearly as broken as I had thought! Not only had he contacted Luca Testa as per my instruction but he had stolen this most insidious of props from the Barker and kept it on his person as a sacred talisman. I held the marble to the rain and gave it a jeweler's inspection. It was my duty to keep it safe. No matter how long my death dragged on, this lad's troth and valor could not be forgotten.

No mere pants pocket or vest pouch could protect so priceless an object. I slipped the aggie onto my tongue and swallowed. I had to massage my throat to force it all the way down, but when I could feel the marble lodged inside of my stomach I experienced a wash of warm feeling. It might have felt like one of the ill livers or coiled tapeworms that Dr. Whistler's products claimed to cure, but it was just the opposite.

I slid away from Johnny and took the revolver from my pocket.

The Barker was right where I expected, not far from where he had limped from the field of honor with Professor Bach. The chemist, of course, had deserted him, as had everyone else. The bedraggled soul had not even Silly Sally Kitty Catty to stroke. He sat in the rain with his back propped against a tree and to me looked rather insane, aristocratically costumed but with an eye full of boggy sod and a waterfall crashing down from his top hat's brim. The gauze packed around his injured foot was soaked purple and I wondered if it had been trampled in the commotion.

Regardless, he was going nowhere. I stood at the feet of the defeated madman, the weight of the revolver and its single remaining bullet dragging down a right arm bothered, but no more than bothered, by two fresh bullet wounds.

I raised the gun.

The Barker grinned. Brown rain sluiced from his bloody teeth.

"Congratulations, Finch."

Those two words contained far more than mere acknowledgment of an underdog victory. Dr. Whistler's Pageant of Health was finished. An event of doubtful legality had resulted in injuries, deaths, shots fired into a civilian audience. The law would clamp down hard. Before the morning was through the rest of the company would have fled. Only the Barker would remain, crippled by his own hand. Not that he would have deserted. This was his shore-blown ship and he was the seasick captain.

Testa had left me alive to suffer and so I chose to follow suit.

There was nothing worse I could do than leave the Barker beneath this tree, bleeding and deranged and waiting for the police to end his storied career. Ah, the number of customers he'd rooked! The hundreds of bottles of sludge he'd moved! How he would miss them all when he was sealed off behind bars. I wondered if he might miss me, too, in somber moments of reflection, the way I took those needles like a champion, the fevered excitement I had raised among the reverent. Had it not been glorious?

There was a forest just over the rise. I turned toward it. That was where I would disappear for now. I pocketed the revolver and took several steps in the direction of the tree line before the Barker again spoke.

"Finch."

Through the gray mesh of rain he looked like a specter.

"Remember when I called you a cleaver? When we first met? You remember that?"

I did not respond.

"I was right. You *are* a cleaver. That is what you do. You shall cut the world in half, Mr. Finch. Believers on one side, heretics on the other. So split, they shall fight, and the losses will be significant. I regret I may not be there to see it. Do you have any idea, good sir, the chaos you shall cause, the killings that will happen in your name?"

The forest tugged at me but I gave this man a moment more.

"There will be chaos and killing without my help," said I.

The Barker's smile was wan.

"Maybe so."

With that I left Dr. Whistler and his Pageant of Health and dove into a blackness of trees and thorned underbrush that within minutes made mockery of the pedigree of my imported suit. Once deep into the timber I buried the gun; I was safer without it. The tree cover meant less mud and I was able to move apace, and with every step I cycled through a fresh emotion: hate, hope, wrath, heartbreak, charity. But most of all there was fear. My fate might be the bright, cornpone one dreamed up by Johnny; it might be the apocalyptic one suggested by the Barker. I knew it could not be both. I resolved therefore to keep that fear in my heart and use it, forever and ever, amen.

For now, I had a destination. It was not back to Chicago and Abigail Finch; I was too debauched to ever again defile that pristine mausoleum. I had a card in my pocket, you see, a gorgeous, sharp-cornered, ivory-and-gold rectangle, and on it was printed an address where lived a man who had sworn to take me in, who might, in fact, be qualified to answer the very question of my existence. Come see his People Garden, he'd said. I meant to do just that. One day soon, I was sure of it, I would stroll down Jefferson Street in Boston, lift a brass door knocker, and introduce myself to the butler: *Sorry to bother, my good man, but the doctor has requested my presence.* Dr. Cornelius Leather would then arrive, teacup in hand, confused because this filthy transient was in no way recognizable as a gentleman. So I would stand tall and speak in full voice, for I would not be ashamed of my true identity ever again:

My name is Zebulon Finch.

PART THREE

1902–1913

———◄◉►———

It Transpires That Your Hero Learns Strange Etiquette,
Meets A Girl Of Significance, And Performs An Act Of
Unforgivable Betrayal.

I.

FANTASIES.

Indulge them at your peril.

How long did it take me to reach the good doctor's doorstep? Thirty-seven months. Call it impossible if you like. Was I not an impossible being? Yea, for three long years your hero wandered America's eastmost column—good seats, it turned out, for watching the battered battalion of What Was lock bayonets with the spiffed army of What Was to Be.

The field of combat? Why, it was the town in which you lived! The weapons? Cable cars and automobiles and improbable new flying machines. The ammunition? Riveted steel, scorched black oil. And the blood? The blood, no surprise, was blood, from men too slow to keep pace with these steaming, iron-toothed engines; from animals too dumb to evade sleek new methods of mass slaughter; from unremembered idiots caught flatfooted in the crosshairs of progress. Only from a distance could one appreciate the warfare for the clownish, bruising waltz that it was, and, indeed, it was at a distance I remained.

My first weeks emancipated from the Pageant of Health were wasted hopping trains. Boston was my objective but the trains were snakes and slithered where they pleased. I hunkered near the open doors of storage cars, let the wind tussle the nongrowing hair of my

171

head, and grinned as a vagabond should. America, this woozy smear of gray and brown and green, existed only for me to master!

Instead my tale became a demon's travelogue. Railyard men pointing flashlights made hobo travel perilous. No matter, thought I. A horse I would steal and into Boston I would ride like Paul Revere! But what did a city boy know of horses? Everywhere I spied riders my own age and yet could not bear to approach them. How carefree they were in their plots and pleasures! Their diverse, stimulating futures I could visualize far more clearly than my own.

Unable to stomach the galling unfairness of it all, I took to the byroads familiar to me from Pageant routes. But Mother Nature knew I was unnatural and she maligned me. In early summer 1902 my foot lodged between boulders in a creek and I stood in rising water for two days digging out the rocks with my fingers. That fall, torrential rains sank me so deep in mud that it was several days into the monsoon before I realized that I was screaming for it to stop, for *everything* to stop, either that or let the wet Earth swallow me whole. Wave after wave of such woes beset me as Gød did His holy best to remind me that I was not human but scavenger.

Like a wild dog, I came to want nothing but to defend my solitude. I drifted with ill winds among the detritus of a changing nation, a rising trash heap of outdated material that included warped wood in favor of iron, then rusted iron in favor of steel. By and by, it included men, too; women and children, as well, each one a casualty of progress. I would come upon these forlorn convalescents squatting in spaces that should have been mine: slouching old barns, moss-coated caves, dewy timber.

One cold day my legs refused to go farther. It happened at the edge of a Pennsylvania mining town. There I spent the last few months of 1904 standing in the trees behind a one-bedroom shack housing a stoic coal-heaver, his dejected wife, their deaf and dumb son, and between three and four diaper-loading gremlins. (I never got a reliable count.) Each night in the weeds, the wife wiped coal dust from her husband while he murmured about bosses fixing to poison him with firedamp gas; of that eight dollars a year they'd stupidly pledged to the Catholic Church; of coalworker strikes being plotted that never matured beyond blueprint.

So absorbed were they in workaday indignities and a twelve-dollar rent that I went unnoticed for months. It was Christmas when I was discovered. The mute child ambled out back clutching Santa's gift, a dime novel with a lurid science fiction title. As he thumbed through his book and wandered nearer, I reminded myself that I was a tree, outfitted in wet leaves, brown as bark, moss plugging each of my unhallowed holes.

I prefer to believe that the boy was able to see me because his mind was awhirl with alien invaders and other preposterous things. His stare was not meant to be accusatory but that is how I took it. The boy was eleven and condemned to a miner's lot. In the blink of a sooty eye he would be seventeen and wedged into a shelter shabbier than this one. His lungs would rattle with the bronchitis of the underground enslaved. His offspring, and there would be several, would repeat the impractical cycle. It was *he* who was the tree, rooted to this rotten soil, and I owed it to his dime-novel sense of wonder to remember my purpose.

Thus I moved. The silent boy stood as wide-eyed witness. I moved and moved and moved, under snow and sun, through mist and moon, instinct my sole propellant, until I passed a placard marked with glyphs enigmatic yet somehow familiar to my depleted brain:

173

MASSACHUSETTS
Population 3,003,680

    Given the rabid specificity of this census, the Boston of my frazzled fantasies had to be real and I, fantastical creature, would at last take my place in the long-anticipated fantasia.

    And what have I said about fantasies?

II.

AWAY! WE OFFER NO CHARITY HERE!"

Three years after Johnny's death I kicked through a wrought-iron gate, pitched across a manicured walkway, and collapsed upon the front steps of a three-story manor of Gothic villa design—the residence, hoped I, of Dr. Cornelius Leather of the Medical School of Harvard College. My dumb skull served as knocker against a quatrefoil door panel. 'Twas the witching hour, black as ink, soupy as a dream, and the unhelpful reprimand tied a black bow on the nightmare. A foot heel shoved at my hips.

"Find another family to leech!"

The maligner who plagued me became encircled by a small assembly of whisperers, gaspers, and grunters. Their noises fluttered about like butterflies. I smiled and indulged these kissing little insects until a woman's strident voice cut through the rabble.

"Mr. Dixon, unhand that boy."

"He's a no-good panhandler, Mrs. Leather. He'll wake up the whole block."

"He's not making a peep. We can spare some bread."

"They're like cats, ma'am. Feed them once and the yard will be crawling with kittens."

"My word. He is in a bad state, isn't he?"

Her voice was gentle enough to inspire me to concentrate.

Nightgowns of various colors surrounded me: gray, blue, plaid, and white, the last being of such sophistication that I became embarrassed of my all-fours position. I planted a shoe for standing; it was weatherworn to the texture of rotten fruit.

Feet thundered down an interior staircase. A harsh voice crashed and echoed.

"Listen to me, everyone! I am not a plant! I do not fold into sleep at the setting of the sun! An inconvenient fact for you to consider on this long night, but nevertheless I insist that you try."

From a distance, the barking of a dog, then two, then three, then too many to count. Of course an urban castle like this would have hounds, and soon they would come in slobbering attack.

In response, a baby began to cough from an upper floor.

One of the nightgowns, a gray one, flitted away.

"Forgive me, Dr. Leather, sir, there is a guttersnipe refusing to leave." This was Mr. Dixon, baritoned bully. He took two handfuls of my clothing but the cotton came apart like cobweb. He muttered in disgust and tried the thicker material of my collar and belt.

"Stop, Dixon. Stop at once."

Dixon stopped.

The doctor's pajama-bottomed knees bent to a kneel.

"Divine Providence," whispered he. "If I believed in it, now would be the time to invoke it. Mr. Finch, is it really you?"

A simple but bedeviling question. *Was* it still me? Had it been me since I'd devolved into a scrounging phantom? Had it been me since my murder eight years antecedent? If anyone could sniff out the base falsehood of my being, it was this scholar, so I nodded with a plainness befitting a bedraggled itinerant: it was me, all right.

"My heart," said he. "It is bestirred. Bestirred mightily."

With great hullabaloo, Leather shooed his servants back to their chambers, crooked my arm about his neck, and launched me to my feet, all the while shouting for Dixon to quit gawking and take the opposite arm.

We plunged into a darkness unbitten by wind and devoid of precipitation and needled not by stars but by funny yellow lights. Indoor electricity? A house, by Gød! I was inside a modern, electrified house! The din of the howling dogs faded as I was hustled through a hallway lined with portraits of ancestors and beneath the tiled voussoir of an archway. My dragging toes registered the change from polished maplewood to silk Ottoman carpet. We passed beneath a pendant-laden chandelier and alongside a luminous grand piano, whereupon a magenta méridienne swam up to us and into its upholstered embrace I was placed.

The dim parlor glowed with opulence. Leather issued hushed orders to his gaunt manservant (who in my fazed state I estimated as fifteen feet tall), and Dixon bolted away with as much decorum as is possible for one sporting a tasseled nightcap. Leather exhaled, smoothed his hair, and took a knee before me.

He was older, of course, but still absent of the whiskers that, in those days, were *de rigeur*. This nakedness of face made his surprise all the more fascinating to observe. He attempted to master the moment, bright eyes scouring my every inch until I was rubbed quite raw.

Dixon ducked back into the parlor and set a silver serving tray upon a needlepointed foot rest. Poking their heads through the distant doorway were two women, one the white-gowned Mrs. Leather, or so I assumed, and the other the gray-gowned nursemaid who held against her shoulder the coughing newborn.

Leather snapped his attention from me long enough to glare at Dixon. "You are expecting crumpets?"

Dixon bowed. "Very good, sir. I'll leave you to it."

The doctor raised his voice over his shoulder.

"To bed with you, Mother! There's a good girl."

The wife I had yet to lay good eyes upon nodded her assent. Instantly I felt shame. Look at me—I was on a *fainting couch*. This was out-and-out castration! The infant blared as it was transported from servant to mother. Mrs. Leather departed, patting the child's back, while Dixon took the nursemaid by the elbow.

"This house grows stranger by the day," groused he.

"That it does, Mr. Dixon," replied she.

Leather ignored the minor rebellion. From the tray he lifted teapot and cup. His excitation was betrayed by the ting-a-ling-ing of the china.

"Something to drink. You must be parched."

I shook my head.

He replaced the china and lifted a plate of cake.

"A bite to eat, then. You are starving."

I met the man's gaze and spoke.

"Neither activity holds interest for me."

A shrewd grin wove across the doctor's face and I understood his offers to have been a test. He dropped both his act and the plate of cakes.

"Untrammeled ground. This is untrammeled ground upon which we lurch."

He consulted a pocket watch. Dissatisfied by the data, he interrogated a grandfather clock only to receive the same bad news about the lateness of hour. The rudeness with which he glared at the ornaments about us conveyed a distaste for the formalities of honorable society. He literally swallowed his excitement; I watched his throat bob.

"You must rest, of course. Rest for as long as you require. Tomorrow the both of us shall rise renewed and together determine how we might best assist each other. This is agreeable?"

Sleep was limp bait but I nodded to put his hammering heart at ease. He helped me to my feet and together we passed through the veranda, dining room, and drawing room, and into the great hall where we found Dixon vulturing beside a wide, upswinging staircase. The butler's overgrown eyebrows knotted at the sight of physical effort being expended by his lord.

"Ready the chamber sidewise to the laboratory, and be snappy," ordered Leather. "I expect it prepared when my guest and I attain the third level. And no more servants on the third floor until further notice. None at all, is that understood?"

Dixon stammered compliance and bounded upward, his stone-heavy shoes reverberating about the vortex of two hundred stairs. I became delirious watching his ascent until a hand affixed itself to my back. My frame wilted like an underfoot dandelion. Never had I known the sensation of a touch so firm and supportive.

"First step." Leather's voice was soft in my ear. "First step is the most difficult."

III.

THE LABORATORY WAS CHOCKABLOCK WITH breakables. Fragile pieces of glassware and dainty pipettes in racks, atembic and ampoule vessels fastidiously stoppered, innumerable jars of biologic matter stacked atop cabinets. From my gut rose a young hoodlum's anarchist yearning to render every fussy shelf into so much bright, gleeful shattered glass. It was a good feeling that reminded me of life. To destroy is to be human, no?

Leather sparked a trio of Bunsen burners and I tore my gaze from the delicates. Morning sun diamoned through a frost-gilded window and did wonders to the sterile white room. The doctor looked similarly refreshed, clean of coat and stiff of shirt, fingernails clipped and spotless, midnight hair stylishly swept. He titled back my chin to examine my jugulars.

"Zero hair growth upon face and neck. Interesting." He took microscopic notes upon a pad, perfect parallel lines. Next he pinched my bottom lip. "Zero blood rush. Most interesting." He pulled the lip downward so as to open my mouth, and peered inside with the help of a magnifying glass. "The tongue evidences anemia, though is not cyanosed, deviated, fissured, or afflicted of leucoplakia buccalis. It is sealed by lingual frenulum to the floor and epiglottis. Cause: lack of saliva. Most interesting indeed."

Up popped a set of forceps with which the impertinent fellow snagged my defenseless tongue. He torqued it to and fro as if wringing a damp rag.

"Wuh ah oo ooing?" protested I. "Et oh ah ee!"

I raised my hands in dual fists. Regardless of the man's heritage or pedigree, I'd knock his block off! Leather favored me with a dry look before releasing the forceps in favor of his pen and pad. I glared at him while limbering my poor, molested organ. Of course this treatment was preferable to the needles of Dr. Whistler. But what on Earth had happened to bedside manner?

"Glands: neither small nor large, hard nor soft, discrete or conglomerate. Head: no tender spots, no fontanelles. Face: neither hemiatrophic nor acromegalic nor adenoid. Eyes: no evidence of conjunctivitis, ophthalmoplegia, or edema of the lids."

And that was just my head! The catalogue of my flesh kept pace with the physical intrusions. Cotton probes burgled the debris of my ear canals. Hot droplets lubricated the troposphere between eyeball and eyelid. A small electric light illuminated the grappling-hook chasm of my neck, from which he attempted, and failed, to gather sputum. Next came tests of reflex (the irritating snapping of fingers all about my head like moths) and perceptivity (a triangle rung behind each ear in aggravating alternation).

Bodily examination was next on the docket, which meant a side jaunt to the laboratory's washroom. I'd never encountered a tub with running water and ran my hand along the porcelain surface. Why, it was as zaftig as a well-endowed female and almost as pleasant to pet! Leather cleared his throat for my attention and explained the workings, more complicated than I would have preferred, but, alas, frustration so often presages pleasure.

Clothing peeled from me like stale rind. Twenty minutes later I was sliding my backside down the tub's sensuous curve, indifferent to the questionable wisdom of submerging a corpse in water. I might have stayed there for a good decade if not for the odor. I parted my eyelids to find that I bobbed within a brown tarn of mud, leaves, and pebbles, while translucent sloughs of dead skin floated about me like ghosts of the lives I'd left behind.

Leather had not seen fit to provide me with towel or gown so I entered the lab dripping wet. Each step came with the audible squirting of bathwater through my freshest wounds. I leaned side to side to rid myself of trapped water.

Leather snapped his fingers.

"Stop playing around. Come here."

I stood with arms outstretched as my personal physician took up sharp bits of ironmongery and prodded the stiff musculature of my body from the top down. He was most interested, of course, in Pullman Larry's pistol shots through my shoulder and abdomen, not to mention the 1896 kill shot straight through my heart.

When the novelty of poking fingers into wounds wore out, the doctor grabbed my pecker.

"Does this function?"

Seventeen years of life, nine years of death, and still the world was full of surprises.

"Excuse me, sir!"

"In either excretory or ejaculatory capacity. Does it work?"

"Release me! Or so help me!"

"Stop behaving like a child. The question is routine."

"It is not routine to me, I assure you!"

"You do know what the penis is for?"

"Do I . . . ? Why, you . . ."

"Indicate that you understand, Finch. Indicate!"

Dearest Reader—oh, Dearest, Gentlest, Most Compassionate Reader. My incredulity masked a truth so dreary I have thus far avoided sharing it with even you. I had, of course, explored my carnal capabilities during those years alone in my monkey cage. No sooner had my hands been trained on liver pads and tapeworm pills than I began to, well, handle myself to throbbing memories of Wilma Sue. Understand that sexual desire stirred within me then; it stirs within me even now. But fie! Without the froth of pumping blood, my favorite appendage was but a dangling tumor, benign except for how it taunted me with memories of merriment.

Leather, crude besmircher of my cocksmanship, gestured at the table. It wormed my self-worth. This was no Pageant of Health! I was obligated to obey neither beck nor call! Naked though I was, I struck the cross-armed pose of a bullheaded Black Hander before, after a minute, burying my indignation and yielding to his request. He traversed thin ice, this doctor, but hearing his findings was the reason I'd come. The results might be worth an ounce or two of servility.

I reclined. He hovered over me with a handful of menacing tools. With eyes a-spark and lips a-twitch, he set about removing the two bullets still lodged in my corpse. What fun he had, pinching and digging and extracting! "*Amazing*," whispered he with each cold screw of the blade. "*Wonderful*," sighed he with each plunk of bullet into pan.

He pressed his fingers into my stomach and lingered.

"Something here. Not a bullet. Bigger. What? Tell me."

"A marble," said I.

"A marble?"

"A golden aggie."

"What do I care of its coloring? You wish me to remove it or not?"

183

I closed my eyes against the rising glare of his scalpel.

"Please don't," said I.

He did not forget to test the old bean, either. Hours later, he pestered me with riddles.

"If Dick has fifty cents and Christopher takes thirty cents, what does that leave for Dick?"

Seventeen years old, impatient, and rankled was I.

"It leaves Dick to track down Christopher and take that thirty cents out of his thieving ass."

Even my flippant responses had a home within his reams of notes. By dusk he had loosened his tie and rolled back his sleeves and his waxed hair flopped across his forehead in hard sickles. So absorbed was he in study that he'd bade Dixon begone at three separate mealtime occasions. He sacrificed every human comfort, and he did it for me. Even a pissiness as practiced as mine wore away in the face of such dotage.

"Let me save you paper," said I. "I am a freak. That is the sole note you need take."

Leather looked up from his notes and squinted as if a fungal sample had begun to yodel. He set aside pad and pencil and stood, shorter than the average fellow but as forceful as a footballer, and he took my shoulders, firmly and with both hands, and raised me so that we stood more or less eye to eye.

Men had held me before, but only in headlocks or so that I might be socked in the stomach by their accomplices—certainly never in kindness. Dearest Reader, may I divulge to you something most unusual? It felt so good that I began to tremble. Brusque though his surgical prodding might be, thought I, might it not be its own type of tenderness?

"I am not in the habit of repeating myself so take the following statement to heart," said he. "The label upon that two-bit carousel of yours was not 'Freak Show.' It was 'Gallery of Suffering.' I will venture a step further. You do not 'suffer' from your affliction at all. You radiate in it. You drift upon the effervescent water of life. Anyone—everyone— would turn over his last possession for but a single drop of this water."

The doctor's confidence vibrated through the tightened fists upon my shoulders.

"Your time believing yourself a freak or somesuch drivel? It ends. My plans for you do not befit a freak. It is most fortunate that I am the surgeon with whom you have become affiliated. Those who share my operating theater at Harvard flee the study of death like rats from a flood. Why? Because death cannot be provoked by solution or scalpel; it is purity itself. And they, with tobacco in their lungs and rotgut in their stomachs, with their manhoods stuck inside one another's wives and reductive notions stuck inside one another's minds, they are *not* pure. No, not nearly!"

I found myself grappling to understand. Zebulon Finch, the hoodlum, the killer—pure? Surely the doctor had misspoken. But his conviction was evident in his locked jaws, and from those flexing muscles I took strength. I had expected many things from this man. But belief? Validation? Respect? These had not been among them.

"Do as I say and I shall shine light into your dark," said he. "So illuminated, you will become what you least expect: an angel. But an angel of science! For what need have we of Gød? We men who have plucked lighting from the sky, quarried energy from the Earth, placed false breath into breathless lungs?"

Spiting good old Gød? Was that what this defender of mine was up to?

Why, yes, doctor, I do have some interest in that pursuit.

He yanked straight my lapels, pounded flat my collar, and ripped the thorns from my frowzy breast. I puffed my chest, proud to be subject to this vigorous smacking. Yet another shock awaited: the man offered me his open hand like a gentleman. I blinked at it.

"Your solemn promise is all I ask. Your promise to remain with me until my dowsing of your mysteries divine their secrets. Promise me that you are mine until then, Zebulon Finch. Let me be the architect of your angel wings."

Ages had passed since Johnny had clung to my cage and begged that I serve as his guardian angel, a concept so preposterous that I'd turned away. Here, now, presented to me by a clean, manicured hand, was an opportunity to become the thing the noble lad had believed I could be.

"Imagine it," spoke Leather. "I, a new kind of father. You, a new kind of son. Together building a new kind of family, not upon the tilting foundations of womb and placenta but upon a much firmer, broader, deeper bedrock."

"Father," "family"—the words cut to the bone. Bartholomew Finch had been the last man to shake my hand; they were the only physical touches he ever distributed. A father? He hadn't deserved the title. And the Barker? A sadistic stepfather at best! Dr. Leather, however, was benevolence itself. Yes, I could expect his fathering to be strict, but perhaps strictness was what a feckless youth like myself needed.

Ah, the molasses of emotion. How it sugars the most dangerous of decisions.

The cold, slack meat of my palm was encircled by a warm grip.

Actually, now that I think of it, the grip was feverish.

L O, HIS PARENTHOOD WAS ESTABLISHED. For me, those first months were a brand new childhood, quickened so that I might make up for all I'd never shared with my real father. Leather obtained a leave of absence from his work, something Bartholomew would never have contemplated. Like a child, I was shy beneath his focused attention; like a father, he encouraged me, advancing me past the detestation I held for my own body. He toiled night and day; day and night I learned to tamp down my chronic impatience and let him toil. When his investigations overwhelmed, I mounted brief rebellions, but he had a patriarch's poise, honoring my hesitations before reassuring me that it would all be worth it.

Zebulon Finch was valuable raw material—about that there was no debate—but a finite one able to be harvested in only the smallest allotments. A carefully plucked hair. A fine scrape of cheek tissue. A hairline peel of elbow flesh. Each bodily theft I bore with what I felt was grown-up stoicism. *Make your new father proud,* I told myself. *Show him that you are worth his regard.*

Each sample then suffered the laboratorial gauntlet: submersion in colored oil, heated to steaming, decolorized with alcohol, and counterstained with Bismarck brown. Rapidly the samples outgrew our storage. So it happened that I found Leather one morn dressed as a sous chef, wrapped in an apron splotched with sawdust and paint and gripping a straightedge. His chin was elevated in what I would come to know as his posture of self-congratulation.

"You slumber like an old dog, Finch. Look fast upon my latest creation so that we might be nimble and make hay of it."

The western wall had been cleared of tables, shelves, racks, cabinets, and lamps, and painted a blinding white. Atop it had been drawn Leather's latest shrine to organization, a black grid dividing the wall into five hundred squares of equal size. The X axis was inscribed with cryptic biologic descriptions (*Vascular; Reticular and Lymphoid; Generative*), while the Y axis comprised a list of chemical procedures (*Staining; Purification; Recombination*). Some boxes already had occupants: flimsy bits of my body in capsules held aloft by small shelves.

"Here we will record our advancement with the breadth of a farmer's almanac. Before these boxes are filled we will have our response to religion's Revelations." He sighed in gratification and slapped the operating slab. "Off with the shirt. Let us place another piece upon the Revelation Almanac."

This quantification of our progress nearly made tolerable the fact that I was not permitted beyond third-floor boundaries. For a time, I took the cloistering in stride. Leather's brain was an organ so further developed than my own that it was folly for me to doubt his decree. But my everlasting nemesis, Boredom, did at last hunt me down and commenced hectoring me across days of material preparation; weeks of interminable experiment; months of tedious note-taking, note-erasing, note-reviewing, and note-appreciating; and an unremitting silence more oppressive than the Pageant of Health's obstreperous jabber.

To this tedium, the doctor was impervious.

In fact, he whistled.

The same tune, over and over. And over and over. And over.

It made me want to jump through the goddamned window! I reasoned with myself that it was human nature for fathers to frustrate sons, though that did not prevent me, one fine spring day, from letting go with a groan loud enough to rattle the room's beakers.

"Enough! This aria of yours is relentless!"

Leather stopped buffing his favorite centrifuge.

"I must have been whistling. I did not realize."

"Not realize? Here, examine my ears, what is left of them!"

"A reaction to the arts. A hostile one, at that. This is noteworthy."

"It's noteworthy for how it's driving me raving mad!"

Leather took up a pen.

"Describe the emotions the music makes you feel."

"Is murder an emotion? Because I could murder someone right now. Anyone, really."

"Is there no upswell of ecstasy? No euphoric transport? No rumble of transcendence?"

"There will be a rumble, I expect, when your damn whistling head rolls down the stairs."

Leather tapped a finger against his chin.

"I wonder what might be learned if we put a finger to art. To see if it quickened your vitals. Yes, it's a champion idea."

"A night at the opera? But I haven't the right bow tie."

The doctor hurried out with such speed that the shelves upon the Revelation Almanac chimed in his wake. Ten minutes of curious noises followed: clumsy thumping from the first floor, crotchety words with Dixon at the second, and then the doctor's pained gasps as he scaled the final flight.

Had he not been so famous an abstainer, I would have taken him for stinking drunk. He was as flushed as a wino, struggling against the weight of a lustrous mahogany box affixed with an enormous horn at least three feet in diameter. It barely fit through the door. Huffing with exertion, he mustered a last burst of strength and lifted the awkward thing onto the examining table. He panted his explanation.

"Victor VI. Deluxe model. The best, Finch. The absolute best."

I eyed the device with suspicion.

"Does it grind meat? If you tell me to stick my arm into that thing I shall refuse."

Leather mopped his brow with a handkerchief.

"See this disc? Through vibration of sound, a modulated groove has been cut into the wax. See this crank? It powers the circulation of the disc. This, Finch, is a steel needle. Observe its insertion. One simply releases the hand break—and look. The platter turns. Cunning, eh? They call it a Victrola."

"I've got it! It's an alchemy machine. You piss into the horn. The wheel turns the pee into milk."

He arranged the disc upon the platter with persnickety precision.

"The public wishes to hear opera blowhards bellowing aggrandizing codswallop. Enrico Caruso? That Italian gasbag? His 'Vesti la giubba' is broken glass to the ears! But I am in personal contact with the Gramophone Company. They are, after all, Englishmen. I arranged and paid for an acoustical stamping. I gathered the best performers. No expense was spared, I assure you. The composer: Carlo Gesualdo da Venosa. Rescue your reputation, Finch, and tell me you know of him."

"A composer? Of music?"

Leather touched his temples as if my words brought him pain.

"It is not your fault. You have been brought up, no doubt, on the pabulum of Mozart. You have heard nothing like this before, of that I assure you."

He operated the machinery with confident hands. The steel needle found its place in the revolving disc and a deep grumble rolled from the giant horn, five voices in grieving unison. For a moment I was horrified. These were no less than the moans of persecuted spirits! And we'd invited them into the house? It was only by remembering my own status as persecuted spirit that I was able to resist lobbing the contraption to the floor.

The music was a winter gale howling through a breach. Then it lifted, individual voices darting apart, the soprano flighting skyward away from the sinister sawing of the bass. Even through the thick walls, the horde of hounds out back heard the song and began to howl. Leather closed his eyes to shut out their protest.

"Listeners of the seventeenth, eighteenth centuries called this madrigal licentious. Disgusting, they said."

His right hand sailed invisible tides.

"From Gesualdo's sixth book of madrigals: 'Moro, losso, al mio duolo.' From 1611. His masterpiece. Mozart came over a century later and remained centuries behind. Can you feel it? The chromatic tension? You might interpret it as dissonance. It is close, Finch, ever so close. For the entirety, it totters at the edge of ruin. And where but ruin, I ask you, is there more beauty? The brightest colors of nature we find in carcasses swallowed back into the loam. In short, Finch, the beauty of Gesualdo is your beauty. They were right, those eighteenth-century pundits. The music is disgusting."

Leather, though, was rapturous, afloat in the phonic vapor. I confess that I was curious to feel what he felt. I crossed my arms in

191

the discriminating manner of a critic and leaned into the palpable vibrations. The Victrola flattened the music so that it sounded as if it were being performed from the cellar, yet still I could picture berobed singers going through the pious undulations of an impassioned recital.

Alas, the score held no power over me. As it reached its final fermata, Leather rested his tired conducting hand upon his breast. Before him, the boxes of the Revelation Almanac held steady like five hundred pairs of hands waiting to applaud.

"This piece is a threnody. The word originates from the Greek *threnos*, to wail, and *oide*, an ode. It is a hymn to the dead. Quite different, you will agree, than an elegy. There is no mourning here. Here there is only love. You must love death to live inside of it, to call its black canals home, to willingly turn over exorbitant fares to the purgatorial boatmen."

The black beetles of his eyes, forever skittering, were for once at peace.

"Gesualdo makes no sense to you. No matter; he will. In the meantime I have purse enough to pay both of our fares through the Underworld. What we shall find there will change you and me forever."

Cast what aspersions you will about the doctor, but he was correct.

It happened overnight.

V.

THE LEATHERS' SLEEPING QUARTERS WERE located beneath the lab and it was commonplace for me to hear the murmurs of nuptial debate. That night, however, the interplay was turbulent. I removed myself from bed, opened the chamber door with a surplus of caution, and crept on bare feet to the staircase bannister, where I adopted the time-honored position of eavesdropping child.

Up drifted the protestations.

"You have a child to think of," pleaded Mrs. Leather.

"No," corrected the doctor. "*You* have a child to think of. I have my work."

"And I am thinking about her. She's been choleric since birth."

"All infants are bilious."

"I think we should consider the possibility, that is all."

"That is all, eh? The possibility that this patient of mine, this patient of historic import, is somehow to blame for this child's niggling cough. It's preposterous, Mary, and offensive."

"I do not mean to offend. But he's . . . this patient of yours, he's . . . unclean, isn't he? It is what the maids say."

"You're listening to the maids? Their conniving minds and rutting bodies are what are unclean."

"You can't blame them. They saw Mr. Finch when he arrived."

193

"What they saw was mud. You are aware that mud washes off?"

"Please don't be cross. Mr. Finch looked unwell. And a baby is so susceptible to disease."

"You wish to teach me about biology? You, the wife? To me, the surgeon? This is how you would like to expend your energy tonight?"

Hip-hip-hurrah, Dr. Leather, good show! This complaining woman's attempt to force me back into a roofless life was unwarranted.

"Of course you know best," said she. "But you did recommend a sterile environment."

"Yes, and did you follow my instructions? Good girl. Let that be the end of it."

"Will you at least examine her? Can't you find a minute for that?"

A hard object smacked down upon a harder surface.

"I have given you free hand in household affairs. What else does an American wife want? Do you wish to be tyrannized? Is that it? Not every baby you sprout will die inside your womb, you know."

"Oh!" It was an inadvertent squeak.

"Two babies you have lost, and now you worry that you might yet find a way kill a third. This is distracting twaddle. Children die. I hold you blameless for the deaths. Should our current child die, I would hold you blameless for that as well."

"The way you talk! It's so . . . heartless."

"You know me, Mother. My constitution requires me to speak the truth."

"I don't want the truth! I want you to *care*. I want you to care for your *daughter*."

Leather's final word on the matter was the cracking open of a leather-bound book.

The lady wept. Even after I returned to bed, her soft sobs troubled my dormant chest. Too many times I'd tracked careless mud into Wilma Sue's chamber, peed in her convenient sink, spat in the corner of the room because it was there. Boorish behavior that I now regretted! Mrs. Leather was a fine enough woman; it had been she who'd prohibited Dixon from ejecting me from her doorstep.

The longer I dwelled upon it, the firmer became my opinion that Dr. Leather had behaved with undue harshness. Our accord as father and son had thus far been a successful one, and it distressed me, as it might any child who overheard a parents' quarrel, that our family might be poisoned by discord. I determined to present myself to Mrs. Leather, and to the house staff as well. In all likelihood the pack of them believed me to be a half-man, half-myth locked away in a tower of fairy tale dimension.

Morning brought the doctor as reliably as it did the sun.

His bright eyes assessed the fists of resolution carried at my sides.

"A simple observation, Finch: your muscles are unsuited for pugilism."

"I want to go downstairs. I want to be introduced as would a normal person. I see no reason for me to be jailed up here."

"Is your experience of me that I make decisions without reason?"

"My experience of you doesn't go beyond this room!"

"Have you considered that you might best be studied in a pure environment?"

"In a pure environment? Like your sickly daughter?"

Leather tapped his teeth together thrice.

"I see we have us a snoop."

Well, Reader, I was caught out. I pressed my fists into my thighs and within a smog of shame bore his disappointed inspection. But the intractability of youth remained. I might have even stuck out my bottom lip.

Three more taps of his teeth were followed by a single, curt nod.

"You believe that you are ready? Then let it be so."

My cold muscles relaxed, my fists unclenched.

Was he not the most generous and trusting father?

So crossed the antithetical paths of Zebulon Finch and Mary Leather. We met over dinner, the details of which are lost to me for how rabid I was to see a human face, any face, other than that of the doctor. The infant child, Gladys, referred to by Leather as "his progeny," was the same indistinct potato as any baby, but Mrs. Leather herself I eagerly catalogued. She was not beautiful by any stretch, though in her ardent brown eyes, prominent cheekbones, and tightly bunned hair she was as handsome as a mother should be; handsomer, anyway, than Abigail Finch simply due to her absence of malice.

Mrs. Leather spoke only a smattering; how could she manage more past her husband's dynamic discourse? Leather had met his wife, said he, at the hospital. She had arrived there suffering abdominal swelling and heavy feminine bleeding. By chance, it was Leather who found her stumbling about the hallways begging for help, and later he requested a report from his colleagues, who recommended the full removal of her uterus. Leather, swaggering wunderkind, scoffed at the dramatic diagnosis, doused Mrs. Leather with chloroform, and went in himself.

What he discovered was an apple-sized tumor extending from the uterine wall into the pelvic cavity. It required no great logical leap for me to attribute Mrs. Leather's miscarriages to the resultant surgery. Ah, but the tumor, rhapsodized Leather, the tumor was *magnificent*; it resembled a human head, complete with nodules for ears, eyes, and nose.

It was a ghastly thing to bring up at dinner. Leather's enthusiasm made me wonder if he'd saved the tumor for his future wife to appreciate. Was it even now stored in one of the lab's specimen jars? The idea sickened me, even though I did not deserve that luxury. It was I, after all, who'd once cupped a handful of bloody teeth before the man from whom I'd knocked them and then gloated about it later to cronies.

Mrs. Leather, as bad luck would have it, was stuck with the both of us. Leather's leave from Harvard had achieved farcical length, and he was being forced to return several days per week to lecture alongside the "rust-gathered automatons." Not being a proponent of relaxation time, he seized upon the fact that Mrs. Leather and I had been successfully introduced. (Laugh if you will; I did.) Soon enough, swore he, I would be the recipient of great gobs of attention and it would behoove me to be fluent in the necessary, if tiresome, formalities of the noble class. Mrs. Leather would teach me all I needed to know.

Leather was master of the household, and as his subjects neither of us had a say in the matter. On the morning of his first day back to work, he convened the three of us in the great hall, where he gave me a pedant's final audit and fluffed the ascot he'd provided to cover my gaping neck wound, for Mrs. Leather was not privy to the truth of my spectral condition. Satisfied, Leather took his leave, stranding his wife and me in the echoing space, wondering what in Gød's green Earth we were supposed to say to each other.

Mrs. Leather was the first to try.

"Ethel Barrymore is winning great praise in *A Doll's House*. I should like to see it, wouldn't you?"

"You wish to see a doll house?"

"It's a play."

"Ah. You mean a stage play?"

"It's Ibsen."

"Absinthe?"

"*Ibsen.* He's a playwright."

"Ah."

A crackling start! For a while we searched the corners of the room for clues regarding how to proceed. Mrs. Leather produced a cloth and ran it across Gladys's muculent nose and glutinous mouth. I shuddered and Mrs. Leather saw it. I regretted it. My opinion of babies hovered somewhere between disinterest and disgust, but that did not excuse my poor timing.

Her voice, louder now, tripled from the marble floor and timbered walls.

"I understand that you are to live with us indefinitely, Mr. Finch."

I shrugged. "It would appear so, ma'am."

"That must mean you are very important to the doctor. I do not know why; that is not a wife's business. I do know that previous guests have been kept to the dining and drawing rooms. *Strictly* kept. I have been given word that you are to enjoy free rein inside the house. That is quite a surprise. Forgive me; all I mean is that it is unusual. I shall do my best to make you comfortable, of course."

"Good of you, ma'am."

Her smile was tight and distrustful.

"Why don't I give you a proper tour, then?"

Eager to kill, cut up, and bury this monstrosity of a conversation, I nodded. It wound up a questionable decision, as the next several hours were given to an overlong survey of late eighteenth-century New England interiors. From room to sumptuous room we crawled, maids with brooms scurrying before us like startled mice, as Mrs. Leather recited flavorless trivialities about aluminum light fixtures, armorial stained glass, and how exactly the library's previous medieval tapestry wallpaper was inferior to the Chinese-influenced cinnabar that ousted it.

She might have well recited her screed to a blank wall. Her cold suspicion angered me, and by and by I ached to break from decency and show this woman the true quality of Zebulon Finch. I'd smash that red-brass perfume mirror! Set fire to those French drapes! Such mischief would at least provide her the excuse to have the ever-lurking Mr. Dixon throw me to the street. I'd have liked to see the doddery old bugger try!

Thankfully for the decor, as well as my brittle bones, the doctor burst into the drawing room around two, catching his wife mid-monologue. She could barely execute a curtsy before Leather began pouncing about, ripping at his tie as if it were the noose binding him to Harvard.

"Everything you see here is camouflage, Finch, the baubles and enamels beneath which insecure humans huddle, both here in this ridiculous house and there at that ridiculous college. Do fish pack themselves inside such beautiful crystals? Yes, they do—when they are dead!"

"Welcome home, Doctor."

Mrs. Leather was not as relieved to see her husband as I would have guessed.

"The world is not so symmetrical as all of this, is it? Life's natural state is the jungle, the twist of roots, the tangle of the nerve system. Gødliness is where? In chaos, in chaos! Not in the gilded homes of the well-heeled or the spired churches of the devout." He gave his wife a condescending smile. "Listen to Mrs. Leather, Finch, but do not take her to heart. I wouldn't want you corrupted."

In seconds the doctor had dismissed his wife's entire day of work. Her placid mask went untroubled; she knew, as I myself was coming to know, that Leather was as unmindful of his cruelty as a spoiled child is his privilege.

"Shall we luncheon?" asked she. "I know you do not favor hospital meals."

"Gruel steeped by sloppy sots with unwashed paws! Never do I touch a morsel."

Mrs. Leather's knowledge of the doctor's palate was encyclopedic and her instructions to the cook intensive. She was an impressive hostess at lunch, more impressive still at dinner. And so on: breakfast, lunch, dinner, week after week, month after month. What I remember most from that grinding stretch is not the doctor's careening about the attic of the world nor his filling of the Revelation Almanac, but rather the wife's unflappable fortitude in the face of ongoing banality. Isn't that curious?

Mrs. Leather took care never to seem thankful for my company, and I, perhaps seeking a parent's approval, began to give her lessons my full attention. Manners were a lost cause. Which fork went where? Not that I could eat. When to bow, or shake, or kiss? Not that I ever would. My innate shortcomings exhausted the both of us and her lessons took on a bent more personal and, therefore, far more enjoyable.

She shared with me the most important sections of *The Ladies' Home Journal*, to date my favorite publication. She commandeered the kitchen and taught me the workings of the eighteen-dollar refrigerator, a two-hundred-pound brass-hinged leviathan constructed of northern elm. As a blithesome aside, she mixed a bowl of Jell-O, a bizarre orange gelatin with a jiggle that reminded me, deliciously, of décolletage.

After a time, we had exhausted what the rooms of the house had to offer and she dared take me outdoors. Oh—that lemon light! The nattering of birds! Those winged maple seeds in their eternal spirals! Like a puppy I chased after her. Outside she pointed out to me the building's notable details, the curved transoms and stepped parapets, and introduced me to the doctor's Pierce-Racine touring car, eight hundred dollars worth of machinery that no one had any clue how to operate. And so forth, until I got to know quite a bit about her without ever learning much at all.

It was in April of 1906 when Mrs. Leather showed me her collection of bicycles and velocipedes corroding in a shed alongside the dog kennel. These were unintuitive contraptions featuring one to six wheels in all manners of combination. She gestured and named a few—"Manuped," "Rover," "Leipzig"—before her arm sagged in dispirit.

"I mentioned at our wedding that I should one day like to ride a bicycle. The doctor, wishing to please me but short, as always, on time, bought every one on the market. Then there were too many to choose from. I never rode a one." She shrugged; her unperturbed mask did not alter. "That is the doctor's way. He pours a gallon when but a drop would do."

I reached out and wiped dust from a particularly lethal-looking machine, a metal gargoyle with dual five-foot wheels and two wooden seats connected by a curved pole to a tiny third wheel at the rear.

"That is the Renn Tandem Tricycle. It was nicknamed 'Invincible.'"

"I'm sure it was ironic," said I. "Obviously, it is a sort of torture device."

"Oh, no. It is quite safe."

"Is that right? Put your feet onto these pedals, near those mean-looking gears. Then I'll collect your severed legs and we'll see if the doctor can sew them back on."

Mrs. Leather turned to me, lips so tight that I thought she was about to let me have it. But the buds of her cheeks plumped and her lips opened into the pink shock of a smile, and a laugh tumbled out of her, all topsy-turvy. She tried to capture it with a silk-gloved hand but it was out of reach. It was funny to see and so I laughed, too, a papery, breathless noise that surprised me into laughing some more, which in turn incited her to laugh even harder.

Before it was over, there were tears in her eyes and a warmth at my core that I knew couldn't be real, for I was a creature to whom warmth was disallowed. Mrs. Leather panted for air, her face to the floor for decency's sake, and escaped locks of her bunned hair tapped at her flushed cheeks. In that moment, I could see the young woman she'd been, one who'd linked herself with the brightest of hopes to a clever English physician.

"Let us ride," said I. "There are seats for two."

"No." She put a hand to her chest. "The doctor forbade you from leaving the grounds."

I make no claim to being an oracle of female longing—my life story, in fact, can be read as a testament to the contrary—but the truth of how she felt was there to be read on her face. And who could blame her? Each morning I craned my neck out my chamber window to see Boston but the view was obstructed; I could see an elaborate cornice and rooster-topped weather vane, nothing more. Mrs. Leather, too, had an unsatisfying view; never did she leave the house, always saddled was she with Gladys and, yes, me. Weren't we both trapped inside the castle's firmaments?

"We can ride and we shall." I took command of the thing's handle-bars and gave it a push. Flakes of rust scattered down into the vacated tire ruts. "'Invincible,' you say? *We* shall be the invincible ones and it is this absurd contraption that will be subject to *our* tortures. Come, be my co-pilot."

To this moment, as I scribble these words from down here in my author's tomb, I find myself incredulous that she accepted. What fettle it took to collect her skirts and position her matronly form upon the front seat, what dash she showed as we jounced from the garage and rumbled down the gravel walkway, what courage it took to let me steer our comical three-wheeler onto Jefferson Street and out into the golden open.

Boston! We had found her! Perched high upon our seats, we analyzed and conquered the bustling, laneless streets. Laggard horses and herky jerky cars threaded between unyielding trolleys, as did an undulating mass of pedestrians, shoppers, newsboys, and bootblacks, every male figure duly hatted, for such were the demands of modern fashion. Mrs. Leather shouted the highlights over her shoulder. Over here, the Crown Jewel of the Back Bay, the awesome steel-framed juggernaut of the Berkeley Building! Over there, the Castle Square Hotel, advertising two-dollar-a-day doubles with a telephone in each and every room!

Fellows my own age threw horseshoes, wore college sweaters, or zipped by on modern two-wheelers. I waved, as if I were no different from they. Indeed, this fool's ride had taken on a time-traveler's importance. I was a normal boy; this woman, not Abigail, was the mother I deserved; and we were doing that thing I had heard tell of long ago: *having fun.* We swerved and wobbled; smashups were staved off by shavings of luck. Mrs. Leather whooped at every near-disaster and I hollered just to holler. At length her hair came loose and whisked my face. I did not mind such blond whips of sunlight.

We both knew it when we had gone too far. Gruff, sweaty Bostonians gave us a parson's scrutiny from beneath derbies and stuffed-bird-decorated hats. Their surveillance was a danger to both of us. I turned around the tricycle and Mrs. Leather lodged no protest. What's that, Reader? You expected a ride into the sunset? It is pleasant to consider such romantic notions. But Jefferson Street, with its science and semblance of family, awaited. Which of those two factors was of greater importance I was beginning to wonder.

VI.

WE STOWED THE INVINCIBLE WHILE the hounds voiced their botheration. Mrs. Leather was brown with road dirt yet ablush with invigoration. While she did her best to pound grit from her dress, I monitored the house. At least one face watched from every window that I could see, eyes as blinkless as those of crows. One by one, the faces disappeared. It left me with a foreboding feeling.

"I should prepare for the doctor's return," said I. "You will excuse me, Mrs. Leather."

"Mary." Her hair was uncivilized, the set of her lips firm. "Please call me Mary."

I was speechless, but more than that I was concerned. Such proffered forwardness required reciprocation, but what had I to offer aside from the story of my unsavory origins both as criminal and as corpse? I faltered; I hawed; I took a backward step toward the house.

Even this coward's retreat came too late. Marching across the back lawn was Dixon, dressed, as always, to the nines and frowning, as always, with disapproval. Trailing him by thirty feet was a bombinating hive of secondary servants, seven or eight in total, close enough to overhear but far enough to escape collateral damage.

Dixon executed the slightest of cursory bows.

"Mrs. Leather, if I may, I request an audience."

"What is this about, Mr. Dixon?"

One could not help but be moved by the courageous set of her shoulders, the ostentatious manner in which she gathered her loose cords of hair.

Dixon hit me with a disdainful look.

"It would better be discussed in private."

"Would it? And what's more private than this fenced and hedged plot?"

Dixon tugged his vest and drew himself upward.

"The staff is bothered, quite bothered, and they have prevailed upon me to speak to you regarding—well, if I must say it, I must say it. The squiring about of you by this . . . lodger."

"You refer to Mr. Finch? Our *guest*?"

"I remind you that I speak on the staff's behalf. Master Finch flusters the ladies under my direction. To be frank, the men as well. They exist in such disconcertment that carrying out their duties has become a challenge. Now the boy is spiriting you into the city? It is a shock too many."

"Have any one of them been asked to wait upon Mr. Finch? To serve him food or prepare his room?"

"That is precisely the problem, Mrs. Leather. They have *not* been asked. Perhaps you are unaware of how this undermines the well-being of a servant. Furthermore, they complain of a, let us say, *unnatural feeling* upon encountering the young master."

The favorable smile I had affected dried from my lips. Kow-towing domestics this crowd might be, but they could sniff out my aberration as sure as mosquitoes. In downtown Boston I'd enjoyed a fleeting dream of guileless boyhood, but the dreamer had awakened.

"More than one of the young ladies have come to me afflicted with anxieties about their virtues as well as their souls. Their fears include divine retribution coming down upon this house, a house for which they feel, if I may say so, great affection."

Mrs. Leather's cheeks had grown cherry red.

"I stand here aghast, Mr. Dixon. You do realize that Dr. Leather holds Mr. Finch in the highest of esteem? He would endure none of this, not a word. And neither shall I. You have in remarkably few words offended me, the doctor, and our guest. Mr. Dixon, I thank you for your years of service and I wish you and the rest of the staff the best in your future endeavors."

The sole sound accompanying this astonishing declaration was the la-ti-dah melodies of house wrens, orioles, and sparrows. Dixon's fabled eyebrows lifted high into his forehead and his jaw, typically locked, lowered to approximately chest level. Nearer to the house, the servants went into a panic and asked one another if they, too, had heard the same unbelievable words coming from Mrs. Leather.

Dixon tried to reassemble his wits. "I . . . I shall need to speak to Dr. Leather, of course, before delivering such news to the others. He is lord of the house and he must know of this before—"

"Of course." Mrs. Leather appeared unimpressed by the implicit threat. "I will have the doctor send for you when he is comfortable. Afterward, you may inform the staff that I will be pleased to offer them written recommendations. That will be all for now."

Her sugared smile was a cobra's poison.

For the record, I have long been a fan of poisonous women.

It was the sort of performance that made one drunk with admiration. We conversed no further but I nigh floated through the next few hours, as proud as the lad whose mother had scolded the class bully into tears. The mood, of course, did not hold once Dr. Leather arrived. I heard him issue sharp words, though official matters were postponed until morning, when Mrs. Leather, the sniffling Gladys on her lap, and I took seats in the parlor while the doctor met with Dixon behind closed doors. We could hear but murmurs. Again, neither of us spoke; what of consequence could be said that wasn't already felt?

We were on our third listen of Gesualdo's "*Moro, losso, al mio duolo*" (Mrs. Leather seemed to care for it no more than I, but it passed the time) when we heard the opening of the drawing room door. What followed was the proud plodding of Dixon going about his way. Mrs. Leather clawed at her sleeve cuff, which she'd nearabout unstitched over the past half hour.

Leather came into the room without a word, fell into a chair adjacent to the low-burning fire, and massaged his forehead.

"Have either of you heard that an earthquake of enormous magnitude destroyed much of San Francisco this morning? No, I suppose not. You were off operating a tricycle."

Until that moment, I knew not the trampling shame of disappointing one's father.

"The city, they say, has been torn asunder as if by a pride of giant lions. Harvard speaks of nothing else. Bored surgeons filled with patriotic poppycock were fighting to catch a train west to help sop up the blood and, perhaps, feel better about their misspent careers."

"That is dreadful," managed Mrs. Leather. "Are there many dead?"

"A few thousand, give or take. What does it matter when we have a few hurt feelings to dress right here at home?"

Mrs. Leather looked down at Gladys's head. Seeing this firecracker of a woman so easily defused left me feeling bereft.

"I have reinstated Dixon," continued Leather. "He is now the most handsomely compensated butler in the Northern states."

"Retain them all," blurted I. "Mrs. Leather let them go on my behalf. I will live elsewhere. In the shed out back. Or off the property entirely."

Leather's eyebrows rose.

"A white knight. Here in our own home. How novel." He gestured lazily at his wife. "No, you shall have your way, Mother. What difference is it to me? Fewer prying eyes and thieving hands, I say. The staff, save Dixon, will be gone before lunch. Which reminds me: you'll need to prepare lunch. You'll also be on your own with the child from this point forward. I presume you thought all of this through before firing our entire staff."

Mrs. Leather continued to study Gladys.

The doctor slapped his thigh.

"So much business so early in the morning! But as I feel no quakes suggesting the imminent rending of this half of the continent, I bid you, Finch, to meet me in five minutes' time, not in the laboratory but upon our back property. Reassure me, why don't you, that you do not require a leash."

He exited as briskly as he'd entered. Gesualdo's loathed madrigal came to an end, the steel needle of the Victrola snapping at the center of the disc. I brought myself to my feet, levered the needle, applied the brake, and turned so as to follow the doctor.

Mrs. Leather stood blocking the doorway, Gladys held to her bosom.

"I know why the staff feels as they do," said she.

It was not a subject I wished to address, not while I was needed for some mysterious purpose out back. But women are a nuisance to sidestep, Reader, what with their hips and chests and countless other parts you dare not nudge.

"It is your eyes," said she.

"What of them?"

She offered me a sad smile.

"You do not blink, Mr. Finch."

You are no stranger, I'll bet, to being told that a wad of salad leaf resides in your teeth. The sensation that settled upon me was similar. I'd not realized that I'd deserted the practice of blinking, and now that the fact was voiced I was quite dismayed. Blinking was so basic a hallmark of Mammalia.

With her free hand she reached for my face. I flinched but she was quick, her thumb touching one eyelid, then the other, pulling both over my eyes. The friction against my eyeball was unpleasant. Mrs. Leather pulled the eyelids open again, then shut them, then did it several times more, until much of the stiffness worked itself out.

"A small detail," whispered she. "But it will help put others at ease."

Mrs. Leather, then, knew the truth. Had she figured it out on her own? The doctor would never have shared information above what he considered her intellectual grade. Even knowing what she did, there she stood, trying to help.

"Every time you have a child, Mr. Finch, you lose a piece of your soul. I believe that. It's right there in the blood and tissue. Souls do not come apart cleanly; it's a surgery. You of all people understand surgery. You understand that even when an operation is successful, it brings the patient closer to death." She caressed her daughter's wispy hair. "Gladys is my miracle. I must do what is necessary to protect her, above myself, above you, above anyone. I do hope that you understand. The doctor's interest in children is nonexistent."

Lies still came easy to me. "That's not true."

"It isn't, not entirely. He did enjoy each pregnancy for as long as it lasted. He enjoyed examining me. In the beginning he'd even warm his instruments before using them. It's why he married me, you know—the tumor. He knew there would be miscarriages. And though the good doctor does not care for babies, he is rather fond of miscarriages."

"Why are you telling me this?" asked I.

"Because you are but a boy. Until you are not, you are vulnerable."

I would never *not* be a boy. Never, never, never.

Leather's voice echoed into the great hall.

"I see you need a leash after all, Finch. Join me now and I shall fashion you a strong one."

Thank you, Mary. The words waited at my lips but I knew better than to grant them passage. The gift of her first name had been given to me on careless impulse. But not even Dr. Leather could control how I used the name in my mind. From that moment on, Mrs. Leather would be "Mary," and though never once did I speak the name aloud, it is how I think of her to this day, these many long decades after her death.

VII.

THE BACK LAWN WAS VAST, immaculate, and cultivated into a green parade of absurd geometric formations. The grass was silvered with morning dew and by the time I caught up with Leather my pants clung hard to my shins. We passed the pitted moonscape of the kennel, a barbed-wire coop too small for the ten dogs packed within. (As a former cage-dweller, I sympathized.) The hounds were not for sport—they were flabby, overgrown, and irritable—nor were they proper pets—they scratched at unkempt fur, rampant fleas, who knew what else.

They whined as I passed.

Leather paid the animals no mind and together we skirted a thick frontier of trees and, to my surprise, emerged into a garden of spectacular arrangement. A flagstone path guided us beneath a lattice arbor tossed with creeper vines as tumultuous as a girl's hair after a romp in the sack. This sylvan tunnel exited into flower beds of kaleidoscopic color. Even I, creature of dulled senses, was jarred by the heady perfume of rich jasmine, chocolate cosmos, stimulating gardenias, sweet lily-of-the-valley, and feminine roses.

There was another odor, sweet but unidentifiable. I could not place it.

Leather pointed. "This way."

He tromped across the terrace and hooked a right by a lily pad—

laden fountain. Then he bent to unlock a short wooden door all but hidden between shrubs. Through it, he disappeared; I ducked and followed. When I surfaced, brushing hyacinth from my sleeves, Leather was shading his eyes with a hand.

"Lovely, isn't it?"

"Yes, most. But I do not understand why we have come."

"Is it not obvious? Your tricycling adventure betrays a desire to intermix with the general populace. You have not progressed to that point, not quite, but that does not mean I cannot introduce you to others like yourself to whom I've become close. It is my hope that you will become close to them as well."

He drew a magnific breath. I followed suit and good lord! The *odor*! The sweetness I'd detected before had become an inundation. I looked about and saw spread before us on a small patch of trellised lawn a Victorian garden party in progress. A congenial party it was indeed, excepting the fact that the partiers were, to an individual, dead.

To our right, three bonneted corpses were perched in rustic cast-iron armchairs, empty eye sockets and lipless grins tilted toward a checker board gray with bone dust and featuring the additional playing pieces of fallen teeth. White parasols had been wired to the ladies' gloved hands. Finger bones poked through the silk.

To our left, a croquet game. A man in a beanie stood with mallet cued up to the ball. *Hurry, take the shot,* urged I, for his buttoned shirt was about to pop from putrefaction. His body was held erect by two fence posts dug into his mottled flesh. Spectators watched from basket chairs and marmoreal benches, legs crossed, hats jaunty, shriveled hands secured to teacups or tumblers.

Closest to us was a septet of musicians. Soft chords hummed

213

from their instruments but it was the breeze that cajoled the strings. Together they made for a handy timeline of decay, beginning with a violinist of greenish tinge and ending with a cellist whose black suit was but a sack to contain his crumbling bones.

The name printed upon their sheet music?

Carlo Gesualdo da Venosa.

Here was the doctor's long-promised People Garden, the sunny-weather project of a deranged landscaper, and one does not witness such outright depravity without bolting away and screaming the entire while. But Leather had me by the elbow and, beaming with pride, forced my stricken legs to stroll with him down a gravel path. We were assailed by slow, overfed flies that bumped into our faces before continuing about their feast. Leather gestured at a particular spoiling body.

"Ah, relaxing with a decanter of port, are we, Mr. Two Weeks? Was the refreshment tent out of *pâté de foie gras*? How tragic, my good man! Then I insist you try the lobster salad. I swear it was imported from the shores of Eden itself!"

Leather chuckled, then spoke *sotto voce* as if Mr. Two Weeks might overhear.

"Watch, now, as I roll back his sleeve—roll, roll, roll. There, that translucid skin, see how it peels away by its own volition? Touch it; it crinkles in a delightful way. You refuse? Tut-tut. You embarrass me in front of our guests."

Whistling Gesualdo, Leather unbuttoned the man's vest and shirt.

"Note the fissure in the fatty tissue? From there is whence the foul stench cometh! Few sights are more educational than that of a self-devouring intestine. Shall we take a closer look?"

Long have I been lousy with names. I cannot reliably report if it was Madame Four Months whose bug-eaten neck had been propped open by silverware, or if it was Professor Three Weeks whose monocle had been cracked by an outgoing tide of maggots, or if it was Lady Eight Weeks whose body was ringed by serving trays collecting every category of bodily slurry. At the edge of the garden I tore myself away from Leather and found ballast against a flowering urn.

"Did you murder these people?" pleaded I. "Is that it?"

Leather's lips twitched in amusement.

"You are quite certain you do not require a sherry? You look more peaked than usual."

"You think I'm not capable of doing something about this? I could run. I could try. I could tell everyone in Boston."

"What, indeed, is stopping you? Besides our promise to each other, of course. And what else do you possess, Mr. Finch, aside from that promise? Why, the clothes on your back are not even your own."

"Is this your end game? To put me here?"

He laughed! The psychopath laughed!

"Finch, you ox. I am no murderer. Harvard is the recipient of a stream of fresh cadavers, a number of which I spirit away from the unimaginative dicing of my colleagues. They are happier in my garden, I assure you, and twice as useful. Here I inventory the active, transformative process of death in ways never before considered. Indicate that you understand."

"I indicate nothing!"

"At least consider Mr. and Mrs. Five Weeks here, enjoying their soda waters. Charming couple. Lost in an equipage accident. In five weeks of death they have given our world more than if they'd lived ten tedious lives. Unlace their clothing and you shall find the expected degeneration. Her aorta, though—pristine! His prostate—healthy as a boy's! So: questions. Where does death choose to feed and why? Where are the loci of the body's strongholds? The body produces curatives in life; does it produce other curatives in death?"

"And I help you in this, do I?"

"Help? Finch, you are the polestar! With my People Garden, I isolate effect. With you, I isolate cause."

"You must show me this for a purpose."

His smile showed a touch of affection.

"Our work has yielded preliminary results."

Distraught though I was, I experienced a rush of woozy excitation.

"It has?"

Leather caught a butterfly in his palm and studied its throes.

"You are dead, Mr. Finch. Officially, medically dead beyond any stretch of doubt. Yet here you are, walking and talking. What I have done—what *we* have done, together—is comb, at an atomic level, for the spark that, though hidden, feeds your animation. Look at the results. Your skeletals and cardiovasculars: nothing. Your lymphatics and endocrinals: nothing. But in your sensories I have found tracks, the same as if left by a colony of ants, of a self-generating energy originating in your prefrontal cortex."

"My brain," said I.

That is all I said, but what I saw was the Barker and his velveted box of pins, so many that he'd pushed through my eyeballs within shaving distance of my brain. He'd been no academic and yet he'd sensed the seat of my vitality, the same as Leather.

"What, then, do we know of your brain? Radiological imaging confirms behavioral analysis: your capacities remain absolutely consistent with those of a seventeen-year-old male. You have the capability to learn, that much is obvious, but one need only study your superior gyrus and precentral sulcus to observe the lack of frontal-lobe neuron growth typical to anyone alive for thirty years. Your cortex should have thinned; you should be drifting in the calmer tides of adulthood, enjoying the increased capacity for reason. Your brain and hypothalamus, however, continue their excitable, impulsive, youthful twitch. I'd go so far as to say that you are trapped in your seventeenth year, caught like the engine of that infernal motorcar of mine."

I felt like an untethered boat knocked about harbor stones. At seventeen years of life, I'd been a Black Hand bandit, an exuberant maimer, a dabbler in minor mutilation, and deserving of my friendless death. Leather's findings sent me into ecliptics of distress. Was I forever doomed to relive that fate? I swore I could hear the pitiless clang of another monkey cage slamming shut.

Call me, if you wish, "Mr. Seventeen Years."

"Remedy the long face, Finch, for you are not completely lacking inertia. That stiffness you feel? The Romans called it *rigor mortis* and it is, in its own way, a maturation. You are rotting away the same as our friends here. There are differences, of course. I've graphed them and they are extraordinary. Your decomposition is moving at zero-point-eight-three percent the rate of a typical cadaver. Why, you could last over a century, maybe twice that, given variables of climate, wear and tear, et cetera."

"No," whispered I. "I'll never last that long. I can't."

Leather squeezed the butterfly and dropped it; the breeze stole the lifeless thing away. His voice became the soft shush of the grass.

"Just know that it is my mission to keep you *out* of the People Garden. Do you understand at last? I said I would remake you and I

217

will. So I beg of you: no more tricycling, no more trifling. You must do as I say the instant that I say it, and trust that my lead is true. This household cannot sustain another disobedient."

The source of my revulsion shifted from this ghastly display to my precarious future. I lifted my nose and tried to smell the lush flower beds that served the purpose, I now realized, of shrouding far gamier scents. What was the doctor if not unbalanced? Yet I, when placed upon Nature's scale, was more unbalanced than he. Perhaps it was only our combined, if oppositional, weights that would tip the final judgment away from monster and back to human.

VIII.

"MEAT ETIQUETTE" WAS THE CUTE nomenclature Leather coined for the phase of experiments that were to consume the next few years of my death. The nickname was apt if satirical. Flesh, you see, has secrets. To be granted access to those secrets, one must approach the flesh with the appropriate manners. Which is to say, no manners whatsoever.

It was a messy affair. The sterile room to which I'd grown accustomed transformed, day by night, into a volatile, disorganized birthing room where together we conceived, delivered, raised, and euthanized the unspeakable offspring of Leather's mind. How did the slaughter commence? Reader, there was no mistaking it. The discharge of the household servants freed the doctor from the last bindings of civilized decency and he swiftly succumbed to his wildest abstractions.

Both my hopes for inner tranquility—to understand who I was, why I was here—as well as more narcissistic instincts—to attain global glory for helping to eradicate death—depended upon the continued brilliance of my adoptive father. So it was with quiet but mounting dread that I watched his obsession with my brain begin to debilitate his own. I knew something was amiss the very first morning of meat etiquette, but could not put a finger on it until I entered the lab. But of course: the dogs. For the first time since I'd arrived, there had been no crack-of-dawn braying.

That is because the dogs were inside the lab, at least in a manner of speaking. Lined ear to fuzzy ear, their severed heads sat upright within pans of their own congealed fluids. Dual electric pumps sat elevated on either end of the table, powering the flow of blood from a glass container suspended above a burner. Tubes ran from this container into the first dog head; a tube ran from that head to the next; and so on, linking all ten heads in a single chain.

Between each industrious *chug-chug* of the pumps came pitiful whimpers, as the remains of each dog tremored, nose jerking at its own fresh-meat odor, ears twitching as if ducking through thorned underbrush, and tongue lolling upon the table within a plash of sizzling froth.

Leather spoke without turning from his work.

"Death, life. Black, white. In this lab, Finch, we shall invent the color gray."

Two hours later, the last dog head went still. Leather took it well. So many notes to be taken! So much knowledge to process! I grabbed hold of the window frame for support and saw Dixon down below, his tall old body wrestling with a shovel as he turned bloodsoaked kennel dirt into a mass grave. Leather, meanwhile, had moved on; the heads had been stacked inside a metal tub for later disposal and he maintained a stream of excited chatter regarding what he'd learned and how he'd apply it.

Meat etiquette was not inspired by mere nightmare. It was formulated upon the pioneering work of physiologist and obstetrician Luigi Galvani. Galvani, I gathered, was the Carlo Gesualdo of eighteenth-century science, whose scandalous experiments had been all but discredited by generations of cognoscenti. Leather, contrarian to his core, had modernized Galvani's ideas—twisted them, one might say—beginning with the concept of *elettricità animale*, the idea that massive sources of self-sustaining electricity hid among internal organs.

Leather's hypothesis was that my superior electrical flow originated with my brain but was patterned into my every cell, not unlike the way a waffle iron imprints its lattice into batter. His job was to agitate the samples that filled the Revelation Almanac, box by box, to exaggerate this code until it could be reproduced.

He was deep into the rabbit hole, the singularity, the labyrinth, and I, despite my growing fear for the doctor's sanity, continued to hold the map.

Winter 1906: I remember them well, those wide Erlenmeyer flasks in which slivers of my skin darted about catalytic solution like minnows; the electrified heating plates, too, upon which the diced cubes of my muscle fiber popped with life like bacon in a pan. My body offered none of the satisfaction of spilled blood, but my tissue incinerated and boiled and froze well enough to placate Leather, with every ensuing emission of smoke or steam seeming to me like Indian smoke signals. What was this figmental tribe trying to tell me? To trust in my father's wisdom? Or to flee from his horrors?

Summer 1907: had only you been there to see this one, Reader! The lobe of my right ear was sacrificed to Leather's scalpel so that it could be bolted with zinc to the underneck of an ethered cat. The unfortunate feline was girdled for the passage of electricity and when the lever was thrown it did catly things, quilling its hackles and yowling and looking as discombobulated as any cat in the history of cats. My earlobe, however, acquired no pulse, and like a sad grape withered on its feline vine.

Autumn 1908: while the first of Henry Ford's Model Ts were

being manufactured in Detroit, Leather was putting the finishing touches on his own paradigmatic machine. Equipment of longheld primacy—the hemoglobin scale, the blood oven, the stacks of litmus paper—were shoved about the perimeter to make room for what he called the "Voltaic Bed," a wide sheet of metal studded with copper rivets. When powered, it hummed with such force that dust danced an inch off the floor. I, of course, was too delicate for this uncomfortable bedding. Enter Miss Nine Days, hailing from the People Garden via first-class wheelbarrow. Leather had a hunch that when the current reached critical level, her cadaver would achieve a deathless state akin to my own.

Instead she roasted like a duck. Meat etiquette was a speculative business.

While gods and devils fought for supremacy upon the third floor, Mary took advantage of the inattention paid her. She kept to her word and poured her energies into teaching Gladys lessons she might one day need to live a normal life apart from this madness. Mary and I still saw each other most days. She would ask me how I was and I would try not to shiver while lying that I was well, very well indeed. It was a pointless game; my problems, unlike hers, did not evolve. She was raising a girl, soon to be a young woman, while I was, ever and anon, a lost and fearful boy.

I did go on reminding myself to blink, though there was no one left to appreciate it.

IX.

EW RECOGNIZE THE MOST IMPORTANT events of their lifetime as they occur, so occupied are we with silly complications and sillier distractions. Chart the roadmap of your life and you will find a profusion of overlong routes and hellish switchbacks, salted patches of Earth crossed repeatedly until stomped to ruin, while the pastures of pleasure are but skirted, peed onto from the side of the road without you having an inkling of their majesty or significance.

So it was that in April 1910 a piece of my past came home to me.

Visitors were uncommon at Jefferson Street but I was hardly disturbed when I heard the late-night clanging of the brass door knocker. Dixon, slow and deaf though he'd become, remembered the path to the front door and I was comforted by the usual disapproving tone of his voice and the ensuing slam.

The following morning was drizzly but nevertheless heralded the return of the stubborn visitor. Dixon, too, knew how to be stubborn. But the visitor returned again during stormy midday, and again at showery suppertime, and then once more amid the pounding rain of night. When Dixon cleared his throat outside the laboratory door, I was shirtless and supine on an unwashed table with Leather poised to tweezer a bit of white matter from my eyeball. The room stank of smoke and cold corpse blood.

Go away, old man, thought I. *This is no place for the living.*

But Leather grumbled, set aside his tool, and cracked open the door.

"Out with it."

"Do forgive me, sir," said Dixon. "But a young lady insists upon being seen."

"Who is she?"

"She will not say, sir."

"This is hardly a dignified hour."

"She is not a dignified young lady, if I may be so bold, sir."

"Do you require a reminder on how to do your job?"

"I have issued warning upon warning, sir. This is her fifth visit in two days. I know you frown upon bringing police to this house but I am at wit's end."

"No doubt she is a relative of a patient who died on my table. Extend the usual sympathies but inform her that I am utterly indisposed."

Leather began to close the door but Dixon raised an arthritic hand.

"The young lady does not ask for you, sir. She asks for Master Finch."

I slid from the operating table and stood. Plasma, someone else's, oozed down my spine. A guest? Me? I seized the idea with unexpected enthusiasm. A reprise from hell's chimney, even for a mistaken call, was worth taking.

Leather shot me an impatient look.

"A devotee of your sideshow act?"

"Show her in," said I.

"Do not show her in, Mr. Dixon. Whoever she is, she is after money."

Seventeen was more than old enough to stand against any father figure! I snapped up my shirt, buttoned it, threaded my arms through jacket tweed, and, as was instinct, patted the pocketed Excelsior.

"Put her in the parlor, Dixon," said I. "I shall be down directly."

I had to endure history's most violently gritted teeth, but endure them I did, and ten minutes later I was stealing down the stairs breathless (I know; it makes no sense) with the sensation of a pounding heart (again, a lack of sense). Dixon, wheezing from effort, was exiting the parlor, and I tipped an invisible hat to him before sliding into the room's bourbon light.

The girl heard me enter. She stood in a puddle of water and whipped around so fast her hair sprayed the bookcase with rain. The hair was black with damp but I could see that in its natural state it was light brown. I took a step closer. She was around my age and beautiful, though skinny, with regal cheekbones and nose, enthralling eyes, and a determined underbite. I grinned and it felt good—the old Zebulon Finch charm, thought I, emerging from hibernation.

Instead of reacting in kind, her brow tightened in bewilderment and she took a hesitant step forward as if trying to see me in a better light.

"It can't be you," whispered she.

I extended my grin.

"Zebulon Finch, at your service. Have we met?"

She prowled lightly, as if upon clawed paws.

"Impossible," said she. "How are you so young?"

The question set off a bell of warning. My smile faltered and she appeared to take it as an admission. She thrust a hand inside her topcoat, a shabby thing sized for a grown man and slathered along its bottommost inches in mud, and withdrew a square of paper. With damp fingers she began to unfold it. It was old, rubbed pale, splitting apart at the creases, but with walloping shock I recognized it before she held it up for me to see. After all, I'd kept my own copy in a scrap-book twenty-four years earlier.

It was my favorite "Wanted" poster from 1895, the one that made me look like John Wesley Hardin. My first reaction was a bloom of elation as if spotting an old friend; seconds later, the feel-ing downturned, for the vibrant young man in the picture was but fourth or fifth cousin to the crippled dead thing I'd become. Finally I felt apprehension, for while there were numerous reasons one might track down a Black Hand rowdy, none of them were good.

I took a step toward the door.

"You are without towel," said I. "Allow me to fetch one."

The girl shook her head. More rain spattered my skin and burned like hot oil. She lurched closer and I stumbled against the humidor. Her eyes lit up as if sensing weakness.

"You think I wanted to come?" asked she. "Crawling like a mutt for your mercy? I would do anything to avoid it. But I'm hungry. I'm *starving*. Look at me."

With her wrongly gendered coat, faded dress, bony shoulders, mud-crescented nails, and overall uncleanliness, the evidence was indeed damning. But in these crimes against her, what part had I played?

"Miss," said I, "I believe there has been a misunderstanding."

"Misunderstanding? No. Misfortune, yes. Of the father to whom I was born!"

She'd come so near that her sharp cheekbones and underbite threatened my neck. I might have presumed that we were about to kiss were it not for the look of her eyes. In them waged a battle between pleading and resentment over having to plead. This iron mask of stub-born pride was a strangely familiar sight.

All at once, I recognized it.

I'd seen it before in mirrors.

This girl was my daughter.

I cried out, an unbidden bleat, and elbowed past her bony arms so that I could bury myself into the fainting couch. That aquiline nose and those patrician cheeks—I admired them because they were my own! That underbite, though, owed its existence to none other than Wilma Sue. It was she who I saw in the girl's beguiling body and cunning face; she I smelled, that aroma of black tea and cheaply laundered sheets; she I tasted in the air, face powder, and fresh rain; and she I touched—only, no, this was not Wilma Sue I touched, it was our spawn, grabbing me by the shoulders, trucking me from one nightmare to the next.

"Leave me be!" demanded I. "Liar! Deceiver! Gorgon!"

"She's dead," said the girl. "Do not pretend that you care."

"But I do! I loved her!" Once it was out of my mouth, I believed it. Had it always been true? I tried it again: "I loved her. Yes—I did!"

"You *paid* her. That's not love."

In the heyday of my carnality, I'd allowed the possibility of impregnating a whore or two, given drunken lapses and the primitive state of prophylactics. But cathouse cabals had methods of addressing such sticky wickets; few prostitutes would be so gauche as to pester the inseminating customer. The idea of having a child? A real, live child? It cudgeled me with confusion, hammered me with panic. I was but seventeen!

I weaseled myself to sitting position. "It wasn't like that. I gave her far more money than required. It was to help her. I was trying to—"

"Is that right? Explain to me how you *helped* her. How you

227

loved her *so much*. I'd enjoy hearing about that. About everything that you did right."

"But why in heaven did she not tell me? Why—"

"That I can tell you. I've heard the story a thousand times. She planned to. The last night she saw you, she tried to tell you. But you—"

I pressed my palms over my ears.

"Stop, stop, stop!"

No repetition of denial, regardless of volume, can eclipse a memory that awakes screaming. I was back in Wilma Sue's arctic chamber, bleeding from the head, only this time when she called to me from her warm bed, it was not just for tea but to divulge to me a secret that must have been eating her alive. She was pregnant and knew that it was mine. What did this mean? That she had stopped sleeping with other men. And what did *that* mean? That she trusted me, believed in me, was risking life and livelihood on my reaction. And what had been my reaction?

To run out on her. To vanish. To prove that I was a delinquent punk more interested in cracking skulls for petty cash than forging any relationship beyond the casual. Wilma Sue left because it was the only logical path forward. She was alone and always had been.

Oh, this cloudburst of repellent truths! How long had it been since I'd felt even a twinge of guilt for those whose lives I'd ruined? In a savage minute this wicked girl had reminded me that no one, including you, Dearest Reader, should ever make the mistake of rooting for me.

"How?" begged I. "How did she . . . ?"

"Die? Was it painful? Was it from slow disease? Could it have been prevented had we had any money? Yes, yes, and yes! Would you like me to paint a more colorful picture? The weakness and the sores, the not

228

sleeping and the total confusion? All of that came well before death."

"Did you not consult a doctor?"

She struck the pillow next to my head.

"Don't you dare give me advice!" Spittle clung to her lip. "There was the matter of payment, don't you know? Though the doctors were happy enough to offer scoldings while carting away her body."

"No more. I solicit you."

"No more—yes, I've tried saying that myself. To those who threw us out of our home. Who wouldn't help her when she was sick. Who wouldn't help me when I was picking through trash on the street. Why else would I come here? There is no one on Earth left for me to beg."

She craned her neck to take in the ceiling fresco, the gilt metal chandeliers, the etched crystal shades. Such affluence had become banal to me, but I saw the surroundings through desperate eyes. To this girl, each accent of refinement signified money, warmth, food, and safety. The ramifications frightened me.

I could be assured, at least, that so glorious a residence contained pockets of solace where I could mourn my darling Wilma Sue out of range of this virulent woe-bringer. I attempted to stand but the girl crooked her body over mine, her muddy coat flapping like buzzard wings, her claws digging into the cushions. Her bright birdie eyes, I hated to see, were the same as mine.

The "Wanted" poster, Wilma Sue's sole heirloom, crinkled against my ear.

"You owe her, don't you think? But she's gone. I'm the one left behind. So now you owe me. And you're going to pay up. Mr. Mystery. Mr. Jefferson Street. Mr. Zebulon Finch. Or should I call you Aaron?"

X.

WILMA SUE HAD NAMED OUR daughter Merle Ruby Watson. As names go it was sturdy enough, though it was the "Watson" that moved me. *Wilma Sue Watson.* Her full name, I knew it at last. Surely a more alluring one has yet to be concocted—go on, say it aloud. The pronunciation forces the lips and tongue to kiss, gasp, and kiss again.

The four shots blown through me by Pullman Larry were nothing next to the twin impacts of Wilma Sue's death and Merle Ruby's birth. Just as I tried to come to grips with one idea, the other one took me by the throat, as a dog does a rabbit, and gave a killing shake. The wounds therefore remained fresh as I bumbled through breakfast, during which the stoic Mary explained the entire situation to the doctor. I felt like a teenager caught in the act—which, I suppose, I was.

"Some girl off the street? In this house?" Leather was baffled. "Finch, have I taught you nothing? Human offspring carries no more inherent worth than does a beslimed tadpole or fresh spot of fungus. I see no reason to open our doors. Not to mention that there is not one court in the land who would believe you fathered this girl, considering your similar ages."

Mary's longstanding control over household affairs was nevertheless a difficult token to rescind. After much berating, Leather regarded me across the table as he chewed. I squirmed. His eyes had

230

of late narrowed to red coals, yet I detected a scintilla of sympathy. If Zebulon was the son, Merle was the granddaughter. Leather would endure her presence for my sake and, by extension, the sake of our experiments.

"For a short time, then," said he. "*Short*. Indicate, both of you, that you understand."

He left for the college, whistling Gesualdo for inspiration.

I considered running out the same door.

I considered forcing the girl from the house at knifepoint.

I considered many a malicious reaction. But each confirmed Merle's meanest presumptions—that I was capable of only the most irresponsible of behaviors, and therefore belonged inside this fine home no more than she. Because there was truth in that, and plenty of it, I instead chose to honor Wilma Sue by displaying kindness toward our daughter. Within reason, of course.

Merle had been stashed in a chamber down from the master bedroom. When I dared peek across the threshold, I was greeted by a vision. In place of the scraggly diabolist had materialized a young icon of porcelain skin and cornsilk hair prettily arranged with ribbon, sporting a dress too short for her tall, hungry frame but nonetheless stunning. She was wiping a languid finger along the bureau as if mesmerized by the absence of dust when I pushed open the door.

"You enter a lady's room without invitation?" She gave me an unreadable smile. "How brash of you, Papa."

I grimaced. What a word! Overnight she had come to accept my impossible youth. Perhaps, in the scheme of her wretched life, it was not the most inconceivable thing she'd encountered.

"Last night you had me at disadvantage," said I. "Now we shall talk sensibly."

231

Merle shrugged and ambled about the chamber, petting this and pawing that, looking for all the world like a princess deciding which items to purchase and have sent back to her castle. With her new clothing had come, it seemed, a new persona.

"Let us get down to it," said I. "Tell me, for starters, what you want."

With the kind of jarring movement that was becoming her trademark, she dropped her body to the silken bedsheets and struck a coquettish pose.

"It was the comet!" exclaimed she. "It was a sign."

"The what?"

"Don't you read the papers? Halley's comet! They say it passes once every seventy-five years. I know, science—what a bore! But this comet came on Sunday night and all the poor people were climbing roofs to see it, and so I did, too, and there it was! A little rider in the sky."

"Wonderful. May we return to our agenda?"

"It had to be a sign, don't you see? So I told myself to be brave and came to you, and here we are! Do you know what yesterday was?"

"Tuesday. Yet another Tuesday."

"It was the day we passed through the comet's tail. So! How about that! It was meant to be."

"Nothing is meant to be. I shall ask again: what is it you want?"

She rolled her eyes.

"You are *such* a father. Nag, nag, nag."

Before I could raise my voice to compensate for the disquiet brought to me by the f-word, she slithered from the bed and drew herself up to the lancet-arch window, parting the curtains with drama enough for a leading lady. She gasped at the view. Or was the gasp staged? With this girl, it was difficult to tell.

232

"Why can't we make a life together, Papa?"

"I beg of you to stop calling me that."

"Oh! I had the most amazing bath this morning, let me tell you all about it!"

"Please do not tell me about your bath."

"I think this place suits me. Suits both of us."

"Understand me: none of this is mine."

She sashayed from the window with a mischievous pout.

"Not yet it isn't."

"What is that supposed to mean?"

To my horror, she patted my cheek with fingers slender and white, but also calloused. The sound was flat and sarcastic.

"I mean only that you are in magnificent shape for a man your age. You might outlive the doctor, his dumb wife, all of them. You never know, this whole place could end up ours."

I knocked her hand away and she trilled with laughter, twirling away until she happened to catch a glimpse of herself in the boudoir mirror. Her eyes went wide as if seeing the approach of a momentous chocolate cake. She hopped this way and that, preening and primping.

"We could tell everyone we are sister and brother," said she.

"What?"

"We could be the toast of the town. The papa who looks forever young and his equally sensational daughter."

"Listen to me. I am engaged at this residence for purposes of work. Important work, if you must know. Furthermore, I cannot be a father. I would not have the first idea of how to behave. I am sorry for that. Believe me, I am. I will speak to Mrs. Leather and see if the family can offer some package of assistance, so that you might begin again in the world amid circumstances more favorable. Would that be agreeable?"

233

I thought it was an amicable enough speech. But it brought an end to her ballet as rudely as a bucket of cold water. Her arched posture wilted into a self-protective hunch. Her haughty airs floated away to reveal the narrowed eyes and sullen underbite of one used to fighting from a corner. She leaned into the mirror, her harder face an inch from the hard glass, tracing her fingertips across her forehead. Even I could see the finespun wrinkles of a girl who'd spent her young life squinting against driving snow in soup lines, coveting the shopping baskets of the rich while gnawing week-old bread, stealing what she needed to survive only to face down condescending men of authority.

How strange: a crumpling sensation in my chest.

Was this what the living referred to as empathy?

I opened my mouth but was a moment late. Merle drove her fist into the mirror. It exploded into silver daggers. For one second, reflections hung upon the air: raging, red eyes; spinning rose petals of blood; my own face turned to a broken puzzle, each twirl of glass alternating a frozen instant of shock. Glass, then, dropped everywhere, a thousand minuscule explosions, while she remained in her lupine hunker, her fist pumping red streams.

By some primeval instinct I found myself at her side, wrapping a silk sheet around her wounded hand. Merle's torso hitched with dry, raw sobs that I could feel in my very bones—and why? Because I had taken the girl into a full embrace. Her sopping injury was warm and damp, and it reminded me, for a soaring moment, of the painful thrill of actual life. Her blood, after all, was part mine, and in that moment we shared it, assailant and victim, beast and beauty, father and daughter.

XI

T HE UNSPEAKABLE RIGORS OF MEAT etiquette continued above, while below began an arduous process of acquaintance. Though Merle and I had launched our ship at an acrimonious port, we paddled somewhere more complex. Our quarters were close and we saw each other at vulnerable moments. Example: while dragging myself from the third-floor funhouse of horrors, body and soul equally sundered, I found Merle peeking from behind a door and judging my stoop of despair as genuine enough not to mock. Example: Merle, humiliated at the dinner table by Leather when caught holding her steak knife like a dagger, calming a bit when she saw me, in solidarity, give my knife the same murderer's grip.

Even more affecting were the moments of gladness. After an umpteenth snooping, I spelunked from Leather's cabinets an old medical study featuring photographs of one hundred naked women, and the sincerity with which I collated my top ten made Merle laugh out loud. She, meanwhile, experienced moments of true bliss upon Mary introducing her to any number of modern luxuries: the telephone, through which she jabbered at switchboard operators; an air-conditioning unit before which she danced in disbelief; teabags, the first of which she sniffed and grumbled about before dunking it and discovering that *it tasted just like real tea!*

The doctor bore his interloping grandchild like a foul odor. Mary, reactive as always to her husband's mood, repeated to him at night that Merle intended to leave as soon as she'd made a determination of what she—a girl with no pedigree, no means, and no education—was going to do with herself.

Did Merle also want cash, as Leather had suspected? Yes, she did, but I told myself that it was a reasonable reaction for one raised under fiscal fatigue. Mary, generous of heart, indulged the lass with a weekly allowance to help her find her footing. What Merle found instead was a row of the best shops in Boston, and rare was the week she did not promenade into the dining room wearing a new dress or accent of jewelry, to the constant captivation of five-year-old Gladys. Mary suggested that Merle take advantage of the new clothing to apply for a position as a nurse or a secretary. Merle said she'd think about it. There the discussion croaked, for the tantrums of Merle Ruby Watson were on the way to becoming legend, and keeping them at bay was key to a happy household.

I felt that Merle and I had achieved, if not closeness, at least a wary respect. Still, she would reveal nothing about how she had tracked me down (I suspected my infamous municipal tricycling), though plied with the right coins, puddings, or flatteries, she would on occasion reveal patches of her mother's story. Dearest Reader, I had to know; the agony was a parcel of mine to claim.

Wilma Sue had left Chicago pregnant in 1895 and lived with Merle for stretches at a time in different Midwestern cities. With authentic agony, Merle described Wilma Sue's final decade at a garment factory, cutting fabric for skirts and blouses she'd never afford until her hands doubled in size with swelling. Details were manifestly withering. Wilma Sue never once rode in a car. Never ordered food at a restaurant. Never bought an item of clothing off the rack.

Hers was a checklist of a life devoid of dignity and desserts.

Merle intended her stories to hurt and repel me, but they had the opposite effect, especially given the status of meat etiquette, which, like its namesake, had begun to spoil. For months Leather's arsenal of electrical toys had ripped apart People Garden corpses for no apparent gain, and the blood-spattered doctor, I feared, was losing all sense of direction, not to mention decency. I lived in apprehension of what atrocity he might dream up next, what part I might be forced to play in it, and what might be done to my own corpse if I refused.

I believe it was natural at so taxing a juncture to search out a better fantasy: taking care of Merle as I had failed to take care of Wilma Sue. Week by upsetting week with Leather, my belief in the new course grew stronger: I *would* take care of her, I *had* to, for she was the sole product of a perished pecker, the only thing I'd ever made instead of destroyed.

First, however, she would need to know the truth about Zebulon Finch.

So it transpired one late-summer eve that I escorted Merle Ruby Watson to the domed veranda, where the two of us could commune in private. She moped most strenuously, as her preferred routine was to prance about the lower floors in her latest gown, tipsy from a smuggled bottle and guffawing at the imitations of the adoring Gladys. I guided her to the chair boasting the best view of the three-sided bay window and took for myself the opposite.

"Your arrival," said I, "has brought to mind many things long forgotten."

Her head tipped back and she giggled at the ribbed vault of the ceiling.

"It looks like we're inside a giant whale."

I counted to five before proceeding.

"Merle, listen to me."

"All I ever do is listen to you."

"Be that as it may. I have something important to say."

She propped herself up on one of her sharp elbows.

"If a whale swallowed you," said she, "I'd try to save you."

I frowned.

"Would you? Truly?"

She snapped her fingers. "Changed my mind. I can't swim. You never taught me."

"You are not making this easy."

"Hey, what goes on in that lab up there? Mr. Dixon never moves from that landing. I've given him the sad eyes, I've tried tickling his chin, but he's too old to care. I know something strange is going on. Why won't you tell me, Papa?"

"In fact, I am trying."

"Are you?"

She made a show of planting her triangular face into her open palms. It was impossible to know if her interest was honest or farcical.

"Something happened a year or so after your birth. I was the target of—"

"I know what you were." Her chill was back. "Mother told me everything."

"Not quite everything. I—well, there is no best way to say this. In May of 1896 I was shot and killed on a stretch of Lake Michigan beachfront."

Merle performed upon me a long, careful study. Being the focus of her stare never failed to distress. It was the look of a butcher, hatchet in hand, determining where best to chop.

"You have my attention, Papa." She sounded as sober as Leather. "Please continue."

With a big balloon of a breath, continue I did. The moon had sailed halfway across its black sea by the time I finished my macabre tour, which began at the bottom of a lake, advanced to a monkey cage, and terminated in a Boston laboratory. At appropriate plot points, I revealed the gaping wound in my neck and the bullet holes in my shoulder.

Merle was silent, her only movement being the painful-looking coiling of a strand of brown hair about a pitiless finger. I concluded with an abstract of the principles of meat etiquette and petered off, having prepared for my story neither satisfying climax nor sorely needed cliffhanger.

Merle tapped her teeth with a fingernail.

"I was right," said she at last.

"How so?"

"That all this"—she gestured to the estate surrounding us—"could be ours."

Greed, greed, greed! Did this daughter of mine have a second emotion? Yes, Reader, I, too, was well-versed in material gluttony but her assessment felt so tawdry after my earnest unweighing. With a wave of my hand, I attempted to erase the comment from the record.

"What we might gain from my condition is a lesser consideration."

"You told me you used to live on the streets. You know how it is."

"We could leave here. The two of us. That is what I want to say."

"And live happily ever after? In what? A ditch? A cave?"

"I do hope those locales can be avoided. But even those fates would be sufferable if you and I suffered them together. Don't you agree, daughter? Our unification might mean absolution for the both of us—even, perhaps, for your mother."

She scrambled to her feet as if my skin had begun to ulcerate with plague. Her chair crashed to the tiled floor between us and I flinched as if I'd been pinned beneath it. In a way, I supposed that I had. For when does Zebulon Finch consider anything through before reeling headlong into it?

"We are *not* the same," cried Merle. "I am *not* like you. I need shelter. I need warmth. I need food, I need water, I need clothes—did you consider any of this? If your secret business on the third floor no longer brings you satisfaction, then I suggest you behave like my mother, like any person with a child ought to: keep quiet and keep working. You, strange and sick as you are, might not need this roof above your head, but I do. I do! I will not let you ruin it!"

Merle bolted from the veranda, kicking aside a set of wrought-iron firetools and shoving from a pedestal a rare seventeenth-century jug. Between the clanging of tongs and poker and the shattering of valuable stonewear, she disappeared, leaving in her wake a wincing medical marvel and his bindle of unwanted secrets, two seafarers locked inside the great whale that ate us and that might spend the next century or two over our digestion.

XII.

APERMANENT RIFT SOON ROSE BETWEEN Cornelius Leather and the Medical School of Harvard College. For some time, the doctor's afternoon homecomings had become fire-bombings from which the rest of us shielded ourselves. Harvard's *witless dunces*, shouted Leather, alleged that his private undertakings were coming at the detriment of his lessons. The doctor was livid. He could no more hold rational discussions with these *dripping idiots* than he could pull pinecones from his ass!

"They call me secretive!" His jabber was the same at both operating and dining room tables. "Well, indeed, gentlemen! Indeed I am! Only a *feeble-minded twit* would share his world-altering discoveries with *lethargic plagiarizers*! Oh, yes, they smell breakthrough all over me and they long to be the second, third, and fourth cooks named in my published recipe!"

This was not the same paragon of sober intellect for whom I'd journeyed to Boston. But how could I flee if it meant leaving behind Merle, not to mention Mary and Gladys, who would then become subject to his concentrated wrath? I dwelt upon the workings of this elaborate trap while Leather boasted about daring the medical board to take away his classes, his title, and the research funding that the *bleeding ignoramuses* had written in black ink upon his contract!

So take them away they did.

No one, I believe it is safe to say, had ever defied the doctor with such temerity. He kicked through the front door that day, hoarse and howling, and raced to the third floor, where in a myopic fit he upended old jars of pickled eyeballs and testicles into the lovely bathtub. He then ripped off his shoes, socks, and trousers, and in his underwear stomped the organs until two inches of green mash coated the porcelain. I watched in silent shock as he pulled his trousers back on and strode away, trailing ocular and testicular residue. In the great hall, he damned each of us in turn.

"How can any sapient man produce results in such a monkey house? You, wife, are a chimpanzee, canny of deception and clumsy of decision! You, child, are a howler monkey, hooting after your milk-giver and reveling in your aggravating blare! You, young woman, are a gibbon, the long-limbed prankster, palming your own shit in preparation to throw! And you, Finch, are the orangutan, so close to human that you have mistook your position as one of entitlement!"

He shook his fist at the bronze candelabrum, the ebonized tallcase clock, the satinwood display cupboard, all the trappings of wealth and position he so despised.

"Gesualdo himself could not have composed in such a zoo! Henceforth all disturbances will be eradicated! Total concentration shall be mine!"

He disappeared into his lab for five days, corresponding with Dixon via notes slipped beneath the door. On the sixth day a massive wooden crate arrived at the house and Leather surfaced to greet it, his unwashed hair snarled into Medusa whips, his extremities trembling from lack of sustenance. He ambushed the crate with chisel and hammer, removed from the straw padding several smaller boxes, and struggled back up the steps as he'd once done with the Victrola.

This inaugurated several more days of tense secrecy. From the lab I heard the thudding of heavy objects; from below I heard the anxious pacing of Merle and the alphabetical recitations of Gladys to her mother. It was as the females slept one night that I thieved down the hall, pressed my ear to the laboratory door, and detected the most peculiar sound. It rose, it fell; it was reedy and high-pitched; it was twice as unsettling for its oceanside softness.

Hweeeeee . . . fweeeeee . . . hweeeeee . . . fweeeeee . . .

I assessed the door's dark maleficence. The filaments of straw poking from beneath it recalled the bed of a Highly Intelligent Monkey—and hadn't Leather just cursed our domicile as a monkey house? This pairing of evidence was portentous but courage was the night's directive; I cleared my throat and spoke.

"Dr. Leather? It's Mr. Finch. I wish to enter."

Hweeeeee . . . fweeeeee . . . hweeeeee . . . fweeeeee . . .

I rapped my knuckles against the door. I could tell by the rattle that it was unlocked.

"I am coming in, Doctor. I hope that is tolerable."

Hweeeeee . . . fweeeeee . . . hweeeeee . . . fweeeeee . . .

I entered upon straw, much more of it, tossed with mangled remnants of the delivery vessels. Naturally I had presumed the shipment to contain medical equipment, instruments toward the elongation of our etiquette; for that I was prepared.

This, though, was much worse.

A single operating table had been situated like a desk facing the Revelation Almanac. Behind it sat Leather in suit and tie. Or who I assumed was Leather, for the motionless figure wore a tall bullet-shaped helmet wide enough to cover both head and sternum. The helmet was constructed of iron but lined with yellow felt so that it might rest comfortably upon the shoulders. The face was smooth and feature-less except for two circular windows at the position of the eyes, both of dark, reflective glass. Just below these windows, a tube snaked out to connect with an oxygen tank set upon the desk. With fearsome slowness, the helmet titled upward and fixed me with a blank stare.

Hweeeeee . . . fweeeeee . . . hweeeeee . . . fweeeeee . . .

It was the sound of the contraption's inhale and exhale.

For an overlong moment two blinkless beings regarded each other.

"Dr. Leather," ventured I, "are you quite all right?"

His muffled voice came in fragments between sucks of air.

"It is called the Isolator. Direct from New York. Genius device. Sounds penetrate only from. Six feet away or less. Narrows the vision to a. Single line of text. Just what I need—" He paused, winded from the brief monologue. The needle on the tank danced upward. "—to concentrate."

Upon the table were arranged not the handsaws and forceps I'd envisaged but tall stacks of musty books. These tomes were of low mint and I could but make out scattered words from moth-nibbled spines: "Magick." "Daemonologica." "Grimoire." "Inquisitorum." "Chiromancy." One volume was splayed open, its foxed pages bearing the fresh wounds of ink-pen incisions. Leather tapped one of these notes with a finger.

"Already the Isolator has bred. Lush fruit. I was correct to eschew. Modern methods. For methods more historical. In nature. My fault in our meat etiquette. Was not reaching back. Far enough. Back to the ancients. Men unprejudiced by things moral. Or proper. Men open to the fear. That lives in the dark. The dark of their hearts."

It had been a cool December at the Pageant of Health when I'd met a proud heretic who'd spoken to me of "saving humanity" and making the world "retch religion and superstition." What, then, to make of the man's swerve toward supernatural balderdash? I had the notion that Leather would be happy, in fact, to *destroy* humanity if that's what it took to plant his flag upon science's highest peak.

Yet he was the father and I the son.

I measured my words through clamped teeth.

"Tell me how I can be of assistance."

The dead black lenses offered nothing, but the body beneath beckoned me with a slow hand that appeared to crest upon an invisible wave of oxygen. I took a step through the straw, a single step, and only as a gesture of goodwill.

"I have missed your. Buoyant contributions, Mr. Finch. You will, of course, accompany me. During my interviews. Here at last we reach the. Homeward stretch of our journey. A stretch you and I shall cross. Together."

As little as you like the sound of these "interviews," Dearest Reader, I liked it less. But I saw no space in which to wedge alternate terms. I nodded assent to the featureless mask and he clapped softly, his two palms barely striking each other as if the smallest of noises might defile the Isolator's well-won solitude. I figured that he might well be smiling beneath that helmet and so I forced a smile of my own. In turn, Leather fiddled with a knob on the tank. The little red needle leapt higher.

That needle—my twitchy little grasshopper friend.

I would grow all too accustomed to seeing it jump.

XIII.

L EATHER CONDUCTED THE FIRST ROUND of interviews as would a sane man. One, he greeted his visitors decked out like an *au courant* gent of the 1910s: fitted three-piece suit with thigh-length double-breasted jacket; shirt starched to hell and back; fat-knotted tie; trousers creased like shark fins; hair slicked back to an otter's specifications. Two, he met them in an urbane setting: a drawing room beautified by a crackling fire and fresh nosegays from Mary's garden, as well as a table of tea, crustless sandwiches, jellies, and pound cake.

Three, he did not wear a large metal mask upon his head.

For these reasons, the early interviewees were the lucky ones. The New York phrenologist, for example, who canvassed my skull with tape measure to appraise what he insisted were the twenty-seven different organs of my brain. Or the French hypnotist, who claimed that, through suggestion alone, he could deliver me from *folie de doute* (my apparently piteous lack of self-confidence), thereby facilitating the memory of the events that led to my *petite problème*.

It was all I could do not to kick these shysters in the nuts. Leather, of course, took boxes of breathless notes. His professionalism began to erode only with the arrival of the spiritualists. Still he wore the suit, still he used the drawing room. But his face and neck were an alarming pink from last-minute treatments of the Isolator. The seers and clairvoyants put on their best shows regardless, and we were treated to lively seances and amusing memoranda from the spirit realm. Leather tried to keep up with his notes, but it was a challenge, what with those fat droplets of sweat smearing his ink.

You are a perceptive reader. You see where this is going?

Away went the tie. Then the coat. Next the tea and sandwiches. At last went the drawing room itself. Soon Leather was receiving each aspirant fraud in the lab itself, devolved by then into a grotto of haphazard, broken instruments and a Revelation Almanac in disarray. No wonder the tarot card reader, a turbaned Italian matron, could not complete a reading of me before gathering her deck and scuttling away. Leather paid her little attention. His hand kept straying to stroke the Isolator, its sumptuous felt surface, sensuous eye windows, and long, ridged oxygen hose.

Mary sent me looks of panicked appeal when we crossed paths. Merle, herself an untamed bitch, sniffed the alpha dog's rabidness and laid low. Even Gladys sensed the bad juju and kept clear of her father, dragging away her ceramic dolls by the feet, their once-beautiful heads of hair serving as mops for floor dust.

Better than the dust of the street, thought I. *I must make the doctor see the family he is driving to bankruptcy.*

The idea of forcing a tête-à-tête gave me misgivings, but so did watching the devolution of the single man in history who'd extended to me both sensitivity and respect. A truthful, if uncomfortable, encounter might make me a better son; was it too much to hope that it might inspire the doctor to be a better father?

Severed from Harvard, Leather had nothing but time, so I needed only follow the disconsolate strains of "*Moro, losso, al mio duolo*" to find him during a spell of repose. The Victrola had been moved to the laboratory and was the single piece of equipment kept spotless. That night I found the doctor draped across a hardbacked chair, the Isolator perched high upon his head like a welder's cap. His eyes dragged and his skin was yellow and glossy.

I stood there until he gasped.

"Right there, you hear it?"

Saliva ribboned his lips. It was a nauseating but common sight; the excess of oxygen acted as low-creeping fog, filling his lungs with dew.

"I did not," said I.

"It was the sound of a single sense split into multiple nonsenses, and then those nonsenses fornicating in orgy to conceive a new sense. Gesualdo, he understands me. The question is, Finch, have you found your way to understanding him?"

"My ears, I think, have heard too much burlesque."

A bleary smile stretched across his flushed face.

"That's Harvard talk. They would be the first to damn my dear Gesualdo. Did I tell you he murdered three people?"

"Dr. Leather, please forgive me for saying so. But it is you, I worry, who is murdering three people. Your wife. Your daughter. Yourself? That is, if you do not patch your broken path."

"A few small deaths in a wider war. What difference could it make? Now, Gesualdo, the story goes, returned from a fabricated hunting trip to catch his wife *in flagrante delicto* with a duke. He killed them both, of course, and displayed their corpses outside the castle for passers-by to enjoy. There was much to enjoy, too; the conniving wife had been stabbed twenty-eight times and her body was shortly violated by a passing monk—so it goes, Finch, so it goes. There was a son, too, whom Gesualdo suspected as being the offspring of the duke. Gesualdo swung the boy on a high swing, back and forth, back and forth, until he was rattled to death, while below a choir sang madrigals exalting the beauty of death."

"Back and forth, yes—this is the futile motion of the cheats and shammers you bring to this house. Have you lost your way so badly?"

"Lost my way? Gesualdo himself was an alchemist as well as a composer, and did not shrink from human experimentation. Had *he* lost his way? These passions led to his lifelong insomnia, further so-called insanity, and death at the hands of his servants, whom he ordered to flagellate his body with maximal barbarism. Had *he* lost his way?"

"You compare yourself to this musician again and again, and to what end?"

"Gesualdo's madness *was* his genius. The Harvardians think I am mad, and, indeed, I hope that I am. Mad as Eratosthenes, as Darwin, as Columbus!"

My efforts were useless. Had I urinated in the doctor's face, he'd have likely applauded my inspired lunacy and taken fevered notes upon piss-soaked pages.

The Isolator clamped down over his face.

"I wonder." (*Hweeeeee . . . fweeeeee . . .*) "If I might use a hose. To attach the Victrola. To the Isolator." (*Hweeeeee . . . fweeeeee . . .*) "Create a pristine capsule. Of musical enlightenment." (*Hweeeeee . . . fweeeeee . . .*) "Do you, Finch. Suppose that I might?"

Limits of decency exist even for walking corpses. So I shan't tell you of the voodoo priestess the doctor shipped in from Haiti to distill from me a driblet of Death, a woman of copper skin and gray bristled hair whose feats included having foretold the recent sinking of the *RMS Titanic*. No, I shan't tell you how she dappled my face with sweet-smelling paint and danced along to a tuneless drum. I shan't tell you how she kissed my ear, how her tears moistened my flesh, and how I felt rising from her body a warm sorrow that extended backward to include countless sympathetic ancestors.

Because what service would such information provide but to depress you? Instead I shall tell you how, partway into the woman's ritual, the doctor took up the Isolator, asking, "You don't mind if I . . . ?" and then suctioned so hard that the hose crimped. I shall tell you how he scoffed as this woman performed an augury that any damn fool could see was legitimate; how he giggled at the vial of Death she presented before he dashed it to the floor; how he lifted the oxygen tank and brought it down upon her back; how she scrabbled away on all fours while he chortled laments about the charlatanism of the Negro hegira; how she made it away bleeding only because I entangled the legs of the helmeted maniac.

That I shall tell you because it is important.

XIV.

I N THE FALL OF 1912 the creditors took the furniture.

Merle came alive; in fact, she was incensed. A typical young miss of the era would have shrunk from the burly menfolk bashing their wide shoulders through our narrow archways. Not this daughter of mine. While the lady of the house wept in the corner, Merle nipped the workers' heels. One minute she foamed with new-fangled curses: "You meddlesome boob!" "You swinish dingbat!" The next, she affected a faint as they hauled away a favorite piece: "Oh, Dearest Lord, not the bedframe! Anything but my Italian bedframe!"

Merle's frenzy might have possessed some absurdist humor (none of the furniture, after all, belonged to her) if not for the poignant path of her fall, and rise, and fall; having at last settled onto a summit of luxury, she was now being inched back toward the precipice of poverty. Exhausted, she collapsed onto a six-legged gilded French sofa; they took the sofa. Demoralized, she crumpled onto a Persian rug of curvilinear motif and raspberry color; they took the rug. From there she trembled upon the bare floor, the only thing she, or any of us, could count on.

The Leathers, after all, had to eat. The doctor watched dispassionately from the third floor, where he held himself against a bannister and gnawed upon a stale wad of bread. Three stories down, Dixon, just as silent, swept each crumb into a white-gloved hand.

In the winter of 1912 they took everything else: the Pierce-Racine touring car, the four-in-hand draft horses, each urn and lamp and mirror, every last piece of family silver. And, of course, the art: earth-hued neoclassical nudes, glowering portraiture, and countless marble busts, each of which glared in disappointment as it was packed into a crate.

In the spring of 1913 they took the clothes. Wardrobes were halved, then halved again. Mary became emotional as she made the calculations of which gowns would fetch the most at resale—the prettiest ones, always the prettiest ones. Gladys handled it with less poise, sniveling as she watched her favorite items of pink and lavender being dragged away as if to the gallows. Merle, of course, was the worst. My, how she shrieked when Dixon came asking for items to sell. She gave up nothing, not a single damned glove or garter.

In the summer of 1913 they took Gladys—or, at least, they tried, a delegation of concerned womenfolk from a local orphanage who came knocking. I watched from an upper window. The woman in charge apologized to no end as she relayed the leaves of gossip that had blown their way, stories regarding the doctor's severance from Harvard, fantastical experiments, corpses in the garden, and, of course, the drain of assets that had been streaming from the front door for months for all to see. Might it not be best to remove the child from so toxic a situation before harm befell her?

It was Mary's breaking point. Though her face burned in shame, she cast away the meddlers. That night, for a change, I was not the only sleepless one; Mary's forceful exhortations to her husband stretched on for hours, no doubt every second of it necessary, for the doctor had behaved of late as if the only plane of reality was the third floor.

What an address Mary must have delivered! For the first time in two years, Leather materialized for breakfast. Mary, Gladys, and Merle stopped mid-chew and Dixon dropped a bowl of fruit. Leather ignored the reaction and sat, his red eyes the most vivid accessory of a colorful ensemble, the last one he owned: a white shirt with high collar, bold orange-and-brown tie, long white-on-black-striped jacket, and matching pants turned up at the cuffs.

"A good day to all," said he, reaching for the bread.

Appetites all around were lost. Never having had one, I leaned over the bowls of hominy and lyonnaise potatoes (our meals had gone downscale) and scrutinized the doctor. Without his oxygen tank, he labored to breathe, yet managed to display that stiff upper lip we Americans had heard so much about, pushing morsels of food past antagonistic teeth despite how they nauseated him.

Mary, oh intrepid one, chose to downplay the event.

"Doctor," asked she, "will you be having tea?"

"Tea." Dixon echoed the word from a stupor. "Yes, very good!"

Leather lifted a hand to halt him.

"I wish, instead, to have a word." He brushed his sleeves in a fair facsimile of refinement. "This morning I shall travel to the college to see Dr. Obediah Cockshut. You may recall his name, Mother; he is the last man in that crumbling asylum who possesses even a grain of vision. His study on congenital cataracts is a landmark, and few men in the world know as much about syphilis. If anyone will hear me out, it is Cockshut."

"And what," ventured the wife, "will you ask of him?"

"To come here." The insolent tilt of his chin dared anyone to complain. "To dine with us." He cut his eyes at me. "To see for himself the metaphorical goldmine I work day and night to excavate. I do not relish bringing another miner into my quarry. But I no longer see a choice. Cockshut, of course, will agree with my assessment and use his agency to convince the college to reinstate my funding. He must!"

If you desire an unabridged catalog of Dr. Leather's failings, I can supply it, free of charge, provided that your shelves are strong enough to bear the weight. There is no doubting, however, that he was a master persuader. That same eve he returned to our nervous lot victorious from what he portrayed as a superlative presentation, though he made us wait an hour to receive that news, having staggered inside as he did, gasping for the Isolator.

After some oxygen, though, how he paraded and puffed and whipped us into militarism! Dr. and Mrs. Cockshut would arrive at our house the following night and everything, absolutely everything, stressed he, rested in the balance.

Leather snapped his heels at Dixon, who shot up to his full height of twelve or fifteen feet. What satisfaction the old butler found in being ordered about again! Cockshut, barked Leather, would require the finest whiskey! The best cigars! Playing cards, too, and do not shy from ribald designs, for Cockshut fancied himself an accomplished lecher as well as player of lansquenet. Naturally we would need a full staff, too, so Dixon would need to hire and train, for tomorrow night only, a housekeeper, underbutler, two valets, two maids, two footmen, a cook, and a scullery maid. Such an expense would leave the Leathers without a cent to their name, but this was the ineludible gamble.

Dixon and I had our differences, but by Gød, his "Yes, sir!" stirred me to my bones! This event might mark the household's last stand, but we would make that stand as a family. Leather clapped and the butler shot away as if he had shed thirty years.

Leather spun upon his heel and faced his astonished wife. Mrs.

Leather, said he, was tasked with marshaling what few pieces of furniture and finery remained and reorganizing them into a few key rooms, while shutting off routes to emptied spaces so that the Cockshuts would find no evidence of desperation.

The doctor widened his focus to include me. His individualized attention typically clenched me inside an invisible fist of fear, but this time I chewed that fear, swallowed it, and stood tall.

"Mr. Finch, you are tomorrow's centerpiece. Yours is the part of Dapper Young Man, if you think you have the chops to play it. None of your dissension, please; remember what happens should you fail. The city street will become our operating table, broken glass our set of scalpels. Concentrate, Finch, upon who you could be should you prevail in this performance."

Performance. The word poked at me.

"Should there be seating cards?" he asked himself. "Aye, there should! On yours, Finch, let us indulge in showmanship."

Showmanship. That word poked me as well.

"'The Revolutionary Zebulon Finch.' No, that connotes rebellion. 'The Trailblazing Zebulon Finch'? No, not enough. 'The Thaumaturgic Zebulon Finch'? Well, that's too much. 'The Astonishing Zebulon Finch'?"

At last I found my tongue.

"No," said I. "Not that one."

"And what of me?"

We turned as one to find Merle, her fine chin pointed at the chandelier, her hands clasped knuckle-white. She had not made a direct address to the doctor in what might have been a year. Her chest, as usual, rose and fell rapidly, out of anticipation or wrath it was eternally difficult to say.

"You?" Leather's inspirational timbre flattened. "You are to stay away."

Her eyes slitted.

"I'm not invited to dinner?"

"Young lady, you are not invited to anything. Your entire presence here has been uninvited."

Her cheeks darkened to scarlet.

"I have every right to sit alongside my father."

"You crave our food, nothing more. For once you shall not have it."

"Papa." Her lip quivered. "Tell him that I may join you."

Relations between Merle and me had been on gravel footing from the outset. But since her veranda outburst, I'd made it my purpose to shield her from Leather's aberrations until I earned her trust, at which point together we might abscond. Taking a stance between Merle and Leather was a delicate proposition.

"I . . . see no real harm," said I. "Can't she—"

"*Papa.*" Leather mocked her plosives. "A cat mimics affection better. You are sub-cat; I'll grant you status of leech. Except leeches have value in a laboratory setting, whereas your style of bloodsucking is futility itself."

Long had my pride been abraded when a man showed indifference to my opinion. I might be weak of limb, but not too weak to take up an iron paperweight and bludgeon the doctor's egocentric skull! What prevented me was simple confusion; I had little experience acting on the behalf of anyone but myself. Into the space left by my inaction tumbled the quick-tongued Merle.

"How dare you say this to me," said she.

"I am sure you have been called much worse," said Leather. "Show your face at this dinner and be very sorry that you did. Have I made myself abundantly clear? Have I used words small enough for you to decipher? Indicate, girl, indicate!"

"You are the one who will be sorry. You have no idea how sorry."

With that, she turned and ran. Her lovely skirts made a colorful fuss, putting to shame my continued silence; I stood there mouthing the air like a beached fish.

"Mr. Dixon," called Leather.

From the next room: "Sir?"

"A third footman for tomorrow. Stationed outside the brat's room. There's a good man."

Activity hastened the afternoon and evening. The quietude of the house at night supplied me additional hours to consider my duties, both to Leather and Merle. I got up, as I was wont to do, and commenced upon my usual directionless wander—perhaps the last of its kind should the next day's event go awry. I got no farther than the second-floor landing. There stood my daughter in a sleeping gown, her hair brushed to perfection and her pale face aglow through a veil of moonlight.

I advanced so that we stood upon equal footing and adopted a smile, defense against what I feared would be castigation for failing to land her a dinner invite.

"I see you have inherited my insomnia," said I.

Merle snatched the lapel of my bedshirt and her sharp little underbite gnashed at my chin.

"I'll stay away from his hoity-toity affair. What choice have I? But that means you have to succeed on your own. Think of Mrs. Leather if my welfare isn't enough for you. Think of her daughter. Think of them on the street eating garbage. Make Dr. Cockman, whatever his name is, make him see who you really are, see everything you're really

257

capable of. You show him that, he can't deny us anything. No one can."

Johnny had not been a son, but even at his besotted end he'd been more childlike than this girl. Had scar tissue hardened the raw vulnerability that had once caused her to shatter a mirror with her fist?

"Of course," said I. "I shall do my best—"

"If you are my father, then you will do what is *required*. Anything that is required to take care of me."

Small, simple, sensible words, were they not? Yet they burrowed into me like metal screws, leaving unsealable gouges that blooded with a single repulsive fact. Daddy's little girl? Perhaps. But Merle Ruby Watson was, by then, older than her papa.

And, as you shall see, craftier as well.

XV.

THE COCKSHUTS WERE FIFTY-FIVE MINUTES late. With a brigade of queasy servants lined behind him, erect and tensed for the bugle-blast call to arms, Leather had arrived at, as you might imagine, quite a state. He had spent the previous eight hours in the lab hooked to the Isolator in an attempt to bloat himself with oxygen enough for this oceanic plunge, and now labored to relearn how humans breathed. I sympathized to a point; I, too, could barely remember.

Just when I thought he might start gnawing upon the carpet, the door knocker broke the silence. Dixon bolted from the parlor. Leather gave us, his servicemen in this sortie, a hard final inspection. The doctor himself looked as if plucked from the Paris *beau monde*, his rented formal wear finished with soft-toe pumps bowed with corded silk, a boldwing collar with piqué bow tie, and hair parted so fiercely that his white line of scalp burned like phosphorescence.

He nodded at Mary and Gladys. "Yes." He looked at me; I'd left the Little Miracle Electric Mexican Stuttering Ring in my room following his earlier complaints. He nodded. "Yes." He exhaled and stared down the doorway. "Yes, yes, yes."

Seconds later the parlor was violated by a man in his late fifties the size of a nine-drawer bureau. His garish ivory oxford coat strained at his dimensions and he had not yet bothered to remove the matching bowler. He wore his hair in long carrot-colored curls and, though facial hair fashion in 1913 had caught up to Leather and me, Cockshut proudly displayed two fluffed muttonchops, which swooped to connect beneath his nose. His cheeks looked patted with a touch of blush.

When this effeminate behemoth saw Leather, he rapped upon the floor with a walking cane topped with an alabaster monkey head.

"There he is—the young lion! At last I enter his den."

Leather broke forward and took the man's goliath, ringed mitt in an overeager, two-handed handshake.

"Obediah. You honor me with your presence."

"Squeeze my hand harder, Corny, and fifteen of your most strapping servants will be tasked with lifting my fat body from the floor."

Corny. Mary cringed. I did, too, a common reaction, or so I assume, for sons first witnessing their fathers subjugated. Leather ate his pride and shaped his lips into a self-effacing grin. It was at this point that Mrs. Cockshut entered. Though in bodily shape she recalled the soft, thickish Mary, she was swathed in a chiffon dress inwrought with gold, one shoulder of sapphire netting, the other of strung jewels. With one hand she hugged a spotted mink stole; the other she extended to Leather as she approached.

"Olive, dear." Leather kissed her fingers. "You are radiant."

Olive and Mary exchanged obligatory kisses; the three long feathers of Olive's headpiece bobbed about. Mary could not prevent a slight sinking of her shoulders. Long has it been my experience that no woman enjoys discovering her fashion to be obsolete.

You would think it choreographed how the Cockshuts turned to address me.

"This must be the famous Mr. Finch." Cockshut pounded his

monkey cane and sauntered up, eyeing me in a manner almost lewd. "Corny has told me the most enchanting things. I do look forward to learning more about your strange and unusual body."

"Obediah," scolded Olive. But her eyes twinkled.

Cockshut held up a finger.

"I am crassness incarnate. We will arrive at the, shall we say, meatier matters in due time. How about an aperitif? Corny, if you tell me that your house is as dry as your office, I shall weep like a widow."

Enter the untested footmen! Thanks to Dixon, they were models of competence, blending into the background like veterans. Mary relaxed and held court with Olive alongside the prettiest window, while Leather chased around Cockshut, who, despite his weight and cane, liked to stick his nose into every cranny of the room. I resolved to remain seated at the center of the room, a parlor game none of the guests had yet figured out how to play.

Dixon interrupted my woolgathering to announce that dinner was served. Cockshut cackled in glee, removed his bowler at last, and charged ahead of the women past a cortege of straight-backed servants. Leather gave a signal and two musicians positioned in the connecting alcove took up their lute and clavichord. While we sat and napkined ourselves, the duo struggled through their first pages. It was, of course, the music of Carlo Gesualdo, and the notation was, of course, reproduced by none other than Leather himself. In no time at all Gesualdo's dementia began to infect the players. They plucked and struck every note with tortured fealty.

Leather took the head of the table. I sat to his right while Cockshut took the foot. Gladys joined us, quiet as instructed, and the women filled the table's gaps. For several magnificent minutes, the entire evening, predestined for disaster, shimmied along a high wire of success. Even I became caught up in our audacious plot until, quite abruptly, I remembered how Leather had categorized this piece of music: a threnody, a hymn to the dead.

The living among us had their spoons poised above the first course of green turtle à l'Anglaise when Cockshut tipped an ear to the air.

"Thunderation! What is this cacophony?"

Mary and I looked at each other in alarm.

Leather's attempt at an easygoing air was horrific.

"It is the work of an Italian named Gesualdo."

"This is composed? I thought the musicians were tuning their instruments."

Olive snickered into her hand. A daub of turtle soup escaped her lips.

"Amusing," said Leather. I watched his every tortured twitch until, at last, he bent to the pressure.

"The truth is," said he, "I find Gesualdo to be undervalued."

Cockshut nudged his wife.

"Young people and their music, eh, dear? It takes a good many years for the palate to detect fish from fowl."

Cockshut clapped his hands above his head.

"Players! I say! Players! Goodness, Corny, did you gas them with nitrous oxide? Yes, you two! Do your audience the cardinal favor of advancing to the *finis* so that we may dine without fear of choking. Let's hear something of quality. Mozart!"

Mozart! The cracking of Leather's teeth could be heard from across the state; I imagined his spoon emerging from his mouth as a lump of chewed silver. The players, though, nodded their gratitude and dove into something cheerful. Leather closed his eyes for the first several bars, his nostrils quivering for additional air.

The soup was removed. In swept the small plates—olives, celery, radishes, salted almonds. Now that Gesualdo no longer drove our party to gradual psychosis, the harmonics of a traditional dinner party emerged: gregarious chewing, convivial slurping, the satisfying shiver of cutlery; and from the hallway, the murmur of footmen and whispers of maids. The sole disruption was a single, unsuitable sound that grew in prominence: a chronometer pacing from the room directly above. Merle's room. Merle's designer footwear, too.

Click click, click click.

Cockshut was old but missed nothing.

"What have you got up there, old boy? Another mystery guest?"

"Forgive the noise. It is a visitor."

Click click, click click.

"The step has a feminine cadence, lest mine ears deceive me."

Leather nodded in reluctant capitulation. Cockshut twirled his orange hair in relish.

"Ever the private one, aren't you? If this visitor of yours is of the concubinal variety, for heaven's sake do not speak it aloud! The ladies present would be forever scandalized." He leaned over his plate and affected a stage whisper. "But tell me in private later, yes? I myself am a man of irregular appetites."

Olive's snickering lips wore a mustache of almond salt.

It was this gross detail that drove home the scene's outrage; Leather's hand reached for the Isolator that was not there, and I, for once, shared his asphyxiation. The doctor had come to America to create counteragents against ingrained ideas and behaviors. Now these plebeian perverts were injecting into his world the bacteria of dismissive doubt.

Leather knew how to fight disease: operate quickly or lose the patient.

"Here, here." Leather pushed away his plate. "Let us cut to the core of it."

"Striped bass!" Cockshut clapped his hands like a schoolgirl upon spying the incoming course. "Noisettes of lamb! Virginia ham au champagne! Oh, Corny, thou dost know the way to my big, blubbery heart!"

Footmen, young and overeager, stole the small dishes that had barely been touched. Leather knew that if he could not resuscitate life back into his dying cause, he and his family might never see such placeware, or such food, ever again.

"Your heart, I hope, Obediah, can be reached by roads more systematic. Allow me to speak of Mr. Finch and the wonders he contains."

"Ah-ah, but you know what they say! Politics before science, and we shan't upset convention. Let's see, let's see. What make you, an Englishman, of our Woodrow Wilson? Does our commander possess behind his spectacles grit equal to that of the Kaiser? Now this is conversation, eh? Run with it, my boy, run with it!"

Cockshut turned his jubilant attention to his plate of fish.

"War will rage," growled Leather, "men will die, graves will green, ad nauseum. This, right here at this table, is what is important. The secrets I close in on are beyond war. They make war irrelevant."

"War irrelevant? Why, war is the only relevant thing! Oh, but I forget that you are young. Too young, perhaps, to understand the necessity of war. Definitely too young to solve the mysteries of life and death—too young, even, to handle your whiskey or grow a proper beard! As a man of advanced age, I urge you to slow down. Enjoy life or die trying, I say."

Mary was well-trained in the role of wife. She knew the scent of disaster.

"The potatoes en croquettes," chirped she. "Are you quite sure, Obediah, that they are not over-seasoned?"

Leather pointed at a sideboard.

"A stethoscope rests behind you. Put it to Mr. Finch's chest. Listen for yourself."

"Put it to your own chest," said Cockshut. "For your heart beats to exhaustion, methinks."

Leather thumped the table with a fist; silverware jumped.

The doctor had begun to wheeze.

"Six feet away from you sits the greatest medical find of the century! And yet you natter away at claptrap! You, sir, are supposed to be a surgeon."

Cockshut deposited flakes of fish upon his tongue and crossed his eyes in ecstasy.

"And you, Corny, are supposed to be a human being. One cannot subsist on knowledge alone. Claptrap, so it happens, is essential to the diet."

Leather, then, did something unexpected.

From the plate of ham he took up an eight-inch, two-pronged serving fork, and turned to me.

"Mr. Finch, I am going to stab you."

Gladys dropped her butter knife.

Cockshut's vigorous chewing ground to a halt.

Olive gasped—a low, but elated, inhalation.

I became aware that everyone awaited my response to this crazed proposition. I gave Leather a cold, steady look.

"And where is it you intend to stab me?"

"Can this not wait?" asked Mary. "Let us delay this . . . demonstration until after dessert."

Leather's face was a quivering mask of asthmatic resolve.

"The forearm. 'Twixt radius and ulna. You may roll up your sleeve if you wish."

Cornelius Leather was a better, truer, nobler man than the Barker. Wasn't that what he had assured me? Wasn't that why I had fled the body-strewn field of honor and its bulleted corpses and crossed thirteen colonies to find him? Now he asked to play butcher upon me, and in front of others, as if I were once more upon a lit stage.

"I would very much prefer that you not do this," said I.

"I will do it and you will allow it."

For a terrible moment we stared at each other.

The musicians finished a movement of Mozart.

Then my daughter, expert conniver, reminded me of a father's duty:

Click click, click click.

Were those damnable shoes made of metal? I swore each step shaved splinters of pure guilt from the ceiling, each of which stabbed my cadaver flesh. I thrust out my left arm and rolled up my sleeve with hateful haste. My skin was whiter than the fish.

So cut it up in similar fashion, you greedy bastard. Serve it up for all to gnash.

Leather, to his credit, did not hesitate.

The fork lifted toward the chandelier.

"For heaven's sake," said Cockshut.

There was no heaven to be found on Jefferson Street no matter how many floors you climbed. The fork plunged and dinner, for the most part, was ruined. The prongs sunk into my forearm and the tips hit bone with dual clicks. Olive yelped, covered her eyes. Cockshut patted her shoulder to calm her, or, perhaps, himself.

266

Mary grabbed the shoulders of the slack-jawed Gladys and shouted at the kitchen.

"Miss—Miss—I don't remember your name! Maid! Maid!"

In seconds a maid stumbled into the room, pushed along by Dixon. Her dress was unfit for the dining room setting but she made up for it by curtseying six ways to Sunday. While Dixon stared dumbfounded at the serving fork vibrating in my arm—not proper table manners, not at all!—Mary steered Gladys into the maid's bewildered arms.

"Take my daughter."

"Ma'am? Where . . . ?"

"Just take her from here."

The maid did as ordered, rushing Gladys past the iron statue of Mr. Dixon.

Cockshut's carrot locks jounced as he whirled his attention from his distraught wife.

"I did not come here against the advice of my colleagues to watch some kind of sick parlor trick, to suffer through your promotion of this con man's budget bedazzlements! You're just as they say, Leather—cracked!"

The cords of Leather's neck thickened as he strained for ever more oxygen.

"Obediah! Consider what is in front of you! See how he feels no pain? He is, by every medical standard, clinically dead and yet—"

"Would you like me to list every disorder that can block the perceptivity of pain? You are a poor physician, sir. My first piece of medical advice to you—after resigning from the profession at once!—would be to remove that damned fork from your patient's arm!"

Leather yanked the fork from my flesh and brandished it.

"See? The boy does not bleed! Still disbelieve? Then I shall stab him again! Name the location!"

"Mr. Dixon!" Mary snapped for the butler. "Remove the course immediately. Do not forget the cutlery."

Dixon reacted as if doused with ice water. His long arms reached out but he was halted by a gesture from Cockshut. With shocking disregard for conduct, the man used his bare hands to rip a hunk of meat from the ham and fling it upon a plate. He then tossed the plate across the table where it landed before me, breaking into four pieces.

"Eat that, Mr. Finch, if you please."

"He cannot eat," said Leather.

"He can eat," snarled Cockshut, "and he will."

"I tell you, he cannot!"

"Your invited guest insists that he do! He shall eat as does a mortal man and you—my poor, misguided Dr. Leather—will, with any luck, extract yourself from this delusional web in which you are caught."

"Have it your way!" Leather gasped for air, white froth gathering at the corners of his mouth. "He shall swallow this portion at your request, and then, my dubious friend, at *my* request you shall probe the portion lodged within his stomach, feel it unspoiled by digestive acid!"

The doctor picked up a dining fork and enclosed my hand around it. I looked at the ham but could ne'er well imagine putting it inside of my mouth. Out of morbidity I pressed upon the meat with the fork and watched the juices rise.

Leather's bloodshot eyes were the latest two bullets I had to face.

"You embarrass me in front of our guests," muttered he, "pushing around fine food as if it were dead rat. Elbows, Finch! Napkin, Finch! You leave no doubt of your graceless age."

Lifting my eyes from the fractured dish, I found Dixon paralyzed against the far wall, Mary watching me through a well of tears, Olive peeking from behind spread fingers, and of course, two Harvard professors awaiting the outcome of this different sort of meat etiquette.

Click click, click click.

Was there any doubt of what I'd do?

Teeth long unfamiliar with the textures of food began their mastication. Strings of fat caught between molars; my out-of-practice lips slobbered grease; a warm coat of ham slime coated my cold tongue. Yet I forced down that moist blob of pig and thumped my chest with a fist until I felt it settle into my unresponsive belly.

"There you have it," said Cockshut.

Leather heaved for air. Sweat popped from red pores.

"Now feel his stomach!"

"I try to make it a habit not to paw the bodies of young men."

Leather kicked back his chair. It struck Dixon, who hobbled aside in fright. With a tremendous sweep of his arm, Leather cleared half the table clean of dishes and food. The crashing surpassed any noise the house had ever witnessed. China split and resplit, somersaulted and split again, each white dagger imprinting itself on my vision like lightning. And the food! An entire market's worth, for which the Leathers had spent their every last cent, turned to carnage. We were spattered.

That was but one second. In the next, Leather lifted me by the lapels and pounded me down upon the cleared table. The back of my head shattered a glass and my hair soaked with wine. I struggled against this domestic attack, adoptive father to adopted son, but his arm was braced against my chest. I heard Leather's free hand sift through the nest of silverware and saw silhouetted against the ceiling

269

what he found: a knife, a good sharp one. It hovered over my stomach.

"WATCH! I'LL CUT HIM OPEN! YOU WILL SEE THE DRY MEAT!"

The Cockshuts were on their feet. The alabaster monkey was raised in defense.

"For the love of what's holy, stop this!"

"YOU'VE WATCHED ME CUT A THOUSAND CADAVERS! YOU DOUBT MY HAND?"

"I doubt your *mind*, sir!"

Leather let fly a tear of laughter and then, Dearest Reader, he began to cut, through my shirt and into my stomach, a C-shaped flap. My gut opened with a rubbery sound, a squirt of vestigial moistness.

Screams of horror spread with wildfire fleetness, through the dining room, down the hall, into the kitchen. Bedlam erupted. Olive was tripping her way toward the door and Cockshut was scrambling to help her. One musician had his mouth clasped as if holding back a tide of vomitus while the other had lifted his lute for use as a shield. Olive managed to shove open the dining room door and beyond it I saw the gaping faces of incredulous footmen and valets, the fleeing forms of maids. Dropped glass exploded from multiple locations. Dixon ran off after something, anything, everything.

Gladys, abandoned by her keeper, cried from afar.

The cosmetics of Cockshut's cheeks had smeared; he was a back-pedaling harlequin.

"Not only will you never return to Harvard, I'll see to it that no institution upon this Earth will have you! If I have my way, sir, you'll be behind bars come morning!"

It was enough to distract Leather. I took his wrist and whipped it to the table, where it came into rough contact with a candlestick.

The knife spun free and when he reached for it, I shoved him over and scrabbled for the table edge. The flap in my gut yawned open; I faltered and that gave Leather time to take hold of my shirt. Across the table we paddled in circles. I snatched his ear and pulled. There was a ripping sensation; there was blood.

He blink-blinked at me as if surprised by my company, indeed by his own presence atop the dregs of dinner. He was purple from lack of oxygen. His cheeks were war-painted with gravies, his hair spiked with jellies. Yet through this animalistic rawness rose an expression of dawning dread as he began to read the story told by these chaotic runes, one of a once-promising family and once-limitless career. Everything now was broken, and to pieces so sundry that no scientist, no matter the extent of his patience or brilliance, could hope to mend it.

XVI.

BY THE TIME THE CLOMPING of Cockshut's cane had faded, I was on my back upon the befouled floor. No student of Luca Testa let his guard down for long; I lifted myself to a defensive crouch. It was a bad idea. Organs inside me shifted as if about to spill out of my stomach flap.

If history's worst dinner party had proven anything, it was that my innards were my only real possessions, even if just nostalgic ones. I leaned back against the wall, gripped tight my abdomen, and searched out my abuser. He, too, had slid from the table and now stooped over the far end. Food was painted across his every inch of clothing.

We sized each other up.

Mary could suffer no more violence. She wiped her splashed face with an arm of equal soilage and addressed her husband.

"Give those simpleminded scholars no more of your spirit. We'll take your findings to New Haven. Or Philadelphia. Or New York. The doctors here mistrust you for the silliest of reasons. You're not as ancient as they? You can't grow a beard? These are the accusations of fools. We do not need them."

Leather took her by the throat. Panic soared inside me and I rose, an isolated moment of true valor, but my guts betrayed me by rolling toward freedom. I leaned backward, else I lose my stuffing.

Mary's back hit the wall. She pulled at the doctor's arm.

His fingers turned white as they sunk into her neck. Short of breath, he hissed.

"I can grow a beard, wife. I choose *not* to. It is a *choice*. Beards are *unclean*. They are as *vain* as a medallion. It is *you*, I think, who *believe* me to be a child. The way you *patronize* me. How you claim we don't need these people's *help*. Indicate, wife, that you understand."

She could do nothing of the sort. Her face purpled and her eyes reddened with popped vessels. I slid down the wall to the floor and began to slither closer with one arm wrapped about my stomach. I floundered with such energy that my chin struck the patterned tile and a piece of my eyetooth shot outward.

It was noise enough to knock Leather from his furious blank. His hand unclenched from Mary's throat. She screeched for air. *The Isolator*, thought I, *someone bring her the Isolator.* She dropped to her knees, hands pressed to scarlet cheeks and saliva bubbling as she fought for sweet air. I could almost taste it myself.

Leather adjusted his vest despite its trashed state. He tromped to the entryway, lightheaded and weaving, before turning to deliver a final pronouncement between gaggings.

"Come morning, Finch—I'll repair your abdomen—you in turn—will repair your attitude—in the interim—I'm afraid—you will need to hold those—precious organs of yours—just as you will—learn to hold—your tongue— it is your fault, not mine—your refusal to cooperate—that holds success—at arm's length—tomorrow at dawn—we demonstrate at Dock Square—why, I'll run you through— with a sword—shopkeepers, the bourgeoisie—those unburdened by learnedness—it is they—who shall save me—who shall demand—my fame, my funding—who shall beg me—with purses outstretched—to fix what—in the human machine—is broken—oh, how they shall beg."

Sauce, gravy, cream, wine, and blood marked the path of his exit.

Mary and I behaved like the two surviving worms of a post-rain playground stomping. I recommenced my pitiful writhe in her direction while she edged along the wall closer to me. Five minutes later we'd found each other. She rested against me, rubbing at her bruised throat. When at last she spoke, her rasp smelled of hot, bloodied spit.

"The doctor must be right. Let him sew you shut. Then go with him to Dock Square. Don't cross him. Please don't, please. For the same reason I don't take Gladys and run. He'd never stop chasing us. Do you understand? Do you?"

It was for the sake of her merciful visage that I smiled.

"You wish me, ma'am, to indicate?"

Mary blessed me with a single hoarse laugh that peppered her chin with dark blood. Nevertheless, I captured the sound in a hand and tucked it away inside of me, in a place where there were no open wounds through which it might float away.

No one had bothered to attend to Gladys. The child's woeful moan experimented with a louder volume. Mary gathered her strength and, with the wall as her guide, brought herself to two feet. She did not offer me a hand but that was all right; the doctor would be most favorably met come morning should he find me right where he'd left me.

Before exiting, she turned off the electric lights. It was a small blessing.

From the lightless room I listened. I heard Mary open and close doors in her search for Gladys; I heard her find the girl inside of a closet; I heard shushing, anodyne words, promises that all would turn out for the best; I heard mother and daughter lock the house doors as if it were any other night; I heard them go upstairs. I did *not* hear them lie in bed and dream of what was to become of their wrecked lives, and for that one mercy I was grateful.

The house, exhausted after such upheaval, slept, and there were no sounds, not for hours. Not until what my Excelsior insisted to me was two in the morning did some indestructible thing stir from the ashes.

Click click, click click.

My daughter, alive and pecking.

The pair of shoes chuckled their way into the room. There was no mistaking the silhouette of a genteel dress, a stylish arrangement of hair—and what was that in the figure's hand but a leather port-manteau bulging with packed clothing?

Merle knelt, arranged her skirts, and whispered.

"Once my father asked to start a new life with me as a family. Fathers know better than daughters. I was wrong to say no. I am sorry, Papa."

Was she crying? I cursed the darkness, for I could not tell.

"You say this now," said I. "Now that the Leathers are ruined."

"I know I can be harsh; it is a stain from a hard life and I promise to scrub it away. You are my father and nothing can change that. You are the boy of whom my mother spoke the most tenderly. Her tender, understanding, forgiving Aaron."

Even better than Cornelius Leather, Merle Ruby Watson knew where to stick the knife.

"The doctor plans to take me into town come daybreak," said I. "Mrs. Leather believes there is gain to be had from it."

"Of course she said that. She's protecting herself. Is this what *you* want, Papa?"

I shrugged; even that smallest of motions rocked my entrails.

"It might mean money," said I. "I know how fond you are of money."

"I am not fond of money; I am averse to starvation. In this suitcase I have a dozen fine dresses. Plus silver. And jewelry. Anything I could take from upstairs. We'll sell it. It will get us far from here."

"Mrs. Leather is not often wrong. Our fortunes may indeed improve when the people of Boston see that I cannot be hurt."

I heard the teacup chime of Merle's underbite parting to show its lethal fangs.

"Oh," purred she, "but you can."

Who knew this better than she? The girl had seen me cower upon her first arrival and later beg understanding of my abhorrent existence. Both proclaimed my pedigree of pain, and pain was something that Merle was skilled at delivering as well as receiving.

She stood and offered her hand as Mary had not.

When I showed her my opened abdomen, she looked away to gather herself before lifting the crumpled tablecloth from the floor and wrapping it around my torso snugly enough to keep my insides intact. She knotted the cloth and hoisted me to my feet. It was a courageous field dressing and yet I found myself thinking of Mary and her swollen, contused neck. What would become of her if the doctor, my second failed father, that oxygen-slurping maniac, awoke to find me absent, a runaway child yet again? I was abandoning Mary to a bad fate as I had abandoned so many before her.

The excuse that came to mind was from Leather himself:

A few small deaths in a wider war. What difference could it make?

By the time Merle let go of me to open the front door, I could stand under my own power. She fiddled with the locks, cursing like a sailor, as I gazed one last time upon the beautiful, upsweeping stair-

276

case. The Little Miracle Electric Mexican Stuttering Ring waited, patient and hopeful, upon the bedside table near my third-floor berth. For an unimaginable fifteen years I had worn it as a reminder of the rogue possibility of goodness in the world; that itself had been a little miracle. Without the talisman, worried I, the modest grace I'd since acquired might be lost as surely as if there were a C-shaped flap cut into my soul. Also upstairs, nailed to the Revelation Almanac, were the hundreds of scraps reaped from my body in Leather's attempt to pare me down to a Nothing in Particular. Did this daughter of mine have what it took to make me whole once more?

Merle's grip tightened around my waistcloth and drew me from the winking furnishings of the once-great hall and into a limpid sea of night. This was the real world; I recalled Mary's advice and commanded myself to blink, to blink again. Merle pulled me down the flowered walkway as if I were a stubborn cow, past the front gate, and into the street. I hugged my guts and followed as best I could.

Capably steered though I was through a night world muddled with late-night drunks and grousing inkeeps, I could not relax. I would have sworn that behind us advanced the muffled panting of a madman trapped within the cage of a metal mask, a father terribly disappointed by his fostered son, halving the distance between us with every city block, impatient to impart a new etiquette. He was an apparition impossible to outrun; indeed he would chase me throughout the night and following day, then the following weeks, the following months, the following years.

Listen.

Can't you hear him even now?

Hweeeeee . . . fweeeeee . . . hweeeeee . . . fweeeeee . . .

PART FOUR

1913–1918

————•((•))•————

*To War We March!; Also, Your Hero's Education
Into The Nature Of Sacrifice And The Possibility Of
Brotherly Love.*

I.

TOGETHER MERLE AND I RODE out a single stormful year. What occasioned our fracture? No less than the pointiest wedges civilization knows how to whet: money, sex, and war. Indeed it was a brief period, and yet that year is etched with permanence upon the foil of my memory for the hopefulness it brought me; the disappointment it brought, too. And the grief. Let us not forget the grief.

Our escape route was knotted as only practiced criminals can knot. Merle led us through alleyways of seeping trash, fields of whispering tallgrass, and underground tunnels through which rackety streetcars ground upon rails. We emerged, to our shared horror, in Cambridge, home of the execrable Harvard College. We banked northwest and so traveled for three days while the vengeful specter of Dr. Leather grasped for our ankles. We bartered for rides when we could and otherwise journeyed by foot, across a bridge spanning the Boston Harbor; through humid, buggy areas adjacent to the Broad Sound; and at last into the green hills that precipitated the end of the continent.

Lake Michigan was a mutt's water bowl when compared to the gnashing teals and grays of the Atlantic Ocean. The tide's magnet pulled at my skeleton; surely so titanic a water had the power to drag me down for good! But Merle was damp and miserable and we had shot too far, and thus we backtracked to Salem, Massachusetts, and procured a two-bed chamber suitable for a young husband and wife—the only relationship we could mimic without rousing suspicion.

For days we did nothing but stare at the walls. Our backstreet window offered no visual relief but a sizzling gnarl of telephone wires. Meanwhile, we suffered the phonic enticement of automobile wheels thudding over brick, the whisper of women's petticoats, awnings snapping with the come-hither promise of fresh buyables. But the terror of Dr. Leather had us hobbled. We were afraid to leave the room, and when I slunk out overnight to gather food for Merle I found myself flinching at shadows. Jefferson Street was but twenty miles distant.

For three days, Merle ate what I brought her without objection.

After that, her loyal governess—discontent—returned.

"I can survive only so long on bread and water," said she. "Look at my skin. It flakes. Look at my hair. It breaks like straw."

"We need to remain hidden. For three months, perhaps four? I'm afraid that this is our lot."

"It doesn't have to be. I have a suitcase full of dresses. We could sell one."

"It would mean going outside during business hours. I suppose I could try."

"You? You don't know the first thing about women's clothing! How would you barter?"

"Teach me, then. It is too dangerous a job for you."

"I'll not wither to an old hag before I'm twenty. I'm going out."

"You are not! That is my final word."

"You don't get a final word, Papa. I'm older than you, you know."

Dearest Reader, you see? Futility, thy name was Merle! She did, in fact, shove her way out with portmanteau in tow, after which I sat and fretted that she, the last person I had on Earth, might not come back. But she did, in fact, sell a dress, and she did, in fact, bring back to the room a feast of beef tenderloin and mushrooms, roquefort cheese, assorted cakes, port wine, and cigarettes. It was an irresponsible way to spend the money, but that, in sum, was Merle—forever clinging to the fantasy that her veins pumped blue blood.

Fattened and tipsy and reclined like a slattern, Merle leered with wine-stained teeth and withdrew from her suitcase a sewing kit she had purchased with her remaining few cents.

"And you thought I brought home nothing for my papa bear."

She bade me to remove my shirt and untwine the squalid tablecloth that for days I'd kept around my torso. The flap on my abdomen bulged with misplaced organs and with tremendous shame I pushed them back into place. Merle looked as though she might faint but instead took a hard drag on her cigarette, thrust out her underbite, pushed me down onto the bed, lifted her skirts, straddled my legs, and unsheathed the sewing needle from the kit.

One need only see how she glared to understand what, to her, the act of sewing represented: her mother and those final years at the garment factory. Operating this needle verged on giving in to a kindred fate. Merle flung her cigarette, grabbed the wine, took a pull for strength, and then, with startling effortlessness, licked the thread and passed it through the needle's eye.

I told myself that each pinch upon my skin was proof positive of affection regardless of my daughter's corresponding oaths of disgust. Upon finishing, she hurled the wine bottle out of the window and guffawed when she heard it crash, and then kept on laughing, shaking her head in disbelief at the repellent act she'd just performed. Not thirty minutes later she had left again with the portmanteau. Perhaps to sell another dress? Perhaps to buy a replacement bottle? Perhaps never to return?

It was a torture of incertitude and she a most capable torturer.

We hated Salem, each in our own way, but, alas, it became the only home we ever shared. That the town's infamy sprang from seventeenth-century witch trials did not escape my sense of humor. Who was the witch now? 'Twas I!—hunted by a fanatic of different puritanical stripe but who'd still love to see me burned at the stake, not to prove my allegiance to any particular demon but to continue tearing my body apart, just for fun, all revelations irrelevant, all almanacs be damned.

Fortune gave us a rare gift: a month, then another, then another, with no sign of Leather. Autumn eclipsed summer and our vampiric fear of being caught in the sun began to dissipate. My preference was that Merle cordon herself within arm's length of me, her dutiful protector, but she was newly twenty and had no intent of abstaining from the invigorating click and clack of an industrialized nation. Like any child phasing from her teenage years, she was insistent upon unencumbered freedom.

Our diminishing funds necessitated the continued peddling of her dresses, with each sale hitting her like an amputation. What she saw in our mirror delighted her less each week, yet through her face's sour contortions she still managed to force cheap wine.

I did not like to see my child sulk and tried everything a father might. In October we dared to attend our first motion picture, a silent one-reeler called *Calamity Anne's Inheritance*. Now *this*, thought I, gawping through the theater's flickering cone of cigarette smoke, was

entertainment fit for Zebulon Finch, requiring none of the consti-
pating analysis demanded by literature or art!

At the conclusion, I rose to my feet and applauded.

"Run it again!" roared I. "Brava! Brava!"

"You," groaned Merle, "are a constant embarrassment."

The girl appreciated nothing. In November, I prevailed upon her
submit to a photographer. Decades ago, a portrait of Bartholomew
Finch, Abigail Finch, and my five-year-old self had graced our Chicago sitting room, and though I had detested the picture for its
fraudulent depiction of fraternity, I longed now for my own proof of
bloodline. Merle, keeper of our purse, was reluctant. By then she was
down to three dresses, each spectacular in form and scandalous of
neck, but scrubbed so often in a rusty tub that you could see through
the fabric to the undergarments beneath.

But the Finch strain of vanity was strong within her, and one
chilly afternoon we spent our last coins on a photograph of Merle in
portrait. She was in snarling spirits, challenging the photographer's
choices of lighting and posture until the very moment of exposure,
when the shell of two embittering decades split open and a blinding
radiance shone forth. When I saw the photographs I was struck anew
by her beauty; Wilma Sue was alive in the girl's underbite, which for
once looked not like the belligerent jaw of a piranha but a feature of
highborn dignity.

By 1914 we were stone broke. I worried constantly that Leather
might yet materialize, so I found a job that would not arouse attention: mopping a stockyard floor. Merle, meanwhile, dithered with
flights of fancy. She wished to play the piano at the nickelodeon—
although she could not play. She wished to sell gloves in a department
store—although she could not make proper change. She wished to

operate a telephone switchboard—although she balked at the hard wooden barrels upon which the women sat.

Consequently she chose as her profession the harvesting and dispensation of my income. No matter that every cent I brought home stank of swine blood; it was accepted anywhere and soon Merle had dolled herself quite nicely. She was not circumspect about her mission: she was out to nab herself a man, preferably a rich one.

"They won't approach me with you hovering about," griped she. "If I want them to pay for food and amusement, I will have to go find them myself."

"Do you know what kind of men wait for a woman's proposition?"

"Yes. Men like you."

Blast it all! The girl had me there.

Janitorial obligations brought me home late but Merle began returning even later, three sheets to the wind and rubbing her crumpled dance card across her bosom, mumbling of the dozens of faultless men who'd taught her the quickstep and the Brazilian tango. Frightened that Leather might spot her, I handed out stern warnings and then could not believe my ears. Me, warn someone else against impulsive behavior? And yet I felt a squeezing that must be the same for all fathers regardless of age, that this child of mine was being stolen from me by males who were my inferiors.

After a time she began to enjoy our sham marriage, as it permitted her the thrill of cuckolding me. Various mendicants she kissed so near our chamber door that her inebriated giggles passed right through the paper-thin walls.

"Shh," some scoundrel or other would say. "Your husband will hear."

"I hope he does," she'd laugh. "Let him get a big, long earful."

Feminine strategy, as best as I could figure it, was to trade upward, but perhaps due to her dirty clothes or caustic manner, Merle was unable to progress past groping lowlifes. Those pretty red dance cards were replaced by phone numbers scribbled on horse-racing schedules. The twinkle in her eyes was replaced by a volcanic gleam. Some early mornings she would arrive with her dress in disarray or lips smacking with a bad taste. The situation worsened in spring, when she began to come home with more money than with which she'd left. She'd sit hunched over the booty, her face distended into a loose red grin that I did not for one second believe.

In June of 1914 I was roused from my nighttime meditation by the hallway hullabaloo of a physical struggle. *Leather!* thought I. *He has found us at last!* I threw open the door with the only weapons at hand, two wine bottles, and found Merle on all fours and reaching for the doorknob while a man, sloppily intoxicated and bleeding from the lip, clearly no surgeon, grasped at her naked calves. I smashed the bottles together above his head. He shrunk beneath the storm of shards and I might have stabbed him in the neck—hadn't I done similar to my old pal Fratelli?—had not Merle landed a heel to the fellow's teeth.

I rolled the unconscious sot down the outdoor stairs like a laundry sack and repaired to our room. Merle was curled into a ball upon the bed. I locked our door, turned off the light, brushed glass dust from my hands, and dropped down next to her.

"Listen, you drunk," said I. "If you expect me to cope with your boo-hooing all—"

Her arms coiled around my torso with so much force that I interpreted it as an attack upon my sewed stomach. But her fists clutched my nightclothes and she was crying, this daughter of mine, *sobbing* if you wish to know the truth, so violently I worried that the worn seams of her dress might not survive it.

My hands did not know where to go. I'd not held my daughter since the day she'd broken the Leathers' mirror, and being neither woman nor physician, the protocols of comfort were foreign to me. Much simpler would be to refund her months of spite and shove her to the floor. But I could not. Her unraveled brown hair, black now with tears, hid a bruise upon her temple; there was grime behind her ears, evidence of inferior soap and cold bath water; and her hitching body was little more than scaffolding—the girl was once again starving.

I took the back of her head in my hand and stroked her hair. I felt a spiritual soaring. I pressed her face against my chest until her nose was flattened in the most darling, pitiful way, and she held me all the tighter and wailed with abandon until my shirt was wet and warm against my cold skin. I savored her supplications, not the usual pointed "Papa" but rather the heartrending "Daddy, Daddy, Daddy." Yes, she was drunk, her allowance, pride, and probably her virtue bespoiled one way or the other, but if that was what it took to smelt this steeled female, then I'd take it, and with gratitude.

I believe that things might have ended up different for Merle and me had not, the very next day, a disaster of historic magnitude swept across Salem. While I chased animal guts with my mop, an agglomeration of combustible materials exploded at a nearby leather factory. The town, parched from summer drought, was greedy for fire. By the time my slaughterhouse was evacuated over one hundred acres were in flames. It was the Great Salem Fire of 1914 and before it was through there would be a loss of twenty thousand homes and ten thousand jobs—mine among them.

The building in which Merle and I lodged had survived; what burned to cinder was our moment of opportunity. In one stroke, I'd lost our income and Merle had lost her assorted haunts. Three days later, as stunned Salemites sifted through the ashes, an Austrian archduke named Franz Ferdinand was assassinated far across the world in a European province called Bosnia. When the news reached Salem, only two details impressed themselves upon me. One, the Serbian assassin was but nineteen; I was downright jealous of his well-publicized feat! Two, the organization he worked for was called the Black Hand.

That should have signaled to me the coming global, and personal, armageddon.

With Salem a ruin and our lives likewise smoldering, Merle began to retract from me. It was on a fateful mid-July night, the air still bitter of smoke, that she came home tearful with rage, perhaps humiliation, perhaps both, and began pacing about our room, swiping up stray chemise suspenders, gloves, and strings of costume jewelry as if intending to pack them. I panicked; if I could not cement our bond that second, thought I, she would leave me. So I moved rashly, and the rest, I regret to say, is history.

"There is no more time for tarry," said I. "We must sensibly discuss our future."

"Our future!" echoed she. "Isn't it bad enough that I, a young woman of marrying age, must live with you in our *present*? In this stinking hovel? Who knows what diseases you carry? Or this whole town carries? It is an open wound, this entire place, and you are but a single, teeny little scab whining to be picked."

Merle unlatched her portmanteau and stuffed the accessories inside.

The Excelsior against my heart skipped one second. My hands lashed out and took my daughter's slim white wrists. She pulled back from the icy touch but I held firm. To my surprise, she abandoned her struggle and instead fixed me with a taunting sneer.

"So forceful and commanding. I declare."

"Merle. You cannot leave me!"

"Can't I? And why would you have me stay?"

"Because I am alone!"

The confession, oh, how it flayed me!

"Alone?" Merle laughed. "Is that all?"

"You do not understand! I am more alone than any being who has ever lived!"

"I understand perfectly. *You* have a responsibility to *me*, Papa. Not I to you."

Though she would not give me the satisfaction of crying out, she winced in pain from my gruff grip.

"Then I will show you," raved I. "All of it. Every part."

"You forget, I have seen your insides. What more is there possibly left to show?"

"Much. Look into my eyes, daughter."

Merle peaked an eyebrow. I yanked her wrists and brought her so close that our noses nudged. She twitched her muzzle like a cat, annoyed but amused, and it frustrated me, this disrespect, this insouciance. What I was about to do I did for her, only her, even though nothing so painfully raked the shreds of my soul than the reckoning of *la silenziosità*.

Down it sank, and down she went with it. My wade into the resplendent pool of obliteration was for me, as always, a heartbreaking peek at the nirvana I was not allowed. Every second I spent in this, my teasing void, was a second Merle spent in hers, but I tried not to worry. In glimpsing her future end, surely she would find the gentle contentment won by a lifetime alongside her doting father.

For one minute I bathed in the sensation, and then indulged one minute more. When I did at last break through the night surf of that blackest of oceans, I found Merle's eyes fastened to my own, her lashes quaking before a burden of trapped tears, her face vacant of color.

I chanced a hopeful smile.

Her features curled like torched newsprint.

"WHY?"

She ripped her wrists from my hands and went sprawling across the table, upsetting dishes and lamps, though she seemed unaware of anything beyond my putrescence and the need to get away from it. Her white cheeks flooded with blood and she flattened herself against the wall, howling for air, her bosom pounding in irregular gasps.

"Why did you show me this? My death?"

"Merle," stammered I, "please, calm yourself, I only wished—"

"My horrible, worthless, lonely death? Have you known it all along? What kind of father are you to show it to me? How much you must hate me!"

"No! There is no hate, I didn't mean for—"

Teeth bared, she lurched forward, snatched up the portmanteau, and retreated to her wall. With one hand she dug her fist inside of it, fishing about while keeping her avid eyes upon me. Before I could manage another soothing word, her arm withdrew in a poof of expelled scarves, and from her hand extended a revolver, an old one, though its dents indicated it had seen its share of action. I identified it by its distinctive trigger and ejector rod as a Colt Lightning, a later cousin to my lovely departed Peacemaker.

Yes, thought I. *This is my child, all right.*

"Stay back! You ghost! You goblin!"

Merle slid across the wall, stomping fallen dishes and clutching the suitcase like an armored chestplate. She rattled her Lightning and I shrank from its explosive promise.

"You see this? This belonged to my mother! And I should have shot you with it the day I found you!"

"I am glad you did not. Instead, you and I, we found—"

"You and I *nothing*! I needed shelter; you had a house! It goes no deeper than that. Now I have no need for you, for you have nothing—nothing but a heart of lies! The same as all men everywhere! I don't need *any* of you!"

Merle had nearly achieved the door. With the portmanteau braced beneath an arm, she patted around for the knob. I reached out for her, a feeble, pathetic gesture. She was as good as gone and it had been I who'd hastened the abandonment. With what stunning speed had I ruined everything!

"If I only had the strength to pull this little trigger. I blame my weakling mother, don't you? Gød, the parents with whom I was cursed." She kicked open the door, backed into the hall, and, realizing escape was imminent, bore down upon her own body, a savage contraction, before screaming out to anyone close enough to hear.

"MERLE RUBY WATSON WILL HAVE EVERYTHING! WILL *DO* EVERYTHING! NO MAN IS GOING TO STOP HER! DO YOU HEAR ME? THIS IS ONLY THE BEGINNING!"

II.

SOOT MARKED MY PASSAGE FROM the ruins of Salem back into the wilds of America.

I did so cursing Cornelius Leather. 'Twas his actions that had provoked Merle's ugliest urges; 'twas his threat that had sent me running with no destination in sight. With Salem behind me, I felt exposed and shrank from every male voice I heard, certain that it came from behind a metal mask with glass for eyes and a hose for a mouth. Perhaps, thought I, all sons felt their fathers were this omnipresent, this omnipotent, and there was no hope to be had from fleeing what was part of you, too.

That did not stop me from trying. I plunged southward, a solitary monster left once more to muse upon his monstrosity. A vagrant without need of grub can travel at ten times the typical pace, and via forest and footpath and rides stolen in the backs of trucks I made great time in an unspecified general direction, with each stop of my journey commemorated by fresh news of armament across the Atlantic.

That pesky dead archduke? His assassination had caused a bit of a kerfuffle. By August, the Austrian-Serbian conflict had roped in the protective big brothers of Russia and Germany. By September, Britain and France had joined in on the side of the vodka-swillers and Europe was locked into a two-front war. Did I give a hoot? Great balls of fire, Reader, I was an *American*. What did I care of lands I'd never see, peoples I'd never meet? I cared for one single human upon this Earth and she was gone.

This incessant jawing about war stirred up many an old codger's memories of Civil War glories, which brought to mind thoughts of a certain former cellmate. Without making a rational decision about it (why start now?), I began to drift toward Xenion, Georgia, where I'd been jailed on November 11, 1901, for Ungodly Acts alongside the Negro thief John Quincy and the lunatic known as the General. After Merle, I longed for such straightforward, if lousy, relationships and wondered if I might get a peek at the General, see if he'd clung to the speck of sanity *la silenziosità* had brought him.

Xenion was filthier than my prisoner's recollection, broiled albino by the sun, the dirt from its uncobbled roads coating the skin of the whites and coloreds who shuffled about in two separate, wearied streams. I arrived in October and made a single inquiry, and a discreet one at that, for I worried that someone might recognize, as local villain Sheriff Nelson had put it, "The Astonishing Amazing Dingdonged Aaron Stick." As it happened, I'd overestimated my fan base. I was directed to Sweetgum, the plantation home of the Hazard family.

Sherman's 1864 March to the Sea had charred and cratered the palatial estate. Nothing grew at Sweetgum aside from rebel patches of wildflowers and a few balls of cotton that pushed through the dirt like pustules. The house, however, remained imposing; the patchwork repairs to the transoms and the gunpowder burns upon the porchway frieze instilled the place with a battleworn courage. I passed beneath a pebbled pergola of ivy, periwinkle, and wisteria and between the Greek columns that toothed the porch. I felt quite small indeed when I knocked upon the gigantic four-paneled door.

From inside came micelike scurrying.

A woman answered the door—just what I did not need. She held a rifle at her side—another thing I did not need. Behind her arrived a second woman. Why vex me in this way, Fate? Then, impossibly, a third woman arrived. Here are my outstretched wrists, Fate; here is a blade! Then came a fourth, a fifth, and a sixth. Certain now that I had lost my mind somewhere back in the Carolinas, I covered my face with a hand and laughed into it.

The first woman looked to be in her mid-sixties; the others were younger by scant degrees. Through owlish spectacles this sextet gave me identical looks of distrust. They were sisters, and not a one of them, I was positive, was a general.

"May I be of some assistance?" asked the eldest. Her elocution was pure Georgian, though pricklier than the peach-mush to which I'd become accustomed.

"Who knows?" groaned I. "I am a great fool on a fool's errand. I was looking for man called the General but I think I might as well add to my list King Arthur's Avalon and the lost city of Atlantis."

The younger five sisters twittered. The eldest raised a hand and they shushed.

"You must mean General Joseph Thomas Hazard. If you like, you may walk one half mile southeast, where you'll find him buried."

I fit my fingers into the flutes of the nearmost Roman column and had a laugh at my one thousand miles of folly. It was 1914; of course the crazy old coot was dead. He would have been in his mid-eighties and had hardly been what one would call a model of good health.

The woman scowled at my apparent mirth.

"Excuse my directness, young sir, but here at Sweetgum we don't laugh about so great a man. Do us a kindness and remove yourself

295

from our portico. I assure you the Hazard sisters can fire a rifle truer than most menfolk."

Punchdrunk with rue, I nodded and began stumbling down the steps.

"I say! Young man!"

I swiveled upon the middle stair and raised my arm in a sarcastic soldier's salute.

"What is your name?" demanded she. "I wish to report you for dishonoring a Confederate hero."

"Finch, ma'am!" I executed the salute. "Zebulon Finch."

It was a handsome wine-colored carbine breechloader rifle that she dropped. No wonder it had been the cornerstone weapon of the Civil War—fifty years later, it did not disassemble or discharge when it hit the floor.

The women swarmed me and with fluttering hands ushered me inside before I could make heads or tails of this startling turn of events. Introductions were rapid: Polly, Lucy, Nelly, Patsy, Peggy, and Susannah—Susannah being the eldest—and within sixty seconds of entry I learned two important facts. One, there was a seventh woman tucked away in a distant room. She was their mother, Patience Hazard, though she preferred to go by her married name: Mrs. Joseph Thomas Hazard. Two, it was not the "Civil War" at Sweetgum; rather, it was "the Late Unpleasantness," and I needed to remember that unless I wished to throw the aforementioned Mrs. Joseph Thomas Hazard into a furor.

I was brought before the hoary old matriarch straightaway. So old was she that I could not discern where the flaps of her shawl ended and those of her face began. While Susannah introduced me in a voice loud enough to pierce any deafness, Mrs. Joseph Thomas

Hazard smacked her white-haired lips and planted a foot to halt the see-sawing of her rocking chair.

"C'mrr."

Susannah was discreet in her deciphering.

"Mrs. Joseph Thomas Hazard asks you to come closer."

It was with some hesitation that I did so. True, the old woman had no teeth with which to bite. But who, I ask you, wished to be gummed?

Her voice was a syrup that slopped together all words.

"Zhuhahchunglezubbalafunch."

"Terribly sorry," said I, "but I did not catch all of that."

"The Archangel Zebulon Finch," translated Susannah.

"Ah, thank you," said I. "Wait. The what?"

"As I live and breathe," sighed Susannah. "You haven't aged a year from the General's description."

The mummified old broad smiled. Her opalescent eyes disappeared into a vortex of wrinkles.

"Zhuyunka."

I looked to Susannah, who shrugged an apology before translating.

"'The Yankee.' But do forgive Mrs. Hazard. We at Sweetgum have had an altercation or two with Yankees in the past."

There was no doubting this statement, as the rifle she carried bore the handprints of routine usage. I learned later, in fact, that it had been my highfalutin' Northern accent that had nearly gotten my head blown off at the front door. Now Susannah could not stop offering hospitalities. A change of clothes? A bath? A cigar? A brandy? Oh, and I must join them for dinner—would I prefer quail or duck? I took a step away. None of this could do me any good.

"Stop yer grovelin', Susie." Picking sense from Mrs. Joseph

Thomas Hazard's verbal swamp became easier after inundation. "The Archangel Zebulon Finch is sad. Gravely sad. Cain't you tell? He needs him some time to mourn proper."

Gnarled claws extended from their place upon her lap; I had no option but to take them. She pulled me close with the strength of old, stubborn sinew. Her lips rippled into a Basset Hound grin and her whisper smelled of pickles.

"The General spoke of you right regular. You brung him peace when there wuddn't nobody else who could. You saved his mind *and* his soul, and cuz a you, my husband died quiet. You are welcome here, good suh, for as long as you require, you hear?"

That is how I became the first, and possibly only, Yankee to stay at Sweetgum Plantation, as good a place as any to tuck myself away from Dr. Leather. Because my angel attribution (the third, if you're counting, after Johnny and Leather) was so crassly unearned, I made an effort to wander the grounds each day, offering short, surface pleasantries to the sisters. My, but they were a peculiar flock of birds! The parlor was filled with chess sets, not such an unusual thing, thought I, until the day I realized that these strange, unmarried women did not, in fact, play chess, but rather unrolled large maps by candlelight and placed the rooks, knights, and kings atop them to represent Union and Confederate soldiers as they restaged the Late Unpleasantness, or the War of Northern Aggression, or Mr. Lincoln's War—whichever bitter euphemism they preferred that night.

"Look, Nelly, General Bragg wins at Perryville if he takes advantage of these train lines."

"Wonderful, Peggy. And do you see what I have done with Stonewall Jackson's march at Chancellorsville? I think it will be a most decisive victory."

"It will, Nelly, it will drive out the damned Union Blue!"

Increasingly I kept to the solitude of the second-story guest room, three walls of which were filled with shelves containing, of all things, novels. Reader, I hope you are sitting down, for I, Zebulon Finch, began to read them. Each spine I cracked only to distract from my lingering fear of Dr. Leather as well as my foolish yearning to hold Merle close one more time. How was I to guess that within the gray gutters of ten thousand brittle pages I would discover golden glimmers of enlightenment? Had I not, I cannot say I would have the wherewithal to write these pages you now hold.

It was as though I'd landed back in Abigail Finch's second-floor study and once again my playmates were of the bookish bent: E. M. Forster, L. M. Montgomery, O. Henry, H. G. Wells, H. Rider Haggard, and even a few authors bold enough to admit their full Christian names. This time, however, their frivolous fantasies provided insight into the dubious decisions I'd made, particularly concerning the General, his wife, and their six daughters. Thrice a day these women prayed for me with a sincerity that ought to have earned my ridicule. Fiction, though, helped me to understand those whose natures were unfamiliar—a most interesting development.

I might have indefinitely played the disreputable role of "Reader" (no offense, Reader) had not, in May of 1915, a British luxury liner called the *Lusitania* been sunk by a German submarine off the southern end of Ireland. Yes, I know, frightfully boring. But the victims included over one hundred Americans, women and children among them, and their deaths stoked the coals of war in the hearths of those who, thus far, had been content to rock their chairs within a cool quiet.

The Hazard sisters began receiving visitors. The chevrons

upon their shoulders told me that these were military men, and the snatches of conversation I overheard told me that they had come with dual purpose: to pay homage to the General and to consult with the sisters on the conflict in Europe. Little had I suspected that these biddies with their chess sets were encyclopedias of modern warfare and repositories of wisdom when it came to predicting the tides of war.

And their prediction?

America would take up arms and fight.

Thus an audacious notion burrowed into me like a screwworm into a People Garden party-goer. That notion laid its eggs and those eggs began to swell, and the resultant maggots squirmed about my brain until I could think of nothing else. By April of 1917, when our high-minded country at last declared war upon Germany, I'd made my decision. I wrapped a suit around my stiffening body, topped it with a tie, and came downstairs while the women were weighting down their maps for that night's campaign. I cleared my throat.

"I wish to enlist."

Blame, if you like, the harebrained conviction of all the novels I'd read, that even the weakest of plots deserved a smashing conclusion. War offered what I most desired: extinguishment. My body and, if I was lucky, my brain would be scattered across Europe by some well-placed bomb, and never again need I check over my shoulder for Leather, never again need I grieve the loss of Merle. Dying for my country meant nothing to me, but who knew? It might mean something to that pernicious bean-counter Gød.

Susannah took hold of her skirts and circumnavigated the entire Southeastern United States.

"Mr. Finch, you mustn't."

"I have not the proper identification. Nor serial number. Nor family who can vouch for me."

"You're just a boy. Didn't you say you were seventeen?"

"Believe me," said I. "I am old enough."

"Sweetgum without its guardian?" cried Nelly.

"War is no place for an angel!" cried Peggy.

I drew strength from the kings and queens bravely leading their platoons of pawns.

"It is what I intend to do, ladies, and my request is that you assist me."

Until then I had asked for nothing and, in fact, believed that the sisters were waiting to be called to duty. Susannah, though, was distraught and brought me before Mrs. Joseph Thomas Hazard, who, older now than Planet Earth, still held court from her rocking-chair throne. It was she who stayed her eldest daughter's hand.

"Tarnation," slurred she. "A-course he must go. There'll be boys out there just like my Joseph, good boys, and they'll need them a guiding hand, a torch in the night."

"Can't it be anyone else?" pleaded Susannah. "Sweetgum has never been so charmed."

"You know well as me there isn't no one in this world who can do what this boy here does. He's got himself a long journey and we Hazards are one little stone in the path. Be a good girl and send word to Colonel Luckman. He been begging to do me a turn since the General dug him out of that hole at Pickett's Mill."

Mrs. Joseph Thomas Hazard was not mistaken. For the balance of 1917, Colonel Luckman conducted himself like a harried suitor, making repeated calls in his bright suit and yellow-tasseled slouch hat and displaying with pride the various signed letters he was receiving from trusted armed-forces colleagues. I only met the colonel once before deciding further encounters would be counterproductive; he knew how a young soldier looked, moved, and sounded, and I did not fit that bill.

Sweetgum rang in 1918 with good news, a telegram from Colonel Luckman. He began the note by restating his confusion as to why I wished to hide my identity or avoid the standard physical; nonetheless, he was as good as his word. He had smoothed a path for me to join an overseas warring unit as part of the first deployment of the U.S. Marine Corps.

While I speculated upon what constituted a "Marine" (did it involve water, and, if so, did I need to learn how to swim?), the sisters gathered outside and fired their rifles into the night air in celebration. Even the old matriarch took a shot from her upstairs window. Only Susannah kept her firearm cold. She alone doubted my divinity; it made sense, then, that her concern over my well-being was stronger. I chose not to look at her. I was getting what I wanted and I would allow myself this rare flourish of positive feeling.

One morning before the break of dawn, a driver arrived to take me to Savannah, Georgia, where I would catch a boat headed all the way to New York Harbor. There I would transfer to the *U.S.S. Glorybound*, headed for the shores of France, where I would then take ground transportation to the Western Front. Each step of my journey was below-board and padded, probably, with cash, but none of that was my concern. My job was to heed poet Alfred Lord Tennyson's words regarding a certain wartime brigade:

> *Theirs not to make reply,*
> *Theirs not to reason why,*
> *Theirs but to do and die.*

Susannah was there to see me off. She was wrapped in a shawl for it was dewy and cold, and she reached from beneath it to straighten my shirt as if spiffing the military dress I had yet to acquire. She was nearly seventy by then, an old maid if ever there was one, but even in that bleary morning mist she saw more clearly than any other woman I'd ever known. In other words, Susannah Hazard had a good idea what might happen to me on that battlefield.

She kissed my cold cheek.

"Be careful, Archangel Zebulon Finch. My brave young Yankee."

I gave her the Zebby grin that used to work wonders with women and, so help me, I lied.

"Careful—that's the idea!"

III.

WELL, WHAT I HEARD IS they make greenhorns serve on firing squads right when they show up, cuz don't nobody like shooting their own soldiers, and greenhorns generally ain't got the balls to refuse. Just, you know, a friendly warning, Private. You want to prepare yourself mentally."

His name I never learned, for he did not stop talking long enough to give it. He was my driver, assigned with taking me from Orléans, a city south of Paris, to the Marine Corps troops gathered near Château-Theirry. He reveled in calling me "Private" even though his rank was no higher. He was a "doughboy," one of the army recruits that made up the bulk of the American Expeditionary Forces. His uniform was several sizes too large, but oh, was the rosy-cheeked kid ever proud of it, taking any excuse to steer our truck toward an officer so that he could stand up, display his drab-colored service coat, breeches, leg wraps, cap, and dogtags, and fire off a crisp salute. Miserably, I had to follow this routine every time.

It became easier to ignore him the closer we came to the field of battle. The French countryside looked as if a giant had tromped through, swinging a sequoia bat. Churches were reduced to pagan circles of brick. Green grass festered with ruptured clay. A shredded British overcoat flapped from a treetop. I shuddered, for the war was

Dr. Leather, the mortar shells his scalpels, and the land but more cheap flesh hauled in from the garden.

The horizon boomed with thunder. Rain—the one thing my dead body hated above all else.

"First day here," muttered I, "and I'll be soaked to the bone."

The driver laughed as we swerved past a truckload of chickens destined for soldier bellies.

Our final destination was *Bois de Belleau*—Belleau Wood—a mile-and-a-half seahorse-shaped forest reserve, a right pleasant place, or so claimed the driver, where well-to-do Frogs (his affectionate word for the French) vacationed to shoot deer and wild boar for taxidermic reward. Unfortunately for the aristocracy, and the wildlife too, Belleau Wood was all that stood between German forces and Paris, a city that the Huns had been trying to breach for four years. In this, the *Kaiserschlacht* offensive, the 461st Regiment of the German 237th Division had taken the woods a day ago and were closer than they'd ever been to the City of Lights. The French alone could not hold them off.

More thunder in the distance.

"If there is one thing I despise," said I, "it's rain."

The driver laughed again. I did not see what was so funny.

He eased up on the gas as we passed through an Allied bivouac camp. Hundreds of neat little tents had been set up in orderly rows, and along the byways I saw men slapping one another on the back and drinking what looked to be beer. I say! This did not look so bad! I felt a surge of confidence that the rain would stay away. Then, indeed, I could count my first day as a part of the U.S. Marine Corps a rousing success.

The driver, however, continued past the camp and into hillier areas. The storm in the distance grew louder. Thunder cracked and I gripped the French Chauchat rifle I'd been issued so that I did not jump and embarrass myself. Inside I felt a twinge of—could it be?—nervousness. I had come here to be destroyed in fine fashion; what on Earth was there to be afraid of?

The driver let the truck roll gently off the road and jerked it to a halt upon trampled grass.

"Belleau Wood, ladies and gents. Grab yer guns and grab yer nuts."

We were met on all sides by golden fields of wheat, rolling green hills, and charming stone-built barns. I stepped from the truck and slung over opposite shoulders my rifle and haversack. The latter I arranged carefully to hide the old grappling hook wound before checking that my personal .45 was snapped into its holder. Near the edge of the wheat, marching to and fro in their brigades and regiments, were over one hundred Americans of every size, shape, and hue. It was possible, even likely, thought I, that there was diversity enough among such rabble to offer a place for even a being like myself.

The driver wheeled the truck into a three-point turn, then idled beside me before heading back up the country road.

"Look, Private, the leathernecks are gonna be tough on you. You ain't gonna know who to trust, who to avoid, when to say something, when to shut up, none of that shit. Just obey your officers, listen to your noncoms, keep your socks dry and your bayonet sharp, and you'll be fine. And Jesus, ditch that Frog piece-a-shit rifle for a better one soon as you can. They flash real bright in the dark—you want the whole German Army converging on you?"

I nodded at this dervish of nonsense, then squinted up at the black, churning clouds.

"Suppose I'll not be lucky with the rain after all."

The driver laughed so hard that he had to pound his fist against the truck door. He wiped at his eyes and grinned at me as he put the machine back into gear.

"That ain't a raincloud, Private. And that bang-bang sure as hell ain't thunder."

IV.

T WAS LIKE THIS: THE U.S. Second Division was being moved to plug the hole Germany had punched through the French line. The alliance included the Twenty-Third Infantry Regiment, the First Battalion, part of the Sixth Machine Gun Battalion, and the whole damned Fifth and Seventh Marine Regiments. This final group was the one to which Colonel Luckman had assigned me. But there was neither time nor daylight enough for me to work upon these men my charms. Our boots were on the Paris-Metz road. It was night and we were on the march.

My fellow Marines, the whole polyglot lot of them, made no secret of their suspicion. I was an intruder into a brotherhood. As we moved through a bug-sung darkness, I gleaned from the nervous chatter that these Polacks, Dagos, Jewboys, Micks, and Crackers (their words, Reader!) had trained together at the bases in Quantico, Virginia, and Parris Island, South Carolina, before shipping over to here and drilling some more. Together they'd bayonetted many a scarecrow, pretended to shoot with broomsticks when real guns became scarce, and taken leaves into French villages where shapely *mamselles* were eager to learn "Americaine."

So unified were these men that they'd taken pains to weigh down their helmets, caps, and tunics with the globe-eagle-anchor emblem of the Marines, so as not to be confused for common doughboys. These

308

were no GIs; rather, they called themselves GI-Marines, or "gyrenes," though even fonder were they of the term "leatherneck." I ran a hand under the strap of my haversack. My lifeless neck, too, had a leathery feel—was that not enough to earn entry into their club?

It could not have been two miles into our hike that I began to fall behind. Soon my only marching partners were the dead animals strewn across the countryside: gut-shot horses, cows blown to pieces, dogs assassinated for reasons one could not guess. I began to panic. In my rush to war, I had forgotten the demonstrable fact of my limited physical strength.

The terrain was treacherous and the gear I carried was over one hundred pounds. In addition to two firearms, I carried ammo, a rolled-up blanket, and a number of bags containing, in part, a periscope, gas mask, set of tools, shovel, first-aid pouch, tin of foot powder, aluminum mess kit, ration bags, collapsible wash basin, sewing kit, spare underclothes, mittens, and, buckled across my back, a folding trench lantern the size of an eight-year-old.

The full canteen I had managed to empty and the useless shaving kit I'd managed to drop into the elbow-high wheat. These subtractions made little difference. I staggered; I tripped; I fell to a knee and then fought gravity until I was wobbling about on bended leg. To my relief, a hand snared the gray wool of my coat and steadied me. I would have thanked the fellow had he not planted his big, flushed face in front of mine and screamed. Let me clarify, for our march was a clandestine one: his was a whispered scream.

"What is your *name*, Private?"

Honestly, he should have known, for I'd been introduced to him not three hours earlier. His name was Major Hugh Horstmeier, and he was a lean, tobacco-spitting hyena of a man, fifty years old if a day, though if his energy level was any indication, he'd been waiting all his life for this war.

"PFC Zebulon Finch. From Xenion, Georgia? You remember me, Skipper, we just met."

The men referred to him as "the Skipper." I thought it might help to adopt the informality.

Horstmeier kneaded his haversack as if it were the only thing keeping him from strangling me.

"Good Lord, son! I don't know where to begin! Number one, you call me Major until you figure out your place in this regiment! Number two, you end your sentences with *sir*! Number three, if you're from Georgia, I'm a goddamned elephant in a tutu!"

"Georgia by way of Chicago," said I. "Sir."

"Did I ask which rock you crawled out from under? Now get those boots moving!"

"I would prefer not to just this second," said I. "Sir."

"Jesus on his throne, *what?*" He spat tobacco at my feet and head-butted his helmet against my own. It made quite a clatter in the old skull. "Private Prefer-Not-To, fall in! That means march, soldier! That-a-way, on the double, before I raise my voice and the Krauts light up the whole sky! Move, move, move!"

I spent the remainder of that six-mile march feeling quite sorry for myself. Even here among a tribe fighting for a single cause, I was once more alone, and worse, being threatened with a court martial by a red-faced fool, who matched every slow step I took with a furious tongue-lashing about how I had apparently learned nothing at boot camp, how I had no respect for rank, how I had all the mettle of a four-year-old girl, how the gyrenes had their own way of dealing with men like me who put the rest of them in danger.

310

The ground shook with explosions as we closed in on the village of Lucy-le-Bocage, where we were to regroup before morning. By then the rain I had feared had arrived and when my foot landed in a gully and I fell into several inches of muddy rainwater, I knew I would not be getting up. No, this was not exactly the glorious death I had pictured, but it would have to do. I waited for the point of a bayonet against my neck, the muzzle of a .45 to my temple, however it was the gyrenes "dealt with" flunkies like me.

Hands dug into my back. I braced. I felt fingers moving quickly about my torso until the folding trench lantern was unstrapped. Two arms wrapped around my body and pulled. My face disengaged from the mud with a sucking sound.

"Get up." It was a whisper.

I put my hands flat to the ground but they sunk into the mud.

With a grunt, the man lifted me from the ditch and planted me feet-first upon firmer ground. I blinked some mud from my eyes to get a look at him. He was an Adonis, broad-shouldered and tall, his handsome blue-eyed face capped with white-blond hair and grounded by the kind of cleft chin that exists only in comic books. In his right hand he held the trench lantern as if it were nothing. He hissed between perfect white teeth.

"You gotta walk. Can you? We're nearly there."

Walk? Could I? It was an exemplary question.

He grimaced at our phalanx, which had all but disappeared into the timber. Without further discussion, he threw my left arm over his shoulder, gripped my wrist with his hand, and began dragging me in the right direction. Halfway there, I found my footing but my measly pace could not keep up with that of the Adonis, who carried me through the woods and back in line with the others before Major

311

Horstmeier realized that we were gone. There was a barn at Lucy-le-Bocage, by some miracle intact, and inside it we troops knelt in a semicircle while the officers stood shoulder-to-shoulder in debate.

Cigarettes had been banned during the march for their tell-tale glows, but now everyone dug into their sacks for their Luck-ies. The rustling lifted chicken feathers from the hay; they twirled in the moonlight as if they had all night to dance. You could hear the tobacco burn, that's how many butts were lit. The exhaled smoke sailed upon sighs of relief; we had made it without a single man being picked off by sniper.

I felt safer as well and in possession of the majority of my wits. I slopped mud from my face with my sleeve and turned toward the Adonis. Here, at last, was somebody possessed with an open heart.

"My deepest gratitude, chap. If there is anything I can do—"

"You don't belong here."

He hissed this from a clenched jaw unencumbered by cigarette.

"Stay out of my way," said he. "Out of everyone's way. You'll get us all killed, you stupid bastard."

V.

FROM THE BLASÉ TO THE petrified, the logical to the scat-ological, no soldier in any condition spurned the improvised morning service of Sunday, June 2, 1918, not even I, Gød's sworn rival. We pressed our bodies against a slender knoll, clutching our helmets with every detonation. Here at last was the famous Western Front and here, unexpected, was a chaplain, what they called a "devil dodger," looking the same as us but collared in white. We tried not to compare the whistles and booms of mechanized death with this reedy recitation from the pages of a pocket Bible. We all, by the way, had been issued pocket Bibles.

"Amen," said he.

"Amen." It was a dispirited murmur. These men, for all their bluster, had yet to witness a single minute of war. One soldier was throwing up in the wheat; another squatted over a pile of diarrhea. The colonel had assured us that we would have adequate cover and a safe distance to establish our position, but no one believed it. How could you believe anything on a day when birds were falling out of the sky fully cooked?

The chaplain closed his Bible in defeat. The men looked at the forlorn mud. It was a moment of pure despondence until the Adonis changed everything. He stood, all six-foot-five-inches of him, with his handsome head above the edge of the knoll where, we imagined, invisible bullets went whizzing. Then he did his brave gesture one better, sweeping off his helmet and flashing a rakish grin while his blond hair whipped in the wind.

"You call that an *amen?* Now, boys, that just won't do, not for the Seventh Regiment it won't. What say we give the good padre here an amen he can write to his flock about?"

The soldiers blinked up at him. One nodded, then another.

"Okay then," the Adonis said. "Let's hear it!"

"Amen!"

Stronger? Yes. But not strong enough for this blond idol.

"These Squareheads are dealing with the United States Marine Corps now! When we say *amen* it's like scoring a touchdown! Let's hear it!"

More nodding, a few lionhearted grins.

"AMEN!"

"Let's send 'em to hell where they belong!"

"*AMEN!*"

Major Horstmeier knew when to grab a moment. He scrambled atop the knoll, blew the raid whistle he wore about his neck, and waved his arms at the field beyond.

"Dig in, men! Dig in!"

The Seventh Regiment erupted in hurrahs as they bounded to their feet and vaulted over the knoll. Without that damned trench lantern I could move as well as any of them and in seconds I was lost in a funnel of gray uniforms so thick I could make out only slivers of nature: golden wheat, a perimeter of trees still reeling from some recent assault, and skies as blue and infinite as the water off the Salem coast—only here the cloudless azure bore the black scalds of artillery smoke.

We had been briefed that the Huns of Belleau Wood were driving back the French in droves, and by the time we dropped to our knees and withdrew our shovels, that truth was underlined by the distant whoosh of German flamethrowers, the bone-jarring blast of the dreaded "Big Bertha" howitzers, the insatiable *TAC-TAC-TAC* of the Maxim machine guns—weapons our boys had speculated upon for days, I knew, and years, I suspected. Punctuating the blasts were the isolated screams of injured Frogs.

I dug. We all dug.

Raw remnants of a French trench provided a base from which over half of our soldiers began to excavate their own workable system. The Third Battalion, to which I belonged, was directed by sergeants to dig two-man foxholes facing the edge of the Wood, and fast, and, goddammit, quit bunching up, we don't want a single shell taking out the whole mess of you. No further encouragement was necessary. Dirt and clay shot into the air from our shovels.

I was paired with a disfavored twenty-four-year-old Irishman from New York named J.T. O'Hannigan, though everyone who had endured his tedious Roman Catholicism and the kissing of the cross round his neck called him "Piano," for he was strung tight as piano wire. He certainly attacked the ground with a maestro's fervor, slicing through green grass without wondering, as I did, what sort of unfortunate fertilizer had made it so green, and sawing through roots without wondering, as I did, if sawing through a man's ankle with my bayonet would feel the same.

For the next few hours we dug. The Third Battalion was spread to my left and right, and courtesy of the back-and-forth of vulgar ribbing I was introduced to the closest contingent.

Corporal Frankie "Peanut" Capella was a thirty-something

315

Italian chef from the Florida Panhandle, whose nickname, one can only assume, came not from a favorite recipe but from some incident at basic training starring his pecker. Peanut was the size and furriness of a black bear but gregarious as a puppy, given to laughing so loud it made everyone on the battlefront duck. Nothing bothered Peanut except the word "wop." Some poor private who knew no better told Peanut, "You greasy wop, quit laughing before you attract every Jerry Squarehead in a ten-mile radius." It ended in an interlude of blood and bruisings, the world at war be damned.

It is law, I believe, that every unit in every war must have a fellow who goes by "Professor," and the Seventh was no exception. Sten Ehrenström taught at a college in Wisconsin, and before work on our holes was through, he'd used his full-throated lecture-hall voice to expound upon everything from the historical precedent behind Pope Benedict XV's recent plea for peace to Germany's unrivaled status as the home of expressionist playwrights. Not once in my tour of duty did I witness the gray-haired Prof complain; instead he used any unfavorable situation to discourse on the "historical forces" that "led us to this nexus," and what, if anything, we, "as a people," could learn from it. Most astonishing was that he did not even mind our infamously ill-fitting boots. The Prof, a Swede, had been raised in wooden clogs, which had prepared his feet for such unforgiving footwear.

PFC Alfred "Mouse" Bartosiewicz, a bespectacled Jew of Polish descent, lived in Kansas City with his family and worked as a typesetter, and that, my friend, was all we knew. So quiet was Mouse that even these specks of information were suspect. Mouse was of gray complexion and could not have weighed more than 125 pounds; if you let your eyes lose focus he would evaporate into the dirt, or smoke, or fog. Yet Mouse was never mistaken for dumb. His fine, bespectacled features were so expressive they approached the prehensile; with but a twitch of his eyebrow or curl of his lip he could communicate more than the Prof could with two hours and a willing audience.

Even now it is difficult for me to even think of Jason Stavros without feeling as if I am liquifying at the joints. Officially the twenty-year-old Utahan was a part-time student of literature and a part-time florist. Unofficially, however, he was a poet and dreamer, too gentle for this war. Everyone loved Jason Stavros with a jealous ferocity, and when they told him to put away the volume of Percy Shelley poems he kept as close as his gun, they hated to do it, for the study of beauty was what Jason Stavros was meant to do. Yes, they called him "Jason Stavros," the first and last name strung together as if each repetition of it were an appeal to Gød to spare this one most of all. He would survive because he was charmed—the men were sure of it.

And then, of course, there was the Adonis. His name was Burt "Church" Churchwell, and though his documents declared him a good Baptist boy from Iowa, he was from *America*—as simple and profound as that. Unlike the rest of our accented masses, Church was astonishing in his lack of inflection; his voice was as tall and ubiquitous as corn. Where Jason Stavros toted poetry, Church toted a football, deflated but who cared? He could nonetheless throw the same spiral he was throwing at Grinnell College when Uncle Sam had come a-calling. To him, the war was "the Game," and his all-purpose substitute for *damn* or *shit* was "Merry Christmas!" In short, he was the sort of sky-eyed, teetotaling goody-goody I had joined the Black Hand to avoid becoming. Major Horstmeier might shout the orders, but the men of the Seventh Regiment fought under Church.

I attribute to loneliness my ache for a nickname of my own.

317

Would I have to be patient and earn one? Hellfire! How I loathed being patient. I stabbed my shovel into foxhole clay and felt my pocket for the hard nodule of the Excelsior and the crinkle of Merle's photograph. Memories of family lost were the only cohorts I had, and those memories, as you well know, were of sour vintage.

Feeling quite low, I leaned back into our rectangular foxhole. It took me a couple of minutes to see it, but when I did, I could not help but smile.

I'd just dug my own long-awaited grave.

"Boy-o! What's the problem? We got sand here that needs packing!"

It was Piano, shouting to be heard over the timpani of battle. He stood at the front end of the dug-out, slapping into place a ridge of protective sandbags. I adjusted my helmet and tried to reorient. It was midday. Word had been passed along that the U.S. had secured a line all the way to Les Mares Farm (wherever that was) thanks to the Frenchies who, despite apparent decimation, would not stop bombarding the Germans. The report from the Eighteenth Company was nevertheless bleak: the Wood seethed with Krauts and sooner or later we'd have to do something about it.

Our neighboring foxholes were finished and their occupants had progressed to checking, rechecking, oiling, and stroking their cherished weapons. Their love of their pieces was fast and faithful, almost lustful; to these steel ladies, they had pledged everything. Feeling derelict, I crawled next to Piano and got to work on the bags.

"Look here, ye going to have to pull your weight! I need to depend upon this wall if I'm going get work done on me maps!"

"Maps?"

He sighed, removed from his side pouch a stack of paper, and shook it at me.

"My da was the best mapmaker in Ireland, and it's in me blood as well, ask anyone. What I'm going to do is map these entire woods, show the major what I can do. It's my ticket right up the ranks, wait and see. I'll leave this war a captain!"

"How pleasant for you."

"Is that brass ye giving me? There will be nothing 'pleasant' about it if I have to spend every waking moment arranging these bags! You're the sand man of this foxhole. You got that, Private Prefer-Not-To?"

My face fell, as did my hopes; worse, they fell right in front of this maligning Irishman. How could I have forgotten that the Skipper had already nicknamed me during our march, and the name was nothing of which to be proud? I was disappointed, and embarrassed that I was disappointed, and the infuriating cartographer gave me a smug grin before removing his papers, rulers, and pens.

The sky all at once exploded with sound and light; smoke trails of orange, red, and gray cutting through the blue, followed by concussion blasts so resounding the cold guts behind my sewed stomach listed to one side, then the other. Though the salvo was to our west, terrified soldiers grabbed their helmets and ducked in their holes.

Not Church. He bounded from his foxhole, planted his shovel, and leaned upon it with an elbow so as to better enjoy the streaming bands of fire. Peanut, that big, friendly Italian, roared with laughter at this fantastic display of swagger. The Prof applauded and Jason Stavros stuck his pinkies in his mouth to whistle. Mouse's head barely cleared his rifle pit, but he, too, was smiling.

Church flashed us a million-dollar grin.

"Will you look at that, boys? Jerry organized some Fourth of July fireworks just for us! Now that's what I call German hospitality!"

VI.

WERE YOU BORN ON JUNE 6? Renounce it. Choose another date. I have heard June 5 is lovely; June 7, too, cannot be so bad. But the sixth day of June has been the passageway for too many souls, and to be born on that day is to clog the conduit between heaven and Earth, to risk being forced on the wrong path, the one to Hell.

The Germans, the Krauts, the Huns, the Heinie, *le Boche*, Fritz, Jerry—call them what you will—the entirety of their 237th Division had advanced upon us on June 4, four or five lines of them appearing like specters from the fog, spaced twenty-five yards apart and firing for hours until sand from ruptured sandbags scoured the skin beneath our uniforms, until we were half-buried in clay from the flexing trenches. We, the mud-crunchers of the Third Battalion, were crouched in a supply trench, removed from the action, which, I began to wonder, must be worse than being fired at, for all you had to go on was the quake of the entire planet.

At 1500 hours on June 5, the French Sixth Army general had sent us our mission: Hill 142, the highest spot in the Wood. At 2245 hours, Field Order Number One was issued. The Marines would attack between Hill 142 and the Champillon ravines to prevent the Huns from opening flanking fire against the French 167th Division. Confused, Reader? That, I am afraid, mirrors our own state. Only the juiciest meat of the order was tastable: we were to overwhelm the German position with hundreds of charging Americans, infiltrate their trenches, stick any living Huns with the points of our bayonets, and at all costs, take the goddamned hill.

On June 6, 0500 hours, we gathered in the frontline trench for our first true test. A wand of dawn blazed the horizon over the German stronghold. Look at us in the light. Painted boot-to-helmet with dirt, eyes blazing whiter than white. We were stripped to the basics—weapons, bandoliers, grenades, gas masks—and looked fragile without our packs. Someone remind us how had we ended up in rural France? Men whispered to crucifixes and fiddled with wedding bands, every follicle attuned to the sergeant atop the ladder peering through a periscope at what we could only imagine. We were a single suspended breath: inhale, inhale, inhale.

Even I, breathless creature, was lightheaded with fear.

The call went down the line, captain to captain.

"Fix bayonets!"

We did. They slotted in just fine. Sharp, too. We'd tested them on our own thumbs to our own horrors.

Footsteps—fast—hurtling down the line.

Our runner, that suicidal screwball, sprinted by, shouting two terrible words:

"TAKE COVER! TAKE COVER!"

And then the trees were obliterated. Great oak gods, black from rain, became white butterflies, a million of them trapped against the ugly brown sky before diving as shrapnel against our turned backs. Severed treetops suspended in midair before dropping with the sound of a giant broom swatting a giant rug. Into our noses shot the hot odor of burned powder and fresh dirt. The stink of nervous sweat leaked from the men like urine.

The sergeant turned, made curt hand signals. Smoke parted to reveal Major Horstmeier squatting on the aboveground turf like an ape, pendulating his arms toward the swirling silver fog while blowing the whistle clamped between his teeth.

"Over the top! Over the top, men! Over the top!"

Church was first, of course, his broad back the dreadnaught behind which we might advance. Here was the moment I'd envisioned in Xenion, Georgia—noble annihilation—and yet I could not move my legs. Regardless, I surged upward, pushed along by crazed soldiers, boots to the ladder, knees to the sandbags, elbows to the grass, belly to the dirt, and then I was crawling on my stomach as someone—who?—had instructed us.

No matter; this was it! The fabled no man's land upon which thousands of troops from a dozen different nations had been pestled into dust. We took to our feet, against orders, but who could resist running when every second was spent as a target? We hurtled into unknown terrain so thick with smoke that I could see only the flash of wet boot heels from the soldier in front of me, the gleam of an oiled rifle stock from the soldier to the side of me, the fires from downed trees burning red through the coarse, woolen world.

Horstmeier's whistle was still blowing.

The Marine Corps responded with the cry learned in training; it came natural even now.

"EEE-YAH-YIP!"

Bees flew past my ears. Even insects were fleeing the scene! No, idiot, not bees but *bullets*, melted down from excavated street pipes in German villages made destitute by four years of war, shaped in a

Berlin foundry into slugs, shipped on trucks and horse-drawn wagons across the hills and mud of Europe, and for what purpose? To be shoved into a rifle and shot out at me, Zebulon Finch, Marine and Madman, sprinting blind through a pea soup of scorching smog. These bullets nicked at my extremities like a scalpel.

Perfect little pieces for the Revelation Almanac.

A sucking void of sound and pressure lifted me from my feet and dropped me down, still standing, yards away, followed by a deafening *thump*—Gød's indifferent backhand shoving me from a blast zone. My brain punched against my skull and clods of clay dropped upon my shoulders, and then there were cries—*First aid! First aid!*—that no one listened to, because we were still running, still hooting our cry, still without a single visible checkpoint.

Flesh against my fingers. I grunted with instinctive rage, wrestled with a man for control of my rifle. But it was Peanut and he took a handful of my collar and shouted into my face. His gums were packed with moss, his tongue black with dirt.

"Bottleneck! Bottleneck! Bottleneck!"

He pointed a finger into the gloom and then began to search for an alternate path.

It made no sense to me. I shoved past the Italian and kept on until I began to make out the five-foot-tall barbed-wire bulwark separating us from Jerry. Our artillery had launched a torpedo to destroy this barricade but either it had failed or we soldiers were off the mark.

A gust of summer wind blew by with the same stink as my slaughterhouse in Salem, and for thirty terrible seconds I could see beyond the soot. Some brave gyrene had managed to cut a narrow path through the wire. The wire clippers, in fact, still hung suspended in the wire, as did the dead solider who had plied them. The bottle-neck Peanut had warned me of was a single-file line of soldiers that might as well have been raw meat pushed into a grinder. A Maxim ripped them apart with ease: *TAC-TAC-TAC!* The leathernecks became leather, the doughboys dough.

Before the black fog rolled back I saw the blurry red glints of German bayonets flashing from a trench not fifty feet away. I dropped to my stomach and rolled to the left, through the mud of a shell crater, over a warm pile of human flesh, across a Hotchkiss rifle abandoned because its action bolt had been melted by fire. My roll was stopped by the body of a gyrene, a dead one, I assumed, until I made out the voice of Church. If there was a soldier still kicking, it had to be him.

He was lying flat and shouting into the face of a downed Marine. Bullets had torn through the soldier's biceps, which now dangled in gray and red braids of uniform and flesh. Church had managed to extract a tourniquet from the soldier's utility pouch, but the man's writhing complicated its application. He cried out in pain; Church pressed a hand over his mouth and ducked. The dirt spat around us from a spray of bullets.

"It's the Game, soldier!" shouted Church. "It's fourth down and inches! You gotta hang tough, do it for the team, push it on through to the end zone!"

"I don't—" came the casualty's anguished response, "know shit—about your damn—football."

The Italian accent was familiar. I propped myself on an elbow to get a look.

It was Peanut; I could be certain only because I'd encountered him mere minutes ago. His nose was gone—I could see the pink channels of his sinuses—but there was no mistaking the thick bil-

324

lows of hair popping from his chest and arms. Church ignored the sensational face wound in favor of the biceps, and for good reason: while Peanut's cauterized nose shed ash, his biceps fountained blood.

"Lemme go." The absence of a nose muffled him. "I gotta kill me some Kraut."

Church set the tourniquet aside, reached into his front pouch, and removed two lemon drops. With his other hand he pried open Peanut's clenched jaw and shoved in the candies.

"Suck on these, Peanut! Mmm, good, right? Sour as heck, huh?"

Peanut drove his head back against the dirt in a wild kind of nod.

Church patted his chest. "Good boy! Now hold still, all right?"

The end of the tourniquet passed through the buckle and wrapped around the biceps twice before Church cranked the wooden handle to tighten the pressure. Peanut sucked the candies with abandon; lemon-colored froth fizzed into the abscess of his sinuses. I looked away. No injury I'd witnessed under the Black Hand compared to this. How many others out here were in worse condition?

I gripped Church's arm.

"There's a bottleneck. We have to fall back!"

He gave me an incredulous stare.

"We fall back when the Skipper tells us to fall back."

"How would we know? We can't hear him!"

A man shrieked in agony off to our right.

"Merry Christmas!" Church glared at me. "You hear *that* well enough, Private?"

Steeling himself with an elongated inhale, he dug several more lemon drops from his pouch, clenched them inside a fist, and began crawling on his elbows in the direction of the cries. I launched myself the opposite direction, parallel to the German barricade, anything to separate myself from disconcerting displays of doomed heroism. The Maxims pursued me; plumes of dirt geysered at my heels like rawboned devils shooting up from an underworld.

I sprawled face-first into a patch of wheat ornamented by bright red poppies. Lead swept over me with such force that the chaff was severed from the wheat, the poppies from their stems, leaving the foliage with a military crewcut. While lying there, arms over my head, I heard the telltale *EEE-YAH-YIP!* of Marines flooding in behind me, searching for another path through the wire. Had I become their inadvertent leader?

They stormed past, half of them dropping from Hun fire to become black lumps beyond the curtains of yellow wheat. The other half, though, hurled themselves at the bastions of barbed wire and, from what I could see from my low vantage, some of them were making it through. The assault from the enemy trench became more erratic, as the Germans were forced to divide their fire at dozens of moving targets.

This was no way to go out. I lifted myself and skulked into the blasted farmland. There they were—Germans! Scattering in pale green costumes and bowl helmets, hurling grenades from behind trees, firing Lugers from the hip, and making aweless stands in the clear with submachine guns firing 450 rounds per minute. I jostled sideways behind the line of advancing Marines, many of them taking bullets that otherwise would have been mine.

Having dashed to the northern edge of the flank, I found myself alone in an orchard. I kicked through dank mulch that had recently been tree bark and took a sharp turn westward. There I collided with another soldier. Our rifles clacked together and we both fell to kneeling positions. I pushed my helmet up out of my eyes and the first thing I saw was a brass belt buckle imprinted with three words:

GOTT MIS UNS

It meant "Gød Is With Us," or so I would later learn, a pretty good joke, seeing how the German crouched before me looked as abandoned by divinity as anyone in history. His rifle was leveled at my chest but his eyes were wide and frightened. He looked nothing like the *Übermenschen* spoken of by German agitprop; rather, he looked like the Hun equivalent of Jason Stavros—deerlike, barely of drinking age, and equipped with fingers accustomed not to his engine of death but to pen and paper.

A battlefield end, I told myself. *Here it is, just as I wanted.*

But the German delayed before doing me the favor.

Was it my face, young as his own, that stilled him?

I shall never know.

For thirty seconds he did not fire, and then his rifle exploded in his hands, a crack shot from a leatherneck coming in from my right. The German yipped in pain, tucked away bloody hands, and withdrew along a retreat path that put him directly into my line of fire. I aimed, an easy shot, but found that I, the same as him, could not pull my trigger. *Do it!* I scolded myself. *You shot how many innocent men in Chicago?*

The soldier dropped from sight into an enemy hole.

Marines overwhelmed my position; I took a seat lest I be tackled. Later I would hear that it was the Eighth Machine Gun Company, joining us at last, and with their additional firepower our column

327

pushed the Huns with renewed gusto. Men roared by and I swear to you, Reader, I heard through the chaos the famous shout that would put Belleau Wood into the history books:

"Come on, you sons of bitches, you want to live forever?"

A funny question for me, when you think about it.

Inside the bedlam it was difficult to string together rational thoughts. How could I have let the dirty Heine live? Was I a traitor? A weakling? Or was there another, deeper reason? I thought of Church, his unflinching rescue of Peanut, his lemon drops of deliverance. Doubtless he was right here in the thick of it, saving Americans and taking down Huns. What right to be in these particular woods on this particular day had I, a grunt who could not claim a single German?

Church had been right.

I did not belong here.

I ran straight toward home base, heedless of the tongues of fire overhead and the mortars bashing holes to my left and right. Our trench coalesced from the gloom like a battleship. I shouldered against what remained of a sandbag stockade and flipped over the edge, falling six feet into the rainwater puddled below.

Boots were plugged into the mud right beside me. I extracted my face from the ooze and saw that they belonged to no less than Major Horstmeier. Good—he was the man who needed to hear the full, treasonous truth behind the lies that had brought me to France.

I fought to a standing position but the major did not notice. He, too, had returned from the field, his sleeves charred and his face tenderized from shrapnel. He barked orders at a seasick-looking captain while moving his finger along a homemade map. And who held that map? None other than my foxhole friend, Piano, his cheeks paled with

328

the same shock as everyone, though suspiciously free of soot or dirt.

The Skipper finished his order. I snapped off a muddy salute.

"Sir!"

Horstmeier knocked my hand aside.

"We don't salute out here, son! You want every mother-loving Jerry knowing who the brass are?"

"No! I'm sorry, sir."

The Skipper squinted so hard that beads of blood squeezed from his abrasions.

"Private Prefer-Not-To? What the hell are you doing here? Do we have Hill 142? Do we?"

"No, sir, but—"

"Then get out of my trench, soldier! Get back in that wheat!"

"I'm not supposed to be here, sir! I'll explain! There were these women in Georgia—"

"Not supposed to be here? Well, no shit, Private! I could've told you that the second I laid eyes on you! Here, let me give you a tip! There isn't *no one* supposed to be here, besides a few fellas who were born to kill, and those are the same fellas who are going to take home the medals, run for office, and someday sign your paychecks. Next to those kind of men, you're always going to look yellow, Private. So get your ass back out there and start doing whatever the hell they say, because that's going to be the rest of your life, son, if you're lucky enough to live it! Now get out of my goddamn face!"

VII.

FIELD ORDER NUMBER TWO WAS issued at 1405 hours. Far sturdier Marines than I had taken Hill 142, but it was a tenuous ownership, and we survivors were told to redirect our assault to recapture the strategically located Bouresches, a blameless little burg caught in the middle of the worst war the world had ever seen.

It was no good, no good at all. We had conquered not even one mile of deformed forest that no man in his right mind would want, and the fight coming from the Huns remained resolute. The first line of our afternoon skirmishers was naked to what we later learned were *two hundred* machine guns; every last man of this first wave drowned in a choppy sea of German lead. Shielded by these corpses, our second line made it farther, only to be picked off by snipers perched in trees. Clean red arcs of American blood capered across blue skies.

Predictably, I suppose, our staunch, methodized offensive rived into smaller skirmishes. When dusk came at last, men from all nations were mishandling their weapons, discharging fire into their own countrymen, or dropping their firearms altogether due to numbness. The scene had the absurdity of a clown revue.

It was with great relief that I received the passed word that operations were winding down along with the sun. I crawled from the crater where I'd cowered for a shameful amount of time—let us not speak of how long—to hear the exciting news that Hill 142 remained

330

in our control. Huzzah! And while a superior field of German fire had put up a fight, Bouresches was mostly ours as well. Hear, hear! Of course, the loss of life had been catastrophic—but that's the wrong way to think, soldier! Why not look on the bright side? We Allies were the proud new owners of a cute little corner of Belleau Wood, a pitiful foothold, for sure. But a foothold nonetheless!

None of us grunts, I promise you, gave a shit about this pile of dirt versus that. Massacred bodies created their own piles, and those were the hills that concerned us.

Peanut had been evacuated by ambulance and the word was that the Prof was missing in action. By now Sten Ehrenström could be one of the thousands of pounds of carrion being feasted upon by scavengers, or he could be caught behind enemy lines with a carving knife to his scrotum. Would he sob forth our secrets or would he forge a filibuster out of one of his memorized lectures?

No one had time to consider every gruesome possibility. There were fresh foxholes to be dug and a new trench to be twisted to our means, for nightfall would give *le Boche* updated conditions under which to launch bewildering new counteroffensives. Church was hip-deep in a hole to my left and I ogled his relentless action. I'd seen a lot of dead men that day, half of them with lemon stains upon their tongues. No feat of sharpshooting impressed me as much as that.

Unlike Piano, beside whom I again dug, or any soldier for that matter, my body suffered none of the travails of the fatigued: uneasy stomachs ejecting the blandest of biscuits, eyes bleeding from shrapnel filaments, muscle cramps felling men as surely as if by sniper. The single but significant aftereffect I endured was that my dead bones continued to vibrate from the day's shellings. With each stab of my shovel, this buzz reverberated in my skull and from it came a whisper.

(((How does it feel, Finch, the electric charge of my Voltaic Bed?)))

Like that, I was swept back across the Atlantic. The spoiling corpses around me were but a repopulated People Garden, the steaming heaps of red guts an advanced stage of meat etiquette, the entire forest an expanded Jefferson Street laboratory.

(((Oxygen gives your brain a bone-chisel sharpness, doesn't it?)))

No, non, nein! I stabbed the walls of the foxhole with my shovel. Leather could not have a single additional piece of me!

(((A piece here, a piece there, I shall get all of you eventually.)))

Leather's mocking echoes did not let up. Neither, then, would I. I attacked the foxhole until the blade of the shovel began to wiggle from its wooden hilt. As the last kernel of sunlight winked out behind our line, I threw down my shovel and leaned back against the hole, body a-tremble not from exhaustion but from terror. That contemptuous voice! For now, I seemed to have buried it, but the strike to my confidence had been true.

So shaken was I that I recoiled at the sight of a page of newspaper somersaulting along the edge of the trench. I collected myself, picked up my rifle, fixed the bayonet, and stabbed it—a direct hit.

I began to unwad the mess.

"Boy-o." Piano snapped his fingers. "Give that to me."

Though the Irishman had spent the day out of enemy range holding his map for officers, he had nonetheless been rattled among the worst. His left cheek had acquired a violent tic. With each crack of distant fire, the cheek contracted like a fist, swallowing his eye inside a vulgar wink.

"For maps," insisted he. "I'm running low on paper. Hand it over."

The paper was French. My fluency had rusted since childhood, but surmising the gist was not difficult.

So the Marines had saved Paris, had we? I was sure that would come as a surprise to us trench-cowerers, who disassembled our pieces to give them a quick oiling before the night sky lit up with more payloads of TNT. I was certain the news would also surprise those poor saps stuck up on Hill 142—Target Number One for rebuked Germans. The paper was propaganda, a hurried attempt to recast a bloodbath to boost morale, but I was appreciative of it. My indignation, at least, pushed Leather even further from my mind.

A bayonet at my throat ended that line of thought.

"Maps," hissed Piano. "I need to be making more maps."

I was tempted to lean into the blade so that it pierced my neck straight through, for no other reason than to give this Irishman a good scare. But far too many holes weakened my corpse, so I folded the paper, taking my time, and relinquished it. His face spasmed so forcefully that tears shot from his eye, then he drew back his bayonet and retreated to his end of the pit.

Though I should have detested him, the worshipful manner in which he fondled the newspaper struck me as poignant. His cheek convulsed; as a result, his hand jerked and the newsprint tore, causing him to cry out like a frustrated child. Before I could think better of it, I removed that day's rations from my kit and tossed it onto his lap.

He glared. One of his hands touched his rifle, a bolt-action Springfield I coveted.

"What's the catch, boy-o?"

"Not hungry," said I. "Eat up."

No further encouragement was required. He cranked open the tin and with filthy fingers tore into the sow-belly and gravy. The sight dredged up opposite memories: the gold-gilded chandeliers and silver candelabras of Abigail Finch's dining room, Mr. Dixon's spotless trays and finicky ballet of decorum. Repulsive as were Piano's eating habits, I preferred them to the endless sheathed daggers of civilized manners.

The Irishman sucked a finger clean but offered nothing resembling gratitude.

"Yes, I'll be needing lots of grub. For energy, you know. For making maps."

VIII.

JUST AS THE SPECTER OF Dr. Leather would not let go of
me, neither would the Germans abdicate the sixth of June. The
lions came by night: poison gas heralded by the bells, rattles,
and green rockets of U.S. alarms. The wind drifted it to our north,
out of range of the Third Battalion. We suffered only an atonal chorus of high-pitched wheezes, the croaking pleas for medics. Was it
mustard gas? Chlorine? Phosgene? Whatever it was, it was heavy; it
groveled along on its belly before sinking into the trenches. We lit the
sky with flares; in the light the creeping gas became a preposterous
pink. But it helped our artillery hang a curtain of fire, beneath which
our gassed brothers could flee for the safety of higher ground.

At midnight, the colonel, a short man with a pointed goatee,
walked the lines escorted by the banged-up Major Horstmeier. At
the call of "ten-hut!," men drooping from the twenty-hour clash were
forced to stand upright and salute. I was one of the lucky few the
colonel chose to directly address.

"A good day, eh, Private? A famous day!"

There was a blot of shaving cream on his neck. It smelled clean,
like mint.

"Yes, sir."

"Tomorrow will be even famouser! We've got intelligence coming in from the Tommys. We've got rebuilt mortars rolling in with

a twelve-hundred-yard range. If we're lucky, a Renault tank. That would be all right with you, wouldn't it, Private?"

"Yes, sir."

"That's the spirit! Say, how many Krauts you kill today, soldier?"

I pictured the one I did not kill.

"Private!" barked Horstmeier. "The colonel is asking you a question!"

((((Indicate, Finch, indicate!)))

I bucked the voice as if it were a rat landed upon my back.

"I . . . I am sure I don't know, sir."

The colonel gave me a prankish squint. "Too many to count, eh? That's what I like to hear! That's what the *world* likes to hear!"

Morale was in the shitter and there was nothing a colonel with time enough to cultivate a goatee could do about it. Duckboards had been placed in our trench to protect us from moisture, but most were critically split. For a while we used pumps to drain the trench of brackish, blood-swirled water, but it was no use, and besides, we were tired. Eventually we sat, our trousers and underwear soaking through.

How had the French, British, and Russians withstood *four years* of such conditions? It had taken but a single day for the Marines to become infested with "cooties," a cute term for the lice that hatched eggs into the seams of our clothing and itched so that we clawed ourselves raw. I, as always, was rejected by bloodsucking pests, though I was not immune to the plague of frogs—yes, literal frogs—that moved by the thousands into our ankle-high water. This moat soon became creamy with stomped amphibian guts.

But no beast was as intimate to us as the rat. The black rats were bad enough—should one doze for thirty minutes, the little assholes would chew through tin and steal one's rations. But the brown rats!

Those cat-sized rotters feared neither bomb nor bullet, and not thirty seconds passed when you did not see one paddling our canals. It was easier, sometimes, to just tip your helmet and let them swim past.

What a tableau the Third Battalion made! Faces gray with ash, eyes Satan-red, sweat-blacked uniforms accented with crimson-stained white gauze. There were fewer of us now—it was a shock how many fewer—but the Prof, at least, had returned, armed with a story about playing dead within a tangle of dead German soldiers, only to discover that one of the Germans was playing dead, too. The Prof laughed about it, too forcefully for comfort. Our thoughts returned to Peanut. No doubt, said the boys, he was in some Paris hospital under the care of a horny nurse, loopy with morphine and not thinking at all about what kind of chef could find work without a functioning nose.

For once I was not the only one who could not sleep. One reason was the dead body of a well-liked Marine named Morgan. He was spread-eagle atop an embankment of barbed wire in full view of our line. It killed the men to see it. By the time binoculars revealed that crows were pecking at Morgan's eyes, the Skipper had had enough. He directed three men to crawl out there and cut Morgan down. But Jerry was waiting and our would-be rescuers were driven back. Men in the trench became edgier. Racial epithets were spewed and hung in ugly clouds. Chaos was close.

Fllllppppp.

It was the sound of cards being shuffled. We looked to find that Church had pulled out a sweaty leather billfold and was sifting through the enclosed photographs. He collated a small selection, elbowed our unit's collective little brother, Jason Stavros, and handed over the pictures.

"Lillian Eve Johnson. Lilly. Nineteen. Hair like silk. Clever as a fox. She's in Iowa, waiting for me."

Jason Stavros handled the photos as if they were ancient scrolls. In a solemn whisper, he read aloud the notes penciled on the back of each one.

"Lilly at beach. Lilly on pier. Lilly at church picnic. Lilly in car."

Church sighed. "She does take many a fine photo."

"Exquisite," said Jason Stavros. "Look at those lips. Those delicate rosebuds."

"Easy does it, boy-o." Piano's face clenched, unclenched. "That's a man's woman you're talking about."

Church waved off the warning. "The kid's right. Lilly's lips are as red as the day is long. Soft as the night is black."

The Prof affected the posture of a lovelorn matinee idol. Church grinned.

"We'll be married when I get back," said he. "The *day* I get back."

"Perhaps the day after," said the Prof. "You might be a little busy that first night."

The men chuckled—a startling but melodious sound.

"Hey, I've got one too." Jason Stavros rifled about his pack until he brandished that beloved volume of Shelley. A single photograph served as the bookmark. He plucked it out and passed it to the man on his left. "Her name's Cassandra. She's sixteen and perfect."

"She's waiting for you, too, I suppose?" asked Piano.

"Well, she's wearing my ring! It's just a class ring, but that's got to mean something, doesn't it?" He smiled, for a moment lifted away from this cesspool. "*Cassandra Stavros*. Gee, doesn't that sound grand? Doesn't it, guys?"

Church wrapped an elbow around the boy's neck.

"Sure it does, kiddo. Match made in heaven, by the sound of it."

The photos were passed around until I found myself in possession of the lot. Zebulon Finch might have commanded little esteem in that hole, but who there had more experience evaluating a female's merits? I gave Lillian Eve Johnson and the maybe-future Cassandra Stavros careful consideration—in other words, I undressed them, piece by piece. Well! Neither were the sort to launch ships! I began to pass the pictures when something caught me in the twist of Lilly's lips. There *was* a slyness there; she might, after all, be a hellcat beneath the sheets. And Cassandra, though plain in face, *did* have favorable measurements—and by gum, was she ever pleased with them!

Ladies, oh ladies fair, your boys are here, waiting in the dirt!

The arrival of a tin pitcher interrupted my latest round of anguish regarding my nonfunctional sex organs. A yawning corporal explained that the poison gas had tainted our water, so here was some rum, courtesy of a French runner. The boys of the Third were struck dumb by this fantastic stroke of luck. They fumbled for their metal mugs.

Church, as always, abstained; even so, the bounty amounted to but a half-cup per man, hardly enough to get one drunk. Yet, like Mr. Christ and his fabled fish and chips, the boys willed it into being enough, and as the tales of girls back home grew in number and overall raunch, the men took hold of one another and sang limerick odes to easy women and wiped away so many tears that their cheeks became pinstripes of dirt and salt. They *were* drunk; drunk on death, perhaps, but drunk all the same.

"Your turn, Prefer-Not-To! Come on, show us what you got!"

Every wearied but hopeful eye glimmered. Except Church's; he, friend to all, still refused to acknowledge me.

"I am sorry," said I. "But I have nothing."

"Everyone else shared," snapped Piano. "That's not fair."

Jason Stavros took a gentler tack. "They don't let you get on the boat without a picture of a pretty girl. A magazine picture. A pin-up. *Something.*"

Emotions were fragile. One face crumpled into disgruntlement, then another. These men believed I thought myself too good to join their ribaldry, when nothing of the sort was true! Without other option, I reached into my pocket, past the Excelsior, behind the page of the *Atlanta Constitution*, and withdrew the single photograph I possessed.

Piano snapped his fingers and gestured for it.

I handed it over, sure that he would rip it up, toss the shreds into no man's land.

Instead he shrugged.

"Not bad."

The private to his left hooted. "Not bad? Prefer-No-To, is this your girl?"

How wondrous it sounded. Merle *was* my girl, in a manner of speaking.

"Yes," said I. "Well, she's a friend."

"Yeah?" The private whistled. "I sure wouldn't mind a friend like that!"

Machine-gun fire rattled off. The Marines hurled themselves to the mud of the eastern wall, slapping on helmets and clutching their rifles. I scrabbled about the muck until I found Merle half-buried, her radiance unbothered by the boot prints across her face. I picked her up, wiped her against my coat, and peered over the parapet.

Morgan, the dead Marine, was being shot at by our own sniper.

Hot disbelief quickly gave way to grim understanding. The Skipper was ordering him to shoot the crows off the corpse. The sniper wiped away tears and aimed. One crow burst into feathers but the rest did not react. Horstmeier muttered a new order and subsequent shots were taken at Morgan's arms and legs in hopes that he could be cut down from the wire—anything so that we did not have to look at that damn corpse for a single minute longer.

One thousand eighty seven of us had died that day, and every man left alive was watching when a shot hit Morgan's head and it mushroomed into bone, brain, and blowflies. Would that, wondered I, help us sleep any better?

N O ONE WANTED BURIAL DUTY but an awful lot of us got it.

Slews of bodies were unobtainable, dangling from low-hanging trees or sunk head-first into hardening mud. Hundreds of carcasses, though, had been dragged behind our line on stretchers and were to receive a quick burial. Yet another trench had been dug, a nice long one even narrower than most, and after the removal of identifying badges and papers, our compatriots were laid head to feet while the chaplain did his thing. Men wore gas masks against the odor, yet rushed back and forth into the wheat, the only place where one could vomit in peace.

Team A, which included Mouse, was tasked with picking through the clothing of the dead and, if a body was falling apart, securing it inside a tarp. Mouse, spectacles fogged from the heat of spilled innards, had his right hand shoved up a dead man's ass. *Poor Mouse,* thought I, *he's gone batty!* I was wrong; Mouse's courage was something to behold. He extracted from the rotten bowels a swollen rat still clinging to a tube of intestine. Mouse took the offending animal by the tail and smashed it against a rock, again and again, and then, after it was dead, forty or fifty times more. This tender scene was scored by cornet; the kid who did our morning reveilles stood at the end of the trench playing "Taps," his cheeks washed clean with tears.

Team B carried the bodies to the trench and stacked them with as much dignity as possible. These were two-man teams, one fellow at the shoulders (when there were shoulders) and one at the feet (when there were feet). Major Horstmeier approached and, because we were safely behind the front, I saluted. The bandage on his face had come loose and flapped in the wind.

"Private Prefer-Not-To?"

"Yes, sir!"

"I've got you with—well, shit, that won't work. You're weak as a damn stick, aren't you?"

"I'm afraid so, sir!"

"Let's get you a partner with some meat on his bones. Corporal Churchwell!"

My salute fell several inches.

Church jogged over and snapped off a salute much crisper.

"What can I do for you, Skipper, sir?"

"I'm sticking you with Private Thumb-Up-His-Butt. See if you can teach him how to lift a few pounds. I don't want to hear about one single goddamned dropped body, understand?"

"You got it, sir."

Horstmeier slapped Church on the shoulder and moved along, leaving the two of us in the shadeless sun, alone for the first time since he'd rescued me on the march to Lucy-le-Bocage. I stared at my crusted boots and counted artillery blasts. There had been a time when I'd delighted in staring into the eyes of those who hated me. Dr. Leather, I feared, had chased off that Zebulon Finch for good.

Nevertheless I designed a nice expression of hostility, only to unveil it after Church had taken off for the bodies. I trotted after like a dog, on the way devising a script of biting remarks that I believed might cut even a legend-in-the-making down to size. Smart dialogue, indeed, but it was for naught. I came upon the noble warrior embracing a blubbering young radio operator and assuring him that all this, too, was part of the Game.

Behind him, I scuffed at some dirt-weeds.

"You." Church took a body by the shoulders. "You're on legs."

Weight is concentrated in the upper body; carrying the soldier's lower half required no special physical effort. The ground beneath us, however, was a calamity of throatlike chasms and spiny ridges, and though Church navigated the blasted geography on a backpedal, I was a blundering lumberer, toppling to knee or hip or elbow while still taking care that not a single pinky finger of the dead man grazed the ground.

It slowed our progress, giving Church more time to inhale the stench of decay, more time for his fingers to sink into pulpous flesh, more time for his hatred of me to reach a boil. At last we straddled the wedge-shaped burial trench, Church on the west side, myself on the east. Together we lowered the soldier as far as we could before letting him drop the final two feet. The *whump* of his landing was no different than that of a sack of potatoes.

I was still stooped over the trench when I felt a hand push against the back of my head. My balance pitched. I reached backward to snag the offending hand in hopes of staving off a fall, but it was Church, he'd been the one to do it, and he was too quick for me to grab. I landed atop two corpses. Hard, smooth objects were beneath my hands—exposed bones? Squishy things, too—tongues, eyes? I tried to stand but tangled with a soldier perforated by machine gun, his raw pink flesh studded with embedded black slugs.

Church smirked at me from high above.

"Oops."

Wan faces of other Marines appeared over the edge. They'd been trained since Quantico to follow Church's lead and on cue they showed me their best disdain. An oppressive wave of self-hatred sealed me to the trench-mud. Go on! Abhor me! Condemn me! Where else does a fiendish divergent like myself belong if not this grisly abyss?

Ah, but do not fill the hole with dirt just yet—for what is this? Zebulon Finch is climbing! Up the west wall, no less, and when Church prods at him with a boot, it is knocked aside with a fist. This is interesting, no? Look how our young renegade, drenched though he is in gore, closes in on his larger antagonist, how he bumps his fair chest into that much broader wall of muscle. Dr. Leather hadn't drained all of Finch's verve, not quite.

"Upset, are you?" taunted I. "That your lemon drops have limited influence?"

"Say what?"

"That these men died and there wasn't a thing even the great Corporal Churchwell could do about it."

Here they came now, the sycophants, the toadies, the bootlickers, encircling us to protect their daredevil demigod. Church, of course, raised a hand to halt them. No one need fight his battles. From my side vision I saw the Skipper at the rear of the pack, arms crossed, letting this conflict play out.

Church poked me with a finger as hard as a 7mm bullet.

"You listen here, Private. No one loved these men like I did. *No one.*"

"Then what is it? Do I pose a threat to your little common-wealth?"

"I'll be burying thirty more of my men tomorrow because of the likes of you."

"If you wish to perform an act, Corporal, I do wish that you would get on with it. Childish games waste the valuable time of these men you profess to love, and quite frankly they grate upon my last nerve."

"You're going to question how *I* protect my men? What do *you* do for them, Private? Is the rumor true? Did you let a Kraut go when you had him right in your sights?"

My mouth, somersaulting along a fun, familiar roll, found itself wide open before the specifics of the accusation reached my brain. I faltered and the hesitation was damning.

"How about that other rumor, while we're at it. That you spent the afternoon playing possum in a crater. While these men in this hole right here got their guts ripped out. Is *that* one true, Private? Because if it is, I think it's something the rest of us deserve to know."

The mood blackened. Church's apostles edged closer with confused, infuriated expressions. I understood; I wished myself back into the catacumbal pit. It was by rare good fortune that these encroaching revengers began to be shoved aside. It was Major Horstmeier, having spent enough time watching the fester of this boil and in the mood to lance it.

"All right, soldiers, that's more than enough of this shit. How about we all have a little respect for the dead? You got beefs, you deal with them on leave, not on duty. That understood, Churchwell? That nice and clear, Finch?"

"Yes, sir," growled Church.

"Yes, sir," growled I.

"Then quit eyeballing each other. These bodies won't bury themselves."

The Skipper aimed his fanatical eyes at a dozen or so individual troopers, each of whom led the retreat back toward the objectionable obligations of Teams A and B. Church gave me a frosty look before stomping back to our designated stack of stiffs. I exhaled, a long-held habit from being human. My cowardice being voiced aloud was bad enough. But a public disavowal by Church? That was the kind of thing that might turn a grunt's life into a living hell.

X.

O N THE FIRST DAY OF a renewed four-day Allied assault, shortly after machine guns repelled our 0430 northward push, around the time that pesky mustard gas once again came creeping, the Gods of War reached down and handed me a way out, not just out of Belleau Wood, but out of the whole cockamamie mess of life itself.

The Huns that morning owned the sky. Floating observational "sausages" had enjoyed a bird's-eye view of our maneuvering while taking ne'er a single hit, while Fokker planes shepherded the German artillery with ease. A sequence of dreaded *minenwerfers* (that's "mine-throwers," Reader; do keep pace with my jargon) were landing with terrific accuracy about my frontline foxhole. Americans to my left and right had been blown right out of their pits; even more astonishing was the number of them who rose back up, shooting.

Then, with no warning, the bawling, bellowing, banging, bursting world went silent. A great pressure quashed my chest and a black wall of dirt came rushing at me. My position had been hit—at last, a direct hit!—and not by the wee 77mm mortars we called "whizzbangs," nor the 88mm "quick dicks," nor even the 150mm "Jack Johnsons." This was a 210mm "sea bag," the big, dumb brute of German weaponry, and for a split second I was suspended in a sensory vacuum, a lovely, peaceful place to be, all things considered.

Then: entombment. The weight of a horse upon my back—no, Leather's Pierce-Racine touring car—no, one of those Renault tanks the colonel had promised and never delivered. Not a dot of light cheapened the solidity of my burial within trench mud. Transferred through the packed soil were the startled grunts of men throttled of their last breath. Also, at a higher pitch, rats—viler animals but no less panicked.

The cool, damp tonnage was not unpleasurable. I tried to relax. From so far beneath dirt, war sounded like a kindergarten playtime: a full brigade's charge became a delicate pitter-pat, the boom of howitzers became no louder than a pop-gun's cork. Yes, it was time to rest, old boy, and to let the children play. Down here, I was no longer Private Prefer-Not-To but instead a stack of buried bones as meritorious as any Church and I had laid to rest.

My thoughts drifted first to Wilma Sue. If there was a Heaven, I would not be seeing her anytime soon, though perhaps Hell, located just down the block, was near enough that she might hear me when I screamed her name. I thought, too, of Abigail Finch. If word reached her that her boy, Zebulon, had been lost at Belleau Wood, would she feel pride? Would she feel regret? Or would she think only that my French lessons had paid off?

The long-promised solace of my demise was impeded by memories of those who'd shown me the kindness that Abigail had not. What if it were Johnny here fighting for his country? Why, he'd tape his cane to his wrist and learn to shoot one-handed. And what of Mrs. Joseph Thomas Hazard, daughter Susannah, and the rest of those screwy broads at Sweetgum; what would they say about my decision to lie fallow amid the loam? They relived the Civil War each night due to a belief that some ideals were worth the fight.

My brain, that inexplicable organ that had bedeviled Leather, now bedeviled me. This, I knew, was a coward's way to expire. For the sake of those who'd given me solace, I had to do better.

My gray fist rose from the mud.

The soldiers of Belleau Wood are long dead. Scores died during the three-week battle, scores more died in the subsequent months of war, and the survivors kicked the bucket in humdrum ways over subsequent decades. But I wonder if there isn't one timeworn old soul still out there, slurping down creamed corn in a nursing home rec room, haunted by visions of war, none more jarring than the time a U.S. Marine buried for over half an hour clawed from the earth like a goblin, black water draining from his mouth and ears, blobs of clay plopping from his eye sockets. This man-thing rose from the depths as if he were the golem of a million dead men, still clutching the rifle they'd handed him in Hell—and what was it that he did?

He charged the line.

The horizon tilted before me like an ocean seen from a ship's bow. The forest looked melted, leaves sizzling down in stalactites of ash, black bark peeled from pale trees like burned-off skin. Fire was everywhere except for the camouflaged boulders and gullies where Jerry hid. The Germans had painted their skin with soot, and their guns too, to prevent glare, and the disguises worked well.

So did mine.

Wherever I ran I looked like just another splash of mud. I bolted right past a unit of four infantrymen swearing in German as they tried to repair their jammed Maxim. They wore respiratory gear and only then did I notice the stench of mustard gas. I kept going; straight ahead there was a clearing, the familiar din of men shrilling through pandemonium, and a plume of flame taller than the trees.

350

Ten stories of dirt hung in the air as wide as a great brown elm, tossed up by an underground mine. I was transfixed until flamethrower fire tore across the trampled wheat, flinging me to smoldering grass. I rolled sideways and came to my knees. Black smoke billowed down from the crackling blaze, but not enough to obscure the green dye staining the air. By bad luck of wind, the gas sat stagnant over our position. To my left I saw a soldier fumbling to affix his gas mask, fretting along the edge of the imperfect seal. Out of habit I lifted my own mask from where it dangled upon my chest and I tightened it to my skull. The sound of my breathing filled the mask—no, I had no breath—then what . . . ?

(((*Hweeeeee . . . fweeeeee . . . hweeeeee . . . fweeeeee . . .*)))

Forever he was there, a sadistic father deriding my every decision!

I lifted a hand to rip off the mask but hesitated, for such an act would reveal me. I looked to my right, hoping for a ravine into which I could delve, but the forest was flat and crawling with injured Americans. Two retreated on their elbows due to the horrible machine-gun strafing of their shins. One sat with his back against a tree, his gas-blistered fists balled over his bleeding eyes. Yet another lay motionless upon his back, choosing to watch the swirls of gas and fire above rather than consider the wet, purple hole in his stomach.

It was a massacre.

What luck I had blundered right into it.

Machine-gun fire poured from the enemy trench like jets of water. Go ahead, Fritz! Shoot me, I dare you! I leapt to my feet and legged southward toward downed doughboys while opening fire with my inhumanly steady hands; helmeted Krauts ducked one after another like tots at a nursery game. Ten feet I ran, ever closer to the fallen. Finally, a German with a spine took aim and a bullet struck me in the right side. I staggered. But did I fall?

Hell, no, sir, I did not fall!

A flamethrower's inferno mushroomed into my path, a second too early to envelop me. When I dove through its shimmering vapor, I felt the edges of my hair frizzle and the skin of my left shoulder shrivel. In a living man, the burns would be unbearable. But did I falter?

Hell, no, sir, I did not falter!

Here, at last, was a GI squatting in the mud, barely older than I, the red blotches of his infected skin beginning to suppurate into yellow blisters. I dropped into the crater and crawled on my belly while Kraut fire tore the trees limbs above, pelting us with daggers of wood. The GI fumbled at his mask with his teeth and feet, a ridiculous stunt.

My judgment, I admit, was rushed. His attempts were valiant, actually, seeing how his hands had been reduced to fingerless nubs. I grabbed his mask, tightened the straps, but before pushing it onto his face noticed the green condensation streaking down the glass. Mustard gas—I hurled the mask toward the German line, a tiny poison bomb, and a machine gun shot it to pieces midair. Oh, to hell with it! I whipped off my own mask and tightened it around the GI's face. Life was so much improved without that Isolator wheeze!

"Can you walk?" shouted I.

He shook his head. A yellow blister on his nose burst.

I slung my rifle over my back, looped one arm beneath the boy's shoulders, and with the other lifted his knees. In the same motion I snatched up my .45. I mounted the hill in full view of the Germans and let loose with a war scream, burial dirt tumbling from my mouth and firing the .45 with an accuracy Pullman Larry would have coveted. Huns dove for cover.

A full round is what it took for me to achieve total astonishment. I was carrying the soldier with no more difficulty than Church had once carried me. Somewhere beneath the dirt—or when choosing to rise from it—I'd rediscovered the strength that had deserted me after death. Could it be because the task in which I was involved was, for once, a virtuous one?

It was a moment ill-suited for reflection. Still roaring, I crashed through the woods until I spied a group of masked Marines holding a position behind a bastion of sandbags. I heard one of them shout, "*Covering fire!*," followed by the chunky rattle of just that. Beneath their bullets I slid around the bags and let them catch the injured boy. The soldiers stared at me in disbelief; even the medic paused in shock before taking a look at the GI.

I holstered my .45, brought down my Chauchat, reloaded, and began to scale the sandbags. A hand gripped me. It belonged to an incredulous private. His voice was muted behind his respirator.

"You can't go back out there!"

"Let go of me," said I.

"You need a mask! It'll burn you alive!"

I grinned; I could not help it. *This* was why I had been brought to this ruined hunting preserve in northern France. Thank you, Death, for burying me deep enough so that I might remember.

"Then burn I shall," said I.

Jerry won my respect. He shot right at me, unlike the coward who'd assassinated me in 1896. But no combination of Central Powers could match me that day. Bring on the Germans, the Austrians, the Bulgarians, the Turks! I'd take on all of them with this single French lead-hucker despised for its lousy calibration. With it I ripped rifles from the hands of snipers, shot grenades while they still hung the air. My first trip back across the field of fire cost me some machine-gunning of my left calf, but I brought to the medic an officer with a bayonet blade in his neck. My next trip involved taking a slug to my left hip and wading through a thick new stew of gas, but I came back with a legless private tucked beneath an arm.

On and on it went. Impervious to bullets, able to play dead to perfection and then dart forward like a rabbit, unaffected by the sounds or tremors that had normal soldiers pissing their pants, I saved those men with the riskiest jobs of all: the chaplains, the stretcher-bearers, the runners. Had I a free hand, I'd collect firearms along the way. Yes, yes, bits of flesh were blown from my body, but hell, Reader, I'd suffered worse.

A dozen rescues later, the soldiers of the sandbag citadel fell upon me and swore that they'd recommended me for the Croix de Guerre and Silver Star, even a Medal of Honor, provided I halt my demented redemption. The rest of my long existence would have been different had I listened. But the deafening peals of back-and-forth bombardments were pierced by a cry of pain close to the German line, a voice that each of us recognized, though never had we imagined it could sound anything less than unshakable and unafraid.

Church.

XI.

WHAT A SOUND. IT BLED resolve from every American who heard it. Reader, I petition your patience. I bolted from the arms of my friendly detainers, vaulted o'er the sandbags, and charged one last time into the crossfire. I veered rightward of a spattering patch of bulleted clay and lunged against a berm of earth tilled by gunfire, behind which I might deduce Church's position.

I was not the only soldier to claim the spot. A GI was crouched there, running a thumb over the pin of his grenade. It made me a tad nervous, so I crawled ten feet northward until the diminishing hill forced me to my stomach. There I stopped and listened. Nothing. Nothing, nothing. Nothing, nothing, nothing—wait, yes, there! You couldn't call it a sob, not from Burt Churchwell you couldn't, but the hiccup of pain was unmistakable. He was alive, and close, but in a direction that was, shall we say, inconvenient.

I took my helmet in my hand and nudged it above the hill.

Sniper fire—*zing!* 'Twas shot right out of my hand.

I contemplated this event for a moment, then looked to the man fondling the grenade.

"You! Private!"

Languidly he turned his head.

"Sergeant," clarified he.

I gestured my apology to his chevrons.

"I wonder, Sergeant, sir, would you mind terribly throwing that egg?"

He regarded it, stroked it.

"It's the only one I got," mused he.

"Oh, they're bringing more, sir, wagons of them," lied I. "Throw it due west, twenty yards, at my say-so. Go left of that and you'll blow up a corporal. Go short and you'll blow up me. Got it? Sir, I mean?"

He pondered the request long enough for Church to hiccup again.

At last the sergeant sighed.

"No one here lets you keep anything. Fine, I'll throw it."

I drew myself into a squat and pressed my Chauchat to my chest. Why wait?

"Now, Sergeant! Throw it now!"

His arm reared back in a perfect arc and I bounced to my feet, filling the forest with bullets. The grenade whizzed past me as I ran, and behind bee-swarms of enemy fire I saw it drop. A sergeant indeed!—'twas a bull's-eye right at the edge of the German trench. I veered, emptying my clip, until I saw a man in U.S. fatigues hunkered behind a boulder. The surroundings were littered with unidentifiable body parts, random cuts of meat in beige casings.

I collapsed myself alongside the one living body.

A bayonet blade came jabbing at my face. I batted it away with my own.

"It's me! American! Marine!"

Church moaned through a gas mask caked with dirt.

"Private Prefer-Not-To? *You?*"

Bullets cracked off the edge of the boulder. I pressed a finger to his lips. He was whole as far as I could tell. Then his leg spasmed with pain and I saw a foot-long strip of fatty skin lying in the dirt like a dead snake. It had been carved from the back of his right calf by a piece of shell shrapnel that lay black and smoking in the weeds. The exposed muscle, as if in shock, barely bled. A mortal wound it was not, yet walking out of here in full view of the Germans might be impossible.

I unlatched my full canteen, pulled the mask from his face, and poured the water at his mouth. He gulped, coughed, and spewed before replacing his mask. I looked for somewhere to set the canteen and, finding no better option, hung it by its strap on a severed arm wedged into the boulder. Yes, I know—not my finest moment.

"Dirty Squareheads tricked me," rasped Church. "Guy was yelling 'medic' in perfect English. Bunch of us gyrenes came in for evac and *boom*." He punched the ground with a fist. "*One* dang Squarehead. With *one* dang submachine gun. Then they started shelling."

"Submachiner? Where?"

"Dead." He jerked his chin at a half-empty bag of grenades. "I been tossing these every couple minutes. Won't last, and I'm throwing blind. Out of ammo, too. Got this bayonet, though, so I might take one or two with me." He grabbed my collar. "Hey, Prefer-Not-To. Do something right for a change. Tell Lilly Eve Johnson from Dubuque, Iowa, I loved her to pieces. Right up till the end I loved her. Will you do that for me?"

"I most certainly will not. We're going to get you—"

"Then go on, crawl your yellow belly out of here! I gotta be ready when they come."

He angled his bayonet against the boulder, the perfect position should a German face pop over the crest. With his free hand he reached into his pouch, extracted a lemon drop, lifted aside his mask, and placed the candy into his mouth.

No soldier, alive or dead, knew the significance of this action better than I. I hurled myself on top of him and pinned down his arms with my rifle. He made fists and tried to raise them but I had the advantage of not just surprise but my returned strength. I pushed aside his mask, dug my fingers into his cheek, forced open his lower jaw, reached inside his mouth, and Reader, call me crazy if you wish, but I dug that yellow son of a bitch out of there and tossed it into the grass.

"You are not going to die, Corporal. You are going to listen to what I say and—"

"Get off me, you coward—"

"You say you love your Marines? If you lie here and die, it is going to kill them. The Third Battalion will fall. The whole Seventh might not hold. So I must insist that you try. Not for me, for I give far less than one damn, but for them, the leathernecks. Your boys."

Church's bloody teeth ground and his big left arm, seaworthy as ever, slipped out from under my rifle and took my neck so hard that two of his fingers sunk into my grappling-hook wound. He pulled until my forehead knocked against his own.

"Call the play, then, Prefer-Not-To. Let's finish out the Game."

He secured his mask and then, ever so gingerly, we arranged our bodies into low squats. A hundred rubies of blood gathered on Church's exposed leg muscle, each one matched by a pearl of sweat upon his face. I reloaded and wrapped an arm around his back, the same way he'd supported me on our first march. I nodded at the grenadier bag.

"I need you to throw a couple of those and then we'll—"

"I'm not some tenderfoot, Private. I know the routine."

He tossed aside his useless rifle and took up the bag. Four grenades remained.

Four measly grenades, one piece-of-shit French rifle, and two hobbling Marines against a full trench of furious Huns. Then, just to top it off, mad orders from a crazed commander:

(((*Run away on tricycle or battleship, but dissection awaits you everywhere.*)))

(((*Here, let me open you with knife, so much more exacting than bullet.*)))

(((*And look! Your invitation to the People Garden, it has at last arrived!*)))

Of course this malevolent mentor impugned me; upon his laugh-rollicked tray he arranged not his favorite kit of scalpels and sutures but rather syringes of toxic doubt, bonesaws of intimidation, chisels of misgivings. I was but a boy playing at being a man. Success of any kind was beyond my reach.

"Counting backward!" shouted Church. "Three—two—one!"

He pulled the pin of a grenade, whether or not I was ready, and hurled the pineapple with the speed and accuracy of a bow-shot arrow. Before it buried itself into German mud, he'd pulled the pin on the next, changed his target, and thrown another blistering fastball.

Mud and men exploded from the trench; Dr. Leather and his paraphernalia of paralysis were simultaneously blown away. I moved, dragging Church's weight behind our cover of black smoke and into the trample of wheat. An outcrop of stone rose fifty feet away, though it might have well been a mile. From the edge of my vision I saw the redirecting muzzles of Jerry's guns, yet rather than falter I thought again of the Hazard sisters. Perhaps one day they'd replay this battle, hatch a better plan, map for me a superior path. In the meantime? This was the way Zebulon Finch wanted to go out.

I opened fire with my Chauchat, but with only one arm to steady the gun the shots did little more than distract. Church, however, planted his injured leg, cried out in pain, and hurled a perfect spiral into the face of a machine-gunner. Then he was pushing off again and so was I, loping along in artless concert as bullets carved visible paths through the tall grass. Our grenade exploded and German helmets, some with heads strapped in, rocketed from the trench. Church's bellow was automatic.

"MERRY CHRISTMAS! MERRY CHRISTMAS!"

We had halved the distance to the outcropping when we heard the *whizz* that preceded the explosion of a whizz-bang. On instinct we threw ourselves to the dirt. When the *bang* came it scooped a gorge in the field, the charred ground belching a truckload of virgin dirt that then fell heavy as cadavers. My Chauchat was torn from my hands and I revoked every bad word I'd said about that Frog hunk of junk—I wanted it back!

I whipped out my .45 and began popping off rounds, a waste of ammo, though the dirt cloud hid us long enough for me to drag Church back to his feet. We stumbled through the freshly carved ravine and up over the side, then dashed for the outcropping while four or five Huns rushed along their trench to match us step for step.

Church threw the last grenade sidearm, a movement of inexpressible grace, and it cut across the wheat with just enough backspin to make it over the lip of the trench and into the laps of our pursuers. Instead of shots fired there was a German babble of panic, followed by detonation and screams—and then our outcropping was right there! A steep bank of stone promised to slow us, so I took Church in a bear hug and with all of my might flung him to safety. He landed on his back, screaming through his gas mask, clutching his raw, open calf.

He made quite a bit of noise. So much so that I did not hear the *whizz*. Church did.

"Down, Private, down!"

In many respects I was fortunate. The shell was not a direct hit. The field behind me surged upward as if it were an ocean wave. Moist clay bestrewed Church's appalled face before I felt a mallet blow to my right leg. I teetered, then looked down to see a snarled wad of shrapnel stabbed into the dirt, pinning beneath it a hunk of bloodless gray meat. Feeling only a dull disturbance, I decided to take a closer look at my legs.

My left leg was fine, but a hole the size of a baseball had been punched through my right thigh; I could see through it to the scorched grass beneath. With no muscle to support it, the flesh walls began to crumple. I pitched forward, right into Church's arms. He wrapped me tight and yanked me behind the rock, shouting self-evident silliness.

"You're hit! Aw, Private, you're hit bad!"

I propped myself against the rock. It was a fine enough spot to sit until they approximated our new location and launched another mortar.

"Stop moving, Private! Medic! *Medic!*"

One could excuse his agitation. Mine was, without doubt, a killing blow. Major arteries had been more than severed; they'd been blown out entirely. Even were there a doctor close by armed with tourniquet, he would not bother, for there was not a man alive who would not bleed out in thirty seconds. Church knew this and yet, despite his pain, despite the knock-knock of Death upon his own chamber door, he dug out a lemon drop and offered it as distraction from what he believed must be unimaginable agony.

"Save it," said I.

The forest floor was blanketed with dry wheat and sloppy mud. I gathered both by the handful and began to stuff them into my thigh cavity. Behind the window of his gas mask, Church's eyes widened. Once the thigh was full enough to support weight, I gave Church a polite nod.

"Your belt, please?"

He asked no questions. In seconds he had it unbuckled, wrapped twice around my thigh, pulled tight, and knotted. While I tested my reconstructed leg against an embedded rock, Church fought against twenty-two years of rational convictions, even, perhaps, against the abrupt and irrecoverable loss of Gød. I did not have the time required to feel bad about any of it. For now, we had to move, and fast, before the Huns, those angry wasps, sunk their stingers.

"Grab onto me," said I. "I shall do the crawling."

He pointed at my face in expanding wonder.

"You're not even wearing a mask. How . . . ?"

I held out my .45.

"Can you shoot? I need you to do so, Corporal, and with precision."

Though the mask hid much of his face, I could see enough to follow the cycle of his abhorrence, repudiation, and denial. But was this not war? Did not each new day shine its torch upon some rare abomination? Resolution diamoned Church's eyes and then his body.

He snatched the .45 from me, popped the rod, thumbed the cylinder, and counted the remaining bullets. With practiced flash, he whipped shut the mechanism and yanked the hammer.

His teeth were blood-splattered, mud-spattered, but still, when he flaunted them, objects of American splendor.

"Can I shoot? Heck, Private. I was born to shoot."

XII.

CHURCH WAS CARTED AWAY, ALONG with scores of others, to a med station set up inside a barn near Marigny. That night, I emptied the wilting straw from my thigh, improvised sticks as replacements for the missing bone, packed the hollow with clay, and tied it with bandages.

With Church left the regiment's capability for transcendence. That does not mean the boys did not fight well. Through morning mist, we captured two-thirds of the Wood on June 11. The whispered word was that the Marines were holding at a seventy-percent casualty rate. The Skipper requested reinforcements; it did not happen. The next day at 1730 hours we launched an offensive in hopes of breaking through into the northern third of the Wood; that, too, did not happen. The lines of fire clotted, the paths of attack coagulated. The rough arithmetic was one inch gained per life lost.

On the night of June 15 our runners brought the overdue word that we were to be relieved in the morning. Such news would have ushered in celebration if not for Mouse. He was lost somewhere in no man's land, laughing out beneath the stars. The sound was so unexpected from Mouse that a few of us chuckled, too. Hours later we figured out that he was dying, his lungs shot up so that his screams came out like giggles. By then it was too late. Jerry lit the skies with magnesium, making rescue impossible. Mouse, the quiet one, was not quiet near the end. He damned soldiers by name, mine included, for not coming to save him, damned the whole regiment, the whole military, the whole war, the whole world.

Our march to bivouac grounds was a glum one indeed. What few of us were left humped across the same gutted landscape we'd come in on and tipped our helmets to the same dead farm animals. They were in worse condition this time, but then again, so were we.

We made camp at dawn, a miraculous sight: clean gray tents, a pond for bathing, warm chow for the eating, tables for card playing, men who still dove at the whistle of distant bombs, and their good buddies who pretended not to notice. The Skipper left us at ease near a sentry tower, returning a few minutes later with a surprise.

With his crisp laundered uniform and easy grin, Burt Churchwell was ready to model for enlistment posters. That calf wound of his had been a "blighty," an injury serious enough to put him on the next westward boat. Church, though, not only walked upon the leg but swaggered. A shocked silence prevailed until someone let out an *EEE-YAH-YIP!* and the battalion, maudlin since Mouse's death, erupted. Church was swarmed. There came a percussion performance of back slapping and all the best expletives. The Prof hoisted two bottles of French wine. Where had he acquired them? Who cared! The starstruck scene, thought I, had to remind our guest of honor of his days leading home-coming parades as a Grinnell College Pioneer.

Celebration made it a challenge, but his eyes found mine. He was of meat-and-potatoes Iowa stock and it clearly bothered him to accept so much adulation while I, his deliverer, stood friendless to the rear. But I understood that this was the necessary order. Were these boys to survive, they needed a leader, and that leader's shine could not be smudged.

I left them to their rejoicing and wandered the camp. Everywhere I saw men trying to recall ordinary behavior. I saw them sit for haircuts and wince at each *snick* of the scissors—Jerry crawling through the wheat with his bayonet. I saw them sunbathe, donning sunglasses as if that might help shield them from the clanking of artillery shells being unloaded, the moans of despair from the medical tent, and, worst of all, the hyperventilations of troops fresh off the boat. How prematurely we'd become the grizzled vets.

Only Piano rejected the chance for R&R. He usurped a corner of the camp and paced it until dust clouds rose, his left cheek clenching as if from invisible jabs. Every five or ten minutes he dropped to the grass, unrolled his tube of maps, removed his colored pencils, and added clarifying granularities. War had stripped most soldiers of their patience, and to preserve sanity they repeatedly ejected Piano from earshot, often by force. At last the Irishman spoiled the isolated nook I'd claimed.

"...arseholes be *lost* without me maps...those woods are bleedin' *thick*...they gonna *die* out there if they don't *listen*..."

The blather needled me the same as any other. I gathered my gear and walked away. Evening had arrived and guys everywhere were burping compliments to the best corn willy they'd tasted in weeks. They waddled about, overfed and dazed, dousing firepits so that German biplanes could not isolate our location at night. In fifteen minutes it was as black as a trench but for the million or so glowing cigarettes flitting about like fireflies.

"Finch."

I was strolling between dual rows of tents. Against better judgment, I ducked down and parted the flap of one of them.

Church sat alone, his back straight, his legs crossed like an

Indian. Before him lay a collection of French pin-up girl postcards and a perspiring bottle of Coca-Cola, though both had the feel of untouched props. He was shirtless except for his bandolier and his guns were arranged close for quick access. His face was difficult to read. He pointed at the space in front of him.

"Sit," said he.

"Nice of you to offer. But I think I shall—"

"*Sit.*"

The tent flap swept shut behind me.

Church positioned a piece of beef jerky between his teeth and watched my right thigh as I manipulated it into a sitting position. The jerky was tough and he wrenched his head side to side to bite off a hunk.

"I've seen you give Piano your rations. My thinking was always, well, he's a bully, you're a chicken. I didn't think any more of it."

"Thank you."

"Why are you thanking me? I haven't done anything for you. Not a darn thing." He flung the rest of his jerky into the tent wall. "I've been sitting here five days now and it's like there's a grenade in my brain with the pin pulled. Listen—will you just listen? You saved my life and I can't go on like it didn't happen."

"Rest assured it was not personal."

"Here's the problem. I can't just go to the Skipper and have him write you a commendation. Because I've got a hunch you wouldn't want me to. He'd find out about your—you know. Your leg. What you *are*. Not that I know myself, because I don't, but I sure as heck know you're not normal."

"Who's normal?"

Church barked once in laughter.

367

"That's true. Out here they blast the normal right out of you." His smile withered and he peered at me with raw curiosity. "Why in the world are you here? Someone like you?"

Call it battle fatigue, call it a hunger for the sort of conversation I'd not shared in twenty years, but in that tent I found myself willing to release the burden of my secret.

"It seemed a fine place to die," said I.

"Huh. Golly. I don't really know what to make of that."

"Why are you here, Corporal?"

"Me? Fact is, I read a story in a magazine: 'A Soldier's Glory.' All full of pomp and circumstance. Got me riled up, I guess. But now I'm thinking different. Maybe what it did was make a sucker out of me."

"If anyone is supposed to be here, it is you."

"See, that's the thing." He tapped his chest. "I'm still here because of you, Finch. You and me, we're connected. I owe you. My folks owe you. Lillian Eve Johnson owes you. We Churchwells, we pay our debts."

It did not escape my notice that he was at last using my real name. This moved me more than I would have guessed, but it did not mean I would drop my guard. One need only peruse recent history to find that affiliation with me was hazardous.

"There is nothing from you that I want," said I.

"C'mon, fella. You've got nothing to hide from me. Tell me how you got this way. I've never begged for nothing my whole life and I'm begging you now."

Dickens had it right: this dream of life was an undigested bit of beef, a fragment of underdone potato, more gravy than grave. Me, fighting for a country instead of for myself? Me, happy to be inside of a cramped tent beside an armed man? Me, in *France*? The pure farce of it dictated that it mattered not a pinch what I told to whom. So I began with the Black Hand escapades from before Church's birth and then toured him through such popular destinations as Dr. Whistler's Pageant of Health, a bona fide secret lab, and a plantation full of southern-fried whangdoodles.

It was a fable without a discernible moral, and at its completion Church swallowed hard, as if General Pershing had informed him that the moon was made of stinky green cheese and he'd just have to accept it. Church chose to believe, I think, because believing was, for him, the easier path. Now he could go about reimbursing what he felt was owed.

"If you're . . . dead, like you say . . . what would put you at peace?"

It struck me as a penetrating opening question.

"I used to believe it would be revenge against he who killed me. What else but revenge can drive one for so long?"

"But you said you came here to die."

"The trail went cold. All things, to me, grow cold."

"Maybe there are better things to live for."

I thought of Merle, out there somewhere, still wilding.

"Perhaps," said I.

"I got another question. This *la si . . . len . . . sio . . .*"

"*La silenziosità.*"

"Right. It lets people see their own death?"

"It is more akin to *feeling* their own death. The state of their soul at the end should they not alter their path." I shrugged. "Or so I believe."

Church slapped his bandolier. "Do it to me. I'm ready."

I gave my head a mild shake. "I will not. It saps all energy and willpower."

"For you? Or for me?"

"Both. *La silenziosità* is not something to trifle with."

He considered this for a moment.

"All right, another question. How many minutes did you say you were dead?"

This question, on the other hand, struck me as offbeat.

"Seventeen," replied I.

"And how old were you? Are you, I mean."

"Seventeen."

"Merry Christmas, Finch! Don't you think that's a clue?"

"How do you mean?"

"Look, how many people did you hurt with the Muddy Fingers?"

"The Black Hand."

"Right. Make an estimate. Any chance it was seventeen?"

This resourceful young man! I was sad to let him down.

"More. Much more."

"Then how many people have died? From your *actual hand*, Finch. Could that be seventeen?"

"I suppose."

"Well, you ever think that's why you're here? To *save* seventeen lives, to pay back as many as you took?"

Dr. Leather, for all his vials, calipers, and annotated bits of fastidious flesh, had never struck upon an idea so crystalline as had this cornfed corporal. Math: nothing was simpler or more profound. Could my resistance to shooting the young German be linked to a tacit inkling that I remained here on Earth not for murder but for salvation?

In the end, of course, the idea was no more than a rose-tinted fancy. What Church had not calculated into his tempting Theory of 17 were the recent figures that weighed the equation against me: Johnny, Pullman Larry, perhaps by now Mary and Gladys Leather, or even Merle, not to mention the troops who died on June 6 while I cowered in a crater with an unspent rifle.

"Maybe," continued Church, "I'm Life Saved Number One. And if you're, you know, rotting away like you say, then I'd wager there's no time to waste."

"'Tis an attractive notion," said I, "but I should need to save the entire regiment to compensate for all I have taken."

"Heck, is that it?" Church chuckled. "If anyone can do it, it's you."

We were interrupted by a tipsy, red-eyed GI passing word that some musical son of a bitch had himself a gee-tar and a bunch of jackasses were singing songs and it was all sorts of god-danged fun and if we Marine bastards liked fun we ought to do ourselves a favor and get our butts over there. Church shot me a raised eyebrow. Our conversation was hardly finished, but then again, if we were as bound as he claimed, would it ever be? He grabbed his Coca-Cola and crawled toward the door.

"C'mon, Finch, let's see if we can kill Jerry with the worst singing this side of Berlin."

Indeed it was a racket unrivaled. The Army guitarist, a captain, was an able plucker, but the brawling conglomeration of off-tune louts gave the inharmonious Carlo Gesualdo a run for his money. Their cause went unassisted by the snappy pap of wartime rags: "Over There," "Pack All Your Troubles in Your Old Kit Bag," and that counterintuitive classic, "Oh! It's a Lovely War." Reader, it drove me out of my skull until Church slung an affectionate arm around my neck. Every Marine present witnessed the gesture and promptly lost track of the lyrics.

Their faces said everything. This pairing of brash American hero and unpopular ghoul was unnatural and they would not stand for it. I wished to retreat, but Church gripped me more fiercely. Soon enough, the music rediscovered its pace, the intoxicated Marines grew tired of holding mistrustful glares, and Reader—it pangs me even now to say it. Gød help me, I put my arm around Church, my *friend*, whom I resolved to treat better than Johnny if it was the last thing I did, and I lifted my voice until it chased away the final vestiges of Leather's phantasmal scorn, until I sang just as poorly and loudly as Church, as the Professor, as Jason Stavros, as all of those doomed fools.

XIII.

NEVER AGAIN DID THE DOCTOR'S oxygen-smothered voice ring inside my skull. Four days later we were back at war and within the half hour a lieutenant brought the bad word that I was to appear before Major Horstmeier. The sun had not yet shown itself and many a disgruntled grunt grunted as I jostled their dozing bodies on my way through the trenches. I ducked into the officer's hutch, an underground bunker complete with tables, chairs, lamps, bookshelves, radio equipment, a liquor cabinet, and a bowl of goldfish.

I saluted.

The Skipper glanced up from a map on which rested pawns similar to the Hazard sisters' chess pieces. He looked, as usual, as if he'd been eating a two-by-four that did not agree with him.

"Private Prefer-Not-To, it has reached my hairy old ears that on the tenth of June you rescued several of my boys pinned down by machine gun. I find this pretty hard to believe. So I'm asking you man to man: is it true?"

"It's true, sir."

But it was not me who responded. The Skipper and I turned to discover Church standing at the entryway. Four days now he had proved muttlike in devotion, but this was a bolder maneuver. 'Twas a good thing indeed that being Burt Churchwell came with certain privileges; Horstmeier did not bother to chew him out.

"All right, Prefer-Not-To. You've got a pair of legs and a talent for dodging bullets. So happens that's just what I'm in the market for. A couple of runner positions have opened up and I'd like you to consider the job."

"Opened up, sir?"

"One boy got bit in half by a bear trap in the woods, and the other caught fire when his signal flares ignited. Neither got shot in battle, if that makes you feel any better."

"Not really, sir."

"Position's voluntary. Command won't force this on anyone."

"May I have a few days to think about it, sir?"

"A few . . . ? Hell, no, you can't have a few days! We're at war here! I need your answer now!"

Let me summarize all that I knew about being a runner. Better known as "suicide detail," our squad was comprised of six crazy-eyed, punch-drunk renegades who were our best method of communication between Allied positions. It was a primitive age, Reader; common was the use of signal lamps and carrier pigeons. A runner worth his salt, however, could ford smoke, fog, mud, and razor wire to deliver attack orders or casualty reports from captain to captain, to lug food and water to soldiers dying of hunger and thirst. Runners were the veins and vessels that tied units into a single body.

They also got blown up a lot.

"He'll take it, sir," said Church.

"Good," said Horstmeier.

I, of course, opened my mouth, just to, perhaps, get in a word or two regarding this brisk sealing of my fate. But before I spoke I considered Church's Theory of 17, which was not so far-fetched after all, was it? Being a runner might provide me a non-killing role in this

War to End All Wars—a position of appreciable irony, seeing how I'd once gorged upon three square meals of violence a day.

"And I'll take it, too, sir," said Church.

So surprised was the Skipper that he dropped the proper salutation.

"Church, I didn't ask you."

"I accept anyway, sir. You said you were down two runners."

"But your leg."

"Good as new, sir. You saw me march this morning."

Church's grin was more persuasive than a howitzer. The Skipper looked lost before staring back down at his map.

"Report to Captain Rockwell, both of you," muttered he. "Dismissed."

Once we had surfaced amid a peach dawn, Church clapped me where, some years ago, I'd taken two slugs in a duel. He looked giddy. It was the fourth quarter and he wanted the ball.

"You and me, little buddy. The Game begins anew, eh?"

The truth was that whatever sport my friend chose, I was willing to play it. From June 22 to June 26, we did just that, though one would need to untangle the bodies to tally the precise score. French command, slap-happy, reasserted that we were to drive from the forest every last stinking Kraut, and thus the Americans continued to shoot and slash while Church and I sped about, vital messages poised upon our tongues or folded into our pockets.

Other runners—mere humans!—were subject to the sonic confusion of battle. My advantage was a silent, still body; I had space to listen, to gauge each danger, and to proceed in kind. I was a *runner*, and so I *ran*, away from cowardice, from intimidation, from fear. The path I forged on June 24 was my finest; it twisted through smoky ravines, across fetid streams, and beneath fiery barricades all the way from Vaux to Torcy. Dozens of times that day I zigzagged it, saluting each of the three dead GIs who served as my signposts. Their faces, melted off, supplied me with whatever I needed: approval, encouragement, or pardon.

Uniquely adapted though I was, it goes without saying that Church was the finest runner the Marine Corps had ever produced. In late June, soldiers fell in such abundance that two hundred ambulances were called in for evacuation. What minor breakthroughs there were became critical, and most came courtesy of the touchdown speed of the valiant Iowan.

You could feel it, how a single man began to tip the scale in our favor.

We reached the northmost end of the forest on June 26. There, Belleau Wood was officially declared captured at the bargain price of two thousand dead, eight thousand injured, and sixteen hundred captured. As surrendered Germans filed past, I searched for the boy I had spared in battle but did not find him. Most likely he had been killed. Still, he counted toward the Theory of 17, didn't he? Even if his eventual death had been an extended torture involving slugs in his stomach and crows at his face? I tried not to dwell upon it; it was cold calculus indeed.

While men wrote letters home about a victory that would, with alarming speed, be forgotten by history, I toured an emptied German trench. Compared to our slop-holes, it was the Taj Mahal. These charming environs were well-stocked with comfortable seating and small tables on which lay unfinished games of cards and dominoes. I took a seat and toyed with an ivory six/six as well as a treasonous thought: if *Der Vaterland* was anything like this trench, it could not be so bad.

A boot connected with the table and the dominoes sprang into the air like shrapnel. I leapt to a fighting stance before recognizing the leer of Piano. He wiped the remaining dominoes from the table and dropped into the very seat I'd vacated. He was fatter than the rest of us, fed for too long on my extra rations. In one hand, naturally, he clutched a roll of his maps, while with the other he tapped ragged fingernails across the scarred table surface. It was a tetchy sound.

"You get an earful of that wallop a while back? It was one of those pile-o'shite Jerrys who done it. Had a grenade stashed up his arse, threw it right into a tent of officers."

I could have shot him for his glibness.

"How many dead?" asked I.

Piano looked bewildered. His left cheek clenched, unclenched, clenched.

"Who bleedin' cares who and how many. It's the *maps*, Prefer-Not-To. Those chinwagging cans of piss were carrying every last map we had. Now we're walking blind."

"We can acquire more maps."

"Can we really now? From who, the French? Ye thick as a brick, boy-o. You ever laid eyes on a French map? Here, let me show you something."

For the first time in our short military history, there was no superior around to tell us to report for muster, stand guard, et cetera. I sighed to communicate that I would grant him a brief moment, nothing more, and sidled up to the table. Piano, in caricature of a saboteur, shifted his eyes about to verify that we went unobserved before unrolling ten inches of the topmost map.

Could this be what he'd been laboring over for so long? Instead of a legible background of white or pale green, his map was a patchwork of bright reds and yellows and oranges, each delineating a geographic or political feature beyond my understanding. While some iconography, such as rivers, hills, and towns, were recognizable, others

377

were alien: dotted hexagons, slanted crosses, triangular flags, and rainbow-colored bridges that spanned the entire Wood, a fantasyland of easy access. Atop good old Hill 142 was an obelisk with a lidless eye.

I backed away.

Piano's eager smile, in one second, curdled.

"Now don't you be getting ideas, boy-o. Don't you go nattering about this."

Whether he feared theft of his proprietary brilliance or tattling of his madness I did not know.

"Whatever could I say," spoke I, "that would do it justice?"

His frantic hands crumpled the paper, and he rocketed upward, knocking over the table with a knee and jabbing the rolled maps at me like a bayonet.

"Bleedin' hell, I shouldn't have showed you a thing! I knew I couldn't trust you, you daft molly!"

He elbowed me aside and made for the nearest ladder. Halfway up it, he swung to the side and shook his fist.

"I won't be eating *your* rations ever again!"

As threats went, it was a weak one, but still it gave me pause. Piano's body might have emerged from Belleau Wood untouched, but you could not say the same about his mind. My Dearest Reader has no doubt made her or his diagnosis: J.T. "Piano" O'Hannigan, with his crippling anxiety, clockwork diarrhea, facial convulsions, and rampant paranoia, suffered from a paradigmatic case of shell shock and needed to be hospitalized before he hurt someone. Sadly, this was a number of years ago—1918 to be precise—when the most dangerous issue related to this perilous disorder was that very few people believed it to exist.

XIV.

TAKE ONE CORKSCREWED, CLIFFBOUND MEUSE RIVER, add to it an impenetrable, underbrushed Argonne Forest, sprinkle within its ruined ravines a few thousand folk willing to bomb one another to kingdom come, and you have the Meuse-Argonne Offensive, the Great War's final battle. The luck of the Seventh Marine Regiment, Third Battalion—always in, always bad—brought our battered leftovers to the front just as it was getting good.

Over the latter half of 1918 we had contributed to offensives stretching ever northward toward the waffle-sugar air of Belgium, from Soissons to Saint-Mihiel to the Blanc Mont Ridge. Along our way, we waded through stinking rivers of fleeing refugees, picked paths through entire towns of torpedoed châteaus, suffered weeding by snipers through monsoons of rain until the overhead zipping of bullets had us marching with permanent hunches. We lost boots in the mud and were too tired to care, then picked up other boots as we found them, praying each time that they did not contain feet. Never did our objectives become more than arbitrary geographical quirks. Take that crest, that hill, that rail station. We did, dying all the while, if not by lead than by typhoid, diphtheria, dysentery, malaria, measles, smallpox, or influenza. One way or the other, Death found us.

Our boys had arrived at a town called Verdun exhausted past

reason and complaining of high fevers, empty stomachs, and blistered feet. I, meanwhile, felt not a single one of these hardships, and so was quite awake when, at the cockcrow hour, my foxhole position became surrounded. At first it was but a single figure materializing from the fog. I patted around for my rifle. My pledge to not kill anyone did not mean I was unable to deliver a bayonet poke. Then my hand stayed, for it was Church, my friend, the one person in this historic mess I was invariably glad to see.

Before I could raise a hand in greeting, other wracked figures emerged from the brume and fanned out to Church's sides: the Professor, Jason Stavros, the other four runners, a dozen more faces I'd come to know as well as my own. Steam rose from their unsmiling mouths. For the first time, I felt the November chill. These men looked to be a vigilante firing squad hoping to break their curse by sacrificing the company's monster. No, they were too clever for that; they would hang me, something quiet. I held my tongue. I would not beg for mercy.

Church squatted and spoke, voice low so as not to disrupt the fitful sleep of nightmaring soldiers.

"This battle smells bad, Finch. Squareheads been dug in here for years. It's a fortress. Heck, I figure we'll take the Hindenburg Line, but it ain't coming cheap. Guys are going to get shot up, no two ways about it. That's why we're here."

"You wish me to draw their fire. I accept."

"What? No, me and the boys, we talked it out. We don't want you in this hash at all."

"Because of inglorious conduct. You wish me court-martialed. I shan't protest."

"Would you shut up? It's like this. Lots of guys, they take wounds, they get sent home. There's no shame in it. I heard about these three doughboys who mailed each other a bandage with gangrene on it so they could all catch it. Probably lost their legs, the nitwits. Fact is, Private, you been wounded worse than any of us. But you just keep on fighting."

I looked from face to grubby face.

"They know?" whispered I. "About me?"

"Marines ain't dumb. They've seen you take bullets, take gas."

"And they don't want to . . . destroy me?"

Church chuckled.

"Merry Christmas, no. We want to *protect* you, Private."

The lips of one of the soldiers began to fluctuate in a manner so erratic that I blamed it on my disequilibrium. This same symptom infected the man to his right, and then another, and another, and soon I was surrounded by the strangest sight yet seen in a very strange war: a detail of quiet, grinning soldiers.

Church fired me a signature wink and swiveled on his boot heels to face his men. Gray dawn made an opalescent backdrop of treetops as he stood before them and began to speak. That morning there was no doubt of Church's greatness; it felt to the assembled as if he'd spent all twenty-two of his years preparing for this moment.

"Listen up, Marines. You heard the Skipper last night. You know what we're in for. It's going to be hard. And guess what? I'm here to make it harder. I'm here to give us a second mission. It's one we don't do for the brass hats, one we don't do for country. We seen a lot of things in this war, you and me, things we'd never have believed. So what's one more? See, there ain't any real difference between us and Finch. Maybe he don't bleed, but what is our blood now, exactly? I say our blood is mud. I say our blood is smoke. It's lead, it's fire, it's

381

mustard gas. That's what makes us brothers. Boys, one of our own is injured. He doesn't say it, he doesn't act it, but he's injured all the same. And what do we do for a fallen brother? Heck, I don't have to tell you. You're Marines. You know what we do. We rise up. We are unafraid. We laugh in the face of enemy fire. Private Finch will not exit this war in pieces. He has saved too many of us already, and now, Marines, we're gonna save him. Are you with me?"

"Yes, sir!"

"Now *we* save *him!*"

"YES, SIR!"

Neighboring gyrenes were jolted from slumber by the shouts but I heard not one grumble or curse. Cries of camaraderie so late in so grueling a campaign moved their emotions by instinct and summoned quick tears to their addled eyes. My own dry eyes could not respond in kind; too bad, for I longed to express this brand-new, unexpected, and unbelievable sensation of true belonging.

Wilma Sue, Johnny, Merle—they might be gone but I was no longer alone.

At that moment came a hollered report that the Browning rifles of lore had at last arrived. No, not enough for every man, but who cared? Optimism bounded back to us like lost dogs. Hoots of joy rose up. Sunlight cleaved the ashen clouds and we gasped at the sight before us: hoarfrost blanketing a rolling valley yet unsullied by boots, or craters, or flame. Even German barriers of razor wire shimmered as if bejeweled.

This was how the world looked before war.

Don't you remember it?

XV.

B

Y NOVEMBER 10, 1918, THE final night of World War I, when Armistice was but a formality for the morrow, the leathernecks huddled about Church as if he were holy fire. How else had they survived the past ten days of ferocious fighting? We Americans had taken the forest and commandeered the Sedan railway center, the heart from which Western Front German rail support flowed. Steal it and you steal Hun initiative, they said. Own it and you own the war, they said.

They had a knack for making objectives sound like a cinch, didn't they?

Instead, the Meuse-Argonne affair had been the whole war tidied into a synopsis: black rapids of artillery fire; poison gas so heavy you had to slop it aside like mud; grenades fat as rats plopping into peopled pits; the chugging of airplanes dipping into our world only to spit iron. Ridge after ridge after ridge was taken as easily as one takes a handful of beef from a living cow. (Not easily.) But the Hindenburg Line had shattered and Germans were everywhere, flapping white handkerchiefs and shouting, "*Kamerad! Kamerad!*"

True to their word, the Third Battalion had shielded me. Whenever the skipper delegated me to a ticklish task, another runner, often Church, would intercept and trade me a low-risk objective like leading captured Jerrys back to HQ. My fellow runners trudged through rain and mud the likes of which we'd never seen and they did it all for me. They died for me, too; I do not know how many. I was a novice to largesse and knew not how to refuse it.

The pup tents pitched atop the open bluffs and bustling with French and American generals said everything about Allied confidence. Goosed by the promise of peacetime promotions, these dignified, selfless leaders of men determined that their troops should run, shoot, and stab till the last second—and then, perhaps, one second more. This was how we of the Seventh became involved in a most unfavorable final assignment: traversing the river in order to rout one or two last machine gun nests.

One hundred Americans were to cross while a French regiment flanked us. We were told that the doughboys had improvised a bridge earlier that day under fire, but once the sun had set none of the runners could find it. As had become routine, I'd been safely stashed in a thicket, yet I could hear what the other runners, distracted by their noisome bodies, could not—namely, the hiss of river water against an obstruction. With each passing minute this knowledge brought me greater upset. This was my last chance to help those who'd so selflessly helped me.

I alighted toward the telltale sound and within ten minutes had isolated it. I whistled the signal and the runners converged, and before they could scold me for my involvement, they squinted into the fog and saw evidence of the bridge.

We spread out so as to guide the troops. By the time we brought up the rear, soldiers by the dozens were making their way across the river in single file, new Brownings slung across their backs. It was far from the silent crossing we wanted. From the murk came the splashes of boots into water, disbelieving mutters, and fearful curses.

I searched the hills of the opposite bank but fog concealed all.

Church gestured for me to return to my hiding place but I would not have it. I planted a boot upon the first plank only to realize that "bridge" was a generous assessment. The GIs had gathered whatever scraps of semi-floatable wood they could find and tied them together, so that each step sank beneath the surface the moment you put boot to it. The only way to remain afloat was to keep moving. A knee-high rope had been strung from bank to bank, reassurance that we were not wandering into an abyss.

Even this late in the war, the Germans were patient.

They waited until all hundred of us were in motion before opening fire.

Towering columns of black water jetted upward as mortar bombs drilled into the riverbed. No direct hit but the water swelled and men were thrown asunder, clinging to the guide rope, clutching planks too measly to support a man's full weight. Before the first scream, the deafening TAC-TAC-TAC of Maxims ripped through the night, chopping the fog into geometric shapes. White mist was striped with red blood. Hands, arms, legs, and scalps went skipping across the water, only to be gobbled by machine-gun piranhas.

Our queue mimicked the river's chaos. Men bunched and collided; the planks sank with the multiplied weight; adjacent sections of bridge were sucked down with them. I found myself sunk to my knees yet still searching for the next underwater step. It was no use and I splashed down into a clumsy dog-paddle. I threw aside my brand-new Browning in order to swim and so did dozens of others, and the river, already boiling with bullets, began to spark orange as those same bullets struck our discarded weapons.

Hands of drowning men grasped at my ankles but it was fruitless because those clever Huns had lined the bottom of the river with barbed wire. I paddled through warm red water, slapping aside the algae of shredded flesh, before my foot found a solid step, then another. I was grateful until I realized that these steps were bodies, piled so high that they created a new, and frankly much improved, bridge.

The far river bank was in sight but the shallows blistered with thousands of rounds of gunfire. Each of us dove in a different direction. Some lived for but a second, dropping face-first into the purple mud, while others like me found ourselves pressed to an embankment embedded with body parts.

Between my legs rested a detached head. It did not seem unusual, so accustomed was I to seeing this particular face. It was Sten Ehrenström, the Professor, his body abolished, including those clog-trained Swedish feet of which he was so proud. That perfect tenured brain, however, was undamaged. If I had more time, swore I, I'd dig it out and slide it into my pouch, for it was an organ that deserved to outlast this war even if I did not.

Yelling—more yelling—but this was a single word repeated, so I unplugged my face from the mire and saw Americans pointing toward a ravine cut into the hill above us. In progress was a creeping advance led, no surprise, by Church, who crawled up the bank on his belly. The rest of us followed.

In the ditch we huddled like rodents, soaked and shaking, each shocked face a mirror of the next. Our limbs were raveled; it was difficult to tell which wounded part belonged to whom. I stilled myself, made a count. Five, ten, fifteen, twenty, twenty-five—that couldn't be right. Twenty-five men out of one hundred? All told, the Third Battalion had made out well. Church was peeking over the crest and at his side lay Jason Stavros, gasping for air. The last one into the ravine had been none other than Piano, and he paid no attention to the bullets owning the air above us. Instead, he spread one of his wrinkled maps across his lap and began scribbling revisions.

"Boys, we gotta move," said Church. "They'll drop a potato masher in here sooner or later. There's a hillside up apiece, a bit of ground we can put our backs to. So we're gonna hump through this gulch till we can't hump no more, and then we go topside and run like heck. Everybody got it?"

Grim nods from all around.

Piano chewed on his pencil eraser, made another edit.

Church crammed his helmet tight and wormed northward. The ravine, narrow to begin with, constricted until we had to turn sideways. By then we were being buried in dirt falling along with every shell impact. Church tried to lock eyes with each of us before jabbing upward with his rifle.

"Two hundred feet, soldiers! Let's go, let's go, let's go!"

He lifted himself over the top, letting rip with his best Marine yap. The rest of us poured from the ravine like ants, screaming to alleviate the fear and hurtling through a darkness lit only by yellow bursts of gunfire popping from the hills. I heard the dull slap of flesh being hit, the wet crack of bodies slammed to the dirt. Troops who'd made it from the river with guns intact returned fire in a crazed attempt to buy a few more seconds.

It was a bowl-shaped indent at the base of a steep rise and we collided with it at full speed. If all twenty-five of us had survived the charge we would not have fit, not even shoulder to shoulder, but that was not the case. We were five or six down, and a good deal more were asphyxiating with the shock of new injuries—fingers blasted off, a kneecap hanging by ligaments, a bullet hole straight through an ankle.

Even these sufferers dared not move, for we enjoyed a buffer no more than ten feet; beyond that, a waterfall of bullets poured down so near we could smell the hot gunpowder and the incineration of autumn leaves. Several gyrenes emptied ammunition into the forest behind us until their guns overheated and their palms glistened with burns.

"Where's the French?" cried Jason Stavros. "Where's our French flank?"

"Telephone!" shouted Church. "Telephone! Telephone!"

An egg-shaped gent began shouldering past troops to make his way to Church. A ripple of excitement spread man to man. Our signalman had survived? Was it possible that the telephone cable laid by this intrepid paladin remained intact? We craned our heads to watch as the signalman planted his telephone box in the mud, removed the spool, and gave the cable a tug.

It was taut and from our bellies ejected laughs of relief. But then the cable dislodged from whatever twig or stone or corpse had snagged it. I held up the frayed end to wallow in the tragic absurdity. After being unspooled across the entire river and up the bank, our lone connection to base had been severed by a single goddamned bullet. We were cut off and *la Boche*, to be sure, was inching closer.

Piano chose that moment to exit the ravine. It was not that we had forgotten about him but that we'd assumed he'd been killed. Instead, there he was, sauntering through the firestorm without a single bullet hitting home. He reached our hollow and took a seat without a word, too busy scratching at a map to notice our appalled disbelief.

Church turned to me.

"I gotta go back."

The telephone cable slipped through my fingers.

"The fire is too heavy," said I. "The bridge is out. You'll never make it."

"It's these soldiers who won't make it. We don't get backup and medical in the next hour, we'll all be dead."

"Wait. Please. Reinforcements will come."

"Private, we're way off course. They won't find us before sunup. We don't have the ammo to last. Look, I'm the fastest runner. I've got the best shot of making it out."

Grab his pistol, put it to his head? Conjure *la silenziosità*, paralyze him to the spot? There had to be some rash action I could take to keep my friend alive! But Church never hesitated; with a wag of his eyebrows he was crossing the laps of men all the way down the line, until he crouched at the westernmost edge of our hollow. We watched in awe as he calculated our coordinates, scribbled them into his runner's log, tightened the straps of his gear, and armed both of his guns. Satisfied, he lowered himself to his belly and gave us a thumbs-up.

The caution with which he crept confirmed the peril of our position. An inch. Two inches. Trying not to disrupt a single branch. We tracked his every move until he slithered beneath a fallen tree and became mystery. The Krauts, meanwhile, were ruthless with the Argonne—it wasn't, after all, their forest. Bullets continued to rain. We made caves of our helmets and backs and resigned ourselves to trusting the one man who'd never let us down.

"Psst. Finch."

I cracked open an eye. In our huddle, Jason Stavros's helmet rested against my own. Our part-time florist had celebrated his birthday at Soissons with a tin cup of wine and was now all of twenty-one years.

389

His face was unrecognizable beneath a layer of dry white mud but those pale brown eyes were unmistakable.

"You want to hear a poem?"

Come up with six more unexpected words, I dare you.

"A poem," said I.

He forced a laugh.

"In case Church doesn't make it. Poems are meant to be heard, right? I got one I been working on and I'm afraid if I don't tell it now, I won't ..."

I was nodding, nodding, nodding. The war did awful things to everyone; one need only evaluate a human face from Monday to Tuesday to know that much. Jason Stavros, though, was the least corrupted of us all and that was worth perpetuating, if only for a few more minutes.

"Tell me," begged I.

"It's not good or anything, I just—"

"*Tell me.*"

Jason Stavros learned that the pressure of public performance was not so unlike that of battle. He inhaled, exhaled, wiped his forehead, cleared his throat, and slitted his eyes so as to look into an unclaimed middle distance somewhere between our position and the last known location of Church. Genuine fright lent his recital a cutting poignancy he'd never again capture, not even if he went on to recite his work in the world's grimiest (and thereby most celebrated) book stores.

> *From shallow holes inside which none dare move*
> *Here is one thing more we cannot prove:*
> *How poppies beckoned us with dusky slander,*

The sultry moss, silk bedgown clay, the oleander
Of weddings between men and their ghosts.
Thunder, rain: a seedling, let the doctors boast
How they birthed countries from thighs of blood,
And from them rebuilt a world.

But a ghost sometimes rolls over.
He shakes roots to show his displeasure.
What sways there is a tree, gnarled and tall
Over his grave. Is that enough? Is that all?
Will it be noticed when the smoke is not men
But industry, returned here again?
Hear me, down here, infinite in my mud;
Remember when what I died for was good.

He regripped his rifle to arm himself against my opinion.

"What do you think?"

What basis had I to judge literary merit besides a handful of overwrought ransom notes that had probably gotten me murdered?

"Beautiful," said I.

His lips twitched toward a shy smile.

"Really? You think so?"

I nodded. "And so upbeat. Just what we need right now."

He laughed, eyelids pearled with tears, and gripped my shoulder. A revived round of shelling rocked the forest floor about us. Lend an ear, Jason Stavros—is not imitation the truest shape of flattery? Recitations of bullets fell in meters and Maxims in complete stanzas, each brought to the exclamation-point finish of sniper fire or the full-stop period of a mortar blast. I half shut my eyes and settled into the abstract poetry. There existed entire catalogs of annihilations worse than this, so quieted was I by the lyrical iambics and the steady hand of a brother.

My thirst for a dazzling destruction was quenched to such degree that I failed to notice, dragging himself toward us on bloodied elbows, the mangled remains of Church.

XVI.

NOTHING BUT HONED INTUITION COULD have brought him back. His face was blown open, the right cheek excavated to reveal a neat row of molars still snug in their gums. The boys moaned. They wept. They reached for their fallen hero but I ripped their hands from his clothes. The arms of the living were blunderous, wobbling things and I would not trust them to honor the delicate injuries of the greatest friend I'd ever had. I dragged Church into my lap and stared helplessly into the brown stew of mud, weeds, and griotle, within which two frantic blue eyes goggled.

I raced through the standard pat-down for mortal wounds but all that I could see in the dark was the pale spotting of melted lemon drops against black blood. From his throat came a thick death-gurgle, so I flopped him on his side and jammed my dirty fingers down his clotted throat. What I would have given to hear, bubbling up from the blood, that asinine "Merry Christmas!"

Hands pulled me away so that a soldier more experienced in resuscitation could take over. I kicked in protest, good sense be damned, driving my boots into the mud until I'd motored myself to the far point of our hollow, the same beachhead from which Church had set sail. His brave belly marks still scored the forest floor.

I did not have to think about it for long.

Running was my job, too.

I planted my heels and launched, only to be dropped by a pair of hands around my good thigh.

Piano had lunged for me at the last instant.

"Ye can't go, boy-o!"

"Dolt! Unhand me!"

I kicked at his hands but the cuckoo kept contriving new grips. He offered me an obsequious grin and pulled from his pocket the wad of paper over which he'd been slaving.

"It's for you, Prefer-Not-To. Take it and travel well."

"Give me your gun instead so that I may shoot you!"

"Ye won't make it no farther than Church without an O'Hannigan map. They're the best. Always have been."

How I would have liked to give the Irishman a brisk strangling! But time was paramount. I swiped the farcical drawing, stuffed it into my uniform, and then gave the dunce a good kick in the stomach. From his shoulders I propelled myself with the opposite of Church's inchworm discretion, racing in four-legged style through moist clay dredged up by a hundred shells. I felt the pause of German surprise, then felt a hot gust of Maxim fire coming up from behind. Unburdened by the weight of a rifle I made it to an oak and fixed my spine against it. Presently the tree was torn to pieces as if by the tiny hands of a hundred feral children.

From there I writhed through underbrush, lost but for the knowledge that downhill equalled riverward. Soon I was out of rifle range, probably sniper range, too, though shells, of course, continued to drop. I was not a good soldier but none in any nation's history moved with my sort of stealth, and when I spied my first German crouching in the weeds, he did not, in turn, spy me. I lay there for a time, without weapon, without breath, without pulse, perfectly undetectable and just as perfectly harmless.

Despair can direct one to do the oddest things.

I dug out Piano's map and peered at it in the moonlight.

The schizophrenic universe he'd invented was pink and populated with both gray and gold saucer-shaped objects, each sprouting red limbs crosshatched with blue. Though the night's abortive charge had speckled the map with mud, I could see that painstaking attention had been paid; eraser burns marked where blue hatches had been removed from one side of a red line and added to the other, along with a particular sort of serif.

A bomb exploded one hundred feet to the west and its flames brought sudden illumination. The German squatting before me was reconciled with a gray icon upon the map, itself rather squat.

These were not geographical features that Piano had been notating. These were bodies, live and dead, American and German both. And those hatchmarks upon each one? Those were weapons, estimated quantities of ammunition. Which meant that I could, if I wished, crawl twenty feet south where laid, according to Piano's bookkeeping, a dead American, and take up what Piano indicated was a bayonet, and, if I wished, use that bayonet upon this unsuspecting Hun to effect a soft death that would go unnoticed in a thicket of such unnatural commotion.

If I wished.

For doing so would mean splitting from the covenant, Church's beguiling Theory of 17, to which for months I'd been true. What needed answering, and right now before Church bled out, was a question viscid enough to have mired every race of people since the dawn of consciousness: whether defending the life of a loved one was worth the destruction of others.

Since Church's befriending, I'd packed away my fear, fool that I was, and now it leapt back to my heart where it belonged, more painful then ever, for this fear was not for myself but for another. *This*, I declare to you, is the fear above all others, the field on which the least forgiving of combats are waged.

I took up my task with an Aztec's ardor. I found the bayonet where Piano's map placed it, made my silent advance, and drove it through a ribcage hard enough to affix the torso to a tree, and while the Kraut quivered and drooled I consulted the map for my next prey.

Reader, oh, Reader, I was *born* for butchery. How was it I'd believed anything else? So gratifying, the release of life from one of these fragile humans; so invigorating, the gush of warmth over my cold hand. I killed and killed, and when I reached what remained of the bridge, I consulted the map, my murderer's handbook, and located the resting place of two Americans. I took up their rifles, nice ones too—one of the coveted Brownings as well as a swell bolt-action Springfield—and loaded them. Stealth would not be required for this final spree.

The last bastions of German hope had pillared themselves atop a riverside knoll, a smart enough position were they not besieged by so proficient an assassin. I scaled the least expected face and caught one sleepy-eyed Jerry picking his nose. Give him credit; one handed, he managed to bayonet me as I returned the same favor through his right eye. The soldier's aim had been canny; from my stomach popped Johnny's golden marble. *Let it go*, thought I, but I, if you have not noticed, was unstoppable, and I fired the Browning to jar it free from the soldier's skull while using the recoil to power my pivot. As

I sailed into view of the dozen or more dumbfounded Germans, I juggled the rifles, snatched the aggie from the air, tossed it back into my mouth, and opened fire with both guns into every last Heinie on that hill.

I left no survivors. Not even myself.

Reinforcements escorted the GIs and gyrenes of that harrowing hollow back to HQ around eleven o'clock that morning, the same time Armistice took effect. Even men missing limbs or blinded behind bandages lifted victorious fists into the air or cried through masks of mud, while the healthy gave a cheer that I figure still echoes through the valleys of the Meuse and circles the summits of the Argonne. At 1101, the woods came alive with happy Huns, their arms raised the same as ours except to signal surrender.

Church was rushed from the forest on a stretcher and lifted into an ambulance. I reached to take his hand, but it was bloody and, to my horror, slipped through mine. I shouted his name. Four medics, three more than allotted for the average man, thumped me aside as they tried to stabilize him. For the moment, Church was alive; his stripped-naked chest pounded in uneven jags. What was unknown was what, exactly, remained of his big, handsome face, for his head had been swaddled in thick cloths that already were soaking with gore.

Someone had scrounged his deflated football and tucked it under his arm. The Game might be over, but a long solo contest was about to begin.

The ambulance left. My shoulders became gallows and from them I hanged. Some time later, I cannot be more exact, an elbow nudged at my ribs. It was Jason Stavros, helmet vanquished, hair swooped into a coiffure of hardening mud. His precious volume of

Percy Shelley was lodged in his armpit, riddled with bullets. Poetry, it turned out, had saved him.

He handed me a lit cigar while, from behind one of his own, he sang along to some patriotic drivel. I hated to puncture his pleasure but a question of consequence needed asking.

"Did Piano make it?"

"Piano?" He frowned as if he did not believe in so preposterous a name. But artifice would never work for Jason Stavros. He looked through his cigar smoke to the broken earth beneath his boots. "Nah. Didn't work out for Piano."

I bit down upon my cigar and searched the horizon. It would always be the horizon for me, wouldn't it?—never a proper end in sight. I straightened my back until I felt the comforting crinkle of Piano's map alongside my heart. On that sheet of paper had been transposed each of the Gød-loving Catholic's many scars, the same as my body bore each of mine. Yes, you might call it crazy. Or you might call it a conscientious document of survival, not unlike the manuscript you now hold.

Over the bacchanalia of exulting Americans and capitulating Germans I lifted my gaze. At last I settled upon a sight I shan't forget no matter the decades I spend spoiling down here in my tomb. Unattended Maxim guns on tripods sat high along an empty ridge, black scarecrows against a tangerine sky, dormant but deadly, just like me.

PART FIVE

1919–1931

———◆———

Herein The Twenties Cavort And Crash, And Your
Hero, Of All People, Is Called Upon To Catch A Killer.

I.

W E CROSSED THE ATLANTIC in a repurposed German battleship and in May moored at the city of Newport News, Virginia. Other termini were more common (New York City, Philadelphia, Charleston, and—forgive my shudder—Boston), but this was the straw we drew, and when we stepped upon the dock we girded ourselves for the homecoming that had become part of the military narrative: limp girls ready to be dipped into deep kisses; confetti cast from above; high school bands muddling through nationalistic atonalities; and a slow ride down Main Street in a roofless auto.

But the nation, poor thing, was tuckered out from parades. The only welcoming parties were those gathered to reclaim the lost luggage of their households' males. I knocked through the theatrics and joined across the street those of the Seventh Marine Regiment not yet met by family. We numbered seven, including Jason Stavros, who had wired his Utah kin that he was taking the long train home so that he might prepare his diary.

Their presence placated me. Long past Armistice, these men had made good on Church's promise to protect me, enacting subterfuge after subterfuge so that I might sidestep dicey administrative hurdles, from physical evaluations to discharge paperwork. Our silences were common and comfortable. Here, though, on American soil, they felt gawky, and we fussed with our packs until a scab-faced grenadier grunted, "Beer?" and we all nodded, grateful that one of us remembered what men did when not busy killing.

We found a brass rail and put our feet up on it. The saloon was a muddy-floored sewer populated by dockyard slobs, and they bought us round after round while we mishandled basic public behaviors. We spoke too loudly as if over mortar fire; we whispered too softly as if crawling beneath enemy wire; we reacted stoically when what was called for was easy laughter. The mirror behind the bar reflected our panic.

Thanks go to that scabby grenadier, who again saved the day by mooning at his glass of ale and saying, "Enjoy it, mates, it might be your last."

I, of course, could not drink, but felt party to their pain. While our boys had been bayonetting Huns and burying the corpses of their friends, what thank-you gift had America wrapped? Why, they'd bowed a ribbon of legislation called the Eighteenth Amendment, which would soon illegalize intoxicating spirits, and, as long as they were having fun, passed a postscript called the Volstead Act, which would extend the ban to the most harmless of lagers.

What rabid curs had orchestrated these waylays upon our full-flavored foams? Priggish prudes acting under such disquieting titles as the Anti-Saloon League (horrors!) and the Woman's Christian Temperance Union (I think I shall be sick!). These "Drys" blamed we "Wets" for every social ill under the sun, but let us not be coy. The brewing industry was run by lions of legend named Budweiser and Busch and Schlitz, all of them German—Kaiserites!—and that was reason enough to shut them down. Our nation never asked we who fought the Germans if we also wished to drink their beer. *Ja*, Reader, *ja*!

In the wee hours, we Marines stumbled from the bar as if gut-shot. Ever sober, I guided us to a hotel destitute enough to contain such destitute hearts. Ribaldry ran out as we unrolled sweaty rolls of cash, paid for berths, and then loitered in an ill-lit lobby, embarrassed at night's end the same as we'd been at the beginning. It was gentle Jason Stavros who dared ask the unasked.

"Anyone heard from Church?"

I shuddered at the name. I'd lost him, and it was less painful to let him stay lost.

The grenadier scratched loose a few scabs.

"Few of us went to the hospital in Paris," said he, "but he made us scat."

"How was he?" asked a private.

"Bad." The grenadier tried to think of a better word but could not.

"I heard they shipped him back in January," said Jason Stavros.

"Here?" asked the private. "Shipped back here?"

We exchanged looks of terror. What if Burt Churchwell was right here in Newport News? We'd be honor-bound to track him down and lay our frightened eyes upon what was left. My own slow corrosion I could stomach, but strong, proud Church's abrupt one? I did not believe I could withstand it.

"Nah," said Jason Stavros. "New York. He's back in Iowa by now, for sure."

We sighed in relief. Iowa was farther away than Europe, Japan, and the North Pole combined. Backslaps were manufactured, good-night adieus delivered, and promises made to breakfast together and exchange addresses in the morning. I nodded agreement, and they, my steadfast chums, were good enough to play along; surely they'd noticed that I hadn't paid for a room. These fine men had more than fulfilled their duty in regard to Private Zebulon Finch.

At ease, boys, thought I.

Dawn found me on a southbound train. Marine garb does wonders for a traveler and I was given every deference. Two days later I was back in Xenion, Georgia, the only real home I'd ever known. The lane to Sweetgum brought me solace. There was the ivy-strangled pergola, the Roman columns, the four-paneled front door. Best of all were the plentiful patches of white cotton scattered across the field. At last, Sweetgum was returning to life.

I proceeded no farther than the front gate. Those patches of white were not cotton—not even close. They were paper surgical masks, the kind worn by every American back home suffering through the Spanish Influenza Pandemic of 1918–1919, which, before it had dried up, had killed more Yanks than the Germans and with no more fanfare than a quick bedtime smothering. Why so many of these masks here at Sweetgum? No sooner had I posed to myself the question than I surmised the dreadful answer.

I slunk back into town, found a neglected tavern, and gestured for a drink; I required a glass to grip if I were to make it through the next few minutes. The bartender curled his lip and offered me a milk. A milk! I presumed he believed me underage before I noticed there was not a barrel of beer nor bottle of spirits on the premises. The South was overstocked with Christian zealots—just ask ol' Mr. Stick—and it looked as though all worthwhile beverages had been hauled off to the stockroom of that lucky son-of-a-bitch Saint Peter.

The man planted before me the glass of milk. He looked as disgusted as I, so I capitalized upon our shared dysphoria.

"What happened out at Sweetgum?"

The bartender smirked at my aristocratic accent.

"Who's asking? You even know what clan live thereabouts?"

"Lucy, Nelly, Patsy, Peggy, Polly, Susannah, and the honorable Mrs. Joseph Thomas Hazard."

It was a convincing enough reply. The bartender swiped up his towel and searched for something to wipe clean, but again, there were no barrels, no bottles, nothing upon which dust might settle.

"Tell you what. Them ladies are saints. The flu hit, there wudn't room in no hospital for miles, and them ladies opened their home to folk who wudn't kith or kin. Took care of my Adelaide, too, and brung her through the worst of it. She got a cough now here to stay and she can't see right no more, but she's alive, ain't she? Them Hazard ladies did that."

"Did they . . . ?"

"Die? Four of them did. It's a awful thing. But how many like my Adelaide lived because of them? A hundred? That's a debt no one round here can pay."

Four of the seven gone. Which four? No, I could not bear to know! I pushed aside my milk, slapped some money to the counter, and stood.

"Look here, son," said the bartender. "I got me some gin 'neath the floor. Sit down, I'll pour you one on the house."

I waved him off, exited, and blundered around the back. Trash bins blocked my way; I kicked them over and out spilled more whiteness— masks or milk, both were ill omens. Farther back was an outmoded privy that still stank from regular use. I sat in the scrub-grass with my back to the whorled wood, as much in sorrow for the good sisters of Sweetgum as for myself, alone again, evermore.

Hours passed before I heard the voices. They rose from behind the rusted hulk of a junked automobile fifty feet up the hill. Unwilling to field human contact, I crouched behind a bank of tall weeds and watched two Negroes, biceps bulging beneath large crates, head toward the tavern. The first was old and bearded and the second no older than thirteen. They entered the tavern through a back door and minutes later emerged with empty arms but thick pockets.

"Ain't our fault some a' them bottles gone missing," grumbled the kid.

"Boss Man gonna have our necks when he hear—"

"Well, what do he expect? You give a man a car full a' shine, he gonna drink some, ain't he? It just be human nature."

"You know I don't drink a damn drop. Boss Man count every bottle."

"Me neither, Paw-Paw." The kid grinned. "Not while we working anyways."

Moonshiners! They ran thick as ticks in agrarian Georgia, or so I'd heard; even the Hazard sisters had indulged in fiery backwoods bootleg on occasion. With Prohibition about to squeeze the last drops from a long-liquored nation, an empyrean age had arrived for these black marketeers. Their cauldrons would bubble at accelerated rates and their desperado dealings could become legend, if they employed the right kind of scofflaw with the right kind of disregard for personal safety. Now, let's see—did I know anyone who fit that description?

I rose from the weeds, tipped my cap.

"Allow me to introduce myself," said I. "My name is Zebulon Finch."

The duo, believe it or not, was not overjoyed to meet me. Their first instinct was to run; their second instinct, upon seeing my

Marine emblem, was to fix in place in fear of being fired at; their third instinct, the prevailing one, was to draw into a crouch of defense or retreat, whatever my next action provoked. To put them at ease, I smiled, though I expect it was unconvincing. I could not pretend to be comfortable around their kind.

"Forgive the intrusion. But I overheard remarks regarding troubles in moving your moonshine."

"Ain't no one said nothing about no shine, mister," muttered the kid.

Paw-Paw snatched his grandson by the overalls. "We'll just be going about our way, sir."

"Discussion of your work is verboten, I realize, but might we suspend the taboo here in private? I believe I am uniquely suited to your profession. Briefly, my qualifications: One, I have no affection for the Anti-Whiskey Bunch or the League of Upset Ladies or what-have-you. Two, I am discreet, as you can plainly see. Three, I am handy with a gun. Four, you need not fuss over bottle count for I do not drink."

The kid possessed a twinkle of nerve I recognized from my own misbegotten youth.

"What do a man who don't drink care about selling drink?" asked he.

"It is a matter of philosophy, I suppose."

"Harold," warned the elder.

"Hold on, Paw-Paw." Harold examined me. "You can drive a car?"

"Drive a car?" I had no idea how to drive a car. "Of course I can drive a car!"

Paw-Paw glared at Harold.

"You can't bring no white boy back to Boss Man!"

407

"Think what we could do if we had us a white boy in uniform. You just said we about to lose a runner."

A *runner*?

My chest nearly burst with pride!

"Gentlemen," spoke I, "do forgive the forthcoming boast. But when it comes to running few men upon this Earth are my equal."

Five minutes of lavish hyperbole later, I found myself hunkered low in the backseat of a jalopy as it rollicked along bad roads to worse roads to no roads at all. Phone cables crisscrossing overhead gave way to woodland sunshade and the parting curtains of gangly kudzu. The car wheezed to a halt in a dark copse, from which we hiked a trail marked only by the sly placement of white stones at the bases of certain trees. Before I saw it, I smelled it: the bready aroma of rye, the sweet smoke of burnt sugar, the flat caramel of warm whiskey.

The distillery was an impressive wooden lean-to built against the incline of a hill. Steam mushroomed from steel vats and the ingredients of the trade were stacked high enough to act as walls: sacks of corn, potatoes, and yeast, and crates of corked jugs, pint and quart jars, empty wine bottles, and wide wooden barrels. At least twenty people, most of them women, stirred and tasted and bottled, while a few more sat on tree stumps and sang along to a man strumming a gap-toothed banjo. Every single one of them was colored. Foreboding, indeed, but what was even worse?

Each one toted a gun.

Weaponless and pale as I was, I began to postulate that I had made a critical blunder. Before I could escape, Harold, that purposeful whippersnapper, led me by the elbow through clouds of smoke and presented me before a figure who needed no introduction as Boss Man.

He was forty years of age, unremarkable of height and lean of build, and reclined upon a log bench with hands laced behind his head and shirt unbuttoned to the breeze. His oaken face was channeled by a life spent in the hard sun, but was, at this instant, placid as a sleeping newborn's. Hair, once dense and black, had grayed and withdrawn, allowing for an angelic golden gleam courtesy of the noonday sun. Nevertheless I recognized the crook at once and my stomach sank like a ship into the sea.

Boss Man was John Quincy, the corn thief, that secretive, insolent Negro with whom I'd shared a jail cell alongside General Hazard eighteen years before.

"You!" cried I.

John Quincy yawned.

"Boss Man," said Harold, "this boy here say he want to run for us."

I'd once belittled this man to cure my own battered ego. To appear before him as a subject made my cold skin crawl with shame. An obnoxious feeling; I shielded myself with indignation.

"I withdraw the offer!" declared I. "I would sooner work for the Kaiser!"

"He say he the best runner ever been," continued Harold. "But I don't know. He look pretty regular to me."

Though a few workers remained in place to funnel liquid, churn syrup, and waft steam, the bulk of the Negro Militia had drifted close to watch, no doubt with their pink palms to the butts of silver guns.

"Is it your claim that you don't remember?" demanded I. "That onslaught upon our jail?"

"Boss Man been in lots of jails," crowed Harold.

"Well, I am not surprised to see that he's resumed his life of crime."

"You can't talk to the Boss Man like that!" Harold tipped his hat back so I could see his thrust bottom lip. "Ain't you never heard of Booker T. Washington? Marcus Garvey?"

"If these are playmates of yours, rude child, I hope never to meet them."

"Ain't you never heard of black pride?"

"*Pride?* Oh, Alice, I have joined you, my dear, through the looking glass, into a land where two-bit bandits expect praise for their contemptible thievery."

"Yeah, my poppa stole. So? He good at it, mister!"

"Your poppa? I might have guessed."

"Boss Man can steal a hundred dollars worth a' potatoes while you stand there talking school talk. By the way, mister, I don't want to meet your friend Alice no more than you want to meet my friend Marcus Garvey."

"Seeing how your father is dumb, if not deaf as well, I shall direct my final query to you before taking my leave. What does your group do, then, Boss Boy, with your old man's stealings?"

"What do you think? Boss Man seen them Prohibition fools coming a mile off. Pretty soon we be making a hundred gallons a day easy. Look at our alky-cookers. We got the best still in the South. Can't you see good out them eyes?"

The quip elicited a scattering of chuckles and I looked over my shoulder. What I saw were endless brown faces beaming with pride at their quick-lipped upstart. Banjo plucking continued undaunted, and the women at the tubs swayed their hips with a wantonness rarely seen beyond bordello walls. I could not help but admire the gyrations.

The entire still, in fact, was testament to these women's tart humor. Nailed to the posts were handbills deriding the evils of alcohol ("Progenitor of Folly, Misery, Madness, and Crime!"); medical charts associating each type of spirit with expected Vices, Diseases, and Punishments ("Egg Rums" led to "Gaming, Peevishness," which led to "Puking, Bloatedness," which led to "Jail"); and magazine adverts based on doubtable claims (an infant in a high chair paired with the rhyme, "The youngster, ruddy with good cheer, / Serenely sips his Lager Beer").

I studied John Quincy.

"Is this why you stole that corn all those years ago?"

Harold smacked his forehead.

"How else you think corn whiskey get made?" He counted off on his fingers. "You has to soak it, sprout it, dry it, grind it, ferment it, distill it. You want to add juniper juice, that up to you. Boss Man got his own recipe. You want a swaller? Naw, you said you don't drink. Too bad. It's the best mash since the Plymouth Rock Pilgrims brought theirs over, isn't that right, Poppa?"

John Quincy at last showed a tinge of emotion, a slight uplift of lip, before apportioning to me that rarest of his products, his voice.

"You look the same, Mr. Stick," said he. "Got the same fight, too. Let's see how we get on."

No further slander crossed my tongue. Try as I might to tap wellsprings of resentment, the Negro's quiet confidence brought to mind the Soothing Foursome brother who'd lugged my body to the field of honor in 1902 without a word of thanks. To whom else had I to turn? My massacre in the Argonne had burned down Mary Leather's efforts to build me into a gentleman. A hidden forest cove was where

I belonged; running rotgut was the job I deserved. So I gave a curt nod. I'd move his moonshine. Perhaps for only a few days, maybe a full week if I was struck by the urge to grandstand. I'd show John Quincy which one of us was the natural-born sinner.

II.

HAROLD WAS RIGHT. DRY DAYS were here and Boss Man was bottling a flood.

Prohibition inaugurated its historic farce at 12:01 in the morning on January 20, 1920, beneath the lifted baton of six months of jail time and up to one thousand dollars in fines. Before it was done, it would flip social orders, rob power from some and stuff it into the pockets of others, squash industries here while giving rise to others there, and inject new life into folks who'd been living on the brink of ruin.

You could not hope for a better example than John Quincy and his brood. Yes, those many workers I had met were his extended, expansive family, ranging from great-great-aunts, step-nieces, and half-brothers to the beloved First Lady of mash liquor, his wife, known across hill country as Mother Mash. Viewed in isolation, each individual was a puffy-haired, singing, dancing ne'er-do-well possessed of not a single ounce of ambition. Together, though, they locked like cogs and cranked out, with the efficiency of Ford, enough drinkable alcohol to fill an ocean.

Forget the shade of your skin—you could not buy better hooch. Who couldn't recall their first nip of Stuck-Shoe Cider or Tin Tub Recherché? John Quincy used purest ingredients, cozying up to priests to purchase sacramental wine and entering into relationships

413

with druggists still permitted to dole out whiskey prescriptions. And who was sent to reassure these professionals of our honorable status? No less than a freshly scrubbed white boy in smartly pressed Marine fatigues!

Xenion and its neighboring anthills could not contain us. In 1922, I was graduated from horse patrol and formally introduced by Harold to the family's venerable Model T. I figured I could conquer it, but came close to dismantling the transmission before Harold quit his guffawing and taught me how to drive. We filled it with liquor crates stenciled "Choice Meats" and "Fresh Fish," and Harold gave me directions to a speakeasy in Savannah that wanted the whole lot.

She was a hell of an auto, that Tin Lizzie! Electric starter motors and colorful pyroxylin paint jobs were the rage, but our dull black, hand-cranked clunker better concealed our success. John Quincy had tinkered with the engine and, boy, was she fast. High-speed pursuits were common, and, being unafraid of roadside crashes, I took blind corners and jumped ravines that no Prohibition agent would dare. The wind against my face was not unlike the rush of Death I'd experienced that one time back in 1896. It was grand.

City work was not for the timid. Agents deputized by the Volstead Act would shutter a gin joint one night only for it to reopen twenty-four hours later under a new guise, and it was my job to know where. Dozens of times, while unloading clandestine crates of liquor, I watched these half-wits, right across the damn street, confiscate beer barrels and axe them on the sidewalk. Little starvelings would then dart out with buckets to gather the beer from the gutter, either for their parents or some Faginlike sort who tipped them a few cents. Such displays lifted my spirits. Now *that* was the sort of youth I would have enjoyed!

John Quincy was coining money. His organization remained backwoods by locale but not by description; his lean-to had matured into a chimneyed warehouse replete with locked doors, blacked-out windows, and a surrounding forest armed with booby traps. My cut was not ungenerous, but I had little use for it. I kept my uniform in prime states of tidiness and repair, paid for adjustments upon the Model T of which I had grown so fond, and that was it.

So why, if not for personal gain, did I keep on for five years? Reader, I can confide in you. The truth is that I discovered at that lawless Negro distillery soft bits of tranquility that helped me forget my failures with Johnny, Mary, Merle, and Church. The place was family personified, closeness incarnate: an office at which business was conducted; a community kitchen wherein kinfolk might offer one another comfort; and a safe zone in which one might let the indignities of America evaporate from one's skin and kick back with a hammered-tin stein. So, too, was it solace for a creature like me.

The daily glow of the frothing pots was joined each night by bon-fires over which roasted stuck pig or egg-stuffed biscuits, and around which danced the whole whooping lot of Quincys, displaying a lack of inhibition that I found by sequence appalling, puzzling, and envi-able. Mother Mash lifted her skirts and stomped about with the best of them, while Harold (by 1925 older than I) made his girl-cousins blush with his fast-talking flattery and even faster feet. They knew that I wished to go undisturbed and respected it, though Mother Mash kept ceremony by approaching me nightly, calling me "child," and offering plates of strange delicacies I could not accept: ox tail stew, fried fatback, and vinegar chitterlings.

There was one other who refrained from the celebrations: John Quincy. Each night he sat across the clearing at the exact opposite of my position, sipping at a single glass of wine with a grandchild bouncing upon his knee, gazing with satisfaction at the tribe he'd lifted from poverty. Near the midnight hour, his slumberous eyes would meet mine and he'd do me the great favor of a single nod. My role, I suppose, was to feel honored. But a young white man like myself had nothing so invaluable as his dignity, and thus I made no response. Let me whisper into thine ear, though, a long-kept secret: honored, Dearest Reader, is how I felt.

III.

T WAS DURING THE LAST two years of my tenancy that sinister forces began to encroach. During city stopovers I always made time for movies, and I took in, as did thousands of others, a picture called *The Birth of a Nation*, put out by a chap named D. W. Griffith. It was advertised as a "Mighty Spectacle," "The Eighth Wonder of the World," "The Supreme Picture of All Time," and starred no fewer than eighteen hundred people and three thousand horses. (When was the last time you saw horses receive top billing? I was excited.) I slapped down hard-earned moonshining moolah and told the ticket boy to make it snappy. I claimed a front-row seat before a thirty-piece orchestra.

The picture ran for well over two hours—and it was not nearly enough! During the intermission, I pouted; when it was over, I shook the hands of the musicians. For weeks while dodging Prohibition officers I imagined myself as the movie's dauntless Ben Cameron, wounded in the Civil War, pardoned by Abraham Lincoln, and founder of an energetic bunch of crime-fighters who wore dramatic white hoods.

Much time did I give to imagining the rescue of fainted maidens and the gunning down of would-be defilers. Little thought, indeed, did I give to the motivations of this masked group, which was called the Ku Klux Klan. It came to pass that *The Birth of a Nation*, the best picture I'd ever seen, stoked red the gray embers of the KKK, giving rise to a revived movement that, in a snap of the fingers, swept the country by the millions, each chapter defending their "Aryan birthright" against the invasive species of the Negro.

I witnessed KKK marches firsthand while delivering goodies in Albany, Augusta, and Macon, and the men in the pointed hats took every opportunity to flaunt their fealty to Biblical mores. Was it any wonder that they were obdurate backers of Prohibition?

You have a capable mind, Reader.

I need not warn you where this is heading.

The Klan's arrival in Xenion was marked by a burning cross planted high upon a hilltop. Local infiltration was swift and deep. Fresh KKK inductees attended church services in full regalia, and fundamentalist Gød-botherers were happy to accept their anonymized parishioners as both rod and staff. Sunday school teachers signed up lads to the Junior Klan and gals to the Tri-K Klub. Teachers began lecturing about the hierarchy of races, and white children began to look at their colored playmates through a newly scratched lens.

The atmosphere at John Quincy's place clouded, darkened, and chilled, and for good reasons. A local Negro family, proprietors of a flourishing cabinetry business, was dragged from their beds to watch while their lawn was scorched with a cross. A colored boy alleged to have been forward with a white woman had the KKK symbol branded into his forehead. A black man caught with jugs of rum was covered with tar, and then, in an inspired ad lib, that tar was set aflame. Businesses were burned to the ground, children kidnapped, women flogged, men murdered.

Intimidation, though, was not among the repertoire of John

Quincy. Even when tragedy touched his family, he pushed toward expansion, slapping the backside of any worker caught gossiping instead of fermenting, bottling, and shipping. In such high esteem did his blood-relative underlings hold him that they kept up the singing and dancing; they even snagged copies of the Klan's newspaper, *The Searchlight*, and included them in their ongoing satiric collage.

It all left me quite conflicted. I was not one of those bleeding-heart Negro activists; my past aligned more with that of the average Klansman. Yet the Klan's single-minded pursuit of the dark-skinned offended me with its lack of logic—I knew firsthand that Negroes were our intellectual peers. It was a quandary I kept quiet, though I wondered what I might do if the KKK's Imperial Wizard paid me a visit and asked for cooperation regarding the apprehension of a certain local moonshiner.

In October 1925, John Quincy made the greatest gamble of his career. Word of his liquors had reached all the way up the coast, and a player in New York City's illegal trafficking racket wished to purchase an amount to distribute to the high-class clientele. Were the reaction enthusiastic, he would enter into a contract that would enable John Quincy to produce his moonshine up North and under the best protection. After one year his family need not worry about money ever again.

Harold was our most reliable driver (my affection for speed sent bottles helter-skelter), but given the current climate, a white envoy was the wisest choice. Only John Quincy, Mother Mash, and I knew the stakes, and after sardining Lizzie with thirty crates of their latest and greatest concoction—Dog Bowl Debbie—they counted out, with solemn ceremony, cash enough for nine hundred miles worth of gasoline, repairs, and bribes. Then came two words I shan't ever forget.

"Be careful," said John Quincy.

This gnarled old root of a man rarely spoke to me, much less offered cautions. Having no suitable responses at hand, I lined my pockets with the cash and blustered through a reply.

"I shall not be careful. *Careful* would require a much higher percentage of the sale and I am in no mood right now to haggle."

But decamp I did not, for Mother Mash reached out with her skinny arms and bound me within a sinewy embrace. I could not bury my ladylike gasp; I wrestled myself away only to find her smiling as if she had expected nothing less from me.

"You come back to us, Mr. Finch," said she.

Her eyes glimmered with what might have been tears of affection. It was an emotion I hadn't the tools to handle; I harrumphed, straightened my uniform, planted my cap, and turned away to crank Lizzie's engine. After she began coughing forth her black clouds, I discerned the distant leaf-crunching of the husband and wife ambling off, the latter's low, musical humming dwindling into the woods. I put the automobile into gear while grinding my teeth. What the devil were these colored folk so worried about?

Minutes later as dusk settled upon Georgia like soot, I rocketed from the forest at impressive speed only to be flagged down by an old fellow standing alongside his parked auto. I was annoyed, but idled Lizzie. He doddered near, his face obscured by the plummeting sun.

"If you're carrying hooch, partner," panted he, "you got to skedaddle."

Part of my profession was playing the innocent.

"Hooch?" asked I. "Does that mean alcohol? Never would I touch such poison!"

The man scoffed. He wore a scraggled white beard; I recognized him as a past customer.

"There's agents up the road a piece and they're stopping cars, giving them the full search. You ought to go round the long way, you know what's good for you."

This bewhiskered galoot might be my senior by four decades, but I was in no need of advice when it came to evading lawmen. Still I kept in mind the task with which John Quincy had entrusted me and wrestled down my tongue—quite a rascal, that organ.

"I thank you for the advice," said I.

"How about Boss Man? I'd hate to see any y'all caught out."

"I am the last one departing tonight. Again, I thank you."

The miser grinned, all four teeth of it, and legged it back to his auto. I wheeled Lizzie around to head off in the revised direction. True to the man's word, this alternate path contained no checkpoints, and for an hour I chugged along in peace. At last, a true adventure! I was overdue for one. I took a corner at top velocity and listened to the reassuring rattle of bottles against their wooden restraints.

It was this chiming that led me through a disconcerting cogitation. It had been peculiar, hadn't it, how the man on the road had used the name "Boss Man"? Most Xenionians were either ignorant of it or knew better than to speak it aloud. What's more, the fellow had been standing outside of his car when I exited the forest path. Had he been waiting for me? For how long? That was a good deal of effort expended by a casual customer, one who, come to think of it, hadn't even asked for the customary free nip for his trouble.

The old codger had outsmarted me.

Grow up, I begged myself. *Please, please, one day soon.*

I jerked Lizzie's wheel. The shatter of breaking bottles pierced the squeal of rubber. Her two rightside wheels left the road but, weighed down by the crates, she slammed back to the gravel, her engine gagging as I shifted to a higher gear. I ignored the low-speed pedal and the reverse pedal; I would require neither.

When at last I roared back down that familiar forest path, I had settled upon definitive answers I would give to the Imperial Wizard should he ever come offering me my heart's desire in exchange for information on misbehaving blacks. The answers were my boot in his face, the blood that would choke him, the cold fingers I would slide beneath the white flaps of his hood and around his throat. I'd perform this murder upon a hilltop if one was handy, kicking aside the charred remains of a burnt cross in order to make known to his followers that masks could not hide you from your fate—believe me, I had tried.

Harold was collapsed in the autumn leaves outside the still, howling to the sky, runners of blood and spit giving his face the gloss of a fresh wound. That told me everything I needed to know. I did not have to put Lizzie into a neutral gear, though I did; I did not have to climb out; I did not have to approach the warehouse to catalog the damage done. The man on the road had once been a customer of ours, yes, but his current allegiance was with a larger, more lethal power.

John Quincy was dead, of course, dangling from the rafters of the distillery he had built, lynched on a rope so long that his feet dangled but an inch off the ground. Two details jumped out: broken fingernails and a tightly shut mouth. He had fought, there was no question of that, but he had not screamed. Mother Mash was hung much higher, her skirts fluttering in the October breeze. The ropes of husband and wife made the same death creak, and both bodies made a circle in the same direction, a final waltz in which they both joined in perfect accord.

This home, and a *home* was what it was, had been torn apart as if by cyclone, furniture quartered, banjo busted, glassware shattered, barrels hatcheted, cauldrons overturned, bins of ingredients upset. The ground was a sweet-smelling bog through which bloodied family members struggled to cut down their murdered loved ones. I headed back to the door and not a single Quincy cared—and why would they? Like that, the years I'd spent with them were erased. I knew that I was, and would always be, an ivory outlander sporting vestments symbolic of a country that did not give a shit, not about this lynching, not about the lynchings previous, and not about the lynchings yet to come.

My backpedal became a dash. Harold, collapsed outside, saw me flee and likely tagged me as a Klan conspirator. Not true, but why dispute it? I'd been just as culpable in their demise. What mattered most was that Lizzie continued to vibrate beneath her forest canopy. That greasy machine carried the final hundred gallons of Dog Bowl Debbie, the South's finest shine, and people in New York City were primed to pay a price that would go a long way here in the South.

My mission had not changed. I forced myself to picture my boss—I was prepared, too late, to accept the Boss Man as just that—not hanging from a rope but tapping his bare foot to a banjo beat, and promised him, loud over Lizzie's engine, that I would deliver his drink as we'd planned, and when that was done, send the fat stack of cash to Harold to disperse among his woebegone kin. It was both the very most and the very least that I could do.

IV.

NEW YORK CITY WAS KNOWN by the nation's Drys as "Satan's Seat," and, at last, the devil Zebulon Finch was there to sit. Highways did not exist in 1925 and it took me a week to reach the outskirts. By then, the punishments I'd brought down on Lizzie had taken their toll. She whimpered during our nighttime crossing of the Hudson River, distracting me from a spectacular cityscape, and passed away as I coasted along West Street. I steered my dearly departed into a narrow L-shaped alley behind a factory. It was a dark and disused space; I concealed her with scrap metal and said good-bye. I'd loved her more than most humans. Make of that what you will.

A few blocks south was a sidewalk-spoked riverside garden called Battery Park. I secured a bench and spent the night staring up at columns of yellow lights reaching twenty, thirty, forty stories into the sky, a man-made Appalachia of steel and glass. Even during the moon's reign, New York hammered and hollered and honked. This was most assuredly not rural Georgia or rural France, nor, for that matter was it Chicago or Boston. What was I to do with no way to transport the crates? With limited cash and no assistance? I hugged my arms and felt quite lonesome indeed.

Morning dawdled, for it was a beastly, drizzling day, and I, lacking a better strategy, slouched northward along a street called Broadway, so bluffed by tall buildings that it felt like a canyon. It buzzed with quacking trucks and ringdinging trolleys and intersected with byways that I'd read about in papers, like Wall Street and Park Place. Were I not a waterlogged corpse without a friend in the world, I might have experienced wonderment.

I halted my futile march in Times Square. The place was throttled with cars and fungal with umbrellas. Here I claimed a random corner and peered through the rain at awesome signs shouting about everything from Squibb's Dental Cream to the Ziegfeld Follies. When a taxi blew by, everyone on my curb stepped back in a single motion: the shy stenographer in the checked wool skirt, the tussled university student holding a textbook over his head, the laborer in a grease-stained jumpsuit, the dead teenager. I realized that this metropolis might as well be a necropolis, as its residents were as faceless as stones in a graveyard and just as private regarding their states of decay.

The unexpected relief of anonymity pounded me harder than the rain. In this city I could exist completely unnoticed. Was that not the ideal situation for a being such as myself? I was eager to put this opportune revelation to the test, but first there was the matter of the giant cache of liquor stashed near Battery Park. I cheeked some rain and spit it out in a happy fountain. Well, I had a plan for that as well!

Four blocks east I stomped until I came upon Grand Central Terminal. There, inside the vast, echoing rotunda, I found a pay phone and, with nervous fingers, inserted the required silver. The hello-girl had a clipped, businesslike tone; no doubt she hoped for each call to be a simple A-B connection rather than an exhausting investigation. She had rolled snake eyes that day, for I was in need of assistance, possibly a lot of it, in locating the only person on Earth I knew who had, at one point, been right here in New York City. Call it a hunch, but I did not believe that he'd repaired to the hushed plains of the Midwest.

"Ahoy-hoy," greeted I. "I need to find a man by the name of Burt Churchwell."

V.

SEVEN WARLESS YEARS HAD PASSED since Armistice. Gizmos like the pop-up toaster and the hair dryer had been invented to rescue women from domestic doldrums, and, thus freed, they'd fought for, and won, the right to do that silliest of things—vote. Men, deprived of nations to destroy, contrived a succession of absurd challenges: the scaling of Everest, the disinterring of old King Tut, the masteries of polo, yachting, fencing, and all the other inscrutable hooey of the Paris Olympics.

Seven years had frayed my sleek nation into a million wild briars and yet, when entering that busy Manhattan diner, I thought that I understood how much had changed.

"Merry Christmas, you're a sight for sore eyes."

My heart, dead as it was, squeezed, as if my ribs had made a fist.

Burt Churchwell, my once-best friend, rose from a padded booth and, when he offered me his hand, wobbled upon a bad leg. By instinct, his other hand reached for the walking stick against the wall. A cane? A limp? I focused on the white-blond hair and cleft chin, for everything else was wrong. Church looked to have lost a foot of height, and what of those oak-tree shoulders? They curled now into a guarded hunch. His torso, honed on the gridiron along perfect Charles Atlas flexures, paunched inside a striped sweater. And his face—that keen, clear, strident balefire—was seamed with shrapnel's errata as sure as if he'd slept on a tennis racquet.

My years spent imagining how he might look had prepared me for even worse. There was no getting around it, though: the man was hard to look at. If one human being deserved to remain forever young, forever unscathed, it was Church, and I outraged at Gød's latest sucker punch.

Church's hand still waited. It was a worrisome thing to behold; what if I felt in his grip none of the camaraderie we'd once shared? I gave it the quickest bob before dropping into the opposite seat. Our conversational ease had been left behind in France and we were bashful.

He gestured at his plate of meatloaf.

"I told the girl you wouldn't be eating." He tapped his scarred temple. "No rations for Private Finch, right?"

Spellbinding though the tablecloth pattern was, I lifted my eyes to meet this stranger's eager gaze. His ice-blue eyes, at least, showed a familiar melt, despite being sunk inside purple chasms and trapped behind eyeglasses. Egad—eyeglasses? On Church? It might as well have been a condemned man's blindfold. How do two people like us, wondered I, begin to speak of the level of terrors we'd seen?

It was easy: one does not speak of them at all.

"You," said I, "are not in Iowa."

"No sir. Once you're used to the big city, you can't go back to them cornfields."

Men like him—*good* men—made awful liars.

"You have been here all the while, then?" asked I. "Doing what?"

He shrugged. His sweater was frowsy. Dirt encircled his neck.

"This and that. How about you? Where the heck you been?"

It was my turn to be imprecise.

"Here and there. Odd jobs, that sort of thing."

428

"Sure. Yeah. Right."

Silence joined us like a third diner. Church rediscovered his meatloaf and went at it with knife and fork, but his chewing of it seemed a forced endeavor. He swallowed like it hurt; it hurt me, as well, and I rushed to rescue the poor guy from his social suffering. The condiment of nostalgia was closest and I grabbed for it.

"Your Theory of Seventeen—you remember it?"

Church smiled at his plate. Oddly, the right side of his face did not crinkle.

"How many you down to?" asked he.

Likely he knew nothing of the nest of Huns I'd slaughtered; certainly he knew nothing of John Quincy and Mother Mash, the latest two numbers I'd been forced to add to the cumbersome total.

"I'm afraid," said I, "that I am up."

He messed with his food and sighed. Again, the right side of his face did not move.

"Don't hold any stock by it. I didn't know what I was saying back then. I mean, I was a kid, right?" He peeked over the top of his glasses. "I guess you still are."

If only I could tell him otherwise. In a handful of years Church would be double my age. Prove to me, Dearest Reader, that there is a monster more unrelenting than time and I shall slay that monster and bring you its head on a pike.

In keeping with the meal's short history of artless questions, I asked another.

"You did not go home to Lillian Eve Johnson?"

Church fumbled his fork and it clattered. He gestured at his scarred face with his knife.

"You think any girl deserves to live with this? Jesus, Finch, come

429

on." He glared at the world beyond of our streetside window, the tainted mud filthing the pure snow. "This here's the only place for me."

So Church, too, had recognized New York City as a trench through which a careful soldier might crawl unnoticed. I leaned forward, keen to tell him that I understood. Before I could, he wiped at his moist eyes and readjusted his glasses and the most appalling thing happened—the entire right side of his face adjusted too.

Burt Churchwell was wearing a prosthetic cheek. It was the size and contour of a chicken cutlet, molded to replace the bone missing from his upper lip all the way to his right eye. It bestowed upon the right half of his face absolute tranquility, a vivid contrast to the quaking emotions of the left half. The glasses, I realized, had no relation to eyesight but rather held the apparatus in place.

It is possible that, once upon a dream, the prosthetic had been dapper. But the years had rubbed it to a golden sheen and textured it with its own craters and scrapes. Worse, a line of shadow marked where it no longer fit snugly against his face. It was pitiable, Reader, little more convincing than the gent who pastes three strands of hair across a naked dome. Oh, my handsome blond knight! Why had Gød forsaken him?

He tapped a fingernail against the false cheek. It gonged.

"Galvanized copper. Nine ounces, one-thirty-second of an inch thick."

"You'd never notice it."

"Don't feed me that baloney. They painted it with this enamel, right? It matched my skin pretty good at first, but heck—we fought that war in the sun, you know? Now I'm all pale but this thing is brown as an Italian. Plus I gotta shave all the time or it looks uneven."

"Are those eyelashes . . . ?"

He ran a gentle fingertip through his right-side lower lashes.

"Real hair. Not mine, though."

"Whose?"

"It could be a Jerry, right? One of them who trapped us in that pocket. Ah, heck. I guess who really cares anymore."

"Right. Of course."

"It's over now. The whole dang thing is over."

The waitress came by and asked if Church was done with the half-eaten meatloaf. This time my eyes were open to the interaction. The girl did not look at Church's rearranged face, nor did Church look at hers. It was a jig of avoidance at which both had developed skill. Only when she was gone did Church watch the waggle of her cutely packaged backside. His hand, in need of something to fondle, found the salt shaker and rubbed it as if it were a charm capable of taking him back to a former life.

"In Europe they had these blue park benches where soldiers were supposed to sit if their faces were messed up, so when people walked by they had time to, you know, prepare themselves. They don't got no blue benches here. You never know what's going to happen."

"I am sorry," said I, "that I did not come to see you."

He offered a half-grin, defense against his unresponsive right cheek.

"It doesn't matter. I didn't want you there. But I tell you, little buddy—I'm glad you're here now."

We looked anywhere but at each other, as males do when unutterables are uttered.

"Hey, I bet the doctor who did me could do a real number on your"—here he lowered his voice—"your leg."

"Oh, I don't know," said I. "I have become quite adept at packing it."

The comment was bleak enough to make him laugh. Out of sheer surprise, I laughed too. Tears had again mobilized at the edge of his eyelids, though these were happy ones—you could tell by the quality of shine. Back when I had been alive and capable of crying, I'd never been able to make such fine distinctions.

"So." He clapped hands still big enough to crush a football. "You called about moving some boxes? Anything I can do, you don't have to ask twice. I got an honorable discharge the week I landed. I got nothing but time, Private."

Having just endured several painful pins of truth, I, the Astonishing Mr. Stick, endured a few more, presenting to Church an abridged narrative of how I'd come into possession of thirty crates of A-1 moonshine yet hadn't the means to bring it to the big-city bootlegger for whom it'd been allocated. Church rubbed his powerful chin.

"You say it's well hid?"

"As well as an entire automobile can be."

"Maybe we'll rent a truck. I don't have the bankroll at the moment, but I'll get there. You and me together—we'll get it done soon, I promise."

I nodded. "Soon, then."

He stuck his hand across the table and this time I shook it with assurance. He signaled our girl for the check.

"Hey, Private. You think you and me could grab one of those crates right now? Battery Park ain't but twenty, thirty blocks from Chinatown. That's where I live. It'd be easy as pie to sell it there. Truth is, I've got this landlord about to kick my butt to the street. I could really use a little cash right now."

The bodies of John Quincy and Mother Mash twirled on their

lynching ropes in my mind's eye; my mind's ear, if such a thing exists, heard the sobbing of the aggrieved Harold. Every single cent of Dog Bowl Debbie profits belonged to them, I knew that. But this man asking for a favor was my friend.

"Yes, of course," said I.

"Aw, great. You're saving my neck here. I'm behind in rent like you wouldn't believe. Two crates might be better, actually. You think you can spare two? This guy's charging me three bucks a week, a whole arm and a leg."

I swallowed, a silly human habit.

"Sure," said I. "Anything you need."

VI.

AND I'D THOUGHT THE SALEM apartment I'd shared with Merle had been vile! Church's fifth-floor flat was a suffocating sty of moldering brick, tortured floorboards, ceiling cockroaches, and mice that took their time trundling beneath furniture at the turning on of each electric lamp. Stronger in smell than the single toilet shared by six units was the constant, wafting aroma of eccentric dishes like chop suey, chow mein, and pu pu platter. The unwelcome sound, meanwhile, was the Chinese language coming through the walls like Maxim fire.

I moved in right away.

I had nowhere else to go, so why not? Church had been spot on about selling the Dog Bowl Debbie. Cane and limp notwithstanding, he was still strong, and we'd lugged two crates across the south side of the city, stationed ourselves in the alley behind Foon's Occidental Restaurant, and sold it by the bottle in under an hour. Even after Church stopped by his landlord's unit to pay off the previous month's rent, a stack of cash remained in our possession. Church fanned the bills and made a rhapsodical announcement.

"Little buddy, you and me are hitting the town!"

What of the balance of his tardy rent? My, how I despised being the cautious one!

"Should we really?" asked I. "I did just arrive."

434

"Aw, come on! We've got a reunion to celebrate!"

"And celebrate we shall. But only—"

"Dang it, Private, this is a direct order!"

The Marines had trained me to obey ranking soldiers. So it happened that I found myself opposite Church in New York's grimiest kitchen as he flung my arms to and fro to teach me a distressing but evidently important dance called the Charleston. Church, that oversized lunk, kneed countertops and elbowed cabinets as he jigged in place, flailing his arms side to side in the manner of an epileptic ape.

Rodentia aside, we were alone, and still the degradation was unbearable. He kept at it until balls of sweat raced down his face, clocking faster times on the false cheek than the real one. When this former leader of men paused from his swaying serenade, he said that the best speakeasies required the sort of tuxedos we did not own—not *yet*, he stressed—but that still left thousands of places we could talk our way into with any halfway decent suits.

"Alas," said I with relief, "I own no such garment."

"You know old Church has you covered! I've got two. Little bit stained, little bit torn. But these clubs are dark."

"Look here. You are twice my size. No item of yours will fit."

"You're in luck, Private, that's the fashion now—baggy!"

You see how my best efforts were rebuked? We danced, if that is what we must call those kitchen-floor convulsions, for the better part an hour. While the sun sank from the bitsy porthole above the stove, Church taught me a slow two-step. He did not seem to register the abnormality of our man-to-man embrace, but hummed along to a private song, perhaps dreaming of Lilly Eve, while we moved in lullaby rhythm, my cold cheek resting aside one of even colder copper.

Church shambled without the aid of his cane, yet maintained a spirit of *bonhomie* as he led me through Manhattan, down an unlit lane, through an unmarked entryway, and up to a black door with a cut-out window, behind which sat a rotweiler of a man masticating a double-decker sandwich. Church recited the password with obvious relish.

"*Salesmanship.*"

The man chewed, narrowed his eyes.

Church tried again: "*Salesmanship.*"

The man jerked his chin at me.

"How old is the kid?"

Church looked bewildered and crooked a thumb at me.

"Him?"

"No, the little green man on your shoulder. This kid looks like he should be wearing short pants. I can't be letting in juveniles."

"I'll have you know that you're talking about a United States Marine, a soldier who took wounds at Belleau Wood, Soissons, Saint-Mihiel, Blanc Mont—"

"Oh, Christ, another trench tale. Fine, get in, just shut up already."

We paid the entrance fee. The man eyed Church's golden cheek as we passed.

Down a tar-black hallway we plunged, feeling our way toward the noise, until we pushed open a door that cracked the muffled darkness into a kaleidoscope of sound and color. Radiant teardrop-shaped bulbs winked along every border and gusset of the floors, walls, bar, and ceiling—a magical grid through which scuttled an impossible number of roaring men and women. Bartenders in black vests lifted into the crowd steins sloshing with foam and delicate glasses bobbing with cherries. Women drank—right there in public, alongside men!—and each sex clawed to the other with an orgiastic disregard for decency. I was struck stupid until I felt Church clapping my back.

"You ain't seen nothing yet, Private."

Smoke blown from a hundred cigarettes formed a chimerical curtain. It parted and we were in the middle of the seethe, the rims of men's hats fencing our own, female arm flesh swabbing sweet perspiration upon our jackets. The squabble was overpowered by a capering music that rose and fell, rose and fell from the end of the room. Church cut a path into a beehive of sweaty dancers who jerked about in incoherent sequence. Again he had to rouse me from a stupor; he planted me onto a tiny metal stool at a tinier table.

He pointed at the stage and I turned to find ten musicians in matching black tie pound away at an unprecedented volume and pace. Horns shouted, then shout-shouted, then shout-shout-shout-shouted in pealing unison, while a saxophonist made cat-in-heat moans that writhed to the rafters. The stage was held down on either side by a burly male drummer and a turbaned female pianist, both of whom grimaced at each other with a sexual strain. Oh, and perhaps I should mention—though every last patron of the speakeasy was white, the musicians, down to the lissome lady massaging the ivories, were black.

I stared at Church in disbelief. He laughed and spoke a short, silly word.

"Jazz."

Had mischief-making of this magnificent measure been going on while I'd puttered along Georgia's dusty, boring byways? I looked to the floor to clear my head and saw near my feet a splendid brass spittoon—a spittoon, I say! More than anything else, this engilded saliva repository drove home the scope of our country's post-war prosperity. It was as if the millions of recently dead had to be exorcized if normal life were to be resumed, and here in this room were enacted the forbidden rites.

Church had ordered drinks at some point. A fizzy soda for the constant abstainer and for me, of course, a seltzer I would not touch—both of us wastes of space in this bedlamite market of freely flowing firewater. He snatched his cup and waited until I lifted mine. Together we clinked our glasses and he, after drinking, chuckled.

"Stop mooning at the gosh-danged band! The dancing girls are *right there!*"

Imagine it, Dearest Reader, if you do not mind an aphrodisiacal blush. These prancing pretties followed every physical urge no matter how licentious the thresh, their shingled bobs frolicking about their jawlines with the same shimmy as their sequined dresses, smoking all the while from long, slender cigarette holders. They were skinny and flat and plated by waistless dresses a-swing with pearls.

Church shouted over the din.

"They call themselves 'flappers.' That the 'garçon look.' It's French. Not bad, eh?"

"They look quite unlike the mademoiselles I remember."

He slapped my back.

"You got that right, buddy. Take it from me, these girls are a whole new breed. They stay out all night and dance till daybreak. See their fingernails? That's polish—they polish their fingernails! And, boy, are they ever crazy for gin! Some of them carry flasks in their dang garter belts. It's a good way to meet them—just ask for a gulp. You can spit it out on the sly. They'd go wild for that Dog Bowl stuff we sold today. Anything to get blotto."

"Blotto?"

"Drunk! Tipsy! I tell you, this town's a bachelor's paradise! I'll

438

teach you everything." He stopped, his face falling. "You *can* still like girls, can't you?"

It depended, of course, on how liberal one was with the word *like*, but this was neither the time nor place to get didactic about the function, or lack thereof, of my nether regions. I nodded.

"Great. All right, see that Jane there, just coming in? See how she's got mirrors sewn into her dress? That's a custom job, and you know what that tells me? *Nouveau riche*, loud and clear."

"*Nouveau . . . ?*"

"New money. They dance faster and kiss longer. They're not hung up by all those old-time traditions."

"Their standards are lower, you mean."

"Well, that's a lousy way to look at it. They're more fun is all. They *want* to pet. It's Prohibition, I'm telling you. A girl's gotta be a little bit bad to go to a gin joint, and once she gets a taste—bam! She can't get enough. It's like Frood says, girls are animals the same as us men."

"Frood."

"What, you haven't heard of Frood?"

"A famous caveman, perhaps?"

"He's a head doctor. These girls are over the moon about Frood."

Ah—Sigmund Freud. I'd read about that oversexed quack. I smiled and nodded. No reason to fuss about proper phonetics.

"I knew you'd pick up fast. You're an odd duck, Finch, but sharp as they come." He finished off his soda as though it were a bracing pull of whiskey. "Let me show you how it's done."

He clapped his hands, blew out a breath, hopped off his stool, and hobbled his way to the dance floor. I watched with great curiosity as he integrated his bulky shape into the knit of lithe, slinging bodies. His gait, so sure upon fields of fire and football, was as oafish here as it had been in his kitchen, but he commenced with the same nerve, heaving his shoes hither, tossing his arms yon, and soon enough his conquered oval of floor space intersected with that of some gamboling gals. In the heat of the brawl, in the delirium of jazz, one partner was as good as another, and I observed with admiration and envy as his paws pressed upon slender hips and twirled them away only to reel them back via lanky, bejangled arms.

Only when the band collapsed and took five did Church wipe his face with his sleeve, take his current partner by the elbow, and pull her in the direction of my table. I sat straighter. By then the flapper had gotten a good look at Church's face and had put on the brakes. She pointed over her shoulder at friends, probably imaginary. Church hooked a thumb my way and tugged her closer. She laughed to be friendly but her eyes flashed with alarm. Church's next advance brought her within ten feet of the table but by then she was wiggling off the hook, no longer smiling, and as she hurried away I heard his last plea:

"But don't you want to talk about Frood?"

I cursed myself out loud for not having corrected his earlier pronunciation. The girl brayed; I winced; Church's shoulders fell and he limped his way to our table a good six inches shorter. He hit the stool hard; his empty soda glass skittered into my full glass of water.

"This ain't the same country we left. I suppose it's better. It must be. I mean, look how happy everyone is."

It was true that you could not number every instance of revelry, of decadence, of flaunted illegality. Surely this was behavior befitting a nation at the edge of empire.

"Guess I gotta learn to present myself better. Both of us do. We gotta learn to sell our good sides."

440

I recalled the club's password, spoken by Church with such pride.

"*Salesmanship*," said I.

Church cracked a grin. The band kicked back into gear with a syncopated shriek and that grin truncated into a wistful twist of lip, while his eyes drifted after the smoke churned up by romping bodies.

"The Cotton Club."

His whispered words were a magic spell.

"That's where we'll go, little buddy. It's up on Lenox—the finest place around. Got the finest girls, too, none of the gold diggers you get at holes like this. At the Cotton Club it's first-class all the way. Chorus girls, more than you could pet if you had all week—even the hat-check girls are tony. And the bands? They make this one sound like a bunch of geese. You ever heard of Duke Ellington? Louis Armstrong? Well, you will. We'll hear them play, you and me, watch how the crime guys give them thousand-buck tips just to play a tune."

This was more than a dream; it was, for Church, the Dream, and for a time I too dreamt of mingling among perfumed heiresses, listening to the melodious repartees of personalities of radio and screen, and seeing sawbucks fly from the wallets of captains of industry. I thirsted for specifics.

"You have been there, then?"

"Well, no. Not yet. But, heck, you don't need to go no further than the line out front to know it's pure swank. There ain't any Plymouths parked outside, you catch my drift? Only Stutzes, Dusenbergs, all the best. You can't walk into a joint like the Cotton Club in duds like these. No, we gotta make some dough first, we gotta look sharp. A few months, if things go good? Wait and see. We'll dance the night away."

VII.

YOU ARE WISE TO WONDER how long an unwatched car full of liquor can last in a given megalopolis. Call it luck, if you wish, for an otherwise unlucky chump, that week after week after week, no one came across my dear Lizzie.

That does not mean the delectable Dog Bowl Debbie found its way to the intended buyer. John Quincy had provided no instructions beyond showing up at a certain warehouse across the East River. That distance became the difference: Church and I continued to sell the bottles piecemeal to pay for food, heat, and rent. These were the barest of necessities, I knew that, and yet I couldn't look for long at any coin earmarked for the Quincys. I tried to convince myself that my duty toward them was finite, that Zebulon Finch was unbeholden to any man.

Except, perhaps, Church. Month after month the city beyond our ramshackle walls crackled with gunfire, much of it coached by a brash impresario named Lucky Luciano. Crime, ever profitable, boomed to historic proportions. The stock market, too, rose, and rose, and rose, making everyone, or so it seemed, rich. I could not go a day without reading breathless advice from columnists ("Put Your Small Capital Into Niles-Bement-Pond if You Wish to Live Like Rockefeller") or fielding tips from shoeshine boys ("Psst, buddy! Invest in Allied Chemical and Dye!").

Church and I had no bank account with which to gamble—nor shoes worthy of a shine, come to think of it. In 1926 the Dog Bowl Debbie ran out, and until 1929 we held the most menial of jobs: packing newspapers, freighting auto parts, selling Juicy Fruit gum on the street. Where Church's disfigurement did not make him unhireable, his mood swings earned him the boot, and I, in solidarity, followed him toward the exit.

He was everything I had in the world, even though our life together felt inconsequential compared to the spectacular feats we'd brought off in the Great War. Such battlefield glory haunted both of us, but especially Church. It did not take an Einstein (or a Frood) to see that war had rattled something loose inside him the same as it had Piano, and that this dislodgment, not his cheek, was his most dominant wound.

The Dream of the Cotton Club remained just that, for Church dared not darken its hallowed doorway until he'd made something of himself. My primary purpose was to buoy my friend's sinking spirits, so I encouraged our continued attendance at more plebeian dives. To maintain my own disposition, I saved cash enough to purchase a terrific ten-dollar Knapp-Felt fedora—second only to the Excelsior in my history of favorite accoutrements.

From beneath its ivory petersham band and laughably long brim, I screened flotillas of flappers for a girl kindhearted enough to look past Church's face. Sensing that I was not on the make, females gravitated into my jurisdiction. As much as it anguished me to be a nonsexual object, I discovered, to my surprise, a great deal of pleasure in chatting up these browbeaten but brazen babes who worked in steno pools, department stores, libraries, and schools in jobs far more interesting than any Church or I had ever held. Who knew that women had so much to say?

So fond of them did I become that I could not blame them for spurning Church. The odds stacked against these young women were enough without him lopsiding the equation.

This phase of our life came to an end in May 1927. The fad *du jour* was dance marathons, endurance contests in which the last couple standing won a cash award. These "bunion derbies" held every hallmark of an event ideal for Church: he needed money, longed for situations in which a girl could not flee before getting to know him, loved to dance, and had a minotaur's endurance. So when he shook an advertisement in my face and said he couldn't lose, what could I feel but gladness at the return of his swaggering gasconade?

It went, of course, poorly, as did everything he attempted that decade. The tin-roofed Coney Island amphitheater was sardined with hundreds of numbered contestants, and I watched from the bleachers as Church and the gal with whom he'd been paired—Couple #281—spun within a sea of individual whirlpools. The first day and night cut the frenzy down to thirty couples, but these were the desperate diehards. A full week later, most of them fought on, their snappy tangos abased into the slouches of half-snipped marionettes.

Some men dragged semi-conscious girls; some girls passed smelling salts before the faces of their drowsing men. Shoes had long since been kicked off to make room for blisters, and the hardwood was smeared with blood. Given that the swelling of his problematic right knee was evident from one hundred feet away, Church's violent crash on Day Fourteen was almost a relief.

From the filthed floor, his glasses and copper cheek askew, he sobbed.

"I won the *war*. I won the *war*. And I can't even win *this?*"

It was a slow advance past the noisy good times of the beaches

444

and amusement parks, with me bearing half of Church's substantial weight as he had borne mine during the march to Belleau Wood. Coney Island was stocked with every pleasure a person could want, from sailboats to cotton candy to, shall we say, more adult diversions, and Church broke from my grip to keel toward one such house of whoredom. I grimaced but had no choice but to draggle after. Such establishments had once brought me considerable joy, but ever since Wilma Sue, the sight of one disheartened me.

Two women led us down a dingy hallway and into a grubby bedroom, where they took from Church two dollars and began to peel off their clothes. It had been thirty years since I'd been privy to such an unveiling, and there were myriad details to note regarding contemporary undergarments, the most jarring of which was the tubular elastic used to flatten the breasts. (Yes, Reader, I know—a criminal intent!) These girls had precious little meat on their bones; the point of the style, I think, was to make ladies look forever young. As someone with just such an affliction, I ached after the kind of soft, luscious flesh of which you could take hold. Oh, Wilma Sue, how I missed her, and in so many ways!

Church's hooker went by Nan, mine Dot. Both affected flapper flash, though a slapdash variety. Instead of the cunning bobs labored over by "beauticians" (a new and hopeful-sounding profession), these girls' hair looked self-lopped; instead of dangling strings of pearls they sported glass beads; and the lockets around their necks contained not swatches of perfumed cotton but cocaine, which both girls snorted from their fingernails, giggling.

Church initiated sexual congress. His bad knee shook, his feet bled into the carpet, and the number pinned to the back of his shirt made his effort feel like another contest. Dot lounged happily upon my unresponsive lap, re-doing her makeup in a compact mirror. On went the rose rouge, the pale powder, the red Cupid's bow lips, the thick black kohl around the eyes. I was too close to appreciate the effort. Her face looked to me like a loosely fitting mask.

While Church went about his business, the girls bantered.

Dot: "Nan, you got a cig?"

Nan: "You've been on a real toot with those. Don'tcha know gaspers will do ya in?"

Dot: "That's a wad of chewing gum. Ain't you read the magazines? It's how all the stars keep their figures."

Nan: "You're all wet. Exercising's what does it."

Dot: "Hah! With all our lays we both oughta be beanpoles. Look, my girl Mabel knows her onions, and she don't eat nothing but spinach and juice—and you'd be happy to have her hip bones."

Nan: "I'd be happy to have her *bubs*. Mine are too big."

Dot: "Well, just keep strapping 'em in, maybe they'll shrink."

Better to sit there, impotent and uninteresting, than undergo the strange suffering of Church. Sweat poured from his crimson face until his glasses began to slide down his nose, dragging with them his copper cheek. This threw off his focus; his thrusts staggered and his grunts stuttered; and then, quite evidently, he began to fail at his task. He tried to nudge his cheek back up with his shoulder and in the doing so stumbled backward.

Nan noticed.

"Aw, what happened, Burke baby?"

Church pushed away from her thighs and retreated to the corner to pull up his pants.

"It's Burt."

"That's what I said—Burke. Come back, we'll try again."

"*Burt.* And that over there is Zebulon Finch. Got it?"

"He your kid brother? He's cute. Dot will give him a round, won't you, Dottie? And you and me can start over."

Church's hands came away from his belt in fists.

"That right there is no kid. That's Private Zebulon Finch of the Seventh Marine Regiment. You got any idea of what this guy did for me? For his brothers? If he doesn't want to be touched, you don't touch him, you got that? You don't *deserve* to touch him, you diseased witch."

Nan's spirits dropped like a nightgown. She raised herself to sitting position.

"You better take a shower, mister. You're getting a little hot under the collar."

"I'm just asking for some respect is all."

"Well, this ain't how you get it. Dot, get your clothes."

"What?" demanded Church. "We're done, just like that?"

"Sorry, bank's closed—*Burke.*"

This kindled within me an angry flame, though whether directed at the raccoon-faced courtesan or the whole sorry situation I cannot say. I stood, bouncing Dot to her feet, and lurched across the room with arms raised, as if scaring away a sidewalk of pigeons. No, Reader, I am not proud of it, but I had Church's shaking fists to consider.

"Get out of here!" shouted I.

Nan got off the bed, swiped up her clothes, and pressed them to her body.

"This is *our* whoopee spot, kid. You can't give us the bum's rush!"

"*Out, out, out, out, out!*"

Dot, the meeker of the two, held the door open. Nan was furious

447

but I suspected this was not the first time a customer had forced a getaway. She shook a finger at us; her cheap strand of beads whirled about like Aboriginal boleadoras.

"You're real flat tires, the both of you!"

The door slammed and we listened to their naked footsteps patter down the hall and retreat inside another room. I leaned against the wall, brain boiling. Church took a seat upon the vacant bed. Tired old bedsprings moaned as he unclenched his hands and studied their scars: maps of Iowan farm land, demolished trenches, the back alleys of lower Manhattan.

"Ever wish you could go back to the war?" asked he. "Keep fighting it?"

I sighed.

"I admit," said I, "there was a certain satisfaction in inching forward, ever forward."

"There ain't no Skipper out here to tell you what direction to go."

"I shall not abandon you. We will find the optimal path."

"Easy for you to say. You got nothing but time. Me, I'm gonna be *thirty-two* in December. Life's just dropping away from me, Finch, I'm bleeding it out everywhere I go. I ain't had a job in I don't know how long. I ain't had a girl since Lilly, not one I didn't have to pay for. I used to be somebody but now I'm nobody. I'm nobody."

He pulled off his glasses, the prosthetic along with it, and rubbed at his tears. The exposed pit of his cheek caught me unawares. The bone had been dug out as neatly as if by an ice-cream scoop, and the pink flesh inside had been layered by surgeons in the style of a croissant. The overall effect was that the right side of his face was being sucked into his skull.

I, too, was pulled by the vortex—I could stand to see my friend like this no longer! I bucked from the bedroom wall and snatched the prosthetic from his hand. Church blinked at me with all the surprise of a child robbed of his birthday balloon. The apparatus was shockingly lightweight. How flimsy a thing to hold control over such a man.

I snapped the arms off the glasses. The rims split too and one of the lenses fell to the floor and broke into two clean halves. Church was aghast, confused, buffaloed.

"Stop? Finch? Stop?"

The prosthetic was of solid copper but, as Church had said, only one-thirty-second of an inch thick, disqualifying it for any Revelation Almanac we might encounter. I hurled it to the ground, spotted an umbrella left behind by a client of this substandard whorehouse, picked it up, and used the point to stab the lifeless copper until skin-colored paint chips began to scatter. It produced ten times the satisfaction of jabbing a bayonet into something living.

My next stab sent the cheek skittering across the floor.

It was halted by the dropped obstruction of a shoe.

Church stood there with a heaving chest and the cave of his cheek glistening. He lifted his shoe, evaluated the heel. Like him, it was old and beaten, but not without strength or sharpness. He looked, probably for the first time since 1918, like he knew what to do. He raised the heel and took aim, the same as he had against untold scores of armed Germans.

"I got you," said he, "you little son of a gun."

VIII.

S O ATTUNED WERE OUR EARS to the minimalist music of spare change dropped into our coffee-jar coffer that we barely noticed the murders at first. Daily news was, for the most part, inapplicable to our social station: stocks we could not buy, fashion we could not afford, events we could not attend. Freed of his false face, Church became a better man and found better work, and our rent, believe it or not, began to be paid on schedule. This left him little time for current events.

He'd instead narrowed his interest to celebrity gossip. Once a month he'd scrape together the change to buy *Photoplay* and read it front to back, responding to every article with adolescent credulity. "Wow!" he'd cry. "Mary Pickford really *is* just a regular girl at heart!" The glum irony was that we were smack in the middle of the age of the movie palace—lavish, air-conditioned, Egyptian-styled temples designed to give proper deference to the new wave of "talkies" starring the likes of Charlie Chaplin, Joan Crawford, Tom Mix, and Bridey Valentine—and we could ne'er afford two tickets!

For me, the dull diversion of fact-addled newspapers had been superseded by the squawking fluff coming from our secondhand Radiola. It mattered little if the program was morning calisthenics, sonorous scripture readings, malefic weather reports, musical show-cases, children's prattle, or even Betty Crocker's Gold Medal Flour

Home Service. If it babbled, I was there to clap my hands in moppet delight.

Only when coppers began raiding our scurvy saloons, not to arrest us for illicit imbibing but to pat us down for weapons, did we hear rumors about a killer. Forthwith I found a newspaper slicked with gin to a tabletop and flapped it about so that it might dry. On the walk home that night I read my first account of the Bird Hunter.

The *New York Herald Tribune* had an edge over the *Times*, the *Sun*, the *Evening World*, the whole inky glut, for the *Herald Tribune* had on the case one Kip McKenzie, soon to be known as my favorite writer. It was McKenzie who'd nicknamed the killer. After the third murder, each of them young women returning home from speakeasies, he wrote, "If 'flappers' are so named for chicks yet lacking the adult feathers to leave the nest, this executioner might well be called 'the Bird Hunter,' so intent is he to clip those wings."

Even when the killer went underground for months at a time, not one week passed without McKenzie boasting "exclusive scoops" from "top-secret sources" on one of these variants: a) The indomitable police had a suspect and were about to make the collar; b) There were additional unpublicized victims and the police were bungling boobs; or c) An eyewitness had surfaced to describe the killer as a very tall man, or a very short woman, or perhaps a circus-trained gorilla.

It was a lurid decade, you understand, and print outlets strove to outdo one another in both the size of their hollering headlines and the carnality of their content. We readers expected fresh, frequent, hot plates of sex and death, and shivered in delectation when McKenzie held back the goriest details to instead repeat his simple, teasing refrain:

"This girl, too, was gutted."

The affair offended Church's Midwestern decency, and so, feeling like a Judas, I stole away so that I might enjoy exchanging wild hypotheses with strangers on the street. The Bird Hunter was a moralistic madman out to punish our reckless youth. No, he was a Dry delivering atonement to those who dared to draught the Devil's drink. Any madness was possible in the world of Lucky Luciano and Al Capone. Even yours truly, typically dazzled by wanton bloodshed, had disfavored February's execution-style St. Valentine's Day Massacre in Chicago. Truly, could things get any worse?

Hah! Funny rhetorical, that.

Appreciate the caustic couplets of that drunk poet, Gød. On October 24, 1929, Kip McKenzie was back on the front page with the slaying of another young flapper. But his story had been booted below the fold to make way for the only thing worse than bloody murder—the bloodying of one's own pocketbook. The entire country was shaken on "Black Thursday," a frightening enough label were it not for the Black Monday and Black Tuesday that quickly overshadowed it. No, it was not a spate of solar eclipses but the implosion of the anything-goes stock market. Boring stuff, yes, unless it was you who had your entire fortune dashed in a matter of hours.

The initial impact upon Church and me was minimal. The Dream of the Cotton Club remained just that; what little money we had fit into our wallets. But, oh, how the city moaned. We opened the windows to the mournful music while our Radiola supplied the numerical lyrics: American Telephone & Telegraph down 106 and 3/4 points, General Motors down 36 and 3/4 points, the whole market drained of billions of dollars, ninety percent of its total value. The imagery conjured was of tycoons in three-piece suits standing amid loops of ticker tape as tangled as battlefield entrails before opening their fiftieth-floor office windows and taking the plunge.

"There won't be any jobs," said Church. "Finch, what'll we do?"

I thought of the bottles of fallacious promises once sold by the Barker.

"This is what happens," said I, "when one trusts in false prophets."

The United States reeled as if socked by a Jack Dempsey round-house. New York City in particular hit the ropes, but at least we had a hero, the intrepid Kip McKenzie, and over the next two months he assaulted his clackety Underwood with the single-minded mission of elevating the moods of we millions of sad-sack suckers. Behold, his latest mobilization:

MARKET PLUNGE SQUELCHES SERIAL MURDERS
"Bird Hunter" Threat May Be Over, Says Our Reporter

Leading theories regarding the Bird Hunter had suggested that he was doling punishment for declining American ethics. The breaking waves of the crash, wrote McKenzie, had tossed the Roaring Twenties against the cliffs; give it a year, two at most, and necklines would rise and hemlines would fall and liquor would stop pouring in such volume. The Bird Hunter, in short, would have no more cause to kill. Wasn't it wonderful?

It was! It really was! I know that McKenzie's millions of readers took solace that, as bad as things were, there were worse things that had been sated. Too bad, then, that, beginning with the very first day of 1930, girls once again began to die, quite a lot of them.

IX.

O N A COLD DAY IN February the bastards came for me.

Church was out, having found dollar-a-day sledge-hammering work alongside colored folk. Consequently I answered the door alone, prepared to give our censorious landlord an entertaining spiel excusing our latest default. My story involved, if I recall, the rescue of a dog from a snow drift and a pending commendation of valor from the mayor.

Two policeman—twins, no less—awaited.

"Zebulon Finch?" asked the one on the left.

I hedged, an old technique.

"And whom might I say is calling?"

The one on the right grinned.

"Look at his skin. White just like Fergie said."

"Blame the grayness of the day," said I.

"You're coming with us, kid," said the one on the left.

"How unlucky, for I am previously engaged. Shall we reschedule?"

The one on the right rattled his handcuffs, and that was that. I sighed, fetched my fedora and coat (no reason to announce to the world that I did not feel the cold), and allowed myself to be pushed, none too kindly, down the stairs and into a waiting patrol car stenciled with "POLICE N.Y." and "5 PCT." Seeing as the buggy had no backseat, I sandwiched between the twins and posed to them polite queries regarding what it was that I had done and where it was that I was being taken, while they, helpful officers of peace that they were, held a debate about the New York Yankees. The left one was a Lou Gehrig man, the right one allegiant to Babe Ruth.

The Fifth Precinct was nothing to look at; besides, I kept my eyes to the slush-filthed floor. I was railroaded into an interrogation room with a table and two chairs, where Lou Gehrig told me to sit, the same as you'd tell a dog. I sat; Babe Ruth handcuffed my left wrist to the table, just above the old serving-fork wound from Dr. Leather. Now I insisted on knowing my crime. Lou Gehrig responded right away. Yankee Stadium, declared he, was the best ballpark ever. Babe Ruth, though, missed the old Polo Grounds. In verbal combat they were locked; so, too, was the door behind them.

One hour later, I was joined by a cop who looked as if his former career had been as a rock at Stonehenge. He was a brawler by all indications, complete with crooked nose and missing front tooth. He slapped down a file folder and crashed down into the other seat. His unruly red hair and explosion of freckles gave him a boyish, pugnacious look at odds with his watchful black eyes. He wore not the buttons, badges, and boots of his fellow garbage collectors but rather a smart suit and a stylish brown-and-black spotted silk tie.

In short, he looked like the sort of combatant who might toss a nobody like me into the slammer on general principle. So sick was I of life upon the nethermost social rung that the old Zebulon Finch insolence bubbled from my throat like bile.

"Detective Fergus Roseborough," said he in an Irish brogue. "You got something you need to say to me, you goddamn skullamug?"

"Well, Fergie," said I, "I suppose I should like to be let go."

His coal eyes glowed and he formed fists as big as medieval maces.

"Tell me your whereabouts New Year's Eve. Or January tenth. Or January sixteenth."

"This is a Prohibition matter? I assure you, I do not drink."

He huffed in disdain, picked up the folder, and glanced at a sheet.

"Charlotte Weidenheim? Lucille Schrubb? Beulah Olson?"

One of his fists uncurled, an invitation for response. I shrugged.

"Your favorite baby names? I vote for Beulah. Congratulations, by the way."

"You're telling me, to my ugly face, you don't know them."

"I should *like* to know them. Are they waiting outside? Why, the shy darlings."

"You think this is a joke? In about two minutes I rearrange your face, see how funny that is."

"If it is a joke, dear Fergie, I have yet to be let in on it."

He slapped the file to the table with enough noise to make me jump.

"They're dead, all them sweet girls. Dead in the worst ways. And I know you did it, you rotten kid."

Silence filled the room as muggy and malignant as mustard gas. I wiped it from my ears so that I might believe what had just been alleged. I, New York City's serial murderer? It was beyond comprehension. Roseborough's face had turned a pink so vigorous it swallowed the freckles. He cracked his knuckles. I took the flicker of panic I felt and attempted to gentle it to a controllable ember. I knew that I was about to behave in a reckless, immature way—but wasn't it progress that I at least recognized it?

"I knew an Irishman in the war," said I.

"Yeah?"

"*Yeah*," said I, mocking his street dialect. "He was insane, too."

It was foolproof bait; in the New York of 1930, hate was endemic. Italians hated Jews, Jews hated Irish, Irish hated blacks, and everyone hated the Roman Catholics. Roseborough slammed his meathooks to the table and the file folder jumped. I took little joy in his fury, for though Piano had indeed been an insane Irishman, his insanity had saved many an American butt. An instant later, the file folder touched down and spilled forth an array of photographs, some locket-sized, others wallet-sized, still others the size of a framed portrait.

"You know them, you filthy whelp," accused Roseborough. "Don't you?"

Ever willing was I to compare and contrast females; sadly, this flock would turn few heads. This one had a nose like a ripened strawberry. That one had a chip in her tooth she could suck spaghetti through. That other one's goony glasses could not, despite their efforts, distract from a walleyed stare. I was about to complain that I deserved a sharper selection when something about the walleyed miss caused me to take a closer look.

I *did* know this girl; I knew *all* of these girls. The names the detective had mentioned came into alignment with faces and I remembered exchanging pleasantries with them at various déclassé gin joints. The names of the others came back to me too—Josephine Harris of Fargo, Elizabeth Stearns of Oskaloosa, Audrey Rice of Santa Fe—each of them charming in her own way, each of them dead.

I blinked my astonished eyes at Roseborough.

"That's right, dumb fuck," said he. "I tracked you down. Skinny guy? Pale face? Hat brim out to here? Spotted talking to every single one of these young ladies? You weren't hard to find."

I touched my beloved fedora. Its soft, comforting realness gave me heart.

"Were they killed on the same nights that I met them?" asked I.

"You confess? Good, we can wrap this up nice and easy."

"Were they killed on the same nights that I met them?" repeated I.

Roseborough crossed his arms.

"I surmise that they were not," said I. "I submit to you, then, that I am being framed."

"Framed? Kid, if you think you're worth somebody going through all this trouble, you've got delusions of what-do-they-call it."

"Grandeur," said I.

"Goddamn right."

I squared my shoulders.

"You have the time and dates of the murders in that file? Very well; I will provide you with the names and addresses of my past employers. Surely some of the nights in question I was working. There will be records."

The twitch of Roseborough's lip indicated how he felt. But a splinter of doubt had penetrated his dinosaur skull, and he had even less patience for doubt than he did the due process of law. He withdrew from his suit pocket a pen—he would have rather drawn a knife—and took down my information. Then he took the photos and the file and left me without so much as a glass of water or a bathroom break, neither of which I needed but both of which seemed reasonable given my cooperation.

It was hours before his return. By then, his freckles had resurfaced and competed with the red glint of afternoon stubble. He did not sit; he tossed the file to the table and paced about like a lion, running his claws through the snags of his orange mane while sizing me up for dinner. At last he spoke—"Motherfucking goddamn son-of-a-bitching cunt" I believe was his artful idiom—and did the last thing I expected. He unlocked my handcuffs.

While I surveyed my wrist for permanent scarring, he gripped the back of his chair and muttered his next question.

"You ever worn a Van Dyke beard?"

Were that I could! Instead the smooth cheeks I died with became an advertisement of my eternal teenhood. This fellow knew how to get my goat.

"We are friends now?" snipped I. "We are to exchange fashion tips? Clearly you are pressing no charges; I demand you let me go!"

"It's the one thing that didn't line up. There was a survivor, see. This hasn't gone public. She didn't make it, not with what this monster did to her, but she lasted long enough to give us a description. Big sunglasses, a long Van Dyke. Sang a little ditty. I figured you could've grown a beard. Worn a fake one. Everything else pointed to you."

"I suppose that is as close as I will get to an apology."

He lifted his chair three feet and slammed it back. Two legs snapped off and the chair went toppling in a clatter of lumber.

"*This is not a fucking game!* Girls are being butchered! Your stories check out, so maybe you didn't do it. But the fact remains that every fucking girl you meet ends up dead. There's a killer pointing a finger right at you, and I'm asking you why that is! Think, why don't you? Someone who goes around singing the same little song all the time, someone you know who wears a Van Dyke, someone who's got it out for you—none of that rings a goddamn bell?"

"It does not. Even if it did, I do not believe I would tell you, not after such treatment. Now, may I be excused?"

Patches of pink rage again blotted out his freckles. He swiped up the folder, withdrew a stapled packet, thumbed through the pages.

"There's no record of you prior to 1925. I turned up a Zebulon Finch who fought with the Marines, but you're too young. You know what that makes me think? I think you're using a stolen name. I think you're covering your real identity. I'd hate to think you were an anarchist, friend. I'd hate to have to turn you in as a dirty Red."

I'd been accused of everything else in my time, so why not this as well? The blubbery bear of Russia had fallen in the war's Bolshevik Revolution, and the clouds of dust that had shot up at its collapse were called Communism. Under the principles of such radicals as Leon Trotsky and Vladimir Lenin (both of whom, incidentally, sported the Van Dyke), the ideal of an anti-capitalist society was taking hold across the world, and America, big and bad though she was, had begun to fear it. The Red Scare was spreading like the Spanish flu, and American men—white men, mind you—had been lynched for Communist sympathies.

"Help me out," said Roseborough, "and I won't dig any further."

To say the least, it gave me pause. If so committed a detective panned my past, he might turn up truths he could scarcely imagine.

"I don't give a shit if you're a commie or a socialist or a suffragist or what-all," continued he. "What I care about is getting this killer off the streets, and if that means I have to do bad shit to you, that's what I'm going to do. So what do you say? Work with me? We figure this out together?"

Even you, Dearest Reader, as far in the future as you might exist, must know of the youthful hotheadedness that compels you to shout down a caring parent, an apologetic lover, a recalcitrant friend, when but a single pill of humility is all that need be swallowed. Alack!—I

460

gagged on good sense, a self-thwarting reprobate to the end.

"An alternate proposal," said I. "How about you take that file of mine, roll it up good and tight, and insert it into your ass?"

I shall spare you a detailed catalogue of the phrases, gestures, and jets of spittle that followed, and remark only that Roseborough swore he was not finished with me, that if I so much as ate a sandwich (the joke was on him) or took a piss (ditto), he'd be there to arrest me for doing it wrong. He turned away before he went too far, neck pulsing and fists clenching, and kicked open the door hard enough to splinter it from the hinges. I took this as a signal to show myself out.

I, too, fumed as I clomped into the snow. That warthog in a suit knew nothing about me, how my time was occupied with protecting Church! I passed a line of dirty children three blocks long, each mutt clutching a frost-sparkled pail, tasked by their jobless parents to purchase a bucket of skim milk for the price of a nickel. Farther down the street I passed a vacant lot that had sprouted a shantytown for those who'd lost everything in the crash. I looked away, always away. Zebulon Finch did not, could not, would not care for those who could not care for themselves. The flappers of New York City were on their own to survive the modern mechanisms of murder, as was everyone else. This was America.

X.

ROSEBOROUGH DID NOT DISAPPOINT. OUT with Church buying bruised fruit, there was Babe Ruth pitching potatoes to Lou Gehrig. Waiting at the box office while Church counted change for a cheap matinee, there was Lou pantomiming "va-va-voom" to a movie poster while Babe dropped me a wink. Taking my turn at the grocer, there was Babe and Lou in a parked patrol car, laughing along to a luxury gadget the police were the first to get—a car radio.

Their eternal presence guaranteed that I could not forget my involvement in the ongoing murders. Even unarmed, I was lethal, for any shop girl, laundress, or female domestic with whom I interacted might end up dead. Thus I became a recluse. I withheld from Church my reasons out of concern that, should he find out, his fragile capacity to hold down a job might deteriorate. He frowned at my every convoluted deferral, cycling through surprise, hurt, and resentment before finally, perhaps to prove something to himself, heading out each night without me.

Yes, it disheartened me, but I was trapped. While I watched from the window his large form limp down the block, I kept an eye out for anyone casing the building. Would I recognize the Bird Hunter as a former Black Hand rival? Or would it be one of my past victims—one of the tattooed Triangulinos, perhaps? Or had I been chosen by the killer at random, the latest of my luckless strokes?

In May, Church and everyone else picking up hours at the Worthington Steel blast furnaces contracted an itchy toe fungus. I atoned for my immunity by offering to go out and buy for Church a jar of soothing petroleum jelly. In truth, I liked Chinatown best at night. Without the glare of sunlight to enervate you, the babble of Chinese became a burbling brook; the lit signs were divertingly haphazard in the time-honored way of immigrants; I even enjoyed the sewage stink emblematic of such rainy evenings. Most importantly, I need only interact, and therefore endanger, a single female—the store clerk. A jar of petroleum jelly versus a human life? Everything had become a game of odds.

For these very reasons I took a back route to the store, and that is how I ended up getting the drop on my pursuers.

Lou and the Babe lounged outside their vehicle, the latter examining a map while the former shelled peanuts. I retreated behind a trash bin stamped, wouldn't you know it, "Worthington Steel." Eavesdropping was not my aim; I wished only to wait them out and get back home with the petroleum jelly. But the meeting offered the sort of serendipity at which the frothing pot of New York City excelled.

"You hear about the old feller they got caged up in the thirtieth?" asked Lou.

"They got nothing but old fellers in the thirtieth," said the Babe.

"Not like this old feller. They got him trying to blow up a candy store."

The Babe sighed. "Fergie's going to serve our asses on a plate. How we'd lose the kid at one a.m. on a Monday? Who even goes out at one a.m. on a Monday?"

"Besides us?"

463

"Good point. So the old feller blew up a candy store?"

"He tried. Bomb didn't set."

"Sheesh. The Charleston Chews live to fight another day, eh?"

"The good part is why he did it."

"Let me guess. The Dum Dum company owed him big."

"Crazy old feller said there ought to be a road there. Quicker path from the Fort Lee Ferry to the Queensborough Bridge."

"Crazy old feller was right."

"Said it was his *job* to make the road. That's what he did—demolish buildings."

"We ought to hire him. Sic him on Chinatown, clear out a few of these chinks."

Surely the dig won the Babe a chortle, but I no longer listened, so paralyzed was I by the fiercest of hunches. I remained crouched for another thirty minutes before an upsurge of rain convinced the twins to pack it in. I stood, thankful for my fedora, and checked my pockets. Just enough change for cab fare north.

Amid the scarlet blear of wet streets and brake lights, I disembarked at the Thirtieth Precinct station, brushed off the rain, and presented myself as best I could to the on-duty officer. I was nervous but nevertheless asked after the prisoner, and though the officer surveyed my jar of petroleum jelly with suspicion, he conceded that they did have a jailee by that name, and, after some time spent conferring with superiors, announced that he was free to release the prisoner into my custody. The man was, after all, more senile than dangerous, and they were holding him only until they tracked down a family member.

A family member—the phrase was exotic to me.

The "crazy old feller" was my father.

Spewing words is my forte—this document attests to that—but I fear I shall flounder at describing my emotion when they brought forth the dynamitier Bartholomew Finch. The last I'd laid eyes on him had been in Chicago. I'd been fourteen and the circumstance had been one of those blustery-breeze visits that were his trademark. He burst through the front door, ushering in sunshine or leaves or snow, and clapped his hands to announce his arrival. A servant stripped his coat while my mother began her way down the staircase with me peeking from behind. Pop looked hopeful at her approach; I recall feeling the same. All she did, though, was angle her cheek to receive the perfunctory kiss. Then Bartholomew spotted me and offered a formal, if soot-stained, handshake. Diminished by the cold reception of his wife, he never had much vim left over for me.

A day or two later he left.

This night's script, rehearsed in the back of the taxi, was to be a short scene for two players, one heavy with theatrical cliché. I, the spurned son, would look into the eyes of my serial abandoner and unleash the words my audience was impatient to hear. I would hold this pitiless patriarch accountable for what he'd done, or not done, and how his absence had propelled me toward the unqualified replacements of the Barker, Dr. Leather, and John Quincy. I'd raise a fist and demand redress. He might even beg for mercy before the curtain fell.

The playwright, though, struck the pages, for the actor before me had been miscast. Where was his waxed mustache? The stylish chapeau? This Bartholomew Finch was jaundiced and saddlebagged, bowlegged and pigeontoed, lopsided of shoulder and contorted of torso. His collapsed chest cracked with phlegm. He was in his mid-seventies with the accoutrements thereby afforded.

The officer loathed playing nurse. He waved me near and, flummoxed, I took the old man's elbow; it shook badly. With my left hand I steadied his back; the flesh was feverish beneath the layers of damp clothing. He slumped into my grip, and just like that I was cradling him. I was stunned. Never before had I touched my father with such intimacy.

My emotions, you can be sure, were molten. I tabled deep thoughts and proceeded outside. The trip down seven wet steps was silent, slow, and treacherous. I spotted one block away the salvation of a twenty-four-hour diner. It took us ten minutes to get there, and once inside I dumped the old man into a booth. His knurled shoulder bone clacked against the wall and he coughed. I took a seat and wondered what the hell happened next. A tired waitress asked if we wanted coffee. I winced; she was female, perhaps a flapper, and was unsafe talking to me. I requested more time, then embarked upon further study of this crumpled ancient. At length I spoke.

"It's me, sir. It's Zebulon."

Sir? An undeserved greeting that came unbidden.

His pale tongue wormed round his cheeks.

"Don't know any Deborah."

"Zebulon."

"Carolyn?"

Descriptions of my father had never deviated from that of a man's man who insisted on doing everything himself, from prepping the TNT to triggering the detonation to observing the explosion at close range for evaluational purposes. This lifetime of blastwork had left him deaf. I raised my voice.

"Your son."

The dark pits of his pupils fought through cataract mucus.

466

"Can't be. You're still a boy."

This injured me in a way I could not specify.

"It is just your eyes, sir," said I.

He shrugged and searched the table.

"There are supposed to be poached eggs. They never remember."

"I'll order you some eggs."

He cocked his head. A lamp backlit his prodigious ear hair.

"Zebulon? It's been a spell. Where you been off to?"

"Everywhere." I felt a sudden need to impress him with all I'd done while he'd been off losing his ears, eyes, and mind. "Down South. Up and down the coast. Boston. France—I was in France, sir, in the war, I fought with the—"

"I'll never understand it. Who starts a war *knowing* dynamite exists? Mark my words, there won't be another one. No one's that dumb. Now where are those eggs? They never remember to poach them."

"I said I'll order you your damn eggs."

"Damage?

"*Damn eggs.*"

"They never poach them."

I shouted across the diner.

"*For the love of Christ, could we please get some fucking poached eggs?*"

I sawed my jaws while the old man sat unperturbed.

"So you have nothing to say to me?" demanded I.

"'To say?"

"Nothing to ask of my life, of what I've made of it?"

He blinked about, probably on the lookout for eggs.

"Here," said I. "I shall provide the dialogue. 'Tell me, dear son, wherever did you run off to all those years ago?'"

"Oh, yes. That is a good question."

"'Are you quite all right, dear son? Is there anything you need?'"

"That is a good question, too."

He waited upon the responses to this scintillating self-interview but I refused to further mock myself. The sizzle from the kitchen grill mimicked the frazzle of my brain until I could not help but break the stalemate.

"Well, you're sitting here, aren't you? Go on, tell me your story, get it over with. You live under some bridge, do you? You have big plans to blow up more candy stores? It's a fascinating life you live; 'twould be a shame if it went undocumented."

His skin was blue with veins brought to the fore by the cold. His fingertips were pink and torn from street scrabbling. So defenseless was he, and still I wished to hurt him.

"You lost all of your money," surmised I, "in the crash."

"Eh. It was Abigail who cared about money."

It should not have jolted me to hear my mother's name invoked, but it did. I saw her again asleep in the bedroom where I'd left her, tasted the saline kiss I'd applied to her forehead. This dodging miser shared none of the burden of such cumbrous memories. Oh, how I oozed distemper! Had he been a true husband and father, I would not have fled home, nor begun a criminal career, nor been shot on the beach, nor become this hopeless, hexed wraith.

"She had to care about something," snapped I.

"Abigail had the house. She had you."

"Indeed, indeed, and she treated both as equals—costly investments to be adorned in the most tasteful of trimmings."

"You know, m'boy, after you left she was never the same."

It was felicitous that this instant paired with the arrival of the

468

ballyhooed poached eggs. Pop mashed the translucent globules into pale yellow gruel that he then transported with a spoon into a gray-toothed mouth. I welcomed each labored step of this procedure, so bewildered was I by his statement.

"How do you mean she was not the same?"

He slurped his slime.

"Every time I came home, she kept up in that study of yours. Checking your schoolwork, reading your textbooks."

I struggled to fathom it: Abigail Finch, dispassionate manne-quin, lingering over the jejune trifles left behind by her escapee son? I pictured her up there, caressing my dusty workbooks, cocking her head in hopes that an echo of recited French might still be whisper-ing about the corner. In one second I was seized by a great, trembling fear that I'd been the wrong one all these years, that I'd been the one to misjudge. Had Abigail Finch loved me after all?

Even more painful to consider: had I, deep within, loved her?

My fork and spoon ring-tingled as I gripped the tabletop with trembling hands. To be a real live boy again, back in that mothballed house, back in those stiff clothes, where mother and child could have another go at the whole shebang. Was all hope lost? No! I remained seventeen! Young enough for a second chance, yet old enough to be bold about it, to wrap my arms around my mother's bony frame, tuck my cold face into her warm neck, and tell her that I was sorry for every foul thing I'd said, sorry for every ungrateful thing I'd done. Why, of course—my childhood room was where I could escape the dangers of New York!

Home: did the English language contain a more hopeful word?

"Mother," said I. "Please tell me where I might find her."

"Dead," blurted Bartholomew Finch. "Rabies."

He licked his fork with a sore-covered tongue.

As swiftly as the rare bird of hope had winged me heavenward, I was dropped back to Earth. I knew that after forty years of negligence I deserved no feeling of loss, but loss is what I felt. I pushed fists into my eyes so that my whole lonesome death might be blotted, but my dead eyes, dry of tears, only reminded me that there was no going back. Love, nourishment, shelter: such bright gems were reserved for the living.

Pulverizing despair clobbered me senseless. I surfaced minutes later still wet from the rain, down a mother, and with nothing to my person except a jar of petroleum jelly. Softly, then, to the slurping sounds of Bartholomew Finch and his eggs, I began to muse aloud, less to be heard by my father than to push myself to a reckoning.

"There is a killer on the loose," spoke I.

"A cow herd?"

"A *killer*. I have been asked to help catch him."

"This cow herd is on the loose, you say?"

"It digs at me, this request. I fear that I am a coward, if you want my confession."

"Your profession?"

"*Confession.*"

Pop wiped his lips with his palm and nodded.

"Glad to hear it, m'boy. There's nothing more important than your profession. Take me. I'm good at one thing, just one thing, and now they don't let me do it. Why? Because of all this so-called progress. Buildings so tall that one day, mark my words, they're going to fall down. Airplanes and zeppelins crashing all over when the roadway is as safe as can be. But no one wants anything destroyed anymore. Maybe it was the damn war, everyone lost their appetite. Take

470

my advice, m'boy. Do your job. Even when you're tired. Even when you're hurt. No matter if you're old like me or a whippersnapper like you. It's the American way: you do what you're good at and you keep on doing it."

The imbecile elder made so much sense that I doubted my own. My true profession was not working a shovel at Worthington Steel. My profession, as I'd learned on the banks of the Meuse, was and had always been *killer*. This did not, realized I, need always be a shameful fate. I could use my ability for good. I could do better than help the insulting Detective Roseborough catch the Bird Hunter. I could catch him myself, kill him myself, get my name and face on the front page of Kip McKenzie's paper, where even Bartholomew Finch, as confused as he was, would see it and know, somewhere in his heart, that I had, at long last, done him and Abigail Finch proud.

What was this mysterious heat warming my limbs of cold clay? Rabies, thought I, passed down through the cosmos, mother to son, all the better with which to poison my bite. I stood and arranged my fedora. We were done, the crazy old feller and I, this time for good, though he had, here at the end, pointed me in the right direction. For that I at least owed him breakfast. I removed my wallet and tossed to the counter my last dollar bill. He stroked it with a palsied finger bolted to an arthritic knuckle.

"To be young again," sighed he.

"No, sir," said I. "To be old. Now that would be something."

XI.

WITH NEITHER MONEY FOR A tailor nor a motherly sort from whom to pull a favor, I swiped a stapler from a sheet-music store and used it to fasten an old sock to the inside of my jacket. Into this sock I slid the sharpest knife in our apartment. On came my fedora and best suit; out came my Excelsior upon a chain so that I might twirl it to nonchalant effect; and northward I bused until I arrived at the city's scorched centrum, that furnace of saxophone and sex known as Harlem. If the Bird Hunter was anywhere to be found, it was here.

I was ill-prepared for the pungent squall of sensuality that clobbered me the second my shoes hit pavement: cotton danked by perspiration, perfume brined by sweat-slicked friction. Insatiate revelers pushed me down the sidewalk, where a lamppost provided bracket against the onset of a million watts: "DANCING" in twenty-foot letters; "LOUNGE" in epileptic strobes that promised anything but; "BALLROOM" bathed in a pink light hinting that the room was, indeed, for balling. "RADIUM," "WONDER," and "PARADISE"— words so hot that moths made love to them and died happy at my feet.

Van Dyke beard, repeated I, *oversized sunglasses, sings a little song.* It sounded easy enough, but each foot of pavement boasted examples of facial-hair foolery, tinted spectacles, and songs on every other lip. What seventeen-year-old had the stamina to remain loyal to his task

472

while Charlie Johnson, Fats Waller, and Jelly Roll Morton flogged their bands so hard that the wails of tortured pleasure bled through solid brick?

I ricocheted from brass-buttoned valet to stage-door Johnny and back again, each of whom had something to peddle: hot peanuts, a swig of coffin varnish, or, heck, how about some "reefer"—two fags for a quarter. I shook my head and bulleted for the swingingest club that might feasibly accept my grade of evening wear and gave them my standard sob story.

The market collapse might have turned Church's *nouveau riche* into the *nouveau poor*, but my, were they ever intent on going out with a bang! The way they hot-footed looked like it hurt. I skirted the upheaval and zeroed in on a table of tomatoes (to use the parlance) recuperating from the hedonistic ordeal. Was the killer watching? I hoped that he was. I patted my stashed knife and told myself that my approach on these girls was no different from a trench rush—some of them might die but those corpses would duckboard the mud for future survival.

As Church had predicted, Harlem girls were thoroughbreds. They sported velvet jackets with leg-o'-mutton sleeves as tenderly folded as bulldog skin; sleeveless tunics as tall and straight as the Chrysler Building; muslin skirts gussied with pearls. But no sooner had they pulled faces over how adorable I was (not the reaction I wanted!) than they were scurrying back to the floor for another round.

That would not do! I plunged after, pulling apart every couple to see whether I recognized an old enemy. This upset both genders, with the females telling me to blow, buster, while the male contingent began clearing floor space for my beating. But the girls swept them away in a silken swirl, leaving me to panic. Curses! Now I'd exposed all of them to danger, too many to possibly protect. I cut my losses and, as the flappers liked to say, ankled it out of there.

In transit I spotted Lou and the Babe exiting the club I'd just vacated. These bunglers were after me again and this time they'd find me knife-handed! I ducked and dashed and surfaced in a lesser joint nonetheless knocked on its ass by a brass brand loud enough to rattle the liquor. There I found a woman slingshotting her knickers into a man's lap before scaling a table and doing the Lindy Hop as if demonically possessed.

I'd paddled from the Styx only to sink into Tartarus; here came Lou and the Babe, tunneling through the mob. Again I swapped locations, this time landing in a humid underground bunker that I realized, too late, was colonized entirely by Negroes. I let go with a weary chuckle; if there were anywhere in Harlem I couldn't hide, this was it! Yet I could not bring myself to leave, so reminded was I of John Quincy's affectionate alky-cooker atmosphere. Enduring alarmed looks, I plodded into the bar morose as hell, commandeered a chair, and waited for the unrelenting twins to accost me.

What I got instead was the earsplitting bawl of a bullhorn.

"ATTENTION. ATTENTION. WE ARE CITY AND FEDERAL AGENTS AND THIS ESTABLISHMENT IS BEING RAIDED. PLEASE REMAIN WHERE YOU ARE."

In other words, giddy-up, and start the stampede! Every Manhattan gin joint, regardless of its backing by Luciano or the NYPD, had a secondary exit for raids, and toward it scrambled the smashed and the scared. A giant black man and I, abrupt allies, clutched each other against the rout. When I did manage to grapple my way up a barstool, I spied Lou and the Babe pointing the way for a coterie of badged invaders led by guess who? Fergus Roseborough, bigger and frecklier and redder-haired than I remembered and boasting the chic new accents of a black eye and a broken thumb.

The detective was using me as bait whether I liked it or not, and now half the black population of Harlem was paying the price. Overhead lights flooded on and the remaining habitués scattered like Chinatown roaches. I took off too, only to find a backdoor bottleneck as thick as any at Belleau Wood. Roseborough already owned that exit, in hopes of sifting from the silt a killer.

I changed direction to follow a skedaddling bar-back. He stormed the ladies room, cutting through a receiving line of women holding their handbags like nightsticks. The bar-back ignored the threat and cranked a coat hook until a section of brick wall swung inward. A tunnel was revealed—a third exit!—and the bar-back took it. I followed, leading a wagon train of women, until one by one we emerged cobwebbed and crudded from an alleyway manhole.

The raids had an immediate effect upon neighboring establishments. Thickset porters linked arms along 131st Street to ensure that hysteria did not taint their Caucasian congregations and that no rabblerouser like me got inside. The streets, thankfully, were a shaken hive of deserters and I fit right in, striding southward as if late for a business meeting set for the curious hour of midnight.

At this rate, luring the Bird Hunter would be a chore indeed. I'd not quite escaped the jazz-time jamboree when a fellow barely my senior caught up to me and popped his red-feathered homburg in salutation without losing pace. He was a stub of a man, measuring to my chin, tow-headed and bright-eyed and spruced in the most youthful of fashions, which is to say he looked like an escapee from Princeton: tan-and-green checkerboard jacket, baggy breeches, and

475

knee-length boots better suited for cropping horses than copping ladies.

"Hot socks, Jim Thorpe! You've sure got anties in your panties! Where's the fire?"

"Pardon, good sir," said I, "but I do not seek conversation."

"Oh, I'm hipped to that. I'd feel the same, chased off by Roseborough and his goons."

I glared in apprehension but kept moving.

"What do you know of it?"

"What do I . . . ? Oh, applesauce! I forgot the glad hand." He stuck out his palm. "They call me Kip, Kip McKenzie."

I tripped over my feet and pitched toward the cement, only to right myself and find that the fast-talking midget was real. Certainly the brawny, ironclad newspapering on which I'd come to depend originated with a sunburned, sleeve-rolled Hemingway. Not this jittery little chipmunk!

"*You* are Kip McKenzie?"

He snapped his fingers.

"Now you're on the trolley! It's swell you've heard of me, we can skip the beauty parlor chit-chat."

"What are you doing here?"

"Same as you, Jim Thorpe, nosing out leads. Roseborough, the big ape, he means well, but he's got all the nuance of a battleship in a mud puddle. He's all over *you*, that's for sure, which means I need to be all over you, too. We copacetic?"

I had no time to reconcile my admiration for this pipsqueak's writing with the immediate problem of my getaway.

"Copacetic we are assuredly not. Yield the sidewalk!"

The gazetteer must have been one hell of a dancer. Courtesy of some fabulous footwork, he hurdled the curb and walked in reverse so that he could look me in the mug as I charged onward. Quite piqued now, I flashed him the knife inside my jacket.

"Wowza, Jim Thorpe," said he. "If a steak falls out of the sky, you'll be ready to eat it. Come on, fella, don't have a kitten. Everything's jake, baby, I'm on the level."

"I'll level *you*."

He yanked his tie to the side so that his collar followed. Beneath his clavicle was a round pink scar.

"Caught a congressman in an affair, real tawdry one, too. Took a bullet for my trouble." Next he pushed back his sleeve to display a white line drawn wrist to elbow. "Exposed some no-bid government contracts. Hardly the Teapot Dome scandal, but I got a scratch for it anyway, plus sixteen swell stitches. So between me and you and the fence post, nothing you're liable to say is going to send me high-tailing. Cripes, listen to me beat my gums! Let's talk about you."

"What do you want?"

"Dirt, details, chin music—whatever you got."

"I refuse to disentangle your gibberish. Tell me what you know."

"Van Dyke, big sunglasses, sings a song. Am I aces so far?"

"Where did you hear all that?"

His grin was so pleased!

"Aw, a good reporter can't kiss and tell. What I don't know, see, is why the Bird Hunter is circling you buzzard-like. If I knew, I could solve this thing lickety-split, make Roseborough and his boobs the laughingstock of the town. Would that be the berries or would that be the berries?"

A hailstorm of running, shoving, and general umbrage rose one block to our rear. McKenzie's playful eyes flicked over my shoulder.

477

"Speak of the devil and here come his gargoyles." He tsked his disappointment and whipped from his jacket, with substantial panache, a business card. "Here, let me prove myself. You take this card, chew it over, give me a ring-a-ding-ding, and I'll head off Laurel and Hardy here. Deal?"

I hated to abet any scheme this sprightly insect hatched, but I relished even less what might happen if Lou and the Babe found that knife in my coat. So I snatched the card and his homburg, too, planting on his white-blond crown my cherished Knapp-Felt fedora. McKenzie's confusion lasted only a second. He grinned and waggled a finger at me.

"The old bait-and-switch! You're a tricky one, Jim Thorpe. Let's gab real soon. Don't take any wooden nickels!"

Kip McKenzie put the breaks on his backward foxtrot, spun upon his ridiculous horse-riding heel, and began to saunter down a cross street, whistling, the fedora banked so that he might be mistaken for me. I wanted to pluck the silly red feather before putting on McKenzie's homburg, but then was not the moment for snobbish adjustments. I crumpled his business card and tossed it to the street. I needed to hoof it, and fast. Everyone in the city, or so it seemed, wanted a piece of me.

XII.

THE NIGHTS! THE RAIDS! THE FIGHTS! Ever through Harlem I crashed. The Bird Hunter terrorized with equal gall, claiming several flappers whose rotten luck had placed them in my path. The bloodbath would have commanded national headlines were our country not tobogganing toward the Great Depression. Kip McKenzie, at least, clung to the story like a tick, and to earn his keep made the news bright, syrupy, and stinking of blood.

Wadded, his pages made acceptable pillows; many a night I spent among the winos of good old Battery Park, so uncomfortable had life with Church become. When not galumphing about Manhattan begging for work that no longer existed, he was frowning at my odd-hour returns from reconnaissance. He was no fool; I was hiding a secret and he knew it. But I would not involve in my dangerous scheme a man who had already survived too much danger.

Hence he and I were riven, left to tiptoe around each other's unarticulated failures. Day by day, I was losing the trust of my only friend.

It rather tore me apart.

Weeks after we'd swapped headgear, McKenzie extended to me an enigmatical entrée at the end of his column:

POSTSCRIPTUM TO "JIM THORPE": CONTACT
ME VIS-À-VIS BIRD HUNTER, VIZ. DESCRIPTION,

LOCALE, RELATION TO SELF, ETC. K. McK. % NYHT.

Indeed it did stimulate me to be mentioned in the *New York Herald Tribune*, an institution even finer than my prized *Atlanta Constitution*. Still, I resisted the flattery. The killer operated just beyond my reach, evident as smoke and equally as hard to catch.

McKenzie, though, proved tireless. His obscure postscript captured the city's imagination and letters flooded in demanding more details about this "Jim Thorpe." It was a publicity coup d'état and McKenzie a clever revolutionary. He lectured his followers on the reporter's code, how he shan't ever divulge a source. Nice speech, but it did not stop him from stirring the pot and thickening it with fresh ingredients.

POSTSCRIPTUM TO "JIM THORPE": IMPERATIVE WE MEET. LIVES HANG IN BALANCE. REACH ME % NYHT.

POSTSCRIPTUM TO "JIM THORPE": LYRICS OF SONG (YOU KNOW WHAT I MEAN) COULD EXPLAIN ALL. LEADS PENDING. FIND ME % NYHT.

POSTSCRIPTUM TO "JIM THORPE": "BIRD HUNTER" ANAGRAMS—"BURRED HINT," "INBRED THRU," "RIB END HURT," "BURNT HIDER." FAMILIAR? CONTACT VIA % NYHT.

This last cryptogrammic clue didn't even make sense, as it had been McKenzie himself who'd invented the alias—not that his rabid readers would pause to remember. At last, on March 15, 1931, McKenzie deviated from the cock-and-bull, though I am sure he did not realize it. I read that day's paper late—perilously late as it turned out—plucking the issue from a trash can after midnight in Battery Park, where I had set up camp away from Church for what was going on three days.

POSTSCRIPTUM TO "JIM THORPE": ANONYMOUS TIP—BIRD HUNTER REQUESTS TO MEET "JIM THORPE" THIS DAWN AT "THE DREAM"—SENSE TO YOU? LET'S DISCUSS. % NYHT.

Slide yourself into my cold corpse, Reader, see if you feel my nausea. The Bird Hunter had more than followed me about New York. He'd been my very shadow, eavesdropping while Church spun fantasies out of aspirational thread. The Dream, the secret he and I shared, had now been parceled to thousands via inky-palmed newsies, though only I had the ability to decipher it.

Dawn threatened. No cab fare.

See how fast I run?

The Cotton Club looked shabbier by daybreak. I'd prayed before its radiant altar many a Harlem night until colored doormen brushed me back to hold limousine doors for fur-coated Shebas and their bow-tied sheiks. But at 5:45 a.m. the iconic letters were unlit and watched the sky like stone relics of some once-important edifice. I crept close, weak with dread.

Parties here raged all night, but between the last ejected debauchee and the arrival of the morning custodians existed this dead zone. I ducked beneath the marquee and peered through the glass. I could see nothing but an obelisk of a red-carpeted stairway. If the Bird Hunter was wily enough to hide inside the club before it closed, he would not be so dim as to invite me through the front door. I slinked into the alley, where I surmounted a locked gate.

From there I climbed a back staircase to the musicians' entrance and found a door thrown wide to backstage darkness—a menacing sight. Yet I entered and from the murk discerned sleeping stage lights, dangling curtain tassels, a centipedal stack of top hats. A windowless tunnel took me deeper, a vein leading to the club's heart.

Now I knew how those English chaps had felt eight years back when breaching Tutankhamun's tomb. Here I was in the Cotton Club at last, a deserted but breathtaking salon of frescoes lording over the country-home facade of the bandstand, from which the stage extended like a tongue. The majesty, however, was sullied by the smolder of early morning, the funk of stagnating alcohol, and the leavings of the aristocracy—widowed earrings, flyaway headdress feathers, each bit of detritus easy to imagine being ripped off by a murderer's hand.

The club mourned along with me: a lost, lonely jazz note scuttled along the wainscot, searching for an exit. No—this note hadn't been birthed by Duke Ellington or Cab Calloway. In a room that demanded a whirling tempest, it was too soft a whistle. It took me a moment to realize that there should not have been any music playing at all.

Fear should have stopped me but I moved as if on rails, following the whistle to a dining room designed in African motif. The joint jumped with the ghosts of cigarette girls, baseball sluggers, gangsters, and actresses. With every squeak of floorboard, I found myself rather longing for the busted-up braggadocio of Roseborough. I'd telephoned the NYPD a message about the Cotton Club on my way there—a fail-safe, nothing more. Should the Bird Hunter manage to dispatch me, too, I wished Roseborough to have a shot at catching him. Charlotte Weidenheim, Lucille Schrubb, and Beulah Olson deserved that much.

The Bird Hunter, when I encountered him, did not spring from the faux jungle like a panther. His was instead a sedate and natural reveal. He stood ten feet away among chairs stacked upside-down by the waitstaff, aglow inside a windowframed bud of sun, cloaked by lingering cigarette smoke, and whistling his song. Roseborough, though, had misunderstood his key witness; this was no "little ditty." I knew this not because I understood the language in which it was sung but because of the frequency with which I'd heard it. Reader, I wager that you, too, remember it.

Moro, losso, al mio duolo.

It was not a Van Dyke beard that hung from the killer's face. It was, rather, a long oxygen tube, furred with mud, filth, and cobweb. Nor were those sunglasses. They were, rather, glass lenses, tinctured brown by the elements and betraying nothing of the man inside the iron helmet. The song, muffled by metal, concluded, and gave way to the sound that had chased me halfway across the world.

Hweeeeee . . . fweeeeee . . . hweeeeee . . . fweeeeee . . .

Two inhales, two exhales—a butterfly breeze that brought with it the pollen barbs of pure terror. Like a dog hearing his master's angry tone, my instinct was rudely physical. My neck shrank and shoulders scrunched, the timorous stance of a domineered son, yes, but also that of a soldier lugging too much gear across a French countryside, alone but for the unabating ridicule of his adoptive father ringing inside his bones.

Four two-top dining tables had been brought together to form an operating platform. Rose-petal wine glasses did the job of beakers; tall beer mugs stood in for graduated cylinders; lit candles acted as Bunsen burners; and substituting for scalpels was a spread of kitchen implements upon a bar stool, arranged by size from paring knife to cleaver. Upon that same stool rested an oxygen tank.

Hweeeeee . . . fweeeeee . . . hweeeeee . . . fweeeeee . . .

Then there was the matter of the body laid out for dissection. It was no flapper, no female at all. It was Church. His presence was so unexpected that it took a while for me to register that he was naked and trussed, his wrists taped beneath his back so that his belly pushed into the air, begging to be carved. Despite this, he was unperturbed, clearly victim to a tranquilizing ether.

Hwee, hwee, hwee—

Three rapid inhales in preparation for speech, then the helmet was pushed to the crown of the man's head. Dr. Cornelius Leather was near sixty, and the years had been cruel to his fastidious features. His eye sockets were foxholes, his cheekbones broken peaks. His nose and forehead bubbled with infection brought about by continual contact with the helmet. Most distressing of all, a transient life had made shaving impossible and thereby proved Dr. Cockshut's accusation: Leather was inadequate at growing a beard. Each straggle was glued inside moist scabs. The humid sickhouse of the Isolator had turned his very face into an experiment.

Church blinked swollen eyes up at me.

"Private?" The voice was thick and slow. "Private Finch?"

Leather petted Church's hair to calm him. Then he took up the paring knife and tapped a wine glass.

"Best instruments I've had in ages," said he. "Clean, sterilized."

484

There was no telling how this bogeyman had kept himself stocked with tanks, but two decades of oxygen sousing had ransacked his bodily systems. Muscle seizures danced him about like a puppet; his left eye did not move, as if its stem had detached; and his lungs snapped with mucus. The gait of his speech was choppier than ever; every short sentence was stolen between gasps of air.

"My hand upon the Hippocratic Oath. Or Ibn Sina's Canon. Whichever trivial pamphlet you prefer. I swear that every dead girl. Has contributed to our goal. With respect to the brain's electricity. I have applied what meat etiquette taught us. Even under the most toilsome of conditions. I have eviscerated cows. So as to warm myself in their innards. Have fed from troughs. Performed operations in sewers."

He grinned. What few teeth remained were black.

"I," proclaimed he, "am a surgeon."

Though I was a creature unbothered by cold, I shivered. Leather was, to a point, correct. Robbed of money, esteem, home, and license, Leather, that rhapsodic slicer of flesh, had contrived new methods of acquiring anatomical playthings. Crowded New York City sidewalks had become his People Garden, the municipal grid his Revelation Almanac. My shiver devolved into a shudder. What had become of kindhearted Mary? And blameless Gladys? Had they, too, become sacrifices to the cause?

I'd been a myopic fool. Murders? No. They'd been *vivisections*.

His chest blasted with phlegm. It was a laugh. He knew what I was thinking.

"Surely you do not consider. My experiments to be murders. Did not you, as well, my brave soldier? Murder for a greater good? I so wished to join you in battle. The British, they were oxen. Typed their rejection onto a form. Subject: my mind. It pains me even now. All those available carcasses. All that anatomy revealed. Had I access to that slaughter? I might have saved millions."

My faltering frame teetered. The idea of rushing around a trench corner to find the leering Dr. Leather was too much to bear. I lurched for the stabilizing back of a chair, and from there gauged that I'd shortened the distance between us to nine feet. For Mary and Gladys I would need to tighten the threads of my loosened mind, distract the doctor with dialogue, and creep close enough to disarm him of that knife.

"Tell me what you want."

My, how insignificant I sounded.

"No less than the Fountain of Youth," replied he. "Herodotus. Alexander the Great. Ponce de León. May our tireless forebears rest in peace. For the Fountain exists. Not upon mythical soil. But inside each brain. Tonight I feel joy. Won't you share it with me? Through many overgrown paths I have carved our way."

I pushed away from the chair. Eight feet now, but I was skittish and my ankle buckled. Church, in his infant state, snorted amusement.

"Yes, Doctor, you have carved," said I. "But the carving has been upon innocent young women. You cannot believe that their deaths were deserved."

He lifted his head as if seeing these girls frolic like fairies among the hanging ferns. He massaged his exposed neck to provoke oxygen flow. One overgrown nail snagged a patch of beard and the skin tore, discharging an opaque pus.

"Their deaths *were* deserved. In a most efficacious sense. For you, Mr. Finch, are the one who chose them. My job was but to dole out their rewards. The opportunity to be like you. To have a chance at eternal youth."

I dared take another step. Seven feet. Nearly close enough, if I were to lunge, to pull Church to the floor. I ordered myself to keep talking, though all I wanted was to run.

"Forgive me for saying so, Doctor—but haven't you failed?"

He shrugged as best he could beneath the Isolator's weight.

"Young women. Were easier to catch. A necessary consideration. For I am not so strong these days. But in the end, it was a problem. Female brains are too small. A quarter-pound smaller than the male. Difficult to navigate. Even for proficient hands. But tonight, a larger subject. Your friend. Doesn't he help convince you? Let us make it so that the two of you. Can be friends forever."

His paring knife floated across Church's body as if blessing it.

While he looked down, I scuffled closer. Six feet, five. I could smell the vagrant sweat.

"Please," said I. "Forego the knife. Join me over here, in this booth. We can sit together in comfort, talk about the old days, for as long as you like." I cringed. "You frighten me, Doctor."

"Frighten? That injures me. My intent is to comfort. The premise, to you, should be familiar. I insert copper pins. Into particular ganglia. Then power them with electrical current. Our female subjects made stunning achievements. One sat up, tried to stand. Another acknowledged pleasure and pain. The last conversed with me. For forty-eight minutes. *Forty-eight minutes, Finch.* Do you see? We stand at the threshold."

There, at springing distance, I paused. The sad misalignment of his eyes made his appeal all the more affecting. The doctor had been twisted, yes, but had it not been the rough washmaid hands of life that had done so much of the twisting? His original plan for me had been pure, and coated though he was in grime, that kind of purity could not be polluted. His was an unsurpassable brain, even drunk on oxygen; he was a hundred horrible things and a liar was not one of them.

Success, then, was a grape at last ripe enough to pluck. Could it be that inside the flayed organs and between the isolated synapses of two dozen dead flappers, Leather had sourced the uncanny embryo of my existence, a feat no sane man could achieve? By this same power, might he reverse my sorry fate? So help me, I believed it. It had been so long since I'd believed in anything.

The paring knife was no more than an educator's baton; he set it down. It was the ideal moment to attack, but I did nothing but observe the doctor pick up a serrated bone saw and place it upon the patient's sternum. Leather knew that this, too, would be a familiar sight to his dutiful son. He'd always required access to the heart when manipulating the brain.

"S'cold," tee-heed Church.

I gazed down at my friend. It was curious, the extent of my numbness. Hadn't I always held that Burt Churchwell deserved a chance at immortality? Middle age and infirmity did not suit such a warrior. If it succeeded, this procedure might return to him all he'd lost: fearlessness, heroism, valor. And so what if it failed? What mattered of Church's life, I told myself, had been lost in the Argonne Forest, and his technical death here would be negligible, of no more consequence than that of Mary and Gladys Leather—cheap fare, on the whole, for a shortcut across what, for me, was a journey of dispiriting length.

"Come, then," said Leather. "Steady an old man's hand."

And I did. There I was. At table's edge. My hand atop his. The fear was gone. How had it happened? No matter. With more tenderness than I'd assisted Bartholomew Finch from the Thirtieth Precinct, I helped this alternate, but superior, father adjust his saw for a truer entry. To my great shock, Leather began to quiver. His lips trembled. His breath snagged. This man, cold as stone, was overcome by my touch. The Excelsior, my closest thing to a heart, ticked so hard I thought it might explode. Leather and I were together again. Anything was possible. Tears ran from his eyes, even the dead one, and embarrassed, he reached up and hid his crying face with the Isolator.

Hweeeeee . . . fweeeeee . . . hweeeeee . . . fweeeeee . . .

He lifted the saw two inches so that he might apply maximal force. Though I knew what sort of spatter to expect, I did not step back, but rather licked my lips, lusting for a tide of blood upon which I might float my hope ever higher, while at the same time stomping into the mud whatever shame still remained.

The saw plunged.

Hweee—

Flesh opened in the chest, but the wrong chest. It was quite a surprise, that plosion of white skin, red meat, and greasy clothing. The cream-colored wallpaper behind Leather was atomized with a black sunflower of blood ripped straight from his waterlogged lungs. An instant later the gunshot reported in my ears and my reaction was not a self-protective dive but rather to reach for Leather and shout—

"*NO!*"

—for this was my personal Revelation, my chance to reach into Gød's guts, squeeze the supernova of His heart, and steal the plot printed upon His pulmonary pulsars. It was not just Cornelius

Leather gored, it was Zebulon Finch, and what bled from him was his last chance for peace.

I scrambled forward, hip knocking one of the dining tables out of position. Upon the floor knives clattered and glasses shattered and something the size of a body fell, too, but I cared not. I pushed past the spoils and fell upon my fallen savior, my torturer, my pursuer, my savior again.

"Get off him, Finch!"

Of course Detective Roseborough had read McKenzie's column. Of course he would have Lou and the Babe on my tail. Of course my uncredited message had reached him via NYPD mobile radio. The lone surprise among these predictabilities was that the bruiser had stealthed through the club without knocking down a single stack of breakables to warn us of his arrival.

Roseborough's command went ignored. I tore the Isolator from Leather's face and pressed a hand to the gouge in his chest. Hot blood squeezed past my fingers. Were only the Cotton Club stocked with actual cotton, so that I might staunch this mortal wound! Failing that, I'd take one of Church's fabled Great War lemon drops, which might keep Leather alive for a few more moments, enough to tell me what I needed to know.

Leather expelled a hellacious liquid and his pale lips made fish kisses.

"Quick!" cried I. "Tell me what you know!"

"Step aside!" Roseborough, closer. "Step to the goddamn side!"

Leather's eyes showed their yellow underbellies.

"The hypnotist," uttered he. "Phrenologist. Priestess."

"Yes, yes, what of them?"

"MOVE, FINCH! OR I WILL SHOOT YOU IN THE FUCK-ING HEAD!"

490

"Please, doctor!" begged I. "What did they tell you?"

But Leather had his own request.

"I only ever wanted to know the end. Might you, dear boy, give me a taste?"

How many of the moribund had so far received my ministrations? What did it cost me, besides psychic upset, to drip onto his penitent tongue the sacramental wine of *la silenziosità*? But I was selfish and in that, our final moment together, cared only about my own answers.

Neither of us got what we wanted. A fist snatched my hair and wrenched back my head, and in this inverted world I saw Roseborough's boulder jaw, hastily bandaged—another fight?—and his extended arm, which ended in a revolver. The gun jutted forth; the barrel grazed my nose. Without ado, it discharged at a distance of a foot, and Cornelius Leather became a string of very small, almost invisible dots upon the vast timeline of American history.

What a mess, thought I, for the janitors to find.

Church had ended up on the floor. The bone saw had done damage. Blood poured from a gash in his chest and globs of gore stippled his naked body, and yet he chuckled. One of Leather's knives glinted and I snatched it, intent to finish what the doctor started. Hadn't I learned the routine by now? I rolled atop Church and raised the weapon, ready to slit him from gullet to groin in hopes that the secrets Leather had isolated in his recent research would be waiting just under the skin, suckling for my attention.

The giddy glaze of Church's eyes cleared like slandered clouds from an uncivil sun. His witless grin wavered. This could not be his best friend ready to murder him, could it? A fine question! Could it, Dearest Reader? Could it?

It was only the lack of time that stopped me from ripping him open. I dropped the knife and pushed away. The heels of my hands slid through brain matter and I collapsed next to one of Leather's ears. Whether the ear was still attached to his head I did not care to know. Up above, a mile away, Roseborough was shouting instructions at underlings still making their way from backstage. Soon the place would be a cyclone of activity as humans once again attempted to wipe away all traces of inhumanity, never caring that inhumanity was all to which some of us had to cling.

I put my lips to the ear. It was already cooling. I had acted too late before—recall the fate of John Quincy and Mother Mash—and so I whispered but one quick confession. I repeat it here, for you, Reader, only you, always you. Keep it, if you dare, at your bosom, so that its arctic secret might be thawed by your beating heart.

"I indicate," said I, "that I understand you."

PART SIX

1932–1941

———◦◉◦———

*Being The Thrills, Chills, Glitz, And Gloom
Experienced By Your Hero In A Beautiful
Make-Believe World.*

I.

M Y CARCASS HAD SEEN livelier days. Pallid during the 1890s and bluish at millennium's dawn, my flesh had, at its dawdler's pace, followed the devolution of the typical People Garden partygoer, and by 1932 I was the shocking white of a fresh piece of paper. My feet and back had adopted a periwinkle hue, thanks to the pooling of old blood when I walked or reclined, and my muscles had begun to sag as if strapped to my bones by weakening elastic bands. My skeleton was becoming assertive; clothing could barely hide the handlebars of my clavicle, the shutter slats of my ribs, the bowl of my pelvis.

Now add to this the mortal offenses. Fishing-hook chasms, pistol-duel holes, meat-etiquette gouges, stomach-flap stitches, a clay-and-straw-stuffed thigh. Each of these gross infractions I had ample time to fret about as the make-up girl clapped powder upon my face and the film crew scuttled about adjusting heavy lights atop telescoping stands. The motion picture camera itself was locked onto the head of a tripod and into it was slotted a mouse-eared magazine. The hooded lens fixed me with its raven stare.

Before the film runs, let me chronicle the *mise-en-scène*.

You may credit the sensational aftermath of the Bird Hunter's death to Kip McKenzie, who parlayed his bit part in the climax into a relentlessly promoted ten-part series of articles that told the entire

495

tale front to back with a librettist's flair for sentiment and exaggeration. The most egregious of fabrications was McKenzie's casting of himself as hero, piecing together clues just in time to stop the killer from striking again.

I was named in the story whether I liked it or not—and I *did* like it, if you want to know the truth. Less enamored of the attention was my roommate. Leather's saw had perforated Church's left lung, leaving him with a clattering cough that soiled his every shirt with blood. Co-starring in a splashy news story came with no financial benefits and we hadn't the war chest for the operation he required. Instead he rambled about the apartment unfit for work and spitting up lung tissue.

Expectoration or accusation? I could not tell. I lived in flinching fear that Church's ether-murked memory of the Cotton Club would come rushing back. Already he'd learned from McKenzie's articles how I'd hidden from him my pursuit of the Bird Hunter, and it had confused and upset him. He'd risked all to protect me in France and still I had not trusted him?

The penance I paid was to navigate the city, night and day, to scrounge paying gigs—and in the interim keep my friend stocked with clean handkerchiefs to tidy his spritzed blood. Just such proletariat scrabbling occupied me when I received a most startling proposal. It manifested as a Western Union telegram from Hearst Metrotone, the newsreel service of the Fox Film Corporation, one of the biggest movie studios in Hollywood. The unbelievable contents were as follows:

MR. ZEBULON FINCH
NEW YORK (NEW YORK)

*READING WITH GREAT INTEREST OF YOUR
RECENT CIRCUMSTANCES STOP DESIRE TO PURSUE
ARRANGEMENT WITH YOU TO APPEAR IN ONE-
REEL FILMED PICTURE ABOUT ROLE IN MURDERS
STOP CAN OFFER COMPENSATION OF $35 FOR YOUR
TROUBLE STOP KINDLY CABLE RETURN LETTER
AT MY EXPENSE STOP YOURS MOST SINCERELY*

ED MANN

CULVER CITY (CALIFORNIA)

You know I am starry-eyed; I do not dispute it. Allow me, though, to dazzle you with a pendant of benevolence. Thirty-five dollars was a goodly sum, and every penny could go toward Church's medical care. Noble enough for you? Good. Now, Dearest Reader, let me to gibber like a little girl. Hollywood! Wanted me! For a picture show! I had to hug a lamppost so that I could bear the imposing vision of myself as a black-and-white god flickering across the colossal screen of some columnated picture palace.

Because the enterprise seemed gauche considering Church's suffering, I kept the news to myself. I cabled Ed Mann that very day, I did, picturing in my mind's eye the broad-chested stallion who might go by such a name. Further briefings followed, each one studded with specifics, the most fabulous of which was that my film was to be one of the fashionable new talkies!

I was sick with nerves on production day. At noon I reported to a gentleman's club on the Upper East Side, a solemn four-story structure that blinded me with its polished mahogany surfaces. Luckily,

497

a club steward presented himself, took my coat and hat, and led me into a well-carpeted smoking room, where I was greeted by the first of what would prove to be three or four dozen disappointments.

Ed Mann was an eel who looked as if owed a year's worth of sleep. He licked stray luncheon off his fingers and offered me a sticky handshake while checking a pocket watch with his other hand. My story, griped he, was the first of three scheduled for the afternoon, so there was not one second to spare. He shoved me out the door with his three-person crew in pursuit, sacking my premeditated plan to impress him with rapier wit.

Our first location was a street corner down the block. For a Depression-era pittance, Mann had availed himself of the services of an elderly Jewess whom I was tasked with helping across the street. Mann snatched the woman's gnarled hand, pressed it to my forearm, checked his pocket watch, and scurried back to look through the camera.

"Terribly sorry," said I, "but what relation has this to the murders?"

"You're a doer of good deeds!" shouted Mann. "We're just establishing that with filmic shorthand!"

Filmic shorthand, eh? That sounded quite elaborate! I took the invigorating deep breath due a saint such as myself and patted the hand of the poor, wrinkled crone. True, I'd be more likely to elbow this slowpoke from the sidewalk rather than help her along, but who cared—the movie mechanism had begun to wind! A burly sort lowered over my head a long pole with a microphone attached on the end while bewildering slang began to sling.

"Sound ready?"

"Ready."

"Camera ready?"

"Ready."

"Roll sound!"

"Sound rolling."

"Roll camera!"

"Camera rolling."

"Zebulon Finch, Roll One, Scene Five, Take One. Mark!"

"Scene Five?" asked I. "What of Scene One through—"

The slate board cracked! I jumped.

"And action!" cried Mann.

The camera purred like a huntress lynx. I, the prey, retracted into a defensive crouch. As luck would have it, the biddy clinging to my arm was a born ham; she clutched my cold fingers and sang, "Oh, *angel*, it is so *kind* of you to help a *sickly grandmother* like me across this *dangerous city street!*"

So that's what I did, feeling as natural as if being filmed toilet-papering my ass. But after Mann bellowed, "Cut! Print! Moving on!" I heard no complaints. I searched about, suddenly hungry for feedback, but Mann was cursing his watch and storming toward the next set-up. Which involved, if you can believe it, me ruffling the revolting hair of some lice-ridden street urchin, which was followed by a shot of me extracting a hissing cat from a tree and handing over the flailing monster to an indebted housewife. This fraudulent flimflam continued until at last, per Mann's schedule, we looped our way back to the club for a concluding interview.

Here, Reader, is where you first joined us beneath the blazing kliegs: your hero caked in women's cosmetics, costumed in a smoking jacket and cravat, and posed just so against a splendiferous hearth while the accessory of a gourd calabash pipe was wedged into my palm. This was a Zebulon Finch whitewashed to fit the vanilla palate of the moviegoing masses—but, gee, anything for the movies!

With camera a-whir, Mann began to toss questions so soft they barely qualified as such. *Can you describe your heroic resolve in catching the Bird Hunter? It was concern for the safety of others that drove you, is that right?* Their design precluded anything but the doughiest of replies. I obliged, feeling a bit peppery, while Mann checked his damnable watch.

At length a displeasing odor permeated the room.

Mann, for the first time, paid attention. He sniff-sniffed.

"What the dickens is that? Smells like turned meat."

The klieg lights—the heat upon my dead flesh—how embarrassing.

"Sorry, gents." I cleared my throat. "I'm afraid that would be me."

Mann's crack team of dunderheads misunderstood. Believing that I had caught aflame, the sound recorder produced a brass fire extinguisher and ran toward me operating the pump. His foot caught on an Oriental rug, the extinguisher went airborne, and he reached for the nearest light stand for help. It was slapstick worthy of Harold Lloyd: the light toppled and smashed to pieces against the hearth, a comical hair's breadth from my casually propped elbow.

Into the room blundered the steward followed by a pride of club elite. An argument about the damage erupted. It was during the top-volume squabble that I noticed a large glass shard from the klieg jutting from my left thigh. I sighed, for they were my best trousers. I removed the glass and held it up so that I might curse it—this was hardly the debut of which I'd dreamt—before noticing that the assemblage had suspended their row to stare.

I hid the shard behind my back like a child.

"It is nothing," said I. "Recommence your quarrel."

Mann's pocket watch made no further appearances. His later appointments were forgotten. A dormant newsman's instinct awakened and when the interview resumed, his questions were of higher quality. Pinned like a butterfly to an entomologist's board, I stammered a series of dodges. Don't you feel pain, Mr. Finch? Of course I feel pain, it's just, you see, my thigh, it has nerve damage from the war. But you are too young to have fought in the war. Did I say war? Well, I meant "war" as metaphor—the war with the Bird Hunter. Ah, so you admit that the Bird Hunter knew of this ability of yours?

Mann promised me a fifteen-dollar bonus when at last he ran out of film.

I nodded my appreciation but felt no elation. What had I done?

Weeks later I received my check, cashed it, and cornered Church while he was taping the handle of his fractured cane prior to heading out on a hundredth futile job hunt. From my pocket I pulled the fifty bucks. The instant steeped to an essence all that was sour between us: he flinched as if expecting a stiletto, and I flinched at his flinching. Still smarting from Ed Mann's shoot, I lied that I had come upon the cash in the park, and wasn't that the niftiest luck?

His eyes, full moon at first, slivered, leaving me feeling smarmy. Of course the honorable Burt Churchwell would never accept money he judged as unclean. His gaze, however, was not one of disdain. Glistening from his concave cheek was a puddle of tears. The display of emotion made me fidgety, seeing how I'd once again hidden from him the truth.

"I thought," said I, "you might put it toward mending that discommodious cough."

He wiped his nose with his sleeve.

"Shucks, Private. I got a better idea. I been talking to some real

501

stand-up fellas in the soup line and they're organizing soldiers to march on Washington in a couple weeks. I been meaning to tell you. Don't know why I haven't. I guess we've both been busy. But how about you and me join them?"

"A march? Whatever for?"

"They're calling themselves the Bonus Expeditionary Force cuz of how the government owes them their service certificate bonuses. That's a lot more than fifty bucks, little buddy, and me and you are owed it too. It ain't American that we starve before they decide to pay up."

"True, but—"

He snatched the cash.

"This'll get us there. And then we can march together, just like old times. You and me, brother. Heck, *all* of our brothers. We took down the Huns, didn't we? I think we can handle them boys in D.C. How 'bout it?"

Months of excruciating suspicion had at last generated this fresh scion of friendship. I grabbed at it and held tight to it, nodding, smiling, and basking in my friend's large, bruising embrace. Had only I recognized the symbolism of the hacking cough that ended the hug and the black spots of blood that spattered the floor.

The day before the march was a sunny, hopeful one. The local chapter of the Bonus Army had reserved a bus destined for the capital, and Church and I had agreed to rendezvous at the station for the 4:30 p.m. departure. He was picking up our pressed Marines fatigues while I'd been tasked with obtaining victuals for the road. I was en route to the market when I made the fateful mistake of lingering before a movie theater.

Ever a sucker for promotion, I was boning up on a Warner

Brothers picture called *I Am a Fugitive from a Chain Gang* when my eye strayed from the kissable lips of actress Glenda Farrell and landed upon a boxed insert touting the "Added Attractions." Squeezed between a "Farce Comedy" and a "Cartoon Comic" was the "Talking News," the highlights of which were fired in bullet points:

• *Manhunt Continues for Kidnapped Lindbergh Baby!*
• *There Is a Vaccine for Yellow Fever!*
• *Meet the Strange Central Figure in the Bird Hunter Case!*

"Merry Christmas," gasped I.

The 2:45 matinee started in minutes, leaving plenty of time to see what Ed Mann had made of me. I slapped down thirty cents for a ticket, claimed a seat near the back for a quick getaway, and drummed my seat so impatiently that a woman summoned a colored usher to beg me to stop. One hundred years later, the projector wheezed to life; one thousand years later, the insipid comedy short faded to black. At last came the bracing fanfare of Hearst Movietone News and "the top news of the day"—*the top news!*—began.

In a snap, it was over. My screen time hadn't exceeded two minutes and yet I sat in the dark stunned while a disfigured moll called Betty Boop hijacked the entertainment. Had it really been me up there, gesturing with my pipe and insisting that I cared deeply about the welfare of my fellow man?

The pièce de résistance had been the glass shard being pulled from my leg. Captured by an unprepared camera, the shot was jittery and off-kilter; moviegoers stroked to complacency by smooth dolly shots cried out in unison. I did not budge when *I Am a Fugitive from a Chain Gang* began. The plot followed an unfairly condemned man pursued

503

across the years, but it was my face I saw lingering upon that screen.

I exited the theater in a fog. Moviegoer chatter centered not on actor Paul Muni's gutsy performance but rather on that curious fellow from the newsreel. Was that business with the shard real or Hollywood effects? They did not know, but agreed it deserved a second look.

The Excelsior ticked like a tapped foot. From my coat I removed it and registered a time of 4:45—fifteen minutes late. If I ran, I might still make the bus that Church was no doubt holding. Taxi after taxi passed the theater; I did not hail a one. The lure of plodding alongside the indignant injured in Washington was no lure at all when compared to the red sparkle of the marquee above, the yellow dazzle of the lobby beyond.

I felt low about abandoning Church like that. I did.

But from my trouser pocket I fished another thirty cents.

II.

ON JUNE 27, 1932, I received by post an invitation to a Fourth of July dinner. It was printed in gold foil upon creamy stock the likes of which I hadn't felt since being handed Dr. Leather's business card three decades prior. I read it over and over, struggling to swallow a single delectable crumb.

I had been invited, or so read the absurd text, to Pickfair, which I knew from Church's celebrity magazines to be the sprawling Beverly Hills home of the first couple of the silver screen: America's Sweetheart, Mary Pickford, and the King of Hollywood, Douglas Fairbanks. The letter, penned by a third party in their employ, claimed that Mr. Fairbanks had viewed my newsreel and was keen to add me to a guest list that, historically, was second only to the White House in its litany of luminaries.

A valedictory paragraph indicated that a reservation had been made in my name for an American Airways flight scheduled to depart from Floyd Bennett Field on July 2. I had to sit down. Zebulon Finch in an airship, dashing among the clouds? For the millionth time since my death, I wished I could have a drink—very stiff, if you please.

When the glow had subsided some six or eight hours later, I confronted a predicament. There had been no word from Church since I'd jilted him at the bus station, even as the papers reported each travail of the beleaguered Bonus Army. After erecting a Hooverville along the Anacostia River with which to shame President Hoover, General Douglas MacArthur's U.S. Army—the irony, it scathes!—set upon the squatters with bayonets and tear gas. One would think that these were Germans saboteurs being dispelled, not American heroes.

Two men had been killed in the fracas and cameras had caught it all. Of late I huddled by the telephone like an Army wife, waiting for Church's cry for help that would, at the same time, indicate his forgiveness. But the bell did not ring. I toggled the rotary dial and drew patterns in the handset dust. Perhaps, thought I, the Bonus Army's strife had trawled memories of the Cotton Club. If so, he might prefer his apartment empty when he returned. In fact, his prolonged absence might be his quiet Midwestern way of holding the door open for my exit.

The notion might have inspired me to jump into the Hudson River were it not for the invitation card's caressable embossment. Wasn't it possible, even probable, that I might better help Church from afar? I'd earned fifty dollars, an astronomic sum, for a half-day's work in Ed Mann's picture. Perhaps in Hollywood, the one town in America unaffected by the Depression, I might work a full day, a full week, a full year, many times over, and mail every penny of it back to my friend until I had purchased his lung operation as well as his forgiveness.

I'd intended to help John Quincy's family and failed.

This time, swore I, Zebulon Finch would come through.

So it was with an anvil heart that on July 2 I put on my last surviving suit and hat, stomped a mouse on my way out of the apartment, locked the door, and slid beneath it my key. It was only then that I agonized that Church, upon his return, might worry. I scrounged the lobby for a handbill and found a chip of coal with which to write. The paper I slipped beneath the door offered two words in a caveman scrawl:

GONE, HOLLYWOOD

My plane was a Ford Tri-Motor—"the Tin Goose," the pilot called it—and in this goose's belly were ten wicker rattan chairs and little else. Take-off was a thing of white-knuckle terror and I might have kicked out a window and dove for land had there not been two delighted children right behind me. Once aloft, the ride was not unlike that of a boat, except for the noise, which was deafening, and the vibration, which was numbing, and the quick drops in altitude, which were pants-pissingly scary—well, it was nothing like a boat. The view? I cannot say. It was bright white panic for twenty-five-hundred straight miles.

We landed in a town called Burbank and I emerged from the flying coffin into a seventy-two-degree heaven of palm trees and blue skies. A taxi took me to Hollywood, where I asked a sunglassed bloke in a straw boater for the nearest hotel. He fast-talked directions but all of the stucco buildings looked the same, and I wound up cutting through an alley. I turned a blind corner and came upon a man squatting amid debris.

"Say, friend," said I, "I wonder if I might bother you for . . ."

I left the request dangling. The man was having himself a shit on the concrete. His mucky clothing betrayed his derelict nature and the twitch of his face conveyed mental derangement. He glanced my way, not much perturbed, and boosted the volume on the song that he was singing: "Who's Afraid of the Big Bad Wolf?" from the Walt

507

Disney cartoon, which, by that year, had become a sarcastic anthem of the Great Depression.

"Tra la la la la," sang he.

He reached for a copy of *Variety* with which to wipe his ass.

Perhaps Hollywood was not so unlike the rest of America.

Independence Day was as beautiful as the two days before it, and in the late afternoon I engaged a cab to carry me to the appointed Beverly Hills address. Through the San Ysidro Canyon we wound until arriving at the kelly green lawns and Tudor stylings of Pickfair. I was let out in a parking lot shining with Bentleys and Cadillacs and Packards. Jumpy as a virgin, I killed a half hour fondling the hood ornaments—griffins, swans, angels, mermaids—before forcing myself up the long paved path, beneath the overhang of a great gabled roof, and into a crowd where I did not belong.

Forty people of paralyzing beauty filled the back veranda with the finest of leisure suits and summer gowns. Men accepted cocktails from servants and slapped the backs of comrades while women giggled at private jokes or looked elegantly bored. Two dashing dans with waxed hair and pencil mustaches saluted my arrival with their drinks but, receiving nothing from me but apparent retardation, resumed their debate.

An infernal force pushed me into deeper waters, one dog-paddle after another. Why, there was Charlie Chaplin—*the* Charlie Chaplin—making as if to club an opponent with a croquet mallet. And wasn't that Lillian Gish, star of *The Birth of a Nation*, outfitted in gloves, matching hat, and an ermine collar despite the weather? And fielding questions by the bookcase, that looked like honored aviatrix Amelia Earhart! And who was that on his knees scratching the chin of a mongrel dog? It couldn't be Albert Einstein. Could it?

This was no throw-your-stockings-into-the-air blowout of the Twenties; here existed codes of conduct no two-bit criminal from Chicago could hope to understand. I shuffled past a grand piano (a Steinway, natch) and beelined for an Edwardian four-panel screen behind which I might cower. A blonde woman in a pale-gold satin dress and a commendable bust clocked me with a swinging hip as I passed. I goggled at her, astonished.

"Relax, kid." She had a Brooklyn squawk. "They's humans. Most of 'em, anyhow."

With a thick-lidded wink, she sashayed into the miller-abouters, pendulating her well-packaged buttocks with enough verve to clear a path six feet wide. I watched her collar two men at once, pulling them from their respective females. In seconds she had herself encircled and I could see no more.

"You there. Young man."

Ye gods! What indignity now cometh? I turned toward a settee festooned with deer antlers but found it vacant. Behind it, however, all but hidden within a forest of ferns, a woman lazed against gold drapery. Though she stood, she had about her the look of a lounging tigress eyeing a warren-load of unwitting bunnies. Any red-blooded (or, for that matter, no-blooded) American male would know her on sight.

Bridey Valentine was no less than the foremost sex symbol of the screen. I had seen her in countless pictures: *The Votes Are In*, in which she played the unstable (and insatiable) eldest daughter of a desperate senator; *The Struggle Buggy*, in which she portrayed a humble switchboard operator determined to burn down a burlesque hall; *Judy Plays the Game*, in which she starred as a card shark who falls for the detective on her trail; and, of course, *All Who Are Wearied and Burdened*, the controversial smash hit about

509

a mute nun forced to break her every holy vow in order to rescue a group of orphans from gangsters.

Willst thou, Dearest Reader, lend me a single paragraph within which I might roll like a pig in the muck of physical desire? Bridey Valentine's hair was a black abyss, forever billowed into chaos begging to be soothed. Her eyebrows, sly as the slots of a violin, butterflied in tandem with lashes growing ever longer from inside to out. So many actresses had large, limpid eyes; Bridey's, though, were small, the better to keep secrets, and smelted by amber irises. Her lips were sculpted so as to smile and frown as one: love, hate, love, hate. Her body, of course, was maddening, and given to onscreen contortions that shoved *this* hip into vulgar altitude even as it sloughed *that* breast against sheer fabric. She breathed in a way other actresses did not, her belly and bosom in constant pulsation, her thighs rocking—tensed, relaxed, then tensed again, so that you, poor boy, were squeezed of all breath of your own.

I, junked piece of human garbage, approached her.

Her golden eyes flicked toward the crowd.

"You were talking to Miss West. How do you know her?"

"Miss West?"

"You didn't know that was Mae West?"

No, damn it all, but I should have guessed. That crackly old Radiola of Church's had kept us abreast (so to speak) of the bawdy performer's exploits upon the New York stage as well as her arrest because of a play called *Sex*, which had exploited the irresistible slogan, "Enjoy *SEX* with Mae West!" I hastened to curtain my spectacle of ignorance.

"Yes, Mae West," said I. "We do not know each other all that well."

Bridey popped a cigarette between her lips and raised an eyebrow. My kingdom for a lighter! She rolled her eyes at my transparent alarm, shook a flint-wheeled gadget from her purse, lit up, and expelled a dragon of smoke in Miss West's direction.

"I have it on good authority she's making eight grand a week. For her first picture. You know what I made on my first picture? Sixty-five."

"That seems quite respectable."

"Sixty-five *dollars*. A *week*. This bitch moans like a cat in heat and they give up the whole bank. They'll regret it when it comes time for close-ups. There's not enough filters in the world for that face. Meanwhile the censors gather like alley cats. Hays is putting watchdogs right on her set, did you hear? There are ways to push the envelope— believe me, I know—but what she's doing is bad for all of us."

"Hays?"

"Will Hays. The Hays Code. For moral decency in pictures. The three-second-kiss rule?"

"But of course," said I. "Will Hays."

Smoke snaked from the corner of her lips. At last she gave me her undivided attention. I fidgeted before the inspection.

"You're not in pictures, that's for sure," said she. "Who are you?"

"I'm nobody. I'm sorry."

"Don't be sorry, I'm sick of somebodies. Your name."

"Zebulon."

Her laugh was a taunt.

"Now there's a name the studios would change. Too many syllables for Mary Moviegoer. Tell me, Z, do I need to introduce myself?"

Hundreds of hours had Church spent regaling me with vapid "exclusives" and silly "scoops" from his gossip rags, and until that moment I'd considered them wasted time. Now those pages provided crisp kindling for a furnace of industry insight. Something at last upon which I could discourse! I cracked my dry knuckles for effect.

"Bridey Valentine got her break in *An Orchid Unknown*, 1925, opposite Norma Talmadge, after which she went on to become one of the screen's pre-eminent tragediennes, starring in a series of dramatic roles that presented her as the opposite of girl-next-door Mary Pickford."

"Today's hostess, so go easy," said Bridey. "But do continue."

"Miss Valentine's career was shaped by a childhood accident in which she damaged the tear ducts of her left eye, limiting how directors could photograph crying scenes. Eventually producers began choosing roles for her that did not include crying at all."

"Hearsay at best. But I remain impressed. Resume."

"Ergo, Miss Valentine became known for tough characters and an even tougher off-screen persona. Among the rumors are that she spends her weekends entirely in the nude, dabbles in witchcraft, wears a locket filled with blood, and puts cigarettes out on the soles of her feet. Her stock-in-trade is the shock."

"Nice turn of phrase. But who would stub cigarettes on her feet?"

"Miss Valentine is best known, of course, for her combustible sex appeal, and has been linked to some of the most visible men in the business. There was *l'affaire* Errol Flynn, *l'affaire* James Cagney, *l'affaire* Victor Fleming—"

"Well, Fleming's a rite of passage. He hardly counts."

"—all of which have given Miss Valentine the reputation of one who goes in and out of relationships quickly."

"Yes, in and out, in and out. Isn't that how you do it?"

"When asked about these romances, Miss Valentine repeats her catchphrase: 'Always a Bridey, never a bride.'"

"I rue the day I said that. Who the hell wants to be a bride?" She removed her cigarette. "Here, give me your foot so I can put this out."

But she smirked when she said it, so goddamn radiant that I beamed. How grand it was to feel the return of the old strut and swagger! I gambled on a grandstanding gambit.

"However, it is my opinion, having known Miss Valentine for such a long while now, that she is not so brambly as all that. In fact, she seems quite likable."

"My word, Z. I'll bet your sweet nothings have unzipped a lot of dresses. But I'm afraid you've much to learn about Hollywood. Truth and reality are intertwined in these here hills. I am what they say I am—and there is nothing I can say about it."

"Such a knot of words." I gestured at the settee. "Please let me assist in the disentanglement. Mind the antlers."

"Sit? In this dress?"

A long, luscious leg that had no business being attached to a woman in her mid-thirties stretched outward to display the gown to best advantage—a snug velvet encasement with metallic leaves embroidered about the collar and down the steep neckline. The dress had no back to speak of, and I longed to warm my cold palm upon the kiln of accessible skin.

"This is my standing dress," lectured she. "There is another version for sitting."

"Your sense of humor goes vastly under-reported."

"I'm quite serious. Ask Mary. She recommended the designer."

Mary Pickford? I'd forgotten the swarm of buzzing dignitaries! Now I inhaled their stratospheric air and felt no correlating queasiness. What volumes of confidence could be won from the most casual of attachments to a woman like Bridey Valentine.

"I should like to meet Miss Pickford," said I. "And Mr. Fairbanks, as it was he who extended my invite. Swell people, I should think— the swellest!"

"I think they'll like you, provided you keep your enthusiasm to a low boil. Just don't ask Mary about her next picture because there *is* no next picture. She's through with acting thanks to that horrible facelift. She can't even smile anymore, poor dear."

"Facelift?"

"Oh, Z. You're a charmer. Yes, you shall meet them. And George Bernard Shaw, if you can find him beneath his beard. And Dietrich too, although don't get too excited about it; she is, as you will see, a raging lesbian. It's all here for you, so go, go, take advantage of it—it's the Hollywood way. I do suggest staying clear from *that* one. The fat fellow staring daggers."

"Fatty Arbuckle! The hefty humorist! Is he still making films?"

"He's mounting a comeback." But she said it through bared teeth. "You recall the rape trial? How he squashed that starlet to death?"

"Oh." This did damper the mood. "Yes."

"They say that the poor girl's girl parts were in a box on their way to the incineration room when the coroner rushed in and stopped it, and that's when they discovered that her bladder had been ruptured by the weight. He almost got away with it."

"But he did get away with it."

Bridey shrugged.

"Fans don't forgive as easily as juries."

"So why invite him? If he is as hated as you say?"

She reached out, stroked the hair above my ears, and spoke softly.

"There are many reasons one might be invited to Pickfair. Some of them admirable. Some of them not. Fatty Arbuckle—oh, how do I say it with any class? He is a star burning out before our very eyes. We have to watch it up close if we are to understand our own demises, which will come, and quickly, because time out here moves double-speed. Make sense?"

No number of printed puff pieces could have prepared me for this introspection. Nor could Bridey have guessed the effect her words would have upon me. As the world's bearer of *la silenziosità*, I knew how one could dangle the secrets of death before any man or woman, and how, regardless of the danger, they would snatch at it.

Her hand slid from my hair (was this a fantasy picture?), down my cheek (hellcat, pray continue!), and to my chin, where it drew to a teasing pinch. She let go; my dead skin took its time expanding. Her lashes fluttered and she blew me the smallest of kisses.

"Be careful out there and you might live to see me again."

And then, Reader, Bridey Valentine took her leave, the shush of her hemline across carpet ten times more effective than Mae West's honking. Everyone turned to kiss-kiss her cheeks. I became jealous, of course I did, for I'd been the hunter to capture her as she'd prowled the greenery. But it struck me that she might be teaching me a lesson: not all women could be captured.

Halfway through a sigh worthy of a silver-screen romance, my allotment of daylight was blotted out by a figure sidling up next to me. There was a yellow suit, acres of it, and squirting from its collar was a perspiring, ham-pink face split by an alligator grin and buttoned with blue eyes that blinked, blinked, blinked like a bird.

"Watch out for Valentine," giggled Fatty Arbuckle. "She'll screw your prick off."

III.

WHAT IS ONE MONTH IN Southern California? Or two, or four, or six? The sun shined until it became a stupor, a daydream of life undelineated by the usual indicators of rain or snow. Los Angelenos lived as if in constant emergence from a dark theater, convinced of their mastery over the smaller, dimmer worlds played out across the rest of the country.

For a time I was their best barnacle. My debut at Pickfair earned me a string of auxiliary invites, from home banquets complete with ice sculptures and balalaika quartets, to lunch parties aboard houseboats and schooners, to private rooms behind velvet ropes in happening clubs like Hawaiian Paradise and the Famous Door. No one in the flea-ridden flophouse where I resided received such summonses, and from that I drew an energy both prideful and, after a time, pitiful.

It took talent to make a splash and I was but a gimmick, sat ever nearer the washed-up end of the table and called upon once per evening to entertain.

"Why, you're that young magician Doug was so keen on," one would remark.

"You *do* look ghoulish," a second would say. "Is that make-up? Max Factor is doing fabulous things these days."

"Do your bit!" a third would add. "Jolly good fun—Madge, wait until you see."

And thus my night would rise to a climax befitting the Pageant of Health, with me borrowing a pin from an adjacent lady and, after a halfhearted spiel, jabbing it into the back of my hand and displaying it as if it were a ring. The sophisticates gasped and clapped, and, oh, how I slurped it up in my thirst to belong to their society, if only for a minute. The flavor was always bittersweet; each time I would spy a starlet so put off by my demonstration that she could not eat.

Bridey had warned me.

There are many reasons one might be invited. Some of them admirable. Some of them not.

My trick became tired. Invites petered and I was friendless. Poorer than I'd been in New York, I hustled work as a movie extra. My bony, ashen face made me an ideal "Mad Villager" or "Freak Number Four" on a half-dozen Universal Studios horror pictures, and I mailed almost everything I earned to Church's Chinatown address. There came no reply, though, and chasing fake monsters like Bela Lugosi and Boris Karloff off soundstage cliffs did nothing for my self-esteem. I was the monster, the real one, and I waited for the other mad villagers, or freaks, to realize and redirect their pitchforks.

I was studying up on active volcanoes into which I might hurl myself when I saw a note being slid beneath my door. In it, the harried handwriting of the proprietor relayed a telephoned invitation to a last-second shindig celebrating the fresh repeal of Prohibition thirteen years after its harebrained ratification. For most, this was cause for a celebration of the guzzlingest kind. I, however, pressed the heels of my hands to my sockets, hoping to suppress the images of John Quincy, Mother Mash, and the alcoholic mud foaming beneath their dangling feet.

I'd half-crumpled the note before noticing the party's location:

517

the San Simeon home of publishing magnate William Randolph Hearst. Shared with his almost-wife, actress Marion Davies, it was rumored to be nothing short of a medieval hilltop acropolis. Only the hasty organization of the event explained my invite. I set the note upon my lap and smoothed the wrinkles. Yes, I'd attend one last bash as a toast to John Quincy, who never lived to see the liquor laws fall.

Perched high above a portentous fog, Hearst Castle was a thing to behold, one hundred and sixty-five rooms situated upon acres of craggy bluffs that looked as if shipped over from Scottish moorland—and given Hearst's fortune, it was possible. I passed beneath the hand-carved eaves and cathedral arches as did everyone else, hushed by the semblant fairy tale and waiting for the royal wedding (or under-bridge trolls) to conclude it.

A butler scowled at my weathered suit and in a self-righteous huff I stormed the so-called Assembly Room, a hall of etched ceilings, ancient tapestries, marble nudes, bronze busts, and a thirty-foot Christmas tree. Sixty-some people mingled in the caramel light, drinking suddenly legal liquors by the steinful. Ignoramuses to a man! Not a one of these ales or lagers could possibly rival the love-punch of Dog Bowl Debbie.

Renaissance-era choir stalls were built into the walls and I claimed a corner one in order to embark upon what I hoped to be a sulk of legend, crossing my arms so that my naked, bony elbows peeked from matching holes. I was the bum in the alley, these people were the big bad wolves, and it was with their grand successes that I wiped my vile filth: *Tra la la la la.*

Mr. Hearst appeared via a hidden door to great applause and he pointed us toward the Refectory, a dining hall in the style of a middle-ages monastery, with tall windows, colorful Sienese banners, and a long table fit for sixty-four fools. Placecards directed me to the ass-end, some forty or fifty miles from our hosts. Painstaking place settings were old hat to me, but this was farcical: three china plates, three glasses, four forks, three spoons, two knives, and a selection of other instruments of dubious utility.

"And paper napkins!" exclaimed the drunkard to my left.

"And ketchup and mustard bottles!" exclaimed the drunkard to my right.

"That Hearst," said the first, "is one of a kind."

I buried the urge to kill. Onward came the soup, caviar, bison tenderloin, potatoes and gravy, string beans, apricot tartlets, and enough alcohol to honor its resurgence. People englutted and imbibed and cackled, and not one of them paid me any mind. My empty veins itched with the maggots of antipathy until I could take no more.

I bolted upright to leave but the cockamamie handkerchief tucked into my collar had found its way beneath my untouched plate. Plate bumped glass and glass overturned, spilling my wine across the tablecloth. Drunkard I and Drunkard II at last noticed me and raised a hearty hurrah at my faux pas while servants rushed to blot and wipe. I sat to dislodge myself and Drunkard I grabbed my shoulder.

"I know this mug! This is that young fella who sticks forks in his arm. It's a riot!"

"Forks, you say?" chuckled Drunkard II. "Like some kind of savage? Maybe Fay Wray discovered this guy on Skull Island! Whaddya say, kid? How's King Kong smell in person?"

The bastards howled until a tray of crab flakes distracted Drunkard II. Drunkard I, though, was undeterred, mussing my hair with every insult until the ladies around us began to laugh as well. Had I really traded companionship with Church for this debasement from

519

self-righteous jackals? My emotions coalesced into a cold fury that burned through the rancid cancers of my torpid organs, and I turned toward the heckling dipsomaniac, flaming with the ice of *la silenziosità*.

Hearst Castle smudged down to a Neanderthal's cave of stone and fire. Time swallowed me down its hot throat. There!—Death!—waiting as always to tease me with vulture claws. This time the pain was worth bearing in order to watch the drunkard's plumped roseate cheeks flatten and whiten and the boozed exuberance of his eyes deplete with horror.

I am the savage, you fat fuck?

Indeed I am, and unto you this I savage.

Adrift in obliteration, I did not hear the cheery voices die out nor see the grins fall, but when at last I surfaced, it was not two or three diners staring at me with their open mouths crowded with cud, but our entire half of the table, twenty or thirty people rudely awakened from their everlasting privilege to the realization of their ugly, encroaching deaths. The drunkard himself was a blubbering wreck, his fountain of tears melting through a flume of snot and beer.

I stood, this time unmindful of my handkerchief, and charged toward the nearest door. *La silenziosità*, dependably as ever, had left me weak, and servants were amassing to warn me that this was not an exit. I shoved past the busybodies, anything to escape from all those film-camera eyes, and if I became lost in the castle? All the better. Castles had dungeons; perhaps down there I might be shackled.

The door fed into a sitting room that looked like a mouth—a long tongue of purple rug, the biting teeth of chandeliers. Past stone sphinxes stood two golden doors, but they were locked, and so I took up a three-foot candlestick and swung it at my pursuers.

So weaponed, I dashed to the right, through a chamber dominated by snooker tables and a Flemish tapestry, then beneath an Arabian doorway. Servants cornered me in a small Art Deco movie theater, but I climbed over four rows of padded seats and candlesticked my way out of a side exit and into a blue evening of tall palms and long shadows.

I expect a night watchman would have shot me down like a coyote had I not happened upon a door that brought me back to the Assembly Room. There I encountered a serving boy ignorant of my escapades. I asked him to fetch a taxi, and make haste, make haste! I bashed through the vestibule and onto the front esplanade, and would have sprinted down to the road to intercept the cab had I not received an abrupt question.

"Still disturbing the locals, Z?"

Behind a veil of smoke stood Bridey in a red dress, tapping ashes into an ornamental urn. Her repose suggested nonchalance, but the bosom heaving within the bodice betrayed that she had hurried to catch me.

"How do you do," said I. "Had I seen you at dinner I might have—"

"Delayed your jailbreak? That would have been a shame. It was the highlight."

Behind rattling doors, a squad of irate servants shouted to one another their scheme to nab me. I needed to vacate, and yet so complimented was I by Bridey's attention that I lingered.

"The truth is, Miss Valentine, that I have had a streak of rough luck. It has made me mindful that I do not belong here, not with people of your stature. The jailbreak, as you say, has only begun. I believe I shall hop a train tonight, or steal a car. Whatever it takes to make myself scarce."

"A pity." She fluttered her bobcat lashes at my groin. "And here I thought you were excited to see me."

I looked down and saw that I still wielded the three-foot candlestick. Such clever ribaldry! I laughed aloud; it surprised the both of us into grins.

"You know what?" posed she. "You're exactly right. You don't belong here. Which is why, in my opinion, it is such good fortune that you *are* here. I trust you got a good gander at those quacks crammed in there like a Busby Berkeley number? They make a lot of money changing—by the role, by the trends, by the minute if necessary. But you? You're as strange as ever."

"You praise me for this?"

"I don't know what it was you did in there, but you might as well have pissed directly onto Hearst's plate. In other words, yes. I am praising you, dear, most highly."

My luck could not last forever. The doors burst open and spit out a butler whose last filament of hair stood straight up in the breeze. He expected a lengthy sprint before catching me and was taken aback by my presence. He glared, pet down his cranial poof, and bowed at Bridey.

"Madam, I must ask you inside. This young man is an infiltrator and crook."

"An infiltrator?" Bridey looked amused. "Why, this is Mister . . ." She extended a braceleted arm in my direction.

"Finch," said I.

"Madam, he has purloined a valuable candlestick."

"Pish-posh. He's stolen nothing."

The butler winced as servants do when tasked with correcting their uppers. He gestured at the antique that I held at my side.

"It is one of a quartet of gilt-brass sticks set with four moonstones. Unmistakable, I'm afraid. The police are on their way."

"Oh, *that*," said Bridey. "I asked Mr. Finch to carry it for me so that I might have a set of my own designed. Did I forget to ask permission from Miss Davies? Blame it on the feminine mind! So flighty, you know. Now be good and call off the police, lest we create a headline about Bridey Valentine's Hearst Castle incarceration."

The butler knew he was being gamed but, well trained, he bowed grimly, returned inside, and began snapping fingers to call off his tuxedoed hounds. Bridey waited until the doors were closed before giving me a most devious curtsy.

"Acting," said she.

"Brava," said I. "But I think I should return the candlestick."

"Out of the question. It's our cover story. In fact, I'll have to get an entire set made just to cover my tracks."

"I am sorry about that."

"Sorry? It can't cost more than one or two thousand, tops."

"Still. If there is anything I can do to repay you."

Bridey dropped her cigarette into the urn and arched her back so as to push herself from the column. She advanced with a serpent's slowness, the diamondback crepe of her dress rasping across the underfoot marble. Inches before me she halted, hands low upon her cocked hips, elbows back, chest forward, and face tilted so that I could see my pale reflection in her lipstick's luster. The lips parted, wet. Behind them, white teeth, pink tongue, nibbling movements, a throaty hum.

"Repayment," mused she. "Yes, I can think of something."

IV.

THE LEBARON CONVERTIBLE, AS CANDY-APPLE in color as Bridey's dress, had been a gift from an MGM honcho, or so she shouted over the lament of wind, purr of engine, and thump of California asphalt zipping beneath us. I hadn't traveled so fast since outrunning Prohibition agents in Tin Lizzie, and held tight as the car nestled corners and blasted through stop signs down the crashing coast and through Santa Monica, slowing only when hitting the fences, hedgerows, and drives of Beverly Hills. She acted as tour guide, hollering who lived where along with a garnish of commentary.

"*Clara Bow! Has a screw loose! Mother used to chase her with a butcher knife!*"

"*Buster Keaton! Serial lothario, new divorcé! Ten to one he's slobbering drunk!*"

"*Gloria Swanson! Couldn't hack it in talkies! Has a really unusual nose!*"

It was too dark to comprehend the Valentine estate beyond how the outdoor tiki torches flashed across row after row of windows. We jerked to a halt inside of a garage, colliding with something. Bridey was unconcerned. She leapt from the convertible, took me by the tie, and led me beneath pepper trees, around a pool house, alongside a tennis court, past the servants' quarters, and through a back entrance made to look like part of the rubblework masonry.

Inside, her pull upon my tie tautened, and in the mausoleum dark

I could catch only major furnishments: the wrought-iron staircase, the opposite balconies overhanging the foyer. We passed through a hallway soldiered with grandfather clocks cracking away at the nut of Time, and emerged into a library lit by a popping fireplace and lined with surrealist paintings of an apocalyptic bent. I felt a sharp tug at my heel and fell to a knee. Hearst's invaluable candlestick rolled beneath an armchair.

The incriminating glass eyes of a bear rug stared up at me. One of its fangs had snagged my pant cuff, yanking the tattered fabric so that the top of my knickers showed. Before I could adjust my virtue, Bridey lifted me by the tie—had I needed air, I would have choked—and appraised the development. With agonizing slowness, she passed a cool fingernail between my skin and the elasticated waistband of my drawers.

"A little eager, are we?" she breathed.

I should not have come. I knew that. But the aftershock of *la silenziosità* was invariably a paralyzing loneliness; had the bear rug offered a fig leaf of companionship, I would have taken it. Bridey curled my tie around her fist to create a shorter leash, and dragged me upstairs until we arrived at a palatial bedroom. With nimble puissance, she untied my tie and skinned my jacket, and with both hands she shoved me between two of the four posts of a blue-and-yellow silk canopy bed. Tasseled drapes did a jig at my landing.

Bridey crawled her way up my body, her small, strong hands taking fistfuls of my shirt. She buried her face in my neck and filled the grappling-hook hole with warm breath. Kisses crested my jaw and continued across my ear. The long-forgotten glories of girl-flesh awakened in me a near-cannibalistic hunger. She bared her beautiful neck and I devoured it, nibbling the lean muscles, sucking the tender skin, licking at coils of hair with my sandpaper tongue.

Her hips rocked in pleasure and she slithered downward with a hiss of fabric. I felt a pull on my torso and gasped—it was Dr. Leather cutting the flap into my gut or Merle sewing it back shut. Bridey's head resurfaced, not with gore in her mouth but one of my shirt buttons. With the gentleness of an obedient doggie, she set it upon my chest, then waited, pleased with herself, for her reward.

For the first time since, well, my *first time*, I knew not what to do. She gave me a sidelong look.

"I don't have to bite *all* of them off, I hope."

Thirty-seven years, Reader! Nearabout four decades since I'd been skin-to-skin! With desperation equal to that with which I'd dug myself from a Belleau Wood trench collapse, I tore at Bridey's dress. Since the Nan-and-Dot episode, ladies' garments had evolved yet again and I could not locate a single damn hook-and-eye. By the time I'd isolated the key to her nakedness—an Oriental gold buckle that pinched the whole ensemble together—Bridey, embodiment of sex to a nation of men, was kissing her way down my stomach.

My rotten, putrefying stomach.

"Stop," said I. "My body—it's unclean."

"Good," hissed she. "Everyone else is buffed and trimmed like show dogs."

"I'm cold. Can't you feel it?"

"So? Everyone else is hot, or so say the headlines they plant."

"I'm pale. Look how pale."

"And everyone else is baked brown like hamburger in the pan."

I snatched both of her wrists.

"What?" gasped she. "Did I do something . . . ?"

Show me a god, any god, *the* Gød, and I would build a ladder tall enough to strangle Him! It was not fair! Not fair! Seventeen I was, a flooded reservoir of potency, but with no pumping blood to steel my enfeebled male organ, I might as well be a toddler. I snaked myself from her torrid limbs and sat against the headboard, feeling downhearted enough to end it all, if only that were an option.

"I can't," said I. "I just can't."

Here was a woman no man had ever spurned, and I braced for her face to adopt the wolfish snarl used to imposing effect in so many of her pictures. She would then scream for a manservant to throw my inadequate corpse to the street, or, to maximize degradation, do the honors herself. For leading her on with false promise, I deserved it.

This unpredictable female instead rolled to the side, propped her head with a palm, and gave me the studious squint of a zoologist struggling to classify a bizarre creature. She clucked her tongue.

"Chastity. Now that's a new perversion."

"It is not my intent," moaned I, "to be perverse."

"Don't say that. I have a hunch you might be the most perverse of them all. Who knows? Abstinence could be a fun lark, provided one is open to a little suffering, which I am. I'll try anything once, and most things twice. For now we'll just—what do they say? Turtledove? We'll do some turtledoving?"

Zebulon Finch, barnstormer of female anatomy, conquistador of copulation, rutter of lore—*turtledoving*?

With an idle hand, Bridey pulled tight my belt and then, to torture me, traced her fingernails in circular patterns across the tongue.

"Polite young man like you. You're holding a torch for some sweet young thing back in Indiana, I'll bet."

The first rule of any carnal encounter is to deny ever having *seen* another woman. Bridey's hypothesis, however, offered an honorable exit from an awkward situation. Moreover, there was truth to it. I had, and forever would, hoist a torch for Wilma Sue, if not a ten-story inferno. From the floor I could hear my darling's heart, the Excelsior, ever patient with my shortcomings, tutting from my jacket pocket.

"Illinois," said I.

"Tell me her name. No, let me guess. Phyllis. Wait. *Lois.*"

"Wilma Sue."

"Two names? She ought to be twice the homemaker, then."

Bridey did not hide her skepticism. For some reason, she believed us cut from similar cloth, incapable of finding any fulfillment in the humdrum of a little house, a little job, and a little lady to bring me my slippers. She had no idea of the type of creature with whom she laid, nor that creature's appetites.

I removed her hand from my belt and slid it up under my shirt.

"Changed your mind already?" pouted she. "I barely even tried."

"Shh," said I.

Over the next half hour, I gave her fingers a guided tour of my damage, every unhealed hole, abrasion, gouge, and burn, supplying no explanation beyond the obvious—that I was far stranger than my newsreel or parlor tricks had made me out to be. I was, just as she'd implied, a perversity.

I took care to make the exploration chaste, but even here Bridey rebelled. At each patch of decay she tickled; at every crossroad of collapse she caressed. It was, of course, sexually aggravating; more than that, though, it was moving—profoundly so. The promoted image of Bridey was that of an exotic who welcomed the uncanny and profane. Magazines, fabulists by trade, were, for once, on the money. My repulsiveness excited her. Perhaps my strange flavors acted as antidote to the perfect blandness of a celluloid world.

Had you burst in upon us afterward, you would have believed

we'd just finished the good deed rather than aborted it. For a time, Bridey lay stroking my cheek and watching the sluggish reaction of my dead flesh. I was not a fellow given to snug-a-bugging, but so thankful was I for her lack of disgust that I could have lain there all night. Bridey, being Bridey, had other plans.

She stood up alongside the bed and all but groped herself as she smoothed from her dress the evening's creases. By the time she bothered to give me her bedroom eyes, I was on tenterhooks.

"You're not sure you have what it takes in the sack. You're still stuck on this Wilma bird, too. Well, that's fine for now. I have but one humble question to ask."

She detached the Oriental buckle and with a shrug the dress fell like rose petals about her naked feet. There in the moonlight shone an aphroditic vision of Bridey Valentine before which the general public would never get a chance to genuflect. She angled an arm behind her head coyly, while sliding the other suggestively across her exposed tummy.

"I wonder if, in the meantime, it might bring you some pleasure to . . . bring *me* pleasure?"

In my decades of keening over the end of my erogenous existence, I'd never considered such a simple thing. It took, I suppose, a woman bold enough to ask for it while her partner remained despicably decent.

I did not debate for long. I had thirty-seven years for which to make up.

"Why, yes," said I. "I believe it would, at that."

V.

EVEN ONE AS DISMISSIVE OF social mores as Bridey could not keep a strange boy nineteen years her junior on the premises. But neither would she allow me to return to my sleazeball inn. So, in an inspired whim, she drew up papers and hired me on as her official "amanuensis"—a term for "secretary" so convoluted it all but guaranteed that no one would be clear what I was supposed to be doing. Turning down the offer was not an option, for the position included a weekly paycheck. That meant I could begin sending Church the kind of money he needed. Surely, before too long, he'd write back to say that all my trespasses were forgiven.

Bridey gave me both an office and a bedchamber at the south end of her two-story, thirty-room Colonial Queen Anne mansion, using the excuse that the servants' quarters were already choked with the butler, cook, lady's maid, hairdresser, Japanese gardener, chauffeur, on-site vocal coach, and the executive assistant charged with shepherding forty-thousand fan letters a month as well as producing the *Bridey Valentine Fan Club Bimonthly*. These minions approved of me no more than Dixon and his gang, for if they knew one thing about their employer, it was that she did not need helping.

In fact, she made me feel like a thumb-twiddling kiddie. Never before had I seen a woman on equal footing with men. Bridey by then was bringing in the criminal-sounding sum of ten thousand dollars per week, and yet she retained no agents, managers, or lawyers. More frequently visited than her closets of gowns or shoes was her fort of filing cabinets, in which she kept, in labeled concertina folders, ledgers enough to make old Mr. Hobby jealous. Between call times, she hunched over these logs with reading glasses and red pencil, tracing every monetary current: furs @ $7,000/year, stockings @ $9,000/year, perfume @ $30,000/year, and onward.

She was, to use a word close to my heart, indefatigable. Bridey woke at four to have her hair done before heading to the studio. MGM's contract stipulated four pictures per year, so invariable that they were shorthanded by season: "Spring Valentine," "Summer Valentine," "Fall Valentine," and "Winter Valentine." In February of 1934 she was Henrietta Hawk, brash flying ace able to pilot her biplane through any storm, until she meets a storm called Captain Schmidt, played by Spencer Tracey. In May she was Babs McCourt, smart-lipped small-town reporter who must team with a down-on-his-luck private dick, played by Douglas Fairbanks, Jr. In August, she was Letty Dekker, British spy who infiltrates Germany as a nightclub dancer in order to free Colonel Tab Candler, played by Leslie Howard. And so on.

Then there were exercise classes, dance practices, script conferences, and charity dinners. By bedtime, though, she was Bridey, my Bridey, and rare was the night we did not lie in bed talking for an hour or two. *Talking*, you ask? For an hour? Or *two*? Zebby, poor sop, how did you withstand so much girl-gabble? With ease, friend; Bridey was the most fascinating person I'd ever met, and yet she had few, if any, real friends. Even more than rubbing her to a frenzy, she relied on me for this—to hear her speak from the heart. What I learned was a backstory for which any scandal rag would murder.

Bridey had a daughter.

It made good sense to tell me about it, for as long as I was under her roof, it was unfeasible that she could hide her periodic phone calls to a nine-year-old girl called Gopher (short for "Margeaux"). With characteristic lack of sentiment, she unleashed the whole dirty truth one morning over breakfast.

"Don't ask about the father," sighed she. "I couldn't tell you. Believe me, had I the money, I would've had an abortion faster than you can say the word. All the top girls have had two or three. There's more abortionists out here than clap doctors."

Lady business of the most distasteful sort! I strived toward a bouncier mood.

"Surely you have found some mirth in motherhood?"

"I'll just say this: an actress should be wary, very wary, of children, and should never, under any circumstances, marry, not if she wishes to control her own fate. Now hand me that grapefruit before I starve."

It was a momentous grapefruit. In the passing of it I weighed whether to tell Bridey of Merle. If there were a stage fit for such dissonant music, this was it. But Merle was older than Bridey, a fact perhaps too weird for even a self-proclaimed connoisseur of weirdness. Bringing up Merle would also bring up Wilma Sue, and that was a subject Bridey abhorred. As ever, Merle was a poison; mentioning her was tantamount to sprinkling arsenic atop, say, a grapefruit.

Young Bridey had known that her role in *An Orchid Unknown* was her ticket to stardom. She therefore concealed the existence of Margeaux and designed to steal the picture from star Norma Talmadge. No matter the costumes presented to Bridey, she scissored them all to hell to more favorably display her assets. She swung her hips in long shots and licked her lips in close-ups until the crew wolf-whistled so loud you could almost hear it—and it was a silent film!

By the end of 1925 Bridey had received the honor of being named a Western Association of Motion Picture Advertisers "Baby Star." Thus was she thrust into the limelight. Overnight, MGM publicists crawled from the crannies to whitewash her past of any dirt, and boy, did they ever find a large clod of it. Within an hour of finding out about Margeaux, a screenwriter had been assigned to concoct a story about a dead GI.

I, for one, liked the sound of it—wasn't I myself a dead solider? Bridey, though, tore the pages from the writer's hand and stomped them with her heels. Never would she allow herself to be defined by a man, much less a fictitious one! A single option remained, and so she took it, bestowing upon Margeaux the untainted surname of "Malone" and sending her off to be raised and schooled at an expensive boarding institution in Santa Barbara.

Marooned in the mansion, I had no choice but to take these stories on faith. Certainly there was no denying Bridey's dedication to the outré. Where other celebrities outfitted their homes in Seurat, Tiffany, and Cartier, Bridey appareled hers in macabre historical relics. A gold-leaf death mask from Ancient Greece. A jade Egyptian mummification kit. An Iron Age cauldron depicting human sacrifice. A death pendant taken from an aboriginal burial box in Newfoundland. In many ways, these morbid *objets d'art* had foreshadowed my arrival.

It was as if Bridey had been waiting for me her entire life.

The most alarming artifacts were an assortment of Middle Ages chastity belts. The gentlest resembled buckled leather underwear, while the harshest were steel-toothed traps capable of scaring away the most determined of deflowerers. Bridey posited the collection as a rejoinder to the censor Will Hays—it was best to keep sex locked up, eh, Will? But as with everything Bridey did, her comedy had a point. It was all points, in fact, all edges.

Roughly once a week, you see, she rededicated herself to my seduction, and my stern deferrals only goaded her gambler's nature. She would win the kitty, resolved she, if she but sharpened her play.

"You are the rarest thing," she'd flatter, "in my entire collection."

There went her hand, creeping up my leg.

"Just try," she'd beg. "I'll help you. I'll be patient."

I required no belt to be locked inside my chastity.

"I am dead," said I, "and that is that."

"Forget Wilma What's-Her-Name. I can be better than her. Let me prove it."

"Are you deaf? I cannot."

"Then I'll borrow a movie camera. Put it in the corner while we do it."

"Why on Earth would that help?"

She tickled my ear and laughed.

"Because pictures never die, silly. That's why I, too, am going to live forever."

VI.

O NE MIGHT PUT ONE'S FINGER inside the Etruscan cinerary urn and wipe the dust of centuries. One might try on the feathered Peruvian burial mask to see if it fit. These lurid curios were for anyone to enjoy. There was but one room that remained locked and unremarked upon; that is, until summer 1935, when Bridey brought me to the threshold with sententious and, to be frank, worrisome fanfare.

She was decked out as if for a premiere, a checked dress with an orange bolero jacket and matching orange hat. From an orange pocket she removed a large key, unlocked the door, and then, with her orange fingernails resting upon the knob, delivered a statement— prepared in advance, one would imagine, though Bridey had a gift of bringing scripted words to life.

"When you first, quote, 'make it,' the twelve months that follow are everything. That's when the studio heads use their big, fancy man-brains to figure out, quote, 'who you are.' For an actress, it's a losing proposition. Should they fail, well, your hit was a fluke and into obscurity you slide. Should they succeed, then you're really stuck, for now they've invented your, quote, 'formula.'"

"I vociferously disagree," said I. "Your roles are manifold and mutable!"

"Oh, a girl can wiggle a bit, like a worm on a hook, but she mustn't delude herself—she's on *their* hook, and they'll make damn sure her formula goes untampered with. If you're Joan Crawford, you're the noble clotheshorse. If you're Ginger Rogers, you're the tap-dancing paramour. Your next career checkpoint? Your inevitable drop from exhaustion."

Rest assured, Reader, that the objective to siphon money to Church remained intact. It is just that, month by month, my purpose in Hollywood had begun to broaden, and it was right then, as Bridey deprecated her many triumphs, that I knew I'd become smitten beyond the mercenary rationales of money or even physical beauty. The woman challenged me as no one since Wilma Sue had dared, and that, more than anything since my death, stimulated me toward a sort of life. I resolved to return the favor and help her through any insecurity.

"I do tell you that you work too hard."

"Yes, but it is in aid of a goal. It used to be, anyhow. For a long while now, I've lost my way. But you've inspired me, Z. I can't tell you how much."

"Me? Inspire you? You are overstressed, all right."

"You have reminded me that life—my life, anyway—is short. If I am to make anything worthwhile of this frivolous profession, there is no more time to waste."

The moment required only lowered lights, orchestral pomp, and rising red curtains to be complete. Bridey turned the knob and flung open the door, flattening her melodramatic form across the jamb like the breathless heroine of a silent-film serial.

The reveal was anticlimactic. Not a nugget of El Dorado's gold, not a hint of Smaug's riches. It was a stuffy storeroom, bigger than a monkey's cage yet smaller than a Chinatown flat. Lining the floor and shelves were dusty reams of paper shotgunned with ink type, the lower strata of yellower age than the higher. Stacks of pink and blue carbon copies provided the only variance in color. Placed high upon a shelf, like Sacco and Vanzetti awaiting sentencing, were two doomed typewriters.

"This is quite . . . What I mean is, this is very . . ." I gave up. "What is this?"

Bridey pressed all of her choicest parts against my back.

"A *script*. Six years I worked on it. Researching, analyzing, revising; days, nights, weekends, holidays; it was everything to me. Then I walked away from it. I thought it had beaten me. But it hasn't, Z, I know it hasn't."

An entire room lost beneath paper like drifts of snow—for a single script?

"If I may ask," said I, "what sort of script?"

"A screenplay. *The* screenplay. The one that will change everything, not only for me but for all women. For all *pictures*."

Bridey had no equal in chutzpah.

"I am listening, and with an avid ear."

"I won't play The Girl forever. You know that's how they describe female leads? Doesn't matter if it's a weepie, a comedy, or a gangster picture, I'm still The Girl, as if my child-bearing organs were my only notable characteristic. A girl, I'll remind you, is not a woman. She's only allowed to have girl-sized problems. If I get a pimple, twenty men get on the telephone to discuss the state of my scabbing. If I raise a stink about it, they call it a tantrum and punish me with roles so bad I'd rather shoot myself in the face. Then at my funeral, they'll say, 'What a woman!'"

"Well, you must tell me all about it."

This I said to push along the conversation, for I'd grown alarmed at the ardor with which Bridey fingernailed my back. She rustled me from the room, locked it, and led me by the hand to the library, where she positioned us on the loveseat and lit a cigarette before taking my chilly hand.

"The title: *In Our Image*."

"A Biblical reference?"

"Very good, Z. First, a preface. Life revolves around three things. Can you name them?"

"I shall follow my instinct. Lingerie."

"Close! Sex. What else?"

"How about a thick cut of steak, bloody as war."

"That's right, food. You're good at this. The third?"

"I daren't push my luck."

"Too bad, the third one is up your alley: death. The bedroom, the table, and the grave. Nothing else matters."

It bothered me that I was incapable of partaking in any of the three.

"The plot?" managed I.

"Forget plot. This is a *story*. The most primal of stories: a woman loves a man."

"And you would play the woman."

"As it happens, yes. Now this man, you see, beneath his human clothes, is a wolf."

I glanced at the bear rug. He looked bemused.

"Is this . . . a fairy tale?"

She puffed at her cigarette.

"Of sorts."

"Is it for children?"

"It's for *everyone*. Shut up and listen. The woman loves her man but decides she cannot stay with him. He is, after all, a wolf and he does what wolves do."

"Eat babies and such."

"So she sets to writing him a good-bye letter but has no paper at hand. What she has are calendars—all sorts of calendars. So she rips off a month and uses the back of it for her note, but it doesn't come out right so she crumples it up and throws it away. She rips off another month, then another, and those months become *real*, and by the time she's finished the note she's crumpled up entire years. She goes outside to deliver the perfect good-bye letter only to find that her wolf has died."

"Because wolves have shorter life spans."

"Exactly! But it's worse than that. All wolves have died, all natural predators, which includes man, by which I mean *men*—leaving women behind in a world devoid of violence. But is that a good thing? It's a vacuum, isn't it? A kind of slow death? So the women begin to create new men by surgically removing from each of them a rib and packing it in clay."

Dearest Reader, I shall respect your time and skip to the end of this brain-scrambling debacle. Among the impossible set-pieces were three consecutive scenes of unexpurgated sexual intercourse and a sequence in which Bridey's character goes feral and is trapped by hunters (with wolf teeth, natch). The film's climax, to be filmed in a continuous ten-minute shot, involved her corpse being disemboweled, divided into cuts of meat, and individually wrapped and sold at a butcher counter.

'Tis a delicate art, being a critic.

"I beg your pardon," said I, "for I am unschooled in matters of business. But I fear the Hays Code would be inflexible regarding the depiction of animal fornication, much less human."

She stubbed her cigarette to death.

"It's only 'fornication' if you're scared of it. In the script I call it 'carnal knowledge.' I use the term deliberately."

"Again, your pardon—one thousand times I beg it. Yet it would seem to me that the ending, too, would need adjusting."

The widening of her eyes felt like a warning.

"That's the whole point of the picture. I am chopped into little pieces, like a roll of film, and shipped all over the world to be consumed."

"Your totality of vision I would not dispute. Which studio, do you think, might permit imagery of such . . . potency?"

"Why do you think I slave as I do? I've agreed to twenty-five pictures over the next seven years. Twenty-five more dopey go-rounds as The Girl. By 1942 I will have made MGM so much money that they will not be in a position to *permit* me anything. They will *owe* me. Frankly, I expected more understanding from you."

Ah, but the ruffled feathers of feminine affront were my most comfortable pillows! I'd antagonized gaggles of gals in the past and knew the best tools with which to coo, cajole, and inveigle. Bridey's barricades were robust but not impregnable, and before long I had her convinced that my enthusiasm for *In Our Image* was the very marrow of my bones. It was a white lie meant as a heartfelt gift, though it was for Church that I tied the bow. Those paychecks had to keep coming.

"Please," said I, "may I read it?"

Her fingers flew to her beautiful throat.

"No! Oh, no, no. I couldn't allow it, it's not ready. But it will be, Z, there's no more question about that. A few more years of acting and then I'll show you—I'll show *everyone*—exactly what kind of woman Bridey Valentine is. Can you be patient?"

I'd been dead nearly forty years.

Patience? Yes, I'd heard of it.

VII.

BRIDEY HADN'T HYPERBOLIZED HER MARTYRDOM at the Metro-Goldwyn-Mayer cross. She succumbed to a fifth MGM seasonal and acquiesced to every lucrative loan-out to Paramount, Warner Brothers, and RKO. What few calendar boxes remained were crossed out by live dramas at Lux Radio Theatre or advertisement shoots arranged by the image department, most of which married a shot of my regal Bridey with blather she'd rather die than utter aloud:

> *"This Face Powder Allows Me to Be Nonchalant About My Complexion."*
> *"Nine Out of Ten Women Have Hosiery Problems—But I'll Tell You My Secret."*
> *"For Now I'm Only a Bridey, But I Still Dream of Rose Blossom Engagement Rings!"*

For the sake of *In Our Image* she accepted these indignities and more. She was absent day, night, and weekend, leaving me oodles of time to wander the mansion's dueling grand staircases, red-wallpapered sitting rooms, bead-curtained verandas, and even dull pantries, dodging servants and, because it was my disposition, contemplating the occasional theft.

In fact, I was pondering the pilferage of a sinister stone carving of Paleolithic origin when I became aware of footfalls advancing upon the drawing room with greater speed than any servant. So convinced was I that a sneak thief was in my midst that I lifted the priceless carving like a bludgeon.

That it was a twelve-year-old girl flustered me. My unnatural silence had scrambled the child's radar and she pulled to a halt. I remind you that it was 1936 and the little lasses of America had been brainwashed by the bouncing ringlets, polka-dot baby-doll dresses, and red Mary Janes of child star Shirley Temple. Even mothers battered by the Depression sewed their daughters copycat costumes. This girl, however, wore an expressionless gray tunic. Her long black hair flaunted not one festive ribbon and was instead held at bay by a nondescript band.

Verily, she was a wholly unremarkable thing save the banker's stack of money she was stuffing into her wee purse. She was caught in the act, eyeing my makeshift weapon, young muscles flexed to flee. I lowered the stone figure and she exhaled. From the other end of the palmette-patterned Mahal rug, she fired a penetrating squint.

"You're Z."

Usage of the private nickname was all the evidence I required.

"And you," said I, "must be Gopher."

"*Nnn*." A hard hum of irritation. "Margeaux."

I postulated that the pubescent's impertinence stemmed from the tragedy of having inherited none of her mother's beauty. Indeed, what traces existed of Bridey—the ember eyes, the natural frown—emphasized the regrettable averageness bequeathed by the uncredited father. The girl was thirty pounds too heavy and bore the weight on a slack, dangling posture. Crooked glasses pinched her nose, and teeth, indeed gophery, shone with the first set of steel orthodontia I'd ever seen.

I attempted a host's smile.

"Your mother forgot to mention your visit."

Her voice was thick from the mouthful of metal.

"My mother doesn't forget anything."

"She wished to surprise me, then?"

"Wow," said she. "You don't know anything, do you?"

She traversed the rug with slow, scuffling steps, making no attempt to hide the cash-crammed purse, and placed her crossed arms across the top of a rosewood armchair.

"You're just like Mother said. You're all pale and sad-looking."

"Sad? No, small child, you are confused."

"There's nothing wrong with being sad. Sadness builds character."

"I don't believe in it," sniffed I. "Never understood the point."

Margeaux shrugged.

"That's what they tell me, anyway."

"Are all modern instructors so cheeky?"

"Therapists. Mother has me seeing a million. They ought to just lobotomize me and get it over with."

"I fail to see how one could be sad with so much money in her purse."

In acknowledgment of the touché, she raised one eyebrow. Just like Bridey.

"You're meaner than Mother's other men," said she.

"I am not mean. I simply do not care for children."

"That's a laugh. You're barely older than me."

"I am older than I look."

"Then why don't you like children?"

The query was fair, but the answer private. My extended death had introduced me to three: Little Johnny Grandpa, Gladys Leather, and Harold Quincy, juveniles with nothing in common except for having left my acquaintance desolated or dead. It was time, thought I, to frighten away this ankle-nipping imp before she began down a comparable road.

"I do not like children because they do childish things like steal money. Now, shall I bother your mother at the studio with a telephone call? I'm sure that director, producers, actors, and equipment operators alike will welcome such a worthwhile interruption."

Margeaux gestured her chin at the stone Austrian I was throttling.

"You weren't planning on stealing *that*, I hope."

"You know, I've had a change of mind. Let me make some calls about that lobotomy."

The girl did not know how to smile (with that orthodontia, who would want to?), but she dropped her shoulders to convey disarmament. The movement pulled at the sleeves of her tunic and I saw dozens of lines drawn across her pudgy forearms in seashell patterns. They were scars—deliberate and artful and the most beautiful thing about her, which was, I realized, a truth of considerable melancholy.

I clacked my teeth in vexation. I did not enjoy feeling sympathy for this funked Ophelia, even though I knew by instinct that she understood me; both she and I had won attention because of our contiguity to death. It was an obnoxious reminder of my intrinsic uselessness and I lashed out.

"Well, girl, are you returning the money or not?"

Her voice was gentler.

"I don't mind that you're mean."

"You have yet to see mean, I promise you."

"Mean is real, at least. Mother's other men had all these big phony smiles and big phony faces. Sure, they were nice. But what's the point of being nice if you're just going to look in a mirror all day? My therapists tell Mother I'm depressed because I'm not pretty, but that's stupid. I'm depressed because nobody cares about anything. Do you know about the Dust Bowl? Farmers are losing everything they have and you think people out here care? They don't even know what farmers *do*."

"Your mother is not like that."

"She is. She thinks she's different but she's not. You watch. I'd rather be dead than be like that. Really, truly. I'd rather be dead and buried."

My eyes shifted again to her armful of scars. This time she noticed and her eyes, Valentine all the way, flared. Rapidly I contemplated adultlike consolations one might speak and—Hail Mary, full of grace, all that drivel—I spoke them.

"Bridey cares about you very much. If things were different, if she could claim you without scandal, I have no doubt that you would be living right here with us."

"Is that what she said?"

"Yes." I shrugged. "More or less."

"Don't forget she's an actress. She's Bridey Valentine and she gets what she wants. We're just two of the people who give it to her."

Such dismal wisdom from so pint-sized a sage might have inspired laughter had not the words cut with so sure a hand. Even I had to admit that I was there at Bridey's pleasure, and that she could dispose of me at first displeasure. The realization rattled me.

It was, surmised I, how Margeaux must feel every day.

Perhaps I would steal the Paleolithic figure after all. It was worth money, and it was always wise to plan ahead.

Margeaux patted her purse.

"I don't suppose you could forget to mention I was here."

"The servants," said I, "have all seen you."

"Yes, but them I can pay off. Mother isn't known for spoiling her staff."

Her accosting stare broadcasted the hope that I, on the other hand, was unbribable. Had you told me an hour earlier that the respect of a twelve-year-old girl would have me burning with pride, I would have booked you a padded cell. Now I was reluctant to see Margeaux go and so delayed her with a question.

"Where on Earth did you get that money?"

But Margeaux had determined that our conversation was kaput and was already stomping toward the veranda exit. She did do me the favor of pausing at the doorway. Her graceless stoop was unchanged; there was something brave about that.

"The walk-in shoe closet. Top shelf. Second-to-the-last hatbox on the left." She shook her head. "Honestly, Z. You need to work on your snooping."

VIII.

PITY THE SWINDLER WHO TRIED to put one over on Bridey. Within minutes of homecoming, she sensed Margeaux's storming of the compound. Bridey was not cross; rather, her brisk manner evinced an embarrassment over the lengths her daughter had gone to avoid her. Nothing more was said of Margeaux until a month later, when I overheard Bridey's end of one of their calls. Before then I'd had no interest in eavesdropping, but now I toed up to a wall well-positioned for espionage and peeked around it.

Scandal rags would have paid good money for a photograph of the invincible Bridey Valentine in a state of such defeat. Her upper body was slumped across a telephone table, hair uncombed, face unpainted, and bundled in a salmon-pink robe.

"I suppose I *did* start smoking at your age but that's beside the poi—. Why, that's a horrid thing to say. Of *course* you will live long enough to care. You're doing so much better, that's what everyone tells—. You're a bright girl with a wonderful future. I don't see why you can't be happy."

She twisted the telephone cord around her purpling finger.

"If only you would engage with people, participate. You used to twirl your baton, what happened to that? Oh, yes. Well, we can't all be coordinated. What about that play you did in fourth grade? You had so much fun. Well, no, I didn't, and I've apologized for that, but what would have happened had I come? There would have been questions, it would've become a three-ring—. Baby, I'm *not* being conceited, I'm—"

Vertebrae pressed through her robe.

"I don't expect you to be interested in acting. That was silly of me. I just want—Gopher, I want whatever *you* want. I want you to be happy—healthy and happy. Just don't smoke too much, will you promise? And do what your therapists tell you. And eat right—baby, I'm not saying a word about your weight, but you must read that booklet I sent about moderation. And sleep—are you getting enough sleep? Do you need another prescription?"

Her head of messy hair perked up.

"Why, yes, Z's here. Is there something you'd like me to ask him? Or if you'd enjoy speaking with him personally, I'd be happy to—"

Ten thousand fan letters a week, Americans spraining their wrists to describe the depths of their devotion, and a few muttered words from an unsociable child had rubbled her confidence. I began to look for a hiding place until I heard Margeaux's mortification blaring from the receiver.

"Gopher, Gopher—all right, I won't put him on—I didn't mean to—I'm just trying to—"

Margeaux severed the connection, and it took thumb-screw levels of endurance to ride out the ten minutes that groveled by before Bridey placed the handset into its cradle. When next I dared look, I found her mourning her reflection in the wrought-iron mirror over the table. I knew what she saw. It was early; she was undressed and without cosmetics; she was not armed to hide from herself the truth.

Bridey was thirty-eight in a town that preferred its ingenues still dewed from their buds of womanhood—in other words, my age. She was furthermore estranged from the daughter whose youth might pull against the ever-nibbling shark of time. Bridey led a life rich of food, rough of tobacco, harsh of alcohol, and late of nights, everything against which she warned Margeaux, and even a face and body like hers could not triumph *ad infinitum*.

Insecurity, as if bid by this bugle, came marching with the September 1936 death of Irving Thalberg. To you the name likely means nothing, but to Tinseltown noblesse, he was "the Boy Wonder," the humble son of German Jews appointed manager of Universal Studios at age twenty and the driving force behind the MGM dynasty. In hindsight, his sudden death at age thirty-seven was the first spot of tarnish upon a golden era.

Not since Rudolph Valentino's passing had Hollywood so grieved. On the day of the funeral, five minutes of silence were held at every studio in town, and newspapers squared their every inch with mawkish eulogies from the crème de la crème. I cared not one stale fig about a dead executive, but Thalberg had been the orchestrator of Bridey's twenty-five-film plan—upon which rested the eventual fate of *In Our Image*. I offered her encouragements: everything would work out, she was bigger than any one producer, that sort of tripe. She was too smart to believe it.

Bridey recounted the funeral through a veil she refused to remove. The street outside of Wilshire Boulevard Temple had been blocked to accommodate thousands of spectators angling to see the parade of sorrowing stars. Everyone was there and even the squirreliest starlet had been forced to wear inexpressive black. The result was a rare leveling of the field. While the rabbi droned, actresses twisted their necks to gauge the competition. There was no hiding who looked great or merely good, who was laudably young and who was criminally old.

Bridey was sobbing by the time she left—I saw the published photos. She was captioned as bereaving a fallen friend, but that was a stretch. Old age, that rat fink, had crept up on her and stabbed her in the exquisite back. It was fitting, I suppose, that the ambush had happened at a funeral.

She'd slipped the valet an extra twenty to fetch her car first, but it did not arrive before she became entangled in a grapevine that, even at this driest of affairs, bore bruise-colored fruit. Thalberg, the gossipers gossiped, had been sure-footed in his career, but boy, he'd sure made a misstep when passing on the film rights to a book called *Gone With the Wind*.

I'd never heard of it; I assumed it to be the tale of an interesting tornado. I came to find that the book was not meteorological in nature but instead a Civil War tear-jerker. The property had gone to David O. Selznick over at Selznick International, and with Clark Gable anointed as the male lead, Selznick was ramping up a global search for The Girl, or rather, The Girl to End All Girls, if you believed the chatter outside the Wilshire Boulevard Temple.

Bridey, for one, believed it. Every female in town (and likely a few males) wanted the role of Scarlett O'Hara, and as "Scarlett Fever" engulfed Hollywood, Bridey began hauling around the refrigerator-sized novel, breaking the spine like she was killing it, dog-earing pages until they snapped, and cramming the margins with minuscule manifestos regarding motivation. While Bridey was on set I gave the book a whirl but put it down around page eighty-million, even though I was rather fond of Miss O'Hara. She was pompous, duplicitous, underhanded, and randy. What wasn't to like?

By those same yardsticks, it was the role for which Bridey had been born. There was but one niggling issue. By my calculation,

Scarlett O'Hara began the story in her teens and was not a day over thirty by the drop of the final curtain. Believe me, Reader, I did not relish summoning the thunder of a Bridey scorned, but neither could I stomach months of preparation put toward an impossible end.

One explosive afternoon the topic forced itself.

Bridey strangled the most recent issue of *Photoplay*.

"It says right here they've got Norma Shearer doing lighting tests, and she's only a couple of years younger than me! I guess they haven't noticed that Norma hasn't any tits, absolutely none to speak of. The falsies alone will send them overbudget!"

She punted the magazine across the room.

"And Tallulah Bankhead? Why, she's just a watered-down me! And Katharine Hepburn, that grandpa in a dress? It makes my skin crawl! And Bette Davis? *Bette fucking Davis?*"

She looked about, probably for a gun with which to shoot the *Photoplay* dead.

"Calm thyself," urged I. "There are other roles."

"Not like this one. This one *makes* me, and it makes my script a reality. I'm not going to sit here and let them hand it to some witless chippy!"

One could not help but recall how Bridey herself had made her name by out-and-out robbing *An Orchid Unknown* from Old Lady Talmadge, but that footnote I kept to myself. Gingerly I proceeded.

"Regardless of outcome, you know that those hussies cannot hold a candle—"

"Oh, don't patronize me. I don't keep you here to kiss my ass."

"That does not sound half bad." I winked. "Let us give it a try."

"You'd like that, wouldn't you? Anything to avoid actual sex. I suppose you'd prefer No-Tits Norma or Grandpa Hepburn."

"Everything I say upsets you. Henceforth, let us speak only in milquetoast generalities."

I bent down to pick up the magazine. She booted it out of reach.

"Of course your beloved Wilma Sue never gets older, does she? She's safe from the ravages of age, perfectly, pristinely *dead*."

Bridey's black eyes blistered. Honed on dozens of sets in dozens of scenarios versus dozens of redoubtable actors, the glower was strong enough to nail me to the wall. Nothing injured me more than base slanderings of Wilma Sue, and Bridey, in her foulest moods, always remembered.

"She wasn't a *goddess*," said she. "She wasn't *perfect*. You've built a pedestal to this girl like she's the epitome of virtue, when she was every bit as faulted and as foul as me. It's a child's viewpoint, Z. You can be such a child."

She turned on her black suede heel and cruised from the room. I listened to her clack across a mile or two of flooring before hearing the smart click of the lifted telephone receiver. A savvy hunter, I removed my shoes before pursuing my game on socked feet. The duty I'd taken on, I tried to remind myself, included administering cool water to my overheated female firebrand.

"Overland three-seven hundred," she barked at the operator. "Yes, hello, this is Miss Valentine. I require you, at once, to connect me with—yes, that's right. Darling, I could not care less if he's busy; interrupt him. Who? I don't care if he's got FDR in there. All right, listen up, girlie. You tell him Miss Bridey Valentine is on the line and she's beginning to feel, let's say, a nervous breakdown coming on, or perhaps a sunstroke—you know, one of those actressy ailments that can shut down a picture for weeks. Why, yes, dear, of course I'll hold."

When I retired that night, I did so alone, aside from the annotated

Gone With the Wind I intended to render into confetti. I did not, though, for as upset as I was, I had to hand it to Bridey—her caveman club still worked. Ten minutes of telephonic tirades had won her an appointment with Selznick for the very next day. I dwelled upon Church, unresponsive to my every cash mailing but no doubt repairing himself toward health. When had everyone begun turning to me, of all people, to maintain mature behavior? Above all, I had to keep the money flowing.

I placed the novel outside Bridey's boudoir, all 1,037 pages intact.

It was a bad sign that she was not carrying the book when she returned the following night. She had frizzed hair and pink skin, evidence that she'd scrubbed away the garish rouge of a twenty-year-old Georgian debutante. We eyed each other, silent as duelists, until she made her way to the library, busied herself at the wet bar, and tossed down her throat a shot of bourbon. She closed her eyes as the antivenom coated her innards. The bear rug, ever mirthful, waited to chuckle at human follies.

"He offered me a part," said Bridey.

I dropped my corpse onto the loveseat.

"Right there? At the meeting? Why . . . that's remarkable! The magazine said one thousand actresses have read for the part—one thousand! When will it be public? We should take out a full page in *The Hollywood Reporter*, thanking everyone for their belief and trust—"

I, blinkered old nag, quit my nickering upon noticing another three fingers of booze being swallowed, glug-a-glug-glug. Bridey wiped her mouth with the back of her hand and gasped at the corollary gut-fire. She steadied herself against the bar.

"The part of *Belle*," said Bridey.

This character I did not recall.

"Belle . . . ?"

"Belle Watling." Glug-a-glug-glug. "The powdered old whore."

Selznick, hoped I, had removed the breakables from his office prior to Bridey's combustion. Further details dribbled out as she anesthetized herself: how the role was contingent upon a screen test, a process to which she hadn't been subjected since naifhood; how the moguls didn't use to wedge her *into* pictures, they built pictures *around* her; how Selznick had interrupted her impassioned pitch so that he could administer an injection of amphetamines to keep himself "glued"; how the whole thing had been an excuse to put Bridey in her place in a post-Thalberg landscape.

I patted her hand, brushed her hair. I assuaged, I consoled. The evening tilted, lost itself in duration, and sometime during the deadest, drunkest hours, Margeaux's warnings snaked like an arid Baja breeze about the room's keystoned arches, corniced ceilings, and dead bear. Mother, she'd said, was a phony like all the rest; Mother, she'd said, cared only for herself and her image. She was a strange one, our little Gopher, but she was not without insight, as I was soon to discover.

IX.

BRIDEY INSISTED THAT IT WAS no big deal. Getting a facelift was no worse than getting your teeth done. Who even remembered Joan Crawford's asymmetrical ivories before she had her jawline straightened? What leading lady hadn't gagged at Clark Gable's tooth rot during a love scene before he had the whole set of them replaced?

My own body brought me regular disgust, and yet I could not stomach her description of the procedure. The crude incisions behind the ears. The stretching of skin as if it were a sheet across a bed. On the day of the surgery I paced the mansion afraid that I might retch the full contents of my stomach—namely, Johnny's golden aggie, a token of another era when science pretended to perform miracles.

Bridey was driven home late the following night to avoid being photographed. When she entered clinging to the chauffeur's arm, I covered my mouth to inhibit a scream. She squinted through the purple custard of two black eyes, her entire face swollen, glossy, and encrusted with blood along the cotton treatments of her ears and jaw. My poor mangled beauty! I took her in my arms, heedless of the staff that watched us, and moaned that we would find a way to reverse the damage, that all was not lost!

It was needless drama. A deep-peel facial treatment was to blame for the burned flesh but it healed rapidly, as did the bruising and inflammation. Bridey spent half of her recovery in front of a convocation of mirrors and the other half updating MGM on her progress. I hated the surgery the same as I would hate a man who had beaten her, so it was with substantial conflict that I acceded that the procedure had, in fact, rolled back ten years of age.

Her tightened skin widened her eyes so that she appeared as startled by her beauty as I. Emboldened by this cut-and-stitch, she embarked upon a bonanza of self-improvement, from a month-long diet of vegetable broth to a programmed series of enemas. How she strutted about, hips swinging with spunk enough to knock the skull of a decapitated Viking from its pedestal.

The role of Scarlett O'Hara had been awarded to actor Laurence Olivier's wife, an English coquette named Vivien Leigh. But the new Bridey no longer cared. She was nine films into her twenty-five-film contract and rededicated to squeezing the next sixteen for every last award and box office record. She had the face; all she needed was a reason to make people look at it. In other words, she needed a scandal, and no one did scandal better than Bridey.

This time, the scandal was me.

To this day I carry upon my bony back a freight of bitterness. I believed, stupidly, that it was affection that compelled Bridey to ask me, at long last, to leave my Beverly Hills confines and visit her upon the set of her new Western, *Die, Banditos!* That morning I could not knot my tie, and for a blissful few seconds I was an ordinary seventeen-year-old kid, anxious for a date at his first upscale restaurant.

Never shall I forget the surreality of the stroll to Stage 19. Women in towering headdresses commingled with fellows skirted in Egyptian gold. Workers moved bizarre props—a jade jaguar, a giant plaster head, a science-fiction missile—on wheeled pallets. A cluster of midgets threw dice outside of a stage, while a truck rumbled by with a medieval tower bound for the backlot. I tipped my hat at a lucky fellow tape-measuring the bust of a girl in a flesh-colored leotard. He gave me a quick scan and made, I suppose, a forgivable assumption.

"*The Devil's Henchmen*, right?" He thumbed left. "Two doors down."

Outside of Stage 19 lounged a rabble of reporters and photographers chewing toothpicks. As one, they gave me a look before judging me inconsequential. I gave them no mind, so eager was I to get my dead flesh out of the heat. Inside it was cool and dark, so long as I stayed clear of the lights aimed upon a saloon set. The surrounding hullabaloo was like Ed Mann's newsreel crew times fifty, bustling with harried technicians all the way up to the catwalks. I felt quite small. Movie people, I'd found, had a knack for that.

Bridey sashayed from the darkness in a plaid frontier dress with fur cuffs, black lace gloves, and a tight black ribbon around her neck. Her baguette of hair bounced about her shoulder as she put my arm across her elbow and steered me back outside. I tried to resist.

"Might we remain inside? The heat is not good for my—"

"I'll simply die without some fresh air."

The moment we stepped outside, the lazy shutterbugs spat their toothpicks and became a well-trained firing squad, lifting their cameras in unison and blasting. I blinked at the strobe effect and staggered, but Bridey gripped my suit with one hand while daintily touching her breastbone with the other.

"Boys!" scolded she. "I swear a girl cannot enjoy a moment's privacy."

It was flirty fibbery, frisky fakery, and the photogs scarfed it, laughing and pressing closer, firing their pulses of light off her smooth new face. Bridey, the obvious orchestrator of the event, pouted and kittened, then trilled with laughter when they shouted what they were being paid to shout. My heart, that ball of mud, hardened and sank.

"Who's the Casanova, Miss Valentine?"

"Bridey, is this lucky fella pitching you woo?"

"What's your name, young man? You in pictures or what?"

I tried to enliven my daft look. Bridey made up for my hesitation by embracing me, not as she did in real life, with pelvis a-pushing and breasts a-plumping, but in an exaggerated stage hug capped by the hackneyed finale of her cheek pressed flat against my own.

"His name is Zebulon Finch and I'm simply mad about him! And you can print that: Z, E, B, U, L, O, N."

I heard the coffin crack of opened notebooks, the dead grass of rushing pencils.

"Miss Valentine! How about a smooch with the new beau?"

Other reporters hoorayed the motion. Bridey dropped her jaw in sarcastic shock before adopting the more familiar suggestive glower. She licked her ruby lips, tilted her face to mine, and drooped backward so that I was forced to sustain her in a romantic dip.

"Someone call Will Hays." Her murmur was just loud enough for transcription. "I think we might break the three-second rule."

I'd long prided myself on being an accomplished and unrepentant falsifier, yet this public kiss caused me discomfort. It felt as though our unique affection was shoved through a gristmill to create a more palatable product. Ten thousand photographs later (the final third of which guest-starred the Marx Brothers, who dropped by to make hubba-hubba faces), Bridey patted me on the head and sent me home like a good little boy. And like a little boy I sulked for having received less than I'd desired. This might be my coming out—the public cotillion long planned by Dr. Leather—but Bridey had choreographed it so as to benefit only her.

Our next stop was Grauman's Chinese Theatre, anchor of the Hollywood Walk of Fame, for the premiere of *Take My Wives—Please!*, Bridey's long-awaited slapstick slugfest with superstar Greta Garbo. Because the agoraphobic Garbo was her usual no-show, the twenty-thousand fans focused on Bridey, who led me about like a colt. Flashbulbs popped; I smiled, or tried to. What else did one do in Hollywood? Here was the fame I'd originally traveled west to find.

"Who Is the Mystery Man?" begged the headline of *Photoplay*.

I was not, as speculated, an expatriated prince from some sunless empire.

"What's Going on in Bridey's Love Nest?" demanded *Screen Romances*.

Not much, aside from one-way erotic servitude.

"A Boy-Toy for Bridey: Does True Love Know No Age?" inquired *Hollywood Low-Down*.

Star-fuckers had short memories. No one recalled my newsreel.

It was a cool autumn day in 1938 when a team from *Life* magazine visited the mansion for a six-page photo feature entitled "Relaxing at Home with Bridey Valentine." She was posed in a series of ludicrous *tableaux vivants*: beaming in the garden with a badminton racket (she had never played); in the parlor running a feather duster over china (are you kidding me?); and in the bathtub, smoldering from within a coat of bubbles (she believed baths were for babies).

I, too, was subjected to staged stupidity. The *Life* squad decked me out in lumberjack flannel and forced me to a kneel atop the accursed bear rug, gripping a log as if I were about to toss it upon the fire. I held the pose for several minutes while the bear, his glass eyes happy with flame, flaunted his tranquil death.

It was from that locked position, with my last crumbs of pride being lapped up by the bear's indolent pink tongue, that Bridey gave me a look I shan't forget. She was pensive, leaning against bookshelves with her pinky nail bit between her front teeth. I'd seen this look before, usually while she searched photos of herself for imperfections she might crush like roaches.

Despite the fire, flannel, and flashbulbs, I was taken by a chill. This body of mine had long titillated Bridey because of its abnormalities, but her study of me told a developing story. Had not surgery perfected her perfection? Perhaps her lover, already a boon when it came to press coverage, might double his value after benefitting from similar alterations.

"Mr. Finch?" beckoned the photographer. "America's housewives prefer you smiling."

X.

HEAR MY CONFESSION: I WORE tights. Gød damn me, I did. Nylon pantyhose had yet to be invented, so these were rayon stockings, but shame made no distinction. Bridey's late scrutiny had made me fearful of bloat, that inevitable phase of decomposition, and just as anxious about odor. My intent was to snare any scent of rot inside the tights, draw them shut like a garbage bag upon removal, and then air them out in a discreet location before asking Bridey's people to launder them all to hell.

California's incessant sun turned every sidewalk, boardwalk, and open-air bistro into a twenty-thousand-watt floodlight. I tried not to care, but Bridey had been right. I'd looked cadaverous in the *Life* spread; I'd practically ruined the whole thing. Thus the tights, the support garments, and the Pan-Cake and blush I swiped from Bridey's vanity and applied with all the artistry of a baboon. In a town full of fruits, I felt the fruitiest, so there was some relief when I was exposed—as it happened, peeling off my tights upon the bed.

The indignity of it all! I dunked my face into my hands.

Bridey glided across the room, nightgown flittering, and encircled my stiff, frigid flesh in the lissom warmth of her own. She cooed and petted my hair, and I recoiled. Her painted nails felt like beetles crisscrossing my scalp.

"There, there. There is no cause for embarrassment."

"No cause? I am attired like a courtesan!"

"You're self-conscious. It's only human."

"Human," rued I. "I thought I'd renounced all that."

"Hush. This is Beverly Hills. There's nothing unusual about a man being vigilant about his appearance. Do you think all those cleft chins come from the Chin Fairy? Why, even Valentino had his ears tucked."

"I am no actor. Such excuses do not apply."

"That's right, you're not an actor, and let's thank our lucky stars for that. What you need, Z, is—well, your needs are unique. But I can help you. I'm *glad* to help you. I know just the man for the job. Oh, darling, darling! I'm so pleased you felt secure enough in our relationship to come to me with this."

Point of fact, I had done nothing of the sort, but Bridey had gone electric. Should I wish to be uncharitable (and I do wish), I'd posit that Bridey had deliberately incited this insecurity so that she might pounce and pamper, thereby luring me up the scalpel-steps of modern glamor. Even cognizant of this, I gestured for her to continue— anything to dig me out from this trench-collapse of pride.

Bridey's cosmetic surgeon was named Biff. Let all six syllables permeate you, Reader: *Dr. Biff Futterman*. You do concur that the name alone was a fifty-foot red flag? Not just any quack could be trusted with my bodily imponderables, so I waffled about scheduling an appointment. Whip-smart, Bridey wrangled us an invite to a dinner party that Dr. Biff was also attending so that I might evaluate him in a looser setting. I acquiesced, despite having a somewhat spotty history with surgeons.

The party was two hours away in the forests of the San Bernardino Mountains. There nestled the hunting lodge home of the hermetical Maximilian Chernoff, Hollywood's most esteemed director. An émigré from Russia's Bolshevik Revolution, Chernoff had gotten his start in war pictures—gruff, virile morality plays crammed with sweaty close-ups of agonized men. He'd since meddled with everything from Westerns to musicals, instilling each with a brawny musculature. He'd worked with Bridey only once, but it had led to her defining role in *All Who Are Wearied and Burdened*. If anyone had the brass balls to direct *In Our Image*, said she, it was Chernoff. Thus the dinner had a second purpose.

We were thirty, a hodgepodge of movie stars and moguls, financiers and family, all gaily corralled by Chernoff's wife, Mercy St. Johns, a handsome broad whose age had abbreviated her acting career and who was starved for some of the old Hollywood pizzazz. Everyone received two welcome kisses, one upon each cheek, except for me—the coldness of my first cheek startled her the same as if I'd muttered a sordid proposition.

Like the rest of the lodge, the dining room was wood on wood and syruped with sconced light that underlit the deer antlers lining the perimeter. The menu was wild game, brought out by servants but cooked by Chernoff himself, who arrived late to the table still clad in a white cooking apron and gesturing for everyone to shut up with their hellos. He could have been the twin of Teddy Roosevelt, some six presidents back: beefy, brusque, and walrused of mustache.

He indicated one glistening pile of meat and spoke with a Russian accent.

"Is elk."

Then the other.

"Is pheasant."

Without another word he took the head of the table and got

564

down to business with fork, knife, and bare hand, stuffing his cheeks so as to avoid answering questions beyond noncommittal grunts.

Mercy St. Johns had, at Bridey's backstage bidding, sat me across from Dr. Biff, where my presence was endured like a fart. Biff was girlish, with feathery blond hair, pursed lips, and buffed nails. He was a grinner and a fawner, tickled to be in high company, and my opinion of him seesawed. That is, until the conversation turned toward the dullest of all topics: politics.

"One simply cannot summer in style these days," sighed an actress. "I had my heart set on Prague before that terrible man in Germany had to go invade it."

"You're quite right," said another. "I cannot imagine crossing the Charles Bridge with those vulgar red flags ruining my castle view. What do they call that thing—the swastika? It sounds like an item from a Polish bakery, something sweet with poppy seeds."

"Poppy seeds!" laughed Mercy. "Hedda, you're a card!"

"Adolf Hitler," boomed a producer, "will be the death of us. People do not realize how many pictures are financed with Reichsmarks. Not to mention our reliance on the German talent pool. America could stand to steal away a few more Fritz Langs, I say."

"Funny Fritzy and his monocle," pouted Mercy. "I should have invited him."

"Excuse me for saying so, but I, for one, am glad you didn't."

All heads turned toward Dr. Biff, deliverer of this churlish rebuke. Upon being illuminated under such light, he pulled a grin so symmetrical it had to have been fashioned upon an operating table.

"I know Lang made that fine robot picture and that's all well and good," said he. "But now is a time for us peaceful nations to circle our wagons and be cautious with whom we consort."

"Fritzy is a fine Jewish boy," said Mercy. "We've nothing to fear from him."

"Don't we?" Dr. Biff, sudden sommelier, swirled his glass beneath his nose. "Who's to say why he left the Fatherland? That Goebbels fellow, Hitler's propaganda man, they say he adored Fritz Lang. Shouldn't that give us pause?"

"Shall we cast aside our every German friend?" challenged the producer. "And what of our Italian friends, now that Hitler and Mussolini have their Pact of Steel?"

"Well," said Dr. Biff, slurping his cabernet, "as long as we're cutting wienerschnitzel from our diets, why not spaghetti carbonara as well?"

Maximilian Chernoff set down his steak knife with a loud *thock*. Everyone bottled up, the same behavior, I imagined, as was common on his sets. Chernoff had said fewer than ten words since his identification of the meats and was clearly not keen to add to that total. But he stood, wiped at his lips with a napkin, and gave his audience a curt bow.

"Please excuse. I have a carcass to dress. Very good to visit you all."

With that, he charged from the room, kitchen apron bunched in a fist. The only sound was the shift of ice cubes in a glass. Bridey looked crestfallen at Chernoff's exit but she recovered, for she was, at the end of the day, a professional.

"If there *is* a war," declared she, "I do hope we stay out of it. What sort of leading men would be left to kiss? Just grandfathers, invalids, and cowards as far as the eye can see." She smirked. "Then again, I'm hardly choosy."

The remark was naughty enough to punch a hole in the pressurized bubble; a heave of laughter tore from each torso and Mercy St.

566

Johns capitalized on it, grabbing the discussion by the nose-ring and pulling it into safer pasture. Only Dr. Biff looked remiss. He turned to the closest diner—me—and put a hand to his mouth to deliver an aside.

"Reality," sighed he. "Picture people can have such difficulties accepting it."

The fact that I'd been forced to snuggle next to this squabbler infuriated me. I took up a handful of untouched elk meat and hurled it at the surgeon's face. Chernoff, like me, preferred his game rare, and Dr. Biff's face was blotched with blood and spattered with savory spices. Mercy shrieked, the producer laughed, and everyone else gasped as two servants rushed handkerchiefs-first to the doctor's side. So frantic was the bedlam that the candles flickered, turning the antlers above into devil horns, ideal to graft upon my evil skull.

I was up and out of my chair.

"Beg pardon," said I to no one in particular. "My elk slipped."

Then I was through a door and down one annex, then another, wondering if I might ever get through a single civilized dinner party without doing something reprehensible. Presently the light sources lessened and with surreal abruptness I became flanked by a stampede of nature's creatures enough to make Noah jealous. It was only after tensing for concurrent gorings that I identified my assailants as taxidermied.

Rigged upon cedarwood panels, articulated inside cabinets, and posed amid naturalistic simulacra was a vast menagerie. Three identical monkey heads stared at one another in incredulity at their absurd situation. A pile of hairless piglets fought for a sow's nipples. From a tree branch bolted into the wall dangled an immense sloth, so that he might enjoy an upside-down view of the kaleidoscope of hummingbirds caught behind glass. There was, of course, a bear—not a rug but the whole damn thing—a hulking Kodiak reared on its back legs and locked in combat with a cougar. Both animals were trimmed with gelatin blood and foam spittle.

"Straight, left, right, straight."

His centrality had concealed him. In the middle of the room sat Maximilian Chernoff in a massive leather armchair, cleaning an elephant gun. At his feel lay an old Brittany Spaniel with a name tag reading "OKSANA"; she rested, indifferent to the fifty antlered and horned heads branching from the wall behind her, each of mythological dimension: the Pan-like ibex, the Bacchus-like bison, the Atlas-like moose.

"The way back," said Chernoff. "Straight, left, right, straight."

He kept his attention upon the gun, which he polished with a gusto I recalled from wartime foxholes. I spurned my marching orders and dallied, anything to delay my return to the Dining Room of Disgrace. I cleared my throat and toed the plank.

"Handsomely furbished creatures, if I may say so. The hippopotamus is quite plump, eh?"

Chernoff slammed shut the bolt carrier.

"You appreciate? This is so?"

Zounds, no. Taxidermy was for ghouls.

"You bet I do!" enthused I.

Chernoff harrumphed, laid his weapon across his thighs, and considered me for the first time that night. His eye, trained through a camera lens, was scrupulous. I puffed my chest and thought imposing thoughts—me, bare-chested, wrestling a gator, that sort of thing. Chernoff reclined into the soft leather and dropped a hand to scratch Oksana's scruff.

568

"Fewer and fewer agree. Victorian décor—not so popular. Is fusty, is gloomy. I myself do the taxidermy—do you know this?"

"You don't say! How charming."

"Is my true passion. But Mercy, she does not like. She behave like *babushka*, tell me, 'Maximilian, you keep your stuffed animals in back.' Is how she calls them—stuffed animals. Eh, is all right. I like it here. Here is my cave."

The mention of his wife shriveled me. It would not be long before Mercy St. Johns told her husband of my tableside antics. Chernoff's paternal sternness inspired me to come clean before my misbehaviors were otherwise outed. Thus I introduced myself and with a fair bit of hawing recounted Dr. Biff's harangue and the heaping helping of elk steak I'd fed his face.

Chernoff boomed laughter and clapped.

"You bring me humor! Very good!"

"You are not cross with me?"

"*Nyet!* Mercy is beautiful sable, but she bring to our home donkey asses. It is they who are the animals. It is they who wait until you are down to feast upon your broken leg." He gestured at the taxidermia. "But these? These are my noble friends. We meet as equals in the Yukon mountains, the African savanna. No malice, no hypocrisy. Is what we all hope for, *da?* A dignified end?"

The director's English was middling but his instinctive grasp of the drama of life dispirited me. Consider, Reader, my own implausible backstory, hinged as it was upon the overused plot device of a bullet through the back, as well as my character arc, which had heedlessly helixed without a conventional three-act structure to guide it. Chernoff was right: I would do anything for a distinguished finale.

So shined upon me a ray of insight.

I needed no surgeon, no purveyor of living tissue.

What I needed was a man who understood the preservation of dead flesh.

Oksana did not bare her teeth when I approached her master, nor did she growl, for the dog was stuffed the same as all the animals around us, her good work on safaris of legend having ceded to a blissful sleep the likes of which I could only imagine.

"Forgive me, Mr. Chernoff," said I. "But I have for you a proposition."

XI.

WHERE THE HALL OF ANIMALS had been a dustless basilica surveilled by unsanctified saints, Chernoff's workshop was a small and windowless rectory. It smelled gamy and alcoholic. Only a fetishistic neatness kept the space from being overwhelmed by its alarming contents. Dangling from the walls were aprons, gloves, and tanning tools; stretched across looms were hides awaiting pickling; crucified upon teensy crosses were skinless carcasses yet to be deboned; and panting from the corner were two large freezers from which curled a white fog.

Chernoff pushed aside a table crowded with wax-sealed jars; the stillborn creatures within bobbed in amber liquids like the Barker's tapeworms. Chernoff freed me of my coat like a gentleman, sat me down, and rolled up my right sleeve. An arachnid light stand was positioned so that I was bathed in yellow light, and he took up my hand, gently, as if to kiss it.

"Here is where we perform test? You are positive?"

Where else, Dearest Reader, but the wound that had started it all in 1896? If Mr. Avery's fish hook hadn't snagged that tender triangle of flesh between pointer finger and thumb, I might still be at the bottom of Lake Michigan, ossified into an underwater shelter for all varieties of innocent guppies.

I had expected Chernoff's disbelief, if not outright horror, but had yet to be shown either. Since I'd shared my portfolio of unhealed wounds in the hall, the sole emotion he suppressed was excitement. Here was a man so built for challenges—obstinate actors, inopportune weather, hundreds of disorderly extras—that he'd accepted me as hungrily as a birthday child does cake. Now he toyed with my fingers, thumb, and wrist, his ear cocked for the murmur of bones.

"Is customary I work with fresh specimens. But is not imperative. Skin is what I need, and yours is intact. More or less."

"I thank you for making an exception."

"I told you, it is my passion."

"Then I thank you for believing me."

He gestured toward the Hall of Animals.

"You saw my platypus? When first platypus brought from Australia, what do naturalists say? Is hoax, they say. Bill of duck, body of rabbit, tail of beaver—is funny joke. *Nyet*. I believe what my eyes see. The eyes, always believe the eyes. Is why pictures so popular."

All the while he was tabulating equipment upon the counter, putty knives and chisels, boxes of salt and bottles of astringent. Next to the these lay a small bird in a middle stage of disembowelment. Its entire outer comportment of skin, feathers, legs, and tail had been turned inside out, leaving behind a moist red head, spindly neck, and tiny blob of organs.

"You're not planning to do *that* to me." Hopefully, I added, "Heh-heh."

"A finch or a Finch." Chernoff chuckled. "What is difference?"

I considered the bird-blob, then my hand. The latter was a-tremble. Chernoff snatched it. He pulled up a stool, sat, and set to drawing an ink circle around my quivering wrist.

"Americans were not always so tender. Where do you think you get leather for your shoes, my friend? I believe the movie screen is to blame. Our violence, it is too clean. A polite edit, snip-snip, and there is no blood, no bone, no pain. What is death in the pictures? It is a dream before our actor awakes to applause. This is not the death I knew in war. Or in the Orient, or on the Nile, or in the African bush."

He exchanged his pen for a small, sharp knife. He rolled back his own sleeves and I saw fat white scars crisscrossing his right forearm.

"Africa," said I. "Is that where you received those?"

"*Da, da.* A lion, two-hundred kilogram. She take my shot and is upon me before I shoot again. Was a nice struggle. I suffocated her with my fist down her throat."

The knife blade was ice against my skin. No icier, though, than my touch must have felt to Bridey. If this alteration would becalm her so that we might again achieve the harmony I could find nowhere else, then it would be worth it.

"You can really do this?" pleaded I.

The tightness of his smile made it difficult to gauge the sarcasm.

"I have yet to receive a complaint."

The knife gnawed at me like a patient rat. I closed my eyes and did not open them as the blade completed its circle; I kept them shut as Chernoff worked a flat tool beneath the skin to loosen it; and I dared not open them when he began to peel the skin from my wrist and palm the way you would take off a glove.

Chernoff was patient. It took over an hour to remove the skin of my hand in a single intact piece—a dry, papery thing—during which time there were footfalls in the Hall of Animals, perhaps partygoers hoping to have a word with the elusive director, perhaps Bridey coming to corral me. Well, too bad. She'd been the one to hurl me at the feet of the buffoonish Dr. Biff. All I'd done was find a superior alternative.

Eventually Mercy St. Johns did knock on the door, but Chernoff shouted a Russian word that sent her running. After that we were left undisturbed for the rest of the night. Chernoff was clearly content. While cleaning, tanning, and salting the flesh-glove, he hummed tunes that brought to mind frozen lakes, rabbit-fur ushanka hats, and brimming cups of vitalizing vodka.

Chernoff next began to cleanse my exposed muscle with warm water. Reader, I've made no secret of the contempt in which I hold Gød. Yet I felt as if ministered by gentle Jesus himself, so baptismal were Chernoff's soft ablutions. He patted dry my rinded hand with a clean white towel, used a hobby knife to nick away tendon gristle, filled the fishing-hook wound with a snug wire implant, applied a resin solution, rolled the skin back on, and sewed the outer wounds shut with the help of a tiny needle and a magnifying glass.

The second he was finished, his stomach, obedient as Oksana throughout the night, roared for its breakfast. It had to be morning. He stepped aside to wash his hands in a sink.

"Well? You like or do not like. Speak."

The hand was supple, pink, and aglow with health, the appendage of a young man not four decades dead but seventeen years alive.

My lubberly stammer was incommensurate to such a triumph.

"How . . . how much? Do I owe you for . . . this miracle?"

"You are guest. Is free. You go home now, you think thoughts. You want more, you come back, we make arrangement. Money—is not so important but is how American gentlemen do business. *Da?*"

Da, da, da! Shall I sing the word indefinitely? I exited the workroom bowing and blubbering praise, then traipsed through the Hall of Animals with my marvelous new appendage held before me like a glowing scepter. Chernoff, that peerless artiste, had even managed to erase the ring-finger scuffing wrought by Johnny's long-gone Little Miracle Electric Mexican Stuttering Ring.

It was dawn and felt like it: a brand-new day for Zebulon Finch! Wrangling a ride back to Beverly Hills took some doing, but by the time I arrived at the mansion I was using the Hand for this, that, and the other thing, and nearly squealing with glee. See how the Hand tips the driver! Look how the Hand opens the gate! Have you ever seen anything so wondrous as the Hand unlocking a door?

Bridey, per her established grind, was in her office. She wore a burgundy dress with shoulderpads wide enough to destroy a doorway, and was calculating gross percentages or net worths or some such tedious bunkum. I vibrated with more stimulating news, but waited at the precipice until she took off her glasses and fixed me with her trademark glare.

"Good of you to drop by. Too bad I am busy."

I rushed the desk.

"The evening took a turn I never could have foreseen!"

"I'd say that's an understatement. You jilted me, Z. Bridey Valentine, left stag at a party. That does not make me look especially good at a time when I am trying to look especially good. Exactly who do you think you are?"

"Your servant, your humble servant!"

"I had to tickle Biff's chin all night to get him to keep my next appointment. It left me with no time whatsoever to talk to Maximilian about my script. It could be six months before I get another chance."

"Yes, Maximilian—that's what I'm trying to tell you!"

"I'm paying you, aren't I? I believe that makes you obligated to obey when I tell you to get out of my office."

Words, ever my ardent accomplices, failed me, so I flung the

575

Hand across the desk, stopping a foot short of Bridey's nose. To her it looked like the gesture for *stop* and her cheeks reddened. I turned the Hand round and round till she began to focus upon the flesh. Her scythe eyebrows unlocked from their clash and her scowling lips parted with a delicate pop.

"All right," said she. "Talk."

She held her sharp tongue throughout. When I concluded with Chernoff's offer for further treatments, she snapped her fingers and pointed at the armchairs facing her desk. I sat in one and she took the opposite, perching upon the edge so that she might compare my hands side by side. The difference was breathtaking. The left hand looked as if grubbed from a grave, while the right looked as if it should be gripping a baseball, hoisting trophies, and sliding beneath cheerleaders' skirts.

Bridey's eyelids lowered.

"Did Maximilian say anything about me? Anything at all?"

It was, you will agree, a moment unfit for candor.

"Only that you were more beautiful than ever." The compliment, decided I, needed more Russian detail. "More radiant than the Caspian Sea, more magnificent than the Kremlin!"

Bridey might have detected the fib had not she been so eager to believe it. She brushed a whip of black hair behind an ear; there was no trace left of the facelift scar. Dr. Biff, that pompous schmuck, knew his business as well as Chernoff knew his. Bridey stood and from her cleavage fished a necklace off which dangled a key, and she used that key to unlock a safe embedded in the far wall. She returned with a thin sheaf of cash. Grover Cleveland gazed importantly from the topmost thousand-dollar bill.

She tucked the money into my pocket. Explanation was not

needed. Bridey had no cause to impede my Hollywoodization, particularly if it bound me to the one director who might realize her script. To her this was a double victory; every step I took into her bright, ageless future was a step away from the darkening yesteryears of Wilma Sue.

Reader, look! Plot, subplots, characters, and theme—at last every one is conjoined.

Buy a bag of peanuts, settle in.

For here comes the twist.

XII.

CHERNOFF CONTINUED TO PLAY KING'S Man to my Humpty Dumpty, first darning Leather's serving-fork puncture in my left forearm, next sanding away the flamethrower burns of my left biceps, and third reconstructing my grenade-blasted right thigh. With every peel, pickle, paste, and patch, I began to see myself, many decades the outsider, as resolutely, proudly American— no, as *America itself*, cobbled from foreign pieces the same as our grand country.

Bridey was too busy to curb my immodesty. Nourished by our fruitful scandal, she labored like a sled dog, dragging her frazzled entourage from soundstage to soundstage, filming one role during the day and a second at night. After our Limey pals got their peckers crossed with those of Hitler's Nazis, displaying patriotism became paramount, so she spent weekends and holidays jetting about to star-studded events to raise money for the British Relief Fund. With the U.S. determined to sidestep another war, support efforts fell to the likes of Fred Astaire, Myrna Loy, and Bridey V.

Thus I took my first fledging flaps outside my nest. The autonomous act of driving myself to Chernoff's lodge vivified me, and each passing moon I handed the director thousands of dollars without equivocation. Bridey's cash advance ran out; prideful like a lad away at university, I asked not for further funds but rather paid Chernoff from my own wages. A boy my age ought to be worrying about pimples and dandruff, not decay! This left nothing to send Church but I was surprised by how little I minded. Not once in a hundred paychecks had he bothered to thank me.

When Bridey did come home, she and I were no more a misalliance. Rather, we were the Wonder Twins, younger and trimmer each time we toweled off from our respective fountains of youth. Her bedtime chatter revolved around a possible new neck, while I pondered my own frontier—a whole new face. We sighed over the prospects until she fell asleep; after that, I sighed some more. Bridey was five films away from fulfilling her contract and the shooting script of *In Our Image*, she said, was almost finished. It felt as though our good fortune might never turn.

On February 29, 1940—Leap Day, a black portent—we attended the twelfth annual Academy Awards, held at the Cocoanut Grove nightclub of the Ambassador Hotel. Bridey had received her third Best Actress nomination, this time for the role of a dethroned, banished, debased, and yet enduringly well-scrubbed princess who falls for the eye-patched ringleader of a band of medieval outlaws. An usher guided us around the indoor palm trees. Clad in a black satin dress and cape flounced with cockerel feathers, Bridey ravened through a field of lilac, juniper, and rose gowns.

While she entertained well-wishers with her jaded eye-rolls, I fulfilled the arm-candy role for which I'd been trained and taxidermied, quiet and dashing in a stifling tuxedo. We landed at a plum table where we knocked elbows with James Stewart and an absolute doll-face named Judy Garland, who I mentally declothed until her unrelenting cheeriness began to make me ill.

It was during the naming of Best Original Score that I became aware of an itch. So I scratched it; what could be more banal? Our host, a duck-faced prankster named Bob Hope, yielded the podium to the songster behind *The Wizard of Oz*. The itch, I realized, came from the Hand; I stopped scratching. The composer's speech was short, and Mr. Hope proceeded to deliver an Oscar to Walt Disney for some bit of cartooning. The room was dark; I drew close a candle so that I might see the source of my itch. Mr. Disney was done; now Mr. Hope wondered aloud who devised the year's Best Story?

My tablemates belched cheer upon the naming of *Mr. Smith Goes to Washington*. Perfect timing! I drew back my sleeve by its sterling silver cufflink and brought the Hand to the guttering flame.

The flesh had buckled inward at the former location of the fishing-hook wound. With horror, I saw that the skin around it had revolted against Chernoff's chemicals and now shone with a banana-peel blackness. I was rotting. Right there at the goddamned Academy Awards I was falling apart.

I turned to Bridey but she was groaning along to Mr. Hope's latest crack. I craned my neck elsewhere for a hallway through which I might escape. What I found instead were film cameras pointed every which way, more than I could tally. Bridey had mentioned this in the limousine, how the ceremony was being filmed for a Warner Brothers newsreel; that was why she had to wear something that would make a splash in black-and-white.

Ed Mann and his capering clowns were after me again! If I fled, those snitchers would film it, toss it up on a million screens, and this time people would remember. Under the table I hid the Hand, that unpardonable traitor, and grafted onto my whirling head a deranged grin. Face by famous face, the grin was mirrored back, each mouth as wide and red as a slit throat. Before my eyes, beauty became disfigurement. Refinished teeth were primitive stones, stained not with wine but Cro-Magnon blood. A tightened forehead was burnished bone. A pert new nose was the hairy black void of a sow's snout.

Frank Capra dropped me a wink—he knew my dirty secret. Mickey Rooney slapped his knee—he'd tell his chums my whole sick story. Bob Hope waggled his long lizard tongue at me and relinquished the podium to Spencer Tracey, who turned the list of Best Actress nominees into a pontiff's gonging: Bette Davis, Irene Dunne, Greta Garbo, Greer Garson, Bridey Valentine. Cryptic names of lesser devils, all of whom howled fealty to their ascendant winner and high priestess, Vivien Leigh—Scarlett O'Hara herself—whose every word of gratitude goaded her frothing minions to orgiastic thrall.

In single slugs, Bridey downed cocktails, blood-red and piss-yellow and pus-white. Ice rattled; I gasped. This ceremony, or necromancy, whatever it was, was finished, having lurched out ahead of me while I roiled in delirium. I came to life with the Hand tucked beneath my lapel, watching Bridey chant ancient incantations to purring cameras: "Always a Bridey, never a bride, isn't that right, boys?"

There!—a dagger of darkness!—a door!—and beyond, the wide-open night! With my unspoiled hand I took Bridey by the elbow but we were blocked by giddy goblins gibbering glorifications regarding *performances* and *realizations*. Here in this hippodrome there was no Depression, no drought, no poverty, no war. Bridey they cheek-kissed but me they offered hands for the shaking, their *right* hands, which meant my right hand, *the* Hand, was required to meet them.

I clobbered my way through the crowd, jilting Bridey for a second time, but what else could I do? Outside, a doorman hailed a cab; that cab spat me out at the mansion; there, I took a car and torched rubber for two hours until reaching the lodge. By then it was three in the morning and the mountains were cold and black and probably teeming with trolls. I attacked the door; there was no response. I shattered a window and clambered through it.

"Chernoff!"

I bolted down darkened hallways, cradling the Hand to my breast.

By the time I reached the Hall of Animals, I was hysterical. These jeering abominations were no better than those monsters at the Ambassador! My flesh was in ruin and thus it was ruin I'd spread. I ambushed a polar bear, took a jaw in either hand, and pulled until the bottom half broke loose and dry straw erupted from the mouth. I hooted, lashed out with the Hand, and snatched a kudu by an ear. It came down with a thump, its braided horns spearing the belly of a fox; rather than entrails, it spilled sawdust. I swiped the sawdust with my hand and licked it— blood of conquest!—before barreling forth, beating the stuffing out of a tapir, tipping dozens of mounted heads cockeyed, and using a decorative arrowhead to slash a bison hide to ribbons.

The storm was me, and I was lost within it. After a half hour of ransacking, I spotted Oksana the Brittany Spaniel snoozing unconcerned amid the slaughter. I sank my claws into her neck flab so that I might rip her skin clean off as a magician whips a tablecloth from beneath full place settings.

A gunshot blasted and the leather chair beside me skidded back ten feet. I looked up and there was Chernoff, his smoking elephant gun quite the accoutrement against his crisp tuxedo. He aimed the gun at me before his face showed recognition. Even then, his rage went unabated.

"What have you done here? Unhand Oksana or I shoot!"

582

I kicked the dog; she glided across the floor like a puck. Chernoff juked it and advanced. I rose to full height and displayed the beslimed cavity of the Hand.

"What *I've* done? What have *you* have done, sir?"

From behind the sight of his gun, Chernoff squinted and frowned.

"Is only decay. For this you break window? Defile dignity of our friends?"

"*Only* decay? *Only?* I am no dead animal you found in the woods!"

"But Mr. Finch. You *are* dead animal. You *are* in woods."

"Take this warning, sir. In seconds I shall ford the distance betwixt us, welcoming any gunshot you wish to contribute, and then, you Soviet scum, I shall play African lion with you. I shall shove my fist, decay and all, down your lying throat."

"Is always Tchaikovsky with you, is always *boom-boom-boom.* Chernoffs are men of honor. Here there is no lie, only simple fact. Your hand, it spoils. The rest of our work, soon it spoils too. Where is the surprise in this? Treated hide cannot live beside untreated. Is obvious to the brain."

"Then you must fix it! This is your fault!"

"*Nyet!* This failure belongs to you, Mr. Finch. A great many hours we waste on foolishness. Little bit here, Mr. Chernoff, little bit there. This is not what taxidermist does. You wish full preservation? Is fine, is good, is no big deal. But there cannot be more of this pussyfoot!"

"Then what do we need to do?"

"Your skin must come off. All of it."

My fury, wilded as it was, went cold.

Chernoff tipped his shotgun at a gorilla that had survived my rampage.

"Gorilla is lovely, *da?* You are same as gorilla. One cut and skin comes off in single piece, like pajama. I scoop out abdomen, remove soft matter, replace with stronger material. Is best treatment. You leave here brand-new. You last for centuries. We do this now or we are through. Is your choice."

He slanted his body so that chest, shoulders, and gun each pointed the path to the workshop. There awaited the alkali stench that to me smelled of ambrosial dew; there awaited the stanchions from which had dried flaps of my skin, or, as I saw them, clothier racks from which I might be dressed for success.

While Chernoff cleared his throat and tapped his tuxedo shoe, I imagined the feeling of liberty that would come with being fully peeled. I expect the sentence sends shivers, Reader, but consider it from my perspective. My body was a filthy haversack I was damned to schlepp through always muddier fields, and when Chernoff shucked a piece of it, the fresh air upon me felt *new* again, how it used to feel when I woke with windows wide and Wilma Sue snoring beside me.

Chernoff clapped his hands.

"Forty-eight hours this will take. Many meetings will need rescheduling. Come, we begin."

His eyes glinted behind Roosevelt spectacles.

I shuffled in his direction.

My path took me past Oksana. Her muzzle was planted into the crotch of a mountain goat. It was indecent, not what the bitch deserved. I lifted my eyes to find a moose, tipped so that its broad antlers were jammed into the mouth of a hyena. Neither would have so bungled combat in life. Behind them stood the hummingbird cabinet, glassless from impact with a thrown anteater. Yet no bird darted for freedom. Such lovely, virtuous animals—Chernoff had been right about that. But also so weak; I'd taken them down without a fight.

You could reap the skin, the meat, the bones.

But what of the fear in the heart?

Is that not what keeps an animal alive?

I stopped walking; I swayed in place. Chernoff's brow tightened.

"We go now. You trust in me, *da?*"

Chernoff's barrages had subdued Hollywood's most outspoken personalities. But they'd been actors, and what, I ask you, were actors of that era? They were trophies for studios to hoist in the same way the actors hoisted their silly statuettes. Fleeing the Ambassador, I'd dodged a dozen Oscars, and in each caramel gleam I'd recognized my contorted reflection. I, too, had become a trophy for Bridey's shelf, placed there to indicate the breadth of her conquests. I was likewise to Chernoff, a handsome dead thing for exhibit.

'Twas better, concluded I, to rot on one's own terms.

True to his stoic character, Chernoff said nothing as I retreated from the Hall of Animals, climbed back through the busted window, and took to the car. I drove and drove, each of my taxidermied parts worming back toward aberrance, until I hit the outskirts of Los Angeles. There I jackknifed the vehicle to a curb, rear-ending a parked Studebaker and dinging a new gadget called a parking meter.

I deserted the sweltry leather chamber and stalked the lonesome streets until high-wattage street signs became tamed by the brighter hues of the rising day. The more dilapidated a cross-street looked, the quicker I took it, until I trod among my own people: not the beautiful and celebrated, but the leprous and depraved.

I pointed at the glimmer of sun and accused it.

"*Won't you remove me from this Sodom?!*"

My plea smacked about the concrete. When it relented, it did so to a jaunty tune crooned by a pitchless singer nevertheless pleased by his rendition. The song I recognized at once as "Who's Afraid of the Big Bad Wolf?"; I recognized the singer, too. It did not much surprise me that it was the same bum I'd stumbled upon enjoying an alley crap just after my arrival in L.A.

He, at least, had gone unchanged by time's passage. He was still larded in squalid rags and quaggy with sores, and I took solace in his dogged durability. He held to life like a parasite, repellent in a town built on the backs of beauties, and unapologetic about sucking from it what blood he needed.

My smile perturbed him. His song went skeptical.

"Tra la la la . . . la?"

If only I'd owned a complete set of *Variety*, that most sumptuous of toilet papers, to gift him! For the scuffling wretch had done me a service, reminding me that I'd once known a man like him, whose mind and body had been so crippled that he'd been forced to begin anew. His name was Burt Churchwell, and I castigated myself for having forsaken him. He'd saved my soul before, so why not again? Yes, the soul—that jejune belief. I hoped it might yet be tucked away inside me, that evasive thing Dr. Leather had tried to unearth and Chernoff had wanted to toss into the trash with the rest of the rubbish.

XIII.

WRITING HAD FRIED ME INSIDE many a pot of boiling oil o'er the decades. Is it any wonder I quailed upon penning this most delicate of summonses? After finding Church's old phone number was disconnected, I lived out a scene from Bridey's script, shredding draft after draft of a letter, each page symbolic of calendars' worths of wasted time. At the end of the day, not to mention wit, I mailed Church not an apologia but a transferrable plane ticket: first-class, one-way, New York to Los Angeles.

All that was left to do was tread water in hopes of staying afloat with Bridey long enough for Church to find me. During those ten months of lies, Bridey added to the household such gadgetry as a "television" and a bug repellant in the form of an "aerosol spray," but these were flaccid distractions. Bridey had disparaged my decision to suspend taxidermic therapy, and after learning from Mercy St. Johns how I'd sacked Chernoff's "stuffed animals," she accused me of undermining the future of *In Our Image*. I believed only two things prevented her from kicking me out: one, her schedule—she'd reach film number twenty-five before year's end—and two, the thought of me, the world's strangest thing, being in another collector's museum.

I feared the worst for Church. What if he'd been arrested as part of the Bonus Army and never released from jail, and every cent I'd mailed had been pocketed by the Chinatown landlord? Low were my spirits that day in December when the butler found me in the library and announced that I had a visitor. I sprinted across miles of mansion to arrive at the eastern drawing room, where a man stood examining a pleasant series of framed medical sketches detailing the Mesolithic skull-drilling process of trepanation.

This was no champion of the gridiron and battlefield. Neither was it the scrapper with whom I'd ridden out the boom and bust of the Twenties. This fellow here was *old*, with thin, graying hair and a back so bent it took him five seconds to turn around with the help of a cane. He wore a beard to effect a comb-over of sorts across the crater in his cheek. It was Church, all right, but a variant I'd never imagined: bone-thin here, lard-soft there, and routed with wrinkles, particularly when he grinned.

"Dang," said he. "You don't ever change, do you?"

A chirping laugh fluted up from lungs that had never satisfactorily healed. The greeting was, in fact, rather funny. Me, not change? What had I done in this ersatz Shangri-La but change? I extended my hand, which had reassumed its pre-taxidermic smutch. Church's hand, meanwhile, was draped in loose skin and freckled with age. But he was Midwestern, not Californian; he would not have blanched had I resembled a pile of hamburger.

We shook, and Reader, it felt fine.

"Gød, Private, I'm sorry, I'm so danged sorry. I got the operation, just like you said, and it helped some, it did—and my rent, it went up and up, and the money helped with that, too—but I couldn't—I just wasn't sure you wanted me to—"

I sealed our continued clutch with my opposite hand so that he did not feel it necessary to complete his statement. It was difficult to believe that I was the son of the unfeeling Bartholomew Finch, so badly did I wish to embrace this long-lost comrade.

"I saw the magazine pictures," said he, "but couldn't ever believe it. How in heck did you end up here?"

I dared grip his shoulder. Far beneath the atrophy lurked a quarterback's girth.

"There is much to say." I indicated two chairs. "Let us say it all."

Hollywood was a fever and Church was the tub of ice that lifted me from it. For hours we exchanged not gossip and aspersions but rather stories of simple struggles: the darn good buck-twenty-five an hour he'd made as a welder before the smoke had aggravated his bad lung; the highway robbery of dental fees that obliged him to home-yank three teeth via pliers; the work he'd recently found helping move an entire graveyard across town—lots of smelly coffins, but golly, he sure enjoyed being in the outdoors.

Church had found peace in hardship, and in his itemized banalities I found something as well: the pain and striving that *was* life, that *was* meaning, as opposed to the mesmeric embalmment of Hollywood. Of course I was lost out here in this fancy crypt—I was Death walking among the dead! Where I belonged was back in the trenches with my dearest friend.

So captivated was I by our future together that Bridey's nighttime return home caught me unawares. She clacked into the drawing room on impossible heels, legs glossy beneath a country-club daysuit, her gloved arms arranged fetchingly as she worked to unpin a hat from her waves of black hair. Even then, hours before the real disaster, I detected my blunder.

We should have already left.

"If you must use this dreadful room," said she, "then I insist that you get off your ass and—"

The heels quit their clack. Bridey flapped surprised lashes at the giant man taking up her satinwood settee. Church, a gent through and through, pushed upon his cane and rocketed upward. Beholden by social convention, I did the same, but found it difficult to meet Bridey's eyes. Never before had I entertained a personal guest; it did not take a person of her intuition to sense that a plot was afoot.

"I don't believe I've had the pleasure," said she.

Church stumbled forward, his leg fighting his cane, burying an inopportune cough in his shoulder while reaching out a quaking hand.

"Miss—I am—it's my—I am very, very pleased—"

I spoke through teeth.

"Allow me to introduce Burt Churchwell. He is a friend from the war. He is from *Iowa*."

The last bit I added for sympathy's sake. Bridey peaked her eyebrows at the exoticism and extended a hand to see what the backcountry brute might do with it. Church stalked it as one would a greased pig, coming at it with two hands in case it darted. Once he'd captured it, he cradled it in disbelief, sliding his thumbs across the pearly silk.

"Are all Iowans aficionados of gloves?" asked Bridey.

Church dropped the hand as if caught licking it.

"Oh, no, ma'am. Not that yours aren't—I just haven't ever met— I've seen so—well, I can't even count—so *many* of your pictures and—"

"Then it is I who must thank you," said Bridey. "Tickets are no longer cheap, are they? I fear one day they'll cost a whole dollar."

Church's flabbergast blinded him to Bridey's unsparing enumerating of his threadbare blazer, unscrubbable shirt stains, and under-nail grease. The plunging basin of his right cheek interested her the most.

"Of course you will dine with us," said she.

"No, ma'am," sputtered Church. "I couldn't!"

"That's right," interjected I. "He is on a New York clock and weary from travel."

"Good, I prefer my men weary, they are so much easier to influence. Wouldn't you agree, Mr. Churchwell?"

"Church. Everyone calls me Church."

"Then I shall call you 'C.' Now, let me rouse the chef. Odds are she's tipsy on cooking sherry at this hour, though inebriation does tend to bring out her genius. Shall we say ninety minutes? I would like to freshen up. Perhaps I'll don a new pair of gloves to feed your fetish."

Quite assuredly the vixen was up to something.

A last supper, I told myself, *and then I am gone.*

Bridey came to dinner late enough to make an entrance. Though how else does one enter when squeezed inside of a blood-red Vera West cut so low that one's breasts receive only the tiniest handholds of crepe? This imposing chest was boosted by an engraved silver girdle, which matched both her sleek turban and the pearled band around her throat. From the staircase she descended like Poe's Red Death into the masque.

Church's thighs thwacked the table when he stood, the first of countless faux pas committed at regular intervals throughout the meal. Bridey, at her most devious, had arranged a menu fit to flummox: peppercorn ox tongue, braised cock's combs, and lemon-and-parsley offal with a side of creamed durian fruit. Church gaped at the spread as would any Heartlander, and with every improper approach, Bridey was there to tut-tut and refill his glass with wine.

Does that sit queasily, Reader? It should. Church, the kid who'd survived a war without the abetment of a flask, the man who'd lived through Prohibition without so much as a curious sip, was so out of his depth that partaking in alcohol for the first time seemed like the simpler road, especially when being offered up by the star of his most outrageous fantasies.

In a click, he was drunk. He sniggered when a sliver of tripe skittered from under his knife and Bridey giggled right along. He went mush-mouthed when saying "I don't got a girl," and the two hammed it up with "I gone dotted a knurl" and "I won't gut an earl" before descending into besotted hilarity. A lesser expert on the Valentine oeuvre might have believed the performance, but not I. Pause the projector. See there, hidden amid the grain? She pretends to drink her wine, only pretends.

Our tiffs had escalated to all-out warfare and the sea of battle was Church.

Then bring the carronades broadside, thought I. *She shall strike her colors before dawn.*

"Say, dear-heart," posed I with acerbity, "why don't I avail you with tales of Church's wartime élan? He is a man twice decorated." Pointedly I added, "The sort of man with whom one *should not trifle.*"

"To the contrary, lover-boy." Bridey matched acid with acid. "I've found that the strongest men are the ones most in need of trifling."

"Eating tongue is hard," slurred Church. "So chewy."

"But *lambkin,*" seethed I, "surely a gentleman who has maintained his innocence despite such odds should be permitted to *go about his way* free of indoctrination into waywardism." I brought out the Excelsior. "My, look at the time. Church, old friend, we ought to be tucking you into bed."

"I pee the bed." Church coughed, shook his head. "No, no, I didn't say that."

"Bed does sound like fun," snapped Bridey. "But before dancing? Unheard of!"

"Dancing?" I gnashed my jaws. "You cannot be serious, *sugar-bun*."

But serious my sugar-bun was. She lifted my punchy partner onto unsteady feet and led him from the room. I lingered to stew until I heard from the phonograph player the sliding trombone of Glenn Miller. I threw down my napkin, charged through the hallway of grandfather clocks, and entered the library, where Bridey's seldom-used Philco unit was refulgent with electrical power. From the cabinet speakers resounded a juvenile ditty called "Chattanooga Choo Choo."

The music had a woozy swing, a perfect match for the loopy ellipses sketched across the carpet by Bridey as she, veteran of untold dance scenes, steered Church away from such tricky obstacles as the walls and floor. It brought to mind, and painfully, the time Church had taught me the Charleston in his kitchen. He'd been clumsy then; now he careened about like a dog on hind legs.

Church had once mastered what he'd dubbed "the Game," but Bridey's game was scored by goals more far obscure. After abandoning fancy footwork in favor of check-to-cheek oscillations, she tickled her fingers along Church's spine. His fists floated, afraid to touch her bare-skinned back. She pressed closer, crawling a hand up his arm, neck, and face, until her red nails tickled that most sacrosanct of private parts, the hole in his cheek.

He gasped, frightened by the intimacy, and gripped Bridey's body with childish desperation. His boozy, disoriented eyes sought mine and he mumbled for help.

"Private . . . ? Is this . . . is it okay . . . ?"

"Private Finch," shushed Bridey, "can't help you now."

"Private Prefer-Not-To," blubbered Church. "That's what we use to call him."

Their slow waltz circled round and Bridey's carnivore eyes caught mine.

"Why, that's a *very* apt name. There are, in fact, a few things he prefers not to do."

She slid her hands down Church's sides and onto his thighs.

Even invertebrate cuckolds had their limits! I sprang forth, snared Bridey's wrist in one hand and Church's in the other, and disentangled them as would a boxing ref. Bridey was hurled into a bookcase; she cried out. Church capsized over the arm of a sofa. She I left to her smarting but he I hauled to his feet. His skin was teal and his cheeks swollen as if with vomit. I tugged him from the library and hollered to the rafters for help.

The butler met us in the hall. While the grandfather clocks tsked our boorish behavior, I enjoined the servant to call a cab, insert Mr. Churchwell inside of it, and supply the driver money enough for a hotel room in which my friend could repair. The butler was guiding Church's arms through his coat sleeves when Church began to register the new drama in which he'd been cast.

"Hang on. Wait. Private, I wanna stay."

"Listen to me as well as you are able. You are being taken to a hotel. Sleep off the drink. Tomorrow I will gather you, I promise. But tonight there is business I must conclude."

"Well, that's some way to treat an old friend. Merry Christmas!"

What I most wished to do was punch his lights out, stuff him into a trunk, and mail him parcel post back to Iowa where he belonged. A hotel was at least a quarantine; every second he spent in Hollywood, I now realized, came at the risk of contaminating the open wounds of his lungs or, more to the point, his heart. This town excelled at finding those whose damaged parts would make the tastiest sausage, provided an unsatisfied customer like myself did not move quick and steal them from the butcher block.

XIV.

BRIDEY WAS FACING THE PHONOGRAPH player when I returned. Her biceps glowed bluish where it had struck the shelf. I heard the moist *whump* of a needle drop, followed by the opening drawl of Artie Shaw's "Stardust." Her naked back rolled with the wistful strain, spine and scapula pressing against her skin like dragon wings wanting to be freed. Her hips swung this way, slow, and that way, slower, so that her blood-colored gown was a dripping wound cut through the air.

Her languid turnabout was protracted agony. Throbbing pale neck, smothered cinder eyes, slippery crimson lips. She sucked on a long cigarette.

"My dance partner. He's run off. I need another."

I became a bull. Lower the head, square the shoulders, and snort. Bridey Valentine always got what she wanted, is that right?

Fine, then, fine. After all, she'd earned it.

Our love story, if that's what you'd like to call it, was never going to end any direction other than horizontal. I took her by the waist and lugged her toward the hearth. A Persian rug fattened before her dragged feet and her hip collided with the end of the loveseat; it splintered and she grunted in pain. But it was she who pushed me over the back so that I landed upon the cushion. Around it she paced a coyote circle, gauging which part of me to eat first.

She ankled off her shoes, worked her hands under the hem of her dress, removed her knickers, and threw them into the fire. She was then upon me with claws and teeth, ripping at jacket and shirt, unmindful of the signatures her nails might forever write across my flesh. She was sloppy and impatient; she left my upper body half-dressed and went for the trousers, beneath which she felt the hardness she'd so long hunted.

Just as rigor mortis had stiffened individual muscles of my body, so had it stiffened the softer tissue of my genitals. I had over the past year grown rigid enough to do a man's work, even though I was not a man, not even a boy, just a corpse who turned this consensual fornication—"carnal knowledge" as Bridey would say—into a rape of all things natural. She snarled and grabbed it, her selfish motivation, after all this time, still intact: to screw the Wilma Sue, and everything else left of my old life, right out of me. She positioned my pecker at the bow of her sex.

I was colder than cold. She was hotter than hot.

White steam crept from under the red skirt.

Bridey bucked her hips and we were locked. She pointed her face at the coffered ceiling and shivered at the deep chill. Then she swore gruffly, directly cursing her icicle invader, and began to jolt back and forth. Faintly I felt a single bead of mercury heat. I dug my fingers through the dress and into her thighs so as to hang on for dear death.

We were foes caught in a playground fight of slapping limbs when things inverted. We fell from the loveseat, rolled, and sprang back in the same position, she on top and crashing her hard pelvis into my fragile own. A general softness cushioned the assault and I turned my head to find beneath me a bedding of black fur. The bear rug, that mocking bane, had me in its clawed clutches! *See?*

laughed the bear. *Even dead things have their uses.*

Bridey dragged her bosom along my chest so that the friction peeled away the bodice. She pushed the dress down to her waist and slid her hands up her naked torso. What looked like sensual self-fondling was anything but; it was a mirror of the tour of my wounds I'd given her our first night together, her own Revelation Almanac—a meticulous account of the damages accrued when playing tug-of-war with Death.

The scars glowed in the orange light. Here, a breast-lift. There, a tummy-tuck. Evidence of Dr. Biff's meddling was curlicued into her navel and tucked into the crevices of her armpits. Bridey lifted her hair from her shoulders and angled her body so that I might appreciate the disfigurements for the war injuries that they were. Church had removed his facial prosthesis to disclose his damage; Bridey removed her gown to reveal hers.

"Stardust" finished. Needle nudged label and made a cyclical thump. Bridey adopted the rhythm, squeezing her lathered legs around my white slabs of cold thigh. Forget the Greek death mask, the Egyptian mummification kit; forget every spookish icon with which she'd styled herself a patroness of the dark. Copulating with the Devil himself, now that was the outermost thrill.

Within this meat-etiquette melding I began to experience uncoiling spires of pleasure. These went far beyond the cheap pumps of blood I'd felt as a youth; this was a lessening of deadness for having been plugged into a furnace of life. I, the gigolo Zebulon Finch, was once again a fumbling virgin. Bridey, voracious vamp, was restored her maidenhood.

It was our first time. It was our last time.

Shakespeare had it right about a post-poisoned Juliet:

She was a flower, but death deflowered her.

"Yes," cried she.

Yes—devastation.

"Yes!" cried she.

Yes—immolation!

"*Yes!*" cried she.

Yes—*erasure, destruction, oblivion, take me!*

Her starved muscles, biting; our quick cadence, disrupted; her flammable sweat upon both of us, sparked and rushing in blue flame. With one brute thrust of her hips, she harvested my root. There was a dull snap. No orgasm on Earth could lighten so heavy a weight, no ejaculation could offer such overdue release. Bridey slid away with my pecker still inside of her and I was glad. She could not keep the whole of me forever, but this single piece, for which I had no further use, belonged to her—it had for a while—and would make, thought I, a nice addition to her museum, a final endowment from me to my cut-up and sewed-back-together patchwork queen.

XV.

RUMORS IN THE DROWSY DARK:

Z will take you.

Not since my death had I been this close to actual sleep, and yet I could not help but rouse myself with speculation. "Take": was the word used in the mortal sense? For though I could not sleep, breathe, or eat, I had proven myself adept at taking. Look to my hands for proof. Sixty-two years since a cursed birth and those merlot spots came not from age but from spilled blood.

He'll go with you, I promise.

Surely the destination of debate was Hades? Though I knew not the exact route, I'd seen multitudes of signposts and might yet be convinced to pathfind.

I'll ask him when he's up.

Up? I'd never be up again! I chuckled the vulgar joke into the bear rug.

He'll meet you at your place at seven. Baby, I have to run, I'll ring you later.

Good! Begone with you! Your nattering distracts from my misery.

Ta-ta, little Gopher.

Gopher?

The voice, then, was not that of a Delphic deity tossing lightning-bolt riddles at my skull. It was Bridey, the human female with whom I'd lain to crippling effect. Bridey's tone that morn ought to have been one of howling horror. She ought to have lurched into the room, pouring blood from her groin, still clenching the knives with which she'd cut out the parts I'd diseased.

Instead, she'd telephoned her daughter. Such calls were usually held out of earshot, so certain were they to degenerate into bickering and wheedling. Today, though, Bridey had exuded maternal control, given sound advice, and, as a bonus, lent her daughter the services of her live-in eunuch as blithely as she might loan out a pair of heels. I glimpsed her for one second, ravishing in a pearl-white negligee, the chiffon frolicking along the versicolored Turkish runner.

Then she was upstairs, ringing the bell for her hairdresser. I drew myself to a seated position upon the bear rug, nauseated by the lack of—well, how else to say it?—*flopping* from my nether regions. From what grade of steel was this Valentine woman forged? Off to the studio she was gallivanting, whistling birdsong, as if it were every day she extracted from her cervix a hunk of hardened corpse.

The telephone began to ring.

How could I mourn my mangling if Margeaux kept bringing her mother back to the phone? To hell with it, I'd set the girl straight myself. The idea of me making a social call was laughable. Truly, I might never leave the house again! I began to stand but hesitated upon hearing an object hit the floor. There, tented upon the bear's head, was a stack of paper bound by three brass fasteners, having been left upon my lap as if in amends for my literal emasculation. I picked up the two hundred pages and flipped them over.

For as long as I might decay, I shan't forget that cover page, not the pyramid of text, not the Underwood font, not the capitalized paranoia of the concluding threat. The date printed on it belonged to that very morning, which meant Bridey had woken early to run a copy—over a decade's worth of work, given to me to read at last.

The foregone farce of the story was beside the point. Instead of a morning-after ejection from the palace, I was being offered a permanent place, a producer's role in the next stage of Bridey's career as she freed herself from studio strangulation, rejected the Hays Code, and roadshowed her opus across the globe. After last night, the two of us shared an unspeakable secret, and was that not indistinguishable from absolute trust?

The telephone was still ringing.

I rolled the script into nightstick shape, wrapped the bear rug around my body to cover my shame, and hobbled into the hall where resided the telephone chair. The phone was baby blue and of hourglass contour, and it convulsed with every cry. I snatched it up and spoke so as to have both first and last words.

"Zebulon speaking. I'm afraid your mother spoke out of turn. I am engaged tonight and every night henceforth. I wish you moderately well. Good day."

Alas, had only I hung up as swiftly as I'd answered.

"Papa?"

The voice was broken glass shaved across concrete.

But I knew that glass; I knew that concrete.

"Merle?" whispered I. "Merle, is that you?"

"Oh, Papa. Papa, help. They say they're going to kill me."

Some shocks the old knees could not take. I collapsed into the telephone chair. Last I'd seen Merle Ruby Watson was a quarter century ago as she'd backpedaled from a crummy Massachusetts hovel with her mother's Colt Lightning revolver pointed, my booby prize for having used *la silenziosità* to give her a glimpse of her fate. Her final shout had been an oath to conquer the world, though it sounded as if she'd gotten it backward.

Her ability to track me down, at least, had not waned.

"Merle. Where . . . ?"

"I'm here, Los Angeles. I'm with—they don't want me to say."

"These people are with you now?"

"They're right here. Please don't be cross with me. I didn't want to bother you but they made me! They made me tell them who you are because they say I owe them money, and I don't have even close to what they're—"

"Do you? Owe these people money?"

"Well, yes, I suppose I do, but—"

"How much?"

"Oh, Papa, I didn't want it to be this way!"

"Merle. How much?"

"They say two thousand, though I don't see how that's—"

"Two? *Thousand?* In what bramble have you become ensnarled?"

"What matters is I don't have it. These people are serious, Papa. They know you have the money and they want it."

"What makes you believe I have two thousand dollars?"

"Papa! Everyone knows who you live with."

"Miss Valentine's money is entirely inaccessible to me."

"Please!" Her rawness thickened with sobs. "*They are going to kill me.*"

Had she called twelve hours earlier, I would have yanked the phone cable from the wall. But the situation, to say the least, had changed. Beneath the bear rug I was neutered, a tangible reminder that I would never again sire a child. Bartholomew Finch was likely dead; my foster-father, Dr. Leather, was the same; Church, my sole brother, was at best sleeping off a hangover at a hotel, at worst prone in a ditch, the hayseed victim of a scheming city.

That left Merle. Bloodsucker yes, banshee for sure, but she was nevertheless the last link I had with life and I could not abandon her as I'd abandoned all others.

"The address," said I. "Give it."

There was a lengthy interim during which I gathered my clothes from the library floor, dressed myself, rolled the screenplay and placed it into my inside jacket pocket, and crouched in the cellar while Bridey called for me, searched about, and finally departed. Afterward I scaled the stairs, entered her dressing room, breached the shoe closet, and found, right where snooping young Margeaux had years ago said they would be, rolls of cash, quite a few of them, waiting inside the second-to-the-last hatbox on the left.

XVI.

THE NEIGHBORHOOD TO WHICH I'D been bidden was a
snarl of railroad tracks called Watts. I had taken the first car in
the garage, Bridey's brand-new Coachcraft Roadster (known as
the "Yankee Doodle"), a snug, roofless two-seater as bright red as her
beloved Lincoln LeBaron. It proved to be a remarkably poor choice;
its futuristic design caught the attention of dozens of directionless
jaywalkers as well as one street preacher clutching a shepherd's staff,
who chased me down the block as if warning me to turn away.

It was an overcast fifty degrees, polar by L.A. standards, when
I parked the Yankee Doodle outside a line of darkened doorways,
the saddest of which was not the smoke-scarred typewriter repair
shop or the glass-shattered liquor store but rather a bombed-out
hollow identified as "Dog & Cat Hospital." This was the landmark
Merle had referenced. Around the corner, clinging by rust to the
brickwork, was a metal stairway leading to the second-story flat.
I patted the two thousand dollars in my breast pocket and made
the climb.

Luca Testa would have had a good chuckle at this sorry stopgap
of a syndicate. For starters, the door was unlocked—I walked right
in. The blue smoke that swallowed me was thick, but still I could
see that no sentinel guarded the door. Instead there were ratty sofas
upon which slumped six or seven listless and underfed deadbeats,

605

some dozing in puddles of their own drool while others scratched at irritated skin. The place stank of tar and sugar. Somewhere, a radio droned on about Joe DiMaggio.

I crept through the living room, across the kitchen, and past three bedrooms, each of which had its windows draped in the faded Chinese textiles of a decrepit opium den. Women clad only in brassieres smoked wrinkled cigarettes that ashed upon their emaciated stomachs. Men with trembling fingers counted out lopsided pills. A boy my age sat in a corner, a soaked handkerchief pressed over his face, inhaling hallucinogenic fumes with religious fervor.

The air crackled with dissatisfied mutters.

At length I arrived at a narrow mud room pillared by ten fidgety men, each in the process of moving toward, or from, the amnesic states of the aforesaid sprawlers. It was not until I shouldered past a man with a black eye and a runny nose did I notice the female in their midst. She languished upon a metal folding chair, stringy brown hair dangling across two arms perforated with bruised needle holes.

I cleared my throat.

"Gentlemen. I am Zebulon Finch."

The men chuckled at my diction and ignored me. The woman, though, raised her head.

Merle had come to me in Boston in a low state, rain-soaked and livid, qualities that had but sharpened the blades of her fifteen-year-old beauty. Even scrawny and sloshed in Salem, she'd smoldered with inextinguishable spirit. This woman, though, was older than Bridey and looked twice that. She'd become as skeletal as a dead tree, shedding desiccated bark and popping apart at the joints. Her hair was sparse; her skin was whey and splotched; furrows cut through her flesh as if tunneled by termites.

The Colt Lightning had long since been pawned away.

"It's Papa." She grinned with yellow teeth. "Look, Sandy. Papa came."

A freckled pig to her left broke off a dispute and turned to me with interest. His silver tie and fat lapels exhibited the catchpenny dazzle that years ago I would have sported myself, but looked passé next to my top-of-the-line tweed jacket, wool sweater, and patterned silk scarf. Sandy appreciated the ensemble before putting his hands to his hips.

"I'll be dipped in shit. It *is* you. I seen your mug in the papers. And here I thunk the skinny little bitch was having me on."

My hands curled into hammers.

"The skinny little bitch happens to be my daughter."

He slapped his thigh.

"That's what she said! You two are nuttier than junebugs in May. Guess you gotta be nutty when you're in pictures, eh? Say, lemme ask you, friend, cuz it's been occupying my mind. What size a' jugs do Bridey Valentine got? I figure they, you know, pad them up big for film, but I still stay she got real big ones. I'm a pretty good judge a' jugs."

The lackeys laughed and smacked their hilarious hero on the back. Merle licked her scabbed lips, looking frail enough that a loud cough might seize her heart for good. What would Major Horstmeier have said? I ordered my fists to hold their fire.

"Her jugs, as you say, are of goodly proportion. Now that this knowledge has been shared, might we get down to it? I understand there is a ransom to be paid to remove Merle from this place."

"Whoa, whoa, I ain't ever said *ransom*. Look, mister, I'm making jack shit off this deal. Two grand, that's just what the skinny little bitch owes me, I swear. The last thing I want is trouble, understand?"

Sandy parted his jacket to show the pistol tucked against his porkbelly. I recognized the checkered grip of a .357 Magnum, too brilliant a revolver for such loathsome slime. The rabble showed no interest in the weapon, as they probably packed their own, but the bulging envelope I produced might as well have been the Hope Diamond. Some went revenant, others jabbered expletives, still another danced a jig. Sandy leered and extended a hoof.

I handed it over. Sandy ripped it open, peeked inside, and whooped. I turned away, gnashing air but wishing it was the man's flabby neck. Extortion was a favorite Black Hand tactic of mine and yet now I found myself appalled at the very notion of trading life, that most ephemeral of commodities, for a pile of paper printed with dollar signs.

"Real nice doing business with you, Mr. Finch," said Sandy. "So I'm gonna give you some friendly advice. Old Merle here is what we call a 'procurable woman.' She's probably got the clap, the syphilis, every VD there is. So you'll want to get yourself one of them prophylactics so you don't bring that junk home to Miss Valentine."

Recall how I'd pounded Mr. Patterson, Wilma Sue's inkeep, into tenderized steak?

All fork-tongued slanderers of Watson girls beware:

There is a Finch bred for the sole purpose of pecking your eyes out.

Sandy's mouth detonated into blood and teeth. My fist ricocheted back, bones ringing, and I paused at the curious sight of one of his canines embedded between my knuckles. That woke up the narcotized ninnies. Hands ripped me away from Sandy, pinned back my arms, and socked me in the stomach. But these rhinos were juiced senseless, and with a few astute kicks I had pulled away and was lifting Merle by her twig shoulders.

"The money, Papa," slurred she. "Get the money."

Darling Merle! Her priorities were nothing if not reliable.

My left shoulder was wedged apart. It was Sandy, back on his feet, choking on pink froth, both fists clamped upon the hilt of his buried switchblade. His gurgle of rage turned quizzical when I evidenced no pain; instead, I twisted his arm round his back, the switchblade clacking against my clavicle. Sandy sobbed and kneeled. Both the envelope of cash and the .357 Magnum hit the floor.

Well, why not make my daughter happy?

The money I put in my pocket, the revolver I displayed to my audience.

"Shoot 'em, Papa," croaked Merle. "Shoot 'em dead."

Supporting my flyweight berserker by the shuddering shoulders, I pushed through the mud room and into the hallway, swinging the gun. Sandy's sycophantic sheep bleated and dove into darkened bedrooms. The only chatter was the radio, finished now with DiMaggio and babbling about the North African battlefront. The moment had the feel of victory until I caught the flashes of gun-metal, ten or twenty times over, drawn on either side of me.

One loathes to pocket a Magnum at such a moment, but I adjudged it prudent. I swept Merle into my arms, the same as I'd done a dozen injured soldiers on June 10, 1918, and sprinted, shouting for the bewildered junkies of the living room to make way. I shouldered body after body and the air became sleeted with pills, beclouded with cocaine, twinkled with pinwheeling hypodermics. I crashed through the storm door, hitting the rusted staircase with almost enough force to bring it down, and then hurtled down the steps, pitching with the topweight of my daughter.

That the Yankee Doodle was roofless saved precious seconds. I dropped Merle into the passenger seat and leapt behind the wheel.

The ignition was cranked and the engine was growling before I diagnosed something awry. How my jacket lay upon my chest was different than during the drive over. The object that I'd tucked into the inside pocket was gone.

Bridey's script had fallen out during the struggle.

That private work of twelve years, deserted among careless thieves.

I looked at Merle. Her sunken eyes were shut so hard her eyelids made butterfly quivers. The glove compartment buckle had scraped her wan cheek, but the wound was dry, as if she had no blood left to bleed. A feeble pair we would have made if not for the words whispering between her chalked lips:

"I love you, Daddy. I love you, Daddy."

Everything else became trivial. It mattered not that I had no friends and no future, for in this woman's throat beat the pulse of Finch blood and that meant that I was not alone.

I placed a cold kiss upon her swampy temple.

She tightened into a ball like a poked caterpillar.

There was no fear, only gallantry. I uncorked the switchblade from my shoulder and pressed it into her fist. She snuffled like the child she'd never been, slight and vulnerable, fully dependent upon her father. I strode past the Dog & Cat Hospital, feeling rather canine myself, though, unlike Chernoff's Oksana, I'd risen from my long-held slumber. For the sake of Sandy and his abettors, I hoped the pet clinic still shelved tourniquets, styptic, other tools to staunch the blood of dumb animals. I also hoped that the Watts street preacher might roam our way, prepared to minister last rites to the immoral, desperate, and dead, or even to myself—all three in one neat package.

XVII.

OW FATIGUED I BECOME WITH transcribing brutalities. Let us just say that I dealt out suffering, a lot of it, and death, some of it, as I, with my discharging sidearm, slouched ever further from the promised land of Church's Theory of 17. But retrieve *In Our Image* I did, and the liberated screenplay recuperated upon the dashboard, orange and snarled with drying blood.

For hours I drove about without destination for no better reason than to let Merle sleep. Even through the discord of a full-service gas station stop, she failed to rise from her twitching coma. I smiled with warm affection and blotted her damp hair with a handkerchief. With but an hour of sun left in the sky, she came to, smacking dry lips and thumbing the leather interior as if it were an elegant ballgown she'd wakened to find herself wearing. We were in a neighborhood even worse than Watts. Nevertheless I parked, filled my pockets with script and knife and gun, shooed aside the brats playing jacks, and assisted Merle from the car. A brisk walk, that's what she needed.

This was no Rodeo Drive. Establishments brawled for air: tobacconists, clothiers, soda fountains, and taverns, each papered with avowals that their wares were the zenith in quality and value. Most were spruced with yuletide trappings of some sort—berried wreathes, sprigs of mistletoe, tinsel—and Christmas shoppers made the best of it, lugging about bags and flipping pennies to the Salvation Army

Santas. Holiday songs feuded from competing doorways.

It felt rather grotesque given the drug addict clawing at my elbow. We walked as geriatrics, with Merle choosing each inch of sidewalk with suspicion. Still, the movement did her good. She lifted her face to the breeze and her brindled cheeks started to pinken. I, too, began to feel the happy rush of once more holding my blood relative in my arms. At length I decreed her well enough to dispense information.

"Merle, my sweet. Tell me why you came here."

"Why does anyone?" Her voice was hoarse. "To act."

It was not entirely implausible. Who could cycle through emotions with the zoetrope speed of my daughter? The hard fact, however, was that her beauty, once upon a time of silver-screen quality, had been scratched to the bone.

"Forgive me," said I, "but aren't you a touch old to make that your métier?"

"No. I've already filmed one picture."

"Give me the title. I am well-versed."

"*Peeping-Tom Picnic*. A fabulous lark."

"If you tell me that this was a stag film," said I, "my heart will fail."

"Yes, it was. And no, your heart won't do *anything*."

I tripped and stumbled while the succubus snorted.

"Merle! Why would you subject yourself to such degradation?"

"It's no different from what Bridey Valentine does. Show a little leg, a little tit, and like magic they give you money. I swear, Papa, you can be such a child."

A delicatessen, packed with upright folk who did not strip in front of cameras, presented itself. On impulse, I ducked inside and pulled Merle along. Here we could sit in a booth, father and daughter, ordinary as you please.

"Your obvious intent is to ruin me," muttered I. "But I won't let that happen. Waitress?"

"Me? Ruin you? Oh, that's right, I haven't told you about my lovely abortion."

A dozen people looked up from their soup and sandwiches. I wheeled about, steered Merle back outdoors, and quickened down a byway thick with men of nefarious leans. Evening had lowered; pink and yellow neon dissipated like dye into the sapphire sky. But darkness provided inadequate cover from Merle's unblushing account of the cold table upon which she'd endured surgery. The abortionist had botched the job and she'd bled for a week, and when she'd finally scraped together the cash to see a qualified physician, she'd learned of the internal scarring that now rendered her infertile.

"Naturally, that's when I started to actually want a baby. If only to stick you with a granddaughter. Seeing how much you enjoy taking care of me."

"These are false fronts," reasoned I. "You love me; I know you love me. You do not blame me for your barrenness."

"Oh, but I do, Papa! I do! Had I had one single pocketful of your money, everything would've been different. There would have been better clothes, and therefore a better job, and therefore a husband, and therefore a child, and therefore no abortion, and therefore no stag picture, and therefore and therefore and therefore and therefore!"

Her yelps bothered the passing unbotherables. I corralled her against the brick wall of a pawn shop. We had progressed into a red-light district of peep-show cinemas and penny arcades boasting lewd photo reels entitled *Hot-Cha!*, *Nude Kisses*, and *Girls of Spain*. Scragged pitchmen jabbered their wares at pedestrians while street-corner

613

twosomes swapped money for illegal goods. It was a Harlem drained of all joy, sapped of all class.

"Looks like my kind of place," said she. "So be a peach? Give me the two grand and we'll call it even."

Merle might as well have carved out my dead heart. Unkind to her though the unknowns of life had been, she still preferred that risk, along with the gift of a couple thousand dollars, over accepting me for who I was—or the prospect of owing me a single damn thing.

"But the money." I sounded feeble. "It was meant for your rescue."

"You really want to rescue me? Then hand it over."

"I don't believe that wise, given the state of your . . ."

"Poverty? My state of poverty? The same sort of poverty as my mother?"

"I try and try to atone for how I treated her, but you refuse to let me."

"*This* is how you atone. You give me the money."

"I might be the child you say I am. But a stooge I am not. In one week you would spend every cent on morphine. I am not blind to those bruises on your arms. I have seen a hundred men, former soldiers most of them, marked by the same addiction."

"I'm supposed to go cold turkey? Papa, that would kill me."

Merle switched on a grin and dug into her skirt pocket.

"I have one left," enthused she. "My last hit. I want you to have it. We don't even need a needle. You can just swallow it or crush it—"

"Put that away."

"Mother told me you drank, smoked, everything. Don't you miss it? Here. Five minutes and you'll feel it in your legs, the back of your neck, and then it's like you're in a secret, safe place where no one can hurt you. Morphine is for *pain*, Papa. Don't you have any pain?"

Reader, what a question.

I seized her arm and wrenched it. The beige tablet hit the sidewalk and bounced. Merle cried out and reached for it but I bounded in the direction of the Yankee Doodle, dragging my child behind. Did I know pain? Introducing Merle Watson to Bridey Valentine—now that would be painful! I could but pray that Bridey would, after stages of shock and disgust, sign a check that would pay for Merle's medical impoundment. And if Bridey refused? Well, those medieval chastity belts and aboriginal pendants could be stolen and sold. Nothing, swore I, would thwart me from righting my wrongs toward Wilma Sue and Merle Ruby Watson.

Nothing, perhaps, except the most unexpected voice in the whole world.

We tumbled past a colorless, paint-chipped establishment beneath the eaves of which crackled a grandiloquent but impish sales pitch; 'twas the sort of voice that could flatten the back row of a crowd to its pew even as it fondled the fragile fancy of a worshipful front-row face. In the forty years since I'd last heard it, it had lost not a blurt of bombast, an edge of erudition, a whip of wickedness.

I turned about. Merle crashed into me and held on, sobbing.

Ashes to apocryphal ashes, dust to doleful dust.

The Barker.

XVIII.

THE OPPRESSIVE URBAN STENCH OF petrol and urine was overrun by the rural odor of dusty straw that had exemplified my tenure as the Highly Intelligent Monkey of Dr. Whistler's Pageant of Health. My limbs went as lame as old Mr. Stick's; my tongue, too, went as dumb.

"Out of your cage at last?" asked the demon. "Or finding your way back in?"

Given enough time, Dearest Reader, all chickens—even headless, spurting ones—come home to roost. The Barker stood at a shabby pulpit beneath a sign promising "GIRLS! GIRLS! GIRLS!," eighty-five years old if a day, a wasted hobgoblin half as tall as the renegade knight who'd once commanded a whole battery of blackguards. His locks still reached his shoulders, though now they were white and the hairline began just north of his ears, leaving his scalp bare but for sunburn peels and purple lesions.

The cut of his jib, though, had suffered nothing. His shoulders, aslant now, were nonetheless thrust backward; his chest, concave now, continued to push forward; his mouth, toothless now, still lazed in grinning anticipation of his next whopper. This two-bit peep show upon this second-rate strand was but a different type of Gallery of Suffering erected upon a different Boardwalk of Chance. Despite having seen his own bleak end in *la silenziosità*, the Barker was still barking.

I could not speak, but given the politics of our relationship, that felt appropriate.

Merle whimpered. I was crushing her arm.

"Conversation was never Mr. Stick's specialty," mused the Barker. "Mayhap this will bring about a verbal reaction?"

He rolled up his right pant leg. The bottom half of the leg itself was missing. Strapped to the swollen knee by leather buckles was a piece of dark maple lathed into the shape of a lower leg but chipped white by years of wear. He'd long ago quit topping it off with a shoe, and the carved wooden toes had been gnawed away by city cement.

The Barker rapped the wooden leg with a knuckle.

"What you see before you with your own eyes, ladies and gentlemen, is a grave wound that Yours Most Meekly suffered in the Great War during the Battle of Cambrai! Alone, I addressed and defeated a German A7V tank, thereby saving the priceless lives of my entire cherished regiment!"

He let the pant leg, and his pretense, drop.

"It has been my delighted discovery that customers respond most generously to that tale. It makes the handing over of twenty cents feel right patriotic, turns the viewing of disrobing young women into moral obligation. Does it have the same effect on you, I wonder?"

You no doubt recall that the Barker had shot off part of his foot to avoid dueling me. Now I pictured the ugly reality: my old foe hobbled, gushing blood into the black Virginia mud, elbowing his way through the rain for help while his open wound was aggressed by an infection for which there were few remedies in 1902, aside from the crude correctives of a surgical saw and a belt to bite.

"You, here?" I had no control over what I said. "*How?*"

"Where else but Hollywood, Mr. Stick, would a cavalier of

617

my character go? Fallen stars of the silver screen have become my twinkling tonic. And my audience? My audience has gone quite unchanged. Niggling ailments continue to bedevil Modern Man, and I, lowly servant, continue to anesthetize the sufferers."

He severed eye contact to bray at two backslapping joes wandering by.

"Twenty cents, good sirs, to see Garter Girl Gabrielle Dumont, the Pacific Siren! Exposed in person! Extra late shows! Free parking! *Viva Les Femmes!*"

The men dithered, lazy trout distracted by colorful tackle, and the Barker reeled them in with a more flattering pitch about the artistic obligation we as Americans had to appreciate the female nude in all of her transcendent splendor—such had been the healthy habit of giants of men like Michelangelo and Cézanne!

He'd sold two tickets before I could begin to piece together my sick, exploded wits. I yanked at Merle's arm but, for some infernal reason, the malcontent had wedged her foot against the podium. The Barker took notice of our feeble struggle and whimsically peaked his bushy white brows.

"Your choice of companions, at least, has improved beyond mischievous midgets."

The gut-burn of Johnny's golden aggie might be the beacon able to guide Merle and me from this overcast imbroglio. I focused upon it too late—the Barker was suddenly holding Merle's slender hand inside his wrinkled paw. I grimaced, expecting Merle to bite, but she showed no reaction, not even to his loose, toothless lips upon her knuckles.

"Gentle contessa," bade the Barker. "Let us forgive your escort's rudeness. I am Dr. Whistler, A.M., M.D., former lecturer on nervous diseases and neurasthenia at the University of the City of New York, fellow of the Boston Academy of Medicine, author of *Every Man Is a Physician*, author of *A History of Groin Injuries*, Medicinal Therapist to the Massachusetts State Women's Hospital, and eternally yours. Would you pay me the indescribable honor of an introduction?"

"Merle." Her voice was flat. "He's my father."

"Oh, truly?" The Barker radiated. "You don't say."

I snapped the bridge of their joined arms with a slap of my hand.

"I care not that you are old and withered," said I. "Touch her again, I will kill you with your peg leg."

The Barker, wizard of provocation, continued to court Merle with lewd looks.

"Merle, from the French *merle*, via the Latin *merula*, meaning 'blackbird.' But which blackbird? I wonder. Are you the opportunistic crow? Or the raven of myth and legend?"

"Raven," she whispered.

"Then, Raven, might you do an old, old man an easy favor and turn your head slightly—ever so slightly!—so that I might enjoy your profile?"

To my sputtering shock, Merle did as he asked, the first time, to my knowledge, that she had ever fulfilled another human being's request. She even blushed. The Barker hummed an appraisal.

"Life has yanked a few of your feathers, hasn't it, Raven? Yet I think you could build a nest here among our flock—given the proper billing, so to speak. One cozy spot might be between the hours of three and six in the morning. Here, I can see the marquee! 'The Ripe Raven of the Sunset Strip.'"

"Daughter," begged I. "This is abject vituperation. Believe not one word. I know this evildoer and he wishes only to infuriate me, which he has done, and degrade you, which he is doing. You are nothing like the noxious tramps he peddles."

"Forever flows the gumption from our intrepid Mr. Stick! You may have known something of my business at one point, but look, old friend, at my face. See the number of years that have passed since then? I can assure you that a woman of, shall we say, maturity can generate a faithful crowd of admirers, provided that she is willing to venture a bit further than her pubescent colleagues. Our Raven is the sort of product of which I've always been most fond: bitter to the taste, tinctured with time, and of dubious veracity, yet salvageable, soluble, and, with a fresh label and a bit of watering down, sellable."

I took Merle by her puny elbow and bared my teeth at the Barker.

"You are abhorrent. I take extreme satisfaction in your looming death."

I bolted down the sidewalk but managed only two steps before Merle's arm ripped from my grip. I swiveled upon my heel, arms spread so as to squash the Barker's brittle old-man skull between my palms, only to find that he was not the culprit behind my daughter's dislodgment. Merle stood at his side by choice, her back straightened for the first time that day, or, for all I knew, since 1913 when we'd slunk from Boston.

She placed a hand upon the rat's shoulder but her eyes kept aim at me.

"I'd love to be one of your girls," said she. "I think you and me could go places."

The Barker's grin revealed brown gums.

"Most certainly," cheered he. "You are packed, I say, with promise!"

Hours ago I'd murdered for Merle and she'd repaid that debt by loving me; I'd heard it, Dearest Readers, with my own dead ears! It was a sentiment she hid too well during waking hours. But suppose I were more softhearted? Suppose I were more supplicating, more submissive? Might it not bring my daughter's latent love for me back to the fore?

Mary Leather, a wise woman, had foretold it:

Every time you have a child, Mr. Finch, you lose a piece of your soul.

I offered Merle a hand from which, to my disrepute, the scuff of Johnny's ring had been taxidermied.

"Please," said I softly. "You do not know this man."

She shrugged. More than anything else, she looked tired.

"There's no other way. Unless you give me that money."

"What I give you is better: a solution. Together we shall wean you from your ills."

"*Wean* me?" Her shoulders fell. "I am what I am, Papa. Can't you accept it?"

That Merle chose to align her life with that of the man who'd worked to ruin mine was its own brand of satiric justice, the beginning eating the end, Ouroboros the self-devouring snake. My life had begun, truly begun, in a brothel bedroom alongside Wilma Sue, and now it was ending, truly ending, outside a brothel with her daughter. I'd lost both of them, and didn't that mean I'd lost myself? If my resurrection had a purpose, it was to fix things in life I'd broken, but look! I'd but broken them further.

Out jutted Merle's fierce underbite. How I adored it.

How I'd miss it.

The Subject, that innominate empty vessel, the same one who'd withstood so many of Dr. Whistler's needles, takes over now so that he might fend off unendurable pain. The Subject turns away, and walks, and does not look back. The Subject bears the holly-jolly music and blinking lights of a new age coming at him like a kettle of hawks. Go ahead, beak from him his family; talon away his friends; leave him a dry pile of carrion. He will put up no defense; that is the Subject's style.

The Subject slides into a leather seat. The Subject cannot think of Merle. The Subject will not think of Merle. The Subject regards the shiny red machine. It belongs to a woman. The Subject pictures her, a series of silvered daguerreotypes. Was this woman as alone as he? Not quite, thinks the Subject; she has a daughter, Gopher. No, Margeaux. The Subject recalls a dour face, extra pounds, forearm scars. There, now, was a girl who understood loneliness. There was a girl who was herself a sort of Subject.

The Subject is pierced by a new pin, one of curiosity. It is to be expected: any monster is intrigued upon learning of a second of its kind. The Subject engages the ignition as imprecise recollections knock about his blank brain.

Z will take you.

He'll go with you, I promise.

He'll meet you at your place at seven.

A facial pinch—has another needle fastened together the Subject's lips? The Subject checks the rearview mirror and finds contrary evidence. What pesters the Subject's face is a smile. The Subject's mission, after all, is to ensure that Zebulon Finch feels nothing. To the Subject, there is no daughter, no pitchman, no dreams. There is only the road ahead, the good-bye waves of palm trees, and the endless black pavement, the vanishing point into which all must vanish.

XIX.

MOTHER PHONED TO SAY SHE'D lost track of you. I assumed you weren't coming. Sorry, but it's nine o'clock, this isn't going to work."

Margeaux's excuse was redundant given that she wore not a gown but a shapeless black tent of velvet pajamas. Even so, her appearance jolted me. My mind had crystallized her as a short, portly, bespectacled, and brace-faced twelve-year-old house-breaker, but this young woman had caught up to me in both age and height. While she was hardly ravishing, her glasses were stowed, her teeth were straight, and her size was at least ambiguous beneath that tarpaulin.

But the second she'd opened the door, I'd felt that shared sense of desolation that had united us upon first meeting. We snapped together now like magnets. Was it any surprise? All night I'd been attuned to a frequency of sadness and here in Santa Barbara was the signal the strongest.

None of that meant I had the courage to be anything but brusque. I'd not driven all the way here, circumventing major thoroughfares in case the police were patrolling for a red Coachcraft Roadster connected to a multiple-fatality shootout, only to be dismissed at a dorm-room door.

"Get dressed," said I.

"Oh, I see. *Fashionably* late is what you are. Did Mother teach you that?"

"Will you get dressed?"

"My, my. This is going to be fun, isn't it?"

Nevertheless she followed orders, stamping into the bathroom to emerge fifteen minutes later transformed from limp-haired druid to gussied debutante, her Bridey-black hair pulled away from a strapless floor-length gown laced with a Mexican motif across skirt and bodice. For certain it was a gift from Mother, who, despite her faults, knew how to pair a dress to a body.

Not that Margeaux was going to be mistaken for a Cinderella. Though thinner, she remained several sizes over fighting weight and her posture suggested a burden that had but grown heavier across the years. She fidgeted nonstop, running a finger beneath her three-strand pearl necklace and tugging at her silk gloves so that they covered every last scar.

"Are you going to stare at me all night or what? It's not like you look so great either. You look dead."

"I am here as a favor."

"When shall I present you with your award?"

"Say what you wish. Let us embark."

"Fine, then. Great."

Neither of us budged.

"Well?" she demanded.

"I confess I know nothing of our destination."

She covered her face with both hands.

"Gød, you're hopeless."

The night was windy. By the time we reached the parking lot, Margeaux had thrice failed to light a cigarette. With nothing to

624

cork her mouth, she grouched the agenda. The last Saturday before semester's end marked the traditional Winter Formal, a dance with no significance beyond that everyone in California was obsessed with being beautiful. In this aspect, Margeaux had not changed: the little girl who lambasted Hollywood fakers and fretted about Dust Bowl farmers had grown into a young woman of equivalent values.

I, for one, was upbeat about our objective. What I knew about high school dances could fill a thimble, but I imagined that they were, first and foremost, dark. The idea that I could be an anonymous teenager for these few hours before my probable arrest had high appeal, and I was relieved that my jacket, untouched in the drug-den massacre, would suffice for such an event.

My happy trance was cut short by a groan upon arrival at the red convertible.

"*This* is the car you brought?" Margeaux whined.

"Will the wind play havoc with your hair?"

"Everyone will *look* at us," hissed she.

She curved her back, squooshing her corpulence against its delicate bindings, and glanced about. Skipping through the lot were half a dozen gowned and suited classmates rushing to overcome their own late starts, and not a one of them paid us any mind.

"Isn't that the point?" asked I. "To be seen? Why else the gown, the shoes, et cetera?"

"The point is Mother. It's always Mother. She wouldn't let me graduate without attending a stupid dance. There's a war going on, you know that? Millions of people are dying in Europe and this is what she decides to care about. She said if I don't go, people will say nasty things."

"What kind of nasty things?"

"Oh, I don't know. That I don't like boys?"

"Interesting. Don't you?"

"I don't like *anyone*. I don't understand why that's so difficult for people to understand." She sighed. "Let's just get into this capitalist U-boat and get this over with, okay?"

She flopped herself into the Yankee Doodle and sank low into the seat. I was about to follow suit when I noticed a minor, but telling, detail. Each girl prattling past on heels wore a ribboned flower pinned above her breast. The boys piling into jalopies cradled similar miniature bouquets intended for their dates. It seemed an important, if subtle, social signifier, and it concerned me that, without it, Margeaux might encounter, as she put it, nasty things.

"One moment," said I, stepping away from the car.

In truth it was a good two or three moments before I returned. I took my seat behind the wheel, tossed onto her lap a small arrangement of flowers, and revved the engine.

"What's this?" asked she.

"It is called a corsage." I swung the car around, honking at horse-players.

"I know what it's called. Where did you get it?"

"From some chap."

"And how did you get it, exactly?"

"I socked him."

"You *what?*"

"Only in the breadbasket. He will yet dance the night away, I promise you."

I swerved from the lot and floored it, hurling Margeaux against her seat, though that did not prevent her observing me with renewed interest. The possibility occurred to me that no boy had ever before

626

done her a kindness; the thought brought me much discomfort. There was a refreshing clarity to Margeaux's absolute disapproval of the world, and I wished not to corrupt it.

She murmured directions. I watched for police lights. She was ruminative. I wondered what in the goddamned hell I was doing. Presently she spoke.

"Congratulations, by the way."

"Be less obscure."

"Mother told me this morning. Look, I don't care. I'm happy for you. It's true, I never thought of you as a plutocrat, but what do I care? People change."

"What are you going on about?"

"The will." She frowned. "Was it supposed to be a surprise? Mother put you in her will."

Let this line upon the page be the proxy for my stupefaction.

"Are you all right?" asked she. "I don't want you to crash this monstrosity."

"Money," stammered I. "I have no right to it."

"Look, don't worry about me, she has plenty for her whole pathetic excuse for a family."

Family: does it not strike you as a pregnant word?

If the script had been a proposal without a ring, the will was marriage without a certificate.

We arrived at the local Elks Lodge, site of the Winter Formal, long before I could begin to process the flustering news. The clamor from inside confirmed that we were indeed late, and yet we sat for a time in the parked car listening to the squawk of muffled jazz and the moan of a building wind, while a single glum balloon knocked its head against a lobby window.

I got out of the car, made my way around it, opened her door, and extended my elbow.

She blinked up at me.

"What are you doing?"

"Don't you think we should go inside?"

"What? You can't come in with me."

Few things are as disheartening as letting a proffered arm fall.

"No, it's not like that," said she. "It's just—it's the school. They have a million rules. You have to register guests and I didn't know that—I mean, Mother didn't—it would create a big fuss. We'd have to find the principal and get his permission, and then—"

That I'd imagined the evening unfolding otherwise was embarrassing. I held up a hand to quiet her.

"Everyone will look. Say no more."

My smile might have even looked real.

I stepped back to allow her to hoist herself from the car. She faced the Elks Lodge as if it were the gallows. I watched from my demoted position as chauffeur as she did a dozen feminine things at which, on any other night, she might have scoffed, rising upon toes to create a straighter back, twisting a bracelet to some better advantage, touching her hair so gently as not to be touching it at all.

Her sigh was loud and defeated; I found myself aching at the heartbreak of the hopeful little handbag positioned as shield over her tender stomach. She gave me a skittish glance.

"Beautiful," blurted I.

"Z," said she. "Lying does not suit you."

But she flushed, and the best way to hide it was to break away across the lot. I followed her progress, from the uncertain stoop of her shoulders as she leaned into the wind to the nervous fists formed

628

inside her silken gloves. Everyone else in sight was coupled, but when a Negro fellow held the door open for Margeaux alone, she nodded with a poise that would have made her mother proud.

I reclaimed the driver's seat. It would take a cop of Roseborough's tenacity to track me to an Elk's Club in Santa Barbara; thus, I had hours to kill. I placed upon my lap the last diversion I had in the world: the bedraggled, battle-pocked copy of *In Our Image*. I smoothed it out the best I could and opened the first page. It stuck to the verso via a daub of dried blood.

By the low illumination of parking lot lamps, I read. And read more. And—by jove—read even more than that. It was as if I were back in that well-booked guest room at Sweetgum, riveted by the expeditionary antics of H. Rider Haggard and the visionary leaps of H. G. Wells. Even if the script were unproduceable (it was), even if the struggle to make it would bring Bridey nothing but professional ruin (it would), the half-baked fairy-tale amalgam of wolves and women that she'd described to me was nothing less than hypnotic when put to page.

I shall never know how she pulled it off. The man-wolf was no hirsute Lon Chaney Jr.-type gnawing the scenery, nor were the sex scenes comparable to the tawdry titillation you'd get from the Barker's twenty-cent peep show. These elements were, rather, the crepuscular internal organs that, through pump and squish, powered the most beautiful of creatures—and was that not life itself? The dark inside that made us seek the light outside? The ineffable paradox of being?

It was symbolic of my own prolonged death that I never got to read the death of Bridey's protagonist. Mere pages before the screenplay revealed the meaning of life—by then, I expected nothing less—

the driver's door of the car flew open. I jerked in surprise, dropping the script. It was Margeaux; I hadn't noticed her approach. But her pounding bosom left no doubt that it had been at a sprint. Her carefully woven hair had disentangled, hanging like entrails about her shoulders. Black daggers of melted mascara carved each cheek and her gloves had pooled to reveal past diagrams of pain.

"Move over," she sobbed.

"Margeaux, what—"

"*Move!*"

XX.

S HE DROVE FAST.

"Faster," she urged herself.

The little engine screamed.

"Faster."

They were the two syllables she'd stressed for an hour, a plea for time itself to accelerate until it drove a period into her long, tortured sentence. She did not divulge what had happened at the Winter Formal, but what matter did it make? Pain, her constant bedfellow, had grown sick of sharing a mattress and had decided to smother her with the pillow. Margeaux's tears mixed with the salt of the Pacific Ocean. Big silver breakers shattered into the moonlit cliffs that propped up State Highway One.

She'd chosen the coastline roadway for no reason that I could discern, but now that we were halfway to Los Angeles, I was determined to make her keep driving. Bridey and I were finished, but that did not mean I couldn't, as my last act in Hollywood, force a mother-daughter reunion; Margeaux deserved better than a boarding school that brought her such misery. To hell with the gossip hounds who prowled Bridey's gates, waiting for just such a scoop to make their careers: *Bridey Valentine's Illegitimate Love-Child Revealed!*

The Yankee Doodle was built for style, not control, and the ocean wind waggled the tail. Margeaux gasped and braced an arm against

631

the dash, but after she straightened she barked baleful laughter into the night. She turned her painted face and shouted over the shrieking wind.

"*What is it you want? If not Mother's money?*"

The gust from a northbound truck throttled our smaller vessel. The steering wheel juddered; she fought it. Meanwhile I fought her horrid question, but it kept after me with the artlessness of a junkyard dog. What, indeed, had I been *doing* for six decades? Were there ciphers to be read in my trail of wreckage?

Ocean blasted cliff, artillery fire from Neptune. I ducked. The tide retracted its claws from the rock and sand with a hiss.

"Tell me what you want!" begged she. "Something! Anything!"

Was the center line of a highway meant to be straddled? It must be 1922, rural Georgia, where such lines did not yet exist and I drove a Model T called Tin Lizzie and could go wherever I wished, at whatever speed, with any cargo.

A car horn blared. Margeaux swerved back to the brink. I spat the salt of years and found that I did, in fact, have an answer to her question.

"I want to fix things," said I. "To make things right."

"And what have you accomplished?"

"Nothing." The truth stung. "*Nothing.*"

"Perfect! Then there's no reason to be here. Is there?"

The logic was indisputable. If Zebulon Finch, reset each day to age seventeen, could not scrape patient victory from this impatient world, then there was no victory to be scraped.

"That cliff coming up," mused she. "We could run right off it. All this wind? People would think it was an accident."

Margeaux's hair had become mythological in the wind, grasping sea-serpent tentacles, writhing snake nest, black fire. Beneath, her face was silver and still. I became dazzled, then agonized, by the smooth vulnerability of youth, how little the flesh anticipates life's coming ruin.

"We could," replied I.

While those like Bridey moved through life as though their every gesture had consequence, those like her daughter were neglected, ignored, uninteresting, and therefore uninterested. Margeaux understood the feeling of importance no better than a scorned stepchild understood a birthday party when heard only through an attic floor. Of course she was apathetic about her mother's will. Money meant nothing to her. What she was desperate for was purpose, but there was none to be found.

I knew how she felt. I, too, could think of no good reason to carry on.

Margeaux braked in the middle of the highway, and then reversed the car across the opposite lane and onto a trailhead leading into the Santa Monica Mountains. Tucked beneath a treed canopy, the Yankee Doodle idled, its headlights shooting across Highway One to incandesce the guardrail before dissipating into the ocean below. The crash and hiss, crash and hiss, crash and hiss of the tide terrified me, reminding me of something awful—but what? To drown it out, perhaps, Margeaux punched the engine, filling the forest around us with growling, encircling lions.

Her eyes swam, her chest pounded.

"Yes," said she, and I heard an echo:

Her mother, on the floor, crying Yes!, cheering a different sort of annihilation.

I prepared to spew the buoying blather required to talk her down from this perilous perch. But the wind whistled encouragements from legions of the Hollywood dead, whose early exits from the stage of life had won rave reviews at so many a gossip-fueled cocktail party. This destructive tide—this crash and hiss—had Margeaux, too, in its grip. I found that I missed her extra pounds. I missed her skewed teeth. I missed her crooked glasses.

"The rocks are craggy," warned I. "They shan't let you go."

Might not they take tenacious hold of me as well?

Margeaux took my hand. Hers was hot, damp, and adamant, and told me that it was *she* who would not let *me* go. That this girl, realized I, was seventeen was not coincidence but a cosmic gift. Margeaux was offering the universe a chance to correct what it had flubbed in 1896. This time, there would be no rescue from the depths.

"You're so cold," said she.

I squeezed so that she might best feel infinity's freeze.

"Yes," whispered I. "Coldness is all there is."

I put my icy lips to her heated fingers and with a kiss transferred Bridey's proposal to her daughter. Margeaux's veil could be seaweed, her dress a bank of undersea sand, her bouquet a fistful of shells, and together we could bask in nuptials of lull and tranquility.

It was then that I identified the sound of the tide.

In it crashed: *Hweeeeee* . . .

Out it hissed: *Fweeeeee* . . .

These soft shushes were loud enough reminders of who I truly was. Deserter of Wilma Sue (*hweeeeee*), maimer of upright Triangulinos (*fweeeeee*), traitor of goodhearted Johnny (*hweeeeee*), bumbler of Leather's revelations (*fweeeeee*), slaughterer of faceless Huns (*hweeeeee*), pied piper of murdered flappers (*fweeeeee*), misleader of faithful Church (*hweeeeee*), disappointer of a daughter (*fweeeeee*). These accusations were the tide, yes, but also the wind in the grass below, the rustle of the palm leaves above, the sigh of the girl alongside me, and the dead skin of my left hand sliding from the live skin of her right as she slotted the car into gear.

Margeaux pounded the pedal. The tires squealed like hogs mid-butcher. For two seconds the car shook as if aboveground of my pop's TNT, and then the tires snatched a wad of turf and slingshotted us forward. We came out crazy, snapping tree limbs and smashing a headlight before thudding down upon pavement. I tensed for north or south collision but the road was ours, and in the second before the grill snapped the guardrail, I took back Margeaux's hand. In near-death she was perfect, invulnerable at last to time's degeneration.

I wonder if anyone saw the roadster fall into the ocean like a shiny red drop of blood.

The crash was so loud it was silent. The impact hurled our hard skeletons against soft muscle. Images disassembled. Engine block driven through hood. Windshield glass sluicing laps with diamonds. A tire bobbing away into the black. A sudden pitch forward, sucked into a spumous hole. Tufts of torn seat leather rising with the water, to my chest, my neck, my chin, because we were sinking, and some things floated while others did not.

A final moon-stained glimpse: two hands still clasped.

Freezing water surged over my head and then pushed me lower. The screeching contortions of the waking world slid into the ebony glue of the depths, and the roadster cut beneath the whitecaps as if piloted. Mighty fists of pressure crushed the car until it made minor-key songs of bending steel. The composer, if I am not mistaken, was Carlo Gesualdo.

His was fitting funeral music and the Yankee Doodle was our

shiny red casket. Yet it suffered a fatal, obvious, and stereotypical Californian flaw—it was a convertible. With a swiftness unexpected within such slow motion, I was suctioned from the driver's seat. The car was there; the car was gone. I flailed, nowhere at all. I had lost everything, including Margeaux's hand.

My spiky panic smoothed the instant I felt soft sand beneath my feet. Here I was, back again, at the basement of it all. Hadn't it been at the bottom of a lake that I had first lost track of Death? Perhaps here, at the bottom of a bigger one, I would find it. A phosphorescent fish twitched by. I reached out, petted it, and it darted away. I laughed and felt the weight of water fill my lungs.

The water itself, mused I, was different from that of my first drowning. Whereas Lake Michigan had been translucid and left to the nautical dead, this stretch was polluted with the detritus of the living: liquor bottles once employed to drown sorrows, pennies wished upon to thriftless end, jewelry tossed away in heavy-heartedness. This sediment of failure and loss twinkled like dull stars in an inverted heaven.

A fresh piece of flotsam: a soaked, sad-petaled flower, Margeaux's corsage, dropping into the hand that had once held hers.

She was alone out there.

Whatever had I done?

A citified landlubber to the core, I'd had little exposure to swimming holes, yet I kicked off like an Olympian, scattering sand and rocketing through its nimbus. Here, blackness; there, blacker shades of blackness. On instinct I aimed for the latter, paddling for what felt like hours. My hunch won out, for there on the seabed lay the hulk of the Yankee Doodle. Its front end had been scrunched into a smile; it seemed glad to have been resettled in the deep. You could not say the same for the body that agonized above it.

Margeaux's floor-length gown had coiled about her legs, giving her the appearance of a selkie yearning for dawn. Her hem was ensnared in the crumpled mitt of the driver's door and she bobbed above as senselessly as the balloon at the Elk's Club. Was she alive or did the flit of the current imbue her with lifelike movement? No time to tell; I clambered over the ruins and yanked at the bottom of her skirt.

Just fabric, stupid silk, worthless lace, and yet without gravity to assist me, I could not gain the leverage needed to tear it free. A dreadful minute passed; there was still a chance. Two minutes passed; miracles did happen, so why would I quit? Ten minutes, twenty, thirty; absurdity now, gruesome folly, the batting about of a sodden corpse. Our little Gopher was gone, Dearest Reader, her acidulous judgments, her perceptive proclamations, all of it swallowed.

Pictures never die, Bridey had said. She'd been right. Everything else did.

I wrapped my limbs around Margeaux as would a squid and let the tide toss us with playful kitten paws. But after a time, the roadster caved in on itself, jerking her downward with a force I could not counter. I swam aside; I did not wish to see how she might be pinned or buried. I heard it, though, the belly-grumble of collapse, which produced in its wake a sudden and powerful current. It grabbed me by the ribs, nothing less than the hand of Gød, and lifted me up toward the thousands of debt collectors I had yet to pay.

No! Greatest of all sinners! Spurner of justness! Release me!

I grabbed a loose fender to weigh me down, but it had been fractured in the crash and fell to pieces in my hands. Up I surged and down I kicked, this time taking hold of a branch of mossy wood, which disintegrated into viridescent dust. I dug rocks from the sand

and jammed them into my pockets to weigh me down, but Gød, impatient now, clamped me in His forceps. Obediently I rose; the world worsened from bucolic black to glowering gray. Once again I was delivered through the Uterus of Time; once again it was an ugly breech birth. Though what other kind could a fellow heading backward expect?

XXI.

B UDDY! HEY, BUDDY!"

Before this invocation, millennia had passed, during which any of my fantasies might have been true. My eyelid dark, for instance, was really ten feet of ocean silt. The hiss of the highway was the undersea tectonics of a rearranging planet. Even the hands that took me by the armpits could have been a coral reef claiming me as feed for generations of fish.

"Jeez Louise! You all right, guy? You okay?"

The sizzling surf slid away as my body was dragged up the beach. My chin cut a tunnel through wet sand, then two hands wiped clean my face before rolling me onto my stomach. One of the hands walloped my back—a surprise—and my mouth voided a gallon of brown water seasoned with stones, twigs, shells, and bottle caps. No mayflies crawling their way out of my throat, not this time.

"Breathe, buddy! Breathe!"

That I could not do, but eject more scree I could. When the pile of vomitus became too much, I elbowed my body, lighter now for being emptied, away from the hands that continued their meddling. I foundered atop a bed of hot sand and, seeing no way around it, opened my eyes to the day.

It was the brightest one ever. The sky was spotless. The December breeze was sugar. Birds made wide circles, enjoying their forever descent. I looked at myself and saw that I was covered with trans-lucent white jellyfish. I welcomed their poison before realizing that they were the soaked slop of screenplay pages.

"You're one lucky son of a gun. Hoo-boy."

Hunkered in the sand a few feet away was a boy my age, blond and suntanned and loaded with blinding white teeth. His ironed trousers and starched shirt had been thoroughly disheveled by his pointless rescue, but he was grinning.

"There wasn't anyone else in the car with you, was there? I sure hope not."

I coughed wet sand.

"I was just driving along up there when I saw the guardrail all busted up, so I pulled over and checked it out. Figured the wind last night could have sent someone over the edge. But I didn't really think—oh, wow!"

He chuckled, leaned back against the dune, and titled his face to the sun.

"Tell you what, I'll never forget today. First what I heard on the radio and then this? Hey, buddy, is that what ran you off the road? You heard what happened and got upset? Heard about Pearl Harbor, I mean?"

If Pearl Harbor was a woman, she'd had the good fortune of evading my warpath.

"Hold on, you haven't heard? The Japs bombed it to pieces this morning. It's all over the news. I was listening to the game when they broke in—hey, look, buddy, I know you been through a lot here, but you better get wise. Pearl Harbor is in Hawaii. It's a military base. The dirty Japs, they sneak-attacked it, killed all sorts of our guys."

With a push-up motion, I raised my waterlogged torso from the

640

beach and prompted myself with the various mechanics of standing. I lifted one knee, but it shook like that of a newborn foal. No, that is too precious a simile; I was an abysmal creature of the sea making its first gawkish land maneuver, uncertain that its soft limbs would hold. But was that not my ongoing struggle writ large? The perpetual waffling between monster and man?

"Buddy? You know what this means, right?"

My prolonged residency upon this planet had taught me a thing, perhaps even two. This Hawaiian incident would goad our fair country into another war. Arsenals on both sides would be sharpened to new classifications of lethality. There would be more casualties, more deaths. Plato, that berobed blowhard, had been no favorite of mine during my childhood tutelage, but he'd written one observation that I could not shake:

Only the dead have seen the end of war.

My knee held; I planted the associated foot. The whole leg trembled. It would never hold my weight.

The boy punched a fist into a palm.

"We'll cream 'em! That's where I was headed when I found you. Me and some pals, we're meeting up at the recruiting office in Malibu to get our physicals. You bet we're gonna whip those Japs. Those Nazis, too! Hey, sorry about your car and everything, but maybe you want to come along?"

This curious death of mine had led me to a surfeit of unexpected places, uncommon people, and outlandish ends, and it was nowhere close to finished. Kneeling there upon that sun-blasted beach, I would not have been totally surprised, I think, to learn some of what was yet to come. That I would meet leaders of men and become a leader myself; that I would go places no human being had ever gone;

that I would come to know, much belatedly, the true identity of my murderer. Can you still not make out the inevitable end to my tale? Oh, you darling thing; were your hand here, I would pat it.

Take heed, Dearest Reader, should you opt to continue with me down this narrowing path. We have spent considerable time in each other's company, you and I, and often such proximity breeds fondness. But throw no arm about my shoulder; fly me no kisses before we meet again. Eye me instead with suspicion. Keep handy a register of the damages I have rained down upon those who have kept my company.

Never forget who I am and what I have done.

My shadow, struck by midday sun, evanesced beneath my feet as though I had never existed. I was standing. My knees knocked, hips teetered, and spine flapped, but I was standing. Perhaps that meant something; perhaps it did not. I rose to full height, a man, at least for now, on some grade of terra firma.

The boy stood too, slapped the sand from his seat, and addressed me square.

"It's a new day, fella. A new world. What do you say?"

I was but seventeen, young for an enlistee, but I wagered that Uncle Sam would be willing to bend his rules for a lad so eager to die for the cause. For any cause, really. So what did I say to this magnanimous challenge? What else *was* there to say, Reader, about a country so generous that it handed to me, free of charge, one more chance at annihilation committed in the glory of its star-spangled banner, its twilight's last gleam, its amber waves of grain—all that fine stuff.

I smiled. It looked good, I bet. I still had a bit of the knack.

"Gød bless America," said I.

END OF VOLUME ONE

A COMMERCIAL SOLICITATION TO THE READER

Provided that you have enjoyed this fancy, we implore you to read the conclusion: *The Death and Life of Zebulon Finch, Volume Two: Empire Decayed.*

A NOTE OF GRATITUDE

Mr. Kraus wishes to convey appreciation to the following cohorts and colleagues: Mr. Richard Abate, Ms. Lisa Brown, Mr. Joshua Ferris, Ms. Eliza Kennedy, Ms. Amanda Kraus, Mr. Grant Rosenberg, and Mr. Christian Trimmer.

READING GROUP GUIDE

DISCUSSION QUESTIONS

1. Zebulon presents himself as the readers' hero. How would you define a traditional hero? Do you think Zebulon is a hero? Why or why not? What is the single most important thing he is trying to achieve?

2. The archetype of the antihero abounds in literature and pop culture. What is the definition of an antihero? What are some of the attributes and motivations they possess?

3. Several traits characterize Zebulon as an antihero. What attributes and conflicting motivations consistently contribute to Zebulon's downfall? What do you see as his greatest flaw? Consider some examples.

4. Kraus has infused his darker, flawed, and highly complex protagonist with enough traditional heroic strengths and intentions to gain reader sympathy. Choose one circumstance from the novel in which you sympathize most with Zebulon's plight. What are his strengths? In what ways are you sympathetic to his point of view? How important is it to you that you can relate to the main character in a novel?

5. How do your impressions of Zebulon change throughout the story? For what reasons?

6. One important theme in the novel is humanity versus science. Zebulon's physically decomposing and mutilated body can be seen as a reflection of everything around him. Discuss how this reflection ties into that theme.

7. What is the tone throughout the novel? Does the tone change as the novel progresses? Zebulon suggests that the foremost attribute of youth is hope. Does the author establish a feeling of hope through Zebulon's perspectives and filters? Or does he express something else entirely?

8. Zebulon describes his story as a "tragicomic opera." Do you think his description is accurate? Why or why not? Are there any other literary genres that you would use to categorize this novel?

9. Examine this novel as a work of social criticism using satire as a literary device. What is the author's purpose in presenting the story through satire? What corruptions of human nature does he expose? What other social criticisms or commentary does he offer to us as readers? Consider a few examples from the text to support your answer.

10. The use of irony often goes hand in hand with satire. Find and discuss examples from the text when Kraus has used irony to comment on the vices of American culture and society. How is it ironic that Zebulon's final act is to write a book?

11. Kraus infuses the criticism of satire and the paradox of irony with humor. What scenes stand out as the most humorous to you? What purpose do you think the humor serves in each of these scenes? How does it impact the author's use of satire and irony overall?

12. What general effect does Zebulon have on the people he meets? What effects do others have on him? Which supporting character most intrigues you? Why? What effect did this character have on you and on Zebulon?

13. What social commentary does the author suggest about each of the following characters: Barker, Dr. Leather, John Quincy, Merle, and Bridey Valentine?

14. Look back at the discussions between Zebulon and Merle. What is Merle trying to convey to Zebulon? Does Zebulon understand? Why does Merle have trouble defending her position?

15. What is Dr. Leather's proposition to Zebulon? What does Zebulon believe about Dr. Leather's motives? How does Dr. Leather justify his own beliefs and actions?

16. Consider the concepts of trust, friendship, dignity, prejudice, and redemption. What roles do they play in this novel? Which concept do you think Zebulon struggles with the most and why?

17. Church becomes a prominent influence in Zebulon's life. Discuss Zebulon's relationship with Church over the course of the story. How does that relationship change? What does it mean to each of them?

18. What is the nature of Zebulon's relationship with Little Johnny Grandpa? How does their relationship impact Zebulon? What are some of the decisions and actions that result from Zebulon's relationship with Little Johnny Grandpa?

19. What moments in the story are the most relatable to you? Most bizarre? Most suspenseful? Most heartbreaking? Most unexpected?

20. What is the significance of the aggie that Zebulon keeps safe in his stomach? What is the significance of the Excelsior pocket watch? What do these things represent to Zebulon?

21. What is "la silenziosità"? When and how does Zebulon use it? What does it mean to the people upon whom he uses it?

22. In the trenches in World War I, what does Zebulon learn about the nature of sacrifice? What does he learn about brotherly love? What did *you* learn?

23. *At the Edge of Empire* provides a study rich in vocabulary. Were you able to infer meanings from the text? Discuss words you might now like to incorporate into your personal vocabulary. What does Zebulon's use of language say about him?

24. As the author prepares us for Volume Two, Zebulon suggests that we "Never forget who I am and what I have done." What does he mean by this? What is his purpose in conveying it?

25. Do you see life differently after reading this novel? Why or why not? Do you think you will do anything differently from now on? How so?

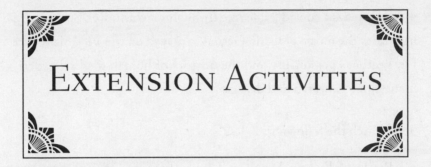

EXTENSION ACTIVITIES

1. In the early 1900s in the United States, the Black Hand was prevalent in organized criminal activity. Create a graphic organizer or write a brief essay on American organized crime to show similarities and differences between Black Hand extortion operations and activities of the American mafia during this time period. Address origins, purposes, participants, practices, and tactics.

2. Research the following: the state of medicine in the United States at the turn of the twentieth century, possible reasons for a proliferation of quack medicine shows promoting fraudulent herbal remedies and poultices, and the charlatans who promoted them. Did these charlatans and quack remedies provide something that was needed by the society of the time period?

3. Investigate the unsavory world of so-called "freak shows" in America at the turn of the twentieth century. The following compelling sources offer reliable research into these violations of human dignity: the 1971 novel, *The Elephant Man: A Study in Human Dignity*, a classic work by psychologist Ashley Montagu that inspired the 1980 semifictional American film, *The Elephant Man*, directed by David Lynch; and the 1977 play, *The Elephant Man*, by Bernard Pomerance, produced on Broadway in 1979.

4. Music plays a considerable role throughout this novel. Specifically, how does the music of Carlo Gesualdo played on the Victrola reflect Dr. Leather's personality and the horrors of human medical experimentation? Research and discuss.

5. Research the following:

+ Battle of Belleau Wood and its importance to Americans in World War I

+ Science fiction pioneer and futurist Hugo Gernsback's invention of the Isolator in 1925, a helmet designed to increase focus

+ The Spanish Flu pandemic of 1918-1919, and its worldwide effects as the most devastating epidemic in recorded history

+ Prohibition in the United States in the 1920s and its historical effects

+ The largest financial crisis of the twentieth century: the Stock Market Crash of 1929 and the global effect of the Great Depression that followed

6. There are many well-known antiheroes in literature and pop culture. Choose one antihero and place him or her in an imaginary conversation with Zebulon Finch. What would be their topic of conversation? On what key issue might they agree? Disagree?

This guide was prepared in 2016 by Judith Clifton, M.Ed, MS, Educational and Youth Literary Consultant, Chatham, MA. This guide has been provided by Simon & Schuster for classroom, library, and reading group use. It may be reproduced in its entirety or excerpted for these purposes.

Turn the page
for a sneak peek of...

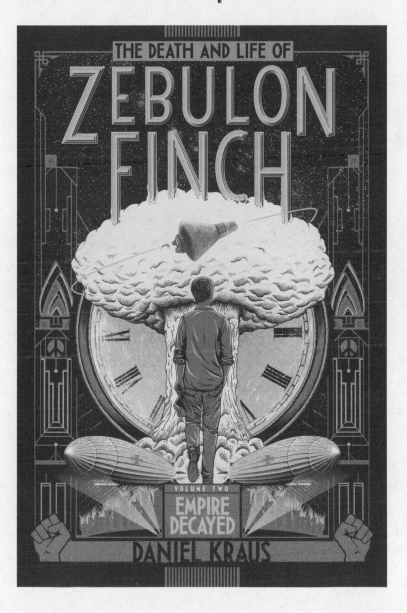

N THE TIME THAT IT took to reach a vacant side street, night descended and I swore that I could see against a black sky the blacker triangles of the RAF. Frau Meixelsperger charged down an alley, through a wooden gate, and into the fenced backyard of a modest bungalow. There she squatted before a flowered hillock, parted a curtain of leafed tendrils, and knuckled a signal upon a steel door embedded in the dirt. The reply was the clang of a thrown lock; the door swung outward. Without a word, she dropped her legs into the hole and disappeared inside.

Another dark, downward path in a dark, downward death. I followed.

Meixelsperger bolted the hatch above while I surveyed the grim scene. Family bomb shelters were not rare, though I doubted that they usually crammed nine people into a ten-foot-long, five-foot-wide, four-foot-tall warren. Corrosion had worn mournful mouths through the corrugated steel walls, which supported, just barely, crooked shelves of dusty canned foods. Damp blankets had been draped to ward off poison gas, and the moldy stink mingled with that of the diesel fumes wafting from the engine powering a triad of flickering bulbs. A pile of World War I gas masks trapped the light in their lenses and turned it into gold. Fool's gold, I was certain.

I turned to the baker.

"Is there time to return to the big shelter?"

"*Dummkopf!*" she spat. "First you strike child in public. Second you complain of shelter. Is this not *gemütlichkeit* enough for Mr. America?"

"I only suggest that we might have hidden just as well in a crowd."

"It is your luck these people do not *sprechen* English. We would be out in ditch. *Mein Gøtt!*" She tossed up her arms. "Direct hit, we die anyway. This make you stop complain?"

The woman interrupted her shaming screed to arrange sandbags as a seat upon the cold dirt floor. I refused to follow suit; I crossed my arms and challenged each inhabitant's gaze. With menfolk out manning anti-aircraft flak, it was an estrogenated lot. A matron recommenced work on a half-finished knitted scarf. A young wife gathered her three children and opened a story book to a marked page. Squatting at the far end, two adolescent girls picked up their game of chess. Only the elderly woman huddled upon a throw rug addressed me, and with spirit; she sent me the sign of the evil eye, or some such juju, before turning away.

Meixelsperger snorted.

"She no more goes home. She stay down here always. You believe this makes her coward?"

The question brought me discomfort. I shrugged.

"You females appear to judge me just as harshly."

"They should! Shelters, they are already full with disease. The measles? How do you say it? The weeping cough? They are old and with children. They are nervous because you are ill."

Oddly, her assessment left me in high dudgeon.

"I am not ill. I am pale."

"I need hero, and America sends me sick child."

"I am no child, madam. I can do everything asked of me. More, even."

She arched her eyebrows. Let us be factual: it was all one eyebrow.

"You look covered with brick dust, like you crawl from rubble. What do you think this make them think? Husbands, sons. Maybe they crawl from rubble as well? A very sad thing to think."

"I make them sad, do I? What do I care? Are these your friends?"

She smirked.

"Down here, Herr Finch, we keep to our own business."

Brief though my London stopover had been, I'd been regaled with tales of English camaraderie, how each Luftwaffe blitz had further stiffened inflexible Brit lips. This shelter brokered no such esprit de corps. Deep in my gut, Johnny's golden aggie, that symbol of rebellion, burned with certainty. Though this wasn't the gadget-rigged spy HQ of which I'd dreamed, each one of these females had something to hide from the Third Reich.

The first bomb fell. Distance reduced the sound to crinkling, but flakes of rust slalomed down the steel siding, and dirt dropped onto our heads. The children cheered this novel precipitation. I, as ever, loathed blemished clothing, and after brushing myself clean, crawled, with inflated reluctance, from the room's center to beside the brusque baker. As if to mock my preening, she refused to acknowledge the dirt clods caught in her hair.

"Begin talk. How do you help us with progress?"

I goggled at her demanding expression.

"Help you? I believed you were to help me! What is this *Geschenk* I heard so much about?"

"*Mein Gøtt!* The world is upside down. You hide away with Pig

Pigtof von Pig so long that all strategy I gathered for you is useful no more. If you get close to der Führer, a thing I now very much doubt, you tell me at the bakery and then, *ja*, our resistance will not disappoint, I promise you. So many little overthrows they will equal one of giant size. You tell me, Mr. American Hero, what you need, and then I rate the difficulty. How about we get rid of your beloved von Pig?"

I bit back a retort in von Lüth's defense. The giant had treated me more than squarely. His chief fault, as far as I could see, was being lost in the hedge maze of academe. I'd suffered similar disorientation as an overeducated youth, and sympathized. Forced to choose between von Lüth and this irritable operative, the decision was simple. Drop all the bombs you'd like—I'd take an open, green rooftop over this crumbling ossuary.

"Leave him be," said I. "Though, he has an SS agent I could live without."

"This is very easy. We will kill this agent for you. All it will do is reveal us, destroy all we have worked for. As long as Mr. America is happy."

"I am doing," bristled I, "what I can."

"This is not what the Americans say. They tell me you achieve nothing."

So swiftly were the winds of indignation stolen from my sails! Had Rigby, who'd pushed for my deployment, been given the lash by superiors for having believed in a lazy malcontent, if not outright turncoat, like Zebulon Finch? Rigby would have been fired; he'd be jobless in a wartime economy; by now, his whole clan would be living on stale bread and powdered milk—Janet, Roy, Sandra, Walter, Patty, Stanley, and Florence. Why did I have to remember every single damned name?

I'd planned to shut up Meixelsperger by crowing about von Lüth's promised confab with Heinrich Himmler, but the boast died in my throat; it would out me as the gullible patsy that I was. Meixelsperger, on the other hand, was a tidal power.

"America," muttered I, "is fortunate to have you."

She made a fist of kitchen-scuffed knuckles, but resisted cuffing me.

"America does not 'have' me. I am not interested in America. I have interest in Deutschland not losing all. Your Americans, they give me transmitter called Joan-Eleanor. I do not know why this name. Code, decode, all night until fingers bleed. Some of what they ask is simple. Ration reports, curfew hours. Is this building bombed? Is that? But revolution is not so small. If you, Mr. America, do your job, all will change. In *one day* it will change. Much danger for me, for everyone, but much rejoicing when—"

Detonations: one, two, four, six, a dozen, guttural throat-clearings from a subterrestrial demon that snatched our ball of soil and rattled it about like a die. We grabbed for the walls, but the steel siding vibrated like mechanical saws. Terror, terror! Meixelsperger, the bravest, cried out. The bulbs winked off, then on, and everyone was on all fours as plates of dirt chunked from the ceiling cracked across our backs. A hole opened above us—through it, a tapestry of stars— and pretty flowers dangled into the shelter like garroted bodies.

The tremors subsided. Blocks away, flak fire boomed.

The mother resumed storytime, but from a page that had been torn.

The girls pushed dual pawns, pieces that now slid through tears.

The knitter traded sweater for Russian phrasebook, practice for the aftermath.

The old lady grinned at the sky, her teeth blacked out with mud.

Meixelsperger was the sort of immovable object to which one huddled for comfort. Unlike the others, she did not participate in masquerade. She remained stomached to the floor, a half-inch forehead slash painting a tidy black stripe of blood down her cheek. She bore it as she did the dirt in her hair, proud evidence of suffering. Her country had been gelded and blinkered, and still she cantered about as she wished and took in treachery with wide-open eyes.

"How do you do it?" begged I. "For I cannot."

Meixelsperger blinked past blood.

"How do I be brave? A stupid question. You are born woman here, brave is only choice. You are 'future mother.' You are 'breeder of the master race.' Poor men—the National Socialists take their minds. But it is worse, I think, how they take a woman's body and soul."

From her deep bosom she fished a silver chain that ended in a golden starburst centered by a blue cross and black-enamel swastika.

"Look! This is greatest honor for a woman in the Reich. It is the *Mutterehrenkreuz*, the Mother's Cross. But it is not so difficult to obtain. Birth eight children, that is all."

Eight children? Though I was confident that this bruiser could cannon out one hundred sucklings without breaking for lunch, I detected no facility for petting and cooing, nor did her eyes sparkle with motherly mist at the mention of her prodigious brood. I knew why. It was all but guaranteed that most of her children were Party faithful and that some of them had already died for their love of der Führer.

A few streets over, a building exploded. It must have been of wooden construction. The splintering made the rather pleasant crackle of a fireplace, and the ensuing drop of lumber had a glockenspiel quality. But we were not fooled. The children sobbed, the girls shrieked, the old woman howled, and I pressed my face to the dirt. Meixelsperger, though, as if perversely inspired, sang through the clamor, the sleet of soil. Just four notes, a radio call sign I recognized.

"*Pom, pom, pom, pom.*" She had to shout; planes were bearing down, buzzing like a stinging swarm. "You know this BBC? Many Germans have what we call 'detector,' an item of wires for our radios. BBC broadcasts in German, for Germans, and now my brothers and sisters, they too know what I know, know of truth, know how the *Wehrmacht* loses Stalingrad. Germans begin to taste the bitters of defeat, and it is stale taste—no *Geschenk*, that is certain. When Hitler speak, what they hear now is lies. When they read newspaper, they think, is this false news? How strange, all these stories of Jews being resettled. Resettled where?"

The skies above popped with gunfire. Orange light strobed through the ceiling fissure. Wind whipped; detritus levitated; pieces of debris darted about our cave like wasps. When struck, Meixelsperger did not flinch. She looked alive, grinning like the mouse who'd outsmarted the lion. The noise was deafening now, and she shouted like a general ordering her troops on a suicide charge.

"*Something is rotten but now we smell it! Resisters grow like weeds, like the White Rose group in Munich—school children beheaded for celebrating free thought! But what happens, Mr. America, when you cut the weeds and do not pull the roots? Weeds grow back stronger! These are the children I mother! These are the daughters of dissent!*"

Meixelsperger raised her Mother's Cross, but it was yanked away when our humble hill was walloped by a wind that slung all nine of us to the eastern wall. The lightbulbs swung and shattered. The western wall caved with a sigh. We were pressed together, a black tangle of flesh, mud, flesh, mud. For a moment, sound was the only sense: down the block, a hailstorm of brick cracking against the street, the muffle of the old woman caught beneath the dirt, the frantic rabbit-scratch of the two girls digging to free her. Was I still whole? I shifted my legs and stirred a lethal soup of broken glass, knitting needles, chess pieces, a set of false teeth.

The gods of war, all of them—Anhur, Ares, Mars, Mixcoatl, Pele, even von Lüth's Wōden—linked arms rugby-style and came straight at us. We curled like snails, some squealing, some praying, and one of us damning Brit and Yankee alike. It was not Frau Meixelsperger, Reader, but Mr. America himself, for I knew that there were good people in Germany, innocents and fighters for right, but after they were tilled into the soil, who would ever know it? Blood and soil, *Blut und Boden*. Here were both elements, expanding not across Europe but into the caverns of hell.

Fingers were pulling my hair. I resisted but was wrenched nose-to-nose with the half-buried Meixelsperger. In the fiery flicker, the oven scars of her forearms were revealed as war tattoos as true as Church's, as true as my own. The Mother's Cross was pooled between us, so close that I could see how all eight corners had been whetted to points. Meixelsperger had turned the unwanted honor into a weapon. Yes, it might prick her breasts from time to time, but wouldn't such stabs only sharpen the fantasy of sinking the cross into the jugular of Hitler himself?

There came a purple flash and the sound of the sky being ripped in half. Meixelsperger's arms wrapped around me and mine around her—instinct, not affection, but oh, how grateful it made me. I thought of Mary Leather, the last truly good woman I'd known, and wondered if she, with her bold buds of feminism killed off by an early-century frost, might have evolved into someone like this mad baker, able to take her life into her own calloused hands rather than let it be manipulated by man's mania.

Dry lips pressed to my ear to croak over the firestorm howl, the same as had Rigby's in the moments before I'd tripped and fallen into a foreign land, and she used my real name, a gesture that, even amid apocalypse, did not go unnoticed.

"*Down here is where myths are born, Herr Finch. The underground shapes the overground, never the other direction. We are counting on you.*"